MOON-LIGHT JACK
or
THE KING OF THE ROAD.

A SPLENDID PICTURE GIVEN WITH Nos. 1 AND 9,

ONE PENNY WEEKLY,   OFFICE, 147, FLEET STREET.

MOONLIGHT JACK,

THE

KING OF THE ROAD.

AN ILLUSTRATED ROMANCE.

LONDON:

NEWSAGENTS' PUBLISHING COMPANY, 147, FLEET STREET, E.C.

1866.

MOONLIGHT JACK

OR·THE·KING

OF·THE·ROAD

"I BRING TO YOU MOONLIGHT JACK, WOUNDED AND FAINTING."

See page 8.

No. 1.—January 13, 1866.]

[Price One Penny.

PUBLISHED BY THE NEWSAGENTS' PUBLISHING COMPANY, 147, FLEET STREET.

BOOK I.—THE VOICE FROM THE GIBBET.

CHAPTER I.

THE GIBBET ON THE HEATH — THE LIVING DEATH—THE VOICE OF THE DOOMED—THE HIGHWAYMAN'S LAST HOPE—SAVED AT LAST— RASPER, THE THIEF-TAKER—FEARFUL FATE OF THE SPY—THE MEETING BENEATH THE GIBBET.

THE sound of wailing went dismally over the dark heath—the sound of a human being in mortal agony or deadly fear.

Yet there was no one there.

Upon that vast expanse of tangled brushwood, bounded everywhere by the black darkness, no living thing was to be seen—no living thing, indeed, was moving, save the slimy toads, and the sky-larks, and the grasshoppers, and the humming beetles.

Heavy gloom was everywhere—a hideous gloom which the presence of a creaking gibbet seemed to render more heavy and hideous still.

Still the voice of woe rang out upon the night—

"Help, help! Mercy, mercy!"

Whence came the voice?

To whom did it appeal for mercy when no living thing was near?

A human form hung amid the clanking chains.

Could the voice come from this poor wretch whose life had been saved by a miracle?

Alive or dead he looked as if no mortal aid could reach him, for the chains held him tight and the bands were around his limbs, and the crows, eager for their filthy feast, were already perched upon his shoulder and pecking at his check whenever his voice was silent.

For it *was* his voice that rang out upon the night; it was from him that came the cry of terrible anguish which told of a heart overcharged with horror, and a mind every moment threatening to give way before accumulated terrors.

The voice might have been the voice of an aged man, so tremulous, so appealing, so full of misery and wretchedness was it.

But the eyes which glared out upon the black night and seemed as if straining to pierce the gloom were the eyes of a young man in the prime of manhood; the form which swayed to and fro in the stormy wind had the thews and sinews of a Hercules.

Yet he might have been a child for all that his strength availed him now.

The wind, as I have said, blew him to and fro like a feather. His arms were strapped to his side; his legs were swathed like those of a mummy.

All that lived outwardly in this wretched being was his voice with which he scared the carrion crows and battled with death.

So the wind roared round him his death knell, and the old gibbet creaked, and the chains clanked, and the toads beneath croaked, and the insects hummed dismally, and the silent stars looked down coldly upon the scene which the moon shadows rendered more spectral and terrific.

Presently, in the far distance, was heard a rumbling sound.

The man hung in chains listened eagerly.

The slightest sound which betokened the presence of human life was like the voice of an angel to him.

The sound approached nearer.

It was the sound of horses' feet.

Then came the sound of men's voices, more grateful still than all; and the horses, leaving the rough high-road, galloped over the noiseless turf.

Galloped eagerly, in the darkness, towards the man in chains.

When they arrived beneath the gibbet the captive's eyes could see that they were well-dressed, well-mounted, and masked.

Any one who was accustomed to the road at night would at once have seen what they were.

They were gentlemen of the road—captains of the merrie highway, with whom the words "Stand and deliver" constituted a kind of dictionary of wealth.

The heart of the man in chains beat high with joy.

So fiercely, indeed, did it beat, that for a moment he could not find tongue to address those whom he confidently believed to be his saviours.

"Moonlight Jack, don't say we've come too late," cried one of the men, in a jovial, cheery way. "We've come from London to save you, Jack, and we've merry work before us."

No sound came.

"Moonlight Jack, awake!" exclaimed another. "In an hour Captain Rasper comes this way."

At this name the man in chains recovered his voice.

It acted like a talisman.

"I am alive, my friends," said he, "in spite of Rasper and the law. I am here safe and sound. But tarry not. Be quick and release me from these chains. They weigh as heavily on my heart and mind, my boys, as ever they do upon my body."

A loud shout rent the air.

"Hurrah for Moonlight Jack!"

The sound rolled merrily over the dusky heath.

No longer a sound of woe, but the loud rejoicings of merry hearts.

Two of the highwaymen stood on the backs of their horses and began filing at the chains.

Two others held the feet of the man below so that when the chains gave way he might not fall too heavily.

Another, with a sharp knife, cut away the ropes and bandages, so that in a few moments the arms and legs of the long-imprisoned man were free.

Rasp, rasp, rasp, went the file.

The highwaymen worked with a will.

Within the hour Moonlight Jack was a free man.

He was at first so stiff that they were obliged to seat him gently on the dusky earth that he might rest awhile ere he endeavoured to walk.

Presently, in the distance, the rumble of a coach was heard.

"Moonlight Jack," cried one of the men, "here's something which will fire your blood and give you strength. He who comes is your deadly enemy. Listen to the sound of the wheels. They are the wheels of Captain Rasper's coach."

The man who spoke these words leaned over the broad shoulder of Moonlight Jack and whispered the words in a tone of eager hate.

It was evidently his wish and his interest to inflame as much as possible the anger of Moonlight Jack against Captain Rasper.

His words had the desired effect.

Moonlight Jack sprang to his feet, and, though still weak, cried out,

"Joe Falcon, have you brought me my horse?"

"Yes, do you not see her bending her head behind you?" cried Joe Falcon. "Poor Rufus! he is here, glad to see you once more in spite of the cowardly shot of Captain Rasper."

Moonlight Jack answered not.

His face, already pale with starvation and cold, was now more ghastly still, and convulsed by the fiercest passion.

He turned towards the horse, was assisted into the saddle by Joe Falcon, and in a few moments the party passed from the shadow of the gibbet and rode over the velvet turf towards the high-road along which the carriage of Captain Rasper was now proceeding rapidly.

The point to which both parties were directing their steps was a spot on the high-road where a dense copse rose on one side, and a deep pool laved the other.

It was about as dismal a spot as the coach to Dover had to pass on its route, and it was with an inward " God be praised !" and an audible sigh of relief that the coachman whipped on his horses after he had passed it, and drove merrily along the highway into the town of Woolwich.

Here Moonlight Jack and his companions posted themselves.

They knew that they could not here be seen ; and the pool in front of their hiding-place was a convenient spot for ducking a refractory coachman.

The carriage containing Captain Rasper approached—Harry Rasper, the captain of the Thief-takers—the spy who had sworn falsely against Moonlight Jack, and consigned him to a scaffold from which a miracle had saved him.

Just as the vehicle was even with the coppice the highwaymen sprang out and seized the horses' heads.

Rasper's servants never travelled without arms, but the attack was so sudden and unexpected that the pistols of the highwaymen were against their foreheads before they could seize their own.

" Fear not !" cried Joe Falcon, to the driver, "be still, and you are safe. Our business is not with you, but with your master."

Moonlight Jack approached the door of the carriage, and taking a dark lantern from the pocket of one of his companions, he held it up so that his face was fully visible to the occupant of the coach.

Rasper, a man with florid complexion, red hair, round twinkling eyes, pug nose, and wiry moustache and beard of a fiery color, was at any time an unpleasant object to look upon.

Now he was worse than usual.

His face, on perceiving Moonlight Jack, turned ashy pale ; and grasping the cushion of the carriage tightly, he gasped forth,

" Who are you and what do you here ?"

Captain Jack burst into a loud and scornful laugh.

"You scarce need ask my name or my errand," he said, bitterly, as he opened wide the door. " Descend at once, or meet your death."

There was no mistaking the sincerity of Jack's words.

His voice and the terrible sternness of his looks showed at once that there was no compromising his anger.

" What want you with me, Jack Tyrrell ?" asked the Thief-taker, as he stepped into the road, " I had thought that you were dead."

"I doubt it not, and hoped so, too," returned Jack. " When you behold a man hanged at Tyburn you naturally conclude him dead. It doesn't do always to believe your own eyes, though. I was hanged at Tyburn, but I am here alive, you see. Seize him, my men, there is no time to parley."

Three stalwart fellows laid hands on the unfortunate Thief-taker.

" Follow me," cried Jack, and he led the way back to the gibbet.

On arriving there, they descended from their horses, and stood ready to obey the orders of their leader.

" What is that ?" cried Captain Rasper, hiding his face in his hands after he had pointed in horror at the gibbet.

" It is the gibbet where I was hung," said Moonlight Jack, " the gibbet, where, for a day and a night I hung in chains, wrung by woe, dying almost with starvation, only saved now by a miracle. Upon that gibbet you will end your days, upon that gibbet you shall learn what sufferings you have inflicted upon me and upon others."

The Thief-taker trembled so greatly that he could scarcely stand.

" You do not mean it, Jack," he muttered, in a tremulous voice, from which his terror had taken away all power, " you can't be so cruel as that."

" Cruel !" cried Jack, " who talks of cruelty ? Can you have the face to talk of cruelty—you who have falsely sworn against me, you who have torn me from my friends, you whom I have to thank for my living death ? Bind his wrists and legs, lads," he added, to his men, " and put a gag over his mouth, for his voice I have no wish to hear."

The wretched man struggled violently.

Two men also, who sprang from the carriage, fought and battled for him.

Terror gave him supernatural strength, and he fought and tore like a madman.

But it was of no avail.

Four strong men were around them, and in a few moments they lay bound and helpless on the ground; their wrists and ankles tied, their mouths gagged ; the only sign of life being the glaring flaming eyes.

There was no hope.

A drowning man they say will catch at a straw. But here even the straw was wanting.

He saw the Eternity he dreaded for himself but forced upon others, stretching out in terrible vistas before him, and the sickening dread of an unknown future fastened upon his heart like the cold clammy hands of the dead whom he had destroyed.

The highwaymen enclosed him in the heavy chains, and hoisted him up, and he was left dangling in the cold night air, while one of his men who had escaped unhurt was sent off to tell the tale.

Moonlight Jack and his companions waved their hands in derision, and galloped away over the noiseless turf, while the wretched man, dying by inches, glared out upon them from amid his clanking chains as the wretched wave-tossed mariner glares at the lights of a receding ship.

When Moonlight Jack and his companions attacked the coach and dragged Captain Rasper out into the road, there was one person whom they did not observe.

This was a boy about fourteen, who crouched in a corner, pale and trembling.

He was the son of the Thief-taker ; his name, Jonathan Rasper.

Most boys of his age, seeing their fathers in

deadly peril, would have rushed forward and done their best to save them.

But Jonathan Rasper was constitutionally timid.

He inherited cowardice from his father.

So he allowed the men to take the captain away, and crawling behind a bush, watched them as they swung him up on the gloomy gibbet.

Then, when the highwaymen had galloped off, he approached his father.

"Father," he cried, "I am here."

There was no reply.

He repeated his words.

Still no answer.

A bright gleam of the moon suddenly revealed to him the fact that his father's mouth was gagged, though his eyes were open.

He approached the gibbet, and being light and active, he had soon climbed to the top.

He then slid down the chain, and tore off the bandage which confined his father's mouth.

"It's me ; it's Jonathan, father," he said.

The eyes still glared with a stony glassy glare.

But no sound came.

Captain Rasper was dead !

The boy, on finding this, shuddered and trembled so that he nearly fell to the ground ; but he at length recovered himself sufficiently to slide down the upright of the gibbet.

He did not stop to fasten on the gag, for he could not bear to touch the corpse again, or to look again into its glassy eyes.

He slid down, and when he reached the earth he knelt down upon it and uttered a vow, a vow of vengeance, vengeance to the death against Moonlight Jack, and the others who had killed his father.

There was nothing noble in the vow, however.

It was a vow of cruel, terrible vengeance ; but it was not the vow of an open and generous brave heart.

It was the vow of a creeping, crawling serpent, the vow of a spy and a traitor.

He was about to go when a hand was placed gently on his shoulder.

He uttered a cry of fear, and leaped aside.

He need not have feared.

The new comer was a young girl, a girl of some sixteen or seventeen summers.

"Who is that?" she said, looking into his face pleadingly and pointing to the gibbet. "I saw you trying to save him."

"It's Captain Rasper," muttered the boy, with a shiver ; "they've killed him."

A smile broke over the girl's face.

"Where's Moonlight Jack, then?" she asked, eagerly.

"They've saved him, and put my father up in his place," returned the boy, savagely, as he clenched his fists ; "but I'll be even with them. I'll hunt them down, only wait awhile."

The girl seized him by both arms, and looked him steadily in the face.

He could see then how beautiful she was.

"So you're Jonathan Rasper !" she cried. "I've heard before what a sneaking, crawling cur you are ; but, mark me, no peaching, no spying on Moonlight Jack, or I'll be the death of you, as sure as my name's Gipsy Bess !"

So saying she darted away from the boy, who had been fumbling in the breast of his coat for a dagger, and left him once more alone, and shivering in the presence of the Silent Dead.

CHAPTER II.

THE STRANGER AT THE INN—THE MEETING ON THE ROAD—"STAND AND DELIVER"—THE RING—THE MISER—THE TEMPTATION—THE ROBBERY—DESPAIR—THE SHOT OF REVENGE—HURRAH FOR THE ROAD—THE STRANGE ADVENTURE—MOONLIGHT JACK'S RETREAT.

THE evening of the following day was just closing in when a horseman stopped at the small hostelry that stood at the extreme margin of the Dover Road, some miles from London, and ere the landlord was aware of the presence of a guest he had dismounted and entered the bar.

"A cold and bad night coming on, your honour," said Boniface, with one of his lowest bows.

He was more than ordinarily polite, for, partly by the fading light, and partly by the cheerful blaze of the large fire, he had already discovered that the cloak in which the stranger was wrapped was of the very finest cloth, and that the narrow gold lace that edged the three-cornered hat was no counterfeit, but the genuine manufacture of Little Britain.

Satisfied, therefore, that the stranger must have money in his purse he proceeded to suggest the propriety of preparing a warm posset for the master, and a feed of corn for the horse.

"No, no, Master Landlord," said the stranger, "a draught of your best ale will do ; I've some miles to ride to-night."

"Surely your honour can never think of crossing the hill?" cried Boniface. "'Tis perilous indeed, and night is coming on."

"Alack, sir," interposed the hostess ; "'tis, indeed, a sad night. It will rain, your honour, and perhaps snow. Farmer Gubbin's lad this time last year went out to seek some sheep on just such a night as this, and he was found next morning, your honour, stiff—quite stiff."

"But, good dame," replied the stranger, laughing, "he had but two legs to help him, and I have four."

"Aye, sir ; but the road is desperately bad," persisted the landlady, determined to make a bold stroke for a guest.

"And truly, your honour," responded the landlord, taking up the cue, "a gentleman's coach and six broke down near the top of the hill, though three boys were scotching the wheels ; there is a great pitfall, too, out yonder."

"But, good man, you forget the moon that is to rise in half an hour," said the stranger.

So saying he drew from his pocket a huge gold repeater, of almost the size and shape of a turnip.

"Your honour had better be cautious," whispered the landlady, pointing to the adjoining kitchen where several rustics were sitting.

The stranger laughed at her praiseworthy caution.

"Nay, good woman, I have no fear of highwaymen."

"Heaven grant your honour may meet none ; but your honour had better stay."

"I cannot, my good woman. I leave England to-morrow : so be quick."

"Then your honour *will* go on," said the landlord, bringing out the pewter tankard and the long-stemmed glass ; "but I trust," he continued, lowering his voice and looking oracular, "you carry but little about you ?"

"Nought but what I can well afford to lose," replied the traveller, with a careless laugh, and a slap on the waistcoat pocket.

A deep but suppressed sigh seemed to form an echo to these words.

The traveller looked towards the kitchen, whence it appeared to proceed.

The rustics, however, who were discussing their ale, were in too merry a mood to notice a sigh; but in the further corner he perceived a well-dressed young man sitting thoughtfully with his arms folded on his breast.

"Please, your honour, gie us summut to drink your honour's health." said one of the rustics, coming forward and making his very lowest bow.

"Well, my lad," replied the good-humoured stranger, "I don't care if I do give you a Queen Anne's half-crown to drink confusion to all Pretenders and Jacobite plots, for they do sore damage to our London trade. So here it is, and much good may it do you."

Not stopping to receive the vociferous thanks of the delighted rustics the traveller threw down his reckoning, wrapped his scarlet roquelaire closely round him, and proceeded to remount his good steed.

"Farewell, Master Landlord," said he. "I have never yet met a highwayman, and 'twill be strange if I do to-night."

Onward rode our cavalier, scarcely heeding the coming darkness.

He was not dreaming of any fair one, however; it was not the age of chivalry.

It was the era of Dutch taste and French poetry, the prosy, matter-of-fact earlier half of the eighteenth century—the year 1728.

And well fitted for the age of our hero.

He was no knight pricking forth in search of adventures, but Mr. John Richardson, the substantial Hamburgh merchant of Mincing Lane.

His thoughts were most probably engaged upon his bales of merchandise, or if a female name arose to his tender recollections amid the softening influences of the twilight hour, it was that of "De Vrow Johanna," the gallant bark which on the morrow was to convey him far beyond the pleasant chime of Bow Bells.

Well, on rode Mr. Richardson towards London.

But hark!

What was that light echo which followed each almost noiseless tread of Strawberry's hoofs on the soft, chalky road?

He looked back, and perceived a well-mounted horseman making directly towards him.

Flight was in vain, for the middle of that desolate road had scarcely been reached, and his pursuer was gaining fast upon him.

"A highwayman, truly," said he. "It is well I have pistols for him."

The well-mounted pursuer soon drew up close beside him.

"I have a request, sir, which you must not refuse," said he, in a low and hurried tone.

Mr. Richardson recognised in his pursuer the young man whom he had but a short time before seen seated in the inn kitchen, and struck with his bewildered air, and the irresolute tone in which he addressed him, his curiosity now almost exceeded his anger.

"What!" he exclaimed, "is this the new method of saying 'Stand and deliver?'"

"I have a ring, sir," replied the other, endeavouring by a violent effort to suppress his agitation, and extending a ring with the left hand, while the other grasped a pistol, "and for this ring I must have twenty guineas!"

Mr. Richardson eyed him sternly.

"This is a bad trade," he said, at the same time that he glanced at the highwayman with a feeling of interest he could not resist. "Here's my purse; off with you, and seek a more honest method of procuring a livelihood."

The young man put back the proffered purse.

"No," he said, "take the ring, I pray you, and give me twenty guineas. Lend—lend it me, I pray, only twenty guineas!"

"A strange highwayman, in all truth," muttered Mr. Richardson, again surveying the robber with a degree of interest for which he could not account.

Then he counted out the gold.

"Well, mayhap," he said, "trouble may have brought you to this. But be warned by me, and seek out an honest calling. So give me the ring, and away."

The stranger eagerly snatched the gold, faintly articulating, "Heaven bless you!"

Mr. Richardson, not sorry to escape so easily from his first encounter with a highwayman, spurred Strawberry onwards, after casting a look behind.

There sat the young man, motionless on his horse, the hand which had been so eagerly stretched forth to secure the golden treasure still half held out, and his eyes with a wild and sorrowful expression fixed vacantly on the lowering sky.

"Poor fellow!" ejaculated the kind-hearted merchant, "I should greatly like to know what hath brought him to this."

He now examined the ring for which he had paid so high a price.

It was of plain gold, with a good-sized mocha stone, evidently not worth much above a pound, but with no inscription or crest or initials or anything that might lead to a discovery of its late owner.

Although baffled and disappointed in this he determined to keep the ring as a memorial of his first encounter with a highwayman; and the next day saw him setting sail from the shores of England.

Meanwhile the young man threw off his apathy, and, instead of remaining in the middle of the road all night as seemed likely to the old merchant, he turned his steps towards a large house which stood between the inn and the spot where he was now standing.

On arriving there he paused awhile and surveyed the place.

It was an old place, built ages before, and surrounded by very antiquated palings and antiquated trees and grounds.

But it was the residence of a wealthy man.

Clement Cormorant was a person of some renown among business men in the neighbourhood.

He had made a fortune in business, and retired to Cormorant House to live out his days and spend his money in company with a niece, Grace Dashwood, and an old housekeeper.

Old Cormorant had a taste for entomology, and might often be seen chasing butterflies and insects of all kinds, tumbling over the briars and rolling into pools, and braving all kinds of terrors from broken noses to broken shins in the pursuit of learning.

In the exercise of this peculiar branch of monomania he had for some time the assistance of Lucien Fairleigh, a young man who had come to him highly recommended.

He acted as a kind of general amanuensis to the old entomologist, who was also a great book-worm, and, being a very handsome as well as a well-educated fellow, he soon ingratiated himself with the niece.

Grace Dashwood was a splendid specimen of female beauty.

Tall and graceful, she possessed an elegant figure, whose finely-moulded limbs and pretty bust was fully revealed by the peculiar dress of the period.

She was very attractive, indeed, and was not at all disposed to reject the advances of young Fairleigh.

They had frequent chances of meeting one another, frequent opportunities of being together, for when old Cormorant was indoors it was very often that he was fast asleep and left them to talk as they please.

The old man had no objection to the match.

He was sufficiently sensible to see that they were well-suited, and, finding that the young man was well disposed and a faithful servant, he encouraged in him the belief that if he remained in his service a certain time, he should marry Grace Dashwood, and receive a very decent sum as dower.

But, in spite of this, he was a miser.

He loved his gold, grasped it whenever he could get it, and never paid any one's wages until he was absolutely compelled.

Of course Lucien Fairleigh had been engaged at a salary, but, though he had been with Clement Cormorant three years, he had never yet seen the colour of his money.

Lucien had an aged father and mother entirely dependent on him.

He had intended, of course, to give them the greater part of his salary in order that, in their declining years, they might live in that comfort which had been long denied them.

But he had been unable to give them a penny.

His father obtained a little work—work quite beyond his strength, but at length, two weeks before our story opens, he fell sick, and starvation threatened both.

Lucien, distracted and heart-broken, applied to old Cormorant for his salary.

The old miser put him off with promises.

He renewed his application, but with the same effect.

Then came his temptation.

His father had had nothing to eat for two days.

His mother had been starved longer, though the son knew it not.

Coming home from them, burning with rage; boiling with indignation at old Cormorant, for not shelling out the salary; wretched and depressed at the scene of woe he had left, he passed into his master's study, and saw him, as he thought, fast asleep.

The room was very quiet; the table strewn with papers—one of the drawers wide open.

He approached Cormorant.

His intention was to seize him by the collar, and shake him into wakefulness, and demand his money.

Ere he proceeded half way, a sight caught his eye.

A glittering, tempting sight.

A heap of dazzling gold!

The temptation was too strong.

On one side, a mother and father starving and dying.

Eyes pleading for help which had watched over him in tenderness.

On the other side was the heap of gold, which was nothing to the miser, and everything to Lucien —a heap of wealth, from which he would miss nothing.

The tempter was at his elbow and he fell.

Into the glittering heap his fingers glided, and counting twenty sovereigns, he placed them in his pocket.

At this moment old Cormorant awoke.

He glanced at the intruder in terror.

He rubbed his eyes.

He could scarcely believe the evidence of his senses.

He rose transfixed with horror when he *did* recognise the robber, and stood there with glaring eyes and mouth wide open.

He could not speak, he could not move, he could not make a single sign to stay the robber.

He watched his retreating figure—he saw that he did not turn his head, and he made up his mind.

Lucien was from that moment an alien.

He acted upon the erroneous idea that he was only taking his own, and that he would repay it as soon as he received his salary.

He went joyfully to his father and mother, relieved their distress, bought them food, and paid their rent.

For a few hours he felt happy.

It *was* but for this time.

When he presented himself once more at Clement Cormorant's house the door was closed against him, and a note placed in his hand.

It was from old Cormorant, and ran as follows:—

"LUCIEN FAIRLEIGH.—I have been kind to you—very kind to you. You have repaid me with base ingratitude. I saw you in the act of robbing me. For the sake of the affection which my niece bears you I will forbear to prosecute you, but never attempt to see either me or her again.

"CLEMENT CORMORANT."

For a few moments Lucien Fairleigh stood in silent misery.

He read and re-read the letter.

But there was no avoiding the one stern fact.

He was discovered!

The housekeeper, who still remained at the door, watched him curiously.

She knew something was wrong, but had not the slightest conception of the truth.

"Can I see Miss Dashwood?" asked Lucien, eagerly.

The woman looked puzzled, but after awhile consented to arrange a meeting outside the house.

The lovers met, and an explanation ensued.

Grace Dashwood did not regard the matter so seriously as Lucien Fairleigh.

She felt convinced that her uncle would forgive him if he would only return the money.

Lucien did not give credit to her assertion; but even if he had, of what avail would it have been?

He had no friends, no one of whom he could ask a favour, and he went away far more dejected than he had come.

So time passed on until the arrival of the rich merchant at the inn suggested a desperate remedy for the evil.

So he scaled the wall eagerly, and acting upon a preconcerted signal tapped at Grace Dashwood's window.

In a few minutes she had dressed herself, and was out with him on the old terrace.

"I have the money, dearest Grace," he murmured, as she clasped his loved form to her heaving breast. "Can you obtain for me an interview with your uncle?"

"Yes; I will make him see you!" she cried. "If you return him the money what room can he have for complaint? Enter through my chamber, I will lead you to him."

"Stay! Where is he? He will be angry if he is disturbed from his bed."

"He is not in bed; he is at work among his insects. He has made a sad mess of it since you have been away."

The young man again pressed his mistress

ardently to his heart, and then passing through the bed-room reached the door of the library.

Grace Dashwood entered abruptly.

She wished to take him by surprise.

The old man was so busy with his insects that he did not observe their entrance.

He had both hands passed through his grey hair, and was staring hopelessly at a confused heap of little animals.

He looked up sharply, but not at all angrily at Grace when she passed her arm round his neck.

"Are you come to help me?" he said. "I am in a terrible confusion."

He had not yet perceived Lucien.

"No!" cried Grace, "I have brought Lucien. He comes to return you your money."

The countenance of the old man changed at once.

He sprang from his chair, his eyes glaring, his whole form dilated with anger.

"Come not near me," he yelled, "base deceiver and thief! Go, ungrateful miscreant! leave my house at once! Do you think I wish for stolen gold? You can have come by no money honestly, you a beggar and a starveling! Leave my presence this instant lest I stain my hands with your blood!"

As he uttered these last words with the fierceness of a tiger, he seized a pistol and presented it at the head of Lucien Fairleigh.

In an instant Grace Dashwood had thrust herself between her lover and the fatal weapon.

"Minion!" shouted the old man. "Minion! Dost thou, too, dare me? Dost thou come between me and my just revenge? Dost thou protect a beggar and a thief who will have no resource now but the highway and the gallows?"

Lucien Fairleigh gently pushed Grace Dashwood aside, and stood boldly before the infuriated miser.

"You have spoken rightly there, old wretch," he cried; "you do well to talk of my only resource, you who forced me to sin by your beggarly rapacity and wretched lust for gold; you who starved my father and my mother, refused me my rightful earnings and compelled me to take what you should have given. You have spoken aright, the high-road is my only resource. Upon the high-road this night I have earned these twenty sovereigns, on the high-road I will earn a fortune and return to claim your niece, whose love even your hideous hate cannot wrest from me."

With these words he rushed through the open door, heeding not the form which knelt and cried, "Lucien, come back, come back!" and only just escaping the bullet which the enraged Cormorant fired at his head.

True to his word he escaped from the house, and, proceeding round to the stables, saddled the splendid brown mare which the old man, in spite of his miserly habits, kept for Grace Dashwood's use.

He then hastily wrote a few lines in pencil on a paper which he attached to the manger.

DEAR GRACE,—I have taken your pet mare Cherry. It will bear me, I hope, through many a strange adventure, and bring me at last back to you, my first and only love.

LUCIEN FAIRLEIGH.

In a few minutes after he was riding merrily along the dark highway.

The white horse on which he had ridden from the inn he left attached to a tree, that its colour might not be the means of his being recognised.

The night was beautiful.

The moon was at its full, and the stars shone brightly everywhere.

The odour of the scented fields struck agreeably on the senses, while the cool though gentle breeze served to brace the nerves and exhilarate the frame.

"A life on the road must be a pleasant one," cried Lucien, intoxicated with anger at his late adventure, and influenced by the beautiful scene around him. 'Hurrah for the road!' has been the cry of others, then why not for me?"

As he spoke he heard a faint noise in the distance, and, in a few moments, he saw a man running hurriedly towards him.

The new-comer wore a mask, and, by the way he held his hand to his side, it was evident he was wounded.

On seeing Lucien he ran towards him.

"Stranger," he cried, "I am wounded and in danger. Will you save me?"

"How can I save you?" asked Lucien Fairleigh, in surprise.

"By giving me a seat on your horse," he said, in a voice which was tremulous with running and weak with pain.

"Certainly," cried Lucien. "Here, I will aid you."

He leaped down and assisted the wounded stranger to the saddle.

He then got up behind, and, turning the horse's head, rode away in a direction opposite to that by which the wounded man had come.

"Stranger," said the latter, "you are generous and kind. You are going out of your way to assist me."

"Not I; all roads are alike to me. I seek adventures."

"Of what kind?"

"Those in which purses are concerned."

The stranger laughed.

"Fortune always leads me right," he said. "I am one whom, perhaps, you have often heard of— Moonlight Jack, the king of the highway. A sorry king, you will say, just now, more's the pity. Yet I can scarcely complain, when it is my own fault."

Lucien Fairleigh felt like one in a dream.

The name of Moonlight Jack had been a bye-word on the road for years.

He was the terror of the timid, the admiration of the brave.

It appeared, indeed, beyond all probability that, having taken to the road but a few hours before, he should have fallen in with such a man.

Then suddenly a shiver ran through his frame.

In those days high and low rejoiced in a superstition which, in some phases of life, entirely destroyed all enjoyment.

He remembered having heard that Moonlight Jack had suffered on the scaffold, and that he had been hung in chains.

Was it his wraith that sat upon the saddle?

Was he riding with a dead man?

Though he trembled, however, he did not lose his presence of mind.

"Moonlight Jack!" he cried, "I heard that he was executed at Tyburn, and hung in chains."

Jack laughed.

"So he was," he answered, "but he was too much for the hangman. Though hung in chains, he was saved last night, and lives to avenge himself. You have said you will aid me?"

"I will."

"Are you willing to join me?"

"I am."

"Then ride right on until you reach the cross-road; take there the road to the right; at the tenth house on the left stop, and, alighting at the door, knock, and ask for Gipsy Bess. You will know—what——"

As he said these words he reeled in the saddle, and would have fallen had not Lucien Fairleigh caught him in his arms.

He had fainted.

"His strength is spent," said Lucien, as he urged his horse to greater speed. "I must be quick, or I shall, indeed, have a dead man to carry."

So saying, he galloped on, and reaching the cross-road, turned sharply to the right.

About a quarter of a mile down he reached the tenth house.

It was a queer, old-fashioned place, approached by a rustic drawbridge.

This drawbridge was now down, spanning a broad deep ditch, full of noisome water.

It always *was* down when Moonlight Jack was absent.

When he was at home it was drawn high up, so that no one could approach the house.

Lucien hesitated not.

He had engaged in a strange adventure, and undertaken to save his companion, and it would have been the worst of cowardice to shrink at the last moment.

So he hurried across the drawbridge, and knocked loudly at the door.

In a moment it was opened.

"What want you?" cried a gruff voice, as a shaggy head protruded itself.

"Gipsy Bess," returned Lucien Fairleigh, "I bring to you Moonlight Jack, wounded and fainting, so aid me in lowering him from his horse."

Three men came out at once, and in a few minutes Moonlight Jack was safe inside the house, where Gipsy Bess tended him.

The door was closed, the brown mare was led round to the stable, and Lucien was detained amid the band of ill-looking, lowering men.

"You'll have to stop here till *he* wakes," said the shaggy-headed party who had answered him at the door. "I don't know how this little affair happened, for you don't look quite the right sort."

"If you don't like my appearance, you can go to the devil," returned Lucien, and, so saying, he stalked towards the chimney-corner, and sat himself down by the fire, which, now in the chilliness of the short hours of morning, was peculiarly acceptable.

These words effectually prevented any further interference, and so, dozing over the fire, we must leave him while we return to the inn where Lucien had met the traveller, in order that the reader may understand how Moonlight Jack fell into so terrible a scrape.

CHAPTER III.

MOONLIGHT JACK AT THE INN — THE ROUND ROOM — THE MYSTERIOUS VOICES — THE CONSTABLES BREAK IN — THE STAIN OF BLOOD — THE PURSUIT — THE BALL-ROOM — THE CHILLY WIND — THE DISAPPEARANCE OF ELLA HUNTLEY — THE SEARCH — THE WHITE SPECTRE — THE RETURN — THE FORCED MARRIAGE.

ABOUT an hour after the departure of Mr. Richardson, the city merchant, from the inn another traveller entered.

Before his arrival the conversation of the guests, now just preparing to go home, had turned upon highwaymen.

Mr. Richardson himself had started the subject, it will be remembered, and many who had some little distance to go began to feel somewhat less comfortable than before.

Several extra glasses of grog were swallowed, and heavy sticks grasped, and each one seemed endeavouring to calm his own fear by casting ridicule on his companions and striving to increase their alarm.

"Well," said Boniface—Sam Groggins by name, "well, there is one thing which we folks can congratulate ourselves upon, and that is the execution of Jack Tyrrell—him as they called Moonlight Jack. He *was* a man, too, a handsome, well-made, noble fellow as ever you clapped eyes on ; but he was a rare devil, and frightened every one off the road."

"Don't you holler afore you're out of the wood," said a steady-looking old file of a farmer, as he buttoned his thick coat up to his chin, and then looked at his pistols, "don't you holler afore you're out of the wood, Master Groggins. Moonlight Jack isn't dead at all."

The company started in wonder and terror.

As for Groggins, he stood with his mouth gaping open like that of a fish.

"Not dead?" he said. "Why, he's been executed and hung in chains."

"Yes, but he isn't dead for all that," cried the farmer. "He was alive when they hung him in chains. His friends saved him, and last night as Rasper the thief-taker was going by in a coach they seized him and hung him up in Jack's place. What think ye of that, my hearties?"

"Why, it's just what you'd have done yourself in the same position," said a loud, manly voice, and as the words were uttered, a tall, commanding figure stood among them.

It was Moonlight Jack !

The company stared at him in complete wonderment, and not a few of them turned deadly pale.

Jack Tyrrell glanced round him in amusement.

The startled faces of the people were certainly enough to make any one laugh ; any one, at least, who could boast such an iron constitution and indomitable courage as he could.

Jack's face was well known.

The landlord who had been congratulating his friends upon the execution of the famous marauder, knew Tyrrell of old.

He had often opened a bottle of wine with him, and had never, moreover, been over-particular as to whence the money came.

Considering, indeed, the many benefits which Groggins had received from the gallant highwayman, he should have been the last to glory in his death, and when he met the eyes of Moonlight Jack the thought at once occurred to him that his ingratitude might be repaid in a way to which he might object.

"Why, Jack," he cried, "who, in the name of all that's sublime, expected to see you here?"

"Not you, at least," answered Jack. "From what I heard you telling the worthy people here, I am no welcome visitor ; but I will not quarrel with you. Let me have a good stiff glass of grog, and when you have mixed that let me have the Round Room to myself for an hour. I've got some accounts to settle."

"What, is the devil coming to square up with you, Master Jack?" asked an old man, with a bent form, and long white hair streaming over his shoulders.

He was Jem Barrow the sexton, and presumed upon his age.

"May be he is, Master Barrow," returned Jack. "He's coming to swear that I cheated him the other night when I changed places with Captain Rasper."

'DO YOU KNOW THESE FACES?'"—*See page* 14.

"How cheated him?" said the landlord, return-ing with the glass of grog.

"Why, you see, the devil was pleased when he thought I was dead, because I was some one worth having; while, as for old Rasper, he knew he could have him whenever he chose. So it wasn't a good exchange, you see. This is good grog, land-lord. Your health, gentlemen all."

So saying the daring robber nodded to the com-pany, drank his bumper off at a draught, and taking the light proffered him by the landlord, walked up to the Round Room as orderly as if he had been the owner of the house for years.

The Round Room was a strange place.

It was absolutely round.

The door through which Moonlight Jack entered was rounded to the shape of the rest of the

chamber, and when it was closed it would have been difficult for a stranger to discover where the opening was.

The furniture in the room was rounded also, and in the centre was a large round table.

At this table Moonlight Jack sat down, and drawing a pair of pistols from his pocket laid them on it.

He remained there so long that at last the landlord began to wonder what he was about.

The landlord crept up, and then the landlady.

They could hear Jack's voice, and another voice too, that of a woman.

How came she there?

Here was the mystery.

She had not entered by the door, since the door had never been opened.

No. 2.

She did not belong to the inn, for, besides the landlady, there was no female in the house but the chambermaid, who was still below stairs.

Who could she be?

They heard her voice raised in entreaty, and his raised in anger, and they were becoming racked by a most violent and overwhelming curiosity, when a noise below attracted their attention.

The landlady crept down again, leaving the landlord with his ear still glued to the keyhole.

The new arrivals were a *posse* of constables.

They were in search of Moonlight Jack.

The landlady, who feared to be inculpated, pointed upstairs.

At the door of the room they found the landlord still listening at the keyhole.

"We come to arrest John Tyrrell!" cried the head constable. "Where is he?"

"He is in that room, I suppose, gentlemen," said Groggins. "He went in there, and has been talking for the last hour with some lady, though the Lord only knows how she got in there."

"Open the door, then," answered the constable. "We will see for ourselves."

The landlord did so, with a duplicate key, and advancing into the room, drew back suddenly with a cry of astonishment.

The chamber was empty!

On the table was a woman's glove; on the floor a stain of blood.

This was all the sign that life had been there.

The window was closed and bolted on the inside; everything was arranged exactly as the landlord had left it.

The landlord stood aghast.

The constable shook him roughly by the shoulder.

"Come, come," he said. "Tell us where this man is, and no nonsense!"

"I swear I know not!" returned Boniface, all of a tremble. "My guests can prove that he came up into this room alone and that no one entered with him or after him. I, and my wife, when we listened at the door, heard two voices—a man's and a woman's. And now they are gone. I shall begin to think it was a spirit. I like not men who are hung in chains and then escape."

The constables were puzzled.

All they could do was to take possession of the glove, and warn the landlord severely.

Just as they descended the staircase there was an uproar outside.

"He is here! He is here!" shouted a voice.

It was that of one of the constables, who had been left to watch outside.

Those who had entered the inn quickly joined them.

Just in time to see Moonlight Jack spring from a plantation near the hostelry out into the high road.

The constable raised a pistol and fired.

The shot took effect, hitting Jack Tyrrell in the side.

But he still kept on running like a deer, until, as we have seen, he met with Lucien Fairleigh.

But the mystery was, who and where was the woman who had been in the room with the highwayman?

A strict watch was kept over every portion of the inn.

Not a single point was neglected to be watched, but no sign came.

Whoever and whatever she was she had disappeared.

From this point we must shift the scene to a house in the same neighbourhood.

It was a splendid place—the mansion of a wealthy nobleman.

The Marquis of Huntley was a man whose riches were the only good thing about him.

He was a favourite at Court; a handsome man, considering that his age was forty, and the keeper of a splendid establishment.

He had two daughters.

The one a dark, stern beauty, with raven tresses, and black eyes and commanding form.

The other, a fair-haired girl of some twenty summers, with a full, voluptuous form, a sweet, lovely face and an expression the very opposite of her sisters.

The one was called Lady Ella Huntley, the other, the dark sister, was named Lady Edith.

More of them we need not say here.

Suffice it to say that in the household at Huntley Castle, Lady Ella was a toy and plaything, the Lady Edith was the queen.

There was no mother, and to the elder daughter the marquis gave over entirely the charge of everything.

He himself moved about the house like a spirit of evil.

He was gloomy, dismal, unsociable at home.

It was only when in the society of strangers that he was affable and sociable.

On the evening in question, the same evening which saw Moonlight Jack's strange visit to the inn, a gay party took place at Huntley Castle.

All the fashion and beauty of the neighbourhood had been invited, and the ball-rooms were full to overflowing.

Both Lady Ella and Lady Edith looked supremely beautiful.

Both were dressed in low ball-dresses, displaying freely their large bosoms and rounded shoulders; those of the one, pale, white and cold, those of the other glowing with the hue of health.

The black tresses of the one contrasted but unfavourably with the golden tresses of the other.

Yet, on this occasion there was a noticeable difference in the behaviour of the two sisters.

Lady Ella was generally the gayest among the gay.

It was the Lady Edith who was reserved and haughty.

On this occasion positions were reversed.

Lady Edith seemed to have stolen from her sister all her liveliness and vivacity, for her eyes sparkled, her whole person seemed impregnated with a new life, while Ella was pale and distracted and seemed to take no pleasure in anything.

She danced because she imagined that it would seem odd if she did not; she talked as if to pass the time, and even made a very feeble effort to flirt with Sir Percy Delaine, a young courtier whom her father had tried to force upon her times out of mind.

But the Marquis of Huntley was too clever a reader of the human heart not to perceive that something was amiss.

Again and again he spoke to her and endeavoured to extract from her the cause of her abstractedness and uneasiness.

But he could not.

In his own dark heart he had suspicions.

He had good reasons for them.

He had heard, he had seen enough to be certain that something was preying upon his daughter's heart.

There had been whispered stories of her wanderings by night when all else were in bed ; of strange meetings with an unknown gallant ; of moaning noises in her room ; of conversations with invisible persons.

Recollect that, as I have said, this was in the year 1728, and superstition was the order of the day.

Remember, too, that Jacobite plots were rife, and you will readily understand that the fair girl's wanderings and mysterious conversations were linked with doings with the evil one and Jacobite conspiracies in addition ; two things, by the way, which some persons considered necessarily joined.

However this might be, the fair and joyous Lady Ella was this night gloomy and sad, and, as the hours wore on she became more sad and gloomy still, until, at last, about midnight, she withdrew from the merry throng and sat down in a bay window which overlooked the grounds.

Suddenly, just after Sir Percy Delaine had left her, the windows were thrown open, a cold wind swept through the room, causing the bare shoulders of the women to shiver with cold, and sending a chill even to the hearts of the men.

Sir Percy turned to close them, lest the desperate and unearthly cold might strike to the soul of his beloved, but as he did so the casement was closed with a slam, *and Lady Ella was gone!*

She had not passed through the dancers, for no one had seen her, and no doors had been opened.

Sir Percy tremblingly sought the Marquis of Huntley.

To him he told his story, and the fears he entertained that Lady Ella had thrown herself from the casement.

The marquis looked grave.

" You have not, I hope, spoken of this in the ball-room ?" he said,

" I have not, my lord," returned Sir Percy. " I imagined that it would be imprudent."

" You did rightly," said the marquis. " These idle stories are best reserved from the many."

" Stay, my lord," cried the young baronet, testily. " You use the word 'idle ;' do you apply that word to me because you deem my story false ?"

" Not so, not so," replied Lord Huntley, " but this is, without doubt, a freak of my foolish child's. She requires some one to guard her, to be her protector —she needs a husband. Sir Percy, if your inclinations are the same as they have been, my daughter becomes your wife this night."

The young man's face flushed.

The hand of Lady Ella he had long eagerly sought, but this unlooked-for haste he could scarcely believe in.

" My lord," he said, " I need scarcely tell you that my feelings are unchanged, but I question whether your daughter will consent to so precipitate a union."

The Marquis of Huntley frowned.

" Her consent having been once given will not be asked again," he said. " If *you* are willing, the marriage shall take place this night."

" *I* am willing, my lord," returned Sir Percy ; " but are you not in fear for your daughter's life ? Do you not fear that she has thrown herself from the casement ? I, for my part, should propose that

your retainers should light their torches at once, and seek beneath the window. Remember, at this very moment she may be breathing out her life upon the sharp rocks."

The marquis thought a moment, repressing the scornful laugh which seemed forcing itself to his lips.

" Well," he said, " Heaven knows what this wild girl may do. Go to Anthony Sleeman ; tell him to accompany you to the Blue Rock, that is the great block of marble which is beneath the eastern casement. Seek there ; but you will find, I trust, nothing. Your bride will be awaiting you here."

Sir Percy did not wait for a second permission.

He at once went in search of the men, and within a few moments they were at the Blue Rock, a mass of marble so called from the broad blue veins which everywhere passed through it.

They examined every nook and corner, but could find nothing.

There was no sign of any fatality, but just as Sir Percy Delaine was about to call back his men he fancied he saw the marble move, and a white figure pass beside it.

It must to all appearances, however, have been an hallucination, for when he looked by the light of the torch all was as before.

The Marquis of Huntley expressed no surprise upon hearing the result of his search.

" I expected as much," he said ; " wait patiently and you will see your bride again among the dancers."

Time passed.

The ball went on without interruption.

No one had observed the disappearance of Lady Ella.

Each girl was too busy with her lover ; each cavalier was too busy with his mistress ; each elderly dame too busy with scandal to take notice of her movements.

Sir Percy Delaine watched eagerly.

Presently his patience was rewarded.

Lady Ella, pale, but smiling, entered by the door, passed through the dancers and made her way to the spot where Sir Percy was standing.

He had not observed her entrance, and seeing her suddenly by his side he started in astonishment.

Lady Ella broke into a low silvery laugh.

" Did I frighten you, Sir Percy ?" she said.

" Well, Lady Ella, you *did* alarm me," he said, hesitatingly. " Your disappearance just now caused both me and your father some uneasiness. I searched everywhere beneath the window and near the Blue Rock, for we feared you might have fallen from the casement. And now, re-appearing so suddenly and without my seeing you enter the room, you certainly *did* alarm me. But, come, since you are returned, shall we join the dancers ?"

Ella laughingly complied.

They were soon amid the gayest of the gay.

Suddenly Sir Percy stopped.

" See, Lady Ella," he cried, in a distracted tone, " there is blood upon your arm. It is dripping on your dress."

Lady Ella glanced anxiously at her arm.

Then she bit her lip with evident vexation.

" It is nothing," she said ; " a mere scratch. I suppose it was my bracelet that wounded it."

" Allow me to bind it up," returned Sir Percy, taking gently hold of the warm plump arm.

He took her fine cambric handkerchief, wiped away the stains, and saw a wide deep gash.

"Why, here is a dagger's wound!" he cried. "What means this, Lady Ella?"

A spasm as of agony passed over her features.

"You see it pains me to speak of it," she cried; "do not ask me more questions, Sir Percy, if you love me."

He bound her arm up tenderly, pressed her little hand to his lips, and said,

"Trust me with that secret some other day then, Lady Ella, when I have more right to ask you."

She blushed deeply, but did not reply.

Sir Percy drew her arm gently through his, and led her out of the throng.

He was just about to address her when the Marquis of Huntley approached.

"Ella," he said, "I wish to speak with you. Sir Percy Delaine, it is now too late to carry out what I spoke of but now. To-morrow evening, however, I wish to see you early."

He bowed to Sir Percy and led Ella away.

What passed at that conference I cannot here relate.

Suffice it to say, however, that within an hour Lady Ella retired to her own chamber, pale, agitated, under the influence evidently of some fierce excitement.

Very soon after this a man, dressed in ball costume, but evidently belonging to the lower classes of society, entered the ball-room, and elbowed his way somewhat rudely through the dancers.

He made his way into the presence of the marquis.

Here, without preparation, he took him by the arm, and hurrying him on one side, said,

"Dismiss the guests. All is done, and you are wanted."

"For long?"

"For this night only."

The marquis mused.

"Why dismiss them?" he said. "Better let them stop and remain the night."

"Then how about your departure?"

"*You* can arrange that. Proceed to the ball-room, tell the guests that I am taken suddenly ill, that I am retired to my room, but I desire them to keep up the festivities, and remain at my house all night. To-morrow evening we shall have fine doings here."

"On what occasion?"

"A marriage."

"A marriage?"

"Yes; cannot you guess *whose* marriage it will be?"

"Not I."

"That of my daughter Ella."

The man shuddered.

"What again?" he said.

"Yes. Why should it not be so?"

"Who is the victim this time?"

"Sir Percy Delaine."

"A thousand pities: a fine, handsome, brave young man, such as he, should be reserved for a better fate; but time presses, I must go."

He left the room and re-entered the bed-room.

In a few moments a whispered rumour went round the room to the effect that some one wished to address them.

The dance and the hubbub ceased.

"Ladies and gentlemen," said the stranger, "I regret to announce to you that the Marquis of Huntley has been seized by a sudden attack of illness. The physician, who is now with him, is confident that it is nothing but what can be relieved permanently by a night of rest. The marquis, therefore, wishes you to continue your festivities to as late an hour as you please, and to remain his guests until to-morrow. To-morrow evening will be the celebration of a family festival.

A few moments were devoted to speculations as to the particular malady which could so suddenly have assailed the host.

Then the guests set themselves again to the labour of pleasure, and music and laughter once more prevailed throughout the house.

When all were so occupied in festivity as to make it safe to move about, the marquis passed down into the court-yard with the new arrival.

They went into the stable, saddled a horse, and led it round to the front gate, where the stranger's steed was tied to a tree.

They then mounted, and in a few moments were proceeding at a headlong pace down the road.

They had not travelled more than a mile when they turned off sharply to the left, and after proceeding about a hundred yards down a narrow lane, stopped before a dense coppice.

"Let us be careful," said the Marquis of Huntley. "I tell you what it is, Dawson; I have a belief that we have been watched times out of number; let us wait a moment and glance round us."

They looked anxiously up and down the lane, and, then, dismounting from their horses, they pushed aside a mass of brushwood, and led their horses through it.

On the other side was an open space, where was a building something like a brick-built tomb.

It was open only on one side, and was covered over with grass.

Approaching this door, the Marquis of Huntley took a key from his pocket and opened it.

The horses were then tied to a tree, and the nobleman and his attendant descended the steps, at the bottom of which they found themselves at a large, well-lighted room, in which a number of men were sitting round a table.

Their presence was eagerly welcomed, and the lower doors were then closed upon the conspirators.

CHAPTER IV.

THE BALL-ROOM—THE MARRIAGE—THE CLOUD OF FIRE—THE WARNING HAND—THE NUPTIAL CHAMBER — THE BAPTISM OF BLOOD — THE MURDER — THE ALARM — DISAPPEARANCE OF THE BRIDE—THE SCENE IN THE GLEN.

THE next night came.

The guests at Huntley Castle were once more assembled in the grand ball-room, and the Marquis of Huntley appeared among them gay and smiling as before.

"Dear friends," he said, during a pause in the dance, "dear friends, I have a surprise for you. This night is to see the celebration of the marriage of my daughter, Lady Ella, with Sir Percy Delaine. There have been reasons why it has been kept so secret. A priest is now in attendance; will you attend us to the banqueting-hall?"

With this brief speech he led the way into the old banqueting-hall, where the portraits of the grim old ancestors, and the coats of mail, looked down upon the assembled guests as if reproving them for their levity.

At one end of the hall, near the huge fire which crackled and blazed up the chimney, the bride and bridegroom and the clergyman, with Lady Edith Huntley, stood ready.

Ella looked very beautiful.

She was dressed in a low-necked robe, displaying her bare white shoulders and her splendid bosom, over which fell the wavy masses of her golden hair.

She appeared under the influence of intense nervous excitement.

Her breast heaved, her hands clenched nervously together, her eyes sparkled, and were surrounded by a broad black rim, which contrasted strangely with the rich carnation of her cheeks.

Sir Percy Delaine looked supremely happy.

If any evil presentiment weighed upon the heart of his bride it did not affect him.

The guests having ranged themselves round, the ceremony commenced.

Nothing occurred to interrupt the proceedings.

Everything went on as it should, and in a few moments Sir Percy Delaine and Lady Ella Huntley were man and wife.

The banquet which followed was of the most magnificent description, and the bride and bridegroom were the observed, admired, and envied of every one.

They would scarcely have envied Lady Ella had they known her real feelings.

Light-hearted as she seemed to any one who did not closely observe her, the wild excitement of her appearance did not in the least subside.

Presently, during an animated conversation, in which the Lady Ella was taking no part, one of the domestics approaching her slipped a note into her hand.

She did not stop to read it.

The superscription seemed enough to convince her how to act.

The marquis, her father, was the only one in the company who saw the servant bring the letter.

He turned very pale, and leaned towards her.

"It has come," she said. "I knew it would."

"What is it?"

"There is a dagger upon it. It is a summons to appear. I am going. Do not seem to observe me."

She turned then to her young husband, and said to him, with a smile,

"Percy, I feel faint. I have your permission, I am sure, to retire for an hour. I will return when the banquet is over."

Sir Percy pressed her hand.

"Certainly, dearest," he cried. "I will lead you from the table."

"No," she said, hurriedly, "that will make people observe me more. My maid, Jessica, here, will accompany me. I will return ere long."

Sir Percy Delaine had had before this many evidences that his beautiful bride had a will of her own.

Yet never until this moment had he known her to speak in a tone so authoritative.

He could make no objection, however.

Ere he could reply she had swept from the room.

She passed swiftly along the corridor, up the broad marble staircase into her own chamber,

pressing her hand tightly over her white bosom, and keeping her eyes fixed upon the floor.

Jessica followed her.

At the door of the bed-room, however, her mistress dismissed her.

"Jessica," she said, "you can return to the servants' hall. I have no need of you here."

She then entered the room abruptly and fastened herself in.

As soon as she had done so she took from a peg a heavy shawl and wrapped it round her bare shoulders.

Then, taking a lamp in her hand, she proceeded to a portion of the room close to the head of the bed, and, holding up the light, brought to view a small round plate of brass.

This she pressed.

A door at once flew open, and a gust of wind rushed up so violently that the lamp was nearly extinguished.

She hesitated not, however.

Evidently the route was not a novel one to her.

Down the steep stone steps she went until she reached the beginning of a subterranean passage, which appeared to wind away interminably into the distance.

She did not, however, proceed far down this underground corridor, but, stopping at a kind of doorway, she passed through it by means of a key, and found herself in some dark and dismal cloisters.

To any one who was unused to the place it was horribly dark and dreary.

The moon was up, and its brightness, as its light lay in fretted patches on the floors, only served to render more gloomy and spectral the heavy shadows that lurked around.

She paused as she entered, and held the lamp aloft.

Its feeble rays penetrated but a short distance into the dense darkness, but it brought a reply.

Immediately the heavy tread of a man's boots was heard, and a tall, broadly-built stranger stood before her.

He was covered from shoulder to heel by a cloak; his gold-embroidered hat was slouched over his eyes, and his features were concealed by a mask.

"Ella, you are here punctually," he said. "Have I come in time to prevent you from committing a deadly crime, or am I again too late?"

Ella shuddered.

"There has been no crime committed," she said; "but you are aware that this evening I have been married to Sir Percy Delaine?"

These words, delivered with some firmness—although, as I have said, the stranger's voice made her shudder—these words appeared to exasperate the stranger to the highest pitch of madness.

He stamped so heavily upon the pavement that the echo went stamping round the entire cloister.

"D——n!" he cried. "Are you not satisfied yet? Do you wish more blood? Have not your two victims sufficed you?"

"They were no victims of mine!" she said, vehemently. "How dare you accuse *me* of crimes, Lord Brandon—you who have been guilty of hideous murders, of atrocious sins, which you have laid to *my* charge?"

"They lie on *your* soul, Ella Huntley!" cried Lord Brandon, in a solemn tone, which resounded dismally in the old cloisters. "If *I* am the dagger which avenges, you are the power which drives the weapon home. You are *my* wife, Ella, in the sight of Heaven, and I have sworn that no other man shall wed you. You may marry a hundred husbands but so surely as the night comes they will die !"

He paused.

"Come with me !" he cried, suddenly seizing the trembling girl by the arm. "Come with me, and I will show you a sight which may perhaps bring you to your senses."

Lady Ella had no power to resist.

The stranger's hand closed upon her arm like a vice, and he dragged her away through the echoing stone passage, till they reached an arched doorway.

Beneath this they passed, and the stranger producing from his pocket a lantern, opened a small, iron-bound door, and led Lady Ella into a small chamber, at one end of which was a huge black box.

There was a small fire in the grate, which proved that some one had been occupying it recently.

Brandon closed the door behind him.

"You see my home," he said.

"Your home ?" exclaimed Ella Huntley, in astonishment.

"Yes," cried Brandon, savagely. "Why should it not be ? I am in my father's house, and have a right here."

"You acknowledge it now then ?" exclaimed Ella Huntley. "You acknowledge that you are my brother, and yet you dare to call me your wife !"

Brandon laughed wildly.

"Acknowledge it ?" he cried. "No, I do *not* acknowledge it. It is a base, a malicious lie forged by the devil and his fiends, to hurry me on to my doom. No, no, I am *not* your brother. I am *not* the son of the Marquis of Huntley ; but since it has been said so, I have claimed as a privilege a residence in this living tomb, where elsewhere I have no place to rest my head. But come, let us finish this scene !" he cried fiercely.

He approached the huge black box and removed the pall which concealed its cover.

Then he raised the lid and beckoned Ella to approach.

She did so tremblingly.

Then she recoiled in horror.

The box was formed into two coffins.

In these coffins lying side by side were two human skeletons.

Upon the breast of each was a portrait and a dagger.

"Do you know these faces ?" cried Brandon, fiercely, as he raised the miniatures and dragged her hands from before her face.

"Yes, yes, take them away !" she cried. "I want not to see them."

Brandon laughed.

"You know them well, I have no doubt," he cried. "This dark one here you married because you imagined he would awe me, and that I should not dare to harm him. He was a fine handsome fellow. I knew him well, and have passed as his friend ; but in marrying him you broke your oath to me, and he died suddenly at the altar. I killed him ; you know it. It was *my* hand which administered the poison ! Was this no warning, that you again tempted me ?"

Ella replied not.

Her eyes were fixed upon the second miniature.

"Ha, ha !" he cried, with his wild laugh again. "Ha, ha ! *He* was fair to look upon, was he not ? You married him in France that *I* might not follow you, and that people might not know of the union. But *I* was on your track. I watched you. I saw you toying with him, and I pitied him, for he was but a boy, and his eyes and his ringlets would have made him pass well for a woman. But you married him, and on your wedding night when you entered your nuptial chamber a man staggered in after you bloodstained and ghastly—a man who had followed you down the dark corridor, but who could not speak from pain and weakness. This was your husband. Still this was no warning. Again you are married ; again to-night blood will stain the hand, which, but for your own obstinacy, might be pure and spotless."

"It is so now !" murmured Ella, "it is so now ! There is no blood upon my conscience, though it must lie heavily upon yours !"

The tall strong man paced wildly to and fro for a few moments, and then, at length, breaking into a softer mood, he took Ella's hand, led her to a seat, and knelt before her.

"Oh, Ella !" he cried, passionately, "why has this come to pass ? Why have you driven me to these deeds of blood ? Why have you made me a bye-word and a terror when I might have been your happy husband ?"

"Brandon," said Ella, gently, "when I knew not our terrible story I was kind to you—I loved you. I married you. When I vowed to be constant to you I meant my oath, and would have kept it. But ere the night of our wedding-day arrived it was proved to me that you were my brother—proved beyond a shadow of a doubt—and I left you. What could I do else ? The hideous crime of being my brother's wife I could not commit, and I will swear, Brandon, here, in the presence of the dead whom your mad jealousy has destroyed, that no sins of yours, no crimes, no threats, shall induce me to change my purpose."

"Then, by the powers of hell, I swear that you *shall* be mine !" cried Brandon, springing up. "To-night, ere the hour when Sir Percy Delaine hopes to clasp you in his arms, he shall die by this hand, and on the dagger which drinks his blood I will swear vengeance on the next victim whom you lead to the altar ! Mark me. I am a man of action—not words—and if you wish to save Sir Percy you have but a short hour before you."

"Save him ! how can you ?"

"There are but two ways. Declare your marriage with me, or fly with me now. In the end you must accept my terms. You know my determined spirit well. Remember, too, there is something due to my clemency. You are in my power at this moment."

Ella rose and drew from her bosom a poniard.

"You know this dagger well," she cried. "You are aware that its point carries deadly poison. One scratch from this would be your instant death. I trust, you see, not to your clemency but to your fear."

"Death ! do you speak to me of fear ?" shouted the wild ungovernable man, drawing his sword.

Lady Ella Huntley stood bravely before him.

"Yes ; fear !" she cried, "or you, a strong man, would not draw a sword against me, a weak, helpless woman. Let me pass. I will save Sir Percy !"

"You cannot."

"I wl bid him leave me for ever."

"If you do so I will not harm him," said Brandon.

Then suddenly a bright idea seemed to strike him.

"Good : send him away. If *he* lives you cannot marry another : but remember," he added, in a fierce whisper, "send him away *at once*, for if you are not mine you shall be no other man's. You see these skeletons ? Ere long Sir Percy's will lie there if you do not obey me."

The girl trembled.

But she had courage to say,

"Let me go, and I will do your bidding."

Brandon opened the door.

"Go, Ella," he said, gently ; "but, by Heaven ! forget not my words."

He let her out, pressed her hand fondly, and disappeared.

Ella Huntley passed again up the corridor and reached her bed-room.

She had scarcely entered when there was a loud knocking at the door.

She threw her heavy shawl from off her bare shoulders, dishevelled her hair as if she had been lying down, and then opened the door.

Sir Percy Delaine appeared.

"You were so long coming, dearest," he said, fondly, as he entered, "that I came hither to see why you tarried."

"Oh ! Percy !" she cried, flinging herself on her knees at his feet, when he had closed the door, "leave me ! leave me ! I am accursed. I have a brand as it were on me. If you remain in my room your doom is sealed. You will die by the hand of an assassin."

Sir Percy smiled, placed his hand upon the handle of his sword significantly, and locked the door.

In a quarter of an hour after this loud screams alarmed the inmates of the castle.

The guests rushed in a body towards the bedroom.

The door was quickly broken open when a scene of terrible disorder presented itself.

A scene of murder in its most ghastly form.

The floors, the bed, the chairs, the walls were spattered with blood while the grand mirror was smashed into a hundred pieces.

Of the fate of Sir Percy Delaine there was little doubt, for the dead body lay upon the floor, its face hideously disfigured, its clothes torn, and a broken sword on the ground beside it.

As for Lady Ella Huntley she had disappeared.

CHAPTER V.

THE RIVER SIDE—SOFT SAM—THE HIGHWAYMEN —THE ATTACK ON GRACE DASHWOOD—THE COMBAT—THE RESCUE—THE HAUNT OF THE ROBBERS—THE FLIGHT—THE COMPACT.

SOME few days after his arrival among the robbers, and while Moonlight Jack was still in bed from the effects of his wounds, Lucien Fairleigh made his way towards the house of old Cormorant in the hope of seeing Grace Dashwood.

His progress had been slow owing to his footsteps being dogged by a half-witted fellow, known in the neighbourhood as Soft Sam, who had often received a kindness from him.

He knew him to be a "safe man," but yet he cared not to be observed.

At length, however, he fancied he had thrown him off, and he accordingly wandered down by the river side, which he knew to be her favourite walk.

The afternoon had gone by, and the brightness of the day had become obscured, not only by the sinking of the sun, but by some large heavy clouds which had rolled up, and seemed to portend a thunder-storm.

Lucien had looked up twice to the sky, not with any purpose of returning home, for the rain he feared not ; and, in witnessing the grand contention of the elements, he had always felt an excitement and elevation from his boyhood.

There had always seemed to him something in the bright light of the flames of heaven, and in the roaring voice of the thunder, which raised high thoughts, and incited to noble efforts and great and mighty aspirations.

He looked up twice, however, to mark the progress of the clouds, as, writhing themselves into strange shapes, they took possession of the sky, borne by the breath of a quiet sultry wind, which seemed scarcely powerful enough to move their heavy masses through the atmosphere.

When he looked up a third time, Lucien's eye was attracted to the opposite bank by the form of the half-witted man, Soft Sam, making eager signs to him without speaking, although, from the point at which he stood upon this slope, Lucien could have heard every word with ease.

As soon as he saw that he had caught the traveller's eye, however, the half-witted man called to him vehemently to come over, pointing with his stick towards a path through the trees, and shouting, "You are wanted there."

Lucien paused, doubting whether he should cross or not ; for though the stream was shallow, and the trouble but little, still the man that called him was, as he well knew, insane, and might be urged merely by some idle fancy.

While he hesitated, however, the other ran down the bank, exclaiming, when he had come close to the margin,

"Quick, quick, Master Lucien, or ill may happen to her you love best."

Lucien stayed not to ask himself who that was ; but crossed the stream in a moment, demanding, "What do you mean, Sam ; what ill is likely to happen to ——"

He was about to add the name of her who had so recently and busily occupied his thoughts ; but suddenly remembering himself, he stopped short, and the half-witted man burst into a laugh, exclaiming,

"What ! you won't say it, Master Lucien ? Well, come along with me quick ; you will find I am right. I settled it all for you long ago, and I said you should marry her, whether the old man liked it or not."

Soft Sam paused for a moment.

Then he went wandering on again.

"Come on ! come on, quick ! There are two of the foxes down there waiting by the dingle, just beyond the park gates. You know what foxes are, Master Lucien ? Well, you never thought to go fox hunting this evening ; but I call them foxes because the law wont let me call them by any other name ; and she has gone down to the old woman at the cottage, and to talk to her. So that she will be just coming back about this time, and then she will meet with the foxes ; though, after all, they are waiting for Master Nicholas, the collector's clerk, I dare say ; but they will never let her pass without inquiry."

While he spoke these wild and rambling words, he walked on rapidly, followed by Lucien, who was now seriously alarmed.

Although what his companion poured forth was vague and incoherent, yet there were indications in it of something being really wrong and of some danger menacing Grace Dashwood.

He remarked, too, that the half-witted man, as he walked along, frequently grasped the cudgel that he carried, and lifted it up slightly, as if to strike.

But it was in vain that Lucien tried to gain any clearer notion of what was amiss, for his questions met with no direct reply, his companion answering them constantly by some vague and irrelevant matter, and only hurrying his pace.

Thus they proceeded through the woods that topped the bank over the stream across a part of the park to a spot where a belt of planting flanked the enclosed ground on the side furthest from the house and the village.

It was separated by a high paling from a lane which ran along to some cottages at the foot of an upland common, and which lane itself was every here and there broken by a little irregular green, ornamented by high trees.

The ground around, indeed, seemed to have been cut off from the park, and probably had been so in former times.

There was a small gate opened from the park into the lane, at the distance of about a quarter of a mile from the spot at which Lucien and his companion approached the paling, and at that hour of the evening they could discern the gate with the path leading up to it ; for though the sun was below the horizon, it was yet clear twilight.

Towards that gate Soft Sam rapidly bent his steps, but they had not yet reached it when Lucien suddenly heard a scream proceeding from the lane on his right hand, and apparently close to them.

The memory of the ear is perhaps stronger and keener than that of the eye ; and, though he had never heard that voice in any other pitch than that of calm and peaceful conversation, the distinctive tone was as discernable to the quick sense in the scream he now heard as it would have been had Grace Dashwood simply called him by his name.

He paused for no other indication. In a moment he was through the belt of planting, and, vaulting at a bound over the paling, he stood in one of the little greens we have mentioned, an unexpected intruder upon a party engaged in no very legitimate occupation.

On the sandy path which marked the passage of the lane across the green stood Grace Dashwood, with a tall, powerful man grasping her tightly by the right shoulder, and keeping the muzzle of a pistol to her temple, in order, apparently, to prevent her from screaming, while another was busily engaged in rifling her person of anything valuable she bore about her.

So prompt and rapid had been the approach of Lucien, that the two gentlemen of the road were quite taken unawares, and the one who held her was in the very act of vowing that he would blow her brains out if she uttered a word, when the muzzle of the pistol he held to her head was suddenly knocked up in the air by a blow from the unexpected intruder.

The first impulse of the robber was to pull the trigger, and the pistol went off, carrying the ball a foot above the head of Grace Dashwood.

Instantly letting go his grasp of the terrified girl, the man who had held her threw down the pistol and drew his sword upon his assailant.

But Lucien's blade was already in his hand, and his skill in the use of his weapon was remarkable, so that in less than three passes, which took place with the speed of lightning, the robber's sword was wrenched from his grasp and flying amongst the boughs of the trees, while he himself, brought upon his knee, received a severe wound in his neck as he fell.

At that moment, however, another terrified scream from the lips of Grace Dashwood called her defender's attention, and, turning eagerly towards her, Lucien at once perceived that it was for him not for herself that she was now alarmed.

The robber whom he had seen engaged in rifling her of any little trinkets she bore about her had instantly abandoned that occupation on the sudden and unexpected attack upon his comrade, and was now advancing towards Lucien better prepared than the other had been, with his drawn sword in one hand and a pistol in the other.

The moment which Lucien had lost in turning towards Grace had been sufficient to enable the man whom he had disarmed to start upon his feet again and to run to the spot where his sword fell, and the traveller found that in another instant he should be opposed single-handed, and with nothing but his sword, to two strong and well-armed men.

He did not easily, however, lose his presence of mind, and, seizing Grace Dashwood's arm with his left hand, he gently drew her behind him, saying,

"Crouch down low, so that you may not be hurt when they fire. I will defend you with my life."

Scarcely had he spoken when the second ruffian deliberately presented the pistol at him and fired.

Lucien felt that he was wounded in the left shoulder, and the blow of the bullet made him stagger ; but, in the course of his life, he had been wounded before more than once, and, as far as he could judge, he was not now severely hurt.

His two assailants, however, were rushing fiercely upon him, and the odds seemed strongly against him ; but at that moment another arm, and a strong one, came in aid of his own.

His half-witted guide had by this time scrambled over the palings as well as his lameness would permit, and, with the cunning of madness, had crept quietly behind the two plunderers.

As soon as he was within arm's length, which was but a moment after the shot was fired that wounded Lucien in the shoulder, he waved his cudgel in the air, and struck the man who had discharged the pistol a blow on the back of the head, which laid him prostrate and stunned upon the ground.

Lucien's quick eye instantly perceived the advantage, and he rushed forward, sword in hand, upon the other man.

"THE BALL WENT THROUGH HIS HEAD." – *See Page 24*

Finding, however, that the day was against them, the ruffian fled, after making an ineffectual effort to raise his companion, and in a moment after the sound of a horse's feet, as it galloped rapidly away, was heard in the road above.

"It is right that every man should have his nag," said the half-witted man, turning over the prostrate robber with his foot, "but thou wilt ride no more, simpleton. I wonder if these clerks of St. Nicholas have lightened the burden of Master Nicholas, the clerk?" he continued, turning as if to speak to him whom he had guided thither.

But by this time Lucien returned to the spot where Grace Dashwood stood, and holding both her hands in his, congratulated her upon her escape.

Grace looked up in his face with an expression that could not be mistaken—

"I would rather be thus protected by you than by any one I ever knew."

After a few words of congratulation and assurance to Grace, he called to his half-witted companion,

"Come, Sam, come, leave the scoundrel where he is ; we have not time to make sure of him, and we had

No. 3.—January 20, 1866.] [*Owing to the great demand No. 1 has been reprinted, and may be had with No. 2, and the Large Engraving, for One Penny.*] [Price One Penny better get into the park, and towards the Manor as far as possible."

Thus saying, he drew Grace's arm within his own, and led her on to the gate of the park.

At this moment footsteps startled him.

He looked up hastily.

Old Cormorant was hobbling along with two servants. Lucien remained no longer.

"Heaven bless you, Grace," he cried, and fled away towards the road.

Old Cormorant, however, had seen him, and came up puffing, and blowing, and swearing most terrible and unholy things against the man he had driven to crime and shame.

We must now return to the spot beneath the park wall, where we left one of the assailants of Grace stunned by a blow from the cudgel of Soft Sam.

At length, however, the sound of a horse's feet was heard cantering lightly along the road, and a goodly gentleman, dressed in a fair suit of black, and mounted on a fat mare, made his appearance in the lane.

The good round face of the new comer was turned up towards the sky, calculating whether there was light enough left to let him get to Fairbridge in safety, and the first thing that called his attention to the object in his path was his mare, who had never before shied at anything on earth, recoiling from the body of the robber so violently as to throw forward the good round stomach of the rider upon her neck and shoulders with a sonorous ejaculation of the breath.

"God's my life! who have we here?" said Master Nicholas, and dismounting from his mare, with charitable intent, he bent down over the stranger.

There were two or three particulars in the sight itself, which made the heart of the collector's clerk beat rather more rapidly than was ordinary.

The stranger had in his hand a drawn sword, and a discharged pistol might be seen lying within a foot of him.

The feelings of the good Samaritan vanished from his bosom as soon as he had made this discovery, and stealthily creeping away, regained his mare's back, and rode off with all speed.

Shortly after the robber began to recover, and, regaining his legs, looked about him with some degree of wonder and amazement.

While busy in recalling all that had passed the sound of some one singing met his ear, and in another minute the head and shoulders of Soft Sam appeared above the park paling.

The half-witted man saw that the robber was upon his feet again, and he clambered over the fence and approached his former antagonist.

"I have come to apprehend thee!" he cried, laying his hand boldly upon the robber.

Strange to say the freebooter not only suffered him to take hold of him, but very probably might have even gone with him like a lamb to the slaughter, so much was he overpowered by surprise, and so little did he imagine that such an act would be performed without some power to support it, had not two or three horsemen at that moment come galloping down the lane as hard as they could ride.

A single glance showed the captive of Soft Sam that the new arrivals were friends.

He accordingly twisted himself out of his mad antagonist's grasp in a moment, and prepared to lay violent hands upon him in return.

Soft Sam, however, looked round him as the others came up with an air of wonder, indeed, but not of alarm, and muttered, "More foxes! more foxes!"

A sharp consultation ensued, of which Soft Sam seemed to be the object; but, at length, one of them exclaimed, "Come along, come along; bring him with you, and do what you like with him afterwards.

This plan was adopted, and two of the robbers, seizing upon Soft Sam, dragged him along between them, at a much quicker rate of progression than was at all agreeable to him.

For nearly an hour they hastened on as fast as they could; but, at length, much to Sam's relief, the whole party stopped before a lonely inn on the borders of a wide common.

The sound of strangers drew out the landlord.

"Quick! take the horses up to the pits," he said, speaking to the boy of all work.

"Why, Master Gliddon, who have you got there? By my life, it's Soft Sam. What, in the devil's name, did you bring him here for?"

"Why, Master Greenford," replied one of the men, "here's Gliddon and Sparks got themselves into a pretty mess. They would go out against the captain's orders to try a bit of business on their own private account, and they have got more than they bargained for, I take it. Gliddon has a cut in his neck, which bleeds like an old sow; and Sparks has had a blow of this same fellow's cudgel whom we have got here."

The conversation had taken place while the party was alighting, but now the landlord pressed them to come in quickly, and Soft Sam was hurried by them into a large room containing a long deal table and several settles and benches for its sole furniture.

Underneath the light, with his two arms upon the table, and his head resting upon them, and his face hidden entirely, sat a boy, and the gang of plunderers had been in the room several minutes before he was aware of their presence, so sound was the slumber in which he was buried.

"Hark ye, Master Douglas," said the landlord, as soon as the door was shut. "I think it a very silly thing of you to bring this fellow up here."

"Why, we did not know what else to do with him, Greenford," answered the other. "Sparks wanted to shoot him."

"You shall do no harm to him in my house, Douglas," replied the other. "The man is a poor innocent whom I have known this many a year, and I won't have him hurt."

"Thank you, Master Greenford, thank you," exclaimed the poor fellow. "Do not let them hurt me, and I will give you the shilling with a hole in it out of my tobacco-box."

"You see, Greenford," replied Douglas, "the thing is, we risk this fellow betraying us. He has seen all our faces, and could swear to us anywhere."

"What signifies his swearing?" demanded the landlord. "He is as mad as a March hare. Nobody will believe his swearing."

"Aye, but he may give such information as will lead them to ferret us out," replied another of the gang. "He must be got out of the way somehow."

"He shan't be got out of the way by foul means, however, Master Douglas," replied the landlord. "Come, nonsense! make him drink with you, and he'll forget all about it. He'll sing you as good a song as any man in the country, and if he promises not to tell anything he has seen you may be quite sure of him."

"Truth, truth, Master Greenford," cried the object of their discourse. "I always tell truth. Did any one ever hear me tell a lie in my life?"

The friendly landlord now busied himself in setting out the table in the midst for supper, and, at the same time, lent a sharp ear to the consultation which they held.

As he went round the table, however, setting down a cup here and a platter there, he gave the boy before mentioned a knock on the elbow, which roused him from his sleep, and, the next time he passed, the landlord whispered a word in his ear.

The boy took no particular notice at the moment, but rubbed his eyes, yawned, spoke to Douglas and the rest, and then disappeared from the room.

Large joints of roast and boiled meat soon graced the board.

Soft Sam was made to sit down between the two men, Sparks and Gliddon, who supplied him plentifully with food and drink, and then Douglas, who was beginning to get merry, insisted upon having one of the songs the landlord had so much vaunted.

The madman required no pressing; the very name of music was enough for him, and, with a full, sonorous voice, he began an old song, one of the many in praise of punch.

"Now I will sing you a song in return, Master Sam," cried the rough-featured fellow called Gliddon, who had been one of the assailants of Grace Dashwood.

And he accordingly proceeded to pour forth, in a voice of goodly power, but very inferior in melody to that of Soft Sam's, a song well suited to the taste of his auditors.

Scarcely had Gliddon done his song, when a step was heard in the neighbouring passage, which made the whole party start.

The next moment the door was opened, and Brandon stood amongst them.

His brow was somewhat cloudy indeed, but his bearing was frank and straightforward, and sitting down in a chair which had been placed for him, he fixed his eyes sternly upon the man who had suffered from the cudgel of Soft Sam, demanding,

"What is all this I hear, Sparks?"

The person he spoke to hesitated to reply, and the one who had been called Douglas answered for him.

"I believe, captain," he said, "the best way when one has been in the wrong is to own it, and to tell the truth. Sparks, there, heard that Master Nicholas, the clerk, was coming along the green lane this evening with all the receipts, and he thought it would be a good sweep for us all if we could get the bags. He asked us all to go, but only Gliddon would have a hand in it. Well, they fell in with a young lady first, and they thought they might as well have her purse too."

Brandon set his teeth hard, but said nothing, and Douglas, who saw the expressson on the other's face, went on,

"Temptation, you know, captain—temptation will get the better of us at all times. As I was saying, however, some one came to help the lady with this poor silly fellow, and Gliddon got a cut in his neck that won't be well for this ten days, and Sparks a broken head."

The brow of Brandon never relaxed its heavy frown, except when Douglas announced the evils which had befallen the two adventurers, and then a grim smile for a moment curled his lip.

"Do you know who it was that came to the lady's help?"

"Oh! I marked him well enough," replied Sparks. "I shall not forget him."

"He is one of your good friends, Captain Brandon. I have seen you walking with him twice, and I think he might have known better than interrupt a gentleman in his occupations."

"The only pity is," said Brandon, coolly, "that he did not send a bullet through your head."

"He has got one in his own shoulder," said Sparks, doggedly, "for I saw the ball strike, and I hope it will do for him."

"If he chance to die of it," said Brandon, in the same calm, stern tone, "I will blow your brains out. I am not a man to be trifled with, and if once more either of you disobey, be sure that I will then be as severe as I am now lenient. Can any one tell," he continued, "who the lady was that was attacked by them? I can only suppose that it was old Cormorant's niece."

"Just so—just so!" cried Soft Sam, from the other end of the table. "It was pretty Mistress Grace Dashwood."

"Why have you brought him hither?" demanded Brandon, in a sharp tone.

It took some time to explain to the leader of the band the motives which had induced them to bring the half-witted fellow up thither.

"And, therefore," exclaimed Brandon, interrupting the speaker, "because he was likely to recognise Sparks and bring him to the gallows, Master Sparks persuaded you to drag him up here that he may recognise us all, and bring us to Tyburn along with him. It was worthy of you, Master Sparks."

"You are wrong for once, captain," said the robber. "If I had had my wits I would have taken care that he should recognise no one. Dead men tell no tales I said then, and I say so still."

"They tell tales that are heard long years after," replied Brandon, with melancholy sternness.

Thus saying he left them, but returned much sooner than they had expected, and when he appeared was evidently much moved.

He sat down at the table, however, and remained for a moment in silence with his brow leaning upon his hand.

"What think ye, sirs?" he said, at length. "I I find that the whole country is astir against us on this bad business. Messengers have been sent out from the Manor to call a general meeting of the magistrates for to-morrow, and nothing is to be done but for each of us to take his own way out of the county till the storm has blown over. Let us all meet this day week at Lenford."

"But what is to be done with him?" demanded one or two of the fraternity, pointing to the unhappy lunatic, while at the same time some of the others came forward and whispered to their captain, apparently on the same subject, with sinister looks.

But Brandon replied, sternly,

"No! I say no! Leave him to me; I know him well, and he may be trusted. Now, to horse, and depart, but one by one."

The tone in which he spoke courted no reply, and the band quitted the room.

A silence for some minutes reigned in the room. Brandon at last broke it.

"Soft, Sam," said he; "do you know what those men pray me to do with you? They say, that if I let you go, you will betray what you have seen to-night, lead people to the places where we meet, or give evidence against us if ever we are in trouble; and they say that the only way is to silence your tongue for ever."

"No, no, no!" cried the poor man, fully awakened to his situation by such words; "pray don't, pray don't! I will never tell anything about it, as I hope for God's mercy."

"If you will swear," said Brandon "by all you hold dear, never to tell any one what you have seen to-night; never to lead any one to this place, as our place of meeting—"

"I will! I do!" cried the madman, solemnly. "I will betray you in no respect."

"So far, so good," answered Brandon, "but that

is not all. I give you your life, when every voice amongst us but my own was for taking it ; you must promise, if ever I call upon you, to do me a piece of service."

The other gazed earnestly in his face.

"What is it ?" he demanded, "what is it I have to do ? I will break none of the commandments. I will neither rob nor murder, nor help to rob or murder."

"I require no such things at your hands," replied Brandon, moved a good deal by his companion's earnestness. "I may only require you to guide me on my way in a moment of difficulty ; to lead me by the paths which, I am told, no one knows so well as you do ; and, perhaps, to guide me into a house."

"Guide you I will, in moments of difficulty ; lead you I will, when you want it ; but not to commit a crime."

"What I shall ask you," said Brandon, solemnly, "is, to commit no crime. My purpose shall be to take no man's goods from him, but rather to restore to him who is deprived of it that which is his own."

"Swear to me that," exclaimed the other, "and I will lead you anywhere."

"I swear it now !" answered Brandon, "and remember that, having sworn it, I shall never ask you to do anything but that which you now agree to do. No questions, therefore, hereafter, even were I to ask you to lead me into the heart of Huntley Castle."

The madman laughed aloud.

"There should be none," he answered, "for I know why you go."

"Indeed !" said Brandon, with a smile ; "but it is enough that you are willing. I trust to your word in everything. Hast thou any money, poor fellow ?"

"Nothing but my shilling with the hole in my tobacco-box," replied the man, looking ruefully in his interrogator's face. "Pray do not take that from me ; it and I are old friends."

"I would rather give than take from thee," replied his companion. "There is a guinea to keep thee warm ; and now thou art at liberty to go, so fare thee well."

As he said this, he turned away and left the room, and poor Soft Sam, gazing upon the gold piece in his palm with evident delight, walked quietly out of the inn, and, although it may seem strange to attach ourselves so particularly to a personage of the class and character of Soft Sam, yet must we, nevertheless, follow him a little further in his wanderings.

On the edge of the moor was a low shed and a stack of fern, which the poor fellow must have remarked in some of his previous peregrinations, for towards these he directed his steps at once, pulled down a large quantity of the dried leaves, dragged them into the shed, and, having piled them up in a corner, nestled down therein.

By daylight he was upon his way, and an hour's walk brought him into the deep woods that backed the splendid dwelling of Lord Huntley, which was known in the country by the name of The Castle.

It was by the back way that Soft Sam now approached the mansion. Here he was met by a person at the sight of whom he bent down his head, and glanced furtively up with his eye like a dog who does not very well know whether it will be kicked or caressed.

The figure that approached him in the long dim walk was that of a tall, thin woman, of perhaps fifty years of age, dressed in dark-coloured garments.

She did not frown, but there was a cold calmness about her compressed lips and tightly set teeth, and a piercing sharpness about her clear black eye, which rendered the whole expression dark and forbidding.

Although passed the usual period of grace, yet she walked gracefully and with dignity, and although no smile curled her lip, and her countenance underwent no change, the tone of her voice while she spoke the first few words to him at once showed the half-witted man that he was not out of favour.

"Why, how is it, Sam," she asked, speaking with a very slight foreign accent, "how is it that you have not been up at the Castle for these six weeks ?"

"Because I got my fill at the town and the Manor, Mistress Martha," replied Sam.

"Aye, that is it," she exclaimed, "that is it, if every one would but say it. Men go for what they can get, and when they can get their fill at one place, they seek not another. The only difference between the madman and the world is, that madmen tell the truth, and the world conceals it."

"I always tell the truth !" cried the half-witted man.

"Yes ; but you are only half mad," answered the housekeeper. "But go in the Castle, Sam ; and if you go along the long back corridor you will find my maid in the room at the end ; bid her give you the cold meat that Lord Henry Davenport left after his breakfast."

"After his breakfast ?" cried the half-witted man. "He has breakfasted mighty early ! But now—oh, I guess it, he has gone to London. I heard her tell him to go."

"Nay, then," said the housekeeper, smiling as far as she was ever known to smile, "I suppose he is gone to buy the wedding ring for pretty Grace Dashwood, and have the marriage settlements drawn up. Methinks he might have told me too."

"Nay, Mistress Martha," replied Sam. "No wedding ring ! no marriage settlements ! Mistress Grace is not for him."

A slight flush came over the pale cheek of her to whom he spoke.

"Not for him ?" she exclaimed ; "not for him ? Does she refuse him, then ?"

"Yes, to be sure," replied Soft Sam ; "every man is refused once in his life."

"Art thou lying, or art thou speaking truth ?" demanded Mistress Martha, fixing her eyes sternly upon him. "Did she refuse him ?"

"Truth," replied the man, "I always speak the truth."

Martha stood and gazed upon the ground for several minutes.

"I do believe," she said, speaking to herself, "I do believe that things possessed without right have a doom upon them which prevents them from bringing happiness even to those who hold them unconscious of holding them wrongly."

"We ought always to do what is right, Mistress Martha," exclaimed the half-witted man, whose presence she had totally forgotten, "and both you and I know that right has not always been done."

"Out upon the fool !" exclaimed the housekeeper. "Hold thy mad tongue. How darest thou to prate of right and wrong, not having wit to keep thee from running thy head against a post. Get thee in before me. Thou shalt give the marquis an account of this refusal."

Soft Sam slunk away before her flashing eye and angry words like a cowed dog.

CHAPTER VI.

LUCIEN FAIRLEIGH REVEALS A SECRET TO GRACE DASHWOOD—HIS ENCOUNTER WITH LORD HENRY DAVENPORT.

TWO evenings after the rescue of Grace Dashwood from the hands of the ruffians, Lucien Fairleigh, leaving the abode of Moonlight Jack, took his way towards the spot where he hoped to meet his mistress. She did not deceive him.

There, at the usual spot, she was waiting, and she advanced eagerly to meet him.

"Dear Lucien," she said, "I am so glad you have come. My life in this house since you have quitted it has been a life of incessant misery. Only these meetings with you make life at all endurable."

"Dear one," said Lucien, "your love alone makes life endurable to me; but even old Cormorant, your uncle, I have forgiven, since his furious anger has been the means of discovering a secret which would otherwise have for ever been hidden from me."

"What secret?"

"I will tell you. It is a strange one, indeed; but I have seen enough to persuade me of its truth. Chance threw me in the way of one Jack Tyrrell, or Moonlight Jack, as he is called. He is a highwayman——"

"And you his friend?" said Grace, shudderingly.

"Yes; for he has proved himself one. He has been seeking me for years. It seems that the old people at the cottage are not my father and mother!"

"Not your father and mother?"

"No. The Marquis of Huntley is my father; my mother was Ella Latimer, the daughter of poor but honourable parents. The marquis married my mother in secret, and I was the offspring of this marriage. A few years after this my mother died. At her deathbed the marquis, who had long ceased to care for her, was not present; but the one who *was* present acted for him.

"This one was a man who had loved Ella from boyhood, but who had been discarded by her for the marquis.

"When he found that she had broken her vow to him he married another, and had one son, Moonlight Jack.

"Though he married, however, he still watched over the one he had loved as a boy, and when my poor mother, on her dying bed, begged him to protect her child, he took a fearful oath.

"This oath was to the effect that he would never cease seeking for the papers which proved her to be the wife of the young marquis, and me his rightful heir.

"'If I die ere I have accomplished this,' he said, 'I will exact the same oath from my son.'

"Moonlight Jack and I were brought up together until I was five years of age; then I was stolen away by some one, and given in charge of those whom I have ever looked upon as *my* father and mother, and whose kindness still claims my love.

"Jack Tyrrell recognised me some time since by the names and initials on my arm, '*Lucien, son of E. L. and H. F. M., of H.*' I was always told that this meant 'Lucien, son of Elizabeth Langton, and Henry Fairleigh, Merchant, of Hurstpierpoint.' It is not so. It stands for '*Lucien, son of Ella Latimer and Henry Frederick, Marquis of Huntley.*'

"Old Tyrrell died when Jack was fifteen, and from him his father exacted the fearful oath that he would see me righted; and, now, since a strange Providence has brought me to him, he will carry it out through fire and water. But, Grace, my dear one, you are sad; tell me, why these sad looks? Will you not wish me joy of my good fortune?"

"Yes, dear Lucien," she said; "but still, I fear for myself."

"Why so?"

"Because maybe this change of fortune may bring a change of heart."

"Why doubt me, dearest?"

"When you are greeted as the Marquis of Huntley, and you are amid the gay throngs of beauty, your heart—yet untried by temptation—may find another."

"My heart will never swerve from you. But methinks Grace Dashwood has attracted other admirers. Since I left your uncle's house, Lord Henry Davenport has been here very often, and they speak of him in the neighbourhood as your accepted suitor."

He said these words bitterly.

"Do you *doubt* me?" cried Grace Dashwood, tearfully. "Has Lucien Fairleigh's heart changed already since he has found himself to be Lord Lucien Davenport?"

Lucien smiled. Smiled bitterly though.

He was fully aware of the hatred which Clement Cormorant bore him, and of the fact, too, that the old man admired Lord Henry, and would eagerly accept him as a suitor for the hand of his niece.

He knew, therefore, that the young lord—his own half-brother—had every opportunity of seeing her, while he himself could meet her only in secret.

"No," he said; "I do not doubt you, Grace; but tell me, has Lord Henry proposed?"

"Yes, and been refused. He seemed very sad, for he has set his heart, I know, on me, but I told him I loved another."

"Did you say whom?"

"I did not."

"That is well. Soon I shall rescue from the Castle the papers which declare my legitimacy, and will wrest from my father what is my birthright. Then, perhaps, as Marchioness of Huntley, you will, as my wife, be received by your uncle."

He threw his arms round her, and pressed her to his heart; their lips met in a fervid kiss of love; and he set her heart at ease by promising to use none but lawful means to obtain even his right.

He still held her gently with one arm thrown around her, and her left arm locked in his, when the sound of a footstep met his ear and he looked up.

Grace's eyes were raised, too, and her cheek turned very red, and then very pale, for, at the aperture at the other end of the bowling-green, appeared no other than Lord Henry Davenport advancing rapidly towards them.

Lucien Fairleigh's proud nostrils expanded, and his heart rose high; and drawing the arm of Grace through his own, he advanced with her direct towards Lord Henry Davenport as if about to return to the house.

The young nobleman's countenance was deadly pale, and he was evidently much moved, but he behaved well and calmly.

"Your uncle wishes to speak—to speak to you, Grace," he said; "I left him but now just awake."

Lucien saw that Grace could not reply, and he answered,

"She is now about to seek Mr. Clement Cormorant, my lord."

"I rather imagine that he has business that may require Mistress Grace's private attention," replied Lord Henry, in the same cold tone which had been used by both. "I have also to request a few moment's private conversation with Mr. Fairleigh. I will not detain him long."

Grace suddenly raised her eyes, and looked from one to the other.

"Fairleigh," she said, aloud, "before I leave you I have one word more to say."

"I will rejoin you here in a moment, my lord," said Fairleigh, calmly.

Lord Henry bowed; and Fairleigh, with Grace's arm still resting in his, walked on towards the house.

Grace spoke to him as they went, eagerly, and in a low voice.

His reply, as he left her at the door of the Manor, was, "On my honour! Be quite at ease. Nothing shall induce me."

As soon as he left her he returned at once to Lord Henry, whom he found standing with his arms crossed upon his breast in an attitude of deep thought.

"Your commands, my lord," said Fairleigh, as soon as they met.

"By your leave, Mr. Fairleigh," replied Lord Henry, "we will walk a little further where we are not likely to be interrupted."

Fairleigh signified his assent, and they proceeded in silence for some way till they reached a small glade in the park, when Fairleigh paused, saying,

"This is surely far enough, Lord Henry, to prevent our being interrupted in anything you can have to say to me or I to you."

"Perhaps it may be, " replied Lord Henry. "I have a question to ask you, which may perhaps lead to other questions."

"I must first know what your first question is," replied Fairleigh, "before I even consider whether I shall answer any."

"The question is simply this," rejoined Lord Henry, in a somewhat bitter tone; "who and what is the gentleman who calls himself Mr. Lucien Fairleigh?"

Lucien smiled.

"Had, I, my lord," he said, "either visited your property, even as a sportsman, in answer to your lordship's own invitation, or had I introduced myself into your family, I might have thought myself bound to give some answer to your question; but as I have done neither the one nor the other, I will beg you to excuse me from replying to it, and I will pardon you for putting it."

"This is all very good, sir," said Lord Henry; "all very good indeed; but you do not escape me by an affectation of dignity. In the first place, sir, you cannot suppose that I shall conceal from Mr. Cormorant what I remarked to day between yourself and his niece."

Fairleigh turned very red, but he still replied, calmly,

"In regard to that, my lord, you may do as you please."

Lord Henry bit his lip, and replied, "I must insist, sir, upon having an explanation on the spot, as to who and what you are; as to what your title is to be in the society in which I find you, and what are your claims to one of the richest heiresses in the county."

"Your pardon, my lord," replied Fairleigh; "you are now going too far. I might give every explanation that I think fitting to the uncle of the lady in question; to you, who have no right to enquire, I shall give none."

Lord Henry again bit his lip.

"The right I have, sir, is twofold—that of one of her oldest friends, and that of an applicant for her hand."

"In neither quality," he said, "can I recognise in you any right to interfere, and you will pardon me if I say, that I will not only give you no explanation whatever upon the subject, but will not condescend to hear you speak any further on a matter with which you have no title to meddle."

"Then, sir," replied Lord Henry sharply, "nothing remains but to bid you draw your sword. I do you honour in taking it for granted that you are worthy of mine," and as he spoke, he drew his weapon from the sheath.

Fairleigh remained, however, with his arms crossed upon his chest and a somewhat melancholy smile upon his countenance.

"Once more," he said "you must pardon me, Lord Henry; neither in this matter can I gratify you."

"Well said, Master Lucien," cried a voice close beside them, "well said, well said. I think, my little lordling, you had better put up your cold iron, and go your way home to your father. To think of a man wishing to bore a hole in his neighbour like any carpenter with his gimblet! Let us look at your skewer in a handle, my lord."

And as he spoke Soft Sam, the half-witted man of the village, advanced, and extended his hand to take hold of the blade of Lord Henry's sword.

The young nobleman pushed him sharply aside, however, bidding him begone with an angry frown.

"Well, I'll be gone," replied the half-witted man, "but I'll be back again in a minute with more hands to help me."

And away he ran in the direction of the village.

"Now, sir, quick!" exclaimed Lord Henry. "If you would not have me suppose you both a coward and an impostor, draw your sword, and give me satisfaction at once."

"Your lordship may suppose me anything you please," replied Lucien. "Having done nothing that can reasonably dissatisfy you, I shall certainly do nothing to give you any other sort of satisfaction."

"Then, sir, I shall treat you as you deserve," replied Lord Henry, "and chastise you as a cowardly knave."

And, putting up his sword, he advanced to strike his opponent.

But Fairleigh caught his hand in his own powerful grasp, and stopped him, saying,

"Hold, Lord Henry, hold! I will give you one word of explanation. If, after having heard that, you choose to draw your sword and seek my life, you shall do so; but remember, as you are a man of honour, to none—no, not to the nearest and dearest—must you reveal the imports of these words," and, drawing him closer to him, he whispered what seemed to be a single word in the young nobleman's ear.

Fairleigh then let go his hold, and, pale as ashes, with a quivering lip and a straining eye, Lord Henry staggered back.

———

CHAPTER VII.

THE ROBBERY ON UPPINGTON MOOR — MOONLIGHT JACK—DEATH FOR DISOBEDIENCE.

THE sun had gone down, but the moon had not yet risen.

The sky, which for nearly a month had been calm and serene, was covered over with long lines of dark grey clouds heavy and near the earth, when a solitary horseman took his station under a broad old tree upon the wide waste called Uppington Moor, and gazed forth as well as the growing darkness would let him.

Everything was vague and undefined in the shadows of that hour, and the long streaks of deeper and fainter brown, which varied the face of the moor, spoke merely of undulations in the ground marking the great extent of the plain towards the horizon.

A tall, solitary, mournful tree could be seen here and there, adding to the feeling of vastness and solitude, and about the middle of the moor, as one looked towards the west, was a small detached grove, or rather clump of large beeches, presenting a black irregular mass, at the side of which the lingering gleam of the north-western sky was reflected in silvery lines upon what seemed a considerable piece of water.

It was an hour and place fit for sad thoughts, and the horseman sat upon his tall, powerful gelding in the attitude of one full of meditation.

Presently, as if impatient, he gently touched his beast with his heel, and made him move slowly out from under the branches of the tree.

Scarcely had he done so, however, when the distant sound of a horse's feet was heard.

His eye was now bent anxiously, too, upon the western gleam in the water, and in a few minutes the dark figure of another man on horseback was seen against the bright back-ground thus afforded, riding slowly on as the road he followed wound round the mere.

In a moment after two or three more figures were added, and all three suddenly stopped.

But a moment after there seemed a sudden degree of agitation in the group.

Then came a bright flash, followed at a considerable interval by the report of a pistol, and immediately after all three horsemen disappeared.

"What can this mean?" exclaimed the stranger, aloud. "I fear there is mischief!'

The sound of his voice seemed strange in the midst of solitude, but he had scarcely spoken when the stillness was again broken by the noise of a horse's feet.

This time it came in another direction, not exactly opposite, but much to the right hand of the spot whence the former sounds had proceeded, and the beast was evidently galloping as fast as he could over the turf.

At length another powerful cavalier became visible, approaching at full speed.

As he drew near he looked round more than once, and pulled up his horse suddenly by the tree.

"Are you there?" he said, in a low voice.

The watcher, who was no other than Lucien Fairleigh, at once joined the new comer, Moonlight Jack.

"Quick, quick, Lucien!" cried Jack. "Put your horse into a gallop, and come with me."

Lucien drew back.

"Hesitate not," cried Moonlight Jack; "no time is to be spared."

"I care not for the business," cried Lucien. "I fear me blood, innocent blood, will be shed."

"Nay, there you wrong me," cried Jack Tyrrell. "Highwayman as I am, no blood is on my hands,

That attack on Mistress Grace Dashwood was not of my doing nor of my men's. It was done by that villain Brandon's hirelings, and even he approved not of it. No fear, then, of further outrage. Brandon, since the murder of Sir Percy Delaine, has fled this part of the country. Come, then, move on with me; I fancy I am pursued."

Thus saying, he put his horse again into a gallop, and Lucien Fairleigh followed.

Two or three times, as they rode on, Moonlight Jack looked back over the moor.

But no moving object of any kind was to be seen, except one of those phosphoric lights which linger on the edges of an old marsh.

At length, when they had gone about two miles further, Moonlight Jack checked his horse's speed, saying,

"There is no one following now, yet they made the signal from the hill. Did you not hear a pistol shot just before I came up?"

"Yes," replied Fairleigh, "I heard it distinctly, and saw the flash. Was that as a signal that some one was following you?"

"It was," answered Moonlight Jack. "But how you could see the flash I do not know, for they were down below the brow of the hill, where one can see both roads to the Castle."

"Oh, no," said Lucien; "the men who fired that shot were upon the moor, close by Upwater Mere, and I very much fear, Moonlight Jack, that some of these accursed evil companions of yours have been again committing an act that you neither knew of nor desired."

"If they have," exclaimed Moonlight, with a horrid imprecation, "I will shoot the first of them, were he my own brother!"

"How many were there of them on the watch?" demanded Lucien Fairleigh.

"Two," replied his companion.

"Then I will tell you what I saw," answered Fairleigh.

"As I sat upon my horse and looked out over the mere which just caught a gleam from the sky, the figure of a horseman crossed the light as if he were going to the Castle; just at that moment two more came out upon him, from among the beeches, it seemed to me; then came the pistol shot, and a minute after they all disappeared.

Moonlight Jack gave utterance to another oath, and then, after thinking a few minutes, he added,

"It can't be any of my people, they dare not; I have told them that I will have no bloodshed. On the head of the man be it, then, whoever it may be, if blood has been spilled this night!"

"At all events," cried Fairleigh, reining up his horse entirely, "had we not better go back and see? I fear very much, Moonlight Jack, that they have shot the man, whoever he is."

"No, no!" replied Jack, "if they have shot him he is shot, and there is no need of our meddling with the matter."

"But he may be merely wounded," replied Fairleigh; "we had better go back."

"No!" thundered Moonlight Jack; "I tell you no! It is mere madness; we are but half a mile from the house. When I have got there, we shall learn who has done this, and I will send out and see if any one is hurt. Come on, come on!"

On reaching Jack Tyrrell's house they passed into a large chamber well lighted, in the midst of which was a large table furnished with a flagon and some drinking cups.

At the further end sat two men playing with dice, while a third, a short, smart-looking personage, stood watching the game.

They ceased when Moonlight Jack and his companion appeared, and the merriment which they had evidently been enjoying was over in a moment.

"But you three left," cried Jack Tyrrell, as he entered, "but you three left? Where are Hardman and Varley?"

"They went out shortly after you, Captain Jack," replied one of the men who had been playing. "I can't tell where they've gone."

"Hark! they are coming," said Moonlight Jack, as the sound of horses' feet was heard stopping opposite the house. "Let them in the back way, Harry, and bring in supper. Here, come with me, Master Lucien."

Moonlight Jack carefully shut the door behind him, and, when he stood alone in the passage with Fairleigh, he unbuttoned his vest and took from an inner pocket a key of a very peculiar and extraordinary form.

"There's the key, Master Lucien," he said, speaking quickly, and with strong passions of some kind evidently struggling in his breast. "Your own fate is now in your own power; manage it as you will."

"But tell me how this has been obtained?" said Lucien.

"I have no time for long stories," replied his companion, sharply; "there it is, that is sufficient. But I will tell you so far, I—I alone, though directed by one who knew the house well, walked through it this night from one end to the other, and within six yards of the old man himself, with nothing but a door between us, took this key from the hiding-place where he thought it so safe, and brought it away undiscovered. Now, Lucien, leave me; I am not in a humour to speak much. I have matters before me that may well make me silent. Since you say you *must* go to the Lake House to-night, mount and begone with all speed. Take the back road," he added, as he undid the door for Lucien; "take the back road, and, for the love of God, go no more upon the moor to-night."

Lucien made no reply, but, mounting his horse, rode away into the night.

Moonlight Jack, on returning to the room, said not a word for some moments, but fixed his eyes upon Varley and Hardman.

He drank his wine in silence, and in silence the supper passed.

When it was over, however, he spoke,

"Now, my Masters Varley and Hardman," said he, "we are all present but two; be so good as to tell me where you have been to-night?"

The time which had elapsed, the indifference and even carelessness which had hitherto appeared in Captain Tyrrell's manner, and a cup or two of wine which he himself had drank, had removed the degree of apprehension which at first mingled with the sullen determination of Varley.

He replied, then, at once, with a look of effrontery,

"I don't think that at all necessary, captain. I rather believe I have as much right to ride my horse over any common in the kingdom as you have, without giving you any account of it, either."

"You hear him, my men?" said Moonlight Jack, "you hear him? Hardman, you tell me."

"I'll tell you at once," returned Hardman, "and devilish sorry am I that I ever went! I certainly would not have gone had I known how it would

turn out. I'll never as long as I live go out again with Varley."

Varley muttered something not very laudatory of his companion, but it was drowned in the stern voice of Moonlight Jack, who exclaimed,

"Go on, Hardman!"

"Why, we went out to the beeches by Upwater Mere," replied Hardman, "and we had not been there long, when up came some one on horseback, going along slowly towards the Castle. It was not the person we were looking for, however——"

"Pray who were you looking for?" inquired Moonlight Jack.

"Why, I think that is scarcely fair, captain," said Hardman.

"It matters not," replied Moonlight Jack. "I know without your telling me. Go on."

"Well, as the young man came up," continued the other, "Varley said we might as well have what he had upon him. So we rode up, and asked him to stop quite civilly, but instead of doing so he drew his sword, and spurred on his horse upon Varley, and——"

"Well," exclaimed the captain, impatiently, "what then? I heard the pistol fired," he said, seeing the man hesitate, "so tell the truth."

"Well," said Hardman, "well," and as he spoke he turned somewhat pale. "Well, then, Varley fired, you know, and brought him down, and we pulled him under the beeches, and took what we could get. We have not divided it yet; but it seems a good sum."

As his companion had been detailing the particulars of their crime, the changes which had come over Varley's countenance were strange and fearful.

He had watched with eager anxiety the countenance of Moonlight Jack, who sat nearly opposite to him at the other end of the table; but being able to gather nothing from those stern dark features, he ran his eye rapidly round the faces of the rest, and after several changes of expression resumed, as well as he could, the look of cunning and daring impudence which he had at first put on.

"Hardman," said their leader, "I shall find some means of punishing you. As for you, Varley——"

"You shall not punish me, captain," interrupted Varley, knitting his brows, and speaking through his teeth, "you shall not punish me. For, by —— if you don't mind what you are about, I hang you all."

Moonlight Jack sat and heard him calmly, keeping his eyes fixed upon him with stern gaze till he had done speaking.

"You hear!" he said, looking round at last.

And, at the same moment, he drew a pistol from under his coat.

Every face around turned pale but his own, and Varley started up from the table; but before he could take a single step, and while, yet, with agony of approaching fate upon him, he gazed irresolute upon the face of his leader, the unerring hand of Moonlight Jack had levelled the pistol and fired.

The ball went through his head. The unhappy man bounded up two or three feet from the ground, and then fell dead at the end of the table.

Moonlight Jack sat perfectly still, gazing through the smoke for about a minute, and through the whole hall reigned an awful silence.

He then laid the pistol calmly down on the table before him, and drew forth a second.

Hardman crossed his arms upon his breast, and looked him full in the face, saying,

"Well, captain, I am ready."

MOONLIGHT JACK
OR THE KING OF THE ROAD

"HE APPROACHED THE BED WITH A STRANGE GLIDING NOISE."—*See page* 20.

"You mistake me," said the captain, laying down the pistol on the table with the muzzle pointed towards himself. "My friends, if I have done wrong by the shot I have fired, any of you that so pleases has but to take up that pistol and use it as boldly as I have done its fellow. What say you—am I right or wrong?"

"Right! right!" replied every voice.

"Well, then," said Moonlight Jack, putting up the weapons again, "some of you take him down. And you, Roberts and Williams, hark ye!" and he spoke a few words to them apart. "Take Hardman with you," he added, "that shall be his punishment."

So saying, he turned, took up a lamp that stood near, and quitted the hall.

CHAPTER VIII.

THE STRANGE FACE AT THE WINDOW—THE DEADLY FIGHT—THE CHAINED PRISONER.

WE must leave Moonlight Jack for a time, and ask our readers to accompany us to Huntley Castle.

No. 4.—January 27, 1866.] [*Owing to the great demand No. 1 has been reprinted, and may be had with No. 2, and the Large Engraving, for One Penny.* [Price One Penny

There is an antique chamber in that ancient house.

Curious and quaint carvings adorn the walls.

There was but one portrait.

The portrait of a young man with a pale face, and a stately brow, and a strange expression about the eyes, which no one cared to look on twice.

There is a stately bed in that chamber of carved walnut wood, and hung with heavy silken furnishing.

The floor is of polished oak.

Heaven! how the hail dashes on the old bay window!

Like a discharge of mimic musketry it comes clashing, beating, cracking upon the small panes.

But they resist it; their small size saves them.

The rain, the wind, the hail, expend their fury in vain.

The bed in the old chamber is occupied.

A creature, formed in all the fashions of loveliness, lies in a half-sleep upon that ancient couch—a girl young and beautiful as a spring morning.

Her long hair has escaped from its confinement, and streams over the blackened coverings of the bedstead.

She has been restless in her sleep, for the clothing of the bed is in much confusion.

One arm is over her head, the other hangs nearly off the side of the bed near to which she lies.

A neck and bosom, fit for the study of any sculptor, were fully disclosed.

Oh, what a world of witchery was in that mouth, slightly parted, and exhibiting the pearly teeth!

How sweetly the long silken eyelashes lay upon the cheek!

Now she moves, and one breast is entirely visible.

Whiter, fairer than the spotless clothing of the bed on which she lie, is the smooth skin of that fair creature just budding into womanhood, and in that transition state which presents to us all the charms of the girl—almost of the child—with the more matured beauty and gentleness of advancing years.

Was that lightning?

Yes!

An awful, vivid, terrifying flash, then a roaring peal of thunder, as if a thousand mountains were rolling one over the other in the blue vault of Heaven.

Who sleeps now in the city?

Not one living soul.

The hail continues, and the wind moans on.

Now she awakens — that beautiful girl on the antique bed.

She opens those eyes of celestial blue, and a faint cry of alarm bursts from her lips.

She sits up on the bed, and presses her hands upon her panting breasts.

Heavens! what a wild torrent of wind, and rain, and hail!

Another flash!

A wild, blue, bewildering flash, streams across that bay-window, and she started back with a wild cry of terror.

"What—what was it?" she gasped. "Was it real or a delusion? A figure, tall and gaunt, endeavouring from the outside to unclasp the window! I saw it! That flash of lightning revealed it to me, standing the whole length of the casement!"

There was a lull of the wind.

The hail was not falling so quickly.

Moreover it now fell straight.

Yet a strange clattering sound came upon the glass of the long window.

It could not be a delusion.

She is awake and she hears it.

Another flash of lightning—another wild cry!

There was now no doubt.

A tall figure stood on the ledge immediately outside the window.

It was its finger nails upon the glass which produced the sound so like that of the hail.

Intense fear paralyzed the limbs of the beautiful girl.

That one shriek was all she could utter.

With hands clasped, a face of marble, a heart beating so wildly in her breast, that each moment it seems as if it would break its confines, eyes distended and fixed on the window, she waited frozen with horror.

The pattering and clattering of the nails still continued.

No word was spoken, but she could trace the form of the intruder against the window, and she could see its long arms moving to and fro feeling for some mode of entrance.

What strange light is that which now gradually creeps up into the air?

Red and terrible—brighter and brighter it grows.

The lightning has set fire to a mill, and the reflection of the rapidly consuming building falls upon that long window.

There can be no mistake.

The figure is there, still feeling for an entrance, and scratching against the glass with its long nails.

The young girl tried to scream again, but a choking sensation comes over her and she cannot.

It is too dreadful.

She tries to move.

Each limb seems weighed down by tons of lead.

She can but in a hoarse faint whisper cry,

"Help! help! help!"

That one word she repeats like a person in a dream.

The red glare of the fire continues.

It throws up the tall gaunt figure in hideous relief against the long window.

A small pane of glass is at length broken, and the form from without introduces a long gaunt hand, which seems utterly destitute of flesh.

The fastening is removed, and one half of the window is swung open on its hinges.

And yet she could not scream—she could not move.

"Help! help! help!" was all she could say.

The figure turned half round, and the light fell upon its face.

It was perfectly white, perfectly bloodless.

The eyes looked like polished tin; the lips were drawn back leaving the grinning teeth visible.

It approached the bed with a strange gliding movement, clashing together the long nails that literally seems to hang from the finger ends.

No sound came from his lips.

Is she going mad, that young and beautiful girl, exposed to so much terror ?

She has drawn up all her limbs.

She cannot now say " help."

The power of articulation is gone, but the power of movement has returned to her.

She can draw herself slowly along to the other side of the bed from that towards which the hideous apparition is coming.

Her eyes are fascinated.

The glance of a serpent could not have produced a greater effect upon her than did the fixed gaze of those awful metallic-looking eyes that were bent upon her face and wandered over the naked beauties of her form.

Crouching down so that the gigantic height was lost, and the horrible protruding white face was the most prominent object, came on the figure.

What was it ?

What did it want there ?

What made it look so hideous, unlike an inhabitant of earth ?

Now she has got to the verge of the bed, and the figure pauses.

It seemed as if, when it paused, she lost the power to proceed.

The bed-clothes were now clutched in her hands with unconscious power.

She drew her breath short and thick.

Her white bosom heaved, and her limbs trembled, yet she could not withdraw her eyes from that marble-looking face.

He held her under a spell with his glittering eye.

The storm has ceased.

All is still.

The winds are hushed, the church clock proclaims the hour of one.

A hissing sound comes from the throat of the hideous being, and he raises his long, gaunt arms.

He advanced.

The girl extended one white and rounded leg from the bed, and placed her small foot on the floor.

The door of the room is in that direction.

Can she reach it ?

How can she break the charm ?

God of Heaven !

Is it real or some dream so like hideous reality as to nearly overturn the judgment for ever ?

The figure paused again.

Half on the bed and half out of it, the young girl lay trembling.

Her long hair coiled wildly over her heaving breasts.

Her eyes glared.

Her whole body palpitated with fear.

The pause lasted but a moment.

Oh ! what an age of agony !

With a sudden rush that could not be foreseen, with a strange howling cry that was enough to awaken terror in every breast, the figure seized the long tress of her hair, and, turning them round his bony hands, held her to the bed.

Then she screamed.

Heaven granted her the power to scream.

Shriek followed shriek in rapid succession.

The bed-clothes fell in a heap by the side of the bed.

Naked with the exception of her night-dress, she was dragged by her long silken hair completely on to it again.

Her beautifully rounded limbs quivered with the agony of her soul.

The glassy, horrible eyes of the figure gleamed with greater brightness, and he gazed on her form with a hideous satisfaction.

Then he dragged her head to the bed's edge, and forced it violently back by the long hair still within his grasp, and held her down by pressing his other hand over her palpitating breast.

The young girl could bear no more.

One last look she gave at the terrible being above her, and then her head reeled and she fainted.

The man then released her, and lifted her back upon the bed.

Then he advanced to the table on which stood the lamp, and lit it.

Having done this he took from his face the ghastly mask which had covered it, removed his long-nailed gloves, and stood before the mirror to examine his appearance.

Divested of his hideous disguise the terrible Beast of Night was far from hideous.

Yet on his features there was a ghastly smile.

" She has fainted," he muttered.　" My purpose will easily be effected, and she can never recognize me."

Taking up the lamp he approached the wall, and examined carefully.

Presently by the side of a picture he observed a small brass knob.

This he at once eagerly pressed, and a door flying open he passed through and ascended a narrow staircase.

This led him into a small room, in one corner of which was a large chest.

Placing the lamp on the table he knelt down by the side of this chest, and drawing a key from his pocket opened it.

Within was a small casket, which he also opened, and taking from it something rolled up put it back in its place.

Then he closed the large chest, and slowly, glidingly, stealthily returned towards the room where the fainting girl lay upon the antique bed.

Placing down the light upon the table he approached and gazed at her.

The sight of her naked white shoulders, her rounded breasts, which still palpitated with agitation, her limbs still as in death, but full and beautiful, and freely disclosed by the disorder of the bed-clothes, seemed to induce other thoughts in his mind.

" She is very lovely," he murmured.　" I have none to love me.　Such a woman as this would serve to make me a different man.　Yet why should I speak thus ?　What is life to me ?　What can it ever be but a blank and a curse ?　Why should I think of any woman when the only woman I ever loved is my mortal foe ?　Yet this girl is very lovely ; it would be a pleasant revenge to make her mine.　Ah ! she wakes !"

The young girl opened her eyes, and gazed at him, but fainted again on seeing him.

He approached nearer.

Bending over her he gazed long and earnestly

and admiringly at her exquisite beauties, and then stooping down covered her lips and her white shoulders with passionate kisses.

"She is mine!" he murmured, as he pressed her closely to him.

CHAPTER IX.

THE ALARM—THE FORCING OF THE CHAMBER DOOR — THE PURSUIT — THE STRANGE DIS-APPEARANCE—THE DEADLY FIGHT.

PEALING screams resounded through the Castle, and the affrighted inmates started from their beds.

Lights flashed about the building, and various room doors opened; and there was the sound of voices calling one to the other.

There was a universal stir and commotion among the inhabitants.

"Did you hear a scream, Henry?" asked a young man, half dressed, as he ran into the chamber of another domestic.

"I did. Wherever was it?"

"God knows! I dressed myself directly."

"All is still now."

"Yes; but unless I was dreaming, there surely was a scream."

"We could not both dream there was. Wherever came it, think you?"

"It burst so suddenly upon my ears I cannot say."

There was a tap, now, at the door of the room where the young men were, and the voice of the housekeeper was heard, crying,

"For God's sake get up!"

"We are up," said both the young men, appearing.

"Did you hear anything?"

"Yes; a scream."

"Search the place, then, search the place! Where did it come from? Can ye tell?"

"Indeed we cannot."

Another person now joined the party.

He was a man of middle age, the steward of the Castle, and as he was about to ask the meaning of the disturbance, a rapid succession of piercing shrieks broke upon their ears.

The housekeeper fainted, and would have fallen to the floor of the corridor in which they all stood, had she not been promptly supported by the last comer, who himself staggered, as those piercing shrieks resounded on the night air.

He, however, was the first to recover, for the young men seemed paralyzed.

"Henry," he said, "can you doubt that those cries came from the room of Emily the lady's maid? I will bear the housekeeper into her room, and then we will begin our search."

Quick as thought he rushed away, and then entering his own bed-room, he returned in a moment with a pair of pistols.

"Now, then," he cried, "follow me!" and bounded across the corridor in the direction of the antique apartment wherein the cries proceeded, but which were now hushed.

The Castle was built for strength, and the doors were all of oak and of considerable thickness.

Unhappily they had fastenings within, so that when the man reached the chamber of her who so much required help, *he* was helpless, for the door was fast.

"Emily!—Emily!" he cried; "speak!"

All was still.

"Good God!" he cried; "we must force the door!"

"I hear a strange noise within," said one of the young men, who trembled violently.

"And so I fancy *I* do. What does it sound like?"

"It sounds to me like some one endeavouring to file through iron bars."

"What on earth can it be? Have you no weapon that will force the door? I shall go mad if I am kept here."

"I have," said the young man; "wait a moment."

He ran down the staircase and presently returned with a small but powerful iron crowbar.

"This will do," he said.

"It will. Give it me."

"Has she not spoken?"

"Not a word. My mind misgives me that something very dreadful must have happened to her."

"And that odd noise——"

"Still goes on. It is like the rasping of a file; but then again, ever and anon, there is the sound of heavy groans, which curdles the very blood in my veins."

The man took the crowbar, and with some difficulty succeeded in introducing it between the door and the side of the wall.

Still it required great strength to move it, but it did with a harsh, creaking noise.

"Push it!" cried he, who was using the bar.

The men did so.

For a few moments the massive door resisted.

Then suddenly something gave way with a loud snap.

It was a part of the lock, and the door at once swung open.

How true it is that we measure time by the events which happen within a given space of it rather than by its actual duration.

To those who were engaged in forcing open the door of the antique chamber where slept the young girl whom they called Emily, each moment was swelled into an hour of agony; but in reality, from the first moment of the alarm to that when the loud cracking noise heralded the destruction of the fastenings of the door, there had elapsed but a very few minutes indeed.

"It opens! it opens!" cried the young man.

"Another moment," said the other, as he still plied the crowbar, "another moment, and we shall have free ingress to the chamber. Be patient."

As he spoke he succeeded in throwing the massive door wide open, and clearing the passage to the room.

To rush in with a light in his hand was the work of a moment.

But the very rapid progress he made into the apartment prevented him from observing accurately what it contained, for the wind that came in from the open window caught the flame of the candle, and although it did not actually extinguish it, blew it so much on the side that it was comparatively useless.

"Emily! Emily!" he cried.

Then, with a sudden bound, something dashed from the bed.

The concussion against him was so sudden and so violent that he was thrown down, and in his fall the light was entirely extinguished.

All was darkness save a dull reddish kind of light that now and then from the burning mill glittered into the room.

But by the light—dim, uncertain, flickering as it was—some one was seen to make for the window.

Henry, although nearly stunned by the fall, saw a figure, gigantic in height, which, to his disordered imagination, seemed to reach from the floor to the ceiling.

The other young man, George, also saw it, and so did Marchmont, the steward.

The figure was about to pass out at the window whence there was an easy descent to a garden.

Before it passed out they all caught a glimpse of the side face, and saw those fearful-looking, shining metallic eyes, which presented so terrible an appearance of unearthly ferocity.

No wonder, then, that for a moment a pain seized them all, which paralyzed any exertions they might otherwise have made to detain that hideous form.

But Marchmont was a man of mature years; and he recovered sooner than his companions.

"Don't rise, Henry," he cried; "lie still!"

Almost at the moment he uttered these words he fired at the figure, which then occupied the window as if it were a gigantic form set in a frame.

The report was tremendous in that chamber, for the pistol was no toy weapon, but one made for actual service.

"If it has missed its aim," said Marchmont, "I'll never pull trigger again."

As he spoke he dashed forward, and made a clutch at the figure he thought he had shot.

The tall form turned upon him, and he saw its face. It was one never to be forgotten.

It was hideously flushed with colour, the colour of fresh blood.

The eyes had a savage lustre, whereas before they had looked like polished tin.

They now wore a ten times brighter aspect, and flashes of light seemed to dart from them.

A strange howling noise came from the throat of the hideous figure, whose open mouth displayed a row of dog-like teeth.

For a moment it seemed disposed to rush upon Mr. Marchmont.

Suddenly, however, a strange impulse seemed to seize it.

It uttered a wild and terrible shrieking kind of laugh, and then turning dashed through the window, and in one instant disappeared from before the eyes of those who felt nearly annihilated by its fearful presence.

"God help us!" ejaculated Henry.

Marchmont drew a long breath, and then giving a stamp on the floor as if to recover himself from the state of agitation into which he had been thrown, he cried,

"Be it what or who it may I will follow it!"

"No, no, do not!" cried Mrs. Adams, the housekeeper, who had returned to the room.

"I must, I will! Let who will come with me, I follow that dreadful form!"

As he spoke he took the road it had pursued, and dashed through the window into the balcony.

"Come, George," cried Henry, "let us go with him! Emily, my beloved betrothed, has been in danger! I am sure you will aid me in punishing her foe!"

The housekeeper, who was the mother of both the young men, screamed aloud and implored them to stop.

But the voice of Marchmont the steward was heard, exclaiming aloud,

"I see it! I see it! It makes for the wall!"

They hesitated no longer, but at once rushed into the balcony.

Thence they dropped into the garden.

They found it far lighter than they had expected.

The morning was now rapidly approaching, and the mill was still burning, and the mingled light made almost every object plainly visible, except where some deep shadows were thrown from some gigantic trees that had stood for centuries in that sweetly wooded spot.

They heard the voice of Mr. Marchmont as he cried,

"There! There! towards the wall. There! there! God!! how it bounds along!"

The young men hastily dashed through a thicket in the direction from whence the voice sounded, and there they found him looking wild and terrified, and with something in his hand which looked like a portion of clothing.

"Which way? which way?" they both cried in a breath.

He leaned heavily on the arm of George as he pointed along a vista of trees, and said in a low voice,

"God help us all! It is not human! Look there! look there! Do you not see it?"

They looked in the direction he intimated.

At the end of the vista was the wall of the garden.

At that point it was full ten feet in height, and as they looked they saw the hideous monstrous form they had traced from the chamber of Emily Dornley making frantic efforts to clear the obstacle.

Then they saw it bound from the ground to the top of the wall, which it very nearly reached, and then each time it fell back with such a dull heavy sound that the earth seemed to shake again with the concussion.

They trembled—well indeed they might as they saw the figure engaged in its fruitless efforts at escape.

"What is it?" whispered Henry, in hoarse accents. "Oh, God! what can it be?"

"I know not," replied Marchmont. "I seized it and it was cold and clammy like a corpse. It can be nothing human."

"Not human?"

"Look at it now. It will surely escape now."

"No, no; we will not be terrified thus. Come on, and, for dear Emmy's sake, let us make an effort to seize this bold intruder. What will the marquis say if he hears of this business, and is told we were afraid to attack him? Who knows that this horrid thing is not the murderer of Sir Percy Delaine and the abductor of Lady Ella?"

"Take this pistol," said Marchmont, "it is the fellow of the one I fired. Try its efficacy."

"He will be gone," exclaimed Henry, as at this moment, after many repeated attempts and fearful falls, the figure reached the top of the wall, and then hung by its long arms a moment or two previous to dragging itself completely up.

The idea of the appearance, be it what it might, entirely escaping, seemed again to move the steward, and he as well as the young men ran forwards to the wall.

They got so close to the figure before it sprang down on the outer side of the wall, that to miss killing it with the pistol seemed a matter of utter impossibility.

Henry had the weapon, and pointing it at the tall form, with a steady aim, he pulled the trigger.

An explosion followed, and with a howling shriek the figure fell headlong from the wall on the outside.

"I have shot him," cried Henry, "I have shot him—he is surely human!"

"It would seem so," said Marchmont. "Let us hurry round to the outside and see where it lies."

This was at once agreed to, and the whole three of them made what expedition they could towards a gate which led into a paddock, across which they hurried and soon found themselves clear of the garden wall.

Following it its entire length they yet found no sign of a human body.

At some parts close to the wall there grew a kind of heath, and consequently the traces of blood would be lost among it.

After traversing the whole length of the wall line they came to the hall and glanced wonderingly at one another.

"There is nothing here," said Henry.

"It could not have been a delusion," said Marchmont with a shudder.

"A delusion!" exclaimed the brother, "that is impossible; we all saw it."

"Then what explanation can we give?"

"By heavens, I know not!" exclaimed Henry. "This adventure surpasses all belief; it is most terrible! Let us return and see how poor Emily fares. God help her; poor Emily! my beautiful Emily!"

CHAPTER X.

THE WATCHERS — THE APPEARANCE OF THE PHANTOM—THE SHOT—THE CHAINED PRISONER.

RUNNING at a swift pace, they very soon reached the Castle, and, when they came in sight of it they saw lights flashing from the windows and the shadows of forms moving to and fro, indicating that the whole household was up and in a state of alarm.

Henry, after some trouble, got the hall door opened by a terrified servant, who was trembling so much that she could scarcely hold the light she had with her.

"Speak at once!" cried Henry. "Is Emily living?"

"Yes, but——"

"Enough! Thank God she lives! Where is she?"

"In her own room! Oh! dear, dear, what will become of us all?"

On reaching the old room they found that several lights had been brought in, and, in addition to the housekeeper, there were two other female domestics who appeared to be in the greatest possible fright, for they could render no assistance to anybody.

Tears were streaming over the old woman's face, while Emily, propped up by pillows, looked like one who had suffered a severe illness.

On her clothing, on her neck and her bosom were some spots of blood, and round her throat was a mark as if she had been nearly strangled.

"Oh, Heaven!" she kept murmuring, "oh, heaven have mercy upon me and save me from that dreadful form!"

"There is no one here, Emily," cried Mr. Marchmont, "but those who love you, and who would, if necessary, lay down their lives for you."

"Oh, gracious God! save me!"

"You have been terrified, but tell us what has happened. You are quite safe now."

"Oh, do not leave me; do not leave me, any of you. I shall die," she exclaimed, "if I am left alone again. Oh, save me! That dreadful form, that hideous face!"

"Tell us how it happened, dear Emily," cried Henry; "or would you wish to sleep first?"

"No, no, no!" she said, "I do not think I shall ever sleep again."

"Say not so; you will be more composed in a few hours and then you can tell what has occurred."

"I will tell now. I will tell you now."

She placed her hand over her face as if to collect her scattered thoughts, and then added,

"I was awakened by the storm, and I saw that terrible apparition at the window. I think I screamed, but I could not fly. Oh, God! I could not fly. It came, it—it seized me by the hair! I know no more!"

"Well, well," said Marchmont, "I think Emily had better get some sleep, now, if she can."

"No sleep—no sleep for me!" again cried Emily. "Dare I be alone to sleep?"

"You shall not be alone, dear Emily," said Henry, "I will sit by your bedside and watch you."

She took his hand in both hers, and while the tears coursed each other down her cheeks, she said,

"Promise me, Henry, by all your hopes of Heaven, you will not leave me me."

"I promise."

She gently laid herself down with a deep sigh, and closed her eyes.

"She is weak, and will sleep long," said Mr. Marchmont.

"You sigh," said Henry; "some fearful thoughts I feel certain, oppress your heart."

"Hush—hush!" said Marchmont, pointing to Emily; "not here, not here."

"I understand," returned Henry.

"Let her sleep."

There was a silence of a few minutes' duration.

Emily had dropped into a deep slumber.

That silence was first broken by Henry.

"Mr. Marchmont," he said, "look at that portrait."

He pointed to the portrait in the frame to which we have alluded.

"Gracious Heavens! How like!" exclaimed Marchmont.

"It is—it is!" said Henry; "those eyes——"

"Yes, and the face and mouth. It is the portrait of one Brandon—Lord Brandon, who was expelled the castle for some false claim he set up. But stay, we will say no more at present; to-morrow we will consult."

"The daylight is coming quickly on," said Henry; "I shall keep my sacred promise of not moving from this room until Emily awakens; but there can be no need of any others stopping. Go, all of ye; I fear nothing."

"I will fetch you my powder-flask and bullets," said Marchmont, "so that you can reload the pistols. It will soon, now, be daylight."

This being done, Henry drew the table by the side of the bed, and sat down, and the others left him.

His situation was somewhat strange.

Impressed as he was by the fearful events of the night, he could not resist fixing his eyes upon the portrait.

He tried in vain to resist the feeling.

At length he shifted his chair, so that he could gaze on it without effort, and placed the candle so that a faint light was thrown upon it.

He fixed his eyes on the face.

It was a life-like portrait.

More than once he fancied that the eyes moved, and he closed his own that he might not see them.

At length the sickly light of morning peeped into the chamber, and Emily awoke.

Her first words sufficiently proved that she had not forgotten the events of the preceding night.

"Help, help!" she cried, and Henry was by her side in a moment.

"You are safe, Emily!" he cried, "you are safe!"

"Where is it now?"

"What, dear Emily?"

"The dreadful apparition. Oh! what have I done to be made perpetually miserable?"

"Think no more of it, Emily."

"I must think, my brain is on fire. A million of strange eyes seem gazing on me."

"Great Heaven! she raves," cried Henry.

"Hark! hark! He comes on the wings of the storm. Oh! it is horrible! most horrible!"

Henry rang the bell, but not sufficiently loud to create any alarm.

The sound reached the ears of his mother, who hastened into the room.

She soon succeeded in quieting the girl's fears, and when the bright sun was high in the heavens Emily slept a calm and refreshing sleep upon the bosom of her whom she soon expected to call mother.

The events above described, having happened in that wing of Huntley Castle which was occupied by the servants, had not disturbed the inmates of the other; and until further was known of the strange apparition, it was decided *not* to inform the marquis of anything.

He was not a man with whom any of the domestics cared to come too much in contact, and upon this occasion, they could scarcely tell what view he might take of the matter.

Marchmont, however, as well as the other domestics, had frequent conversations on the subject during the day, and it was decided by the former that the strange visitant was a murderer.

This Henry refuted.

"If it had been so," he said, "there would have been a wound in her neck and blood upon the bed."

"So there was: her bosom and her night things were covered with spots of blood. But time will prove my words. There was a mark round her neck as if he had grasped her tightly, and we may have disturbed him ere he had time to complete his deadly work. But time will show—time will show."

"I fancy he was wounded last night. Perhaps he will not again trouble us."

"Perhaps; but that is doubtful. At any rate the wound is nothing. To-night when she sleeps in another chamber, you and I and George will watch together."

The night came.

It was within a very few minutes of midnight.

The moon had climbed high in the heavens, and a night of such brightness and beauty had seldom shown itself for a long period of time.

Emily slept, and in her chamber sat the two brothers and Mr. Marchmont silently, for she had shown symptoms of restlessness, and they feared to break her light slumber.

The long continued silence at length became painful, and, when the echoes of the midnight chimes had died away, a feeling of uneasiness came over them which prompted them to conversation.

"How bright the moon is now," said Henry.

"I never saw it brighter," returned the steward; "I feel as if I were assured that we shall not to-night be disturbed."

"It was later than this when we received the visit," said Henry.

"It was," said Marchmont, rising. "Let us go out into the garden. We have two pistols and have nothing to fear."

They accordingly left the room and took a survey of the castle and grounds.

Nothing was to be seen.

It was then suggested by Henry that they should proceed to the park wall—which was broad enough to allow them all to sit upon it—and take a survey of the open meadows.

This was at once acceded to, and ascending accordingly where the strange being had on the night previous made such frantic leaps, they took their positions on the wall, and, although the height was but trifling, they found that they had a much more extensive view than they could have obtained by any other means.

Scarcely had they seated themselves when Marchmont seized Henry by the arm.

"Great heavens! what ails you?" said the young man.

"There is a young lime tree yonder to the right."

"Yes."

"Carry your eye from it in a horizontal line as near as you can towards the wood."

"Yes, yes; I see. Good God! what is it?"

"It is a human form stretched there," cried the steward.

"It is; as if in death."

"What can it be?" asked George.

"I dread to say," said Marchmont, "but to my eyes it seems even at this distance like the form of him we chased last night."

"What, Brandon!"

"Yes, yes. Look, the moonbeams touch him! Now the shadows of the trees gradually recede! God of Heaven! the figure moves."

Henry's eyes were rivetted upon that fearful object; and now a scene presented itself which filled them all with wonder and astonishment, mingled with sensations of the greatest awe and alarm.

As the moonbeams touched the figure, which lay extended on the rising ground, a perceptible movement took place in its limbs.

They appeared to tremble, and although it did not rise up, the whole body gave signs of vitality.

"The murderer! the murderer!" said the steward. "I doubt it not now; we must have wounded him last night, and a long rest has been necessary for his restoration."

Henry shuddered, but he was the first to propose some course of action.

"Let us descend," said he, "and go up to the figure."

"Hold, a moment," cried Marchmont, "hold! I am an unerring shot, as you know, Henry. Before we move from this position we now occupy, allow me to try what virtue may be in a bullet to lay that figure low again."

"He is rising!" cried George.

The steward raised the pistol.

He took a sure and deliberate aim, and then, just as the figure seemed to be struggling to its feet, he fired, and with a sudden bound it fell again.

"You have hit it," said Henry.

"Yes, indeed; but I fear me not mortally."

"No matter," cried Henry, "I can endure it no longer. I will seek the spot where it lies."

So saying, he sprung from the wall.

"Be not rash," cried the steward. "See, it rises again, and its form looks gigantic!"

"I trust in a good cause," said Henry, and pursued his onward speed.

Marchmont and George followed him.

They ran towards the piece of rising ground; but before they reached it, the man rose and made rapidly towards a little wood which was in the immediate neighbourhood of the hillock.

"He is conscious of being pursued," said George. "See how he glances back and then increases his speed."

"Fire upon it, Henry," cried Marchmont.

He did so; but either he missed his aim or his shot did not injure the stranger, for he took no heed of it but passed on rapidly.

On reaching the wood, he took a sharp turn to the left and passed down a long avenue enveloped in black darkness.

Presently, amid the trees, a slight light glimmered.

Towards this he made his way like one accustomed to the spot, though the gloom and darkness of the night was such that one unaccustomed to the place would have stumbled and fallen more than once.

But Brandon, the assassin, held on his way, straight on.

He passed through a thick clump of trees, crossed a plank, which over-reached a small stream, and stood before an iron door which was set in the side of a high mound of earth.

This he opened, and entering the subterraneous abode, closed the door after him.

A second door, reached in a few strides, admitted him to a chamber, supported by rude pillars, and paved unevenly with bricks and stones.

In one corner, chained to a pillar by a steel chain like a dog, was a woman, young and beautiful, whose wild glaring eyes told of acute mental suffering.

This woman was Lady Ella Huntley!

CHAPTER XI.

THE MURDER ON THE HEATH—THE ARREST OF LUCIEN FAIRLEIGH—THE SECRET CHAMBER— THE FIERCE ANGER OF THE MARQUIS—THE UNHOLY COMPACT.

DAY had long dawned, the morning after the scene at the robbers' haunt, ere Lucien Fairleigh woke: and even then he woke not of himself, nor till the servant had twice called him by name, standing close by his bedside, and looking upon him with an expression of much interest, indeed, but with a face from which all colour was banished, apparently by fear and agitation.

"Master Fairleigh!" he said; "Master Fairleigh! No guilty man ever slept so sound as that. Pooh! nonsense, I say."

Fairleigh woke, and looked up, and demanded what was the matter.

"Why, sir," replied the servant, "here is good old Dewberry, the landlord of the 'Falcon,' wants to speak to you immediately. I met him as I was going up the village, coming down here as fast as he could roll."

"Then you have not got the packet I sent you for?" said Fairleigh, coolly.

"He has got it, sir, safe," replied the man; "but he would not give it up, for he was coming on to you himself."

"He should have given it, as he was directed," said Lucien; "tell him to wait; I will see him when I am dressed."

"But he says, sir, he must see you directly—that his business is of the greatest importance—that there is not a moment to lose."

"Oh, then, send him up," said Fairleigh, "if the matter be so pressing as that."

The man instantly disappeared, as if he thought that too much time had been wasted already, and while Fairleigh proceeded to rise, good Dewberry was heard creaking and panting up the stairs, as fast as his vast rotundity would let him.

His face, too, was pale, if pale it ever could be called, and he was evidently in a great state of agitation, though the jolly habitual laugh remained, and was heard before he was well within the door of Fairleigh's room.

"Haw, haw, haw!" he cried, as he laid down the expected packet before Fairleigh.

"IT WAS THEN PERCEIVED THAT THE BODY WAS THAT OF A STRANGER."—*See page* 38.

"Lor a'mercy, Master Lucien, this is a terrible business," he continued. "Well, I never did think —however, it's all nonsense, I know," and he again burst into a loud laugh, ending abruptly in the midst, and staring in Fairleigh's face as if for a reply.

"Well, good Dewberry," replied Fairleigh, who, in the meantime, had broken open the seals in the packet, and seen that various bills of exchange, which it contained, together with equivalents for money, were all right; "well, Master Dewberry, what is it that is very terrible? what is it you did

never think? what is it that is all nonsense? I am in the dark, quite."

"Gad's my life, sir, they won't let you be in the dark long!" cried the landlord of the "Falcon;" "and I came down to enlighten you first, that you might not be taken by surprise."

"As to what?" said Fairleigh, somewhat impatiently.

"Lord, sir, I thought that fellow must have told you something, at least," replied the landlord, "or that his face must, if not his tongue, for it's all black and white, like the broadside of the 'Hue and Cry;'

No. 5.—February 3, 1866.] [*Owing to the great demand No. 1 has been reprinted, and may be had, with No. 2, and the Large Engraving, for One Penny.*] [Price One Penny.

but the matter is this," he added, after laughing a moment at his own joke, "it seems that poor Lord Henry Davenport, who was a good youth in his way, though he was somewhat sharp upon poachers and deer stealers and the like, was murdered last night upon the moor."

"Good God!" exclaimed Fairleigh, clasping his hands. "Good God!"

"It's but too true, sir," continued Dewberry, throwing as much solemnity as he could into his jocund countenance. "It's but too true; and there is poor Lord Huntley, his father, distracted; and, for the matter of that, I think the magistrates are as much distracted too, for after having been with my lord since five o'clock this morning, they came down to my house, and began examining witnesses, and taking evidence, and sending here and there; and the end of it all is—for I heard them consulting over it through a chink in the door—they judge that you are the person who murdered him, only because that mad fellow, Soft Sam, came running down to the village last night for help, swearing he had seen you and Lord Henry with your swords drawn upon each other. So while they were busy swearing in constables, and all that, I thought it but friendly like to come down here and tell you, in case you might think it right to get upon your horse's back and gallop away till the business is over."

"Swearing in constables?" said Lucien, without seeming to take notice of the worthy host's suggestion. "Why, they don't suppose my name is 'Legion,' do they? One constable, I should suppose, would be quite as useful as twenty."

"Aye, Master Lucien," replied Dewberry, "but they vow that you are connected with the Gentlemen of the Road, who have been sporting round about here lately, and they are afraid of a rescue."

"Indeed," said Lucien Fairleigh; "the sapient men. However, Master Dewberry, ring that little bell at the top of the stairs."

The silver hand-bell, to which he pointed, was immediately rung, and the man, who had remained half-way down the stairs, was in the room in a moment.

No sooner did he appear than Dewberry, who put his own construction upon Fairleigh's coolness, exclaimed,

"Quick, Master Geoffrey, quick! Saddle Master Fairleigh's horse for him!"

"No, no, my good man!" said Fairleigh. "You are making a mistake, good Master Dewberry. Take this packet, Geoffrey, and give it into Mistress Grace's own hands as soon as you can. I am going out with Master Dewberry, here, upon this business, which I see you have heard of. What may be the result of these foolish people's foolish suspicions, I cannot tell; but do what you can, Geoffrey, to keep the matter from the ears of Mister Cormorant and Mistress Grace as long as you can. Warn the other servants too, for there is no use in adding fresh vexation to that which your mistress is already suffering. You must all know very well that I have nothing to do with this business, and can make that clear very soon. Say, therefore, that I have gone out for a few hours, but left that packet for Mistress Grace, with my best wishes. Now, good Dewberry, go back to your inn, and tell these worthy men that I will be with them in five minutes—as soon as I have dressed myself."

Our worthy landlord pursued the directions he had received, rolled down the stairs, and laboured along the road towards the village, with his surprise and admiration both excited by the extraordinary coolness and self-possession displayed by Fairleigh under such circumstances.

By the time he had reached the middle of the bridge he perceived a great number of people issuing from the door of his own house, and ere he was half way up the street of the village he encountered ten or twelve constables and special constables, headed by the two magistrates in person.

No sooner did he approach than the stentorian voice of one of the magistrates, Sir Thomas Smythe, all unlike the dulcet notes of Sacharissa's lover, was heard to exclaim,

"Take him into custody."

"Where hast thou been?" Sir Denis Leigh exclaimed, in softer tones.

"You have been aiding and abetting felony!" cried Sir Thomas.

"You have been warning the guilty to escape!" said Sir Denis.

"You have been helping the lion to fly from his pursuers!" said Sir Thomas.

"You have been treacherously giving information of our secret council!" said Sir Denis.

"It is being an accessory after the fact," said his companion.

"It is misprison of treason!" said the other.

"It is levying war against the king!" shouted Sir Thomas.

"It is a gaol delivery!" cried the head-constable, determined not to be outdone by his betters.

"Haw, haw, haw!" exclaimed Dewberry, laying his two hands upon his fat stomach. "What is the matter with your worships?"

"Hast thou not gone down on purpose," said Sir Thomas, "to warn Lucien Fairleigh alias Master Lucien, to evade and escape the pursuit of justice by flying out of the back door while we are approaching the front? Hast thou not done this, Dewberry? And woe be unto thee if he have so escaped! Take him into custody, I say?"

"Well, your worships," said Dewberry, beginning to look a little rueful under the hands of the constables, "I have been down to Master Lucien, I own it; but I went upon other business that I had to do with him. Does not every one know that I had a packet down for him by a special messenger yesterday night, with orders to deliver it into his own hands? And if I did talk with him this morning of what was going on, did he not send his compliments to your worships, and bid me say that he would be up with you in five minutes, as soon as he had got his clothes on?"

"Pooh! nonsense, man!" exclaimed Sir Thomas, growing red in the face. "Do you think we are fools, to be taken in with such a story as that? Are you fool enough yourself to think that he will come?"

"I say, as sure as I am a living man, he will come," said Dewberry. "Aye, more, my masters," he continued, after giving a glance towards the Manor House, "I say, then, he is coming."

All eyes were instantly turned in the direction in which his own had been bent the moment before, and the figure of a man, which seemed to have just issued out of the gates of the park, was seen walking with a slow, calm step along the road towards the village.

The magistrates, the constables, and the multitudinous crowd which followed them, all stood in silence, and what we may call "thunderstruckness,"

So little credence had they given to the assurance of Master Dewberry.

However that may be, the party could not believe their eyes when they saw Lucien Fairleigh approaching.

He came up without the slightest appearance of hesitation or dismay at the sight of the formidable phalanx arrayed against him.

"I am told," he said, "that a most lamentable affair has occurred, and that *I* am accused of being the cause of it. However absurd this supposition may be, I suppose you feel yourself justified in arresting me, and, therefore, I will go with you—the more readily, because I know that I can so easily disprove the charge."

He was led accordingly in a kind of state procession to Huntley Castle, where he was placed in a room to await the coming of the marquis.

Mistress Martha received the magistrates haughtily, and when Lucien Fairleigh had been locked in his chamber, she turned sharply and contemptuously upon them, saying,

"He did not do it. He never did it. You will make yourselves a laughing stock in the country."

Sir Thomas was about to reply ; but she silenced him by ordering one of the servants who followed her to have the cold meats laid out in the little hall, and find the butler for a stoup of Burgundy.

A proposal made by him to leave two constables behind in the ante-room she cut short less pleasantly, telling him that she would have no constables in her master's house, except such as were intended to be thrown out of window.

The magistrates soon saw that it was of no use to contest matters with the haughty and fiery dame, and, for want of other things to do, therefore, they followed the man-servant, and were soon deep in the mysteries of a cold collation.

In the meanwhile, Fairleigh had remained in the solitary chamber which had been assigned to him.

As soon as the door was closed he took nine or ten turns up and down the room in a state of much agitation ; then gazed out for a moment from each of the windows, by which it was lighted ; and then sat down at the table, and placed his hands for several minutes before his eyes.

The room itself was a cheerful and a pleasant one, with a vaulted ceiling richly ornamented, while the thick walls of the tower were lined with oak, very deep in hue, and finely carved with Gothic tracery.

The form of the chamber was perfectly square, and its extent might be six and twenty feet each way.

The furniture, too, was good though ancient, and of the same carved oak as the panelling. It consisted in a large table, and a smaller one, eight or nine large high-backed chairs, and several curious carved cabinets.

But the objects which most attracted the attentions of Fairleigh were two small panels, distinct from the rest of the wainscotting, and ornamented in such a way as to show that they were not at all intended to be concealed, with a small pointed canopy above each, similar to that which surmounted the door by which he had entered, but only smaller in size.

In each of these panels was a small keyhole, surrounded by an intricate steel guard, and it was evident that each covered the entrance of one of those cupboards in the wall, in which our remote ancestors took so much delight.

Besides the door by which he had entered, there was a smaller one on the opposite side of the room, leading, as Fairleigh conceived, to a staircase in one of the large buttresses, and as it might be useful to know all the outlets of his temporary abode, his first action, after gazing round the room, was to approach that second door, and try whether it was or was not locked.

It was firmly closed, however, and he took his way back towards his seat, pausing, by the way, to examine the two small closets we have mentioned, and murmuring to himself, as he did so, " This is very strange."

As he spoke he drew forth from his vest the key which had been given him on the preceding night by Moonlight Jack, and put it in the lock, but did not turn it, though it fitted exactly.

He withdrew it again almost instantly, and replaced it in his bosom, then folded his arms upon his chest, and took one or two turns up and down the room, pausing at every second step, and gazing thoughtfully upon the floor.

By the time he had been half an hour in this state of confinement he heard a key placed in the lock of the door by which he had entered.

In another moment it opened, and the tall, stately figure of Mistress Martha entered.

In one hand she carried several books, and in the other some writing paper, with a small ink horn suspended on her finger.

She shut the door after her, but did not attempt to lock it, and then laying down the books and implements for writing on the table, she turned round and gazed fixedly in Fairleigh's face.

"Have we ever met before ?" she said, at length. Your face is familiar to me, it comes back like something seen in a dream. Have we ever met before ?"

"If we have," replied Lucien Fairleigh, "it must have been many years ago, when the face of the child was very different from the face of the man."

She still gazed at him, and after a considerable pause said, " I have brought you some books that you may read, and wherewithal to write, if you like it. In return for this write me down your name."

Lucien smiled, and at once complied.

Mistress Martha glanced at it with a meaning smile and quitted the room.

Lucien had not been left five minutes alone ere the voices of persons, rapidly approaching, caught his ear.

At first he imagined that they proceeded from the side by which he himself had entered ; but the moment after he became convinced that they came from the direction of the other door, which, as he justly supposed, communicated with a staircase in one of the large buttresses.

At first, of course, the sounds were indistinct, but a moment after, a key was placed in the lock and a loud deep voice was heard exclaiming, " I will stop for nothing till I have seen him face to face ! Where is this murderer of my son ?"

The door was thrown violently open before these words were fully spoken, and the Marquis of Huntley himself stood before the prisoner.

He was a tall, handsome, powerful man, wide-chested, broad-shouldered, and still very muscular without being at all corpulent. He might be about sixty-four years of age, and his hair was snowy white. His eyebrows, however, and his eyelashes, both of which were long and full, were as black as night. There was many a long deep furrow on his brow, and a sort of scornful but habitual wrinkle between the nostril of the strong aquiline nose and the corner of his mouth. On his right cheek appeared a deep scar, round, and about the size of a pistol-ball, and on the chin was a longer scar, cutting nearly from the lip down into the throat and neck. He was dressed in a suit of plain black velvet, with the large riding boots and heavy sword which were common about fifteen years before the period of which we now speak, but which were beginning by this time to go out of fashion.

On entering the room, his teeth were hard set together, his brow contracted till the large, thick eyebrows almost met, and his whole air fierce and agitated. His dark eyes darted round the room in a moment, and alighted upon Fairleigh, who turned and faced him at once.

The moment, however, that their looks met, a strange and sudden change came over the whole appearance of the Marquis of Huntley.

He paused abruptly and stood still in the middle of the room gazing in Fairleigh's face, while the frown departed from his brow, and he raised his hand towards his head, passing it twice before his eyes as if he fancied that some delusion had affected his sight. His lips opened as if he would have spoken, but for a moment or two no sounds issued forth, and the calm, quiet, steady gaze with which Fairleigh regarded him, seemed to trouble and agitate him.

"What is your name? what is your name?" he exclaimed rapidly when he could speak. "Who brought you here?"

"My name is Lucien Fairleigh," replied the prisoner. "If you seriously ask, my lord, for I suppose I have the honor of addressing the Marquis of Huntley, if you seriously ask me who brought me here, I have only to reply, two very silly persons, calling themselves magistrates, who have trumped up this foolish charge against me."

"Foolish charge, sir?" exclaimed the marquis. "It is a terrible—a most terrible charge!"

"You forget, my lord, that I assert my innocence. I assure you most solemnly, by all I hold dear—I pledge you my honour as a gentleman, as a Christian, as a man, that I have no more share in this unfortunate event than you have."

"Yet your proceedings have been strangely mysterious lately."

"In what way?"

"You quarrel with Mr. Clement Cormorant—you leave him because he refused you your money; yet when you leave him you are suddenly possessed of funds, and your father and mother are supplied with every luxury. Stay! interrupt me not. You threatened him that you would turn robber, and you have been seen in company with one of the greatest thieves on the highway—a man called Moonlight Jack."

"Those persons are not father and mother to me," returned Lucien Fairleigh, fixing his eyes upon the face of the marquis; "I claim a higher birth. Yet of that anon. My business is now to swear my innocence."

"I would willingly believe you," said the marquis; "but, oh! young man, if you have slain him by fraud or villany, I will take vengeance on you by making you the public spectacle, and giving you up to the rope and the scaffold. Chains shall hang about you, even in your death, and your bones shall whiten in the wind! But if you have slain him foot to foot and hand to hand, you shall meet a father's vengeance in another way. Aye, old as I am, I will take your heart's blood, and you shall find that this arm has lost nothing of its skill, and but little of its strength. You shall learn what a father's arm can do when heavy with the sword of the avenger!"

So saying he left the room.

When he reached his study he found Lawyer Tenterden waiting for him.

"Well, my lord," he said, humbly, though with some eagerness, "how goes the evidence?"

"I know not," returned the marquis. "*I fancy this man Fairleigh is innocent; but, if you prove him guilty, there is a thousand pound note for you at once!*"

The lawyer turned pale, but he did not refuse.

He was a young lawyer, and needed a patron.

"If law *can* prove him guilty, consider it done, my lord," said he.

"Yes, yes," muttered the marquis to himself, as he strode up and down the room, "yes, yes; he *must* be proved guilty; and yet he is strangely like—strangely like——"

CHAPTER XII.

A CHANGE IN THE SCENE—THE CROSS ROAD—MOONLIGHT JACK AND THE MAGISTRATES—THE DISCOVERY OF THE BODY.

THE Marquis of Huntley was still in earnest consultation with the lawyer when Mistress Martha entered abruptly, leading in Soft Sam.

"Here is one, my lord," she said, "who can give us information. He says that last night he saw the murderers burying their victim."

"Who?" demanded the marquis, who still clung to the idea that Lord Davenport was still alive.

"Why, the boy—the boy," replied Soft Sam, "the boy Henry. I come to tell you where he lies."

"Lead us to the place, then," cried the marquis. "Get out some of the men and let us go at once."

Within half an hour the party started, among which were the marquis, the lawyer, Tenterden, the two magistrates, and Soft Sam.

As soon as they reached the beech trees, a perquisition was commenced in order to discover any ground which might seem to have been recently moved; and ere any very long search had been made, a part of the thin green turf showed, amidst the rank blades of grass which covered the ground beneath the trees, a quantity of scattered mould, clearly indicating that there was the spot they sought.

As soon as this discovery was made, a new difficulty presented itself.

With a want of foresight common to country magistrates in those days, the worthy and worshipful knights who came to exhume the body reported to be interred there had forgotten to order any spades, shovels, or pickaxes to be brought with them; and there they were, in the midst of a wild moor where no implement of the kind was to be found within a mile or two.

On the first mention of this want, one of the more active of the lads who had accompanied the party, set off as hard as his legs would carry him in the direction of the little town of Moorhurst; but as that town was several miles distant, some of the other persons present suggested that it would be better to send up to the farm which had lately been taken by Farmer Tyrrell just upon the edge of the moor; and while this suggestion was actually being followed, a discussion naturally arose in regard to Farmer Tyrrell, his habits, character, appearance, station, fortune, and farm.

"Aye, he has got a bad bargain of it," said a sturdy farmer in a white smock frock, which concealed the greater part of a strong, short-backed pony that he bestrode. "Aye, he has got a bad bargain of it, and if he don't mind what he is about he'll do for himself. I might have had the farm for an old song if I had liked, but I'd have nothing to do with such poor swampy stuff. Why, the place has been out of lease for two years."

" He'll do very well," grunted another of the same class. " I'm sorry I did not take the place myself. He'll do very well ; he comes from Lincolnshire, and knows that sort of land. At least I saw J. Tyrrell, Squash Lane, Lincolnshire, upon one of his carts ; he'll do very well. He has the finest horses in the country, too."

" I wonder you call those fine horses, Master Bornham," said a respectable labourer who overheard the conversation ; " they are no more fitted for hard work than my sick wife, Jane ; and as for the matter of that, Farmer Tyrrell will never be much liked hereabouts, for he's brought all his own labourers with him, and that's a hard case upon the people of the place. They say he has been a soldier, too ; and I'm sure he don't look like a farmer, or anything half as honest. Why, he goes about in a laced jacket like a gentleman ; and I never saw him at market, not I."

" I'll tell you what !" cried a sturdy drover who had joined the group, " he's as good a judge of cattle for all that, as any man in this county. He knows a beast when he sees it, doesn't he ? Why, he bought half a score of me the other day, and paid me down, drink money and all, without a word."

Such were the comments that took place upon Farmer Tyrrell in one of the groups into which the party had divided itself.

Something similar, with a very slight variation, from the different class and character of the speakers, was taking place amongst the rest ; and all the little investigating spirit which is excited by the arrival of a stranger in a country place, especially if that stranger be somewhat reserved in his habits, was exercising itself in regard to Farmer Tyrrell amongst the whole of the assembly on the moor.

Lawyer Tenderden ventured to hint that he suspected Farmer Tyrrell had been a bankrupt in Lincolnshire before he came into their county ; but this was instantly contradicted by several others who had had dealings with him, and who represented him as possessing all those excellent qualities which gold invariably bestows upon its owner.

Two or three of the young men talked of Farmer Tyrrell's beautiful wife, but declared she was as coy and backward as if she had been old and ugly.

Some had only caught a sight of her ; some had heard her speak ; and some had never seen her, but were in raptures with her beauty on the mere report of others.

What between the rumours of the wife's beauty, the husband's wealth, and the report of his wearing a laced jacket like a gentleman, Sir Denis Leigh and Sir Thomas Smythe found the two organs of curiosity and reverence in their respective brains considerably excited regarding Moonlight Jack in his character of Farmer Tyrrell, and they entered into slow and solemn discussion as to whether, under existing circumstances, they should or should not pay him a formal visit.

At the end of about half an hour, however, some one was seen coming slowly across the moor on horseback accompanied by two or three others ; and in due time appeared the person who had been sent for the spades and shovels, accompanied by Farmer Tyrrell himself.

Moonlight Jack was mounted on a fine, powerful horse, full of fire and activity, which he sat in a very different manner from that in which the personages around him bestrode their beasts ; and there was something, indeed, in his whole appear-

ance and demeanour which made the greater part of the men assembled take off their hats as he rode up.

There was only one person present, with the exception of the drovers, who showed the slightest sign of recognition, and that was Master Broughton, the informer, who gave a sudden start, and then turned pale, as the stern fierce eye of Farmer Tyrrell fixed for a moment full upon him, with a meaning, perhaps a menacing look.

He ventured upon no other token of acquaintanceship, however, and, riding up at once to the magistrates, bowed to them somewhat haughtily, and said,

" I am happy to hear from this good man that your worships have discovered the place where this poor young nobleman's body has been concealed ; indeed, I expected no less from your known wisdom as soon as I heard that you had taken the matter in hand. I have now come down at once to offer you every assistance in my power. "

And he and the rest accordingly dismounted from their horses, and directed the labourers whom they had brought with them to dig up that part of the ground which bore marks of having been lately moved.

Shovelful after shovelful of earth was thrown out, and the work had proceeded some way when, cantering quickly along the road, appeared two or three persons, who proved to be Clement Cormorant and his servants.

The countenances of Sir Denis Leigh and Sir Thomas Smythe immediately fell, and the first impulse of the former was to bid the workmen suspend their proceedings, after which he turned to his comrade, beckoned up the clerk and the Marquis of Huntley's lawyer, and held with them a quick whispering conference apart.

In the meanwhile old Cormorant came up and dismounted from his horse, while every head was uncovered around, and every face beamed with a smile of pleasure and satisfaction to see him there.

" I have come," he said, " gentlemen, to be a witness of the execution of that painful task which you have undertaken, and to see, perhaps for the last time, the body of my poor young friend, Lord Davenport, whose death we all deplore. Go on, my men ; do not let my coming disturb you."

The men required no other authority, but with redoubled activity plied their work, and in a few moments a long deal case was discovered, rudely put together.

The labourers tried to take the top off at once, but they could not accomplish it ; and after digging round it on all sides, they lifted the heavy burden carefully out, and laid it on the edge of the pit.

The whole crowd gathered round, pressing somewhat roughly upon the principal personages, who occupied the front stations about the grave.

Sir Denis put on his spectacles, and rubbed his hands, as if arriving near some long-desired consummation

Old Cormorant stood near the foot of the coffin, if it could be so called, and gazed upon it with a brow of sorrow, and something bright glistening in his eye.

Farmer Tyrrell looked on sternly, with his arms crossed upon his broad bull-like chest, and his brow gathered into a heavy frown.

There was some difficulty in wrenching up the top.

But at last one of the labourers, forcing his spade

between it and the sides, tore it open, and exposed to view the ghastly spectacle of death within.

Those who were without saw nothing but the form of a dead man; but amongst those who immediately surrounded the chest, there were exclamations of surprise, which made the rest press forward to get a nearer view, and it was then perceived by all who had known Lord Davenport, that the body was that of a stranger!

In the centre of the forehead was a small round wound, spreading from which on every side was a dark discoloured bruise, and a considerable quantity of blood had run down and disfigured the face, on which it had been suffered to remain.

Still the features were sufficiently distinct to show every one that this was not the corpse that they expected to find; and though each countenance around was pale with agitation and awe, yet on the lips of old Cormorant, and of many others, there appeared a smile of renewed hope.

That smile was almost immediately done away, however, when they could look further, for across the breast of the dead man lay a paper on which was written, in a large bold hand,

"The punishment of him who shot Lord Henry Davenport."

The first who read the paper was the magistrates' clerk, and the words were circulated in a low murmur from one to another around.

But at the same time Master Nicholas, the clerk to the receiver of the county, pressed forward as if moved by some sudden impulse, and getting as near the head of the corpse as he could, he gazed eagerly in its face, exclaiming,

"It is. Yes, I declare it is. It is the very same man that I saw lying on the road that night when the robbers laid hold of Mistress Grace Dashwood, and he was one of them beyond all doubt."

"Doubtless it must be the same," said Farmer Tyrrell, gravely. "I think I never saw a more rascally countenance in my life, or one that seemed more likely to deserve the fate that he has met with."

"His clothes are very good, however," said Sir Denis, "they don't look like those of a robber. Why, I declare there is as much lace as would cost two or three pounds any day."

"It's the same man, however," reiterated Master Nicholas, "that I will swear to, and that he was a robber there can be little doubt, from what happened to Miss Grace. Is it not so, Mr. Cormorant?"

"Undoubtedly," replied old Cormorant, "there is no doubt, there can be no doubt that robbery was their purpose. Nor is it improbable that this is one of them. One man was wounded and disarmed by my former secretary, Mr. Fairleigh, the other was beaten down and stunned by the poor innocent Soft Sam, and he it was, Master Nicholas, whom you saw upon the road. Let all these matters be taken down," he contined, looking round him for some one capable of the task.

Soon after this the company broke up, and each one retired to his respective home.

The marquis, on arriving at the Castle, immediately sought the chamber where Lucien Fairleigh was confined.

"I have seen and heard much to-day," he said, "which induces me to believe in your innocence. Yet I have more to say to you. What is it you demand of me?"

"Justice."

"I never refuse that."

"Well, then, you have in your possession certain papers which will give to me rights long denied me. I cherish the memory of those rights as dearly as you cherish yours, my lord, so restore them to me, and do a tardy act of justice."

"I have them not," returned the Marquis of Huntley.

"Nay, say not so, my lord, say not so," cried Lucien Fairleigh. "I know the existence of those papers, and I am not so powerless as you suppose, if I desired to take them by force. I have had them now two days at my will and pleasure; I have them now in my power, and if I took them should only be doing my duty to myself. But I again entreat you to do a tardy act of justice, and not force me to unpleasant measures."

During this long speech the marquis had eyed him with an expression of surprise and doubt.

At the last words, however, his brow gathered again into a frown, and he replied,

"I am not to be menaced, sir; I tell you you shall never have them, and such menace puts them further from your reach than ever."

"My lord, I use no menaces," replied Lucien Fairleigh. "Consider, my lord: here you now stand at the verge of age, touching upon that cold season when the only consolation for declining years, the wintry sunshine of our being's close, is a clear conscience and the memory of good deeds. If, alas, you are deprived of the power of looking back upon many such actions—Nay, hear me out —if there be in the past much that is painful, much that you would feign forget, much that can never be repaired, remember, oh! remember, that what cannot be repaired may often be atoned. The power of atonement is now in your hand—the power to secure the security of mind you have lost."

"Sir, I never knew it," burst forth from the marquis. "My life has been made up of passions and regrets, and as it began so shall it close."

"Oh, no, my lord, oh, no," cried Lucien, "let it not be so. I must wring your heart, but I trust it may be in some degree to heal it. You lately had a son, whom you loved deeply. For his sake, I believe, you have persisted for years in a course of injustice which the nobler part of your nature, I am sure, disavowed. My lord, he has been taken from you; the inducement to remain in wrong has been removed by the will of God, who, therein, has at once punished and opened the way to atonement. Let me beseech you, let me entreat of you, not to suffer this opportunity to pass by unnoticed."

"And do you make the assassination of my son," demanded the marquis, "a plea for my gratifying one who is accused of murdering him?"

"My lord, I have taken it for granted throughout," replied Lucien, "that you know me to be perfectly innocent of that deed. What I demand of you also I have a right to demand. I ask you not to gratify me, but to do an act of justice; I ask of you to do honour to yourself by taking away a stain from an honourable house that you have wronged."

"Right?" exclaimed the marquis, with one of his dark sneers, as if the recollection of something he had before intended to say came suddenly back upon him. "In what consists your right? And how have you any connection with the honour of the family of Huntley? What right has a bastard to prate of the honour of my family?"

The blood rushed rapidly into Fairleigh's cheek; his eye flashed, and his brow contracted, but it was only for a moment.

With what was evidently a great effort he mastered his own passions immediately, and replied,

"The coarse term you have used is inapplicable to me, Lord Huntley. Your other question I would answer by a single word, if I so pleased; and, did I feel as much assured of your son's death as you do, I would so answer it."

"Doubtless, doubtless," exclaimed the marquis, impatiently, "everything can be explained if certain ifs and buts be removed. But I tell you, sir, until they are removed, I shall listen to you no further; nor shall I detain you long, for I came to tell you what may be told in but few words. Mark me, young man, to-morrow you will be taken hence. A gaol will then receive you. A public trial and a public execution will be the end which you have obtained by measuring yourself against one who never yet failed in the accomplishment of that for which he strove."

As the marquis spoke he turned as if to quit the apartment, but Lucien, who had listened calmly and attentively, exclaimed, ere he laid his hand upon the door,

"Stay yet one moment, my lord; our conference is not finished yet. The matter on which I now detain you is these papers. I am not accustomed to say I will do what I cannot do; therefore, when I told you that if you did not do justice, I would with my own hand right myself and my family, I made no vain boast."

The marquis turned and gazed upon him both in surprise and anger, but his rage and his astonishment were doubled when the prisoner took from his pocket the key, the easily recognised key, which had been given to him by Moonlight Jack upon the moor.

Prompt, however, and decided in all his determinations, the marquis raised his voice and shouted in a tone of thunder to the servant whom he had ordered that morning to remain without.

"My lord," said Lucien, "you raise your voice in vain. I have every reason to believe that the persons you have placed there have been gone for more than an hour; and even if they were there still, those bolts and that lock would prevent them from entering; of that I have taken care."

Even while he spoke the marquis had strode across the room towards the outer door, muttering, "They shall soon return."

But the key of the door between the two rooms, which had been left in the inside, was now gone; and after gazing upon lock and bolt with impotent rage for a moment, he turned fiercely towards the other door, which led by the stairs in the turret down to his apartments below.

Lucien, however, had seized the moment, and, casting himself in the way, was in the act of locking that door also when the marquis turned towards it.

Lord Huntley instantly drew his sword, but Fairleigh was not unarmed, as he had supposed.

His own blade, which had been restored to him by the half-witted man, Soft Sam, was in his hand in a moment, but it was only to show himself prepared that he used it, for waving the marquis back with his hand, he exclaimed,

"My lord, do nothing rashly. Remember, you have to deal with a younger, stronger, more active man than yourself, and with one long accustomed to perils and dangers. Stand back, and answer me. Will you, or will you not give up those papers by fair means, or must I take them myself?"

"I will never give them!" replied the marquis. "I will never give them, though that vile and treacherous woman has not only betrayed my trust, but stolen from my private cabinet the key you now hold. I will never give them, and if you take them you shall take my blood first, and die for spilling it."

As he spoke he placed himself, with his drawn sword still in his hand, between Lucien and the small door in the wainscot which we have mentioned several times before.

Lucien advanced upon him; but with the same degree of calm determination which, except during one brief moment, he had displayed throughout their whole conference.

"My lord," he said, "you do the woman, Martha, wrong. This key was not obtained from her. I beseech you to give way, for I am determined to use it."

"Not while you and I both live!" replied the marquis, and as he spoke he made a sharp quick lunge at Lucien's bosom.

The other was prepared, however. His sword met that of the marquis in a moment, and parrying the lunge he grappled with his adversary, and the same moment wrenched the weapon from his grasp, and, by an exertion of his great strength, removed him from between himself and the door.

He had cast the sword he had mastered to the other side of the room, and the marquis seemed to hesitate for an instant as to whether he should spring forward to recover his weapon, or struggle with the prisoner to prevent him from obtaining the papers.

He felt while he hesitated that the very hesitation was undignified.

He felt, too, perhaps, that either attempt would be vain; that he was in the presence of one superior to himself in bodily power, in activity, in energy; one equal to himself in courage, determination, promptitude; one that was what he had been when a youth, but with the grand superiority of mental dignity and conscious rectitude.

He felt himself reproved and degraded, but not humbled, and the natural movement proceeding from such sensations was to cross his arms on his broad chest, and stand with a look of dark defiance gleaming from beneath his long gray eye-brows; while Lucien, taking the key in his right hand, and changing the sword into his left, stood about to open the door which covered all those mysterious points of his history which he had so long concealed.

But even then his young companion paused.

"Oh! my lord!" he said, "I would fain have these papers with your own will and consent. Again, again I ask you, now that you see I have the power to take them, will you give them to me? Will you grant me that which it is my right to demand?"

He gazed upon him sternly, fixedly, earnestly, and strong passions called up in the face of each a strange likeness of expression; but the whirlwind of their emotions was too strong for either to mark the clouds and shadows, the light or the lightning that passed over the countenance of the other.

Urged into fury, thwarted, disappointed, foiled, the marquis had no longer any command over himself, and the only dignity that he could assume was that of disappointed scorn.

"Never, bastard!" he replied, "never! Take that which you can take, that which is in your power! Fly if you can fly! Use your advantage to the utmost if it can be used; but I swear by Heaven and hell, to follow you henceforth unto the gates of death; to devote life, and soul, and worldly wealth, to your destruction; and never to cease till the dark interminable gulf have swallowed up one or both !!!"

As the marquis ended, the other looked at him for a moment fixedly, while the peer stood with his arms still crossed upon his chest, and a look of resolute, unchangeable purpose marked in every line of that dark, but splendid countenance.

Emotions, strong, but new and strange, overpowered his youthful adversary; and casting from him the sword which had successfully opposed him, and the key of all the treasured secrets of his opponent's eventful life, he sprang forward, as if with a sudden impulse which he could not resist, cast himself at the marquis's feet, and looking up in his face, embraced his knees.

The stern determination of the old man seemed shaken.

At that moment, however, strange and unusual sounds made themselves heard from without.

There were cries, and screams, and the noise of many feet, and there was a violent rush against the outer door, as if by people propelled by terror.

The bolts, the bars, the fastenings gave way, and half torn from the hinges, it burst into the room.

CHAPTER XIII.

THE ATTACK ON THE CASTLE—THE DISCOVERY!

WE must go back for a few hours.

The sky was without a star, and a dull, heavy darkness brooded over the face of the earth, as a strong party of horsemen, whose numbers and appearance might well banish all fears, and laugh to scorn all the tales of highwaymen and footpads with which the county then rang, took its way down the road which first led from the county town towards Huntley Castle, and thence passing under the walls of the park proceeded to the little borough of Penshurst.

Descending slowly from the moors, they emerged into a more open country, and any one who had been by the side of the road might have counted their number as eleven, notwithstanding the darkness of the night, and might also have observed, generally speaking, they were tall and powerful men, and sat their horses with a degree of ease and composure only to be acquired by long acquaintance with the saddle.

We have remarked before that the country in that district is famous for little greens of an acre or two in extent, generally shaded by some tall elms, and often adorned by a bright, gleaming pond.

To one of these the party that we speak of had advanced, and though there was a cottage at the further side of the green, all was quiet and still, when the word "Halt!" was suddenly given, and the voice of the leader was heard in a low tone, saying,

"Spread to the right and left under the trees. I hear a horse's feet."

The evolution that he commanded was executed in a moment with the most profound silence, each horseman separating from his neighbour and taking ground some yards to the right and left without any of that pawing and prancing which gives pomp and circumstance to many a military manœuvre.

The proceedings of the leader himself, however, were even more remarkable, for, advancing perhaps twenty yards before the rest, he also quitted the road for the green turf, and then his dim figure was seen to dismount.

The next moment horse and man seemed to sink slowly down into the earth, and nothing, but what appeared to be a small rise in the ground, was seen through the darkness, marking the spot where they stood.

While all this was taking place the sound of a horse's feet beating the road with a quick trot was heard advancing from that side towards which the party had been going, and, after a pause of about two minutes, a white horse, bearing his rider at a rapid rate, could be discovered entering upon the green.

The horseman advanced some way, unconscious of the neighbourhood of so many others; but apparently not quite insensible to fear, for, from time to time, his head was turned round on either side, and, at length, it would seem that he caught a glance of something unusual beneath the elm trees, for he suddenly pulled up his horse, and gazed anxiously before him.

His eyes were keen, and had been for some time habituated to the darkness; and, becoming convinced that there was a considerable party assembled on either side of the road by which he came, when, suddenly, what he had passed as a mere mound of earth and bushes, started into life, and his retreat was cut off by a man springing upon a horse which rose as if magically from the ground, and darting into the road before him.

"Stop!" cried a stern voice, while the gleam of something like a pistol in the hand of his opponent made the rider of the white horse recoil.

He looked round, however, to see if there were no means of evading obedience to the command he had received; but by this time he found that he was surrounded on all sides, and that the way, even to the low cottage by the side of the common, was cut off.

At the same time the command was repeated,

"Stop! and give an account of yourself!"

The additional injunction, however, of "Give an account of yourself!" was rather satisfactory to the rider, who perceived therein a sort of police tone rather than that generally employed by the worthies whom he most apprehended, and who to the word "Stop!" usually added "Deliver!"

He replied, then, with a greater degree of confidence, saying,

"I am a servant of the noble Marquis of Huntley, and I am riding to the town of Penshurst, by his orders, on particular business."

"Show me the badge upon your arm!" said the person who had first spoken; but the servant was obliged to acknowledge that he had come away in haste, and had not his livery coat on.

"You have some cords," said the same voice, addressing one of the other horsemen. "Tie him and bring him along."

In a moment, the unfortunate groom found himself seized, and his arms pinioned behind his back, while a still more disagreeable operation, that of tying his feet and legs tight to the stumps, was performed by another of his captors, who dismounted for the purpose.

"WE MUST FORCE OUR WAY IN, FOLLOW ME!"—*See page 44.*

Not a word was spoken by any one but the leader of the party, and, when he saw that the commands he had given were obeyed, he added,

"Bring him up abreast with me."

And then, riding on at the same slow pace in which they had been proceeding previous to the little episode which had taken place, he asked several questions of his captive in a low voice.

"We shall soon see," said he, "whether your account of yourself is true or not, for we are going to the Castle   Now, tell me, how long do you say you have left it?"

"About half-an-hour, sir," replied the man, resuming a certain degree of courage on finding that he was not injured; "about half-an-hour, sir; and I can tell you that my lord will be mighty angry when he finds you have stopped me, and brought me back; he will make the house too hot to hold you and the county too, that I'll warrant. You don't know whom you have to deal with. He suffers no one to do anything but what he likes."

"Is the marquis still up?" demanded the stranger, calmly, taking not the slightest heed of the other's intimation.

No. 6.– February 10, 1866.] [Order *No.* 1 *of the* BOY PIRATE, *and receive,* GRATIS, *No.* 2 *and a* LARGE ENGRAVING, PRINTED IN SEVEN COLOURS. [Price One Penny

"Yes, that he is, and will not be in bed for these two hours, as you will find to your cost, perhaps, when he hears you have stopped me," answered the groom.

"Does he not usually go to rest sooner?" asked the stranger, again. "I understood that the whole household were required to be in bed by eleven."

"Aye, he generally does go to bed at eleven," answered the groom, "but he has not done so to-night. You will have to rouse the porter, and most of the other servants, too, for old John came out, growling and damning me, in his shirt when I made him open the gates."

"He must not damn us though," replied the other quietly, but in a tone which moved the groom's astonishment even more than anything which had passed before, so little reverence did his captors show for the awful name of the marquis or any of his dependents.

At length they arrived at that spot under the walls of the park.

There the leader of the party halted, and, suffering his hands to drop thoughtfully upon the saddle bow, he gazed up towards the spot where the Castle stood.

At that dark hour, however, nothing was to be perceived but the masses of tall trees with which the building itself was confounded in undistinguished shade, except, indeed, where a single spot of light was seen gleaming high up like a beacon, and marking that there was the habitation of some human beings amongst the dark and awful-looking blackness which the scene otherwise presented.

After thus gazing for a few minutes, the leader of the party turned towards the groom, and while he reined back his horse to the other side of the road, said, with something of a sneer,

"We will save old John the porter the trouble of opening the gate for us."

At the same moment the well-trained horse that he rode, feeling a touch of the spur, started forward towards the wall, cleared it with ease, and horse and rider stood within the boundaries of the park.

"I can't leap with my hands and legs tied," cried the groom, whose first feelings were those of an equestrian; "that's impossible. I shall break my own neck and the horse's knees."

"You shan't be required to leap," was the reply of the leader, from the other side of the wall; and, then, turning towards one of his companions, he added, "You must manage to pull it down."

"I will leap it first, however," replied his companion, and away went a second horse and man over the wall.

No sooner was this done than several of the other horsemen dismounted, and with short bars of iron, which each of them appeared to have slung at their saddle bow, they set to work upon the wall of the park. In less than a quarter of an hour the space of three yards was laid level between the park and the road.

The whole of the troop then passed in, taking the groom along with them, and, riding slowly up to a clump of old chestnuts at the distance of about three hundred yards from the terrace on which the mansion stood, they gathered themselves together in a group under the boughs, and their leader, advancing a few paces, again gazed steadfastly upon the Castle.

Not a sound was heard but the low sounding of the wind through the neighbouring trees, and the screams of the screech owls which nestled themselves in the old ivy of the Castle.

"Now, my good fellow," he continued, turning to the groom, "I want one or two pieces of information from you; but before you answer you had better take into consideration that you are speaking to a person not willing to be trifled with; that if you do not answer straightforwardly and at once your life is not worth five minutes' purchase; and that if you give me false information you will be as surely a dead man within two hours as you are now a living one. In the first place, then, inform me in what part of the house do the servants sleep?"

"Why, up at the top to the westward," replied the man, "that is where the serving men sleep, but there are others, such as the servers, and the grooms of the chambers, who sleep at the top of Hubert's Tower. Then there is my lord's own man, who sleeps in his ante-room; but to-night there were two or three who were ordered to sleep in the outer room where the prisoner is, in the old tower, that is to say in what they used to call the haunted rooms, for they were always shut up, and no one went in but my lord and Mistress Martha, so that folks said that the ghost of the old marquis used to walk there."

"So there are three men appointed to sleep there, are there?" demanded the other. "You are sure of the fact?"

"Why, no," replied the groom; "if you mean whether I am sure they were ordered to sleep there, I'm sure enough of that; but I am quite as sure that not one of them will do it, for I heard one of them say that the marquis might skin him alive first. No, no; they'll none of them stay there after twelve o'clock at night, I'll answer for that."

"Now, tell me further, how many men in all may there be in the castle?"

The groom paused for a moment as if in thought, but then answered, "Some fifteen or sixteen."

"Not more than fifteen or sixteen," continued the other. "It is scarcely worth while priming our pistols. Are there none of them sleep below?"

The man hesitated. At length he said,

"Why, no; not by rights, except the porter and his boy; but to-night there will be Mason and the rest, who, I dare say, will come down into the corridor and sleep in the arm chairs; and then, too, there is fat Charley, who has got Soft Sam in charge, shut up in the dark room at the bottom of Hubert's Tower."

"Soft Sam!" exclaimed the other. "Why, what does he do there?"

"Why, he would not tell, I hear," answered the groom, "who were the people whom he had seen bury my young lord under the beech trees by the lake, so my lord ordered him to be shut up in the dark room, without either meat or drink till he did; and if he don't tell, hang me if he don't starve to death, for my lord's not one to go back from what he has once said."

As the man spoke, the person who had been thus questioning him moved his hand with a rapid and impatient gesture to the holster at his saddle-bow, plunged it in, and pulling out a pistol, thrust it into his belt, he continued,

"One word more, my good fellow. Is not the small wicket door at the back of the western wing very often, if not always, left open all night?"

The man hesitated, and showed evident signs of a disinclination to reply.

"It is, sometimes," he said, at length, "but not always."

"I ask you," continued the other, "did you ever know it shut?"

"Yes, I think so. I don't know; I can't tell," replied the groom, with evident hesitation at what he felt to be betraying the way into his lord's mansion.

"He prevaricates," said one of the men behind, "he prevaricates; shall I blow his brains out, captain?"

"Not yet," replied their leader, calmly. "Do you intend to answer or not? Did you ever in your life know that door to be shut?"

"No, I didn't, no, I didn't," answered the groom. "It's always open, that's the truth."

"Now, there are two doors, one of which leads to the private staircase going to the apartments of his lordship. Which of those two doors is it—the right or the left, for I forget? Your life is at stake," he added in a warning tone.

There was a sound like the clicking of a pistol-lock behind him, and the man replied without the loss of a single moment, "It is the door to the left. I tell you true, upon my word."

"I dare say you do," replied the other, "If you don't, so much the worse for you. You will remain here till I come back; and you know what will happen to you if you have made any mistake in this business. Twyford, learn from him exactly the way to the room where the poor silly man has been put. You and Harvey must undertake to set him free. Then join me with all speed at the point you know. You, Corbyn and Leslie, stay with this good man and the horses; and if you should have such reason to believe he has told me a falsehood as to induce you to leave the spot, give him a couple of ounces of lead in his head before you go. You understand me? I know a word is sufficient with you."

"But, captain!" exclaimed the man whom he called Corbyn, "why should I not go with you? Curse me if I like to be left here, holding the horses like a groom. Why must I not go?"

"Because I appoint you to a post of trust and danger," answered his leader. "There is more to be apprehended from without than from within. But to end all in one word, Corbyn," he added, seeing the other was about to reply, "you must stay here because I direct you to do so—I, who never yet found you unwilling to obey at once, in moments of action and peril."

"That's the way you always come over me, captain," replied his companion. "However, I suppose I must do as you bid, having stood by your side in many a moment of life and death work."

"And always acted like a lion where it was needful," answered his leader, holding out his hand, which the other grasped eagerly. "God bless you, Corbyn!" he added. "There is something at my heart that tells me we shall not be long together. If we part for the last time to-night, remember, that I love you, and I think even now of the watch-fire of Penington Heath, when, wounded yourself, you brought cup after cup of cold water to your wounded captain's lips."

Thus saying, he dismounted from his horse, and eight of his comrades followed his example.

The whole party then began to descend the hill, with the exception of the two who had been appointed to remain with the horses and the unhappy groom, whose terror had now grown to such a pitch that, had it not been for the lashings with which

he was attached to his horse, he could not have sat the animal that bore him, although it remained as quiet and passive as if it had never known any other stable than that of a farmer's mule.

With eager eyes, and a beating heart, the man marked the party descend the hill, emerge from the shadow of the trees, cross the dewy grass, which glistened like frost-work in the full beams of the moon.

It was certain that the property of his lordly master—that, perhaps, the lives of several of his comrades were at at stake at that moment; but yet the worthy domestic felt little or no agitation upon that score.

All that affected him, all that he thought of, as would too naturally be the case with most of the human worms that crawl about in this state of being, was his own situation, his own danger.

At length his feelings became insurmountable.

There are degrees of terror which give courage. He felt that it would be a thousand times preferable to be amongst his comrades at the castle, sharing their fate and mingling in their danger, than sitting there in perfect inactivity waiting a result which he had no power to change, and he writhed with the bonds that confined him.

As he did so he felt that the knot upon the cords which tied his arms gave in a degree, that he could loosen it still further by a great, but silent exertion of his strength; and, as he made that exertion, it slipped down to his wrists, over which it was easily passed.

The two men who guarded him were gazing as eagerly upon the castle as he had been, and their minds were too full of the progress of their comrades to allow them to take any note of the slight movement he had made, so that, before they were at all aware of what he was doing, his arms were free.

As silently as he could he slipped one hand into his pocket for a knife to cut the cords which tied his legs, and he had accomplished that purpose also, in some degree, while they still continued gazing at the castle, along the windows of which more than one light was now gleaming.

He felt he could do no more without calling attention, but he perceived that what remained to do would be speedily done if he could get away and would not impede his progress as he went, and he gazed round upon the two who remained beside him with a beating heart, longing to gallop down to the castle as fast as he could, yet terrified at the idea of making the attempt.

His hesitation was soon brought to an end, however, for, giving way to the impulse of habit, he put forward his hand, without thinking of what he was doing, and patted his horse's neck.

The gesture instantly drew the attention of those beside him.

"What are you about there?" cried one.

"He has got his hands free!"

The groom stayed to hear no more, but, snatching up the bridle, he struck his horse hard and galloped down the hill.

The report of a pistol rang in his ear the next moment, and at the same time a feeling as if some one had run a hot iron along his right cheek, followed by the trickling down of blood, showed him that the robber's aim had not been far amiss.

The slight wound only added wings to his flight, however, and the sound of a horse's feet following urged him on still faster.

It was, and he knew it, a ride for life or death, but, fortunately for him, his beast felt that it was speeding to its longed-for stable, and, though the hoofs of the pursuer sounded close behind, the groom rather gained than lost ground in that headlong race.

Moonlight Jack uttered scarcely a word as he led his men down the hill, through the deep plantations to the left of the castle, and to the small door which he was aware stood generally unlocked throughout the whole night.

Not a human being seemed to be stirring in the mansion or its proximity; darkness, silence and solitude reigned in all the offices and courts, and the highwayman laid his hand upon the heavy iron latch which was to give him admission into the interior of the building without his approach having been perceived by any one.

He paused then for a moment, however, and spoke in a low tone to his band, saying,

"Remember, to free this young gentleman is the first object. After that take what may fall in the way; money and jewels; nothing heavy, nothing cumbersome; all the rest that is light in weight and valuable in quality sweep off at once. What right has he to such wealth more than we have?" he added, in the tone of one who sought to justify to himself and others acts the justice of which he doubted. "He took many a thing from others with a strong hand, and he shall now feel the strong hand in turn. Your weapons, I know, are never unready, but use them not, unless we are compelled. As little bloodshed as possible! Remember, Hardman, the silly man, poor fellow, must be seen to first; then by the marquis's dressing-room up to the old tower. You may clear the dressing-room as you come, if you like; there are many jewels there."

Those he spoke to heard his directions without reply, though some who were armed with muskets fixed the bayonets at the muzzle, and others loosened their swords in the sheaths, and the priming of some of the pistols was examined or increased.

Hardman and one or two others, indeed, of the more experienced seemed too sure of their preparations to need any investigation thereof, and, without touching their weapons, prepared to accompany their leader with as much easy nonchalance as if he had been leading them to a ball-room.

Moonlight Jack himself neither touched sword nor pistol, but there was no affected carelessness in his air.

It was grave and stern, and full of thought, as it well might be when bent upon an errand in the course of which human blood might be spilt like water; without any of the exciting and animating spirit of martial enterprise which, under other circumstances, might have led him to tread gaily the path to tenfold dangers.

He looked round his companions, however, while the short and fluttered preparation was made, then laid his hand upon the latch, and the door opened easily to his hand.

All was dark within, and the hollow echo of Moonlight Jack's foot, as he crossed the threshold and strode on into the vaulted passage, was the only sound to be heard in the mansion.

One by one the others followed, and, leading them on through the dark corridors, without either hesitation or mistake, the highwayman proceeded straight towards what was called the little hall, and pushed open a swinging door which lay between it and the passages communicating with the offices.

As they did so, a light burst upon them, and dazzled their eyes.

A pistol was fired, and one of the highwaymen fell dead by the side of Moonlight Jack.

The heavy door was at the same moment banged to, and an attempt made to secure it.

"Ha!" exclaimed the highwayman, "we are anticipated; we must force our way in. Follow me!"

With a loud shout the men, headed by Moonlight Jack, dashed at the door, and before the defenders had time to fasten it, it was again dashed open, and the highwaymen rushed in.

But the defenders had retreated.

Moonlight Jack strode on, however, into the midst of the hall, with a pistol in his hand; but the place was tenantless, and he found that the light proceeded from a large sconce over the chimney, and from a lamp standing on the table.

"This will light us on our way," he said, taking up the lamp. "That is the door, Hardman, which leads to the marquis's rooms above. When you have set the poor man free, come that way at once. In the end room of the suite you will find a door opposite to you, leading to a staircase between that room and the top rooms of the tower above. Follow the stairs and join me, but remember, do not hurt the old man. Tie him, if he resists, but do not take his life without he attempts to take yours."

Thus saying, he turned, and took his way through the passage that led towards the foot of the great stairs, which he found dark and solitary.

There Hardman and his companion left him, and with the rest of his followers, now reduced to six in number, Moonlight Jack ascended the steps, and entered the long corridor.

"Hark!" he whispered, after pausing a moment. "Hark! there are voices speaking beyond, and I think I see a light through the door. That chamber lies close at the foot of the stairs which we have to go up, and we must see what it contains ere we proceed farther. Follow me," he continued, and, advancing with a noiseless step, he pushed open the door, which was only ajar, and strode at once into the room.

There, seated round the table, furnished with a large black jack full of strong ale, were, not only the three men that were ordered to keep guard over Fairleigh, but two or three women servants of the house, whom their male companions had prevailed upon to come and cheer the solitary hours of night with their presence, and to banish all fears of the ghost by numbers and merriment.

The sudden apparition of Moonlight Jack and his followers, however, at once put an end to all glee.

The men sat for a moment as if turned into marble with terror and astonishment; but the women, without waiting to see whether the object of their apprehensions was corporeal or incorporeal, fled with loud and piercing screams by the door, and as their retreat towards the great staircase was cut off, they had no resource but to rush up towards the chambers inhabited by Lucien Fairleigh.

No sooner was the example of flight set them than the men hastened to follow it with loud and terrified vociferations, and though Moonlight Jack, irritated by the noise, vowed he would fire upon them if they were not silent, they continued their outcry as they rushed on before him up the stairs and through the outer chamber.

Without calculation or concert it struck each of the terrified servants that they might make their way through the prisoner's room down into the marquis's apartments, where they hoped to find new courage or protection from one to whom they had been accustomed to see all things yield in his vicinity.

Each then rushed towards the door, and when they found it locked pushed against it with frantic vehemence.

It shook, it yielded, the steps of the pursuers were heard at the top of the stairs. Another great effort was made, and so sudden and violent was the rush against the door that it gave way at once, and, darting in, the terrified servants found themselves in the presence not only of Fairleigh but of the marquis himself.

"What is the meaning of all this?" exclaimed his lordship. But scarcely had the word issued from his lips, and before he could receive any reply, when the figures of several strange men, armed, appeared at the doorway, and gave him some intimation of the truth.

No sooner did he behold this sight than he sprang towards the door which led to his apartments below, unlocked it, and calling to his servants,

"Follow me," he darted down the stairs, leaving Fairleigh to act as he thought fit.

Moonlight Jack paused but for a single instant for the purpose of speaking a few hurried words to the prisoner, or rather spoke them as he passed.

"Quick!" he cried, "take possession of the papers if you have not got them, and fly across the park down to Penshurst, and thence to London, where use your advantage, and hire the most knavish, which means the best of that great herd of knaves, called lawyers. I must after yonder old man, or he will get to the alarum bell, and have the whole county up upon us."

"Stop, Moonlight Jack, stop!" exclaimed Lucien. "Remember ——"

"I cannot stop, I cannot remember!" shouted Moonlight Jack, sharply, in return, and darting towards the door he rushed after the marquis, followed by his band.

Lucien Fairleigh, left alone, paused for a moment as if to consider, and then took the same path that the rest had done.

The stairs were all in darkness; but the lights from the rooms below, the noise of many voices, of trampling feet, and of evident contention, guided him; and rushing on through the dressing-room, he came to the marquis's bed-room, where the old man, having snatched up what weapons he could find, with the terrified women clinging to his knees, and the three men armed in haste around him, now stood like an ancient lion brought to bay.

With his white hair floating back from his face, and the fire of unquenchable courage flashing from his eyes. With a pistol presented towards Moonlight Jack in one hand, and a drawn sword in the other, he leaned forward ready and eager for the unequal strife; while the highwayman, with his band behind him, and his arms crossed upon his broad chest, stood gazing upon the old peer with a look, stern, indeed, but not devoid of admiration.

At the same time, in a detached group to the right, were Harwood and Hardman, the first of whom had his foot firmly planted on the chest of the marquis's valet, who lay prostrate before him,

while with his right hand Moonlight Jack pointed a pistol at the servant's head.

Hardman from behind, with a short carbine raised to his shoulder, took aim at the marquis, exclaiming, as he looked towards Moonlight Jack, "Shall I fire?"

Like lightning Lucien Fairleigh sprang forward, grappled with Hardman, and threw up the muzzle of the carbine, which instantly going off, struck the fine gilded ceiling, and brought down a considerable part upon their heads.

"Hold! hold!" shouted Moonlight Jack. "If any one stirs he shall die!"

"I know you, mutinous traitor! I know you," exclaimed the marquis, gazing fiercely upon the highwayman. "I have not forgotten you."

"Nor I you, buccaneer," replied the highwayman. "But this is no time to call such memories to mind. Make no resistance, and you are safe."

But even as he spoke, there came the rushing sound of many feet from the direction of the little hall below.

The door to the left of the room was thrown open, and in poured a crowd of men, grooms, horse-boys, running footmen, all armed, in haste, with whatever weapons they could catch up, and led on by the very groom who had been left upon the hill.

Many of them, pale with terror, but the determination and courage of a few among them served to inspire the whole, and they poured on into the room to the number of twelve or thirteen men, jostling each other through the door, and gazing wildly round a chamber in which few, if any of them had ever been before, and which now presented so strange and fearful a scene.

The eyes of Moonlight Jack flashed as he beheld them, and Hardman, suddenly bursting from the grasp of Lucien Fairleigh—for all this had passed in a single moment — sprang to the side of his leader, while Harwood, coolly firing the pistol at the valet's head, followed his companions, and ranged himself with the rest.

The unhappy valet started partly up from the ground, but ere he could gain his feet, fell back again, and writhed for an instant in convulsive agony, while the spirit quitted its frail tenement.

Then all was still.

But matters of deeper interest to Lucien Fairleigh were going on at the other side of the room.

Fury had evidently taken place of calmness in the breast of Moonlight Jack, and the marquis's eyes were blazing with triumph and wrath as he found himself unexpectedly supported by so large a body of men.

"Now, villain, will you surrender and meet your fate?" the old man exclaimed. "Now, surrender or die where you stand, like a man! Out of the way, woman! Why cling you there?" he continued, spurning one of the women servants with his foot, and striding over her to approach nearer to the highwayman.

But at that moment Moonlight Jack's arms were unfolded from his breast, the pistol in his right hand was raised in an instant, there was a flash, a report, and the marquis fell back.

Consternation for a moment seized upon his attendants, and Lucien Fairleigh's voice was heard aloud exclaiming,

"If you have killed him you shall answer for it with your life!"

But Lord Huntley sprang up again instantly, crying,

"'Tis nothing! 'tis nothing but a slight hurt! Take that, villain!"

And, in the very act of rising, he fired the pistol, which he had never let fall, into the midst of the group of robbers.

He probably intended the shot for Moonlight Jack, and there had been a time when no shot of his would have failed in reaching its object; but he was wounded and old, and the ball hit the man Harwood a few inches below the collar-bone, and brought him to the ground with a wild, unnatural scream. All was now confusion.

A number of shots were now fired on both sides, till the pistols and carbines which had been loaded were discharged, and, betaking themselves to other weapons, the two parties mingled, and bloodshed, slaughter, and determined strife spread throughout the whole apartments.

Some were driven back into the rooms beyond, and prolonged the struggle there; some died where they stood, and some were seen to steal away wounded, or to fly as fast as they could with terror.

Skill, however, and discipline were on the part of the robbers, and, though they were inferior in number, the advantage was evidently on their side.

Moonlight Jack, with all the worst parts of his nature roused and fierce within him, commanded, directed, and fought as if he had been in the field.

His eye was in every part of the chamber in turn, and his voice was heard shouting orders to his different men, which, promptly obeyed, almost always brought success along with them.

Two of the grooms, who thrust themselves between the highwayman and their master, fell by his hand, either killed or wounded, even while he was directing others.

But while he strode on towards the old nobleman, who struggled fiercely forward to meet him, he was encountered by one at least equal to himself.

With difficulty, Lucien Fairleigh had forced himself forward through the scene of strife and confusion that was going on.

He spoke to no one, he assailed no one; though he parried more than one blow aimed at random at his head, for though the lamp above gave abundant light, the struggle and the obscurity caused by the smoke, had got to that pitch that men scarcely knew who were their adversaries or who were friends; but with his drawn sword in his hand, he hurried on to the part of the room where he had seen the marquis, and now seemed to devote himself to his defence.

At the very moment when Moonlight Jack was within another stride of the old nobleman, Lucien thrust himself between them.

But the highwayman's blood was all on fire.

"Out of my way!" he cried, "out of my way or take the consequences!"

"Stand back!" cried Lucien in return, while his eyes flashed too with living lightning. "Stand back, or I forget all, and you die!"

"Out of my way!" again repeated Moonlight Jack, and their swords crossed.

At that moment, however, the loud, long peal of the alarum bell made itself heard throughout the whole castle; rung with such violence and determination, as speedily to rouse all the villages and hamlets in the neighbourhood.

Moonlight Jack heard the sound, and never in the moment of the strongest passion, forgetting the judgment and the skill which had distinguished him even in the most unjustifiable enterprises, he glared upon Lucien Fairleigh, unwilling to yield his victim or to give up the strife; but then, as the knell sounded louder and more loud upon his ear, he turned to his nearest companion, saying, in a low voice,

"Denman, we must make our retreat; tell Hard-man to get the men together. We go by the same way that we came. Get hold of yonder casket, and see what is in that cabinet, while I and these good fellows screen you; and be quick, for we shall have the whole peasantry upon us. There is a tremendous smell of fire! Be quick, be quick!"

He spoke rapidly but calmly, glancing with his eye from time to time towards his antagonist.

Although he felt very sure that Fairleigh would not attempt to injure him, unless he pressed him, still he kept his blade playing round that of his opponent, and when he had done he made a lunge or two to fill up the time, but evidently without any intention of wounding his adversary.

Lucien Fairleigh parried them with ease, and, as rapid in his conclusions as Moonlight Jack, he perceived at once that the ringing of the alarum bell, which struck his ear also, had rendered the robbers apprehensive of their retreat being cut off, and now made them prepare to retire.

The marquis, however, fierce and implacable, rushed forward, but the more eagerly from the sounds he heard, and from the hope of taking or destroying those who had dared to assail him.

With word and gesture he cheered on the men that still stood around him, and pressed forward upon the robbers, who were now ranging themselves in regular line, and slowly retreating to the doorway behind them.

His men, however, were in general of the opinion that it is wise to make a bridge for a flying enemy, and they seconded his efforts but feebly, notwithstanding his reiterated commands, and the fearful execrations which he poured forth upon their cowardice.

Two or three, indeed, rushed forward with him, but they were driven back in a moment by the line of their adversaries, bearing with them some severe wounds to teach them more caution for the future.

They dragged back in their flight their more impetuous lord, and, under cover of the smoke, which was now so dense as to render every object in the room indistinct, the highwayman and his men reached the door by which they had entered, and began to pass two at a time.

As they did so, the eye of Moonlight Jack ran over their numbers, and he suddenly exclaimed,

"Halt! Harwood is down and dead, and where are Hardman and Morton?"

"I am here," said a faint voice, which proceeded from a man who was seen staggering towards them through the clouds of smoke. "Go on, captain, never mind me. I will come after."

"We must leave none in the hands of the enemy," cried Moonlight Jack, starting forward, and taking the wounded man by the arm.

At that moment, however, one of the grooms darted upon Morton, and seized him by the collar, but as instantly fell back on the floor cleft nearly to the jaws by the heavy blade of Moonlight Jack, who, while he was thus remorselessly sending the spirit of an adversary to his eternal account, was shouting out with anxious care to his companions—

"Where is Hardman? I don't see Hardman."

Such is human nature.

"I am here! I am here, captain!" cried Hardman, bursting into the room from the opposite door, and throwing down a man who stood in his way.

"Come, quick, then! Come quick!" cried his leader. "We shall scarce have time to retreat."

"No, by —— we shall not!" replied Hardman, rushing up to Moonlight Jack, and speaking in a low tone, "we shall not, for the house is on fire in every part. I ran through there to see if we could get out by that staircase and the little hall, but the fire seems to have begun there. Some of the men must have knocked over the sconce. Our only way will be up these stairs, down the others from the tower, and through the great gallery. But we must be quick, for the fire is running that way rapidly."

He spoke quickly ; but by this time there was no chance of their being interrupted, for the same tidings had just been communicated to the marquis and those who surrounded him ; but not with the same clearness. And horrified at the thought of the new kind of death presented to their eyes, the whole body of grooms and attendants had made a rush towards the ante-chamber and vestibule, hoping to escape by the same way that Hardman had attempted but found impracticable.

The marquis followed them more slowly, and he might be seen once or twice to raise his hand towards his head, as if either faint from loss of blood, or giddy with the smoke and the fatigue.

Lucien Fairleigh gazed after him eagerly, and when he saw him reach the door, and take hold of the lintel as if for support, he darted forward to aid him ; but he was suddenly detained by a strong and powerful hand which grasped his arm, and turning, he beheld Moonlight Jack and two of his men by his side.

"This way ! this way ?" cried the highwayman, eagerly. "This way, if you would save your life and regain your liberty. This way, if you would recover the papers you have so long eagerly sought. The house is on fire, and everything will quickly be consumed."

Lucien hesitated, but when he turned again towards the marquis the old peer had passed through the door and was no longer visible.

"Quick, quick !" cried Moonlight Jack. "Come, you must and shall. Drag him along, whether he will or not."

Some sudden emotion, however, seemed then to take possession of him, and make him throw aside all hesitation at once.

"My duty first," he cried, "and God's will for the rest."

As he spoke he turned with a rapid step and retrod his way into the marquis's bed room.

Moonlight Jack gazed after him for a moment with a look of stern sorrow, and then said.

"On, my men ! He must perish if he will."

A number of voices now assailed Lucien Fairleigh as he entered the marquis's bed-room, exclaiming,

"Not that way ! not that way ! The vestibule is all on fire ! the stairs are down !" and men and women rushing rapidly down the other staircase.

"Where is the marquis ?" he demanded of one of the grooms as he darted by him.

"I don't know," replied the man. "Gone to the devil, I dare say," and on he rushed.

But Lucien Fairleigh, undismayed, strode forward, passed through the bed-room, and into the ante-room beyond.

The fire was running round the cornices ; the smoke was tremendously thick ; the heat and smell of burning wood intolerable, and the rushing and roaring sound of the flames, as they seemed to revel with demoniac triumph in the passages beyond, was almost deafening to the ear.

Immediately under the lamp that hung from the ceiling, however, and leaning on a table of splendid mosaic work, which was soon destined to crumble into nothing under the jaws of the devouring element, stood the Marquis of Huntley, with the blood dropping rapidly from a wound in his shoulder, and from another in the arm.

There was a sort of fixed, stern, cold determination in his countenance, which had something in it awful, as in that scene of terror and coming destruction he remained there without making one effort to save himself.

"Fly, my lord, fly !" exclaimed Fairleigh, hurrying towards him. "This way is still clear !"

"Sir," replied the marquis, calmly and coldly. "I cannot fly. I am old, and weak, and wounded ; I may as well die here as in the next room."

"God forbid that it should be so !" replied Lucien Fairleigh, eagerly. "My lord, I can bear you forth. I am young and strong, unhurt, and unfatigued. Let me—let me save you !"

"Touch me not, sir !" exclaimed the marquis ; "touch me not ! You have brought this thing upon my head. From the sight of that man's face I know where you gained your information of my former life. He came to set you free. Touch me not ! but go to join your fellows while you may. Here, with death hanging over me, and, perhaps, over you, I tell you I hate and abhor you, and will not have your support even to save my life !"

"Say not so, my lord, say not so !" replied Lucien, casting himself on his knees before him ; "let me entreat you—let me adjure you, to accept my aid ! Did you not see my sword drawn against him in your defence ? Hate me, my lord, you may ; injured me, my lord, you have ; but you know not yet that I love you with a love that may change your hate into affection. And, to show you what I feel, I swear that if you come not to safety with me I will remain and die with you !"

The old man was moved.

"This is strange—this is very strange !" he said. "But, no !" he added, "save yourself, Lucien Fairleigh, save yourself ; and, in gratitude for what you say, let us mutually forgive one another. For me, my hour is come ; I know it—I feel it. My plans are frustrated and thwarted ; the secrets of my early life displayed ; the mansion of my fathers burned to the ground ; my son, my only son, dead by the hand of a murderer ! I am old, houseless, hopeless ! Why should I linger ? I am companionless, childless ! Why should I live ?"

"Not childless, my lord," replied Lucien Fairleigh ; "not companionless, if you will have it so. Your son, Lord Davenport, is dead, but not your only son. One son is lost ; but your eldest son is at your feet !"

"God of Heaven !" exclaimed the marquis. "What do you mean ? You are so like—yes, you are so like——"

"Yes, my lord, yes," exclaimed Fairleigh, "I know I am ! I am like Ella Latimer, your first, your only wife ! I am her son ! I am your child ! But now let me save my father !" and he threw his vigorous arms around him.

The old man bent down his head upon his shoulder and wept, but he resisted him no longer ; and Lucien, with a great effort, raising that still powerful form in his arms, bore him strongly onward through the bed-room and the dressing-room behind it to the stairs.

Until that moment the marquis uttered not a word, and the tears rained heavily from his eyes ; but then he raised his head, exclaiming,

"Stop ! stop ! The papers, my boy, the papers !"

"Not for a world !" exclaimed Lucien. "If we have time it is all that we shall have," and on he hurried through the ante-chamber and down the stairs to the long gallery.

There was an awful sight before him.

The rich carved oak wainscoating was all in flames.

The invaluable pictures which covered the wal's shrivelling and cracking with the fire.

The armour and weapons, either of the chase or war, which had been piled up in the form of trophies between the panels, fallen from the brackets that supported them, cumbered the floor in many places.

The ceiling from above was dropping down with the heat, and in two places the flame might be seen forcing its way through the flooring from below, and curling up the wooden pillars that supported the roof.

It was evident that the whole of the corridors underneath were on fire, and as Lucien, bearing his heavy burden, strode on along the gallery, he knew not but that each step might precipitate both himself and the marquis into the gulf of death.

Twice he felt the flooring giving way beneath him, and twice by a longer stride he reached a spot where the beams were firm and unconsumed.

The vast size of the gallery enabled him to breathe with greater freedom, but still he could ·not see clearly to the top of the great staircase, not only on account of the smoke, but on account of a shower of sparks which came down from the top where the ceiling had fallen in.

If he reached it he knew that he was safe, for it was of stone; so he strode on.

The flooring gave way, however, at the first step, but he perceived it giving way before it was too late, and with a violent exertion he sprang across the chasm.

The effort was so great as nearly to cast him headlong down the steps, but he caught the iron balustrade, and with a beating heart felt that he and the marquis both were saved.

"Thank God!" he exclaimed.

"Thank God!" rejoined the marquis; "I can walk, now, I can walk well!"

But Fairleigh still bore him on till they reached the doorway, and passed out under the arch which projected beyond the building.

Then relaxing his hold, he suffered the marquis to regain his feet, but still supporting him by the arm, led him onward towards a spot on the terrace, where all those who had escaped from the fire were assembled.

Farther on there were two or three people engaged in raising, with difficulty, a long ladder towards the high tower where Lucien had been confined.

But a cry of "the marquis! the marquis!" which burst from the nearest group as the two approached caused them to pause, and the woman Martha, who had been directing their movements, ran up in haste.

The marquis, leaning on the arm of him who had saved him, gazed up for an instant upon the splendid mansion of his ancestors, while in some parts wide black vacuities fringed with fire, and in others a mass of flame and a blaze of light, crowned by a pyramid of red sparks and smoke, showed him the state of that building, from the midst of which he had been borne.

The sight thus presented to his eyes, the memory of all that night's events, the sudden wakening up of old, and dear, but painful associations, the renewal of feelings which had been extinct, and the struggle of wonder and uncertainty, with joy and conviction, were overpowering to a frame weakened as his had been.

He turned from the burning mansion to his recovered son.

He gazed for a moment earnestly, intensely on his countenance, and then casting his arms around his neck, he exclaimed,

"It is, it is my son! my child! my deliverer! But my eyes grow dizzy, my heart feels sick," and as he spoke he fainted from the loss of blood, and the manifold emotions which thronged into his heart.

CHAPTER XIV

THE SEARCH FOR THE PAPERS—LOST IN THE FIRE! —THE DYING PEER—THE SNAKE IN THE GRASS.

"HE acknowledges him as his own child!" cried Martha the housekeeper. "Bear witness all of you that he acknowledges him as his son even at the moment of death!"

"Hush! he is not dead!" exclaimed the full, deep voice of Lucien Fairleigh. "Send for a surgeon, and bring a cup of water, that will restore him fully.'

As they spoke the marquis opened his eyes, and looked feebly round him.

A cup of water was brought, and a deep draught seemed to refresh him.

"I am better now," he said. "Give me your hand, my son, and help me to raise myself, I wish to look at the fire."

"Oh, mind not the fire, my lord," said Lucien Fairleigh, "your safety is the first consideration. There will not be wanting means to raise Huntley Castle from its ashes."

"But is the building all down yet?"

"No, my lord, the whole of the right wing is free from flames, and the people are bringing out everything valuable."

"But the tower!" cried the marquis. "Those papers must be preserved at any risk, otherwise your destiny will be clouded."

He then raised himself up, and gazed upon the burning building.

The fire, running along the corridors, had reached to the second story, and round the frame work of the windows might be seen the red hissing flames coiling like fiery serpents.

But above, in the windows of the chamber which contained matters of such interest to the marquis and his son, there was nothing but the calm steady light of the lamps which had been left burning there, and which still poured forth their pale rays above the raging flames below.

"There is yet time," cried the marquis, "there is yet time."

"What mean you, my lord?"

"I mean that there is yet time to secure those papers. Raise that ladder to the wall; why have you removed it?"

The ladder in question was one of those which had been raised as a means for his own escape.

"Be quick," he continued, in harsh tones, speaking to those who stood by; "by Heaven I will have your ears slit if you stand idly there."

The men, reminded by the tones of his voice that the fiery spirit still lived, hastened to obey.

But notwithstanding the fury with which he urged them to the task, it was a work of some time to raise that tall ladder.

While they laboured, the marquis watched with apprehension the progress of the flames.

One after another the small loop-holed windows of the staircase were lighted up.

At length the ladder was raised; but men hesitated to ascend through the smoke and flames.

"Now! now!" cried the marquis, when the ladder was fixed. "I will give a thousand guineas to any man who will ascend to the room."

"HERE IS YOUR HANDIWORK, AND HERE IS YOUR PUNISHMENT."—*See page 54.*

"What do you want from it, my lord?" asked a voice.

"There is a cabinet door in the wall, and in that cabinet there is a small iron case. A thousand guineas to any man who will bring me that iron case."

"I will bring it, or I will perish in the attempt," cried a young farmer, rushing forward.

"You are a brave fellow," said the Marquis of Huntley: "a thousand guineas I say!"

"I'll go through fire or water or both for a thousand guineas," muttered the man, as he buttoned his coat tightly, and drew his hat down over his eyes. "For if I had a thousand guineas, I could marry Polly Archer, and take that farm t'other side of the river."

"Up with you, then," cried the marquis.

"Has any one a pick-axe?" asked the young farmer.

"Here is a crow-bar," replied one of the servants.

"That will do!" and, seizing the bar, he sprang hastily up the ladder.

But, ere he reached the top, the flames were seen bursting through the windows of the adjoining room.

[Order No. 1 of the BOY PIRATE, and receive, GRATIS, No. 2 and
LARGE ENGRAVING PRINTED IN SEVEN COLOURS.
[Price One Penny.

Every eye followed his daring ascent with wondering interest.

He went on boldly, however, and, reaching the top, smashed through the window frames.

As he vanished through the aperture a flickering flame was seen curling round the woodwork, and then it burst into a flame.

At that moment a scream burst from the crowd behind the marquis, and a pretty girl ran forward, wringing her hands.

It was the sweetheart of the young farmer who had ascended the ladder.

A moment afterwards he was seen emerging from the very midst of the flame.

He planted his foot firmly on the ladder, and descended rapidly, holding a small iron case in his hands.

"He has them! he has the papers!" cried the marquis, as he turned towards Lucien Fairleigh with a smile of joy on his features.

"He is safe!" cried the girl; "he is safe!" and she burst into tears.

With a haste that was almost dangerous the young man descended the ladder; but the reason why he did so was soon plainly and terribly apparent to those below.

During the while he was in the chamber the flames had been curling round the upper parts of the ladder, and, just as he reached the bottom, that part which had been weakened by the fire gave way with a crash.

But, the young man was safe, and, advancing directly towards the marquis, he placed the casket in his hands.

Lucien Fairleigh gazed on it eagerly, as he thought that within it were the proofs of his own legitimacy and title to wealth, as well as of his mother's honour and purity.

The casket opened with a spring lock, and Lucien gazed eagerly while the marquis pressed it.

The cover flew open, but, to the surprise and consternation of both, the casket was empty.

"Gone! lost!" cried the marquis, "treachery on treachery!"

And he fell upon the ground in a fit of raving delirium. They raised him up and conveyed him to the right wing of the castle, which, as before said, had wholly escaped the flames.

There he was placed in bed carefully and tenderly, for he now had a son who watched over him with such care and tenderness as only a loving child can bestow on a helpless father.

Lucien Fairleigh, sitting by the bedside of the Marquis of Huntley in his wild delirium, thought only of the fact that the sick man was his father.

Never once did the idea cross his mind that through this man's death he himself would rise to honour.

But there were others in the castle whose thoughts were of a different shade, and who were enraged that, during the wild and terrible conflagration, their safety had been little thought of.

Chief among these was Lady Edith, the eldest daughter of the marquis, who soon after the return of her father and Lucien to the castle, sent for the latter to her room.

She was seated in her boudoir pale and stately when Lucien Fairleigh entered, and she welcomed his entrance only by a slight bow without rising.

Lucien saw in her at once a deadly foe.

He knew, of course, that the declaration of his legitimacy must necessarily place her and Lady Ella in the position of bastards, and he saw at once that Lady Edith was not the one to give up her long-cherished rights without a struggle.

"You have sent for me, madam?" he said, coldly.

"Yes, sir. I wish to know by what right you have usurped *my* functions?"

"Usurped your functions, madam? I understand you not."

"My words are easy of explanation, sir," said Lady Edith. "You have presumed to place yourself by the bedside of the marquis, you have issued orders to the servants, you have in more than one instance countermanded my commands. What right have *you*, a stranger, to act thus?"

"I am no stranger," returned Lucien, haughtily. "I am the son of the marquis—the eldest—the acknowledged son; and who, therefore, has more right here than I?"

Lady Edith's eyes flashed fire, and her bosom heaved violently.

"This is but a statement yet, sir," she said. "Those papers which prove your words, where are they? Have they been stolen that they may not reveal a falsehood?"

Lucien understood the covert sneer.

But he restrained his anger.

"Madam," he said, "I do not forget, no matter how harsh your words, that I am speaking to a sister. But this I *will* say, that until my father recovers nothing but force shall remove me from his side, and if he dies nothing but force shall tear from me my fortune and my name."

He expected an outburst of fierce anger.

He was wrong.

The Lady Edith was silent for a few moments, and her eyes were fixed upon the floor.

Suddenly she rose with a constrained smile, and, extending her hand, said,

"I may, perhaps, sir, have been too hasty; but you must excuse much in one who feels distracted by the frightful events of the day. Pray remain at the castle; but let us defer for a time all questions of lineage."

Lucien Fairleigh took the little hand thus held out to him, and, raising it to his lips, said,

"Madam, nothing can be more consonant with my feelings," he said; "be assured that in everything I shall be most happy to aid and second you."

He then took his leave.

Lady Edith bowed him out smilingly.

When, however, he had gone this smile was replaced by a scowl of hate.

"By heavens!" she murmured, in a hoarse whisper, "I must find some means to compass this man's death!"

CHAPTER XV.

SUSPICION—THE DEAD ALIVE—THE ESCAPE.

ON leaving the burning castle Moonlight Jack, collecting his scattered and wounded followers around him, dashed along the highway in the direction of his retreat.

When they arrived close to the drawbridge, instead of riding rapidly over it he ordered a halt.

"My men," he said, "go quietly round by the back way, I wish to enter unknown to any one."

The men, without thinking of questioning him as to his object, immediately alighted from their horses and led them round the back way to the stables.

Moonlight Jack delivered to them also his favourite mare, and then quietly, with stealthy steps, approached the front window.

This casement was crossed all over by green trellis-work, and through this Moonlight Jack glanced.

As he did so his eyes glared, and he struck his chest heavily.

Near the fire sat a young man, and by his side a young girl.

The former was talking animatedly, while the latter was glancing up into his face with gleaming eyes.

The man was Lord Henry Davenport, the girl was Gipsy Bess!

"D————n!" cried Moonlight Jack, "this is too much. Yet what can I expect? Woman! woman! ever frail, ever fickle! Let them betray me if they will; but by the bright stars above us *he* shall rue it, though the gates of hell stood between us!"

He strode away as he spoke, and stood for a moment gazing into the waters of the moat.

Suddenly a gentle voice roused him.

"Father, what ails you?"

He turned hurriedly.

The speaker was a tall boy of twelve, with long curling hair.

Moonlight Jack flung himself on the green sward and strained the boy to his breast.

Then he said, suddenly.

"Harry, my child, I thought you were with Brandon; I thought you were watching him."

"Yes; but I crept away to-night to tell you news," said the boy, seriously. "You know Jonathan Rasper, the son of the bad man you hanged?"

"Yes, yes; what of him?"

"He is with Brandon. He has joined his band, and the two men who attacked Miss Grace Dashwood have consented either to waylay you on the road or deliver you up to justice by treachery."

Moonlight Jack seemed impatient.

"More of this anon," he said; "return, my boy, to-night, and see me again to-morrow—here, at the same hour."

He then strained the boy to his breast once more and passed into the house.

When he reached the end of the passage he opened a door before him and entered a room, poorly and scantily furnished, where two persons were with whom the reader is already well acquainted.

The first, who sat near the door, with her small, beautiful foot resting upon a rude stool, and her knee supporting an instrument of music in shape much resembling a guitar, was the lovely being who had the name of Gipsy Bess.

She was finishing a song when he entered—a sweet, plaintive song—and as he came into the room her dark, lustrous eyes grew still brighter, and were raised to his with a smiling and happy look, as if she thought she was doing what would please him best, and that the well-known music would awaken some sweet thoughts in his bosom.

The stern, unmoved gloom of his countenance pained, but did not surprise her, for she was accustomed to his moody temper.

The other tenant of the room was Henry, Lord Davenport.

He was now very pale, and evidently but just recovering from severe sickness, and leaned back upon his chair with his head resting on his arm. The right side of the loose vest which he wore was cut open and tied, so as to give greater ease and space to some wounded part beneath.

So intently he had been listening to the music that he scarcely heard the entrance of Moonlight Jack.

A faint but expressive smile hung upon his pallid lip, showing that his mind was occupied with sweet things far away.

"I see," said Moonlight Jack, looking earnestly at Gipsy Bess, "that you have turned his musician as well as nurse?"

Gipsy Bess started and stared inquiringly into his face.

"Did you not wish me to do so?" she said, with her sweet-toned voice; "did you not tell me to do everything I could to soothe him and restore him to health?"

"I did so," he answered, "and I see you do so willingly."

Gipsy Bess gazed in his face with a bewildered look, as if she did not comprehend his meaning, for though his words were not ungentle, they were spoken in that tone which showed the feelings which prompted them to be bitterer than the expression.

There succeeded a pause for one or two minutes, and Moonlight Jack, moving across the room, cast himself into a chair near the window, and gazed out gloomily over the wide prospect that stretched far beneath his eyes, diversified only by the slopes of the hills, without town, or village, or hedge-row to mark man's habitation or his cultivating hand.

As he sat there, he spoke not to any one, and the silence grew painful, till at length it was broken by Lord Henry, as we shall continue to call him, who said,

"I am glad of an opportunity of speaking with you, for I want to know more precisely how I am situated. I have to thank you, I find—"

"For nothing, sir," returned Moonlight Jack. "I have done what I have done for my own pleasure and convenience, and you have to thank me for nothing."

"Such is, perhaps, the case," said Lord Henry, coolly; "at all events you saved my life when I should otherwise undoubtedly have bled to death upon the moor. You have since treated me kindly and skilfully, have nearly cured a wound which might have proved fatal, and have tended me with much attention. At the same time various things, and my having seen, too, an ill-looking fellow with a pistol in his hand, sitting at the foot of the next flight of steps when I crossed from one room to the other, incline me to believe that you view me in some sort as a prisoner."

"Doubtless the ill-looking fellow, as you call him," replied Moonlight Jack, with a bitter smile, "may find many of the fair and the gay in his own rank of life, who would think him fully as good looking as Lord Henry Davenport. But as you owe to me your life you say, how can you complain of being kept a prisoner?"

"I am sure, sir," said Lord Henry, "there is no Englishman who does not prefer his liberty to his life."

"Then, perhaps the best way of settling it," said Moonlight Jack, "will be to shoot you through the head at once, and thus have the account between you and me as it stood before."

As he spoke, Gipsy Bess had advanced gently to his side.

She laid her hand softly upon his arm.

"Jack," she said, glancing up into his face, "Jack, set him free as soon as he is able to depart."

"What is it to you, Bess?" cried Jack, turning sharply upon her, "why do you wish him to depart?"

Her eyes filled with tears, and her white breasts, gleaming through her light gauzy dress, trembled like the rippling billows of the ocean.

"It is much to me, dear Jack," she said reproachfully, "very much to me. I *do* wish him to depart, for you have twice looked coldly upon me since he has been here, which you never in your life did before, and anything which makes such a change I wish instantly away. Set him free, Jack ; he will swear to reveal nothing, and I will be answerable for it that he keeps his word."

For a moment Jack had thought of setting him free.

Her last indiscreet words at once dispelled this willingness.

"*You* will be answerable for him ?" he cried fiercely. "No, woman, if you choose to betray your lover, do so ; I will *not* set him free. I will neither stop you nor watch you ; but mark you well, the consequences be on your own head."

Thus saying, he turned upon his heel with a frowning brow and hastily quitted the room.

Gipsy Bess fell back in her chair with a low moan, and covered her face with her hand.

Lord Henry gazed at her in pity.

This pity soon resolved itself into admiration.

No wonder.

Gipsy Bess, always exquisitely beautiful, looked specially so at this moment.

Her arms being raised to her head, the whole outline of her person was fully revealed.

The glowing breasts, white as snow, soft as love, fluttering like the bosom of a lakelet ; the taper waist, the sloping hips, and the full swell of the glorious limbs, around which the drapery had tightened so as to reveal their largeness and roundness ; all were noted and admired by the young lord, who, sensual, and taught to believe in his own power and beauty, thought he could make an easy prey of this delicious type of maidenhood.

He approached, and his person trembled with delight as his arm passed around her palpitating form.

"He treats you harshly, lady," he said.

She sprang from him, and glanced at him with a look of anger and indignation.

"Treats me harshly ?" she cried. "It is false ! he is kindness itself and he is right, too. I *have* been sorry for you, I see now I was wrong."

She then quitted the room.

She found Moolight Jack in a lower chamber.

Advancing towards him, she passed her arm round him as he sat at the table and drew his head down upon her warm bosom.

"Jack," she said, "I have done wrong. I should not have interfered with you. I was sorry for him, and thought he might have some one to love him as I love you, and so I wished to send him back to his happy home ; but I was wrong to speak of it. Forgive me, Jack, I won't vex you again."

Moonlight Jack strained her passionately to his heart, and kissed her fondly again and again.

"Oh ! deceive me not, Bess," he said, "deceive me not ! By all the powers of heaven and hell, I swear that I will exact a terrible vengeance if you do ! But, there, my girl, don't weep for me. I love you—remember that, and don't try me too far."

After this Moonlight Jack saw that she was less with the prisoner than before, but he did not see that she was never with him at all.

Yet such was the case. From that hour she went near Lord Henry no more.

Yet within four days of this conversation Lord Henry had escaped with the secret of Jack Tyrrell's home !

CHAPTER XVI.

THE FLOGGING OF THE JUSTICE—THE ATTACK ON THE HOME OF MOONLIGHT JACK—THE BATTLE —THE FATAL SHOT—JACK'S SON CAPTURED— HIS ESCAPE.

"GOOD news, Master Justice, good news," cried Jack Sprott, the constable, as Mr. Justice Folderough was sitting in the room of the little inn at Penshurst next morning.

"Sit down, Master Sprott, sit down, and take a ladleful," cried Justice Folderough. "Now what is your story ?"

"I have found out where this Jack Tyrrell—this Moonlight Jack hangs out."

"Ah ! where is it ?"

"Over the hills by Lorneley. I can lead the way."

The justice rubbed his hands.

"Good !" he cried. "Drink up some punch, Mr. Sprott, and we will start at once. How many constables can you rely on ?"

"Only two, sir. All the rest are drunk or in bed."

"Two are enough ; we can get more on the road. Are the horses ready ?"

"Yes, sir."

The justice went out into the court-yard.

John Sprott watched him out, and then swallowed what remained of the bowl of punch, thinking that such encouragement was well adapted to a long cold ride and a dangerous enterprise.

Mr. Justice Folderough and he then passed on along the road ; but having a good dinner inside him, which was nicely shaken up by the horse he rode, he soon began to grumble about the length of the road.

At the very moment that John Sprott was aiding him in his grumblings, a loud and commanding voice exclaimed,

"STAND ! FOR YOUR LIFE !"

John Sprott, at once recognizing the voice of Moonlight Jack, turned his horse's head, and galloped off as hard as he could go.

The rest would most likely have followed his example had not the same voice vociferated,

"Stop them, Hardman ; don't let them go !"

Four or five men then leaping their horses over the hedge cut off the retreat of Mr. Justice Folderough and the constables; while one of the number fired a pistol down the lane after the retreating figure of John Sprott, which was followed by a sharp, sudden cry.

But the horses' steps were still heard galloping onwards.

The flash of the pistol had afforded sufficient light, however, to show Mr. Justice Folderough that resistance was vain, though, to say the truth, he *was* a brave and resolute man, and would have made it gallantly if there had been even a hope of success.

The leader of the party now threw back the shade of a dark lantern, and poured the light thereof full upon the justice and his followers, and demanded,

"What are you doing here at this hour ? What is your name and errand ?"

"Let me pass, in the king's name, I command you !" said the justice ; "my name is Folderough, and I am one of his Majesty's justices of the peace for——"

"Oh ! you are Mr. Justice Folderough, are you ?" replied the other. "Worthy Mr. Justice, who are those two men behind you, they seem not of your own condition ?"

"We are only two poor constables from Penshurst," replied the men, choosing to speak for themselves ; "we are two hard-working men with small families, and are forced to do our duty."

"Let these poor fellows go," said Moonlight Jack, "they are not to blame. But strip me the justice here to the skin ; take every farthing he has in his pocket, and then tie him up to a tree and give him a hundred lashes with the stirrup leather as hard as you can lay it on. I will not take his life, though I should like to give him only one lash for every false and villanous action he has committed; for every innocent man he has sent to prison, to the stocks, to the pillory or the parish beadle; one lash for each, however, would cut him to pieces. Go, give him a hundred, and let him go!"

The commands thus issued were punctually obeyed.

While the justice was hallooing and bawling under the infliction which was administered in the neighbouring field, Moonlight Jack went on addressing the man Hardman, sometimes commenting upon what was going on near, sometimes speaking of other subjects.

"They know we are on the look out," he said, "and they will not stir so long as that is the case. How the beast roars! Yet you say they must be in this neighbourhood, for you traced their footsteps clearly. Those fellows love flaying a justice in their heart; I can hear the lashes they give him even here. But we had better ride home now, and change our quarters soon. There, there, that will do, my men; stop, now, or you will kill him, if you don't mind. Put his vest upon his fat back, turn his face to his horse's tail, and send him down the lane."

Every item of Moonlight Jack's commands were executed to the letter, and Mr. Justice Foulderough still writhing with the pain of the stripes he had received, was partly clothed once more and set upon his beast again.

His face, however, was turned in the contrary direction to that which is usually assumed in relation to the animal that bore him, and his feet being thrust through the stirrups, a few smart blows were added to send the charger off.

Happily, for the preservation of the justice's equilibrium, the horse was weary, and even in its most frisky moods was a quiet, good sort of beast, so that after having jolted him in a hard trot for about three hundred yards it began to slacken its pace, gradually dropped into a walk, and finally stopped to crop a scanty breakfast from the herbage by the side of the road.

Justice Foulderough took advantage of his delay to right himself on his horse, and departed at a sharp trot to the office of the constabulary.

Here he met some one who, of all others, was the best to aid him, whether in a regular attack on Moonlight Jack's premises or a piece of treachery. This was Lord Henry.

The escape of this worthy, when it was discovered by Tyrrell, threw the men into some consternation.

"So I am betrayed!" cried Jack, "betrayed by those I trusted! Hardman, I think ye are faithful to me."

"Indeed, I am, captain," replied the other, "and so are all the rest."

"You can answer for them?" said Jack, with a sad smile.

"Aye, that I can, captain."

"Well, well, Hardman, don't go bail for them, at any rate. Still, when the moment comes, let them be ready!"

"Very well, captain, we will be ready."

Jack Tyrrell nodded abstractedly, and quitting the room sought that of Gipsy Bess.

Approaching her he sat down, and taking her hand, said,

"You are fair, my Bessie, fairer I think than ever."

Then he kissed her, but said nothing more.

He seemed abstracted—almost bewildered, and would every now and then burst forth into wild murmurings.

At length he said,

"Come, Bessie, come, sit upon my knee, and sing me a song. Who knows if I shall ever hear another?"

Though her heart was sad she made no reply, but hastened to obey.

The music still trembled in the air when Hardman suddenly entered the room, and approaching his captain, whispered a few words in his ear.

Moonlight Jack instantly started up with a dark cloud upon his brow.

"The time is come," he exclaimed, "the time is come. Hardman, I will come and speak with you and the rest. Bess, I will be back in a few minutes."

He then followed Hardman out of the room, and from that moment his whole demeanour was firm, calm and collected.

"Have all the horses saddled quickly," he said. "Each man collect everything valuable that he has, each man, too, have his arms already for action at a moment's notice. Did you say, Hardman, that they had come over the hill?"

"No, only one," returned Hardman; "but he came at such speed that there is no doubt the others will soon follow. We shall have to stand to our arms soon, captain."

"We shall see," he said, as he approached the casement, and looked out. "Oh, here comes another of my men. We shall know more anon."

The first of his watchers who had been left on the other side of the hills soon after entered the room.

"Well," said Jack, "what news, Morton?"

"They are coming up in great force, captain," he answered. "I could only see them draw out from the end of the lane upon the hill-side, but there seemed a good many of them. I did not move a step, however, till I saw Denman begin to canter away. Then I thought it time to come on and give you the first tidings. He will be here soon and give you a clear account."

"You did quite right," said his leader. "If we had all to deal with such as you, my man, we should get on very well. Come, Hardman, we will go out into the court. We shall be nearer the scene of action."

He then walked deliberately out into the courtyard, where the horses were now all brought out and ranged in a line.

"Mount, my men!" he cried, "mount! We shall soon have Denman here! Morton, that pistol will fall out of your holster. Don't you see the lock has caught in the leather? You hold my horse, Henry," he added to his son. "Hardman," he continued to the man apart, as he pointed to the boy, "do you think if I leave him behind—this child—they will injure him?"

"Oh, no," replied Hardman, "certainly not; they might take him away, but we could soon find means to get him out of their hands again."

"Good," returned Moonlight Jack. "Good. But I hear Denman's horse's feet clattering down the road as hard as he can come."

In a minute or two more the man he spoke of rode into the court-yard, with his horse all foaming from the speed at which he had come.

"I am glad to see you are ready, captain," he exclaimed, "for, depend upon it, we shall have sharp work of it. There must be at the lowest count forty of them coming up the hill, and all seemingly well mounted and armed."

"Could you see who it was that led them on?" asked Jack Tyrrell.

"Why, there were three rode abreast," said the man, "and I could see them all plainly enough. The one on the left was a man in a black cassock, but I don't think I ever saw him before. The middle one was a fat, heavy man, who I rather think is the justice that we flogged last night, only, in the darkness, then, I didn't well remark his face. But the third one, on the right hand, is certainly that lord you had up here for so long—that Lord Henry."

The cloud grew terribly dark upon Moonlight Jack's brow, and, putting his hand to his throat, he loosened the lace collar of his shirt.

"Fully forty men, you say?" he went on. "Hardman, you are not mounted? Quick, quick! into the saddle. Morton and Denman, put yourselves to the left. Now, Hardman, mark well what I have to tell you. Lead those men out and take at full gallop across the hill to the right. If you keep Elsie's Peak always a little on the left you will come to a hollow—there await me."

"But yourself, captain," said Hardman, "yourself, and Gipsy Bess. I will never go and leave you here alone."

"Do not be afraid, Hardman," replied Moonlight Jack, with a stern smile. "I will take care of them and myself, depend upon it."

"But I do not like this plan at all," cried the man. "What, to run away, and leave my captain behind me at the mercy of those fellows that are coming up! I do not like it all, Captain Jack. This will never do."

"You surely would not disobey me in a moment of danger and difficulty like this?" said Moonlight Jack. "No, no, Hardman, you are too good a fellow for that; but, to satisfy you, you shall see that I provide in some degree for my own safety. Harry, take my horse down into the narrow part between those two sheds, and hold him there, whatever you see or hear, till I come to you. In the first place, however, open those two other gates at the bottom of the court, and when you are holding the horse keep as far back as possible, that nobody may see you. Now, Hardman," he added, "you see that, are you satisfied? Lead the men out as I have commanded. I trust their safety to you."

Hardman looked down and bit his lip, hesitating evidently for a moment whether he should obey or not.

At length he looked stedfastly in Moonlight Jack's face, and held out his hand to him with a melancholy shake of the head.

"God bless you, Captain Jack," he said, "I obey you, even in this, but I am very much afraid that you are not quite right in your plans. I am afraid, I say, that you are acting under a wrong view; and I wish to God you would think of it before it is too late. Well, well, I will go. God bless you, I say. Come, my men, let us march;" and so saying, he led them all out of the court-yard.

Moonlight Jack saw them depart with stern, unmoved composure.

Then he advanced to the gate himself and while their horses were heard at the full gallop proceeding in the direction which he had pointed out.

Gazing up towards the other part of the hill, he saw a strong party of horsemen crowning some of the summit.

He then spoke another word or two to his son, returned into the room where he had conferred with Hardman, and paused with his arms folded on his chest, pondering gloomily for about a minute.

His next act was to cast himself into a chair, and cover his eyes with his hands, while his lip might be seen quivering with intense and agonizing emotion.

It lasted scarcely a minute more, however.

Then rising up he struck his hand upon the table, saying,

"Yes, yes; it shall be so."

He then took a brace of pistols from the shelf, loaded them carefully, and placed them in his belt.

Then he proceeded to a closet, wherein were deposited several other weapons of the same kind, chose out two with much deliberation, looked at them closely with a bitter and ghastly smile, and having done so and loaded them also, he locked the door of the house, and returned to the room where he had left his wife.

The same dark smile was upon his countenance still, but he said as he entered,

"I have been away from you long, Bess; but it was business of importance called me. Now we will have another song, but it shall be a gayer one than the last."

Bess sang, but it was still a sad strain that she chose, and Moonlight Jack, with his head bent down, and his ear inclined towards her, listened attentively to every note.

When it was done he caught her to his breast and kissed her lips repeatedly, saying,

"They are very sweet. Is there no poison in them, Bess?"

"None, none, Jack," she replied, "If any poison has reached your heart it has not been from Bessie's lips."

Moonlight Jack turned away, and muttered something to himself; but Bessie did not hear that the words were,

"Would it were so."

"Play upon the lute," he continued sharply. "Let us have the sound out of that too."

Again she did as he bade her, though by this time there was a sound of heavy blows as if given by a hammer below, together with the trampling of horses' feet, and voices speaking.

"There's some one making so much noise I cannot play," at length, she said.

As she spoke there was a rush of many feet along the passage, and the next the door of the chamber flew open and seven or eight persons rushed in.

Though Bess had not remarked it, Moonlight Jack had drawn some of the benches and tables across the room when he first entered, in such a manner as to form a barricade, and the moment the door burst open he started upon his feet, and levelled a pistol towards it, exclaiming "Stand!" in a voice which shook the room.

The first face that presented itself was that of Lord Henry, and though his nerves were not easily shaken, yet the tone and gesture of Moonlight Jack caused him to pause for an instant, of which the highwayman at once took advantage.

"Lord Henry," he exclaimed, "you have come to see your handiwork, and to receive its punishment. I saved your life—you taught my mistress to betray me."

"Never! never!" shrieked Gipsy Bess.

"False woman, did you think I could not see? Lo! pitiful boy, here is your handiwork, and here your punishment!"

Then turning the pistol at once towards her, he discharged the contents at her breast.

She fell back with a loud shriek, and Lord Henry in an instant sprang across the barrier.

But ere he could take a step beyond it, a second pistol was aimed at his head and fired by that unerring hand which seemed only to gain additional steadiness in moments of agitation and agony.

Bounding up like a deer from the ground, the young nobleman was cast back by the force of the shot at once upon the table over which he had leaped.

He never moved again.

There was an anguished quivering of the limbs, and a convulsive contraction of the hand indeed ; but, as in the case of Varley, the shot had gone straight into the brain and consciousness and thought and sensation were instantly at an end for ever.

The rest of the robber's assailants shrunk back with terror, and Moonlight Jack, with a fierce triumphant smile, gazed at them for an instant.

While casting down the weapons he had used to such fatal purposes on the ground, he drew a third from his belt and exclaimed aloud,

" Who will be the next ?"

Borne back by the pressure of his companion, and by his own fears, Justice Folderough staggered through the doorway into the room again ; but he did so with a bold and undismayed countenance, and pistol in hand advanced towards the highwayman.

But another object had attracted the attention of Moonlight.

It was Gipsy Bess, whose inanimate body lay there an emblem of his rashness.

Giving one glance towards the only one who remained to assail, he cried,

" Fool ! You are not worth the shot," and thrusting the pistol into his belt again, he sprang towards the window, which was wide open.

" He will escape ! he will escape !" cried the justice.

Then he pulled the trigger of his pistol at him with a steady aim.

Loaded, however, by hands unused to such occupations, it merely flashed in the pan ; and though he instantly drew forth the second and fired, it was too late.

Moonlight Jack was already dropping down to the ground below.

" Stop him ! stop him !" exclaimed the justice, springing to the window, and overturning chairs and tables in his way. " He will escape ! stop him below there ! Run down, ye cowardly rascals ! run down and pursue him in every direction ; by ——, the fellow will be off after all !"

And after gazing for a minute from the window, he rushed out of the room.

On the side where Moonlight Jack sprang to the ground there was not one of the party who had come to take him ; all, except those who had entered the house and learned the contrary, believing that he had fled with the rest whom they had seen crossing the hills, and all being busy in examining the highwayman's abode, the courts, the stabling, and the harness that had been left behind, with open-mouthed curiosity.

The voice of the justice, indeed, called one stout farmer round, and he instantly attempted to seize the stranger whom he saw hurrying forward towards some sheds at the other end of the building ; but though a burly and a powerful yeoman, one quick blow from the robber's hand laid him prostrate on the earth, and springing past him Moonlight Jack reached the spot where his horse was held.

The boy Harry had managed skilfully, constantly avoiding the side from which a sound of voices came.

But now the quick and well-known step called him forth in a moment.

The fiery horse was held tight with one hand, the stirrup in the other, and, by the time Justice Folderough with the troop that followed him came rushing forth from the door, Moonlight Jack was in the saddle and struck his spurs into the horse's sides and galloped through the gates.

Two of the farmers who had remained on horseback without had seen him mount, but not knowing who he was had not attempted to interrupt him.

The appearance of their companions in pursuit, however, instantly undeceived them, and they spurred after him at full speed.

On went the gallant charger of Moonlight Jack, however, faster than they could follow, and when they had kept up the race at about twenty yards behind him for nearly a quarter of an hour, the one nearest exclaimed, aloud,

" I will shoot his horse !"

The words must have reached the robber's ear, for instantly his charger slackened its pace, and the pursuer gained upon him a little.

But, then, Moonlight Jack turned in his saddle, and, with the bridle in his teeth, stretched out his right hand towards him.

Next came a flash, a report, and the farmer tumbled headlong from the saddle, severely wounded, while Moonlight Jack pursued his course with redoubled speed.

Almost all the rest of the party who had come to take him were now mounted, and in full pursuit.

But his greatest danger was not from them.

A little above him on the hill, and nearly at the same distance from the house where he had dwelt as himself, were seen, when he had gone about a mile, several of the party who had been sent to follow his band.

The sight of the horsemen in full flight, and many others pursuing, as well as the gestures and shouts of those below, made them instantly turn and endeavour to cut him off.

On that side, as he was obliged to turn to avoid both the parties, the pursuers gained upon him, and, as if by mutual consent, they now strained every nerve to hem him in.

There was about half a mile further on a chasm caused by a deep, narrow lane, between banks of twenty or thirty feet deep descending from the top of the hills, and those above him on the slope having already passed it once that morning strove to drive him towards it, their only fear being lest those below should not act on the same plan.

Moonlight Jack himself, however, took exactly the course they wished, and as bearing down from above they came nearer and nearer to him, they laughed to see him approach at full speed a barrier which must inevitably stop him.

They urged their horses rapidly on, however, lest he should find some path down the bank into the lane.

Nearer and nearer they came to him as he bore somewhat up towards them.

They were within fifty yards of him when he reached the bank, and so furious was his steed that all expected to see him go over headlong.

But no !

The bridle was thrown loose, the spur touched the horse's flank, and with one eager bound the gallant beast cleared the space between, and though his hind feet, in reaching the other side, broke down the top of the bank, and cast the sand and gravel furiously into the lane below, he stumbled not, he paused not, but bounded on while the rashest horseman of the party pulled in his rein, and gazed with fear at the awful leap that had just been taken.

A part is still pointed out on those hills where the top of the bank above the lane exhibits a large gap, and the spot is still called the Robber's Leap to the present day.

Every one, as we have said, drew in their horses, and some rode up and down seeking for a passage down into the lane ; but, in the meantime, Moonlight Jack was every moment getting further and further out of reach of pursuit.

When Justice Folderough, who came up as fast as his horse would bear him, arrived upon the spot, he saw at once it was too late to pursue the fugitive any further, and he exclaimed,

"Give it up, my masters, give it up ; he has escaped us for the present, but we shall get hold of him by-and-bye. A man who gets into a scrape like this never gets out of it without a rope round his neck. Let us return to the house and conclude our examination there. Though a terrible day's work it has been, for, if my eyes served me right in the hurry, there is that poor young gentleman as dead as a stone, and the woman—who seemed a beautiful creature, too—no better."

Thus saying he turned round and rode back towards the house, while those who followed, and who had not been present at the events which had taken place within the building, eagerly questioned such as had witnessed the fearful scene.

While they listened to the details, magnified as they might be, perhaps, by fear and the love of the marvellous, a gloomy feeling of awe fell over the whole party, and they gazed up towards the house as they approached it, with sensations which made the blood creep slowly through their hearts.

Such feelings were not diminished by the sight of their wounded companion who had received Moonlight Jack's fire in the pursuit, and who was still lying on the ground supported by one of his friends who had remained behind, and bleeding profusely from the right breast.

Several alighted, and aided to carry him towards the house, while Justice Folderough and one or two others rode on and proceeded at once to the room where they had first seen the highwayman.

There were sounds of many cries within, for six or seven had crowded into the place after the flight of Jack Tyrrell.

When the justice entered the room he found it occupied by three groups, the nearest of which consisted of two or three farmers gathered round the head of the table, gazing curiously at the objects which it supported.

A little further on was a constable, holding by the collar the fair and curly-headed son of Moonlight Jack.

The magistrate advanced towards the table, and saw that the object of the farmers' contemplation was the dead body of Lord Henry Davenport, which was now stretched out with the limbs composed and stiffening with the rigidity of death.

Too much accustomed to such sights to be strongly affected by them, the justice passed on, shaking his head and his finger, too, at the son of Moonlight Jack, and saying,

"Ah, you little varlet, I shall deal with you by-and-bye !"

"He's a funny little rascal, your worship," said the constable. "He ran up the hill so fast that nobody could catch him, till he got to a place where he could see the whole chase, and there he stood, and let himself be taken as quietly as a lamb, though I told him he would be hanged to a certainty."

The justice saw that the boy, brave as he was, was struggling against his tears.

If he had a redeeming quality, it was love for children.

"There, there," he said, "don't fear, you will not be hanged."

The boy drew himself up proudly.

"I am not weeping for that," he said ; "but for my dearest friend, Gipsy Bess."

"Ah, the woman ! where is she ?" cried Justice Folderough.

"She be gone," said one of the constables.

"Gone !"

"Yes ; as I come back I looked in, and I see a strange face at the window, and just when I turned to call out to some of my companions, and went into the room, the body was gone."

"And did you make no search without ?"

"Yes, your honour ; but all was as dark as pitch, and as quiet as the grave—not a soul was stirring. But I can see a long distance, and just against the moonlit sky, above Barley Hill, I fancied I saw a horse and rider pass."

"Well, well, let us take this boy with us and begone," said the justice. "You, Grainger and Tomkins, watch the body."

So it was done, and on arriving at the house of the justice, the boy was placed in a chamber with a constable.

When his companion awoke an hour or two after daylight on the following morning, no Jack was to be found, though the door was still locked and the room was on the third story.

There were found, indeed, the window partly open, the traces of small feet along a leaden gutter, the branch of a tall elm, which rested against one corner of the house, cracked through, but not completely broken, and the fragments of glass at the top of the wall neatly and carefully pounded into powder with a large stone.

These were all the traces ; but, at any rate, the son of Moonlight Jack was gone !

CHAPTER XVII.

WHICH TELLS HOW LADY ELLA WAS RESTORED TO HER HUSBAND—HOW BRANDON WENT OUT IN PURSUIT OF MOONLIGHT JACK—AND HOW JACK WAS PLACED IN GAOL.

IT will be remembered that the last time we saw Ella Huntley she was chained to a wall in an old house, and that Brandon, the pretended vampire, had just entered her cell.

She glanced up at him with an eager anxious glance.

Brandon marked the look and gloried in it.

"Ah !" he cried, gazing at her fixedly with a sneering smile upon his lip. "Ah ! you are glad to see me now ?"

"Not glad," murmured the young girl, in trembling accents.

"What then ?"

"Fearful of you. Eager to know my fate."

"It is in your own hands."

MOONLIGHT JACK

OR THE KING

OF THE ROAD

LADY ELLA DELAINE.

"That is mockery."

"Not so; it is solemn truth."

Ella burst into tears.

"Why do you mock me?" she cried. "Here I am, chained and helpless, yet you tell me my fate is in my own hands."

"So it is."

He knelt down beside her, and passed one of his strong arms round her slender waist, took up her hand, and pressed it passionately to his lips.

The glance he cast upon her face was full of voluptuous love, yet full, too, of madness and despair.

"Oh! Ella!" he cried, "why do you thus persist in punishing yourself? In the sight of Heaven you are my wife, for I swear, by all the powers above me, that I am not the heir to the house of Huntley. I am Henry Brandon, son of Lord Brandon of Elmsleigh. The real heir to the marquisate of Huntley is Lucien Fairleigh! As heaven is my witness, I,

No. 8.—February 24, 1866.] [Order No. 1 of the BOY PIRATE, and receive, GRATIS, No. 2 and a LARGE ENGRAVING, PRINTED IN SEVEN COLOURS.] [Price One Penny this very night, entered Huntley Castle, and saw with my own eyes the documents which prove the marriage of the Marquis of Huntley with the mother of Lucien Fairleigh!"

"Where are they, then?" cried Ella Huntley, disdainfully, and incredulous.

Well she might be.

Convinced as she was in her own mind that Brandon was her own brother, she looked upon his present statement only as a ruse to obtain possession of her person.

She was certainly, for one reason, inclined to respect him.

She was entirely in his power.

For more than a week she had been so.

Yet he had never offered her any violence.

But yet in her own mind she was firmly convinced that he knew her to be his sister, and desired her in spite of the fact to become his wife.

"Where are these proofs?" she therefore asked.

"I have lost them."

Ella smiled.

"Then I have no more proof than before?" she cried.

"Yes, yes, you have," he cried. "I swear it, Ella, I swear it before Heaven. I had those papers—I read them—I was pursued, and I dropped them in the gardens of the castle."

"Oh, Brandon!" said Ella, passionately, as she clasped her hands over her white bosom, "oh, Brandon! why do you seek to deceive me thus? Are there no women in the world fairer and more loveable than I that you should seek to destroy both body and soul by wedding your own sister? I cannot, will not believe you. Undeniable proofs were placed in my hands years since that you were my brother. Unless you prove to the contrary I cannot give credence to your words."

Brandon paced the room impatiently.

But he made no reply.

Ella went on.

"You cannot love me. No matter what relation exists between us, you cannot love me."

"Why?"

"Because you keep me here in chains."

Brandon looked at her wistfully.

"Oh, Ella!" he cried, "it will, I know, be difficult for you to believe, but it is through love I keep you thus. But four words from you, and I release you from the bonds you fear."

"And those words are——"

"I will not escape."

Ella held out to him her hand.

He took it and raised it to his lips.

"I will not escape," she said.

"I believe you," cried Brandon.

Then, drawing a key from his pocket, he proceeded to unclasp her chains, and in a few moments she was once more free.

"Now," said Brandon, "for this night and the next you will have to remain in this place. The next day I can provide for you a more suitable chamber; or say, Ella, will you share mine? I ask you, my lawful wife, will you share mine?"

He clasped her to his heart as he spoke, and kissed her cherry lips till the hot blood coursed through her veins like fire.

But she turned pale as death notwithstanding.

"No, no," she cried, "no, Brandon, you cannot surprise me thus. Use violence and cruelty if you will, but I will never consent to what the laws of man and Heaven forbid. I am your sister, such I will remain."

He released her at once.

"Good," he cried, "let it be so. In days to come you will repent this. But now I leave you; a bed shall be provided for you. Adieu; may Heaven bless you!"

And, pressing her hand in his, the strange man went upon his way.

Released though Lady Ella Huntley was, she had but the chill, cold cell to remain in.

Yet she had still the power to move about.

Oh, God only, who sees and knows all things, understands what pleasure it is to the poor prisoner to wander hither and thither in his cell, and to imagine to himself, through this hideous imitation of liberty, what the freedom in the green bright fields must be!

She walked to and fro, quickly and musingly.

She scarcely thought.

Thought, to isolated beings in a prison, is not the same as thought to a person at liberty.

The man or woman walking through the pleasant meadows, or through the crowded streets, can concentrate his or her mind upon one subject.

Not so the prisoner.

He thinks of a multitude of things at once.

What *was*, and *is*, and *will be;* the chance of escape; necessity for patience; the slow passage of the hours, and the slow approach of that day which brings freedom; the eager yearning for sleep that will not come; the restless wishing and hoping for the morrow, and the good it may bring forth; the forced serenity; the quiet, maddening unrest which there is no one to alleviate; these things can be only understood by one who has lived within the iron bars, and heard without the merry boys at play, and the merry birds at song, and the working men at honest, unrestricted labour.

People may pity the unthinking birds for being placed in cages and compelled to sing.

Let them keep a little of their sympathy for those thinking, reasoning souls who are placed in cages and compelled to work!

So for a long time Ella Huntley walked hither and thither restlessly.

Presently she heard a noise.

It was a slight noise, yet it stirred her very soul.

It came from beneath the ground.

It must, therefore, proceed from some one endeavouring to make his way towards her cell.

She listened eagerly.

Whoever this new comer might be it must be an enemy of Brandon's.

Presently, at the side of her cell, a large stone moved.

She clasped her hands and watched.

Presently a man's form appeared.

Then another.

They were both masked.

But when they entered, after glancing rapidly round, they withdrew their dominoes and showed to Ella Huntley the faces of Moonlight Jack and Sir Percy Delaine.

Ella rushed to Sir Percy, and threw herself upon his breast, while Moonlight Jack gazed upon them with a supercilious smile.

He had lost his faith in woman.

"Oh, Percy!" cried Ella, pressing her newly married husband to her heart, "you are indeed, then, safe?"

"Yes," he said, as he kissed her rapturously, "I am safe; but no one but you and my friend here knows it. All think me dead. Let it be so; it is better for the present. But, come, let us fly hence, this dismal cell is no place for you."

He took her pliant and half-fainting form in his arms, and carried her towards the aperture.

Then, Moonlight Jack leading the way, they proceeded slowly along an underground passage, which conducted them at length into the highway.

Here two horses were awaiting them. Moonlight Jack sprung upon one, while Sir Percy Delaine, vaulting upon the other, held his young wife before him in his arms.

Ever since the conflict in which Lord Henry Davenport had met his death, and Gipsy Bess had disappeared, Moonlight Jack had abandoned the old house, and taken up his residence in a strange place

It was situated on the banks of the sea river.

Outside it resembled an old barn.

Indeed, among the country people—we are speaking, remember, of a hundred and thirty years ago—it was known, jokingly, as Barn Manor.

Certainly it had some of the attributes of a country manor.

It had a wooded space behind it, where hares and rabbits abounded.

Before it was a splendid fish stream, where the angler could expend many an hour of pleasant as well as lucrative sport.

Here and there were luxuriant fruit trees and strawberry beds ; wild, it is true, but, nevertheless, showing that the hand of man had once been busy there.

Moonlight Jack and his men, on taking up their temporary residence there, made no alteration whatever in the place without.

They simply contrived it so within as to render it comparatively comfortable, and left the outside as rough and wild as possible in order to deceive the police.

When our fugitives arrived at Barn Manor, Moonlight Jack ushered them into a large well-lighted room in which his men were congregated.

All these men rose and bowed respectfully both to their leader and his friends.

"Comrades," cried Moonlight Jack, "I bring to you two persons whom it is my desire to protect. You understand me ?"

The only reply was a clatter of wine cups upon the table.

Then he turned towards the young husband and wife.

"Come with me," he said, "I will place you where you will neither be disturbed nor molested."

He led the way into an inner room.

Following him, they entered a large and well-appointed bed-chamber.

"A good night's rest and happiness attend you," said Moonlight Jack, as he closed the door and left them together.

Sir Percy folded his blushing bride to his heart.

"At length you are mine," he exclaimed, as his lips glued themselves to hers.

"Yes, dear Percy. Yours for ever," returned the blushing girl, who, in spite of natural modesty, felt a warm and unwonted thrill pervading her whole being.

And more so still, when presently she sank to rest in her husband's arms ; for, say what people will about modesty and maiden diffidence, there is nothing more delicious to a woman than those sweet hours when first she is taught what love is, and when, unrestrained by others, she yields to the eager embraces of the man she adores.

Meanwhile we must return to Brandon.

About two hours after his interview with Lady Ella Huntley, Brandon returned to the cell where she had been confined.

It was quite dark.

He turned on the light of a dark lantern.

It was now some time since Ella had fled, and the bed was, of course, empty !

Brandon glanced hither and thither in fierce anger and despair.

Yet both were of no avail.

Ella Huntley had once more escaped from his clutches.

"D——n !" he cried, standing still at length in the centre of the stone cell. "D——n, who can have done this ?"

Suddenly his eye caught a small object on the floor.

He picked it up.

It was a letter.

Eagerly he opened it.

He guessed its import.

It ran thus :—

"Lady Percy Delaine (once called Lady Ella Huntley) has been saved by her husband, whom you failed to destroy ; and by his friend, Moonlight Jack, whom you have many times striven to ruin also. Seek her not. She is well guarded by those who will lay down their lives to save her."

The face of the strong man grew deadly pale.

He crushed the letter in his hand.

"Oh ! Heaven has punished me at last !" he said. "Ella Huntley, whose virgin purity I have so long saved and respected, will this night become the wife of another—this night she will pass in another's arms those delicious hours which should have been mine. But vengeance shall be mine ! Ella Huntley, you shall be the instrument of my most terrible revenge on Sir Percy Delaine, and Jack Tyrrell shall breathe the air of a prison ere this hour to-morrow night has chimed."

On the following night the Chelmsford mail was to pass Romford at ten o'clock.

There were rumours current in the country round about that a large sum of money was to come by this coach, and Moonlight Jack and his followers, therefore, were early on the alert.

Only four men accompanied him.

He had intended to take with him four trusty fellows, upon whom, in similar times of danger, he had before relied, but, two of these being engaged elsewhere, he had selected two others.

These two, of all the remainder of the band, seemed the most likely to be able to replace those who had been compelled to go elsewhere.

Four stout fellows, with a brave leader, were always reckoned sufficient to rob a mail coach, for the passengers never made any resistance, the coachman was generally half asleep, and easily taken by surprise, and the guard's blunderbuss, from lying along the roof in all manner of positions, generally contained as much water as powder and ball.

So Moonlight Jack and his men set off in high spirits.

Funds were getting very low, and, as our heroes thought of no other method of getting a livelihood, they seemed quite business-like in their manners and equipment as they proceeded to levy black mail upon the king's highway.

It was a splendid night.

The moon was clear, and the stars, too, lent their brilliance towards the illumination of nature.

So much the worse for our knights of the road.

A dark, stormy night was best for their enterprise—a night when they could conceal themselves in the heavy shadows of the great trees, and when they had completed their task of plunder, could rush away over the hedgerows, and escape ere they could be recognised.

But Jack Tyrrell never chose his time.

Moonlight, to him, was the same as cloudy weather.

So, beneath the shade of some lofty elm trees, which leaned over the high road, the five companions posted themselves.

Presently Romford clock chimed the hour of ten.

"Ah, my boys," cried Moonlight Jack, "the hour has struck ; now for plunder !"

His words, which generally would have been given out in a merry tone, were now spoken with bitter zest, as if, since the loss of Gipsy Bess, he felt a delight in preying upon his fellow creatures.

Presently the rumble of the mail coach was heard in the distance.

Then it hove in sight.

On it came, swinging from side to side, the lamps moving about like those of a steam-engine with a decided inclination to run off the rails.

The guard, for want of something better to do, was trying to extract a little melody from a very obstinate horn, to which the voice of a somewhat excited passenger formed a discordant accompaniment.

"They are merry," said Jack Tyrrell. "We will soon make them sing to a very different tune ; but remember, my boys, it is the old watchword, 'Purses not blood.' Two to the horses' heads, another to the guard, one with me."

Just as he had completed his directions, which he invariably repeated to his somewhat excitable companions on such occasions as this, the coach neared them.

In a moment the highwaymen rushed forward, and all was confusion.

The guard was dragged down and bound, so was the coachman ; the traces were cut, and the passengers compelled to turn out of the vehicle, were huddling together in dismay.

But just as the knights of the road were preparing to fill their pockets to a good tune, the tables were turned in a manner which no one in the slightest degree expected.

A number of men, whom no one had before seen, but who seemed, indeed, to rise from the ground, rushed up to the scene of action.

They were twenty or thirty in number, and resistance would have been madness.

Jack's companions, at once obeying his instructions, cut and run.

As for himself, however, just as he was about to follow their example he was seized by four men and made a prisoner.

The mail-coach then went on its way, while Moonlight Jack, whose fortunes at this moment seemed really on the decline, was taken towards Chelmsford Gaol.

The man, Brandon, who had betrayed him, was now gone ; but just as they started a voice whispered in his ear,

"*Jack Tyrrell, remember the gibbet on the heath !*"

Jack turned quickly.

He saw the face of him who spoke, and recognised him at once.

It was Jonathan Rasper.

Jack could not move to strike him for he was bound.

But he was still able to speak.

"Spy and traitor !" he said. "Young emblem of your villain father, remember well my words. I shall escape from the hands of my enemies, no matter where they place me. Beware, therefore, how you act. Let me not hear that you have injured those upon whom my heart's love is set, or by the Heavens above us I will flay you alive !—I will tear you limb from limb !"

Jonathan Rasper waited to hear no more, but darted away along the highway in the direction which had been taken by Brandon.

The man by whose side Moonlight Jack rode was well known in Chelmsford and its vicinity.

His name was Treherne, and he united in himself the offices of broker, spy, and thief-taker ; and would not have been very particular about taking a hand in a hanging match, if he thought that the pocket would thereby have been replenished.

In fact, in regard to trade, he took it (like the thieves) as it came, and was never kept back by any feeling of pride or squeamishness.

He was a man of florid complexion, rather inclined to be stout—a man who always pretended friendship and *bonhommie*, whereas his only friend was himself—a man who always pretended to take people into custody with the greatest regret—who assumed a dislike for his pettifoggging profession, and tried to persuade you that had not adverse fortune compelled him, he would rather have swept a crossing than become a thief-taker.

He was very fond of recounting deeds of prowess of his own, and (on the journey of a prisoner to prison) praising up in no small terms the comforts of the prison to which they were going.

This latter Mr. Treherne did on principle.

He did so in order to prevent the prisoner running away.

Having regard to Mr. Treherne's fat paunch, he did not seem a very terrible opponent ; and Moonlight Jack, being a young and active man—one who was rarely outstripped in the race—could not resist a smile, as the fat thief-taker recounted how he had "run this fellow into a hole," and "dodged this fellow," and "put a stopper on that fellow's wind," and "bamboozled this fellow's wife."

All these were very creditable stories, tending mostly to prove (*from his own mouth*) what a consummate liar Mr. Treherne was.

The "dodges," and the "bamboozlings" generally resolved themselves into simple acts of lying, such as pretending to be the "water rate," or the "surveyor," or the "parish doctor."

Moonlight Jack did not in the least object to Mr. Bounceable Treherne having all the talk on the journey, only he could not imagine how this fat piece of consequence could imagine it interesting to a prisoner.

At length, when Mr. Treherne seemed to have settled himself into a story, which he never meant to leave off, he said suddenly,

"Now, look you here, Master Treherne, as you've been a full hour proving to me what a thundering liar you can be, how can you expect me to believe a word you say ?"

This annoyed Mr. Treherne, who began to talk about his position in society, which, after all, wasn't much, considering that he was more than once seen buying a dead man's clothes from a hangman !

So Moonlight Jack quietly put the pot on him.

"Now, look you here, my fine fellow," he said, "you've been an hour trying to prove to me you're a liar. I thoroughly believe you ; so don't say any more."

Mr. Bounceable looked disgusted.

When he did so you could read his character.

His round little eyes were often purposely screwed up into an expression of comicality for the purpose of passing as a good-natured fellow.

But it was of no use.

No one was deceived in him.

There was a cold glitter in his eye which at once proved what he was.

"Really, Mr. Tyrrell," he said, "you are not polite."

"Who the devil need be polite to a thief-taker?" cried Moonlight Jack. "There, shut up. A little of you goes a long way."

So Mr. Bounceable Treherne said no more.

He had very little of interest to say, therefore he did what he was told—shut up.

Arrived at Chelmsford gaol, he was given in charge of two warders, by name Clapman and Chalk, who inducted him into a cell, a cold, stone affair, where the bright light of day was rendered as thick and as dismal as possible, and where everything in fact was on the " wretched" system.

Huge gates, and massy gratings, and terrible stone walls surrounded him, and when the clang of his door had finished its echo, and the jingle of the warder's keys had died away in the distance, and the cold moonlight spread itself like a coverlet of silver over his hard bed—broken into patches, be it said, by the trellice-work of the iron bars—Jack Tyrrell felt indeed as if the outer wall was closed against him for ever.

But it was not so.

Ere a week had passed Moonlight Jack had escaped.

No one thought it possible.

Yet he did it.

He obtained writing materials, made a key out of his pen-holder, passed through the chapel window, and, ere morning had broken over Chelmsford, he had fled !

We must now follow his fortunes.

CHAPTER XVIII.

BRECKENWOLD—THE ENCAMPMENT—THE FLIGHT — THE OLD HOUSE — THE WEIR — THE DARK RIVER—THE BOAT—THE FATAL INN—A NIGHT OF TERROR.

If the reader wished us to point out to him one of the loveliest bits of rural scenery in our leafy England, so tranquil and secluded and yet comparatively so small a distance from an important and busy highway that any one wishing to live the life of a convivial anchorite could therein combine his retirement with every novelty or luxury that the great world could afford, we would conduct him into the centre of a finely-wooded district in Essex.

It is known as Breckenwold.

The tract of land, broken and irregular, is thickly covered with beeches, presenting some of the finest and most picturesque specimens of forest scenery in the kingdom.

Long shady avenues of velvet turf, spangled with daisies, and teeming with quivering hare-bells, pierce the green wood in every direction, now as small foot-paths climbing up the side and running along the edge of some forsaken and precipitous gravel-pit, now plunging into the depths of the forest, apart from the beaten track, amidst coverts of fern and underwood until they widen into fair glades.

These are bordered on either side by the gnarled and misshapen bolls of trees, venerable in their garniture of hoary lichen, whose moss-covered and distorted trunks, far above the ground, offer natural and luxurious settees to the visitor.

It was now an inclement season.

It was towards the end of January.

A heavy snow lay upon the ground, and was still falling, from which the huge stems of the trees started up like spectres, black and fantastic from the contrast.

Everything was wrapped in dead silence.

This was only broken by the occasional report of a gun, sharp and clear in the freezing air.

Even the waggons and horses, with muffled wheels and feet, went noiselessly across the common, pulling up the snow after them.

Along one of the principal avenues of the beeches, about the middle of the day, any one who had chosen might have seen a solitary pedestrian trying to make what way he could towards the centre of the forest.

Had he been previously acquainted with the person, he would probably have recognised Hardman, the gentleman in ankle-jacks, the friend of Tyrrell.

I say he would probably have recognised him, because he might readily have been pardoned for not perceiving at first who it really was.

Hardman had swaddled himself up in so many worsted comforters about his neck and hay-bands round his feet and legs, as to destroy all leading traces of identity.

His toilet was never very carefully made at the best of times, but now it was more eccentric than ever.

He had a red cotton handkerchief tied over his hat, and an old game-bag, patched and mended with pieces of sacking, carpet, net, and whatever else had come first at the moment, was slung over his shoulders, well filled.

It was snowing hard, as I have said.

The feathery particles seemed to have combined against Hardman and put all their inventive powers to the stretch in order to render his progress as uncomfortable as possible.

They had evidently made friends with the wind, who entered into the joke as well, and blew them into his eyes whenever he opened them.

Then they waited for him in sly corners at the tops of avenues, and, when he came by, they all scuffled out at once and tumbled and wiffled about his head, the more desperate getting into his ears and violently rushing down his neck.

But, by the time he put up his hand to catch them, they had all vanished away.

The idler flakes did not practically assault him, but waved derisively round his hat and then ran away.

In spite of the weather, however, Hardman kept on until at length he arrived (by a sudden turn round a thicket) at a spot situated on the side of a small but deep declivity, part of which had given way in a landstep, and formed the hill as it were into two large steps.

Upon this platform and against the embankment above, a large rude tent had been constructed of poles and ragged canvas, apparently the remnants of some drinking booth of a fair.

Before it a greater part of the snow had been swept away and two fires lighted, round which a large party of individuals were gathered, more or less reputable.

Several had the costume and expression of real gipsies, but the majority evidently belonging to that anomalous class of perambulating manufacturers known as tramps.

A couple of tilted carts with chimneys were stationed near the tent, in one of which a fire was also burning, and to these were attached bundles of the thick sticks used to throw at snuff boxes, as well as poles for building stalls.

One of them also carried a light deal table with three legs, from which an ingenious observer might have inferred that some of the party were versed in the necromantic mysteries of the pea and thimble.

A pile of firewood had been collected and stacked up close at hand, and lower down the slope, in a decayed cow-shed, two miserable horses and a donkey were mumbling such scanty fodder as their owners could procure for them.

"Well, my beaus, here we is," said Hardman, announcing his own arrival, which, judging from the manner in which he was received, was perfectly unnecessary. "How's the times?"

"Brickish," replied one of the party, showing a small piece of wool to the new-comer. "Carter took something in that line the night before last from a farm t'other side of the splash."

"Cut up?" inquired Hardman.

"Safe!" replied the man, pointing to the large saucepan which was slung over one of the fires. "What have you brought?"

With an air of anticipated triumph Hardman unslung the game-bag he was carrying, and shooting out a quantity of vegetables, at last produced a very fine jack of ten or twelve pounds weight.

"There's a jackey!" he exclaimed, admiringly. "I took a pair of them with trimmers in Squire —you know who's fleet—last night, and sold one to him this morning. Wouldn't he swear, just, if he smoked it? But now to business. Is Jack Tyrrell here still?"

The man nodded his head, and pointed towards the cart.

"He's got into a rather okkard fire there," said Hardman. "I've walked ten blessed miles this very morning to get him away, for there's no time to be lost."

"Are the beaks fly?" asked the man.

"Downy as goslings," returned Hardman. "They're coming here all in a lump, you may depend upon it, and won't do you much good if you ain't careful. How about that mutton?"

"All right; the snow hides it," replied the tramp, "and if the frost lasts it will keep for ever; but look sharp if Moonlight Jack's to be got off."

Following his advice Hardman went towards the cart, from whose chimney the smoke was ascending, and knocked at the door, which was fastened on the inside.

It was opened by Moonlight Jack, pale, haggard, a shadow of his former self.

The memory of Gipsy Bess heavy on his soul.

In a few words Hardman explained to him that his retreat was suspected, that he had left word to Lucien Fairleigh, telling him where to come, and that they must "bolt" at once.

"Let us go, then," said Jack.

"I only want to go as far as Deltree," returned Hardman. "I've got a skiff lying there that will soon take us over to Fornden Creek. The river's as full as a tick and will carry us down in no time of itself, only we ain't got a moment to lose."

In a few minutes they started.

The gipsies watched their forms until they were lost in the copse of evergreens, and then resumed their wonted occupations.

On learning the dangers of Moonlight Jack, and hearing, too, that a further force was to be sent against him, Lucien Fairleigh, leaving his father, who now seemed in a fair way to recover, started off, and arrived during the evening at Breckenwold.

There was yet some little daylight before him when he arrived at the end of his journey, and the fall of snow had ceased for a time, although the sky still looked threatening.

He immediately went to the hotel nearest the coach office, and procured a horse, thinking he should travel quicker by that method.

At the same time he was anxious not to be embarrassed by the company of another person.

While the animal was being saddled he obtained all the information he wished respecting Breckenwold, and found out, also, that the constables had not long departed, having stopped there in order to take something "to keep out the cold."

This information induced him to make more haste, so that he was soon riding in the direction of Penington Heath.

As he arrived at the less frequented lanes and bridle paths, he plainly made out the traces of the party who had preceded him, as well as some prints of horseshoes, from which he conceived that they had procured the assistance of the local patrol as guides.

He inquired of every person he met how long the police had passed, and from every one he received the same reply.

They were about twenty minutes ahead of him, but they were not using great speed on account of one or two of them being upon foot.

There was but a slender chance of reaching Tyrrell before them, but still the chance was worth pushing for, and he determined at all hazards to ride on at a quickened pace, and endeavour to pass the officers as a casual traveller.

He therefore took advantage of a favourable piece of road to increase his speed, and soon reached the borders of the common at a sharp trot.

A shepherd was standing with his dog at the gate of a field which he now came to, and he pulled up a moment to ask what road to take.

Several thoroughfares, in fact, crossed one another at this point, and the footmarks were lost among many others.

"Are ye along of them patrols?" asked the rustic.

Lucien hesitated for an instant.

Then he thought it best to answer in the affirmative.

"I seed them go up the hill nigh half an hour back," continued the shepherd. "They're after a poacher, ain't 'em?"

"Yes, yes," returned Lucien, impatiently; "but, tell me, which is the nearest way?"

"Why, if you likes to come over this field," said the man, "and through that gap at the end you'll cut off two mile or more."

"That will do," cried Lucien, "and there's a shilling for you."

"Thank ye, sir," answered the man, touching his hat, and apparently overcome by the munificence of the present; "you'll just put up the hurdle again when you've got through?"

Skirting the copse all the way he passed through the gap as directed, and, then, crossing another long meadow, he pushed down the hurdles without caring to replace them, and entered one of the avenues of Breckenwold.

Fortunately, while he was deliberating which direction to proceed in, an urchin came up with a bundle of dry brushwood, and finding that he was going to the very spot, forming in himself a small member of the gipsy community, Lucien stimulated him to a little increased action by the promise of a few pence, and at length saw before him the fires of the gipsies.

Here he learned that the police had been there ten minutes before.

"They're uncommon crafty them perlice," said

the gipsy, to whom he addressed himself. "I think they'd find a man in the middle of a hay-stack even if he wasn't there!"

"Would there be a chance of passing them?" asked Lucien.

"Like enough, like enough," returned the man; "it's nine miles to the weir, if it's an inch, and they're sure to have a drain or two upon the journey."

"There is hope yet, then," thought Lucien, as he once more rode onwards.

The wind howled mournfully through the naked branches of the copse, while the day was rapidly declining as he quitted the beeches.

On arriving at Essy Bridge, and halting at the gate, he was much gratified to learn from the toll keeper that the officers had not yet passed.

Rushing on, therefore, at the greatest height of speed which his horse could attain he soon arrived at the amphibious habitation on the river side where Moonlight Jack had taken temporary refuge to await the reassembling of his men.

After some delay the owner of this mansion upon piles made his appearance at the door, where he remained, imagining that the noise proceeded from some traveller who had lost his way—interruptions of this kind on such an out of the way road being by no means unusual.

But as soon as he recognised Lucien Fairleigh's voice, he bustled forward and assisted him to dismount, leading the horse round to a small shed at the side of the house, and then with a few expressions of surprise at his unexpected appearance, ushered him into the interior of the cottage.

Moonlight Jack was sitting at the fireside, and he sprang up as Lucien entered.

Shading the light of the solitary candle from his eyes, he gazed anxiously in the direction of the door.

"Ah, Lucien! Is it only you?" he exclaimed, as soon as he knew it was his cousin. "Who would have dreamed of seeing you here at this time of night? I declare I thought it was the constables!"

And with a loud laugh he resumed his seat.

"They are after you," said Lucien; they have discovered your retreat."

"I know it; but we have given them the slip."

"You are deceived. They are now in pursuit of you, and a few moments will bring them to the gate."

As he spoke, a short expressive whistle from Hardman, who was stationed at the window, attracted their attention.

"Look," he exclaimed, "if there ain't a bull's-eye lantern coming down the lane, may I never set a night-line again. Up with the dead lights until we know what stuff they're made on."

He closed up the window shutter as he concluded this sentence, and a few seconds passed of anxious silence, so perfect that nothing disturbed but the quick respiration of the listeners.

Lucien compressed his lips and stood ready for action, while Hardman threw some water on the wood embers of the fire-place, extinguished the candle, and took up his position of sentinel at the door, having put up the bar and assuming an attitude of earnest watchfulness.

"Hush!" he said, after a short pause. "It's them, sure enough—ah! very good, very good," he continued, as the new comers were heard calling out from the lane.

"You must wait a bit; we're all gone to bed and asleep."

"We're taken," said Lucien.

"Get down the river as fast as you can by the back door," whispered Hardman, "you'll find the punt lying there. I'll keep them jabbering here five minutes; but don't lose any time."

Quickly collecting their outer articles of dress, they prepared to follow his advice.

Lucien gave a few brief directions to Hardman respecting the horse, and then, catching up the lantern, which the latter had left on the floor, folded his coat round it to conceal the light, and hurried towards the Thames, in company with his friend.

The punt was moored there, hauled a little way up the bank.

Jack Tyrrell directly entered, and took his seat at the end, while Lucien pulled up the iron spike that fastened the boat by a chain to the land, and pushing it off with all the force he could collect, jumped on to it as it floated in the deep water.

The river, swollen with the flood, was rapid and powerful, and directly bore the punt away from the shore, whirling it round with ungovernable force in the eddies, and then bearing it at a fearful rate down the stream.

But they had scarcely started when Lucien, to his horror, found that in their hurried departure they had forgotten to bring anything with them to guide it, and were consequently entirely at the mercy of the angry waters.

In vain they endeavoured to arrest its progress with a few slight rods (pertaining to some fishing apparatus) that were lying in the boat.

They snapped off like reeds.

In vain he caught at the large rushes that danced and coquetted with the stream as the punt occasionally neared the side of the river.

They eluded his grasp, or were torn away from their stems as if they were pieces of thread.

On, on went the boat in its headlong career.

The rapidly passing outlines of the bare and ghastly pollards on the river's bank proved how swift was their progress.

And now for the first time they heard a deep and continued roar, which increased every moment, as if they were quickly approaching its source.

Neither could offer an explanation of the noise.

They remained in painful anxiety for some seconds, until Lucien, who was endeavouring to peer through the darkness, cried out,

"I can see the barge-piles of the lock! We shall be carried down the weir."

Those acquainted with the course of the Thames from London to Windsor may remember that Penham Hook is a piece of land between Staines and Laleham which turns the river into a narrow and sudden curve, cut off from the shore by the lock, whilst the main body of water flows round it with brawling rapidity, a sharp descent forming a natural weir.

Some strong piles are fixed at the head of the rapid to keep the large craft from being drawn into the current, and about halfway round the Hook it gives off a small stream called the Abbey River, which formerly washed the foundations of Chertsey Monastery, one of the most powerful mitred religious houses of its time.

The worn-out boat carrying the two fugitives was now being drifted by the turbulent river towards the point, and the roar of the water as it dashed between the head piles of the lock became fearfully louder and louder.

Lucien kept at the head of the boat, or rather at whichever part of it were first, as it was whirled about in the eddies, and attempted to throw a little more light around them from the miserable candle in the old lantern they had brought with them.

And Moonlight Jack, anticipating the swamping of the punt, which appeared inevitable, had risen from his seat, and having thrown off his cloak prepared to reach the land as best he might when the catastrophe should arrive.

Sometimes the boat neared the shore so closely that its edge grated against the rough stones of the embankment ; but before either of them could hold on it had turned round again, and was once more in the middle of the deep and rapid channel.

Lucien had plainly discerned the forms of the head-piles stretching across the river towards which they were now hurrying, and in another instant the punt was borne against the foremost one with a violent shock that threw them both from their feet, and partly stove in the side, at the same time knocking down the lantern and extinguishing the light.

But they immediately recovered their position, and endeavoured to cling to the ironwork of the standards, and arrest the progress of the boat.

The power of the water, however, was too much for them.

Turning round the side of the piles the punt rushed with fearful violence down the fall, and into the centre of the rapids below the weir, the water pouring in everywhere through the crevices of its battered sides.

Swift as had been their passage before it was now increased tenfold as they grated successively over the stones of the shallows, or glided swiftly onwards in the deep water amidst the masses of ice which were floating everywhere on the surface of the current.

The country on either side was now more open, and the refraction of the light from snow on the banks enabled them to perceive objects somewhat more clearly than before.

They were quickly approaching the entrance of the Abbey river, the position of which was marked by a few leafless shrubs on a small island or ait at the spot where the stream divided.

"It will be the turn of a straw as to which course the punt takes," said Lucien, hurriedly ; "if she goes into the narrow river we are all right, for she will run her head into the bank immediately."

"She is half filled with water," replied Jack Tyrrell, who had retired to the other side of the well. "A minute more will settle it either way."

The boat appeared to approach the ait, now plainly visible on the dark water, in such a direct line that it was impossible to tell in which course they would be carried.

In another instant it touched the side, and was for the moment fixed there as if balancing which current to fall into.

Taking advantage of the check Lucien leaned forward, and, seizing the branch of a willow that grew upon its edge, pulled the head of the boat before it swung round either way.

Then, jumping on the islet, which was not more than ten or twelve feet across, he dragged the punt still further on the dry ground, and called upon Jack Tyrrell to join him, first taking care to secure their craft by winding the chain round the stem of the willow.

"Well, we may thank our stars that one risk is past," said Lucien, as his friend landed.

"Well, we've escaped drowning," said Moonlight Jack, unconcernedly, "those do, generally, who live to be hanged. I suppose we shall have to remain all night in this wretched place."

"If you can suggest any plan to get away I shall be most happy to try it," returned Lucien. "It is not a spot, I grant, that any one would pick out for a gipsying party in the middle of January ; still we have had a lucky escape."

For a few minutes they both remained silent, nothing being heard but the chafing of the river as it rushed past the ait, and the angry wind howling in dreary cadences over the surrounding wastes.

Lucien felt for a short time slightly annoyed at the little gratitude his friend evinced after all his exertions to save him from the fate that threatened him.

But in this he wronged Jack Tyrrell.

He was literally too exhausted to talk.

The wounds which he had received in recent combats were telling upon him, and wrapping his cloak closely about him, he leaned, gasping for breath and shivering with cold, against the trunk of the willow.

But Lucien's kindness of heart was ever uppermost, and, knowing the state of his friend's health, as well as being aware that he must be suffering acutely from the exposure, his feeling towards him was far more of sympathy than anger.

"You had better move about, Jack, if you are able," said Lucien.

"It is dreadfully cold," said Jack ; "my wounds hurt me devilishly."

"Wait awhile," cried Lucien, as if struck with some bright idea, "we will get a light, and see if there is any way of improving our present condition. It might be better certainly, and cannot be much worse."

"How can you procure a light ? The lantern is half filled with water ! It is impossible."

"Devil a bit," answered Lucien. "Tallow don't soak up much, and we can wipe the candle dry. Where is it !"

The lantern had rolled to the extreme end of the punt, but Lucien recovered it, and, throwing out the water, he struck a light.

There was a little obstinacy and sputtering on the part of the wick at first, but at length it burned brightly, and then Lucien, hung the lantern on one of the short branches of the tree, whence it threw its rays over the ait like a beacon in the dreary solitude.

"There is a bottle of spirits in my pocket," said Jack. "Here you are."

Lucien laughed.

"Come, we shall do very well now," said Lucien. "We shall have a fire directly."

"Oh, we might have been worse off," said Jack.

"Worse ! I believe you, my boy," said Lucien. "You had the choice of two alternatives—the police or the bottom of the icy river. Look at that bright star ; mind how slily he winks at us for having jockeyed them both. Now see what I'm going to do."

To collect every particle of fishing apparatus that was made of wood from the punt was to Lucien the work of half a minute, and these he mercilessly split and cut into small pieces.

Next clearing some of the snow from the ground, he laid the foundation of the fire, which he contrived to kindle with various odd pieces of paper, and the lining of his hat.

The flame crept from one piece to another, driving out the angry and hissing sap, until the whole was in a blaze, and then Jack bent down before it, and endeavoured to draw fresh energy from the warmth.

"Now take some brandy," said Lucien, "and make yourself comfortable ; you will soon be all right. For my part, I shall try a few gymnastics."

MOONLIGHT JACK

OR THE KING · OF THE ROAD

THE RESCUE.—*See No.* 10.

And he began violently to belabour himself with both arms, after the manner of cabmen of languid circulation in the extremities, who have been unemployed for hours on a frosty night, until he was quite red in the face, and breathless with exertion.

"It'll be d——d cold when the fire goes out," said Jack.

"We won't let it go out," said Lucien. "We will burn the old boat first. The outside of the wood is wet, certainly, but it is covered with pitch and will soon catch."

"The wind still cuts terribly," said Jack, as he crept closer to the fire. "I wish we could get some shelter from it."

"I wish we could," said Lucien; "but I don't know what to say to it. The wind is not like the cold. The cold is a low, pitiful sneak, who can't stand fire at all, and whom you may always drive away if you please; but the wind is rather a queer customer

No. 9.—March 3, 1866.]   [*Order No.* 1 *of the* BOY PIRATE, *and receive,* GRATIS, *No.* 2 *and a*] LARGE ENGRAVING PRINTED IN SEVEN COLOURS.   [Price One Penny.

to deal with. Ah ! bellow away," he continued, as a blast of more than ordinary force rushed through the trees and across the ait, whirling some of the incandescent embers into the water, "I don't mind a bit as far as myself goes."

Whether or not the wind heard the defiance and felt affronted at it, we cannot say, but certainly it was lulled all of a sudden, as if it had suspended its power, and the fire, which had just before stood a chance of being carried away into the river altogether, now burnt up again steadily and much brighter from the draught.

"What a merry fellow that star is," resumed Lucien, looking at the clear frosty sky in which the constellations were beginning to appear, "and how he still keeps winking through it all ; I wonder who he is ?"

"I can't inform you," said Jack Tyrrell, vacantly ; "I was thinking of something else at the minute."

"Well, don't think of something else, then," returned Lucien, who kept talking on whatever idea came first to keep up his friend's spirits as well as his own. "Look at the stars and think of them; you cannot help doing so if you watch them."

Moonlight Jack was moody.

His mind was peopled with his own thoughts.

Thoughts of the pleasant past—the dreary present—the unknown future.

Thoughts of Gipsy Bess—her love and beauty—the terrible scene which had been the last of his home tragedy.

"I have both thought about and watched them enough since I left Penshurst," returned he, "and often traced out some particular one that had some connection with my own being."

As he spoke, the star to which Lucien had alluded shot half way across the sky and then disappeared.

"Well, that's a jump, however," said Lucien. "If stars are worlds, how awfully those shots must shake the inhabitants. I wonder what that means ?"

"My fate," replied Jack Tyrrell, gloomily. "I shall fall as that star has fallen, and then all will be darkness and oblivion."

"Nonsense," said Lucien, "have a pipe."

Again diving into the secret recesses of his coat, Fairleigh produced some tobacco and a pipe—then an uncommon luxury.

Then procuring some more fuel from the punt, he heaped it on the fire.

The flames shot up merrily and warmly, and the two friends clearing away the snow, sat down and smoked.

An hour or two passed.

They knew the time by the distant tolling of the church clocks.

They sounded clearly through the silent frosty night, followed by the chimes from the other villages more or less distinct in proportion to their distance.

It was now midnight.

The wind had abated.

The moon had risen, and was throwing her cold faint light over the glistening river, and the desolate tracts of ground on either side.

The fire had sank into a heap of glowing embers.

Lucien still reclining at its side with his back against the tree, wearied by his exertions, and drowsy from the cold, had allowed himself to fall into a fitful doze, although his last speech had been a caution to Moonlight Jack not to give way to the slightest feeling of drowsiness.

From this troubled slumber he was, however, aroused by Jack Tyrrell, who, seizing his arm, cried,

"See, Lucien, see ! There is something moving on the bank of the river ! What can it be ?"

Rubbing his eyes, and hurriedly collecting his ideas, Fairleigh looked in the direction pointed out by Moonlight Jack.

He could plainly perceive the outline of a human figure moving apparently between the bank and the water with a stealthy gliding progress.

Presently it left the shore and advanced slowly into the stream of the smaller river, and when it had reached the centre, it bent forward as if gazing intently upon the deep gurgling waters.

Superstition in those times was, as I have before said, the order of the day ; and to be superstitious in an extreme degree, did not imply cowardice.

"Heaven and earth !" muttered Lucien, scarcely breathing, "what is it ?"

"It is an apparition," whispered Jack.

"I never believed in ghosts," returned Fairleigh ; "but this is certainly more like one than anything I could well conceive."

"Yes, and see what it is doing now."

The figure, still bending towards the river, extended its arms, and apparently drew from its depths a dark form bearing the indistinct outline of a human body.

This it regarded for some moments with fixed attention, and then moved again on the surface of the current in the direction of the ait, dragging the other object after it.

"Well," said Jack, rising, "whatever it is, it is coming here. Why, by all that's sacred, it's Hardman !"

"Aye, as right as ninepence !" cried a voice, proceeding from a man in a boat somewhat resembling a washing-tub. "I thought you'd get into some mischief when I found you'd not taken the punt pole. It's lucky you landed as you've done. But come on, the constables are gone long ago."

"Good," said Jack ; "but the punt is useless. It is stove in."

"Then you must come across one by one," said Hardman. "Now, then, captain," he added to Moonlight Jack. "Duty first. I'll come back for Master Fairleigh."

In a short space of time they were once more at the old house on the river.

"And now," said Lucien Fairleigh, "now what shall we do ?"

Jack Tyrrell thought awhile.

"We will meet again at the old place at midnight, three nights from this," cried he. "To horse now, and remember !"

They were soon mounted.

"Now, Hardman," said Jack, whose elastic spirits had somewhat revived, "now we three take different paths. Adieu !"

So saying, he started first, and galloped away down the dark high road.

Lucien and Hardman gazed after him for a moment in silence.

At length the former said,

"Wonderful man ! He is a model of a good heart and wayward spirit."

"Aye, and knows his way about," returned the more methodical Hardman. "He has told us to go different ways, and he's our captain, so here goes. Adieu !"

And mimicking the gesture of his leader the highwayman galloped off, leaving Lucien Fairleigh alone by the dark river.

CHAPTER XIX.

A NIGHT OF ADVENTURES ON THE ROAD.

ON the night following the strange adventure of Moonlight Jack and Lucien Fairleigh on the river, the coach from the north toiled dismally along the broad highway.

It was a gloomy, dismal night.

It was as dark and snowy and overcast as the night they had spent on the ait.

The guard muffled himself up in his great coat, and forgot, in his contemplation of the cold, the chance of being attacked by highwaymen.

The blunderbuss which, from its position on top of the coach must have been as cold or colder than he, reposed uselessly in the solitude, for the frost had long since deprived it of all its biting or barking powers.

The travellers had gone to sleep in spite of the " Traveller's Guide and Companion," which strenuously forbade people who desired to preserve their health to go to sleep and trust to the Demon of the Storm.

The driver was in a state of semi-somnolency, the horses jogged on as if they, too, were asleep, or half so, and dreaming meanwhile of the hay and corn which awaited them at their journey's end.

The snow was so thick upon the ground that the wheels of the coach could scarcely force their way along as it passed upon its noiseless way.

No wonder, then, was it that no one could hear the sound of approaching feet as a solitary horseman made his appearance suddenly by the side of the lumbering vehicle.

The high-spirited creature had passed as gently and noiselessly over the yielding snow as it would have done over turf.

The new comer, who was no other than our friend Moonlight Jack, cried out to the coachman in a stentorian voice,

" STAND THERE, ON YOUR PERIL !"

" Hullo !" answered the coachman, roused suddenly from a dream of a tankard of hot beer at the " Dresden Arms," " who are you ?"

" You will find out too much about me if you don't be quick," cried the highwayman. " I'm Moonlight Jack, and I've ordered you to stop ; that's quite enough to tell you that you're a dead man if you don't."

The coachman pulled his horses up, indulging meanwhile in sundry curses.

Then Moonlight Jack, quite regardless of the guard and his blunderbuss (two things which he generally considered to possess an equal amount of sense), advanced to the carriage window.

" Ladies and gentlemen," he said, as he toyed meaningly with a handsome pistol, " I am very sorry to disturb you, but, being in want of money, I must trouble you for your purses."

People in those days understood at once what this meant.

Moonlight Jack had the orthodox black mask, and the silver-laced hat and coat, and rode the orthodox black mare.

So, amid many grumblings, the purses were found, and delivered up one by one.

There was a curious assortment of people in the northern coach.

A pig-jobber, a horse-dealer, a widow, a young lady running away with an Irish adventurer to get married (*if she could*), and a lawyer's clerk, who had been fifty miles to serve a writ, and found the proposed victim dead.

These were Jack Tyrrell's clients on the present occasion.

The lawyer's clerk he did not trouble, but the others he mulcted of everything of value they possessed.

The pig-jobber had a hundred guineas, the horse-dealer as many more, the young lady had fifty, while her gallant adventurer was compelled to confess that he hadn't five shillings in the world !

The widow appealed to him with tears in her eyes.

" Sir, good sir," she cried, " I have but the money to purchase my only son's discharge from the army. He is my sole hope in life ; oh, pray don't ask for that !"

" There, say no more," said Jack ; " keep it, and take five pounds to boot. Now, my friends, good night."

At this moment there was a loud shout.

The lawyer's clerk, who had his head out of the window, now drew it in.

" Hurrah !" he cried. " We are rescued !"

Moonlight Jack turned hurriedly round.

He saw at once that he was in danger.

A body of at least six constables, headed by a youth, had surrounded him !

The tables were slightly turned.

The pig-jobber, the horse-dealer, and the Irish adventurer, now recovered their courage and left the coach, while the lawyer's clerk remained behind to kiss the young lady, who, having fainted, he supported in his arms.

Moonlight Jack threw the bridle upon the mare's neck and drew his sword, while the other hand grasped a pistol.

" What want ye, my masters ?" he cried.

" Your surrender."

" Why so ?"

" For robbing the mail."

" Not so ; you have yet to prove I have robbed the mail."

" Yes, yes, he has," cried the Irishman, who had lost nothing ; " he has taken every farthing that we —— "

His further speech was stopped by Moonlight Jack, who drove the handle of his sword into his mouth.

" He is the man ; he is Jack Tyrrell," cried the youth who was with the constable.

Jack knew the voice.

It was that of Jonathan Rasper.

" Come !" cried one of the assailants, " come, surrender ; here are odds of ten to one."

" Let me pass !" cried Jack, swinging round his bright sword ; " at your peril let me pass !"

He made a rush forward, and one of the men was struck from his horse.

But he could not force his way through.

The passengers, the guard, the coachman and the constables surrounded him everywhere.

It was a strange game.

He could not escape, but they could not take him.

" Stay !" suddenly cried the head constable. " Jack Tyrrell, I once more caution you to surrender. I give you time to answer, and then your blood be upon your own head."

As he spoke he raised his pistol, and held it even with Jack Tyrrell's head.

" Fire, and be d——d !" cried Jack ; " I will never surrender."

The man fired, but, as he pulled the trigger, a loud shout rent the air and unsteadied his hand.

The ball sped harmlessly, while, at the moment, several strange figures appeared upon the scene.

Foremost among the new comers were two mounted upon grey horses.

The first was a boy of some twelve years.

The other was one habited as a man, but whose sex was doubtful.

The figure sat short upon the horse, the bust was full, the legs large and rounded were pressed out against the horse's sides.

There seemed, indeed, little question that the rider was a woman.

Female or not, however, the new comer burst into the throng of gaping travellers and constables like an avalanche.

Nor was the boy by her side idle.

He seemed at once to single out Jonathan Rasper.

Rushing towards him he dealt him a heavy blow with the butt end of the pistol, and would have finished him had not he slipped away half-stunned and crawled into a ditch.

The youngster then ranged himself on the side of Moonlight Jack.

Jack knew his face and form well.

It was his own son!

The tide was now turned.

With the unknown Ranger of the Road came a horde of brave companions, who dashed gallantly enough through the paid minions of the law.

They fought as became them and the money they received for it.

But they soon cut and run.

The coachman and guard jumped up in great haste, the pig-jobber and horse-dealer scrambled up aloft, while the Irish adventurer, tumbling inside, found his future wife and the lawyer's clerk so engaged in kissing, and other tender endearments, that they never observed his entrance.

Moonlight Jack, meanwhile, having cleared the coach of its principal valuables, cared no more for it, but turned towards his newly found friends.

But in an instant he was completely alone.

One glance, the moon enabled him to take, of a pale, wan face and eyes, which, with their sorrow, made him close his for very pity, and then all had vanished.

Constables and friends seemed to whirl away in one confused eddy, and he was alone!

He gazed around him in bewilderment.

"Am I awake?" he cried, "or am I dreaming?"

He felt his pockets.

The solid gold was there.

Best token of a successful raid!

"Well, well," he murmured, as he turned his horse's head towards London, "my adventure, truly, in the first place, was real, but its ending was a dream! That sweet, pale face could belong to none but Gipsy Bess, and she is lost for ever!"

Then again he broke out,

"My boy, too—my only son! He was there, and thrashed that villain's whelp, Jonathan Rasper! Where is he? He was with *her*. Oh, Heaven, grant that he is not dead too, or what have I to live for?"

So saying, he spurred his horse on towards London and left the dreary scene of his exploit behind, passing the coach on his way and waving his hand to the coachman as he did so.

CHAPTER XX.

WHEREIN LUCIEN FAIRLEIGH ENDEAVOURS TO GAIN HIS GREAT END IN LIFE, BUT FINDS THAT A CORMORANT IS AN UNPLEASANT THING TO DEAL WITH.

HAVING to meet Moonlight Jack two nights after the adventure on the river, Lucien Fairleigh had but little time to spare.

He resolved, however, to use this time well.

His great object was to induce Grace Dashwood to fly with him.

Accordingly, on the next day, he contrived through Soft Sam to convey to her the following note:—

"DEAREST GRACE,—To-night at eight o'clock I will be in the Chestnut Walk. I shall then ask you to quit me of this suspense. Why should we longer wait for that happy moment which shall make us one? Delay is dangerous. Life is but uncertain; and who can tell whether we shall live until all these clouds which hang over us are dispelled? If we delay for years your uncle will still refuse his consent to our union. Where, then, can be the use of delay? But, come, dearest, at eight, that I may pour my pleadings into thine own sweet ear.

"Yours for ever,
"LUCIEN."

He was at the Castle when he penned this.

He had made his way thither immediately upon leaving Moonlight Jack, and had been received most graciously by Lady Edith.

She had felt disappointed.

Knowing well how strong were Lucien Fairleigh's claims to the marquisate and the property that appertained to it, she had, as my readers will remember, sworn that he must die.

When, therefore, he went away on his errand of mercy to save Moonlight Jack from the clutches of the law, she had imagined that he had contrived to elude her grasp.

She was delighted, therefore, to see his face again.

"Mr. Fairleigh," she said, with a smile which was intended to express her pleasure at seeing him again as well as her sorrow at what was passing at home, "Mr. Fairleigh, I am glad to see you here once more. Since you left us the marquis has been sadly ill."

Lucien took her hand and pressed it.

He knew she was false.

Yet he resolved to humour and deceive her.

"Is my father worse, then?" he asked, with real anxiety.

"He is indeed; I begin to fear the worst. He knows no one; his talk is unconnected; he seems unable to remember anything or to understand anything."

This was true.

Yet he could see that she made the most of it, and spoke her words with no slight zest.

"Let me see him," said Lucien. "Perhaps he will know me."

Quietly they approached the sick chamber.

All was very still.

A nurse sat by the side of the bed half dozing.

The marquis, calm and pale, lay upon his back with his eyes upturned towards the ceiling.

Lucien approached.

The nurse made room for him, and he leaned over his father.

But there was no recognition.

The eyes of the marquis remained fixed upon vacancy.

"Father," said Lucien, earnestly, "do you not know me?"

The vacant eyes turned towards him for an instant.

Then they were again fixed on the ceiling.

"I fear he is lost to all of us," said Lucien, sadly. "What says the doctor?"

"That he cannot live."

"Does he name a time?"

"No; but he doubts his living a week longer."

"And *I* doubt," thought Lucien, as he quitted

the room with her, " whether you desire him to live so long."

At eight that night he was to meet Grace Dashwood.

At half-past seven he quitted the castle, and made his way along the banks of the river.

The place of rendezvous—the Chestnut Walk—was one just suited to the meetings of ardent lovers.

The trees so over-arched and so shaded the ground that even on bright moonlight nights lovers could kiss and embrace and indulge in a thousand vagaries without being observed.

When Lucien arrived Grace was already there.

She flew into his arms.

"Oh! Lucien," she cried wildly, "I am so glad you are here! I have been so terribly afraid."

"Of what?"

"Of my uncle."

"Does he know——"

"He knows all."

"What mean you?" cried Lucien, as the panting girl strove hard to articulate her words. "Has he, then, discovered that I have to meet you to-night?"

"He has."

"What traitor has told him? Have you confided to any one our secret?"

Grace, still clasping him to her palpitating bosom, and speaking hurriedly while she glanced wildly behind her to see if any one was coming, said, quickly,

"No, I have trusted no one; but, unfortunately, to-day, in my hurry, I dropped your letter. Every instant I fear that my uncle will come, armed, and prepared to seize you. Fly, dearest Lucien, while you have yet time."

Lucien glanced earnestly at the face which the black darkness of the winter's night almost veiled from him.

"What, Grace, am I to fly alone?"

"Oh! press me not now. There is danger in my company!"

"Then let them come," said Lucien, putting her gently away. "Since you refuse to fly with me death will be welcome."

"Oh! you are most cruel, Lucien!" cried Grace, as she burst into tears, and clung still more closely to him. "Yes, yes, I will fly with you. Let us go while there is yet time!"

They were just about to pass away beneath the spectral branches of the chestnut trees, when a loud voice exclaimed,

"Hold there, on your lives!"

The voice was one well known.

It was that of old Clement Cormorant the miser.

"What want you, sir?" asked Lucien, in a feigned voice, while he drew his cloak over Grace's head so as to conceal as well as possible her features.

"I want you, Lucien Farleigh!" cried the old man. "It is useless for you to disguise your voice. Fellows, seize that man and conduct my niece home!"

Lucien Fairleigh drew back.

"Stand off!" he cried, "stand off! Come not an inch further, on your lives!"

There was no mistaking the meaning of his words and tones.

They were determinedly spoken, and they knew that any attack would meet with a resolute resistance.

Yet, on the other hand, they were four to one.

It seemed cowardly to fear him, yet they knew well that one among them must, in the mêlée, meet his death.

Lucien saw their hesitation, and profited by it.

"My good fellows," he said, "if you attack me it will not only be foolish, but wrong and illegal. Miss Dashwood is here of her own free will, and there *can* be no reason for seizing me, the heir to Huntley Castle, and the future landlord and owner of this very ground upon which I stand."

Old Cormorant uttered a fierce exclamation of rage at these words.

"Heir to Huntley Castle?" he cried. "My men, he is an imposter! Believe him not; he is a common thief—a highway robber! Seize him!"

There was a confused movement among the men, but not one of them seemed inclined to be the first.

No doubt Lucien Fairleigh might in another moment have fled with his mistress, had not a creeping, crawling figure—a figure that had been working itself on like a snake behind him—suddenly rushed between his legs, and thrown him down.

This was Jonathan Rasper!

Lucien Fairleigh was a friend to Moonlight Jack, and, therefore, an enemy of this miserable sneak.

In an instant the men, seeing they were safe, rushed forward, and two seizing upon Grace Dashwood, bore her away.

The two others grasped Lucien firmly, while he was still on the ground, and Grace had disappeared with her captors and her uncle before he contrived to struggle to his feet.

But they were not destined upon this occasion to capture him.

Again and again he shouted aloud, more for the purpose of alarming those whose strong arms were around him than in the hope of attracting the attention of those who were, for all he knew, many miles away.

But he was agreeably surprised.

Hardly had the echo of his voice died away when there was a rushing sound, and Moonlight Jack and Hardman appeared upon the scene.

In a few minutes Lucien was once more on the high road, and the men returned discomfited to the Hall to tell Clement Cormorant of his flight.

CHAPTER XXI.

THE STRANGER AT THE WHITE HORSE INN—THE SUSPICIOUS BAG—THE CURIOUS LANDLADY—THE IMPLEMENTS OF ROBBERY—THE EJECTMENT OF THE STRANGER—THE PURSUIT—THE SCENE AT THE KING'S HEAD—THE SECOND PURSUIT — MOONLIGHT JACK MEETS THE STRANGER—THE ROBBERS AT THE INN—THE MORNING'S LIGHT!

SHORTLY after dusk one evening, a single traveller, young, tall and gentlemanly, and carrying a black carpet bag, might have been seen wending his way towards the village of Great Badloe, where he entered the White Horse Inn, and politely inquired of the landlady if he could be accommodated with lodgings for the night.

Being answered in the affirmative, he expressed a wish to be at once shown to his bed-room as he had had a long walk, and wanted to freshen himself up with a wash and a brush.

The worthy hostess was of a rather inquisitive and suspicious nature.

It is one of the idiosyncrasies of the sex to be so, and Mrs. Plumline was rather an exaggerated specimen of curiosity and timidity.

Having lately heard of a clever swindle upon an

inn-keeper near Great Badloe, she resolved to "keep her eye" on the interesting stranger, who roused her suspicions in an unusual degree by the time he remained in his bed-room.

She couldn't understand why a man should be so long "cleaning and titivating himself," although there was not a square inch of her own plump person which *she* did not scrub and cleanse every morning and evening.

By and bye, however, the terrible stranger walked quietly into the parlour, partook of some bread and cheese and ale, and lighting a cigar, sauntered out for an evening's stroll round the village.

But our astute landlady was not to be deceived by this assumed *nonchalance*, and no sooner was his back turned than she lit a candle and ran up-stairs to his room with some vague idea that he might have concealed the sheets about his person or somehow made away with the bedstead or the chest of drawers.

Everything, however, appeared to be just as she had left it, except that the stranger's bag—and a very suspicious, swell mobsman kind of bag it looked—stood upon a chair near the bed.

Sure enough the key—no doubt in the hurry and excitement consequent on a guilty conscience—had been left in the lock !

Great criminals, we know, have also been great fools, and it is such errors as these which lead to punishment.

Here, at any rate, was a key to the mystery ; and no wonder that her woman's heart, like that of Blue Beard's wife, at the door of the Blue Chamber, throbbed with a fearful curiosity as she stood for a moment, key in hand, eager, but irresolute—

"Loth to stay, yet half afraid to go."

What "strange eventful history" might not that tell-tale key reveal ?

Confused thoughts of unsuspecting landlords swindled out of board and lodging on the strength of bags and boxes loaded with brickbats, of jem-mies, of skeleton keys, &c., flitted across her brain.

The bag was heavier than any honest bag ought to be.

Besides, when she moved it, there was a sus-picious clinking inside.

Surely there could be no harm in just one peep.

Pressing her hand over her throbbing bosom—a very pretty one, be it said, though somewhat matronly—she approached on tiptoe as if afraid the bag would bite her.

"I will examine it, no matter what comes," she said, with some bravery, seeing that the bag did *not* move.

With trembling hand she turned the key.

She peeped in.

Then she started back in horror and amazement.

Here suspicions were too truly verified.

The bag was full of skeleton keys and other bur-glarious instruments.

What a scoundrel that man must be !

The whole thing was as clear as daylight.

He was a professional swell mobsman and bur-glar from London, and had left his bag of tools there while he skulked, in the dark, round the vil-lage in order to ascertain which house was best adopted for his first attack.

His atrocious plans must be nipped in the bud.

With breathless haste she rushed downstairs to her husband, who, with one or two friends, was seated comfortably in the parlour, and vehemently exclaimed,

"What *do* you think, Joe ?"

"I was thinking I should like some more grog," said Joe, drily.

"Oh ! don't talk like that," said his wife ; "the young man that's engaged the bed is a burglar !—a highwayman !"

"Nonsense !" returned the landlord, who didn't want his conviviality to be disturbed by any such piece of business. "What makes you think so ?"

"Think so ?" she exclaimed, indignantly. "I don't think so at all, I know it. I have proved it with my own eyes, and so may you if you like."

"How ?"

"Why, he's left his bag upstairs, and it's chock full of skeleton keys. Come along with me and you shall see for yourselves."

All at once sprang to their feet.

With many a "Goodness gracious !" and "Well I never !" they followed the good lady upstairs, where she pointed triumphantly to the contents of the open bag.

There was great excitement among the spectators.

They elbowed one another excitedly in their eagerness to catch a glimpse of the mysterious apparatus of robbery.

None could exactly tell the use of the strange things, though all agreed they were suspicious.

One, however, in a husky whisper, suggested that a complicated piece of ironmongery something in the shape of an ear trumpet was a thing used for listening at keyholes before venturing to tamper with the lock.

It was a strange scene !

The gleam of the solitary candle shed a flicker-ing light on the pale, conspirator-like faces of the village worthies as they bent excitedly over their ill-omened task, with the buxom landlady standing with folded arms in the background—

"A smile of sombre triumph in her eyes."

"Well," said Joe Plumline, as he took the bag and locked it, "well, I'll take this 'ere bag down with me, and then we'll see what's to be done next."

So with all the importance in the world they ad-journed to the parlour.

They thought themselves wonderful people now.

The event was quite a godsend to the empty-headed gossips.

Here was a good, dark-looking mystery progress-ing under their very roof.

It was brought home to their fire-side, as it were, and they could enjoy it without the least pain or trouble.

It was extraordinary what a zest and relish it gave to the drink and how it heightened the flavour of the tobacco.

But the question now was—what was to be done?

Time was on the wing, and the stranger might return at any moment.

Various schemes were suggested ; but at last it was decided to pretend inability to accommodate him—send him elsewhere, and then catch him, per-haps, in the very act.

This was determined on just as the intended victim returned, and walked unsuspectingly into the parlour.

Here he called for a glass of ale, and then, taking a memorandum-book from his pocket, he began to make some notes.

This was too much.

It was adding insult to injury.

Here he was, absolutely jotting down deliberately, before their faces, the names and localities of the houses where his midnight spoil was to be ob-tained.

Significant glances were exchanged, and sig-nificant remarks freely bandied one with the other.

One of the company began to talk loudly about

certain persons being different to what they pretended to be.

"Hold your tongue," cried another, meaningly. "Don't you see the *gentleman's* writing? What do ye want to disturb the *gentleman* for?"

"Oh, d—n the gentleman!" was the reply, in a somewhat unpleasant tone.

Charitably considering that they were less mad than drunk, the traveller thought he had better ask for his candle.

"Can I have my candle now?" he asked.

"No, you can't," said the landlord.

The traveller looked at the rustic Boniface in amazement.

"Did you understand me?" he asked. "I said, 'Can I have my candle?' Having engaged a bed here, I have a right to ask?"

"You can't have your candle," said Joe Plumline, "and, what's more, you can't lodge here!"

"Why, pray?"

"Well, the fact is. I—I—I—But, there, it's no use mincing the matter—my wife had let the room before you came, to a regular customer, and had forgotten all about it."

The traveller looked as he felt—extremely annoyed.

"Well, but," he said, "don't you think it's rather queer conduct to turn me out in a strange place like this at ten o'clock at night?"

"I can't help that," returned the landlord, boorishly; "I tell you, ye can't lodge here. There's your bag, and you can pay for what you've had, and walk, as soon as you like."

Finding all remonstrance useless, and thinking, perhaps, that the sooner he was out of such queer company the better, the traveller paid his bill, and took his bag.

"I've no wish to spend my night in the open fields," he said. "Perhaps you will have no objection to direct me to another inn."

"Try the 'King's Head,'" returned the landlord, surlily.

And the traveller walked off.

"Now, then," said Joe, as he returned to his open-mouthed guests, "now's our time. Let's follow him."

They accordingly went out in a body to the door.

Here who should come by but the village constable.

"The very man we want," said Joe, and he at once stated his case.

"Well," said the constable, "this may appear all very clear to you, but it don't to me."

"How's that?"

"I don't know; but I can't see it, I tell you."

"Well, what's to be done? Won't you come with us?"

"Yes, if you like."

So they started.

They kept their quarry at a respectful distance, keeping their eyes upon him, and ready to pounce upon him at the proper moment, hoping to take him, as the expression is, "red-handed."

Presently the stranger took a turning leading directly away from the "King's Head."

On this his pursuers began to increase their pace, and, firmly grasping their sticks, made ready for immediate action.

For a moment they lost sight of him.

But, ah! there he is at yonder corner.

He stops to speak with some one.

This, no doubt, is a confederate.

At any rate, the traveller turns him about, and makes at once for the "King's Head."

Finding that the worthy hostess of this establishment would be happy to accommodate him with a bed, he took his seat among the company in the parlour, still puzzling his brain to endeavour to find out a reason for the extraordinary treatment he had received from the villagers.

His troubles and annoyances, however, were not yet over.

The village gossips—idiots of the vale—having gone so far, did not feel disposed to yield their point.

It would never do to allow a detected burglar thus quietly to quarter himself upon an unsuspecting neighbour.

So presently there came a tap at the parlour-door, and the landlady was called aside, and asked if a gentlemanly young man with a carpet-bag was going to lodge there that night.

"Yes; he's in the parlour now," she said. "What about him?"

"Why, do you take my advice," was the reply, "and don't have anything to do with him. He's a London burglar, and his carpet-bag is full of skeleton keys."

The hostess, on hearing this, was prompt but civil.

She called the traveller into her private bar-parlour

Here she stated her case.

She had some compunction in doing so.

The traveller was young.

Moreover, he was handsome.

No wonder she should dislike the job of insulting him.

She was a widow.

She had not yet passed that time of life, moreover, when the tender passion can be aroused in the breast of woman.

So she looked upon the stranger with anything but an unfavourable eye.

However, what was she to do?

Her reputation, her money, was at stake.

So she stated her case plainly.

The traveller was disgusted.

"Here," he cried, opening his bag, "here are the burglarious instruments you speak of. You should understand music. If you don't I shall not take the trouble to explain."

He had lost his gallantry in his anger.

"See," he added, as he opened the much-abused bag, "these are organ-tuning instruments. I have come hither purposely to tune the church organ. There, pray don't make any excuses, I will not stop here now if you were to give me a bed. I will rather walk on up the lane, and go on to Chelmsford."

So saying he rose, flung down his reckoning, and departed.

He did so amid the jeers of the clever gossips.

"Ah!" thought they, as their broad mouths grinned their satisfaction, "these chaps from Lunnon be main cunnin'; but we're a match for them, arter all."

That was the question.

Meanwhile, the stranger trudged on from the inn, and was just approaching a small beer-house, where he thought, perhaps, the fame of his arrival might not have reached, when three men on horseback suddenly stopped him.

"Your purse or your life!" cried the foremost, who was no other than Moonlight Jack.

The traveller started.

It seemed truly as if he had been turned out of two inns for the purpose of being assaulted on the high road.

"My purse is not much," he answered; "but such as it is you may have it, if you leave me but a guinea for myself. If not I must e'en fight for that, for I cannot go away empty-handed."

Jack Tyrrell laughed.

"Well," he said, "keep two, and be quick."

Suddenly an idea struck the traveller.

"Stay!" he cried; "before you fleece me, allow me to ask you to grant me a favour."

"And what is that?"

"That you will come with me for a minute or so into yonder beer-house, and listen to a few words I have to say."

Moonlight Jack laughed.

"Do you take me for a madman," he said, "that you ask me to thrust myself deliberately into such a trap as that?"

"It is no trap," he answered. "I pledge myself, I pledge my word of honour I will not betray you. You are three to one, there can be no danger."

The traveller's manner was such that the highwaymen were convinced rightly enough that he was speaking nothing but the truth.

So they resolved to accompany him.

Entering the beer-shop, which was now on the point of closing, the organ-tuner asked for a bed for himself, which he was at once informed was at his disposal.

Then ordering four flagons of ale he sat down with the three highwaymen at a side table.

Here he confided to Moonlight Jack the history of the last four hours.

Jack listened attentively.

He did not exactly see in what way the story affected him.

But the traveller did not leave him long in doubt.

"I am the last in the world," he said, "to counsel a robbery under ordinary circumstances; but in this instance I should much like to see these busy-bodies punished. You are knights of the road, so the affair will be quite in your way."

"What do you suggest, then?" asked Jack Tyrrell.

"This simply: that *you* should proceed to the 'White Horse,' and make yourself sufficiently agreeable to the landlady to obtain a bed there, and *rob* the house. In addition to this, one of your friends here should proceed to the 'King's Head' and play the same game."

"In this case they will simply fancy you are one of our band, and that they were very clever in the first instance in turning you out."

"Not so; I will take excellent care that they shall know *who* I am, and what thorough idiots they have made themselves."

Jack Tyrrell eyed the speaker narrowly.

"Now look you here," he said. "I and you are strangers, are we not?"

"Yes."

"Then why should I believe you or you believe me?"

"I don't know why. But I *have* told you the truth, and so I trust you'll believe me."

"What guarantee have I?"

The young man thought a moment.

Then he said,

"Come, my luggage in that carpet bag is, as you know, all I depend upon for the carrying on of my business. I will place these in your hands. My purse here contains ten guineas; take it, and restore it to me if I have told the truth."

Jack pushed back the purse.

"No," he said, "I will *not* do that. Keep them. I believe you; and take my advice, quit this place early."

"I will. And how shall I know how you fare?"

"I will tell you ere morning. And now, since it is getting late, we had better start. Lucien, you and I will go together to the 'King's Head.' You, Hardman, go to the 'White Horse.'"

They rose, paid the reckoning, and went off, leaving the bewildered traveller to go to rest.

Meanwhile, Moonlight Jack and Lucien rode up to the "King's Head," while Hardman went on to the "White Horse."

They summoned the ostler in imperious accents, delivered their horses, and entered with a swaggering gait quite different to the quiet demeanour of the gentleman organist.

They knew the people they had to deal with.

"Can we sleep here to-night?" said Moonlight Jack, twirling fiercely his magnificent moustache.

"I don't know, sir. I think—yes, sir," said the landlady, slightly colouring.

Since the departure of the London organ-tuner, the absurdity of the charge against him had been fully established.

A gentleman, a commercial traveller, who had chanced to see him in the room, had recognised him as the partner in a firm with whom he had done extensive business, and when he heard of his clever ejectment, he at once disclosed the fact to the somewhat crestfallen landlady.

The rustic thief-hunters were finely roasted on the subject; and when Moonlight Jack and Lucien Fairleigh entered the public room, they made their coming an excuse for their own going, and sloped before any one could chaff them more.

The end of this adventure we need scarcely narrate.

Both the "King's Head" and the "White Horse" found their error in the morning.

They had ejected a peaceful traveller and given accommodation to three notorious highwaymen.

Consequently not a farthing of money or a piece of anything valuable remained in the hostelries on the following morning.

Pursuit was about as useless as grumbling, and so while our three knights of the road got clear away with their booty, the landlord of the "White Horse" and the landlady of the "King's Head" thought it best to grin and bear it.

CHAPTER XXII.

A VOICE FROM THE GRAVE!

THE Marquis of Huntley being dead, and the all-important papers being still missing, Lucien Fairleigh had nothing whereby to identify himself with the deceased.

So, for a time, he resolved to wait and watch.

He had seen and heard enough of Lady Edith Huntley to be fully aware that not even his life was safe in the precincts of the castle.

He, therefore, for a time at least, resolved to keep quiet, to remain with Moonlight Jack, and allow his master mind to aid him in his new emergency.

But Moonlight Jack himself was strangely changed. His light-heartedness was gone.

Instead of his old joyous laugh and jest, there was an atmosphere of gloomy silence about him.

He would for hours wander away from among his companions on the expressed pretence of watching the highway.

Yet upon more than one occasion Lucien Fairleigh came across him suddenly, sitting on a bank by the roadside, gazing, not on the road, but upon vacancy, his horse browsing on the greensward near him.

MOONLIGHT JACK

OR THE KING OF THE ROAD

PLANNING THE ROBBERY.—*See page* 75.

The disappearance of the body of Gipsy Bess upon the fatal evening when Lord Henry Davenport and his men attacked the strong-hold of the robbers seemed to afford a convincing proof that she was not dead.

The mysterious figure, too, who, with his own son, had saved his life upon the highway, seemed to give credit to the fact that she was alive and watching over him. Yet, where was she?

This question he could not answer.

Convinced as he was in his own mind that she was faithful to him, and that his suspicions as regarded Lord Henry Davenport—now dead—were groundless, he could not conceive in any way *how* she was now occupying herself.

A strange circumstance about this time cast a new light upon the subject.

He had gone out by night down the lonely lane leading to Penshurst, when a small form emerged from the hedge, and stood before him.

No. 10.– March 10, 1866.]   [Order No. 1 *of the* BOY PIRATE, *and receive,* GRATIS, No. 2 *and a* LARGE ENGRAVING, PRINTED IN SEVEN COLOURS.   [Price One Penny

He knew him at once.

It was his son !

"Harry, my dear child," cried Moonlight Jack, clasping the boy to his heart, "where have you been ? Why have you stayed from me ?"

"I have been with Gipsy Bess," he said ; "I have since been with Brandon's gang. I come now to show you where she lies."

The boy's voice trembled.

Whether from emotion or from some other reason he could not tell.

"Is she dead, then ?" murmured Moonlight Jack, in a hushed voice of sorrow.

"Come with me. You will see."

Jack followed his little leader.

The boy conducted him to the walls of the churchyard.

Here they entered, and approached a spot near the church.

The moon was shining very brightly, and a por-

tion of its radiance fell upon the white head-stone of a grave. On it these words were legible :—

Sacred to the Memory of
GIPSY BESS,
Aged 17.

Moonlight Jack gazed for a few moments in awe and terror at the spot which the stone marked as the resting-place of all he loved best on earth.

Then he turned suddenly towards his son.

Suddenly, fiercely, as if he had just discovered a fraud.

"I will not believe it," he cried. "Harry, you are palming off upon me a lie. I will not, cannot believe that Gipsy Bess is dead."

Then came a voice like the wailing of a summer wind,

"If I am not dead to all I am dead to him who believed me faithless."

Moonlight Jack sought everywhere, but the speaker, whoever it was, had *vanished!*

BOOK II.

THE BRAND OF SIN.

CHAPTER I.

THE BROKEN WHEEL — THE THIEVES — THE THREE DINNER-PARTIES — THE JOLLY ROBBERS — THE ATTACK ON THE OLD HOUSE — THE PATROL NOWHERE — THE BURGLARY — THE MAN IN THE RED PLUME.

IN the back lanes of a village, some two-and-twenty miles from London, there stands, or, rather, lurks, a hedge ale-house, called the "Broken Wheel."

From an abrupt corner of ruined barns and pigstics on one side, and a stagnant pool on the other, in the high-road through the village, a lane opens its ragged bushy mouth, and runs straggling away for a couple of miles, where it widens out into a barren common.

These two lonely miles are enclosed on both sides by squalid hedges, broken fences, the end of a neglected garden-wall, a dry ditch, and a turnip field.

At the right-hand side of the garden-wall stood an old summer-house, built of brick, like a little tower, the upper story being intended as a place to sit in, and enjoy the prospect of seven green fields, and a cowshed, with nothing particular in the distance.

This ruined summer-house was now overgrown with ivy, and had become the delightful abode of owls and bats.

By the side of this part of the garden-wall a pathway through down-trodden thistles and nettles ran sloping and winding till it opened into a narrow lane between dark high hedges, amidst which, and standing rather back, was the little ale-house known as the "Broken Wheel."

It looked just like the ugly, half-hidden nest of some strange bird of prey.

The ale-house stood back in a gap between the two high ends of the hedge.

A ditch ran along the hedge, over which a dirty board was placed as a bridge.

The ale-house was built of old boards and worn-out timbers.

It was thatched, and, in colour, as black as dirt and smoke and rottenness from continual rains and damp could make it.

On a little piece of board had been painted a cart with its wheel broken, which was nailed up close under the projecting thatch by way of a sign.

In front of the lower window was an open space between the house and the hedge, of some eight or nine feet distance, where a flat board, nailed on a tressel, served for a table, and a plank on two low posts for a seat.

A three-legged stool, and an inverted washing-tub, afforded accommodation for two more visitors if needed.

On this plank and this stool sat three men, each with a pipe in his mouth.

A brown jug, with a broken nose, was upon the table, two pewter pint pots, and a tall white mug.

These men were known somewhat to the people round, and more to the county magistrates ; but as the reader cannot be expected to have the honour of their acquaintance, I will introduce them.

Jack Day, the first, was a man about two and forty, rather short in stature, but of great breadth of shoulders, with a deep chest and large arms, and thick, muscular legs.

He was a very powerful man, and of greater activity than might have been expected from his frame.

His features were heavy, and he had the look of a lowering bull.

Sometimes when he spoke, however, his whole face lighted up with a most malevolent and daring expression, as though he was ready to commit any act of ruthless violence.

He had very short, thick, poodle-dog hair, and a sunburnt complexion.

Jem Crow was about thirty-five, of the middle height, narrow-shouldered, and stooping.

His legs were well made upon the whole, but his arms seemed rather deformed.

He had red hair and thin red whiskers, a speckled complexion, a sharp, turned-up nose, very small, piercing grey eyes, and a large mouth, with long, yellow teeth.

The third, Jeremiah Woolton, was fifty years of age.

He sat like a very short man.

But when he stood upright he was six feet two, his height being all in his legs.

As he walked his stride was immense, and he had a gaunt strange look like that of some antediluvian bird.

His face was very sallow, and his large hands were as yellow as a kite's foot.

He had a quiet, grave, somewhat thoughtful expression, and habitually gazed down his knees when he spoke to any one.

He had a bad cast in one eye, and had lost the forefinger of his right hand.

He was continually occupied in blowing a sort of inward whistling to himself as he sat looking at the ground.

The dress of these three men—except that Jem Crow wore a fashionably-cut drab frock coat, with a large blotch of grease in the middle of the back—was of the most blackguardly kind from top to toe, and still worse in its filthy neglect.

It was evident that they had been sleeping in their clothes for weeks without once taking them off, or even washing their hands and faces.

These three fellows were burglars, and they were now engaged in settling the immediate operations of a burglary which they had been planning for some weeks past.

"And *she* told you this?" said Jack Day, uplifting his towering gaze, and staring in Jem Crow's face, half-enquiringly, and partly repeating his words in order to be sure.

"Yes, *she* told me this," repeated Jem Crow, as if put upon his oath, and resolved not to contradict himself.

"Kitchen-maid, is she?" proceeded Jack Day.

"Scullery-maid, I said," rejoined Jem Crow, in correction of the inaccuracy.

"Well, then," said Jack Day, after a pause, "I suppose she knows what she's hup to?"

"Course she does," said Crow, "and more nor that, she told me what they was agoing to have for dinner. Pig's fry and a goose, and three biled fowls and a knuckle o' ham, pigeon pie and roast beef, and soup and cheese, and a salmon and wegetables—all sorts—and roast weal and custards, and a pint of shrimp sauce, besides lots of wine, and ale, and grapes, and nuts and plumpudden, to be put on the sideboard ready."

After this inventory, which, except as to the order of "serving," did considerable credit to the retentive memory of the speaker, the three men's eyes all met in a common centre, and the faces all gave a strange grin of greedy delight, quickly relapsing into a kind of morose gravity and self-restraint as though from the consideration that "work" was to be done before play.

The house they had planned to break into and rob belonged to a tolerably wealthy family, named Crompton, with whom the "squire's" son was to dine that day.

The squire was a rich man, and there were three unmarried daughters in the family he was to visit, so that the parents on both sides thought a match would be a very suitable thing, no matter which daughter he chose.

There were only three large houses in the village, and these were at a considerable distance apart.

The squire's house was at the southernmost end.

The house of the clergyman, who was also the magistrate, was at the northernmost end, three miles distant, and the house of the Crompton's stood just between.

It lay back half a mile from the high road, approachable by a long carriage drive of bright gravel, and was surrounded by lofty trees.

Opposite the white gates that opened out into the high road were the remains of a fourth large house in the village, which, having been the subject of an apparently interminable law suit, had been suffered meantime to fall into utter decay so that no one could live in it at all.

One wing of it had fallen down, and every windy night it was expected the whole would come to the ground.

There was a large lawn at the back overgrown with weeds, and then a great desolate garden of considerable length, terminating in an old vine wall and a summer-house, now thickly overgrown with ivy.

On the other side of this ran the narrow pathway through wet nettles and thistles that led to the ugly little hedge ale-house, bearing the sign of the "Broken Wheel," in front of which the three burglars were now seated in conference.

The family of the Crompton's comprised old Mr Crompton, a retired coffee merchant, his wife, his son Fred, a country-bred youth of nineteen, three marriageable daughters, and numerous servants.

At the hospitable board were now seated Mr. Freer, a dashing young fellow from London, and Frank Besley, only son and heir of Squire Besley, of Besley Hall.

Frank Besley was proud of all field sports, a capital shot, &c., but one who never went to any dinner party without getting blind drunk.

It was now ten o'clock.

Young Besley sat still drinking port wine, and Mr. Crompton had for a long time been passing the bottle to an imaginary Mr. Freer, who was really under the table.

At eleven the latter was carried to bed: Mr. Crompton also retired, after enjoining the housemaid to collect the plate and lock it up, and the young squire went home swearing.

All were a-bed now, and asleep.

How silent the house was after all the noise and eating and drinking and rattling of plates and laughing, and getting young men up to bed.

It was midnight.

It was a dark night in the latter end of October.

The day had been very mild, but it had rained hard since eleven o'clock.

The rain had now ceased, however, and the wind had risen.

The boughs of the great trees round the house shake and swing about.

Showers of leaves fall.

Dry bits of stick are sometimes blown against the windows.

The doors and shutters, and the frames of the casements rattle loudly.

Other strange noises were made in the house as well as outside by the weather.

But in the pauses of the wind other noises of a different kind from all the rest might have been heard had anybody on the ground-floor been awake.

The burglars had arrived, and, having selected the point to effect an entrance, were now steadily at work.

Jeremiah Woolton, or Jerry Sly as he was called, having been round to all the lower windows and found them properly fastened with bells affixed, they held consultation, and unanimously fixed upon the pantry window as the most eligible means of breaking into the house.

The pantry window looked out upon a side lawn where the clothes were hung out to dry.

It was six feet from the ground, but there was no area between the wall and the lawn.

The window was without glass, and covered with a frame-work of perforated zinc.

It was, moreover, protected by two iron bars,

and as the window itself was narrow, the body even of a boy could not have squeezed through between them.

Jerry Sly, being much the tallest, accordingly proceeded to effect his part of the task.

He placed himself against the wall, and with a keen file began to cut through one of the iron bars.

He worked quickly and without noise.

John Day and Jem Crow meantime silently took out their several implements and arranged them for use.

They had with them a powerful jemmy (a stout crow-bar), a centre-bit, screw-driver, chisel, files, a pair of iron pincers of a peculiar shape (made to pass through a hole and turn a corner), and a large knife with several tools in it, such as a small saw, two gimblets, a hook, a pick, and a cork-screw.

To this armoury was added a brace of pistols, three bludgeons, a dark lantern, and three masks— a green one made of an old veil, a white one made of cartridge paper, and a black one of the usual masquerading manufacture, though much bent and maltreated.

One bar being announced by sign to be cut through Crow advanced, and, with the jemmy, adroitly smashed and cleared out half a brick from the wall about thirteen inches below the sill of the window.

He then placed himself close beside Jerry Sly, each bending his back with elbows placed flat against the wall and his head pressed upon his arms.

Upon their backs Jack Day soon mounted.

He then seized the lower end of the iron bar just above the place where it had been cut through, and, planting his left toe in the niche where the piece of brick had been taken out, he thus obtained "good purchase," and by main strength bent the bar upwards and aslant.

He now leaped softly down and made a back for Crow, who went to work at the sheet of perforated zinc, which, in a few minutes, he opened all down one side and folded back.

He then thrust his head and shoulders in at the pantry window and listened.

"Go along," hoarsely whispered John Day.

Twisting his legs round at this exhortation Crow dangled them down into the pantry.

His crouched-up head and shoulders faced his friends for a moment and then disappeared.

But presently his hands re-appeared, and the fingers twisted impatiently in the air.

Jerry Sly instantly skipped up beneath the window with the centre-bit and special pincers, which he deposited in the hands, and they immediately vanished in the darkness.

John Day and Jerry Sly, after waiting a few minutes till certain sounds within indicated that Crow had effected his entrance, moved slowly round to the area at the back facing the garden.

Sly pointed to one of the lower windows inquiringly.

Day shook his head.

"Somebody asleep there," he whispered. "Gardener or boy."

Then he pointed to the back door down in the area.

They descended the stone steps, and Day applied his ear to the keyhole, while Jerry Sly applied his to a crack in the top square of the top panel.

In the course of ten minutes' suspense they heard the gradual grating noise of the slow withdrawal of rusty bolts, the gliding back of the tongue of the lock, and the lifting up and laying aside of a chain.

The door then slowly opened, and the muzzle of a duck gun was protruded !

It came out longer and longer with steady, hostile advance, and behind it appeared not the adroit colleague Jem Crow, but the hobbedehoy figure of Master Crompton in his shirt.

"Rascals !" cried he, "take that !"

With these words he fired manfully about three yards above their heads, and struck the top of an ornamental pigeon-house in the middle of the lawn.

Day and Jerry Sly were retiring precipitately, when out darted Crow, and in an instant pinioned the valiant young duck-sportsman from behind.

He began to bawl,

"Thieves ! robbers ! mur-der !"

But Crow's fingers grasped his throat, and he was thrown down with a knee thrust deep into the pit of his stomach, which effectually silenced him.

Day and Jerry Sly, who had rushed into one of the side shrubberies, finding that the cries had been abruptly stopped, conjectured what the turn was that had taken place in affairs, and emerging from the shrubberies met Crow, who explained in a word what had occurred.

"Go on," said Day.

He was savage at the momentary check.

They returned to where the young man was left.

Thinking he might be troublesome if he came to himself, Day dragged him into the passage, intending to lock him up in one of the cellars.

But as he was searching about, a door opened, and the gardener coming into the passage, cried out,

"Who's there ?"

"Nobody," said Day, foaming, and, striking him a blow with his fist that sent the old man reeling back into the middle of the room, he swung the insensible body of young Crompton along the floor, and then taking out the key from the inside, closed the door and locked it.

Two of the male inhabitants of the house were thus safely provided for.

Day said they must waste no more time, but go to work upstairs at once, for he heard them moving.

The three burglars hastily put on their masks, and hurried to the foot of the stairs, seizing cloaks and capes from the pegs in the passage, with which they assisted the disguise of their persons.

Day led the way with a pistol in his left hand.

Crow followed closely with the other pistol, and Jerry Sly brought up the rear with the dark lantern in one hand and a bludgeon in the other, all according to previous arrangement.

They heard the door of Mr. Crompton's bed-room open, and his voice call out,

"Fred, Fred ! didn't you hear a gun go off just this minute ?"

This was instantly followed by a scream from Mrs. Crompton, who cried out,

"They're breaking into the house, I'm sure they are !"

The words were still on her lips, when Mr. Crompton, who had been standing on the landing-place, rushed back into the room, followed by three men in masks.

He had not even time to close the door.

Mrs. Crompton, with a loud scream, hid her head beneath the clothes, and fainted away, while her husband ran to one of the windows and threw it up.

He was, however, instantly seized from behind by one of the men, and flung violently backwards upon the carpet near the bed.

A pistol was then held to his head, while the ruffian, with horrible imprecations, threatened instantly to blow his brains out if he did not give up all his keys, and tell where his money and plate were deposited.

While this was doing Crow ran down stairs with Jerry Sly, and entered the room in which Mr. Freer had been deposited.

The noise and scuffling had awoke him, and he had just got out of bed and was standing in the middle of the room with an owlish stare, when the two men burst in upon him.

He instantly staggered forward, demanding in thick accents, and a tone of authority,

"What's o'clock?"

He was answered by a blow from Crow's bludgeon, which laid him prostrate, and, if possible, more senseless than before, while Jerry Sly hastily possessed himself of a gold watch and chain, which he put in his pocket.

They then left the room.

Loud screams from above now attracted their attention.

The two Miss Cromptons, who slept on the second floor, had issued from their room, and seeing their father lying upon his back with a man in a mask standing over him, had flown up stairs to alarm the maid-servants and their sister.

Immediately three windows were flung open, and they all began screaming,

"Thieves! murder! fire!"

To how little purpose, when there was no house within a mile of them!

But the maid-servant ran down to the assistance of her master, and, darting upon John Day, who was stooping over him, tying his hands, tore him away.

She was almost instantaneously seized by Crow and Jerry Sly, who tied a handkerchief round her mouth so tightly as almost to produce strangulation, and in this state thrust her into a closet in the bedroom, and locked her in.

Day, meanwhile, had rushed upstairs among the screaming women, whom he seized and struck in a most savage manner, dragging them away from the open window, and, being presently joined by his colleagues, they forced all of them into the room of the young Miss Crompton, whom they threatened with instant death, presenting a pistol at her head and a knife to her throat, if she did not keep all the rest quiet.

Jerry Sly then took a gold watch and some trinkets from a toilet table, and they left the room, promising to return and make good their threats if any one again uttered a cry or opened a window.

The three burglars now descended, and entered the china closet, where they gathered up all the plate.

Mr. Crompton was lying helpless on the floor bound hand and foot.

As to the screams from the windows they had been stopped as a matter of caution, but without much apprehension of results, as the house, as previously explained, lay back half a mile from the high-road, and no other dwelling was near.

The burglars, therefore, proceeded systematically to plunder the house.

Jerry Sly kept guard by walking upstairs and uttering threats, and then descending to the bottom of the house.

This he continued to do while Day and Jem Crow brought down the plate, and entering the different rooms, carried off every small article of value they could find.

They even swept up the whole of the nick-nacks from the drawing-room chimney piece, and threw them into the sacks with the spoons and teapot.

It will be remembered that young Frederick Crompton had been laid senseless by a half throtling process on the first entrance of the burglars, and that the old gardener had also been knocked down.

The old man, however, after a time, recovered himself sufficiently to rise, and availing himself of the absence of the watchful guard, Jerry Sly, when he was upstairs threatening the screaming women, he opened his window (his door having been locked from the outside), and let himself down into the area, which was only four feet below.

He then cautiously entered the house, and went straight to the little room where the boy slept.

The boy was gone.

A thought struck the gardener, and he hurried to the coal cellar and there he found him hidden.

The boy knew his voice and crawled out, and they ran from the house, across the lawn, and into one of the shrubberies, and so along the dark filbert walk till they reached the arbour, and here they stopped to take breath.

The gardener then told the boy to make the best of his way into the high road and find the patrol, and tell him what was going on, while he would hasten by another way up into the village by a lane that would bring him out just opposite the house of the village constable, whom he would knock up.

It will now be requisite to revert to the departure of the young squire from the convivial board of this unfortunate country family, and bear in mind the peculiar condition in which he sallied forth into the dark night, refusing with a flourish all companionship of boy or lantern to guide his unsteady steps.

He had not gone far along the gravel walk before a heavy shower of rain came on, and, to obtain some shelter, he stepped aside, among the trees of a plantation, through which he made his way onwards towards the high road.

It so happened, however, that he emerged very much farther off than he had intended, and being near to a little road-side inn, he commenced a battery against the shutters, which compelled the landlady to appear at the window, and then having ascertained his "quality," to come down and let him in.

He remained for an hour or more, drinking brandy and water, on account, as he pretended, of being wet through and through.

At last she got rid of him.

The young squire again sallied forth into the night in a yet more "unaccountable" state than before, and after a time arrived in the main street of the village.

Here he remembered the house of two old maiden ladies, who kept five cats, through whom he had got a whipping when a schoolboy for fastening a cracker to one of their tails on the 5th of November.

He stopped, looked up at the bed-room window, then down at the dining-room shutters, and finished his vague contemplation by picking up a large stone, and commencing a loud hammering against the shutters.

He wound up by discharging the stone through one of the bed-room windows, while he set up a strange and unearthly howl.

He had the greater pleasure in doing this, because the house was within two doors of the little shop of John Denison, the constable.

This nocturnal outrage quickly brought forth the poor maiden ladies to the windows of their several rooms, which they threw up and began to scream,

"Constable! Constable! Thieves! Thieves! Mr. Denison! Mr. Denison!"

Another stone through the bed-room window of the personage thus summoned, instantly brought that invaluable functionary to *his* window, opening which he heard a similar salute paid to another window further on.

It therefore became a clear case that he must hurry off to capture the offender before all the glass in the village was demolished.

He commenced putting on some clothes with the utmost haste.

Meantime the merry young gentleman had moved on till he found himself abreast of the principal inn of the village, viz., "The King William."

The one faint lamp of the main street was just over the way, and shed a dim light on the benign aspect of the gentlemanly monarch above, which the young squire found quite irresistible.

So he swarmed up the sign-post, and first lifted one hook out of its eye, and then the other, and down fell the great signboard edgeways in the road.

Down slid the pleasant young gentleman, and taking up his majesty on his back with the face turned outwards and looking benignly on all behind, moved onwards with his burden staggering yet secure on his legs, and at a good pace.

It was a cold wet night, and Denison the constable had thought it advisable to put on most of his clothes before he issued forth on duty.

He was soon enough to observe a figure going up the main street at no great distance.

He hailed him, and then quickened his pace.

As he got nearer he saw it was a man walking off with some booty—a large square box as it seemed.

"Stop! in the King's name!" he cried.

But the midnight robber only quickened his pace.

Denison quickened his.

The figure began to run.

Denison gave chase.

Away went the pursued along the highroad beyond the village, and presently turned down a deep lane, and ran scrambling through the darkness with a slushy sound, John Denison after him.

But the house of the poor Crompton's, which is being plundered all this time, with poor Mr. Crompton lying on his back bound hand and foot, as any country gentleman may be even now at any time by burglars, and his wife, and family, and servants all in momentary terror of their lives!

What is to become of them?

A boy had been dispatched by the old gardener to run as fast as his legs would carry him up into the high-road, and try and find the horse patrol, while he himself made his way to the constable's house.

Both of these were to a certain extent successful.

The boy was lucky enough to get sight of the horse patrol.

Being unable to contain himself after his recent excitement, the little fellow instantly began to cry out,

"Patrol! patrol! Thieves! thieves!"

The guardian of the highway pulled up his horse.

But before the boy could reach him, the patrol heard the sound of footsteps of men running along the road through the village.

Making sure these were the thieves the boy meant, who were now effecting their escape, he set spurs to his horse and galloped after the sound of the retreating footsteps.

The old gardener, "dead beat" from loss of breath, arrived at the constable's house.

Here he was met by Mrs. Denison in a large night-cap and a small shift, who informed him that her husband had gone out after some villains who were breaking all the "windies" in the village, and that the horse patrol had gone after them likewise.

"They will soon be back, I hope," she added.

The chase of Denison, however, was not destined so soon to come to a close.

Down the long straggling back lanes did the robber with the great box run most vigorously, and the constable after him, panting and gasping, and with one hand pressed to his side.

And now the sound of a horse's hoof is behind them, and *on* it comes, but not very fast, as the lane is so dark and slippery and down hill.

The patrol's bull's-eye lantern is very useful.

It casts a great stream of light before them.

He soon finds out that the first man he comes up with is Denison.

But what is that which retreats?

It is a large majestic figure, attired in colored robes, with a smiling countenance and a fine high-curled wig, running, too, down the lane backwards.

The lane suddenly becomes yet more precipitous.

Alas! for human power, even in a promising young squire, down falls the figure flat, and flatly lies, but still looks up with a courteous smile, the august semblance of his majesty King William.

They picked up the strange complexity of man and sign, and by this time the man was almost in as insensible a condition of being.

Finding it was the young squire, the two parish authorities did what they thought best "under their difficult circumstances,"

They helped him up, wiped the mud off his face, placed him on the horse—the patrol walking by the side to hold him up, and the constable walking behind, humbly carrying the sign.

In this way they escorted the young gentleman to his own house, four miles from the place where they found him.

How has it fared all this time with the burglars at Crompton's?

Excellently well.

They have collected all the plate, all the watches, chains, rings, and trinkets.

All the money, too, in the house they have secured, and all the light portable valuables.

They have brought all down into the kitchen, where John Day is placing them in a couple of small sacks and a canvas bag, while Jem Crow is setting out the table with the remains of the beef and veal and goose and ham, &c.

He has also found bread and cheese, and cold salmon, and a preserved gooseberry tart, and he is now going with a candle to the cellar for a dozen of wine.

Jerry Sly had issued forth on to the lawn at the rear of the house, passed through one of the shrubberries, and approached a hedge.

He gave a low, smothered whistle.

The hedge was pushed aside, and a rough dirty, dog-like face, with a red nose, and red projecting lips, was thrust through the aperture.

The head had a little grey carter's hat upon it, and the thick red lips were sucking the brass-headed handle of a whip, while the eyes seemed to listen as much as the ears.

Jerry Sly bent forward.

"Give her the rest of the corn."

With this brief order, which at once showed the driver that all had gone well, the brute's face was withdrawn from the hole in the hedge, and Jerry Sly returned to his friends.

The table was by this time well covered with all the dainties of the season, and a squadron of black bottles fresh from the wine-cellar.

Crow was digging out a pigeon-pie, and Jack Day was lying back in a chair, wiping his forehead with his sleeve.

They had worked hard in one way, and now they fell to work in another.

The execution they did upon the various contents of the table in the course of a quarter of an hour nobody would believe.

They swallowed mouthfuls that would have done credit to a clown in a pantomime, and drank port wine (Crompton's best) in beer glasses.

As for champagne, they knocked the necks off the bottles, and let the wine spout down their throats.

At length Jerry Sly, filling his tumbler with a bumper of Madeira, took it in his right hand, and, slowly rising, thus addressed the company :—

"Gentlemen, schoolfellows, and friends," said he, "I rise at this early period of the evening in virtue of my being the h-oldest among you, and, therefore, most qualificationed to state a moral proverb like this, as it's good to be merry and wise. We have done our duties this night ; our carriage and horse, likewise coachman, are awaiting for us under a dark hedge close by ; let us, therefore, take up our little property, and go our ways. But, afore we go, I beg to presume to give you a lyall toast. 'Here's the 'elth and happiness of our noble king, and our worthy host, Mr. Crompton !'"

The thieves drank the toast with due honours, and having imbibed the good liquors until they thought it prudent to imbibe no more, they prepared to depart.

Their arrangements were soon made, and leaving their victims bound, and the house open, they sallied forth, entered the cart, and drove homewards.

Now, it so happened that Moonlight Jack and Lucien Fairleigh, with two or three of their band, were out upon the road, close to the house of Mr. Crompton.

Moonlight Jack was expecting some one.

He would not say whom.

Of late he had been most taciturn.

He seemed changed.

He was moody and reserved.

He would confide nothing to Lucien Fairleigh but the ordinary routine of business.

Upon this occasion he had merely said,

"I have to go to Tentleton Beeches to-night. I wish you to come with me."

Lucien Fairleigh had answered "yes," and asked to know the nature of the business.

But Moonlight Jack had not vouchsafed a reply.

During the time that the jovial thieves were recreating themselves at the house of Mr. Crompton, Moonlight Jack and his friends were waiting near Thorley Brook, which was situated some half a mile from Crompton's farm.

It was a strange place this Thorley's Brook.

It was a place of ill omen.

A place where strange crimes had been committed.

A fearful murder had once been perpetrated there ; and a village maiden, bereft of her honour in the heat of passion, had chosen it for her brief passage into eternity.

It was a dark and dismal pool.

Weeping willows overshadowed it, and nodding reeds and long rank grass.

A large elm tree overshadowed it in one part and showed the darkest and deepest of the pool

where the bank was torn and jagged as if desperate hands had seized it in a struggling fall.

"He whom I expected comes not," said Moonlight Jack. "Will you, Lucien, cross the fields there by Crompton's farm, and see if along the other road approaches a horseman with a red plume."

Lucien bowed.

His word was now " obedience."

He had, since the death of his father, the Marquis of Huntley, been thrown upon his own resources.

What these resources were may readily be guessed.

He had no friends.

Excepting those two persons whom he had so long regarded as his father and mother, and who, since the discovery of the secret, he had treated in the same manner as before, he had none whom he could call a friend.

So, with a feeling of utter desperation, he took to the road as a livelihood.

Moonlight Jack had been his friend.

His more than friend.

Some mysterious influence appeared to unite them.

Jack knew his history and his early friends.

Jack had sworn to reinstate him in his rights.

To whom, therefore, rather than to him, could he apply for help ?

And whom, moreover, having chosen a life in the road, would he rather have chosen for captain

With the utmost alacrity, therefore, he obeyed the order of his leader.

Spurring on his horse, he rode at once over the ploughed land towards the farm.

As he neared it he heard voices raised in fear.

Impelled both by curiosity and his natural bravery, he approached the spot.

As he neared Crompton's farm, he observed that the cries were those of women.

Dismounting he entered the house.

All was still.

Still save the wailings of fear and pain.

Forgetting, for a moment, the errand upon which he had been sent ; forgetting, last of all, that he was masked, and had every appearance of being a knight of the road, he entered, as I have said, and ascended the staircase.

He approached the bed-room.

Here the first sight that presented itself was that of three young girls, ranging from sixteen to twenty, nearly naked, and clinging to one another in fright.

He entered their room, and waved them to be still.

"Peace," he cried ; "I have come to save you."

He then hurriedly explained to them that he had been attracted by their cries, and had come to save them.

He then directed them to retire again to rest, and went into the room of Mr. Crompton.

Here the scene was different.

Mr. and Mrs. Crompton were both lying bound upon the floor.

Lucien knelt down and quickly released them.

"Rise," he said, "you are saved. You have nothing more to fear."

Mr. Crompton eyed him severely.

"Young man," he said, "your conduct may be very specious, but it will not deceive me."

"Deceive you, sir !" exclaimed Lucien, in surprise.

"Yes ; you *are* doing so."

"In what way ?"

"In pretending to defend me."

Lucien uttered an exclamation of impatience.

"It would have been better," he said, "if I had taken no notice of your daughters' cries. I came here to save you and them, and I am accused of deceit. Do you know me?"

"I do not. But, hark! what is that?"

Lucien listened.

There was a loud noise below.

The shuffling of feet, and the mingling of many voices.

The voices at length ceased.

Then the feet came up the stairs.

In another moment the bed-room was filled with men.

At the head of them was John Denison, the police constable.

The others he had sworn in on the road.

"Ah!" cried the sagacious constable—literally, the *Jack* in authority—"Ah! here we are fortunate—here is the thief caught."

Lucien drew his sword.

He eyed Denison firmly.

"Where is he?" he cried.

The constable grinned.

"Ah, where is he?"

"Come, no folly!" said Lucien. "Tell me, where is the thief, that we may catch him!"

"Come, no rubbish!" cried Jack Denison, indignantly. "Put the handcuffs on him, my men, and don't let's have any gammon."

The constables approached Lucien to seize him.

His bright sword described a half-circle round his head, and fell, flat side on, upon the wrist of the foremost.

"Stand back!" cried Fairleigh, furiously. "Stand back, idiots and dotards! What want you with me?"

"We require you to surrender."

"For what?"

"For robbery."

"Upon whom?"

"Upon this house."

"Who is my accuser?"

"This gentleman."

He pointed to Mr. Crompton.

He did so enquiringly.

The old merchant responded.

His wits were never of the very clearest.

Besides, the night before he had been drunk.

So he saw the whole affair, like the sottish cockney, "at a glance."

He pointed with all the majesty which a cotton night-cap and a scanty dressing-gown would allow of towards Lucien.

"Sieze him!" he cried.

The men again advanced.

Lucien waved them back.

He addressed Mr. Crompton.

"Sir," he said, "why is this outrage?"

"Outrage, eh?"

"Yes, outrage upon the man who saved your life."

"Bah! you are one of the gang. Seize him, my men!"

Once more the constables thought it prudent to rush upon him.

They were not cowards.

Their only fault was inexperience.

"Come, my friend," said the foremost to Lucien Fairleigh, "surrender. It will be best for all of us."

Lucien laughed satirically.

Then, dashing forward with his drawn sword, he rushed through them, and had gained the door ere they knew what he was about to attempt.

Down the stairs he went and out into the air, and within a few moments was on horseback and once more dashing along the fields in the direction of the cross road where he was to meet the man with the red plume.

What I have narrated had not occupied any great space of time.

Only a space to be reckoned by minutes.

Happily, therefore, he met the man with the red plume cantering along the road.

He at once accosted him.

"A word with you, sir," he said.

The stranger laughed.

"If you seek my purse," he cried, "you have chosen the wrong man. I am of the road myself."

"You mistake me, sir," said Lucien; "I came from Moonlight Jack to seek you."

"In that case," said the man with the red plume, "let us press onwards, for I am late."

So they sped back towards Thorley Brook.

Here they found Moonlight Jack still motionless upon his horse.

He went eagerly forward when he saw the approach of the man in the red plume.

"My friend," he cried, "you have, then, kept your word."

"I never failed you."

"No, truly. But, my son. Where is he?"

The Red-plume shook his head.

"Alas!" he cried, "I cannot tell you. I know that he lives, but that is all!"

"But who is it that keeps him from me?"

"I know not, except it be himself."

"That is not possible; he would never voluntarily absent himself from me."

"There you are wrong," returned the stranger. "I believe it *is* his own wish."

"Why?"

"From what he said. Young as he is his words and actions have a method in them. But hark, what is that?"

There was a strange rustling sound around and over them.

A rustling sound like the sweeping of the wind over the corn-fields.

In a moment more they were made aware of its meaning.

About five and twenty men were around them.

They themselves were but six in number.

They moved to go on, down the road, as if not understanding the meaning of their enemies.

"Hold!" cried a loud voice.

Moonlight Jack still moved on.

"Hold!" cried the same voice again.

This time more angrily.

"Who speaks?" cried Jack.

"I, in the king's name," said Denison.

"The king and you be d——d together!" cried Moonlight Jack, "let me pass."

But they objected.

There was a general fight.

The constables and their friends being strong in numbers, fought valiantly, which the police, by the bye, seldom do.

Moonlight Jack and his men fought like lions.

But what can one man do against six?

The twenty-five, many of them wounded truly, but none killed, pressed around the devoted band.

"Every man for himself," cried Jack, in a loud voice. "Now fly, my friends, and strike for liberty."

The words had scarcely left his mouth when a blow from the hilt of a sword struck him senseless, and he fell backwards upon the horse's back, still holding firmly by the bridle.

"IF YOU SEEK MOONLIGHT JACK HE IS HERE!"—*See page* 88.

The constables knew him well.

A shout of triumph rose into the air.

But it was inopportune and premature.

The beautiful black mare which Moonlight Jack rode reared, flung forward its front feet, and leaping suddenly, dashed down upon the heads of two of the chuckling constables, who chuckled no more for some time.

Before the other Jacks in authority could stop it, it was dashing down the road and Moonlight Jack was safe.

Not so Lucien Fairleigh.

He fell a victim to treachery.

While defending the person of his friend he was assailed behind, not by a sword, but by a rope being cast over his head.

By means of this he was flung back upon his horse, and before he could recover himself was seized and bound.

So Lucien Fairleigh was borne off towards Dorley Castle, where he demanded at once to know the cause of his imprisonment.

No. 11.—March 17, 1866.] [*Order No.*1 *of the* BOY PIRATE, *and receive, GRATIS, No.*2 *and a* LARGE ENGRAVING PRINTED IN SEVEN COLOURS. [Price One Penny.

"You are arrested on a charge of murder."

Lucien smiled.

"I have disproved it; though Lord Henry Davenport is now in reality dead, he was shot in view of all by another hand."

"It is not of Lord Davenport I speak," said the man to whom he addressed the question.

"Of whom, then?"

"Of Henry Maltravers."

"Who is he?"

The man smiled.

"You're determined to keep up a good show of innocence, then?" he said.

Lucien made a gesture expressive of impatience.

"Come, come," he said, "I have asked you a civil question. I am in a dangerous position, and I have a right to have an answer. Who is this Maltravers, and what is the crime of which I am supposed to be guilty?"

It appeared, from what the man said, that on the preceding night the house of Clement Cormorant was broken open, and a large amount of jewellery, plate, and money was stolen.

The robbery was at once, of course, laid down to the credit of the band of Moonlight Jack.

But there was worse than this.

There had been murder done.

The old miser had invited to his house a young man from London, called Henry Maltravers.

He was the son of a man as rich and as miserly as old Cormorant himself.

He was quite youthful, not bad looking either, and Clement Cormorant had destined him to be the husband of Grace Dashwood.

Grace had given him no encouragement.

She loved Lucien too well to allow another to monopolise a moment of her time, even though it were in deception.

But, at any rate, young Maltravers, innocent and brave as he was, was found dead upon the floor of his room with his drawn sword still grasped firmly in his hand, and the blood welling from a great wound in his chest.

The inference was easy.

Lucien was a member of Moonlight Jack's band.

Lucien loved Grace.

Lucien was jealous of all who approached.

He was also an enemy to old Cormorant.

It was to be imagined, therefore, that he could take this ready opportunity of ridding himself of a rival.

Old Cormorant had discovered by some means or another that Lucien Fairleigh was abroad in the neighbourhood that night, and he resolved at once to fix the crime upon him.

He would thus rid himself at once of an enemy, and of one who aimed at the hand of his niece.

The man in the red plume had been able to render no assistance whatever to Lucien Fairleigh.

But he did what was next best.

He hurried on to Moonlight Jack.

A conference was at once held.

What was to be done?

Lucien was in a fortress of well-known strength.

There seemed no hope of rescuing him from it.

Yet, bold as they were, and united by a strong bond of brotherhood, they resolved to try.

First of all, however, came the question of trial.

Perhaps—frail hope it was indeed—perhaps he might be acquitted.

If not there would still remain a few days between the day of sentence and the day of doom.

Knowing the animosity which existed in the neighbourhood amongst the friends of Huntley Castle against Lucien Fairleigh, and knowing, too, that one of the first acts of the authorities would be to seize whatever property was upon him, they resolved to take time by the forelock, and employ a good attorney.

Mr. Matthew Glover *was* a good attorney, and on the trial he proved himself so.

The barrister whom he retained, Montague Rae, made a most eloquent speech upon the occasion, and won the praise of all, and the sympathy of many.

But there was one whom he failed to convince or pacify.

That one was the judge.

Moonlight Jack had met him some nights before and not only robbed him but pulled his nose.

Moonlight Jack's name was repeatedly mentioned on the trial.

He was spoken of as Lucien Fairleigh's friend.

This was enough.

He summed up dead against the prisoner.

The jury, therefore, taking what he said for granted, found the prisoner guilty, and he was sentenced to die the death appointed by the law for such criminals.

The judge passed sentence with great unction and relish, and the spectators at this hanging festival separated, well pleased with the day's entertainment.

Three nights after this was chosen for the attack of Moonlight Jack's band upon Dorley Castle.

It was not an open attack.

It was to be done by stealth.

It was just at sunset that the band moved onward from the high road, across the meadows and the lanes, towards the broad moat which skirted the prison.

The sun was glancing brightly down upon the hamlet.

The wet grass sparkled in the light.

The scanty patches of verdure in the hedges took heart and brightened up.

The vane on top of the church steeple glistened in the general gladness.

At length the glory of the day was over.

The sun went down beneath the long dark lines of hill and cloud, which piled up in the west an airy city, wall on wall, and battlement on battlement.

The light was all withdrawn.

The shining church turned cold and dark.

The stream forgot to smile.

The birds were silent, and the gloom of winter dwelt on everything.

The men moved slowly on.

An evening wind uprose, too, and the slighter branches cracked and rattled as they moved in skeleton dances to its moaning music.

The withering leaves, no longer quiet, hurried to and fro; the labourers trudged home, and from the cottage windows lights began to glance and wink upon the darkening fields.

The men now, with Moonlight Jack and the man with the red plume at their head, joined together as the darkness thickened, and moved in a solid mass towards the castle.

On arriving, they slid down into the moat, and reaching the other side without molestation, glanced around them to see whether they were watched.

Then they looked up at the castle for the sign which had been arranged between them and Lucien.

A light burned brightly in one room.

"He is there," murmured Moonlight Jack; "see, *there* is his signal."

The men then at once set to work.

Their plan was simple, though attended with some danger.

Between the interstices of the stone huge staples were to be driven.

Upon the first one a man was to stand and drive in a second.

Thus he was, at the peril of his life, to crawl up towards the window of the cell where Lucien Fairleigh was confined, and securing himself by a rope to one of the huge bars, file through the iron work.

A peculiar signal was to inform Lucien of the presence of his deliverer, and he was then to fall upon and bind the turnkey in charge of the cell.

The man at once commenced his work.

He made but little noise.

The mortar crumbled away, and the long iron wedges slid easily in between the large stones, and were firmly fixed.

But a misfortune suddenly occurred.

The moon shone out with unusual brilliancy.

A stream of silver light fell upon the body of the man who was working.

The result was almost instantaneous.

A loud shout resounded in the castle-yard.

Then a shot was fired.

Then another.

These were succeeded by cries of pain, and the man fell from the wall.

In a moment Moonlight Jack and his friends rushed to the spot where he had fallen.

They raised him up.

He was stone dead!

They had no time to moralise over him—no time to utter vows of vengeance.

The guardians of the castle surrounded the little band, and demanded their surrender.

A peal of ringing laughter was the only response.

Springing on the horses which they had led across the moat, the gallant highwaymen dashed through the ranks of their astonished foes, nearly treble their number, and leaped across the broad ditch.

Then a loud shriek rent the air.

"You think to slay Lucien Fairleigh. You cannot! Moonlight Jack will save him."

CHAPTER II.

HOW LUCIEN FAIRLEIGH WAS HUNG ON DARN-BOROUGH COMMON.

ON Darnborough Common, one bleak day in November, 1720, such an assemblage of persons had collected that when you looked from an elevation at the monster gathering, it seemed to extend for miles into the open country, while from every road and lane fresh contingents were each moment arriving to swell the concourse.

There was that day a man to be hanged!

A fellow-creature was to be strangled according to law upon Darnborough Common!

It was not therefore likely that human nature, in its ordinary love of variety, could resist the attraction of such a show as that.

What to them was the cold and biting air from the frozen regions of the north?

What to them were the icy particles that hung upon their beards; or the snow, which seemed every moment threatening to fall?

A man was to be hanged!

That was enough.

It was now near twelve o'clock.

The crowd was impatient.

Presently a cry arose from ten thousand throats, "They come! They come!"

"Here they are!"

"They are coming now!"

Oh! what a stirring, and trampling, and pushing there was now for a better place than those who strove and pushed thought they already had.

The mob seemed to be having, throughout its length and breadth, a fight of its own, for no other earthly purpose than to celebrate the arrival of the malefactor, who then and there was to make reparation with his life to that society which had come roaring and shouting to see him die.

Poor wretch!

But there is the scaffold.

It is worth a word or two.

It had been the custom to hang criminals in what was called a gallows tree.

That gallows tree consisted of an upright piece of wood stuck firmly in the ground, with a piece at right angles from the top of it, and the slanting strengthening bands of timber beneath.

On this occasion, however, an attempt had been made to construct a scaffold.

It was, to be sure, a very rude attempt.

A quantity of planks had been brought from the town and placed on the tops of some half dozen carts, as nearly of a height as possible, so that a kind of platform was made, loose and shifting certainly, but still tolerably secure.

In the middle of this platform, where the boards were left open for the purpose, rose up the awful gallows with its cross-tree at the top, and the rope dangling from it.

The hangman, who was a bit of a genius in such matters, had so managed that by the removal of one board the victim of the day would be suspended in a tolerably satisfactory manner, and from underneath he could remove the board with ease.

A black cloth was laid over a portion of the the extemporaneous platform.

The erection, therefore, looked something like the proper sort of thing, and had quite a professional aspect about it.

The ordinary mode was to bring them in a cart under the gallows, and when they were suspended to move the cart from under them so that the last words the criminal usually heard were from the carter to his horse, and consisted of "come up."

Upon the platform was the sheriff of Darnborough conversing with a gentleman from London, who had come down to see the sight in a kind of amateur capacity.

Around the scaffold were a company of mounted yeomanry with their heavy jack boots and huge bear skins and drawn swords.

They shook again with the cold.

A small knot of some eight or ten officers of the police stood close to the steps that led up to the platform.

The sheriff took out his watch.

As his nose turned bluer and bluer from the cold, he said to the gentleman from London,

"Confound them! how late they are! It is a quarter to twelve now! Why don't they bring him and hang him at once?"

"Ye—e—s," stuttered the gentleman from London, whose teeth went like castanets in the cold. "If they don't come and turn him quickly off we shan't have a bit of feeling left."

"Not a bit," said the sheriff.

What sort of feeling did they allude to?

It was just as the sheriff and Mr. Jonas from London had made these feeling remarks that the cry arose from the crowd of,

"Here they are ! here they are !"

It was said just in the sort of way that the clown in a pantomime says,

"Hooray ! here we are again !"

Nobody at this moment stopped to think whether the prisoner was innocent or guilty.

All they knew was that they had come to see the fun, and they were delighted they were not going to be baulked of their enjoyment.

So they watched the approaching cavalcade in eager impatience.

The procession was of the usual character—a cart with the condemned man in it, and the chaplain with the coffin on which the hangman sat astride smoking a short black pipe.

At his feet was coiled the rope, significant emblem of his accursed trade.

In front of the cart were mounted police with pistols in their hands and swords in their belts.

After them rode the governor of the Old Gaol at Darnborough, and around the procession were a company of cavalry.

Even amid the descending snowflakes the horse soldiers looked gay and bright.

They were the only enlivening features of the sad and gloomy spectacle.

The prisoner, who stood erect, gazing at the crowd with undaunted brow, was Lucien Fairleigh.

Falsely accused, falsely condemned, he came on to die.

The crowd swayed restlessly to and fro.

But there was one who went on steadily with the procession.

No matter how the crowd swayed, no matter how the horses plunged, that man, tall, stalwart, brave and undaunted, pressed still onwards.

He was a man of gigantic stature, and his pale face was full of resolution.

It was Moonlight Jack.

The cavalcade had once stopped near the inn on the confines of the heath.

According to immemorial custom the prisoner was allowed to halt and drink.

Bright eyes had gazed at him there from windows, soft bosoms had there heaved a sigh, white hands had raised the cup to his lips.

But he saw but one pair of eyes, and noticed but one pair of hands.

These were Jack Tyrrell's.

He knew how much depended upon this man.

Life itself, dear life, was in his hands.

During the time occupied by the halting of the cavalcade at the inn Jack had endeavoured to get speech with the prisoner.

But he was driven back.

"I have something important to say," cried Moonlight Jack.

"Say it to the governor, then," returned the soldier.

Jack's lips curled in disdain.

"You'll be hanged yourself some day, my friend," he cried, "if one may judge from your villanous face. It's to be hoped that you'll be served as you are serving him."

The soldier spurred his horse forward, and the animal jumped upon Moonlight Jack.

A dig from the highwayman's dagger, however, made him recoil with such force that he nearly upset the governor, who was looking dignified and solemn.

In spite, however, of the disturbance created by this little contretemps, Moonlight Jack had kept on.

He had a purpose in view—evidently a great one —and he was resolved to fulfil it.

When they neared the scaffold, he made a desperate effort.

A mounted policeman barred his way to the cart.

This Jack-in-office eyed him sternly.

"Back, man !" he cried.

He put his hand out as he spoke, to wave him majestically away.

Jack caught it, and left in it a guinea.

"A word with the hangman," he said. "Just one word."

The policeman dropped back a pace or two.

Jack lost no time.

In an instant he had dashed forward, and with one spring he was in the cart.

In another instant he had locked Lucien in a strong embrace.

Then he raised his hat aloft, and waved it in the air.

The huge multitude was excited to the highest pitch.

One tremendous shout rent the air.

"What is this ? Who is this audacious ruffian ?" cried the governor, furiously. "Seize him and hang him, too !"

Moonlight Jack, who had stooped for an instant and spoken rapidly to the hangman, heard his words, and cried,

"You'll be hanged before me, my friend. They tried to hang me, once, but they failed."

Then he sprang from the cart, and was lost in the swaying of the crowd.

"Who was that audacious rascal ?" cried the Governor of Darnborough gaol, turning to an officer.

The officer was laughing.

"He's the greatest devil out, sir," he answered. "He's Jack Tyrrell—Moonlight Jack, as they call him—the rankest thief, the most notorious highwayman in England."

"D——n" cried the governor. "I would have given fifty pounds to have caught him."

"He'd be no use to you if you had him," said a voice close at hand.

The governor turned angrily to the speaker.

It was Moonlight Jack again !

"Seize me that man !" he cried, furiously addressing one of the head constables.

The man lowered his voice as he answered respectfully,

"I would advise your honor not to try it. There are twenty or thirty of his band in the crowd, and a fight is what they want. That would give them time and opportunity for a rescue."

"Nonsense !" cried the governor, who, in the midst of a cavalry escort, felt an unusual amount of courage. "Nonsense ! These men don't put themselves in danger needlessly."

"You mistake them, sir," returned the constable, "this Jack Tyrell would give his own life at any time to save one he thought innocent."

"Bravo, Constable Beardraker," cried Moonlight Jack. "You're an honest fellow, and if there is a scrimmage, take my advice, don't cover the governor with your body, for I shall shoot him first."

Then with a loud laugh he passed away.

They now reached the gallows, and Lucien Fairleigh was led upon the scaffold.

He walked boldly and firmly in spite of the unsteadiness of the platform, and every one in the crowd who met his brave undaunted eye thought the same—

"He is innocent !"

Such was the one idea pervading the hearts of every one.

Many of them wished to save him.

Yet there was no leader.

There was no one to say, " Let us save him !"

Every man felt as did his neighbour ; but no one said it one to the other.

The sheriff and the gentleman from London being now nearly frozen to death, growled out a kind of welcome to the hangman.

" You've been a devil of a time coming, Crowley," he said, with trembling lips.

" Ugh !" growled the hangman, "don't talk to me. Speak to the governor, if you think anything's wrong."

" Well, well, no offence ; only be quick and let's get back to town. I sadly want something to warm me. Be quick, and let's get the job over."

While the hangman was fitting the rope to the beam the clergyman appealed to Lucien.

" For the last time, my friend," he said, " I entreat you to tell me are you guilty ?"

Lucien smiled.

" Spare yourself this trouble, kind friend," he said, " I have answered you truly, and can answer no differently. I am innocent.'

Then he raised his hand aloft.

It signified his intention to address the crowd.

In an instant the mob was still.

Still as the snowflakes that were whitening everything.

"Friends," he cried, in a loud voice, "I die innocent ! I swear it. I am condemned for the murder of Henry Maltravers, a man I never saw !"

A yell arose from the crowd as the condemned man uttered these words.

" Save him !" cried a voice.

But no one moved to do it.

Moonlight Jack and Hardman and their men were there, but they made no effort at a rescue.

How was this ?

The hangman now approached the prisoner.

" Are you ready, sir ?" he said, respectfully.

" Yes," he cried, firmly.

Then he added, in a whisper,

" Crowley, if you deceive me may the curse of a dying man man follow you to your grave !"

" As there is a living Being above us," said the hangman, " I am *not* deceiving you !"

He adjusted the rope carefully, very carefully the sheriff thought, round the victim's neck.

Then he leaped from the scaffold, and removed the shifting board.

There was one shriek from the crowd, and the body of the doomed man swung by the rope as the board was dragged from beneath his feet.

The snow fell fast and thick, and the scaffold, its victim, and the multitude were powdered with white particles.

And so they hanged Lucien Fairleigh on a cold day in November, 1720, on Darnborough Common, for a murder, kind reader, that he no more committed than you or I.

CHAPTER III.

SHOWING HOW LUCIEN FAIRLEIGH WAS HUNG IN CHAINS.

NOBODY who had thought anything about the matter considered that the young, handsome, and brave Lucien Fairleigh would after all have been hanged upon Darnborough Common.

Those who came to see the sight were not, perhaps, of the most thinking class.

Some of them, indeed—those of the very lowest class—those who had heard that Lucien claimed to be the son of the Marquis of Huntley, felt a secret satisfaction in the idea that the civil law had no respect for persons.

This they thought before they saw poor Lucien's body swinging to and fro in the cold bleak air of November, before, indeed, they saw him standing on the temporary scaffold.

But when they looked into his noble, handsome countenance, and heard his few candid words they could not believe him guilty.

So it was with the deepest anguish that all in that great swelling multitude stood and saw him die ; saw him die the death of a felon, when his words and his looks proclaimed him a guiltless man and a hero.

Swinging to and fro in the keen wind, covering up fast with snow till all outline of the human form was gone, the body hung.

Horrible ! most horrible !

What potent spell will restore life and strength and animation to those limbs again ?

All, all seemed over !

The snowdrift and the north-west wind—it was only the merest trifle westerly—came on savagely now.

Amid a whirl of snow, sleet, and misty vapours the dense multitude took its way from the Common.

To and fro gently swayed the body.

The carts and the temporary platform had all disappeared.

The hangman, however, remained, and, with him a tall, lanky youth.

Crowley, the hangman, drew from his coat pocket a flask containing an alcoholic-looking fluid, and, after he had drawn the cork with his teeth, applied the neck of it to his lips.

Chuck, the youth, or apprentice, looked wistfully at his superior during the time the liquor went gurgling down the hangman's throat.

Crowley returned the look as though in doubt whether he should give the youth a drink or not.

At length, with a shake of the head, he wiped the neck of the bottle, recorked it, and returned it to his garment.

Then, after a long pause, he produced a short black pipe, which he deliberately filled, and lighted with equal deliberation.

Chuck also produced an empty pipe, and made mute gestures to express his wish to have it filled ; but the hangman was inexorable.

Then, when the pipe had been puffed at for some time, he dragged to the foot of the gallows an old sack, which contained the chains in which the law's victim was to swing.

The bars were screwed together as well as the hangman's half-frozen fingers could perform their task ; but he was in a hurry, and so was Chuck, so that, altogether, the work was done in a very slovenly manner.

At length it was finished, the rope was cut, and the body of Lucien Fairleigh was swinging in chains.

The hangman and his apprentice then packed up their traps and departed.

As they retired silently over the snow, the sky darkened.

Dense masses of cloud, fringed with an ominous yellow-looking edge, covered up the southern sky, and seemed to pause over the Common.

For a few moments the air was so still that the wind, which had made itself so very manifest only a little time before, seemed to be completely stopped in its progress.

Then there was a strange rushing sound, and down came the snow like a white mantle over all things.

Over the mute figure of him who, but a few days

before, had been moving in all the strength and beauty of youth—over the innocent suffering for the guilty!

The snow piled itself up a foot high at the foot of the gallows-tree.

It piled itself up on every ridge and inequality in the dress or the chains in which the form was hung.

Into a conical shape it heaped itself on the cross-tree of the gallows.

A few frightened birds screeched past the dismal spectacle.

The dense shower of white flakes hardly permitted the sound to vibrate through the air.

As for the swinging figure upon the gallows, it seemed as though there would have been no difficulty in standing below and touching it with your hand, so much lower had it seemed to drop to the earth.

And now the dim twilight of the winter's day had come.

The brief sun had set, and although the snow-storm had abated, still great quantities were caught up by the fierce wind that had risen, and dashed hither and thither with mad vehemence.

A dull, heavy, booming noise would occasionally, too, make itself heard in the air.

This was the roar of the waters falling over the waterfall at the Crag's End.

As the wind set with a sudden gust from the town, the old clock of Saint Mary's struck the hour of seven.

As the sound ceased, there was another closer at hand.

It was the neighing of horses.

Over the snow it came faintly, and then was seen a light.

A light high up in the air, as if held by a man on horseback.

Waving to and fro, it advanced, until it stopped beneath the gallows.

It could then be distinguished that it was held by a rider, who had a boy seated on the crupper.

The rider was Hardman.

The boy was Harry, the son of Moonlight Jack.

Harry glanced up with a bewildered air at the snow-covered figure.

"Is he dead, Hardman?"

"No, not he; he's warm enough. Crowley took care of that. But see, your father's coming with the other men."

In another minute Moonlight Jack had joined the party.

With him were six companions and a prisoner.

This prisoner was the judge who had condemned Lucien Fairleigh.

He looked pale and wan, though resolute, and his eyes ever and anon wandered towards the path they had come.

Before anything could be begun, a sound as of approaching steps was heard.

Then suddenly three horsemen made their appearance, and dismounting, rushed to the rescue.

These three were servants of the judge.

They had heard of the mishap which had consigned their master to the tender mercies of Moonlight Jack, and they had hastened to the rescue, never remembering that in all probability they would be met by a force, perhaps, three times superior to their own.

They were absolutely staggered when they found in what position they had thrown themselves.

But they were all brave men.

Drawing their swords they rushed without parley upon the highwaymen.

The judge, seeing himself thus reinforced, made a feeble effort to second their attempts.

But he was helpless.

His arms were bound, and it was not many minutes before he, as well as his men, were thrown to the ground and bound.

"Now," said Moonlight Jack, rising and speaking in a cold, stern voice, "now, my men, let me explain to you my motives for not only saving Lucien Fairleigh, but punishing the judge who condemned him to this torture. This man—this judge, who is supposed to hold in his hands the scales of justice—has a son. This son—a reprobate—an unworthy scion of a house which had hitherto been honourable, took to thieving and murder as a profession.

"Nothing could induce him ever to try to obtain an honest living.

"In vain his father forced him to go to sea; in vain he obtained him commissions in the army.

"He refused them all.

"At length, joining a band of desperate robbers, he broke into the house of Clement Cormorant and murdered Henry Maltravers, the man for whose death our friend has been hanged this day.

"This man—this judge—knew this when he condemned Lucien Fairleigh, yet he advised the jury to condemn him to death.

"For this murder this judge is now himself condemned.

"My men, be quick there.

"Let him see the release of Lucien Fairleigh, and let him be placed in chains in his stead.

"Thus I punished the man who procured *my* condemnation, and *so* shall this false judge die!"

His orders were quickly obeyed.

In another moment a ladder was formed from a dozen pieces, and raised against the side of the tree.

Upon this one of the men ascended and proceeded to undo the hooks of the heavy chain.

He proceeded gently with his work.

It was a solemn task.

Perhaps, after all, the man whom they came to save might be dead.

They first removed the mask.

THEN LUCIEN SPOKE!

LUCIEN FAIRLEIGH, THE MAN HUNG IN CHAINS, SPOKE!

"Hardman," he asked, faintly, "Hardman, where is Moonlight Jack?"

"He is down there; he has with him your judge, who will be hung in chains in your stead. Here, drink this."

He placed to his lips a flask of brandy.

Lucien drank it eagerly.

It at once put renewed life into his frame.

Then they carefully unlocked the chains, and cast them upon the round.

Hardman, meanwhile, had severed the rope, so that when the chains were off he was able to bear Lucien's body slowly to the ground.

Here he was released from the smaller bonds which confined his arms and legs, and stood once more alive and free in the face of Heaven!

By this time the judge was bound hand and foot.

He awaited death calmly.

"This is murder," he had said more than once.

Moonlight Jack had always answered the same stern words,

"It is justice. See, there is *your* victim; *that* is murder."

The servants, now bound and helpless on the ground, could not help him.

They could only look on with glaring eyeballs, fearing lest their turn should come next.

When Lucien was fairly upon his legs, Hardman and another of the band led the judge towards the fatal tree.

Then they rivetted upon him the iron chains ere they passed the fatal noose around his neck.

After this one of the number clambered upon the gallows, while another forced the miserable judge upon one of the steps of the ladder.

Then, when all was ready, the ladder was quickly withdrawn, the noose tightened around his neck, and he was dead!

Justice was satisfied.

The father of the guilty—the judge who had wilfully condemned the innocent—had paid the penalty of his crime.

Moonlight Jack and Lucien remained upon the snow-clad heath until the judge's death was certain.

And all this time beneath a mass of furze which was covered with a thick coating of snow, had been hidden Jonathan Rasper and Joe Dulledge, the constable.

The son of the thief-taker, the would-be Jonathan Wild, had gone upon a wrong scent.

He had hoped to discover Moonlight Jack in the commission of crime.

It was exactly this discovery which both Moonlight Jack and his companions courted.

This was soon proved.

"Now, then," he said, to the two servants, "you see what we have done. We have hanged your master."

The men retained a sullen silence.

"Ah, I do not wonder," continued Jack Tyrrell, "that ye like not our proceedings. You have lost a master. But mark me—ye will soon find a better. You have heard and seen all that has passed. Go now, and tell every one how Moonlight Jack punishes his enemies. Tell them, too, that as he once escaped from the scaffold and the chains of the gibbet, so he will again: so Lucien Fairleigh has done to day, and so always will do every member of his band."

Hardman spoke a word to them also ere they departed.

"Seek not," he said, "to disturb the body of this man, or vengeance will be swift upon you."

The men wanted no further recommendation.

They mounted a horse together, the other being kept for Lucien, and were soon out of sight.

They knew their master to be dead.

Of what use was his body?

It could not pay wages.

So Lucien Fairleigh and Moonlight Jack once more rode merrily together at the head of their brave band.

Merrily, merrily over the snow; noiselessly, swiftly and joyously.

None of them cared now for the past.

All they were eager for was to catch the murderer of Henry Maltravers and mete out to him that justice which they had just meted to his father upon the icy heath.

For this purpose they turned towards Denbigh Lane, and made for a hostelrie named the "Black Booth."

CHAPTER IV.
THE "BLACK BOOTH."

THE "Black Booth" was, as I have said, a hostelrie in the immediate neighbourhood of Darnborough Heath.

It had derived its strange name from two circumstances.

In the first place it was composed principally of wooden walls tarred or painted, and in the second place there was a tradition in the vicinity that it had once been a booth or playhouse used by itinerant Thespians.*

The present landlord, Tony Gudge, who, like most landlords, hated his rival at the "Black Lion" most unmitigatedly, was an odd sort of customer.

He was short in stature, with a round, rubicund face, and a body almost as broad as it was long.

He was a great favourite with his customers, drank with them, smoked with them—which not all landlords in these days would do—sang with them, and made himself agreeable, it was hinted, even to the extent of helping them against the constabulary.

At any rate, it was quite certain that he asked no impertinent questions, and was not particular as to the quality or trade of those who bought in his house.

On the evening in question a motley group was assembled in the bar.

In another room a man was seated alone.

The groups at the bar were composed of farmers, labourers, teamsters, and others, sprinkled with a few dashingly dressed gentry, whose "loud" attire seemed to proclaim them *chevaliers d'industrie*, or in modest English—*thieves*.

Thieves at least in that wide acceptation of the term which includes gentlemen of the road, sharpers and pickpockets.

They were all *very* boisterous, very lively, and some very drunk, and, consequently the uproar was so great that it could be heard a long distance down the snow-clad road, on whose white bosom the light from the hostelrie cast a gloom which served only to render more dismal the scene without.

I have said the crowd was motley.

You would have thought it so, had you seen the teamster and the farmer (whose waggon and gig were without) pulling out their leathern purses, and treating the keen-eyed gentlemen in lace-embroidered coats, who would soon ride after them and bawl out to them in the clear night air,

"STAND AND DELIVER!"

But the man in the room—sitting alone by the fire—took no heed of them or the hubbub they were making.

He was a young man, with dark hair, heavy brows, heavy mouth, heavy moustache, and black scowling eyes.

He was as unprepossessing a person as you would wish to see in a week's journey; a man whom you would avoid, even if you met him in the best society.

This was he whom they called Robert Gordon, the son of the judge who had expiated his injustice upon the snow-clad heath.

He was anxiously awaiting some one, and kept nervously watching the door.

It could not have been money he awaited.

The murder and the plunder at the house of Clement Cormorant was but recent, and this man was the chief benefiter by the robbery.

It was evidently fear that unnerved this man of evil.

Fear of some danger which was justly his due.

Presently a man entered.

His boots showed that he had waded through slush and mud, and his coat and hat were thickly covered with the snow-flakes.

*In the account of the trial of Moonlight Jack it is said—"There was at the periode of his greatest successe a place or inne called the 'Blacke Boothe,' situate on the borders of an immense plain or commonland called Darnborough Heath, and it was here that Jack Tyrrelle and his men used to meet, and here it was that he took vengeance on one, Gordon, who had maltreated or injured one of his friends."

He was a young man, younger even than Robert Gordon, and he had a sprightlier look about him, although at this moment he was hurried and perturbed.

"Well, Carver," cried Gordon, impatiently, "what news do you bring me?"

"Well, scarcely news at all, for it is incomprehensible," said the man. "I have been to your father's house. They say that the judge was about to step into his carriage, when six men, accompanied by a boy, rushed up, seized him, and forced him to go with them."

"Call ye this no news at all?" cried Gordon, passionately.

"Well, sir," said Carver, "it seems to me a foolish tale, and the maid, too, who told me, seemed all of a tremble, and scarce able to speak, and she contradicted herself, too, a dozen times."

"Order yourself some grog," returned Gordon, "and wait awhile. We shall have more news anon."

He then relapsed into silence.

The man ordered his grog, and they sat without speaking for some moments.

Then there was a fresh uproar at the bar, and four men rushed into the room, three of them scared, bloody, and with clothes torn and in disorder.

Gordon rose in haste and alarm from his seat.

One of the new comers belonged to his own band.

The other three were unknown to him.

"What have we here?" he cried. "What devil's work is doing now, Danby."

"Your father, the Judge, is dead!" cried the man whom he addressed as Danby.

"Dead?"

"Yes, Captain—"

Gordon stopped him.

In an instant he comprehended the necessity for a change in his character.

"Hold, Danby!" he said, "a word with you."

The man stooped to listen.

"Before these men," whispered Gordon, "drop the title of Captain. I must be simply Mr. Gordon. Now, then, to your tale," he added, aloud. "My father, you say, is dead? What new folly is this? What reason have you for your words?"

"Why, sir, I sent Carver hither to inform you that your father had been seized by six men and carried off. These men with me are his servants; they followed their master across the heath and saw it all."

"All what?"

"The style of his death. The men who seized him were Moonlight Jack and his band. They carried him to the gallows-tree where Lucien Fairleigh was hung in chains; and though these men tried their best to save their master, they were soon overpowered, and scarcely themselves escaped with life. They then—they then—"

"Go on. Why do you hesitate?" exclaimed Gordon, impatiently.

The man glanced at him with a gaze of peculiar meaning.

"I will do so as well as I can," he said, significantly; then he continued, "He explained *his* version of the story, and affirmed that Lucien Fairleigh had suffered unjustly, that he had come to save him, and your father should suffer in his stead."

"Well, there is one blessing," said Gordon, with spiteful utterance, "this Lucien Fairleigh had already suffered."

"Yes, but he was not dead."

"Not dead?"

"No, he was not dead. He was lifted down from the gallows unhurt, and your father was hung and then placed in chains in his stead."

"That man is the devil incarnate!" cried Gordon "But I will have vengeance upon him!"

Then, turning to the servants, he added,

"You remember me, no doubt, as the judge's son? You, Fletcher, I recollect now, though but a moment since you were in such disorder that I knew you not."

"Yes, sir, I remember you," said Fletcher, "though ye have been long abroad. Your mother will be pleased to see you, sir; she is, I doubt not, in great distress at the terrible news."

Gordon bowed slightly.

To this speech he knew scarcely how to answer.

His mother was perfectly aware of all his proceedings, and, though she was ignorant of his participation in the murder of Henry Maltravers, she yet was fully cognizant of his worthlessness, recklessness, and debauchery.

"I have but just arrived from abroad," said Gordon. "Go, tell my mother so. Say I will be with her in a short time to offer her what consolation I can upon this sad occasion. Go quickly, and I will follow you."

The serving-man at once departed.

Gordon paced the room hurriedly.

For some moments he did not speak.

At length he turned to his men with the abrupt manner which always characterised him.

"Meet me here to-morrow night," he said, "at this hour, and bring Gurney and Trefoil with you."

Then he threw a purse of money upon the table and passed out.

The distance between the inn and the judge's house was not great, and it was not long before Robert Gordon was in the presence of his mother and sister.

He could do little to comfort them.

The man who in public was an unjust judge was far from being unjust at home, and to those to whom his untimely death had been just reported, the blow came with the greatest severity.

Much of the rancour caused by old wounds departed when the mother clasped her son to her heart.

But it was impossible for her to forget that much of the judge's moroseness of late had been caused by evil tidings of this very son who had now come with such strange opportuneness to offer her comfort.

When Robert retired to his chamber that night his heart swelled with varied emotions.

He knew that in the lifetime of his father he could have hoped for no money.

He knew, indeed, that all he could make sure of was immunity from punishment in those cases in which his father had a hand.

Now the case was different.

"I shall now," he cried, "be able to appear once more in that society from which misfortune banished me. I shall be able, backed by the money which will inevitably fall to my share, to form a band which shall be the terror of the country. No longer shall I be compelled to be subservient to that fellow Brandon, but be master of my own actions, and wreak a terrible vengeance upon this fellow who, in his egotism, calls himself Moonlight Jack."

As he said these words a hand was placed upon his shoulder.

At the same moment a voice said,

"*If you seek Moonlight Jack he is here!*"

MOONLIGHT JACK

OR THE KING OF THE ROAD

THE COMBAT WITH THE ROYAL TROOPS.—*See page 96.*

Gordon looked round in alarm.

The summons was so sudden, indeed, that under the circumstances it would have shaken the stoutest nerves.

It was, indeed, Moonlight Jack who stood before him.

His face was stern and mysterious.

"You have asked for me," he said, "why, then, be surprised that I am here?"

"I did not ask for you," returned Gordon, with somewhat of his old courage returned. "I said that the day would come when I should be able to take my vengeance upon you."

"Why not now?" asked Jack Tyrrell. "Here we are man to man, what more can you desire?"

Gordon's cheek paled.

This was not his idea.

He had no wish, night bandit and murderer as he was, to cope with one whose bravery was the talk of the country side.

No. 12.—March 24, 1866.]   [*Order No.* 1 *of* BLACK HAWKE, *a new and exciting Story. A Supplement, Gratis.*]   [Price One Penny.

"No, no," he said, "my father being dead through your violence things have changed. *I* have changed too. I shall yet live to——"

"To expiate the foul crime for which my friend was so nearly sacrificed. Adieu! In a few hours we meet again."

"And your mission in this house?" asked Gordon, eagerly.

"Is a secret one," said Moonlight Jack, "which *you* could not understand."

Moonlight Jack then passed out as he had come, leaving Robert Gordon in wonder and alarm.

The next night he was to meet his men at the "Black Booth."

Should he go?

His interest told him "yes."

His fear whispered "no."

Gordon had never been celebrated for courage.

But he knew that his interest in every way told him to go.

Relying, therefore, on the bravery of his companions, he resolved to go.

The evening was dark and gloomy.

He approached by the back way so that he could not be seen.

Then, letting himself in by a small back door, he entered the room where we first introduced him to the reader.

His men were already there.

There were others just without the door of the chamber, too, whose presence they were scarce aware of.

These were Moonlight Jack, Lucien Fairleigh, and four of their band, accompanied by an elderly stranger, whose appearance was entirely dissimilar to their own.

Gordon had scarcely time to commence an explanation to his men ere the door opened, and Moonlight Jack and his companions entered.

Gordon's band sprang to their feet in alarm.

As for their leader, he grew pale with terror.

He recognised in the intruder his night visitor of but a few hours before.

"Lay by your arms!" cried Moonlight Jack, solemnly, as he waved away those who seemed disposed to put his courage to the proof. "I come not here to contest with you; I come to speak to yon craven wretch, who should be ashamed to meet my gaze and the gaze of him who stands by my side."

He pointed to Lucien Fairleigh.

"This," he added, "is he who was hung on Darnborough Heath for the murder of Henry Maltravers. There is the man who committed that murder, and who is to die to-night for the deed."

Gordon's face turned livid with fear.

The slow, solemn, determined manner in which Moonlight Jack spoke carried a chill to his heart.

Yet his hand passed involuntarily to his sword.

"My men," he said, in a voice of command, "stand by me. We must rid the world of these ruffians; these are the men who murdered my father. What ho! there, landlord! A Gordon to the rescue!"

Moonlight Jack and his men at once sprung forward, and a fierce conflict ensued.

The clash of steel soon brought others to the room.

The landlord, with a pale face, peered in.

Open-mouthed customers peered in likewise.

But no one interfered.

The "Black Booth" was Liberty Hall.

Gordon fought well.

He knew it was for his life he fought.

His men fought well too.

They knew that if *he* died, the secret of great wealth died with him.

Gordon, however, was no match for Moonlight Jack.

Tyrrell's huge sword flashed hither and thither like a meteor.

At length, bleeding and faint, the murderer endeavoured to make for the back door, by which he had entered earlier in the evening.

Moonlight Jack saw at once the object of his manœuvres.

But he made no effort to stop him.

He rather, indeed, seemed to force him that way.

At length, when his men were all wounded and down, he stood for an instant pale and fighting desperately like a wild beast at bay, and then dashed through the door.

For an instant all was quiet as the grave.

Then a yell of rage proved that he had made an error.

Moonlight Jack's men surrounded the place at the back, and he rushed right into their arms.

Jack Tyrrell and his men followed, and Gordon was a prisoner.

The elderly man, who was no other than Crowley, the hangman, then joined them, and the whole party moved towards Darnborough Heath.

Near the tree where the old judge had already expiated his unjust sentence, there waited Chuck, the hangman's boy.

He was whistling merrily to keep out the cold, and dancing about, too, close by the chain-bound body.

Occasionally, moreover, he would burst out into a verse or two of a hideous melody expressive of the pleasures and emoluments consequent upon the life of a hangman.

He announced his perception of their arrival by a loud whoop.

"It's time you were here, master," he cried, "for I was just a freezing into an icicle."

And as he spoke he ran round in a mad circle.

"Stop that game," cried Crowley, "and climb up that tree."

The boy at once complied.

He was soon dangling with his legs hanging on either side of the same bough as that which held the dead judge.

"Now, then," said Moonlight Jack, "is all ready?"

"Yes, sir," returned Crowley, with an official chuckle.

Jack Tyrrell then turned to Robert Gordon.

"Gordon," he said, in a solemn voice, "there before you hangs the dead body of your father. You are nearly as guilty of *his* death as you were of the death of Henry Maltravers. It was for you he sentenced my friend unjustly to death; by his side you will expiate at once the murder you committed, and the part you had in your father's destruction."

There was silence on the heath for a few moments.

Gordon, pale and trembling, did not say a word.

"Have you nothing to say?" asked Jack Tyrrell.

Gordon folded his arms.

"Nothing to *you*, murderers," he said. "Assassinate me if you like, but I will say nothing."

"Have you nothing to say to Lucien Fairleigh here, who, through you, suffered all the horrors of a shameful death? Go on, then, Crowley," cried Moonlight Jack; "do your duty."

Crowley immediately pinioned his victim with professional alacrity, talking rapidly all the while.

"Really, Mr. Gordon, this is quite a pleasure to

me," he said. "You nearly dragged me into the commission of a murder when I hung Mr. Fairleigh here, so now I'm going to make the only amends I can by hanging you."

Within a few minutes Gordon was pinioned securely.

The rope was then placed round his neck, and he was led beneath the bough.

Here he was forced to mount upon a horse's back, and the end of the rope was thrown up to Chuck.

The horse pranced impatiently.

It was a dangerous place for a man to stand.

A man, too, with a rope tight around his neck.

It was a living drop.

"Here," cried Moonlight Jack, loudly, "is a statement confessing to the murder of Henry Maltravers, and exonerating Lucien Fairleigh from any participation in it. Will you sign it?"

"Never!" cried Gordon, savagely.

"Crowley, lash the horse away, then," cried Moonlight Jack ; "let the murderer die with a lie upon his lips!"

Crowley raised a whip.

"Stay!" yelled Gordon, "stay, I will sign!"

Moonlight Jack approached, and, telling one of his men to hold a torch, took from his pocket a paper, a portable inkstand, and a pen.

The paper he read aloud.

It was a confession to the murder of Henry Maltravers.

When it had been read one of the hands of the doomed man was released and he signed the document.

When he had done so he glanced round him and said, with an expression of bitter triumph,

"Of what avail is this confession? Who will believe it? It is signed by me, truly, but that might be a forgery, and there is no one here to swear to my signature except men who dare not show themselves."

"There you are wrong," said Moonlight Jack. "Hardman, bring forward the two serving-men."

Two footmen were then led forward.

They were two of those who had seen the hanging of the judge.

"Do you know that man?" asked Moonlight Jack.

"Yes, he is Mr. Gordon."

"You have seen him sign that paper?"

"Yes."

"Then sign this paper as witnesses."

The men signed.

"Go now," said Jack, "and tell your mistress what has happened. Tell her how I regret her bereavement. But tell her also that stern justice must be carried out, and that by this document, which you have heard read, and of which she will receive a copy, she will perceive how little she has lost in their death."

The men bowed and were released.

But they did not depart.

A morbid curiosity restrained them.

They desired to see the last act of the tragedy.

"Now," cried Jack Tyrrell, "Crowley, lash the horse!"

"Villain!" yelled Gordon, "a dying man's curse will follow you."

"A just man's curse I should fear," returned Jack, solemnly, "but not that of a murderer."

Gordon spoke no more.

Crowley struck the horse a sudden blow, and he sprang away.

Down came the body with a dull thud, and Robert Gordon lived no more!

For a quarter of an hour the robbers watched the body.

It was merely a matter of form, for the great depth he had fallen had broken his neck.

After this time the highwaymen, who had scarcely spoken except when they noticed occasional dark figures passing in the distance, rode over the heath at a rapid pace towards the "Black Lion."

Crowley and Chuck followed in their cart.

They had received the wage of their labour, and they now proceeded homewards to enjoy it, since no house of public entertainment would receive them among its customers.

"Now," cried Moonlight Jack, ere they entered the inn ; "now, my men, let us cast aside our seriousness. We have been on a dull errand truly, but now for the foaming tankard, and the merry jest, and then, 'Hurrah for the road!'"

A loud and prolonged cheer succeeded this speech.

Then the highwaymen rode in a body to the door of the inn, and descending from their horses entered the bar.

There was a motley throng there, but though, from the appearance of Jack and his companions, it was easy to see what was their vocation, no attempt was made on the part of the customers to annoy them.

The landlord served them with right good-will, seeing that they paid for good things, and they drank with the rest.

Then they started once more, and, with a bright moon and a frosty road, went out in search of adventures.

Moonlight Jack and Lucien Fairleigh went each in different directions with three men apiece, agreeing to meet again at the "Black Lion" at daybreak.

CHAPTER V.

OUT IN THE WOODS BY MOONLIGHT—THE DRUNKEN MESSENGER — EAVESDROPPING — THE FAIR JACOBITE—LUCIEN'S HEART IS ASSAILED—THE MYSTERIOUS MEETING—THE ATTEMPTED MURDER—THE VAULT OF DEATH.

LUCIEN FAIRLEIGH'S route lay along the highway—broad, open, and clear for some time ; but presently it passed along the skirts of a wood.

This he entered with his men, on the look out for the mail, which was expected in some hours' time.

Knowing there was plenty of time, they unsaddled their horses, tied the animals to a tree, and placing the saddles on the ground, sat in the broad moonlight, drinking from their spirit flasks, and talking of the events of the evening.

The time passed quickly.

No one passed, and the place, therefore, was sufficiently lonely.

But the laugh and the merry jest occupied the fleeting moments, and just as Darnborough clock struck the hour of ten, they prepared their horses for a remount.

Suddenly Lucien's horse pricked up its ears.

Fairleigh glided behind a tree and looked out.

A man was approaching, or rather a tall youth.

He staggered to and fro, and was evidently under the influence of drink.

As he came nearer, Lucien recognised Chuck, the hangman's apprentice, who, sitting down, at length began chaunting again the song of the gallows.

Dismally it sounded over the silent road, though the words went to a merry tune :—

> "Hurrah for the gallows-tree !
> The gallows-tree for me !
> 'Tis the emblem of liberty,
> Then hurrah for the gallows-tree !

> "It merrily carries its load,
> Be it prince or peasant-clod ;
> Full many a sigh,
> As the wind sweeps by,
> It wafts o'er the moonlit road.

> "But it sighs alike for the rich and the poor,
> So the gallows-tree for me,
> Full oft the wanderer over the moor
> Has nestled him 'neath this tree.

> "A noble above, a peasant below !
> 'Tis a pleasant sight to see,
> Merrily swinging above the snow,
> Clanking the chains of the high and the low,
> Hurrah for the gallows-tree !" *

Suddenly Chuck stopped, and rubbed his sconce.

It appeared, even to him, that it was absurd for him to be sitting there singing.

"This won't do, this won't do," he said to himself ; "if I've got to be off to the Marchioness of Loudan with that letter it's no use my stopping here. Now, then, Chuck, hold yourself together, my boy, and go on."

Lucien, laughing, in spite of himself, now passed from behind the tree, and approached Chuck.

"Hullo ! Chuck," he cried, "what's up ? What's disagreed with you ?"

Chuck started to his feet in affright.

But on seeing Lucien Fairleigh he resumed his courage.

"Well, Mr. Fairleigh, you see," he said, "old Crowley gave me a rather stiffish dose of grog to-night, and, then, what should I have to do but to take a letter from my Lord Disney to the Marchioness of Loudan. But no sooner do I get out into the open air but whoop go all my senses. I don't know how the letter will go, for I can't see my way, and I shall never find the house."

"Oh ! don't trouble about that," returned Lucien, "one of my men will take that for you. So give me the letter, and go home and sleep off your grog."

Chuck readily gave up the letter, and as he staggered away, utterly unconscious whether he had acted ill or well, the north mail came up.

To describe the attack upon the mail would be unnecessary.

It was only the old story of brave gentlemen of the road, and brave passengers and cowardly guards and drivers who blustered, and instead of fighting fell down flat upon their faces.

As soon as this job was over, a job effected without any bloodshed, Lucien dispatched his companions to the "Black Lion."

He himself then galloped off in the direction of Loudan House.

Arriving at the palings of the park, which were very low, he leaped his horse over them, and then descending from his back took his way slowly towards the house through the leafless trees.

He had once before been to Loudan House, and he knew that Lady Loudan's boudoir overlooked a terrace which was easily accessible from the grounds.

Tying his horse to a tree he crept stealthily from tree to tree until he reached the terrace.

This he ascended by a number of steps, and on

* These words are orignal.

reaching the window, whence a light streamed out upon the night, a ravishing sight presented itself.

The marchioness was at her toilet after just issuing from the bath.

Around her were grouped three maids.

One of them, Annette, was a piquante blonde, and her companions were not inferior to her in grace.

One of them, named Julia, a tall, delicately slender, and elegant girl, with the air and form of Diana the huntress, was of a pale brown complexion.

Her thick black hair was turned up behind, where it was fastened with a long golden pin.

Like the two other girls, her arms were uncovered to facilitate the performance of her duties about and upon the person of her charming mistress.

She wore a dress of that gay green so familar to the Venetian painter. Her petticoat was very ample.

Her shape was equally sloped with the plaits of a tucker or tippet of white cambric, plaited in minute folds, and fastened by five gold buttons.

The third of her ladyship's women had a face so fresh and ingenuous, a waist so delicate, so pleasing, so finished, that her mistress had given her the name of Hebe.

Her dress, of a delicate rose colour, and of a Grecian cut, displayed her charming neck, and her beautiful arms up to the very shoulders.

The physiognomy of these three young women was laughter-loving and happy.

On their features there was no expression of that bitter sullenness, of that unwilling and hated obedience, or of that offensive familiarity, or base and degraded deference, which are the ordinary results of a state of servitude.

In the zealous eagerness of the cares and attentions which they lavished upon their mistress, there seemed to be at least as much of affection as of deference and respect.

They appeared to derive an ardent pleasure to themselves from the services which they rendered to their lovely mistress.

One would have thought that they attached to the dressing and embellishing of her person all the merits and the enjoyment arising from the execution of a work of art, in the accomplishing of which, fruitful of delights, they were stimulated by the passions of love, of pride, and of joy.

The lights shone brightly upon the toilette placed in front of the window.

The marchioness was seated on a chair, the back of which was elevated rather more than usual.

She was enveloped in a long morning gown of blue silk, embroidered with leaves of the same colour, which was fitted close to her waist, as exquisitely slender and delicate as that of a child of twelve years, by a girdle with floating points.

Her neck, delicately slender and flexible as that of a bird, was uncovered, as were also her shoulders and arms, and all were of incomparable beauty.

Despite the vulgarity of the comparison, the purest ivory alone can give an idea of the dazzling whiteness of her polished satin skin, of a texture so fresh and so firm that some drops of water collected and still remaining about the roots of her hair, from the bath, rolled in serpentine lines over her shoulders like pearls or beads of crystal over white marble.

And what gave twofold éclat to this wondrous incarnation of beauty was the deep coral of her humid lips, the roseate transparency of her small ears, of her dilated nostrils, and of her nails, as bright and glossy as if they had been varnished.

In every spot, indeed, where her pure blood,

full of animation and heat, could make its way to the surface of the skin and shine through it, it proclaimed her high health and the vivid life and joyous buoyancy of her glorious youth.

Her eyes were very large, and of velvet softness; her nose delicately curved, was) slightly acquiline; the enamel of her teeth glistened when the light fell upon them, and her vermiel mouth, voluptuously sensual, seemed to call for sweet kisses and the gay smiles and delectations of dainty and delicious pleasure.

At the moment of her present toilette she looked ravishingly beautiful.

Annette, her arms bare, stood behind her mistress, and had carefully collected into one of her small white hands those splendid locks, the naturally ardent brightness of which was doubled in the sunshine, which reflected golden and fiery rays from numerous clusters of spiral ringlets that fell over her cheeks, and in their elastic flexibility caressed the risings of her snowy bosom, to whose charming undulations they adapted and applied themselves.

Lucien Fairleigh gazed for some moments in rapture at the exquisite creature who was placed before him thus half dressed, and in all the abandon consequent upon a perfect ignorance of a man's presence.

For some time he forbore to disturb the group.

It was seldom one gazed upon anything more purely beautiful than the nude bust and face of the charming marchioness.

But at length he pressed heavily against the French window, and entered the room without giving the lady time to throw a shawl over her charming shoulders.

The three women started and screamed.

Lucien raised his hand deprecatingly, while the marchioness, drawing a handsome shawl over her beautiful person, rose from her seat.

"Pray be not alarmed," he cried. "I am a friend, and have a letter for you which should be delivered in secret."

He handed the letter to the marchioness as he spoke.

She glanced at the superscription eagerly.

Then all the colour fled from her cheek.

A deadly pallor overspread her face and neck.

Then she sank down again upon her chair.

"Sit down, sir," she said. "Retire, you," turning to her maids.

Then, as they passed out, she added,

"See that no one disturbs me."

She broke the seal now, and read the letter eagerly.

Her colour came and went as she read.

When she had finished she turned to Lucien, whom, while she spoke, she surveyed with no ordinary interest.

"Sir," she said, "you know Lord Disney, I presume?"

It happened fortunately.

He *did* know him.

"Yes," he said.

"He speaks of you as a trusty messenger."

Lucien bowed.

"Therefore," continued the lady, "I can rely on you. To-night, at twelve, some friends of King James meet at my house. You must be present at the meeting, and carry news to Lord Disney by daylight of all that transpires. There is an hour for rest."

"I need it, my lady," said Lucien. "I have ridden hard this night."

Lady Loudan rose.

"Follow me," she said, as she walked towards a door partially concealed by the rich drapery of the room.

Through this Lucien Fairleigh passed with the marchioness, who led him into a chamber elaborately furnished, with a broad and handsome couch on one side.

"Here you can rest yourself," said Lady Loudan. "I will awaken you at the appointed hour. You need rest, for there will be work to be done this night."

He thanked her, and she withdrew.

Then he threw himself on the couch.

But sleep visited him not.

Somehow or another he could not drive from his thoughts the splendid vision he had witnessed through the window on the terrace.

Those glorious eyes, those splendid shoulders, that magnificent form, forced themselves upon his sight, and though his eyes were closed no sleep came to him.

More than this, the novelty of his situation was enough to banish slumber.

He was a Jacobite at heart, but he had never dreamed of joining any conspiracy.

Now, through a freak of his own, and the beauty of a woman, he was to be led into one against his will.

What would Moonlight Jack say to his rashness?

While yet these thoughts were passing through his brain he heard a light step, and saw the marchioness enter.

She turned her back slightly to close the door behind her, so that when his eyes were open she did not observe him.

He resolved to feign sleep.

So he closed his eyes almost completely.

I say almost, because he could just catch a faint glimmer of what was passing in the room.

The marchioness placed the lamp upon a table at the extreme end of the room.

Then she approached Lucien.

Had she discovered the trick he played on Chuck?

Was she about to murder him in his sleep?

Would it be best for him to jump up at once and cast off his feigned sleep?

No.

His eyes caught a smile which hovered over the lips of his fair visitant, and he resolved to remain as he was.

The marchioness bent over him.

"He is very handsome," she murmured.

Then she stooped down and kissed his lips gently, as if fearful of waking him.

He opened his eyes as their lips met.

His arms were raised, and pressed her glorious person closely to him, and his lips gave back her fervid kisses.

Half fainting with shame the marchioness strove to rise.

Lucien released her, and rising also compelled her gently to sit beside him on the couch.

The marchioness covered her face with her hands.

"What must you think of me?" she murmured.

Lucien slid his arm around her waist.

"I think only that you are very beautiful," he said.

As he spoke he drew her towards him, and pressed a kiss upon her glowing shoulders.

In that moment Grace Dashwood was forgotten.

He had no time for thought.

He never reflected that the lovely siren might be luring him on to destruction.

The kiss imprinted upon him by her burning lips

during his feigned sleep had turned his blood in a stream of molten fire.

He was but a man after all, and when the marchioness sank palpitating into his arms he forgot everything but the supreme bliss of the moment.

Why the beautiful but frail creature he held in his arms should thus unceremoniously yield herself up to him he never paused to think.

Bliss was within his reach, and he snatched at it.

"I may love you, then," he said, in trembling accents, as the warm bosom of the marchioness palpitated against him.

"Yes, yes," was the eager though whispered reply.

*   *   *   *   *   *

The passionate marchioness had but little time for the enjoyment of her new lover.

Within half an hour they were compelled to take a last lingering kiss.

Then, when she had arranged her disordered toilet, and powdered away her blushes, she said,

"Lucien Fairleigh, since *that* is your name, a strange and sudden fancy of mine has placed me in your power. Honour, reputation, all is in your keeping. Can I trust you?"

"Oh! yes."

"And for the sacrifice I have made may I hope for a return?"

"Command, good lady, and I obey."

"Good," she answered, turning aside her head that he might not see the smile which illumined her face—a smile of complete triumph; "good! ere many hours have passed I will tell you how to reward me."

While speaking she opened a cupboard whence she drew a black cloak and a plumed hat.

These she handed to Lucien, saying,

"Put them on, they are the dress of the League."

She then went to a drawer, and drew out a silver cross, and a number—No. 318—also of silver."

These she fastened upon the breast of his cloak.

Then, handing him a black mask, she bade him place it on and follow her.

Lucien obeyed her mechanically.

He was like one in a dream.

It seemed all unlike reality.

He could scarcely believe that the exquisite creature who was speaking to him had yielded herself up to him almost at first sight.

She led him towards a door which she pushed open and disclosed a dark well staircase.

The small lamp she carried shed a gloomy light over the dismal walls.

Lucien hesitated.

He had heard of women who, satiated with passion, had destroyed their lovers by treachery.

Might it not be thus with the marchioness?

"Why do you linger?" she asked. "Are you afraid?"

Her sweet smile drew him onwards as the loadstone attracts the needle.

"Lead on," he said, "the darkness dazzled me."

They now passed downwards more rapidly.

The marchioness knew her way well, and Lucien Fairleigh kept close by her side.

When they reached the bottom of the staircase there could be heard a confused murmur of voices.

On one side was a door leading to the grounds.

On the other was one half open.

At the door stood a masked man who wore the cloak, the cross, and the number.

"Courage," whispered the marchioness, "we will enter."

Then she passed through the door with him, saying to the man, as she did so,

"From Lord Disney. Courage and forbearance."

The room in which the conspirators were assembled was a long vault supported in the middle by a row of pillars.

At one end, and at the top of the apartment, was a little arched window, through which the pale beams of the moon streamed.

But the light of the orb of night was not sufficient for the party assembled within.

Torches were fixed in iron brackets at the sides of the pillars, and cast a yellow glare on the anxious faces of the assembled body of men.

It was a strange scene, and rendered still more strange by the attire of the conspirators.

Every man was masked, and above the black visor wore a hat, with black plumes.

A long cloak concealed the dress, and on the breast was a cross of silver and a number.

The men lounged about as if waiting for some one to speak.

A loud voice at length pronounced the word,

"Silence!"

Every whisper was hushed, and they all stood in a listening attitude.

"We are met here, as usual, gentlemen," said the same voice, "in the service of *the king over the water!*"

At these words every hat was raised, and a smothered cheer resounded.

"I have good news for you," continued the speaker. "A cargo of arms and ammunition is expected every day on the Essex coast, and an expedition is to set out to-morrow to bring them here. An experienced head is necessary to command such an enterprise——"

"Aye, and a bold heart, too, as well as a strong arm," interposed one of the listeners.

"The appointed leader possesses all these qualifications and many others. Lord Disney is the man."

"Good!" muttered some, while others simply nodded their heads in token of approbation.

"The next thing to be done," continued the speaker, "is to examine and sign the muster-roll."

He laid a large sheet of paper on the table, and placed pens and ink beside it.

The men advanced one after another, and signed, the president keeping his hand over those names already inscribed, so that no one but himself might know who was in the plot.

During this conversation Lucien Fairleigh had remained leaning against one of the large pillars which supported the roof, watching the proceedings with considerable interest, an interest which was not lessened by the fact that many of the assembled conspirators were of the fair sex.

The marchioness had left his side almost immediately upon their entrance into the room.

So he had been quite alone.

Alone among men who, had they known his style of entrance among them, would have thirsted for his heart's blood.

Once or twice one of the cloaked men had walked round him, and glanced at him narrowly.

But otherwise his presence had been unnoticed.

At length the man who had walked round him, or one who might have been he, for they were all dressed alike, stopped near him, and whispered,

"MOONLIGHT ON THE ROAD!"

It was the watchword of Moonlight Jack!

"DARKNESS IN THE WOOD!" returned Lucien, in astonishment. "Who are you?"

"Why, Moonlight Jack," answered the first

speaker. "Lucien, you will never do for a conspirator; why, I knew you at once. You sly dog, how came you here?"

"In the same way that *you* came, I presume—on horseback," returned Lucien, somewhat nettled that Jack Tyrrell should have discovered him.

"Nay, Lucien, be not wroth. By my faith, I am glad to see you here. Had I known you were for King James you might have been here long since. But no more now. The meeting is about to separate. I will meet you at the 'Black Lion.'"

"Not so; I have to carry the instructions to Lord Disney. I will meet you at the park gate."

"Good; I will wait for you, and, may be, we will go together."

Lucien and Moonlight Jack now advanced to the table where the marchioness appeared by the side of the president.

Jack Tyrell signed and quitted the room.

Then the marchioness spoke.

"This," she said, "is the trusty messenger whom my Lord Disney sent to me. He will now sign his name here for the first time, and *I* will answer for his faith."

The president bowed and Lucien signed.

He was now a member of a Jacobite conspiracy, with his name on a muster-roll which might be the muster-roll of death.

The marchioness led him again to her apartments.

The woman seemed either under the influence of a wild and sudden infatuation or acting a part.

She flung her arms round Lucien's neck as soon as they were alone.

"Haste with the papers to my Lord Disney," she said, "and at dusk to-night return to me. I *must* see you."

"Farewell for the present," said Lucien, "it will not be long ere I return to you."

He pressed one more kiss on her cherry lips, and then, fearing to trust himself any longer in her society, hastily left the apartment.

The moon was shining with a pale mellow light over the grounds, the tall trees, and the old grey building, which had a chill look.

Lucien, however, little heeded the beauties of the night; his thoughts were divided between two objects—the marchioness whom he had just left, and the instructions he had to convey to Lord Disney.

He had quite forgotten the existence of Moonlight Jack, who, according to arrangement, was waiting for him just outside the gate.

Moonlight Jack perceived his young friend's pre-occupied looks, and resolved to teach him a lesson.

Following stealthily for some paces along the path, he suddenly leaped out and threw his arms around Lucien's body.

So sudden was the action that Lucien was taken completely by surprise, and had no opportunity of resisting the attack.

"What is the matter? Are you mad?" he demanded, as soon as he saw who it was thus grappled him.

"No, my friend," replied Moonlight Jack. "I am not mad, though I fancy you must be to walk the highway in such a careless and unguarded manner."

"I was thinking."

"So was I. First tell me your thoughts then I will give you mine."

Lucien hesitated and changed colour.

"I was thinking of a lady."

The marchioness, I suppose?" said Moonlight Jack, with a knowing smile.

Lucien made no reply; but his comrade knew well enough that he had guessed aright.

"Well, I won't press the question," he said, after a pause; "but I'll tell you what I thought."

"And what was that?"

"Why, that by your leaving the aforesaid marchioness at such an unreasonably early hour, you must be the bearer of despatches, or at all events some important news."

"You are right. I have letters for Lord Disney."

"Concerning the cause?"

"Yes."

"Then the cause stands in great peril unless you exercise your eyes and ears better than you did as you left yon gate."

"What do you mean?"

"I mean that the whole country is filled with Hanoverian spies, and that for ought you or I know, the dragoons may already be on your track."

"I was very foolish; but I will exercise more caution during the remainder of the journey."

"And I will go with you to see that you do not fall away from your good resolutions. So mount your horse and let us make as much of the time as possible."

Close to the spot where this conversation took place, two horses were tied up to a tree, and in a minute the friends were mounted.

They kept on the soft turf by the side of the path, both for the sake of being unseen as well to prevent the footsteps of their steeds from being heard.

Moonlight Jack kept glancing uneasily about, now throwing his eagle eye over the broad fields on one side, and then endeavouring to pierce the thick gloom of the wood, whose borders they were skirting.

"Do you expect to find an enemy concealed in the bush?" inquired Lucien, in low tones.

"I should not be surprised if such were the case."

Then we stand but a poor chance of accomplishing our journey in safety, for in another hour it will be daylight.

Moonlight Jack glanced towards the east, and at once perceived the truth of his companion's words.

A faint tinge of red proclaimed that ere long the rosy orb of day would usurp the place of the paler luminary.

"Come," he said, touching Lucien on the arm, "let us make haste to the 'Red Lion.'"

"Why would you go thither?"

"That I will explain when we reach the house. 'Tis but a hundred yards or two out of the direct road."

They rode on in silence, and at increased speed, until the old roof and chimnies of the inn met their view.

The house was just being opened as the two horsemen led their steeds to the stable, and then strode into the little sanded parlour.

"Bring a bottle of wine, pens, ink, and paper," said Moonlight Jack.

The articles required were soon placed on the table, and then the highwayman securely bolted the door.

"What are you going to do?" asked Lucien, in surprise.

"I mean to copy your letters, and hide the originals, so that if we are attacked, as I have a kind of presentiment we shall be, there will still be the instructions in existence, even if we are killed or captured."

"A good plan," exclaimed Lucien; "let us both set to work."

They did so, and proceeded as rapidly as possible, though the cipher in which the dispatches were written was extremely complicated and difficult.

"There is one emergency provided for," exclaimed Lucien; "but now where are we to hide them?"

"I know a hollow tree in the wood where I don't think any of the Hanoverian rats would ever think of pushing their sharp noses."

"Good, then, lead on to the spot."

"It would be as well to stay here another hour. You must confess we have a very suspicious look travelling at such an early hour."

"Quite right," replied Lucien, so they remained quietly in the inn until the morning had gained a greater age, and there were more wayfarers on the road.

Then they once more started on their somewhat long journey.

On reaching the top of a slight eminence about half a mile from the inn, Lucien turned in his saddle to look back at the quiet old spot.

Through the trees in which the house was embowered, he perceived the gleaming of arms, and on the still morning air the sound of horses' hoofs on the hard road was faintly wafted towards them.

"We have left just in time," he cried. "Forward! we are pursued!"

Moonlight Jack's acute mind comprehended the situation ere his companion had finished speaking.

Both gave their steeds the rein, and bounded away.

Their road led them across a wide grassy moor, while beyond that was a large wood.

If they could gain that shelter there was a chance of eluding their pursuers, and also of depositing the despatches in a safe hiding-place.

The gallant animals that bore them, as if aware of the danger that threatened their riders, strained every nerve.

But ere they reached the wood the pursuing party appeared on the common not more than a quarter of a mile behind them.

The party consisted of two constables and six men of a dragoon regiment that was quartered in the neighbourhood.

"Courage!" cried Moonlight Jack, "we shall yet have time to conceal the original instructions, and if they take the copy away from us, I doubt whether they will be able to make out the *cipher*."

Lucien made no reply, but urged his horse onwards.

The dragoons fired their carbines, but were going at too quick a pace to be able to take any correct aim, and the bullets whistled harmlessly yards wide of their mark.

With a shout of contempt the two friends dashed into the wood.

"This way," cried Moonlight Jack, turning sharp round to the right, when they had passed a huge oak tree.

Lucien followed, and they then returned nearly to the spot where they had entered the forest.

There, in the midst of a little open glade, stood one of the monarchs of the wood, a giant oak, with its trunk cleft riven and gnarled with age, though its sturdy green branches showed how much of life and vigour still remained in the veins of the forest king.

As they approached it Moonlight Jack reined up his steed, and Lucien followed his example.

Dismounting, the two friends proceeded on foot

to the hollow trunk, and with great care concealed the despatches beneath the bark.

Then, once more returning to their steeds, they proceeded towards the residence of Lord Disney.

Their pursuers had already entered the wood, and had divided into three parties for the purpose of searching out the glades and thickets.

For some time they met with no success; but at length three of the soldiers happened to emerge on to one of the clearings exactly at the same moment that the two Jacobites appeared on the other.

"There they are!" shouted the dragoons, and at the same moment they fired their carbines.

Happily, not one of the shots took effect, and turning their horses' heads, the two friends dashed off in the opposite direction.

Ere they had gone a hundred yards, however, the other soldiers appeared before them, having been recalled by the sound of the shots.

"We must fight for it, it seems," said Moonlight Jack, drawing his sword.

"So it appears," responded Lucien Fairleigh, imitating his companion.

Sword in hand, and side by side, they rode at the opposing party.

Steel met steel as each found an opponent.

But there was the third man, and while his comrades were exchanging cuts and thrusts, he plunged his sabre up to the hilt in the bowels of Lucien's horse.

The gallant animal reared, and, staggering, fell to the ground.

Lucien managed to extricate himself from the falling animal, and, with great skill, continued the combat on foot.

Moonlight Jack's sword fell on the head of the man, whose foul stroke had dismounted Lucien, with fearful and overwhelming force.

Despite the helmet which surmounted the man's head, the weapon went crashing on through bone and brain till he dropped from his horse a disfigured and lifeless corpse.

Lucien, too, had severely wounded his antagonist, and there was just a chance that they might escape.

But others came to the aid of the third soldier.

Moonlight Jack's sword was broken at the hilt, and though he bravely defended himself with a long dagger, it was unavailing.

The numbers of their enemies overpowered them, and they were soon disarmed.

"Bind them hand and foot," said one of the constables, who had evinced no great desire to take part in the combat.

This was done, though both Moonlight Jack and Lucien protested against the indignity.

Their coats and vests were torn open, and rude hands eagerly searched the helpless prisoners.

On Lucien they found the copy of the cipher instructions he was conveying to Lord Disney.

Both constables and soldiers stared with all their eyes at the strange characters inscribed on the paper.

"Oh! you precious villains!" said the constable, who was in command of the party. "Won't you be hanged in a hurry to-morrow morning?"

"What is it?—what is it?" asked the others.

"Why, these rascals are Jacobites as well as robbers, and these are their secret instructions to rob his most gracious majesty, and blow up the Tower."

Moonlight Jack and Lucien could hardly refrain from laughing at the fearful charge thus made against them.

"Away to the lock-up!" cried the constable.

MOONLIGHT JACK
OR THE KING OF THE ROAD

THE DUEL.—*See No.* 15.

CHAPTER VI.

THE ESCAPE FROM GAOL.

THERE are times and seasons when all men are thoughtful, but there is nothing more conducive to meditation than the inside of a gaol after a life of freedom.

Moonlight Jack and Lucien found it so, when, after half an hour's walk in the midst of their captors, the door of Anstey lock-up, or gaol, as the villagers called it, shut them out from the world.

For a long time neither spoke, but though thus silent they were not idle.

Their thoughts were busy with the same subject, and that was a swift and sure means of escape.

Swift, because on the morrow they would be tried by a kind of half military half magisterial tribunal, the chief of which was a strenuous advocate for hanging ; sure, because in case of failure they would be looked upon as guilty, and most probably be condemned without a hearing of any kind.

Hanging was very common in those days, and, therefore, little thought of.

After a long silence, however, Moonlight Jack caught sight of his companion's thoughtful face, and thus spoke,

"I can see, Lucien, that you are thinking about the same thing that occupies my brain—suppose we have a consultation together?"

"With all my heart. I was trying to find out some method of escape."

"The most natural thing to be thinking about. What conclusion have you come to?"

"That our situation is hopeless, and we must submit to our fate."

"Think you so?" asked Moonlight Jack, while his eye ran round the wall to see if there were no loophole.

All was solid and secure, for the place had been built in a great measure by a party of angry farmers for the purpose of incarcerating sheep stealers when they could catch them.

The walls were of granite, and the window was guarded by stout bars of iron at least two inches in thickness.

The door was cased with iron, and the hinges were firmly mortised into the stone wall.

The prisoners had no weapon or tool of any kind to enable them to pick the ponderous lock, for everything had been taken from them by the constables.

"I fear we are in a fix," sighed Moonlight Jack. "There is one way though."

"And that?"

"Is to knock down our gaoler when he opens the door, and then run."

"The soldiers are to remain here till to-morrow, I fancy," said Lucien. "On their horses they could easily overtake us."

"We must take our chance. But, hush! here comes some one."

The door opened, and a pretty girl of eighteen years of age or thereabouts made her appearance.

In her hand she bore a pitcher of water and a loaf of brown bread.

Such a fair vision completely banished the knocking down intentions of the prisoners, and both looked upon her with a kindly smile.

"What is your name?" asked Moonlight Jack.

"Mary Dobson, sir," replied the girl, with a blush.

"Have you many sweethearts, Mary?" continued the highwayman.

"None, sir," replied Mary, the colour on her cheeks deepening.

"Lucky for you, Mary, or you might be a prisoner instead of a turnkey."

"Why, what do you mean, sir?" asked the girl, with a stare of surprise.

"I mean that I and my friend are locked up here through undertaking to carry a letter to a young lady."

"Why," exclaimed the girl, "my father said that you were Jacobites, and had some secret dispatches with you when they captured you."

"All false, Mary, except about the letter; that was written in order that the young lady's father might not understand it if it chanced to fall into his hands."

"What a shame!" exclaimed Mary Dobson.

"Why didn't you explain that to my father when he locked you up?"

"He wouldn't believe me, Mary; and the worst of it is that, in all probability, the young friend from whom I received the letter will not marry the lady to whom I was taking it unless she hears from him to-night."

"What a pity!" cried the girl, who fully believed the romance which Moonlight Jack's ready wit had invented. "How I wish I could help you."

"So you can," replied the highwayman.

"How so?"

"By unlocking the door and letting us out."

"Then I should be discovered and punished severely."

"I should be very sorry to be the cause of any unpleasantness; but could you not lend me a screwdriver and a file?"

The girl reflected for a moment ere she replied,

"I have it; there is an old rusty key which unlocks this door in our house. I will bring that when I bring your supper, and then you can let yourself out."

"At what time will it be safest to venture forth?" asked Lucien.

"Exactly at nine o'clock every night my father goes to the ale-house opposite to bring the night watchman over. They generally have a glass together so that the place is frequently left unguarded for half-an-hour."

"Thanks, my dear Mary, I will not fail to remember your kindness when I get out of this hole."

At that moment footsteps were heard without and the girl hastily withdrew.

The two friends were left to amuse themselves as best they could till their evening meal was brought.

Mary could not then stop to say much, but inside the loaf she brought them was a key wrapped up in paper.

"Not before nine," she whispered, "and mind you lock the door after you come out."

Moonlight Jack nodded, and the door once more closed on the two friends.

The hours slowly passed away, marked as they were by the chimes of an old church clock.

As nine was slowly chimed they heard the footsteps of the gaoler as he left his nook in the hall and proceeded forth to the beer-house in search of his companion.

"Now is our time," whispered Moonlight Jack, as he inserted the rusty key in the lock.

Careful as he was in opening it, the iron gave forth a not very melodious sound as the door swung back on its hinges.

Lucien peeped out cautiously, but no foe was in sight.

"The coast is clear. Let us haste away ere the gaoler returns," he exclaimed.

"Hist! no talking allowed," whispered Moonlight Jack, holding up his finger as a signal for silence.

They locked the door behind them, and passing on tip-toe through the ante-room found themselves in the road.

"Good night. A safe journey to you," whispered a soft voice in the ear of Lucien.

It was Mary, the turnkey's daughter, and she looked so enchanting and so pleased at having done a kind action that Moonlight Jack could not resist the temptation to imprint a kiss on her warm rosy lips.

Time was pressing, so without more delay the two liberated friends hurried away in the opposite direction to that taken by the gaoler.

For some little time they walked on in silence; but at length Moonlight Jack thus spoke.

"Have you made up your mind, my friend, to walk all the way to Lord Disney's house?"

"I suppose we must do so."

"Why should we? Those rascally dragoons have deprived us of our horses, and I see no reason, therefore, why we should not borrow steeds from their stable."

"Is your plan feasible?"

"Certainly; the stable is at the back of the prison, and I have no doubt that it is unguarded. Suppose we try?"

"With all my heart," replied Lucien.

They retraced their steps for a little distance, and then, leaping a hedge, made their way across some fields to the little shed at the back of the lock-up, where the dragoons had stabled their horses.

As Moonlight Jack had anticipated, the soldiers had left no one to guard their steeds, and it was therefore an easy matter for the friends to help themselves.

The two handsomest and most powerful animals were selected, and bridles and saddles were placed on them.

"Why should we go unarmed?" said Moonlight Jack, pointing to the empty scabbard that hung by his side, and then to the dragoons' weapons which hung against the stable wall.

Lucien Farleigh's only reply was to draw one of the weapons from its scabbard and thrust it into his own sword sheath.

Moonlight Jack did the same, and being then armed, the pair mounted their borrowed horses and rode forth.

They kept the fields for some distance, and it was lucky they did so, for in a short time the shouts behind them, and the clattering of hoofs on the road, announced that the soldiers were pursuing them.

After a time the sounds died away, and the two friends proceeded by the most lonely road they knew to Lord Disney's residence.

It was midnight ere they reached the mansion, and the inmates had retired to rest when Moonlight Jack pulled the handle of the great bell at the lodge gates.

In a few minutes the porter appeared,

CHAPTER VII.

A NIGHT ALARM—THE SECOND BATCH OF PAPERS—THE MARCH—THE HARBOUR—THE SIGNALS AT SEA—THE COAST GUARD APPROACH—THE WARNING OF BATTLE.

THE surprise of Lord Disney was great at being so unexpectedly roused from his bed.

Judging, however, that something of importance had occurred, he hastily dressed himself and descended to the room in which Lucien and his companion were seated.

"What, in Heaven's name, brings you here at such an hour?" he cried.

"Business of importance," was the reply, "connected with our cause."

"To that cause I am devoted," exclaimed Lord Disney; "but tell me, is the time come to take up arms?"

"Not yet," said Lucien, "though we were compelled to fight our way hither."

"How so?"

"Why, I had despatches to bring you; but we were set upon by a party of dragoons, and the letters taken from me. We passed the greater part of the day in prison, and only escaped through the kindness of the gaoler's daughter."

"Then my instructions are in the hands of the local magistrates by this time, I suppose?"

"Yes; but being in cipher I suspect they will be puzzled to read the rather curious document. Moreover, the originals are safely concealed in a hollow tree; they have only a copy."

"That is good. Are you ready to go with me to this place and give me the papers?"

"As soon as you have given us a glass of wine and some food," replied Moonlight Jack. "We have tasted nothing but bread and water since seven o'clock this morning."

Lord Disney touched a bell, and a domestic entered the room.

"Prepare supper for these gentlemen as quickly as possible, then rouse the coachman, and have the carriage got ready within half an hour. I fancy," he continued, turning to his guests, "that you will be more secure from molestation in my carriage than on horseback."

"Quite right, my lord," replied Moonlight Jack, "although I might suggest the advisability of carrying saddles with us in case we are compelled to cut our traces."

"What, and leave the carriage behind? That would, at all events, betray my share in the plot."

"Perhaps," said Lucien, after a pause, "it would be better to make the journey on horseback."

"So I fancy," exclaimed Moonlight Jack; "I feel more at home in the saddle."

The order for the carriage was countermanded, and as soon as the supper was finished horses were saddled, and the three conspirators set out for the hollow oak in which the original documents intended for Lord Disney were concealed.

Three well-mounted and well-armed grooms accompanied them that they might be better matched in case of another skirmish with the dragoons.

They saw no signs of the military on their road, however, and reached the hollow oak about two hours before daybreak.

The despatches were safe, and when once Lord Disney had them in his hand Lucien felt that a load of responsibility had been taken off his shoulders.

"We must go to the coast at once," observed the nobleman, when he had mastered the contents of the papers. "A cargo of arms is waiting for us."

"Then let us away at once, for fear anything should occur," cried Lucien.

"We must have more men with us," replied Lord Disney. "Luckily, all my servants are of the same politics as myself, and hate the Hanoverians as the fiend hates holy-water!"

"How many more do you propose to take, my

lord?" asked Moonlight Jack. "It will appear suspicious if we muster too strongly."

"Three besides these. They, however, will be in a covered waggon, so as to appear quite a separate party."

The conversation then dropped, nor was it resumed till they once more stood in the hall of Lord Disney's mansion.

After another brief rest fresh horses were provided, and the party, now consisting in all of nine men, proceeded on their journey towards Wentworth Bay, where the long-expected vessel from France was to land her cargo.

Before starting, however, Lucien despatched a note to the marchioness, explaining why he did not return.

The journey was long and the road rough, but, considering the dangerous nature of the enterprise they were engaged in, the wayfarers were not sorry to see the sun sink behind the hills, and the young moon rise slowly from the ocean as they approached the coast.

The spot chosen for the debarkation of the cargo was in every respect well chosen.

The harbour was good, though at that time only used by two or three fishing smacks or smugglers. Though near the main road, it was some distance from any town or village, and, lastly, there was no custom house, or coast-guard station, within some distance.

The scene which greeted Lord Disney and his friends as they reached the top of a range of hills was singularly beautiful.

Before them lay the waters of Wentworth Bay, glittering in the calm moonlight, while on either side the chalky cliffs reared their heads, looking more intensely white under Luna's rays than the purest alabaster.

At their feet three rude cottages served to shelter as many families of fishermen, while the same number of boats were drawn up on the shore.

The whole party eagerly scanned the face of the water, but could see no sign of the expected vessel.

"Strange that the vessel is not here as it should be," observed Lucien.

"Not at all. It would have been excessively dangerous for a strange craft to enter this secluded nook during daylight," replied Lord Disney.

"That, I grant, my lord; but you must also confess that we run an equal risk in remaining here all the night."

"I hope to be at home ere daybreak," replied the nobleman. "Let us try what effect a signal-rocket will have."

He gave the word of command to his men, and in a moment's space of time a rocket went whizzing up into the deep blue sky.

One minute—two—three minutes elapsed, and the whole party began to fear they had come on a bootless errand, when a tiny spark was seen ascending like a shooting star from the bosom of the deep.

"Our signal is answered!" exclaimed Lucien, eagerly.

"Stay a minute," answered Lord Disney; "we must have other communication ere we bring them into the harbour."

By his direction two other rockets were thrown up.

The vessel answered by firing four.

"All is right," said Lord Disney; "make the last signal."

Another signal rocket was then thrown up, and the party then crouched down among the bushes that grew scattered about the side of the cliff.

"They seem tardy," exclaimed Moonlight Jack, after a long interval of silence. "I suppose they have run aground or are chased by a revenue cutter."

"I hope not," replied Lord Disney; "that would indeed be a misfortune and disappointment."

Again they strained their eyes over the glistening waves, but for some time to no purpose.

At length a black speck shot round from behind a neck of land, and then every heart grew elate as each voice cried,

"Here she comes! here she comes!"

It was indeed the "Hero," the expected vessel, and the men moved nearer down to the beach in expectation of her arrival.

"How close can yon vessel approach to the land?" asked Lucien.

"Within thirty yards with perfect safety," replied Lord Disney.

The object of their conversation glided smoothly though swiftly over the tranquil waves.

The inhabitants of the huts glanced for a moment from their windows at the strange group on the beach, and then, concluding that they were smugglers, hastened down to offer their services.

Lord Disney accepted their aid, promising them a liberal reward.

"Have you any coast-guard near at hand?" he asked one of them.

"None, sir," was the fisherman's reply, "except a small party who occasionally walk over from Wentworth."

"And how far is Wentworth from this spot?'

"Five miles as the crow flies; but as the excise-men have no wings they are obliged to go two miles out of their way when they come round this part of the coast."

By the time the man had finished speaking the vessel was within a hundred yards of the shore.

A boat was lowered, and those on shore stood ready to receive the cargo.

Suddenly a sound was heard at some little distance, and every face assumed an anxious look.

"The coast-guard! the coast-guard!" cried a woman, rushing from one of the cottages.

CHAPTER VIII.

PREPARATIONS FOR A FIGHT—THE COMBAT—FIRST VICTORY—FLIGHT OF THE ENEMY—A PRECIOUS CARGO.

THE wild cry of the fisherman's wife, as she rushed from her little hut, alarmed those who were waiting on the beach, and, huddling themselves together in a compact body, the Jacobite party prepared to resist to the death their, as yet, unseen foe.

The woman's voice reached even to the little vessel in the bay, and Lord Disney observed that the men in the boat hesitated, as though in doubt, whether it would be safe to leave the shelter of their swift-sailing bark.

" Steady, my friends. Be firm, and we shall conquer," exclaimed Lord Disney, as he drew his sword and cocked his pistols.

" Had we not better form two lines, my lord, till we know on which side they mean to attack us ?" asked Lucien.

" Your suggestion is good," replied the person addressed. " But, my friends," continued he, speaking to the fishermen who had volunteered their aid in landing the cargo, " return to your cottages. There is no cause why you should aid us in fighting our battles."

The hardy sons of the ocean, however, showed no inclination to quit the scene.

" If it's all the same to you, good gentlemen," said one of the men, " we'd rather stop and have a blow or two with the excisemen. We have some old scores to pay off."

" May as well swing for a sheep as a lamb," muttered another. " They're sure to search our houses ; they always do whenever a ship comes within half a league of shore."

Moonlight Jack and his friends smiled at this speech, which seemed to guarantee that the king did not collect much revenue at that little port.

" Then, stay," exclaimed Lord Disney, " and if we gain the day I will double the reward I promised you."

Then, under the direction of Lucien and Moonlight Jack, the whole body formed in line, or rather two lines back to back.

Still the foe appeared not.

" A false alarm," whispered Lucien, after they had waited in silence for some minutes.

" No, sir," said one of the fishermen, " old Meggie White knows better than to cry wolf. Depend on it spies are near."

The man spoke so earnestly that all were convinced.

Again they listened in silence.

Presently a slight sound was heard.

It seemed to proceed from the face of the cliffs.

It increased, and they could distinguish the sound of footsteps, and the rattling of pebbles displaced by those who were in the act of descending the rocky paths from the highland overlooking the beach.

" There is the place where they will appear," whispered the fisherman. " That's the only path, except the one by which you came."

Every eye was turned towards the spot indicated.

For a short time longer nothing was visible.

But presently dark forms were seen gathering at the foot of the precipice.

Then a body of men, about twenty in number, rushed forward, and a loud voice cried,

" Surrender, in the king's name !"

" King be d——d !" exclaimed Moonlight Jack.

" Surrender, or we fire !"

" Never," replied Lord Disney.

The coast-guard fired a volley, and the bullets whistled over the heads of the Jacobites harmlessly.

The attacking party had fired too high purposely, thinking to frighten the smugglers into a surrender.

Totally different, however, was the effect of their volley.

As they rushed forward from their hiding-place Lord Disney gave the word of command.

A storm of bullets from the weapons of his party went whistling through the ranks of the coast-guard.

Two of their number fell to rise no more, and three others were compelled to limp homewards from the field of battle wounded.

They were all brave men, however, and the remainder pressed on under the leadership of their captain, a retired naval officer.

" Forward, my men !" roared Captain Smeaton. " Cut the rascals to bits if they resist !"

The party under Lord Disney met the charge with determined courage, though almost overwhelmed with the numbers of their adversaries.

" Bravely done, my men," said Moonlight Jack, as he witnessed the foe driven back like a wave from the face of a rock.

The fishermen had drawn, apparently from their high boots, a short cutlass each, and they proved themselves as skilful in the use as in the art of concealing it.

" D—n it, men !" exclaimed the coast-guard officer, will you let a parcel of London counter-jumpers beat you off in this manner ? Forward ! forward, or I'll give every mother's son six dozen lashes in the morning !"

" He is lashing himself up in a fury," observed Moonlight Jack, as he parried a furious blow aimed at him by the enraged captain.

Lucien smiled, but was too busily engaged with a tall, powerful antagonist to turn his head to reply.

The fight was long and desperate.

Sword clashed against sword, shout answered shout, and occasionally a sharp ringing report told of the the sudden flight of a leaden bullet winged with death.

Presently Lucien found himself side by side with Lord Disney.

" I fear our case is hopeless at present," whispered the nobleman.

" Aye, unless those lazy cowards in yon vessel come to our assistance."

" Why they aid us not is a perfect mystery to my mind," continued Lord Disney. " With the aid of six stout men from the crew we could make short work of these fellows."

" Forward, men, forward !" shouted Moonlight Jack. " The day is ours !"

" Stand fast !" the voice of the captain of the coast-guard was heard to cry. " Will you obey me, you lubbers ?"

Then followed a volley of oaths and abuse, which so amused the Jacobite leaders that Lord Disney almost dropped his sword as he laughed at the old captain's fiery oration.

Then the old naval hero led his forces forward again with such a vigorous charge that he almost drove the defenders of the position into the water.

The situation of Lucien and his friends began to look more gloomy than ever.

Each man made the most desperate exertions to maintain his ground, while the enemy strained every nerve to the conflict in order to complete the victory ere aid could arrive.

" Ha ! you villain ! I have you at last !" exclaimed

the old captain, as at length his sword clashed with that of Moonlight Jack.

"Welcome, old tartub, welcome. You say you have me; I only hope you are man enough to make good your words, so here goes to shiver your timbers and lay you on your beam ends."

So saying, the king of the road parried a furious lunge, and in return delivered a thrust with such force and swiftness that his sword blade passed completely through the old sailor's body.

His victory nearly caused his death, however.

For ere he could disengage his weapon the second in command of the coast-guard, burning to avenge his leader's death, made a furious cut at the head of the gallant highwayman.

Lucien saw the threatened stroke, and interposed his own blade.

"Thanks, Lucien, you have saved my life!" murmured Moonlight Jack.

"Which is as precious to me as my own," replied Lucien. "But see, here comes a boat from the ship at last!"

Moonlight Jack cast a hasty glance towards the sea, and sure enough, as Lucien had said, there was a boat nearing the shore.

Eight men at least were in it, and the hard-pressed friends could see the glitter of the weapons that the boat's crew were bringing to their aid.

"Courage, courage, my lads! Help is at hand," shouted Lucien.

"It shall not avail you," shouted one of the coast-guard.

As the man spoke he discharged a pistol full in Lucien's face.

Half-stunned by the report, and blinded by the smoke, Lucien, for a moment, hardly knew whether he was wounded or not.

In a moment, however, he regained his faculties, and, with a well-directed blow, laid his foe at his feet.

"Are you hurt?" eagerly asked Moonlight Jack.

"I think not—at least I don't feel any wound."

"Thank Heaven for that," exclaimed the highwayman, devoutly.

The coast-guard made one more desperate effort to overcome their antagonists ere the boat which they saw approaching could reach the shore.

"To the rescue! to the rescue!" exclaimed a loud voice, and at the same moment the crew of the vessel leaped to shore.

A moment's hesitation to see who were friends and who foes, and then, with the eagerness of eagles swooping on their prey, the new comers rushed forward against the coast-guard.

The aid was timely, for both the combating parties were nearly overcome with fatigue.

Lord Disney's men felt new hope come into their hearts, while their opponents saw at once that the odds were against them.

The combat was prolonged for a few minutes, but ere long the excisemen were compelled to give way.

They broke, and, despite the efforts of their leader to rally them, fled.

The victorious Jacobites pursued them for some little distance, but soon the loud voice of Lord Disney was heard recalling them.

There was much to be done, and little time in which to do it.

The wounded of his party—for none save of the coast-guard had been killed—were attended to, and their injuries dressed as well as the limited knowledge of surgery possessed by Lucien and his friends would permit.

The boat returned to the vessel, and preparations were once more made for receiving the cargo.

First of all came several long boxes, the weight of which was so great that it took the strength of two men to lift each package to the waggon.

These cases contained muskets, swords, and pistols in abundance.

Then came a boat-load of small casks, the very look of which was sufficient to inform all that they contained powder.

While these were being stowed away in the waggon, Lucien and Moonlight Jack mounted the cliffs to survey the road and discover if possible if any enemy lingered in the neighbourhood.

A body of men crossing the plain in an opposite direction to that by which the highwayman and his friends had come, told them that the coast-guard had sufficient to do to transport their own wounded to a place of safety to trouble themselves about the smugglers.

Five dead bodies left behind on the beach showed how severe the struggle had been.

Of Lord Disney's party, including the fishermen, four only had received any hurt.

When the last cask of powder was lifted to the waggon, preparations were made to place the injured men on the vehicle.

One of the fishermen pointed out where a heap of dried sea-weed stood, and of that a soft couch was formed to protect the wounded from the jolting motion of the vehicle.

"Now, my brave friends, here is the reward I promised you," said Lord Disney, turning to the fishermen; "and with it you have the heartfelt thanks of myself and friends. You have done us a service which will never be forgotten by any of those who have taken part in this night's fight."

"Well, you see, masters," said one of the party, "those chaps are always meddling and interfering, so it sarves 'em right when we lends a helping hand to any body as wants to land a few things without paying custom-house duties. You're heartily welcome to our services."

The boat returned to the ship, the white sails once more spread themselves to the breeze.

Lord Disney gave the word, the wheels of the heavily-laden vehicle slowly revolved on its up-hill road, and soon the scene of the encounter was almost deserted.

Lucien Fairleigh was anxious and impatient to return to the marchioness; yet, when they reached the top of the hill, he could not refrain from turning in his saddle.

A light was seen on the sands, and the young man guessed that the fishermen were stripping the bodies of their late foes.

Moonlight Jack rode in silence.

He was revolving in his head a project of which mention will be made hereafter.

CHAPTER IX.

LUCIEN AND THE MARCHIONESS—THE SECRET
DOOR—THE SLEEPER—"KILL HIM!"—LUCIEN'S
CHAMBER—THE MIDNIGHT VISITOR.

THE night passed away and broad daylight had
asserted its sway some hours before Lord Disney
and his friends reached the destination to which
they were conveying their supply of arms and
ammunition.

When they reached Lord Disney's mansion it
was noon; and all were fatigued with their long
journey.

They washed the stains of travel and combat
from their persons, and then reclined on luxurious
couches with all the air of men who had done their
duty.

Repose was both welcome and needful after the
fatigues they had undergone.

Lucien was the first to make a movement.

Immediately on his return he had sent off one of
Lord Disney's servants to the marchioness to ac-
quaint her with his safe arrival at the nobleman's
house, and to inform her that he would see her that
same evening.

When, therefore, the evening shades began to
lower he roused himself from his recumbent
position, and ordered his horse to be saddled.

"Stay with us," said Lord Disney; "I mean to
celebrate our first victory with due honour."

"I thank you, my lord, but pressing engage-
ment——"

"With a lady?"

Lucien slightly changed colour and bowed.

"Then I won't attempt to detain you; but, at
the same time, I assure you we shall miss your
company."

"I must go also, my lord," said the King of the
Road, rising.

"What is this? A conspiracy, as I am alive!
Why, I shall be left alone!"

"I must go, my lord."

"Why?"

"I have important business to attend to."

"Indeed!"

"And, as it may lead me into the presence of
royalty itself, it must not be neglected."

Lord Disney stared hard at the speaker, so did
Lucien.

"What are you talking about?" exclaimed the
latter.

"About an interview I wish to have with his
majesty, the elector of Hanover."

"Strange!" muttered both the others, while a
cloud passed over Lord Disney's brow.

"Fear not that I am going to turn traitor, my
lord," said the gallant highwayman.

"I can hardly think you would after fighting
with such determined bravery."

"Of my expedition to Court you may hear more
when we next meet; but for the present it is not
safe to breathe a word more than I have done.
Come, Lucien, I will ride a little way with you."

"If you will not stay, go in Heaven's name; but
take care of yourself."

"Never fear, my lord, the fox that has once had
his foot in the trap ever afterwards scents danger."

So saying, Moonlight Jack took Lucien by the
arm, and led him from the room.

In the stable-yard their two noble steeds were
pawing the ground and champing the bit with impatience.

A few minutes the clatter of hoofs was heard
and then a bend in the road concealed them from
the eyes of Lord Disney, who watched their movements.

After riding together for a distance of two miles,
or thereabouts, the friends reached a spot where
the road branched into two.

"Here I must leave you, Lucien," said Moonlight Jack. "This is my road to London."

"Farewell," cried Lucien.

"I shall see you again in two or three days."

Lucien pressed onwards, and soon lost sight of
his companion.

He was already in imagination in the arms of
the fair marchioness.

His noble steed could scarcely bear him along
with sufficient speed to gratify his impatience.

Past heath, past wood, past cottage and field, the
gallant horse flew with lightning speed.

At length in the grey twilight the well-remem-
bered building loomed up clear and distinct from
amidst the surrounding trees.

A light twinkled in one of the windows, and
Lucien fancied that by its radiance he could descry
the form of her to whom he was so impatiently
hastening.

"Softly and quietly, fair sir, such are our good
lady's orders," said the man who opened for him
the gate.

Lucien checked his good steed, and in another
moment a groom made his appearance.

"The side door, sir, if you please," said the servant, pointing to a little porch almost hidden amidst
luxuriant shrubs and bushes.

"Why all this mystery?" thought Lucien, as he
directed his steps towards the entrance indicated
by the groom.

A female servant was waiting for him, and,
beckoning Lucien to follow her, she led the way to
the dressing-room of the marchioness.

Like a discreet damsel, however, she paused at
the door, while Lucien eagerly rushed forward to
embrace the fair siren.

"Thank Heaven, you have arrived safely!" exclaimed the marchioness, as she printed a kiss upon
his lips, while her full and throbbing bosom was
pressed to her lover.

"I have returned to find happiness in your
arms," replied Lucien, as he responded to her endearments. "Here, alone, true joy is to be
found."

Again and again they kissed, till it seemed as
though their lips would never part; and all the
while her glittering eyes were gazing into Lucien's
with an expression of passionate love which few
men would have been able to withstand.

They sat down together on a soft, luxurious
couch, still locked in each other's arms.

"Now tell me," said the marchioness, assuming
a frown, "how dare you absent yourself without
permission, after promising to return to me?"

"Necessity, the hard and stern task-master, who
often compels us to act sorely against our wishes
and inclinations,"

" What mean you ?"

" Surely, sweet lady, you received my message ?"

" Yes, but what it meant was more than I could fathom, except that you intended to break your promise. Now, tell me, what was the urgent necessity that compelled you to be nearly a week away from me ?"

" In the first place, while on my way to Lord Disney, I was captured by soldiers and constables, and locked up in a filthy prison."

" From which you escaped in the night. I heard of that."

" Then, when after many delays, I reached my destination, I was compelled to go on to the sea coast to help in the landing and convoy of a cargo of arms we have received for the cause. That took up the remaining portion of the three days I have been absent."

" I shall never forgive you."

" I humbly beg for pardon," said Lucien, falling on one knee at her feet ; " and allow me to plead in extenuation of my fault that I returned as soon as it was possible to do so."

A self-satisfied and triumphant smile passed over the face of the marchioness as she raised her lover from his suppliant posture.

" As you have been engaged in the service of our exiled king," she said, " I suppose I must overlook the offence this time."

Lucien expressed his thanks in a kiss, and then the marchioness continued,

" Am I to believe, dear Lucien, that you really love me so much as you tell me ?"

" Aye, sweet marchioness, I love you more than words can express !"

" You have before asked me for an opportunity of proving your love and courage," she continued, assuming her most fascinating aspect.

" Try me in what way you will, dearest ; bid me, single-handed, fight a troop of horsemen, jump down a precipice or rob the bank of England, I will do it, or perish in the attempt. Aught that courage, strength, or skill can do I will perform, if you but say the word."

" We will see. Follow me !"

So saying, she rose from the couch and unlocked a door which Lucien had not before noticed.

A long corridor was visible, with doors on each side.

Leading the way down this passage she paused at the last door, and, taking a key from her dress, noiselessly opened it.

" Enter," she said, in a whisper.

Lucien silently followed her into the room.

It was furnished with the greatest magnificence.

Thick carpets prevented the footstep from being heard, heavy curtains prevented the ingress of any light from the outside, rich paintings, in which the artist had done his best to perpetuate female beauty, lined the walls, and gorgeous furniture was scattered throughout the apartment.

On one side was a kind of arched recess, the entrance to which was screened by silk hangings.

The marchioness moved towards this and then beckoned Lucien to follow her.

Silently she drew the silken curtains aside, and, with a queenly gesture, pointed downwards.

Lucien gazed forward.

Before him was a couch, and on that couch reclined a man, half dressed.

At least the attire was that of a man, though the features were effeminate, sensual, and senile, while the slender frame and feeble-looking limbs, as well as the low, narrow brow, bespoke both mental and bodily weakness and deficiency.

The marchioness gazed for a few seconds on the sleeping figure with an air of disgust.

Then, turning to Lucien, she whispered,

" That is my husband."

" Is it possible ?" exclaimed he.

" Aye, to that weak, brainless thing am I tied for life."

As Lucien gazed on the form of the sleeper he no longer wondered that the marchioness had so willingly entered into an amour with himself.

He was roused from his thoughts by a slight touch on the arm.

It was the marchioness.

A blaze of hate and triumph was glowing with baleful light in her eyes.

From the folds of her dress she drew a dagger, the blade of which glittered in the light of the wax taper.

" Take this," she whispered ; " prove your love and your courage by burying it to the hilt in his heart !"

Lucien stared in surprise.

Much as he could imagine she hated her husband, he could hardly fancy that she would take such measures to rid herself of the ties that bound her.

" Quick ! quick !" she muttered, " strike well and deeply ; but one blow will be needed !"

Still Lucien hesitated,

The marchioness saw it, and a sneering smile of contempt curled her lip.

At that moment the sleeper made a slight movement.

" Back !" she whispered, concealing the dagger. " He wakes ! I will defer my vengeance !"

So saying, she let fall the curtain, and beckoning Lucien to follow her, left the room.

They returned to the dressing-room of the marchioness, in which a supper had been laid during their temporary absence.

The marchioness motioned Lucien to a seat, and the meal was eaten in silence.

At length Lucien said,

" I fear, dearest, you are angry with me ; but I could not do such a deed without a momentary hesitation. Forgive me before I go."

" Surely you will not go at this late hour. Stay, dear Lucien ; I will not upbraid you. But can you be surprised that I should wish to be freed from such an incumbrance as yon sleeping husband of mine ?"

" Then I will stay."

The marchioness whispered in Lucien's ear, and catching her in his arms he kissed her fondly.

A few minutes later and he retired to rest in the chamber provided for him, which was somewhat similar to the one occupied by the sleeping husband of Lucien's fair mistress.

Though anxiously waiting for her promised visit his head had scarcely touched the pillow ere he fell asleep.

How long he slept Lucien knew not, but he suddenly awoke with some vague presentiment of evil or danger.

As he opened his eyes the wall seemed to open by his bedside, and the figure of a masked man with a knife in his hand was plainly visible.

MOONLIGHT JACK
OR THE KING · OF THE ROAD

THE DUEL IN THE CHAMBER.—*See page* 107.

CHAPTER X.

WHICH SHOWS THAT THE KINGS WE IMPORT
FROM ABROAD ARE NOT PRODIGIES OF VALOUR
AND ARE SCARCELY GENEROUS FOES.

MOONLIGHT JACK, after parting first with Lord
Disney, and afterwards with Lucien Fairleigh, rode
onward to London.

He reached the great metropolis about the same
time that Lucien made his appearance before the
marchioness, and after stabling his horse at a quiet
little inn, entered the public-room, where he
listened with eagerness to the conversation of those
there assembled.

The increasing power of the Jacobite party was
the most general topic, and Moonlight Jack soón
found that the Hanoverians feared almost as much
as they hated the name of Stuart.

The movements of the German king, whom events
had called to the throne, excited some comment,

and His Most Gracious Majesty George I. was severely censured by some, for passing the greater portion of his time in his Hanoverian domain, while others thought he did quite right to reside abroad, and so preserve his sacred body from Jacobite violence.

One thing they all agreed on, namely, that he would arrive in London from Windsor the following day, or rather evening.

Moonlight Jack listened very attentively to all that was said, and then retired to rest, where he dreamed that the standard of insurrection was already raised.

Next day, after paying particular attention to his pistols, the King of the Road mounted his horse, and rode quietly westward.

In those days the aspect of the county of Middlesex and the adjacent shires was very different from the appearance which it now presents.

Modern improvements and cultivation have altered the face of the land, so that the traveller in the present day can hardly tell the roads by which his ancestors journeyed a hundred and fifty years ago.

Many an old mansion has been pulled down, many a village built, many a hamlet developed into a town, and many tracks of ground are now reclaimed, which then were dense forests, unwholesome marshes, or barren moors.

Even Hounslow Heath, the favourite resort of gentlemen of the road, has disappeared under the spirit of cultivation, and left no trace of places where many a daring deed has been done.

However that may be, the road which Moonlight Jack was following lay not at all in the direction of either of the present roads to Windsor, but after leading the traveller to suppose he was going to Oxford, turned suddenly off to the right, and approached the banks of the Thames.

In so doing it passed over a long range of high hills, and a wide extent of common ground on the top, and it was just this point of the journey that Moonlight Jack reached when his watch told him that it wanted but half an hour to sunset.

The common was bleak as it is well possible to conceive, for the winds swept over it without let or hindrance, save in one or two spots where a few scattered beech trees bravely held up their heads to the blast.

It was uncultivated, but, at the same time, cannot be said to have been unproductive, for perhaps there was never a space of ground of equal size which could show such a luxuriant crop of gorse, heath, fern, and thistles.

These herbs, together with a small quantity of not very rich grass, were the only vegetable products of the ground, and the only tenants of the place were a few sheep, by far too lean to need any looking after.

Occasionally, on the edge of the common, there might, indeed, be seen a stray goose or two, but they were like the white settlers on the coast of Africa, venturing rarely and timidly into the interior.

Vehicles seldom crossed the dreary waste, yet, nevertheless, Moonlight Jack was there for the purpose of taking toll of passing carriages.

In those times forty or fifty miles was a long and laborious day's journey, and at whatever hour the traveller began, he was not likely to reach the end of it without becoming the borrower of a dark hour or two from the night.

If the reader will consider how much more sand, gravel, mud, and clay carriage wheels had to pass through in those days, he will easily see the reason why our forefathers were so slow in their locomotion.

Such was the case with a large, cumbrous carriage which, drawn heavily on by four stout horses, wended slowly along the road over the desolate spot described.

Moonlight Jack had taken up his position in the midst of one of the little plantations, or, rather, groups of trees which stood not far from the road, and eagerly watched the approaching vehicle.

The panels of the carriage were plain, without any coat of arms or crest, though there was a heavy and stately, swaggering appearance about the vehicle itself which seemed to imply a consciousness even in the wood and leather of the dignity of the persons within.

And they were indeed dignified persons who sat in that carriage.

The rather elderly gentleman, who dozed so tranquilly with his worsted night cap drawn over his ears, and one foot reclining on the opposite seat, was George I., King of Great Britain and Ireland.

The precise, formal-looking, well-dressed gentleman, who sat opposite the monarch, hat in hand, was Lord Townshend, principal secretary of state.

His most gracious and sacred majesty had left Windsor after a plentiful meal in which cold cabbage and beer played the greater part, and was now on his way to London to know, if possible, what the people of England were doing.

Unable to converse English with any degree of fluency, the monarch had come to the conclusion that he could not do better than sleep away the tedious journey.

To be woke out of one's slumber suddenly at any time, or by any means, is a very unpleasant sensation; but there are few occasions we can conceive on which such an event is more disagreeable than when thus awoke to find a pistol at our breast and some one demanding our money.

The king had sent his state carriage by another road to mislead any ill-disposed Jacobites, who might entertain blood-thirsty motives with regard to his sacred person, and then, in a private carriage, imagined himself perfectly safe, when suddenly the vehicle stopped, and he started up.

My Lord Townshend had been dozing, too, though he preserved his respectful and courtier-like attitude; and before the worthy pair were fully awake to what was passing on, the door of the coach was opened, and a man of gentlemanly exterior presented himself with a pistol in each hand.

The monarch swore, "donner und blitzen !" to such an extent, that he almost choked himself with his own language.

The principal secretary of state, however, was more calm, and therefore after a good stare at the highwayman, he asked that pistol-bearing gentleman,

"Pray, sir, what may be your pleasure with me?"

"I am very sorry to be obliged to delay yourself and the king," replied Moonlight Jack, quietly; "but I have made bold to stop you for the purpose of disburdening you of a portion of your baggage, which you can well spare, but which I cannot."

"Does he know me? does he know me?" cried the king. "Why doesn't he take off his hat?"

"Yes, I know you, Elector of Hanover!" replied the highwayman, "and still keep my chapeau on my head; but, unless I have that diamond button from your own head gear, I shall send a bullet through you without remorse!"

"Donner !" exclaimed the monarch, who never before in his life had been addressed in such a manner.

The highwayman snatched the jewelled cap and tore from it its ornament.

"Now the contents of your pockets, if it pleases your majesty."

"What? The man robs me!" exclaimed the king.

"May not one monarch rob another?" exclaimed Moonlight Jack. "I am King of the Road with greater right than you style yourself King of Great Britain; so your majesty, having ventured to invade my territory, must pay the penalty. Deliver, or I will try whether royalty is invulnerable or not!"

Moonlight Jack's accents convinced the king that trifling with such a man would be extremely dangerous.

Therefore, with all the haste he could, he emptied his pockets and handed the contents to the robber.

There was a diamond ring, a purse well filled, a gold watch, and sundry trinkets of value.

"Now, my lord," said Moonlight Jack, "I must have your money and valuables."

"Sir," replied the secretary of state, "you ask so courteously that I should be almost ashamed to refuse, even if you had no pistol in your hand. There is my purse and my watch, not, perhaps, quite so valuable as his majesty's, but still worth something."

He held out the booty, which Moonlight Jack soon pocketed.

"One thing more," said he. "That is, I must trouble you to hand over any state papers, or despatches, or documents of any kind you have with you."

"That I refuse to do," replied Lord Townshend, firmly.

"I must compel you to do so, then," said the highwayman, presenting a pistol.

The peer flinched not, and the Jacobite robber could not but admire the chief secretary's courage.

He suddenly changed the direction of the weapon, and held its muzzle close to the king's head.

"Come, my royal brother," he said, "can you not persuade your minister to grant me the favour I ask?"

The monarch fairly shook in his shoes with the combined effects of fear for his life and indignity at being thus treated by a robber.

"The man's mad, the man's mad! Give him what he wants; let him have the papers."

"Do I understand your majesty rightly?" asked the minister.

"Yes, yes. Don't you see his pistol? He'll shoot! I shall be killed!"

And certainly the monarch's life hung by a very slender thread at that moment.

"Make haste, make haste, and let the man go," continued the king.

Thus adjured, the secretary of state drew from beneath the seat of the carriage a bag, which he placed in the highwayman's hands.

It was full of official papers, and Moonlight Jack clutched at it eagerly.

"I fear your majesty will repent this hasty step," said the minister, as he saw his dispatches in the hands of the highwayman.

"Shoot him! shoot him! Where are your pistols?" said the monarch.

Moonlight Jack was so engaged in stowing away his booty that he did not hear the whisper, nor did he see the weapon which Lord Townshend held in his hand.

"Does your majesty command me to take his life?" said the peer.

"Donner und blitzen! yes!"

"But your majesty——"

"Shoot him! kill him!"

The nobleman felt constrained to obey the imperious mandate of his royal master, yet he had some misgivings with regard to the prudence of such a proceeding.

Though only Moonlight Jack had as yet made his appearance, there was nothing to show that half-a-dozen other robbers were concealed behind that clump of trees.

The nobleman thought it most probable that the daring highwayman had some considerable force at his back, or he would never have undertaken such a daring expedition.

Such a thing as stopping the king on the highway had never before been heard of, and it afforded the minister an instance of the insecure tenure on which monarchs hold their lives.

Moonlight Jack was busily engaged in looking over the captured papers.

The king snatched the pistol from Lord Townshend's hand, and fired.

<hr/>

CHAPTER XI.

THE OPENING IN THE WALL—THE DUEL—THE ASSASSIN'S DOOM—THE LADY AND THE DISGUISED HUSBAND—THE SUBTERRANEAN PASSAGE—THE VAULT OF DEATH.

THE moment Lucien Fairleigh caught sight of the strange figure that appeared so mysteriously by his bedside he rolled away, and so avoided the dagger stroke aimed at him by the assassin.

Ere the unknown could recover his balance Lucien caught him by the shoulder and dragged him through the opening.

Then, springing from the bed, he clutched at the trusty sword which lay on a chair by his bedside.

"Villain!" he then exclaimed, facing the masked intruder, "why do you thus seek my life? How have I harmed you?"

The assassin dropped his knife, and, drawing his sword, made several furious passes in rapid succession at Lucien's breast.

But the young man had expected the assault, and parrying the thrusts, he returned the attack with such violence that their swords engaged at the hilts.

But immediately afterwards he recollected that such impetuosity would be dangerous, and, obtaining at once a mastery over both his weapon and temper, he continued the combat with perfect coolness.

The masked man took a step backwards.

"Ah! you give ground, my unknown friend," exclaimed Lucien.

"To give ground is not to fly," said the assassin, returning to the attack, "and is an axiom of the art of fencing which every one should study."

"Then practice it!" exclaimed Lucien, replying by a thrust in *seconde* to a straight thrust of his adversary.

Had not the masked man stepped back again with considerable abruptness, Lucien's weapon would have spitted him like a lark.

That part of the man's face not concealed by his mask turned pale with shame and fury, for Lucien's weapon had just touched him on the chest, though so lightly that he might have taken it for the button of a fencing foil.

His anger redoubled as the conviction asserted itself that Lucien was by far the best swordsman, and his attacks became more numerous and frequent than before.

He entertained a hope that he might be able to drive Lucien into a corner, where, having no room to wield his sword, his destruction would become more easy.

"Stop! stop!" said Lucien, parrying the numerous thrusts and becoming more cool as his foe became more exasperated. "Now you are going crazy with anger, and trying to blind me. Go and pick up your sword."

And as he spoke, with a sudden twist he whipped the assassin's weapon from his grasp, and sent it flying to the extreme end of the long apartment.

The man darted back just in time to avoid a blow that Lucien aimed at his head, and springing across the room regained his weapon.

"You shall die, though, in spite of this," he muttered between his teeth as he returned to the attack, though he at once assumed more coolness of demeanour which made him a more equal match for Lucien.

But still it was easy to see on which side the advantage would be.

The swords grated against each other as the combatants feinted, thrust, and parried, and Lucien, seeing that his enemy was determined to make the combat a mortal one, resolved to take advantage of the next error or neglect on the part of the assassin.

Nor was the opportunity long in coming.

A minute afterwards, and the man's foot slipped on the polished floor.

As he stumbled forward, Lucien's sword struck his breast, and passed through him.

He fell to the ground, breathed heavily, then murmured the words,

"—— the marchioness!"

Then he became motionless.

Lucien stood, sword in hand, for a few seconds gazing on his fallen foe.

"What demon instigated you to attempt my life?" he asked.

There was no reply.

Lucien remembered the last words uttered by the stranger, and bent down over the motionless form.

There was no sign of life, and with a movement he snatched the mask from the still features of his prostrate foe.

An exclamation of surprise burst from his lips, and throwing down his sword he knelt by the side of his late adversary.

It was the marquis whom, but a short time before, he had left sleeping on his voluptuous couch.

Lucien searched for the wound, which he found was a deep one, from which the blood flowed in a torrent.

He endeavoured to stanch the gore by bandaging it with towels, and such other articles as were at hand.

He succeeded, and then lifting the senseless body in his arms laid it on the bed which he had so recently quitted.

No signs of life were visible, and Lucien imagined that he had slain the man, whom, of all others, he least wished to injure, not from any feelings of love, but from a sense of honour.

He then hastily dressed himself, for during the combat he had only worn the one garment which every one is supposed to possess.

He then passed through the open panel by which the marquis had entered the room, taking with him one of the candles which had given light.

A long passage was before him terminating in a door.

On reaching this, Lucien gave a push, and found himself in a long, lofty room containing scarcely any furniture, except a table and two or three chairs.

Holding up the light Lucien surveyed the apartment.

There was no window or any outlet save the door by which he had entered, nor was there any chimney.

Lucien searched in vain for some means of communication with the other parts of the house, wishing to know by what means the marquis had gained admittance to his chamber.

There was no appearance of any door or staircase, and the whole affair seemed shrouded in mystery.

Who could have told the marquis of his presence in the house, or set him on to attempt the murder which the young nobleman had evidently meditated, was another mystery which required solution.

There was only one who could have directed the steps of the marquis to that blood-stained chamber, and that was the marchioness herself.

After what had passed between her and Lucien he deemed it scarcely possible that she could have instigated him to the deed.

Yet such was the case, though Lucien knew it not.

The marchioness, angry and indignant at Lucien's apparent weakness and cowardice in refusing to stab her sleeping husband, had devised a scheme by which she hoped to be rid of the lover, trusting to the future to rid her of the effeminate spouse.

The story in the Scriptures of the Egyptian woman bearing false witness against the Hebrew youth who resisted her blandishments recurred to the mind of the marchioness.

With a look of sorrow and anger well assumed on her face she sought the apartment in which her spouse slept.

A few words breathed in his ear caused the marquis to start up in a passion, and call for his sword.

Though weak and effeminate, the marquis was by no means a coward.

"Show me where is this villain," he cried, "who would dishonour me in my own house."

"Hush!" replied the marchioness. "He sleeps by this time."

"Give me my sword, that I may slay him as soon as my eyes meet his."

"Nay, take this dagger; I will lead you by a secret passage to his bedside; you can then strike without fear."

"Lead on, then," he exclaimed, and the marchioness forthwith ushered her husband into a long passage, from which various staircases ascended to the regions above.

Up one of these the marchioness led the way, followed by her spouse.

On reaching the top of the staircase all further progress seemed barred by a large flat stone above their heads, but the marchioness touched a spring concealed in the wall by their side, and immediately the secret door flew open, revealing to the eyes of the marquis another long passage.

The marchioness motioned her husband to enter, and then again led the way to the spot where the corridor apparently terminated in a stone wall.

Pointing to a slight discolouration in the stone, she said,

"Press your hand here, and you will find yourself by his bedside."

The marquis gazed on her a moment with an eye of suspicion.

"You are not playing me false?" he said.

"No," was the calm reply.

She then retired.

The marquis pressed the spring, a panel flew back, and before him he saw the recumbent figure of Lucien Fairleigh.

How Lucien awoke, and what transpired then, has already been related to the reader; but the marchioness did not wait for the end of the scene.

Returning in haste through the passage leading to Lucien's chamber, she passed through the trapdoor, and regained the staircase before mentioned.

Then, touching another spring, the trap-door resumed its position, and it was impossible for the marquis to retreat even had he been so disposed.

She then re-entered her own apartment, and waited for some time till she judged that blood had been shed, and that either her lover or her husband had fallen.

Which had perished mattered little to her, who intended and resolved that both should die.

After some time had elapsed she softly stole towards the chamber in which Lucien had retired to rest.

Through the key-hole she could plainly see on the bed the figure of a man.

This she imagined was Lucien. But what had become of her husband?

She softly opened the door, entered on tiptoe, and glided noiselessly towards the bed.

Her face flushed, and her bosom heaved with excitement as she discovered that it was her husband.

She gazed eagerly on the body of the motionless marquis. Could it be possible that he was dead, and, if so, where was Lucien, who had killed him?

To satisfy herself on the first point she felt his pulse.

The flesh seemed warm, and once or twice she fancied she felt a slight throbbing.

She then laid her hand upon his heart, and her suspicions were confirmed.

There was a very feeble and irregular beating, which showed that life was not altogether extinct.

A fiendish thought took possession of her soul as she gazed on the helpless and prostrate form of her husband.

She secured the door by a spring, and then returned once more to the bedside.

A hurried glance round the room, and then with a hand which trembled with eagerness, she tore off the bandages which Lucien had placed over the wound made by his sword.

A slight movement was the only sign that life was not extinct; and as the marchioness gazed on the stream of blood which issued from the re-opened wound, she felt convinced that the ensanguined tide must speedily and swiftly quench the remaining spark of vitality in his frame.

She was still gazing on with fiendish delight, when a slight noise caused her to lift her eyes.

Lucien Fairleigh was watching her with an air of astonishment.

For a moment the marchioness was perfectly speechless.

"So, madam," said Lucien, regarding her with a stern look, "this is a scheme of your contriving."

"Aye! why should I deny it?" she exclaimed, after a moment's hesitation. "I hated you both, and hoped that both would perish."

"Unhappy woman. What reason could you have to hate me?"

"You were a traitor—false to me and false to the cause you have sworn truth and fidelity to. Death is your fitting lot, and death I doubt not will sooner or later overtake you."

"I am no traitor," replied Lucien; "but even were I one, it would not be your office to judge or to execute. And now, if he dies, you will have the crime of murder on your soul. Madam, I wish you farewell."

With these words Lucien turned away and walked towards the door.

It was fastened; and being unacquainted with the secret spring, all his efforts to open it proved unavailing.

The marchioness laughed scornfully as she saw him thus thwarted in his purpose.

"You cannot leave without my permission," she said, "and that you may imagine I am little inclined to give you. Only on one condition will I forget the past and allow you to depart."

"Name your condition."

"Take your dagger, and with one blow put an end to the life of this bleeding though still breathing object."

"Never will I be guilty of such a crime. The wound he now bears was inflicted in fair combat sword to sword. I am no assassin, madam, or bravo, whose services can be hired by your smiles, nor will I stoop to such base murder as to strike an unarmed and wounded foe."

"Pretty well, indeed, for the companion of a robber to use such high-flown, big sounding words. You speak of honour and so forth as though no crime had ere casts its darkening influence on your soul. I hate scorn, and contemn such feeble-minded creatures as you, who, though they dare not dip their hands in blood, will not scruple to rob and maltreat a farmer or butcher travelling along the road."

A smile of contempt curled Lucien's lip.

"Your hatred, like your promises of love, has no power to move me to do that which my soul condemns. Once more, madam, adieu. If you refuse to allow me pass by that door I have no doubt I can find some other means of egress in this secret passage."

So saying, he once more entered the corridor by which the marquis had reached his chamber, and began to search the wall carefully for a spring which would open some secret door.

The marchioness remained bending over her husband, nor did she leave his side till every sign of life had vanished from his feeble frame.

Then, with a savage feeling of joy in her heart, she forced her way through the open panel in the wall, in search of Lucien.

After a long and tedious examination the young man noticed a slight projection in the wall of the corridor, and feeling certain that it was a spring connected with some secret door, he pressed the nob with all his force.

He was not mistaken.

A door flew open, and revealed to his eyes a large apartment of peculiar shape and appearance.

Lucien entered, and, at that moment, the marchioness caught sight of him.

Springing forward lightly and nimbly as a tiger, she hastily closed the door which fastened itself with a loud snap.

Lucien turned at the sound, but was too late to prevent the deed.

Cursing his own folly, he endeavoured to find some mode of getting out of the trap in which he had been caught, but without success.

There seemed to be no aperture save a small grating at the further end of the room, and all the light he had was that given by the candle he carried in his hand.

After a careful examination of the apartment he set his candle down on the table, and was about to throw himself on a rude couch which occupied one side of the room, when a slight noise attracted his attention.

It proceeded from the grating above-mentioned,

and once more taking the light in his hand he proceeded thither.

Nothing could he see, and he remained sword in hand for some seconds.

Then a voice spoke.

It was that of the Marchioness of London.

CHAPTER XII.

THE KING AND THE HIGHWAYMAN—A JOCULAR MEETING—THE FORCED PARDON—THE VISIT OF THE MARCHIONESS.

WHEN a man is taken by surprise he naturally does and says things which in more cool moments would remain undone and unsaid.

So was it with Moonlight Jack.

The sudden action of the Hanoverian king, and report of the pistol, for a moment confounded him.

He had no notion that the little man in the night cap could have mustered so much courage.

Yet there was the weapon still in the monarch's hand, with smoke still faintly issuing from its muzzle.

That was sufficient proof who was the author of the deed.

Moonlight Jack turned towards the king with a face full of anger in its expression, and drew one of his own weapons from his holsters.

He cocked it, and levelled the long glittering barrel at the monarch's head.

"What would become of England were the reigning sovereign to die suddenly?" he said.

"Oh! mein Gott, it is murter!" screamed the king, holding up his hands as though to ward off the bullet he expected each moment to feel.

The fingers of the King of the Road played nervously around and upon the trigger, while his dark eyes seemed to pierce the king's soul.

But he did not fire.

A thought struck him, which he resolved to put into execution.

He turned towards the secretary of state, and calmly said,

"You have writing materals with you, my lord, I presume?"

"I have," replied the peer.

"Then I will trouble you to write a few lines to my dictation."

"What will be the penalty should I refuse?"

Moonlight Jack shrugged his shoulders as he replied,

"Nothing very serious would happen; but perhaps you would not fare so well if ever you should again chance to fall into my hands."

The nobleman bowed, and drew from beneath the seat of the carriage a small desk.

"Proceed," he said, dipping his pen in the ink.

Moonlight Jack passed his hand thoughtfully over his brow, and then said,

"Write these words:—

"'We, George, King of Great Britain and Ireland, do hereby grant the bearer freedom from arrest for the space of six months after this date; and all constables, officers of the army, and bailiffs are hereby required to let him go free and unquestioned through all parts of our dominions. In witness whereof we have hereto affixed our sign manual.'"

The king sat motionless in the carriage whilst the highwayman dictated the words.

Moonlight Jack took the paper from the hands of the minister, and carefully read it through.

"Quite correct, my lord; you have performed your task well. Now," he continued, turning towards the king, "I must trouble your majesty to sign this."

The monarch naturally enough hesitated to write his name on such a document.

"Refuse," said Moonlight Jack, "and your son will wear your crown ere long."

"Donner und blitzen!" exclaimed the monarch, pushing back his night-cap to be able to scratch his head with greater freedom, "I can't sign dat paper."

"You recollect the French saying," cried the king of the road. "'The king is dead! long live the king!' That will be the case in England if you refuse to grant my request."

And again the pistol barrel approached the head of the Lord's anointed.

The king, with trembling fingers, dipped the pen in the ink, and in scrawling letters, wrote,

"George Rex."

"Thanks to your majesty. I must trouble you, my Lord Townshend, to affix your signature as witness to the veracity of this document."

The statesman, who began to feel amused at the robber's audacity, signed the paper, and handed it back to Moonlight Jack.

"Many thanks," said the latter, as he folded the document, and placed it in his pocket. "One more favour I have to ask. Write again."

Again the nobleman wrote while the highwayman dictated:—

"*The prisoner,——————, is pardoned for the offence for which he is now in custody, and you are hereby required forthwith and immediately to set him at liberty. And for so doing this shall be your warrant.*"

This, too, was signed by the king after some persuasion, backed by the fear of the highwayman's pistol.

Moonlight Jack placed both papers together, and then reined back his steed from the door of the carriage.

"I have no further petition to make at present," he said, raising his hat; "but where favours are granted so readily, I fear I shall be a constant applicant."

"I won't sign anoder, I won't!" screamed the king, whose rage at the highwayman's cool audacity knew no bounds.

"I have no doubt whatever that your majesty will be moved by my eloquence to grant whatever I ask," replied Moonlight Jack, again raising the pistol.

The monarch shrunk back in the most remote corner of the vehicle, and the bold robber continued,

"But, as before said, I have nothing more at present to ask of your majesty, and so I wish you good evening, and a safe journey to London."

He then set spurs to his horse, and was soon out of sight in the gathering gloom of the twilight.

The king and his minister, as soon as they could find their coachman again, set forward on their journey, which history reports they brought to a safe conclusion.

But Moonlight Jack had far to go and much to perform ere he conceived his task was executed in a proper manner.

His good steed bore him swiftly forward, nor did he draw rein till London was once more reached.

On arriving at the metropolis, he sought out a little inn near the Borough, where he was well known, and where he knew he could take a short rest in safety, while his horse recovered from the fatigue attendant on his long and important journey.

The rider paid every attention to the wants of

his horse, which he saw fed and stabled ere he attended to his own comforts.

The landlord nodded in a friendly and confidential manner, as the highwayman strode through his bar.

"I almost expected you," he said, "because the Bow Street fellers was here this afternoon."

"At what time?" said Moonlight Jack.

The landlord mentioned the hour, which was the same in which he had been employed in robbing the king.

It was impossible that they could have heard of that yet, and for any other charge he was well prepared with the freedom and pardon he had extorted from the monarch.

He remained for a few moments in thought.

"Have my horse saddled and in readiness in case of any disturbance," he said. "Once on his back, and I laugh at the scarlet-breasted slow coaches."

The host gave orders as desired by his guest, and the highwayman, after eating a hearty meal, stretched himself on a sofa, and slept.

He held a pistol in each hand, however, ready to start up at the slightest alarm.

The hours passed by, however, without any disturbance, and long before daybreak the King of the Road was once more in the saddle. He rode slowly over London Bridge, disregarding the suspicious looks which the watchmen cast at him; and then turning off to the right, passed at a rapid trot through Aldgate and Whitechapel.

He had gained the open country, and was far on his road ere the sun arose, and men began to creep forth to their daily labour.

He was on his way to Lord Disney with the despatches he had captured, in which the Jacobite nobleman's name was mentioned as a disaffected person, who should be watched and arrested on the slightest grounds.

Before the sun was high, or his brave steed showed signs of flagging, he had reached Lord Disney's mansion, and ascended to the nobleman's chamber.

"Welcome," said he, holding out his hand, which Moonlight Jack grasped. "You left me under such strange circumstances that I could not help feeling a little anxiety for your return. Have you had your interview with the king?"

"I have."

"Surely you are joking?"

"Not at all; and in, proof of the trust and confidence the Hanoverian prince reposes in me, he has surrendered to me these somewhat important state papers."

As he spoke he produced the despatches.

Lord Disney stared.

"Then you must have gone on your knees to some very influential courtier?"

"Not so. I presented myself on horseback, and pistol in hand before the monarch, who I fancy had never set eyes on a gentleman of the road ere I appeared before him. So well did I employ my time and my tongue that he not only gave up these papers but furthermore presented me with watch, purse and signet-ring as a proof of his esteem. See, here are the spoils of war."

And he laid on the table all the valuable trinkets of which he had deprived the king.

"This," he continued, taking up the ring, "will well grace my own finger, the others go to the treasury, which, Heaven knows, will need replenishing ere long."

"Wonderful man!" exclaimed Lord Disney, regarding him with a mixture of astonishment and approbation.

The two then applied themselves to the task of reading the papers on which Moonlight Jack had only bestowed a hasty glance.

Many important secrets with regard to the measures taken by the adherents of the reigning monarch to defeat the plans of the Jacobites did they discover, and amongst others was a letter of instructions to the military chief in command on the east coast relative to a cargo of arms and ammunition, and the means to be taken to prevent its being landed.

A smile broke over Lord Disney's countenance as he perused the document.

"They are too late!" he exclaimed. "These arms are, as you well know, concealed in my cellar. But," he continued, after a pause, "I should not be surprised were they to search my house."

"The stoppage of these papers will, at all events, delay anything of that kind for some hours, and during that time they can be concealed elsewhere."

"I know of no other hiding-place, and even if I did it would be dangerous to remove such things in the daylight while so many spies are in the neighbourhood."

"At all events, I can release you should you be arrested."

"I fear you over-rate your powers, though I know well your inclination to aid me should such a thing take place."

"I fancy I have the power as well as the will. See here."

And Moonlight Jack laid before his companion's eyes the two papers bearing the signatures of the king and his secretary of state, the Lord Townshend.

"One of these will protect me, while the other will free you."

He then gave a distinct account of his meeting with the king, and the manner in which he had extorted the documents from the trembling monarch.

Loud laughs at the expense of his Majesty George the First rang through the building, while Moonlight Jack became at once a hero of the very first degree in the eyes of the Jacobite proprietor of the mansion, who would have loudly applauded a robbery of St. James's palace while the German prince remained in it.

"But where is my comrade, Lucien?" asked Moonlight Jack, when he had recounted his adventures, "I expected to find him here."

"I have not seen him since you both left me," replied Lord Disney.

A darkly anxious look crossed the face of the King of the Road.

"I hope no evil has befallen him," he cried.

"If so, you have the prescription in your pocket which will set things right."

"The evil I speak of is not the king's evil, and is, therefore, beyond the scope of this royal prescription to cure. I must go and seek him."

"Shall I accompany you? My sword lacks employment."

The highwayman hesitated a moment.

"I think it would be best for me to go alone, though I heartily thank you for your friendly offer, my lord."

But little more was said, and, shortly after, Moonlight Jack once more mounted his steed.

He had left Lucien on his way to the marchioness, and it was to her house he turned his horse's head.

The woman's dark and imperious temper had struck him on more than one occasion, and he feared lest his friend should have incurred her resentment and revenge.

CHAPTER XIII.

THE CELL OF TORTURE.

LUCIEN FAIRLEIGH listened with some amount of anxiety to the voice that addressed him through the little grating.

It was the voice of the marchioness !

"Lucien Fairleigh," she said, in tones hoarse with passion, "you are now my prisoner, and it is impossible for you to free yourself without my consent. So listen to the only terms by which your life can be saved."

"I am all attention, madam," replied the young man.

He kept his hand on a pistol all the while he spoke, to be ready for any sudden act of aggression from without.

"You must swear on the Bible, and whatever else in this world you hold sacred, never to reveal what has taken place this night. Should the death of my husband become known by any unforeseen accident you must take upon yourself all the odium and responsibility ; and, furthermore, you must swear unutterable fidelity and truth to me !"

"These are hard terms, madam."

"They are the only ones I will grant."

" And if I refuse ?"

"Death, which you richly deserve, will be your portion ! Escape, without my permission, is impossible."

"Death ? But recollect, madam, I am well-armed and desperate. Should any of your minions enter the room to attack me it would be strange if I could not hew my way through them."

"Death I have sworn to you, unless you swear to what I propose ; nor will I retract my words. Choose your fate, and quickly, too !"

"To die is hard to one so young and so full of hope," said Lucien, musingly ; "but life is worthless when rusting, corroding dishonour and shame has wormed its way into the soul. Madam, I will not agree to the terms you propose. I defy you ; do your worst !"

"Is this your decision ? For the last time I ask !"

"It is."

"Reflect."

"I have done so, and prefer death to open shame and dishonour."

"Then, false traitor, take your fate ! You may now sue in vain for pardon and for freedom ; your doom is sealed ; these walls shall be your tomb, and on that floor shall rats gnaw the flesh from your bones, unless they are too dainty to fix their sharp teeth in your perfidious carcase. Now, farewell, Lucien Fairleigh, and remember, as death slowly lays his cold hand on your vitals, that you brought down your own fate upon your head !"

The voice ceased, and Lucien was once more alone.

The marchioness was in such an angry mood that Lucien, knowing her inflexible disposition, felt well assured that if he escaped at all it must be by trusting to his own energy and resources.

By the light of the candle he examined the room, which he found was of an oblong shape.

The floor was of stone, but on testing the walls he found at once that they were composed of iron or some other metal.

The door by which he had entered could scarcely be discerned, though after some search he discovered it in the centre of the narrowest end of the apartment.

But there seemed to be no spring on the inside, and after an hour's fruitless search he was compelled to abandon that scheme, and trust to his ready wit and youthful strength to devise some other method of escape.

He lay down on the floor, and drawing his clothes closely round him for warmth, was soon asleep.

For some time all was silent as the tomb.

At length a large clock with solemn tone struck the midnight hour, and the sound vibrated slowly through Lucien's strange apartment.

Then followed a grating sliding noise, and Lucien imagined that he felt the floor of his dungeon tremble during the time that it continued.

Then again in a few minutes all was silent, and Lucien once more slept, despite all the excitement attending his strange situation, nor did he awake till a pale ray of light gleaming through the above-mentioned grating proclaimed that it was day.

The candle had burnt out, and the feeble glimmer through the orifice was hardly sufficient to allow him to see across the whole width and length of the chamber.

He rose to his feet, and walked towards the opening, feeling that even that little spot in the midst of the darkness was a slight consolation.

On reaching the wall his foot struck against something, and stooping down he discovered a loaf of bread, and a stone pitcher of water.

The sight of food and drink brought feelings of hunger to his stomach, yet for some time he hesitated to taste.

The vindictive marchioness he thought might have placed poisoned food there in order to destroy him.

At length, however, the cravings of nature were so powerful that he could not refrain from eating, and after the first mouthful swallowed had taken away the fear of poison he made a hearty meal, despite the coarseness of the materials.

Then, to warm his blood, which was somewhat chilled by the night's sojourn on the cold stones, he walked briskly up and down the length of the apartment.

Suddenly a thought struck him, and he started with surprise.

The room did not seem so long as it had appeared when he first entered it.

After a moment's reflection, however, he smiled at the absurdity of the idea, and attributed it to the constant whirl and excitement in which his brain had been for some hours past.

However, out of curiosity, he resolved to take the dimensions of his apartment, and proceeded slowly to pace the whole length of the floor.

It seemed to be eighteen feet long, and about ten wide.

Its height he was unable to determine, the roof being far above his head.

As to the floor, however, there seemed no doubt.

He resolved to wait another day.

The light waned.

Night again invaded his cell.

Utter darkness prevailed.

It was useless to keep awake to watch the walls, for he could see nothing.

So he sought comfort and forgetfulness in slumber.

Like all men who have accustomed themselves to sleep in the face of danger—in the beleaguered camp, on the eve of battle—Lucien slept soundly.

When he woke, the rays of morning were pouring into the cell.

He at once sprang up.

Suspense was worse than reality.

Without waiting to gather courage for his task, he once more measured his cell.

It had lessened in length and breadth two feet !

MOONLIGHT JACK

OR THE KING OF THE ROAD

GRACE DASHWOOD.

"Cursed woman! hideous monster!" he murmured; "her lustful passion was my ruin. This is a punishment upon me for forgetting my own dear Grace."

The marchioness had resolved that nothing should be wanting to enhance the terrors of his prison.

He was not to be left to faint and die of starvation.

In this case the horrors of his position would have been unrealisable.

As it was he was preserved in his full health and faculties, and able, therefore, to comprehend the extent of his peril.

Food was brought to him as usual.

The day again waned.

A long, weary day.

A day that seemed a week.

Night came once more.

The dusky twilight deepened into darkness at eight.

No. 15.—April 14, 1866.]   *Two Numbers and Two Tales, every Week, for One Penny.*—THE WORK GIRLS OF LONDON, *and* THE CRUSADER; OR, THE WITCH OF FINCHLEY.   [Price One Penny.

At nine Lucien laid down to rest.

But not to sleep.

Scarcely had he composed himself, when loud noises were heard in the castle.

Shouts, and deep curses, and the clashing of swords.

Lucien listened eagerly.

How he longed to be among them.

Presently he heard a well-known voice.

The voice of Moonlight Jack.

He was urging his men on to the search.

Even by Lucien, in his cell, it was easy to perceive that Jack Tyrrell, as usual, was on the winning side.

Hither and thither flowed the tide of combat.

Now here, now there the clash of steel resounded.

Now it approached Lucien's cell.

But though he shouted aloud, it again receded.

Presently, however, there was a rush towards the door.

His heart beat wildly.

"This way, my friends!" he shouted.

There was a confused murmur, then the turning of a key in the lock, and Moonlight Jack rushed in. followed by Hardman, and several others.

For a moment Lucien grasped his friend's hand in silence.

Their hearts were too full for utterance.

At length Jack Tyrrell said,

"Well, Lucien, my friend, you see I do not desert you."

"I never thought you would, Jack; but in this gloomy dungeon I confess I had abandoned hope."

"I do not doubt it; but I was resolved to ferret you out."

"What made you suspect this place?"

"I had an interview with the marchioness. From her manner I suspected that all was not right."

"Where is she?"

"She has fled. I should have killed her had she not confessed where you were concealed. But come, Lucien, there is much to do, and in a few minutes this place will be too hot to hold us."

"Is the place, then, on fire?"

"Aye, in a dozen parts. Come."

In a few moments Lucien once more breathed the air of liberty.

"Now," said Jack, "we have to proceed to London. My men have their instructions; you and I when we have redressed ourselves have to meet a certain noble person at the house of a beautiful lady—the Lady Louisa Annesley. *The king*," he added, in a low voice, "*is in London*. Brandon knows it and will endeavour to betray us, but it will be of no avail. Right against might, Lucien, is our motto, and Heaven defend our king!"

And so, enthusiastic in their loyalty—the most mistaken feeling a man's heart can experience, for what have king's been, as a rule, but men a little worse than others—the two men spurred onwards.

CHAPTER XIV.

THE JACOBITE PLOT—THE MAN IN THE CLOAK—THE COALHEAVER AND THE MYSTERIOUS SINGER—THE CONSPIRATORS—THE ROYAL BET—THE FLIGHT OVER THE HOUSETOPS—THE ATTACK—THE ESCAPE—LADY ANNESLEY—THE CONFERENCE—BRANDON AND THE MARCHIONESS.

THE evening of the next day, which was Tuesday, towards eight o'clock, at the moment when a considerable group of men and women assembled round a street singer who was playing at the same time the cymbals with his knees and the tambourine with his hands, obstructed the entrance to Turner Street, a cuirassier and two of the light horse descended a back staircase of the grand hotel, and advanced towards Dragon's Passage, which, as every one knows, opened upon that street.

Seeing, however, the crowd which barred the way, the three soldiers stopped and appeared to take counsel.

The result of their deliberations was soon evident.

The cuirassier turned another way and walked very rapidly, made for Royal Street, where, arriving at No. 22, the door opened as if by enchantment and closed behind him and his companions.

At the moment when they commenced this little detour a man dressed in a dark coat, wrapped in a mantle of the same colour, and wearing a broad-brimmed hat pulled down over his eyes, quitted the group which surrounded the singer and arrived at the further end of the passage in time to see the three illustrious vagabonds enter the house as I have said.

He threw a glance around him, and, by the light of the three lanterns which lighted, or, rather, ought to have lighted, the whole length of the street, he perceived one of those immense coalheavers whom we see often, sooty-faced and broad-shouldered, resting against a post, while his bag hung on railings near him.

For an instant he appeared to hesitate to approach him.

The coalheaver saw this, and began humming the same tune as the street singer.

The man in the cloak then lost all hesitation and went up to him.

"Well, friend," said he to the coalheaver, "did you see them?"

"Yes, captain, as plainly as I see you; a cuirassier and two light horse. The cuirassier, as he hid his face in his handkerchief, was, I presume, his deposed majesty, King James?"

"Yes; and the two light horse were Lucien Fairleigh and Moonlight Jack, those two arch knaves of the road!"

"Ah!" said the coalheaver, "I shall be glad to meet him again."

"Be careful he does not recognise you."

"Not he; the devil himself wouldn't recognise me, dressed as I am. It is you, Captain Brandon, who should take the caution. You have an unfortunately aristocratic air which does not suit at all with your dress. However, they are in the trap, and we must take care they don't leave it. Have our people been told?"

"I know no more than you. You must remember I am incognito in this enterprise. I quitted the group singing the song, which was our signal. Did they hear me? Did they understand me? I know nothing of it."

"Be easy, captain; these fellows hear half a voice and understand half a word."

Indeed, as soon as Brandon left the group, a strange fermentation which he had not foreseen took place in the crowd, which appeared to be composed only of passers-by, so that the song was not finished nor the collection received.

The throng dispersed.

A great many men left the circle singly or two and two, turning towards each other with an imperceptible gesture of the hand.

Some went one way some went another; but, at any rate, they so disposed themselves that No. 22, Royal Street, was surrounded.

In consequence of this manœuvre, the intention of which it is easy to understand, there only remained before the singer ten or twelve women and some children, and one man, who, seeing that the collection was about to commence, walked hastily away and disappeared.

Almost at the same moment the man in the cloak, who had been the first to leave the group, now reappeared and accosted the singer.

"My friend," he said, "my wife is ill, and your music prevents her sleeping. Pass away a street or two, and here is a crown to indemnify you."

"Thank you, my lord," said the singer, reckoning the giver's rank by his generosity, "I will go directly."

The man then went away, and the few last hangers-on went with him.

At this moment St. Paul's struck nine.

Brandon drew from his pocket a watch, whose diamond setting was strangely in contrast with his simple costume.

He set it exactly and then turned towards Royal Street.

On arriving opposite No. 24 he found the coalheaver.

"The singer—where is he?" asked the latter.

"He is gone."

"Good!"

"And the post-chaise?" asked Brandon.

"Is waiting at the corner of the next street."

"Have you taken the precaution of wrapping the wheels and horses' hoofs in rags?"

"Yes."

"Good. Then let us wait."

"Let us wait, then," said the coalheaver.

An hour passed.

An hour of silence.

Few persons passed.

At that hour the street was almost deserted.

The few lighted windows were darkened one after another.

Night had now nothing to contend with but the two lanterns.

Presently they heard the watch in Turner Street.

Then the keeper of Dragon Passage came to close the door.

"Good," murmured Brandon; "now we are sure not to be interrupted."

"Provided," replied the coalheaver, "he leaves before day."

"If his Jacobite Majesty were alone we might fear his remaining, but the fair conspirator, Lady Louisa Annesley will scarcely keep all three."

"Faith! you are right, captain, and I had not thought of it!"

"Are all your precautions taken?"

"All."

"And your men believe it is a question of a bet?"

"Yes; I have made them understand so. Even though the king will be delighted at our service you desire not to risk using his authority. Such I understood to be your words?"

"Yes."

"Then all is ready."

Brandon clapped him on the shoulder.

"You have done well, my friend," he said. "Now understand. You and your people are drunk. You push me. I fall between King James and him who has his arm. I separate them. You seize on him and gag him, and at a whistle the carriage arrives."

"And Moonlight Jack and Lucien?"

"They are held with pistols to their throats!"

"But," said the coalheaver, in a low voice, "if he declares his name?"

Brandon replied in still lower tones,

"In conspiracies there are no half measures. If he declares himself you must kill him."

"By my faith," said the coalheaver, "let us try to prevent his doing so."

There was no reply, and all was again silent.

A quarter of an hour passed.

Then the centre windows were lighted up.

"Ah! there is something new!" they both exclaimed together.

The two men drew back as far as possible into the shade.

Then the window was opened, and one of the light horse appeared on the balcony.

"Well," said a voice from the interior of the room, which the coalheaver and his companion recognised as that of James II., "well, Lucien, what kind of weather is it?"

"Oh!" said Lucien, "I think it snows!"

"You think it snows?"

"Or rains, I do not know which."

"What," said Moonlight Jack, "can you not tell what is falling?"

Then he also came on to the balcony.

"After all," said Lucien, "I am not sure that anything is falling."

"He is dead drunk," said the king.

"Dead drunk!" said Lucien. "No, your majesty. Come here, sire."

Though the invitation was given in a strange manner the king joined his companions, laughing.

By his gait it was easy to see that he himself was more than warmed.

"Are you sure there is danger?" whispered Moonlight Jack, as the ex-king approached.

"Yes, yes," returned Lucien, in a perfectly sober voice, "I must keep up my character to save him."

Then assuming his intoxication once more, he hurried to James II.

"Ah! dead drunk, your majesty, as I thought. Now, king of England, as you may be, I'll bet your majesty a hundred pounds you will not do as I do."

"You hear, your majesty," said the voice of Lady Annesley, "it is a challenge."

"And as such I accept it."

"Done, then, for a hundred pounds."

"I go halves with whoever likes," said Moonlight Jack.

"Bet with her ladyship, then," said Lucien, "I admit no one into my game."

"Nor I," said the ex-king.

"Lady Annesley," cried Tyrrell, "fifty pounds to a kiss."

"Ask his majesty if he permits."

"Yes; it is a golden bargain—you are sure to win. Well, are you ready, Tyrrell?"

"I am. Will you follow me?"

"Everywhere."

"What are you going to do?"

"Look!"

"Where the devil are you going?"

"I am going to the Royal Hotel."

"But how—how?"

"By the roofs!"

Lucien then seized a kind of fan which separated the windows of the drawing room from that of the bed-rooms, and began to climb like an ape.

"My king," cried Lady Annesley, bounding upon the balcony, and seizing James II. by the arm, "for the love of Heaven do not follow!"

"Not follow?" cried James, freeing himself from the lady's grasp. "Do you know that I hold as a principle, that what another man tries I can do? If he were to go up to the moon, devil take me, if I would not be there to knock at the door as soon as he. Did you bet on me, Tyrrell?"

"Yes, my prince," replied the young man, laughing.

"Then take your kiss, you have won," and the king seized the iron bars, climbing behind Lucien, who, active, tall, and slender, was in an instant on the terrace.

"But I hope you, at least, will remain, Mr. Tyrrell," said Lady Annesley.

"Long enough to claim your stakes," said the young highwayman.

Then he leaned forward and kissed the beautiful fresh lips of Lady Louisa.

"Now adieu," he added, "I am of the king's bodyguard, and you understand that I must follow him."

Then Tyrrell started on the perilous road already taken by his companions.

The coalheaver and the man in the cloak uttered an exclamation of astonishment, which was repeated along the street as if every door had an echo.

"Ah! what is that?" said Lucien, who had arrived first on the terrace.

"Do you see double, drunkard?" said the king? "It is the watch, and we shall all get taken to the guard house. Our enterprise will then be ruined."

At these words, those who were in the street were silent, hoping that the ex-king and his companions would push the joke no further, but would come down and go out the ordinary road.

"Oh! here I am," said the king, landing on the terrace; "have you had enough, Fairleigh?"

"No, your majesty."

Then bending down, he whispered to Moonlight Jack,

"That is not the watch—that is a conspiracy."

"What is the matter?" asked the king.

"Nothing," replied Lucien, making a sign to Jack, "except that I continue my ascent and invite you to follow me."

At these words, holding out his hand to the king, he began to scale the roof, drawing him after him.

Jack brought up the rear.

At this sight, as there was no longer any doubt of their intention, the coalheaver uttered a malediction, and the man in the cloak a cry of rage.

"Ah, ah!" cried James, striding on the roof, and looking down the street, where, by the light from the open window, they saw eight or ten men moving, "what the devil is that—a plot? Ah, one would suppose they wanted to scale the house. They are furious; I have a mind to ask them what we can do to help them."

"No joking, sire," said Lucien. "Let us go on."

"Turn by the next street," said the man in the cloak. "Forward! forward!"

"They are pursuing us," said Lucien. "Quick! to the other back."

"I don't know what prevents me," said Brandon, drawing a pistol from his belt, and aiming it at the king, "from bringing him down like a partridge."

"Thousand furies, captain!" cried the coalheaver, stopping him; "you will get us all hung!"

"But what are we to do?"

"Wait till they come down alone and break their necks, for, if providence is just, that little surprise awaits us."

"What an idea, Darley!"

"Hush, captain; no names."

"You are right; follow me," cried Brandon, springing into the passage. "Let us break open the door, and we will take them on the other side, when they jump down."

All that remained of his companions followed him.

The others, to the number of five or six, were already going round by another way.

"Let us go on, sire," cried Lucien; "we have not a minute to lose. Slide on your back. It is not glorious, but it is safe."

"I think I hear them in the passage," said the king. "What do you think, Tyrrell?"

"I do not think at all," cried Moonlight Jack. "I let myself slip."

All three descended rapidly, and arrived on the terrace.

"Here, here," said a woman's voice, at the moment when Lucien strode over the parapet to descend his iron ladder.

"Ah, is it you, marchioness?" said the king. "You are indeed a friend in need."

"Jump in here, and quickly."

The three fugitives sprang into the room.

"Will you stop here?"

"No," said James II.; "they will be attacking your house, and treating it as a town taken by assault presently. Let us gain the river; we can do so by your garden."

They descended the staircase rapidly, and opened the garden door.

There they heard the blows of their pursuers against the iron gates.

"Strike, strike, my friends," said the king, running with the carelessness and activity of a young man. "The gate is solid, and will give you plenty of work."

"Quick! quick, sire!" cried Lucien, when they arrived at the other end. "I have the key; rush through!"

In another moment all three were on the other side.

"You are saved, my king!" cried Jack Tyrrell, as the huge spring lock shot into its place when the door clanged to.

"Draw your sword, Fairleigh, and let us wait for these fellows."

"In the name of Heaven," cried Moonlight Jack, "follow us! I am not a coward, but what you would do is mere folly. Come, sire."

The two young men led the king to the water's edge, and they were already in a boat, pushing off, when their pursuers battered against the garden gate.

"This man must have a compact with Satan," said Brandon.

"We have lost the bet," said Darley, addressing the men, who stood waiting for orders. "But we do not dismiss you yet; the affair is only postponed. As to the promised sum, you have already had half; to-morrow, you know, for the rest. Good evening. I shall be punctually at the rendezvous."

All the people dispersed.

The two chiefs remained alone.

"Well, Captain Brandon," said Darley, looking him in the face.

"Well," said Brandon, "I have a great mind to ask you a favour."

"What?" asked Darley.

"To follow me into some cross road, and blow my brains out with your pistol."

Darley laughed.

"Why so?" he said.

"Why? In such matters when one fails one is but a fool."

"Then in this, captain, I refuse to obey. I rarely do refuse; but in this I do. But see—what is that? The lanterns of the watch! Amicable institution. I recognise you there. Always a quarter of an hour too late; but now adieu, captain," he continued. "There is your road—we must separate," showing the passage. "And here is mine," pointing in an opposite direction. "Go quietly."

Then Darley passed away at the same pace as the watch, who were a hundred paces behind him, singing carelessly as he went.

As to Brandon, he went on through the passage, now as quiet as it had been noisy ten minutes before.

At the corner of Turner Street he found the carriage of which he had spoken.

According to orders it had not moved.

Through all the long interval it had waited with the door open, the servant at the step, and the coachman on his box.

"To the king's palace," said Brandon.

"It is useless," said a voice, which made him start. "I know all that has passed, and I will inform those who ought to know. A visit at this hour would be dangerous to all."

Brandon, as the voice spoke, had turned round.

Despite the male attire which the speaker wore, he recognised the marchioness—the treacherous woman who had pretended to be a friend to King James II.

Any one could have seen that the speaker was a woman.

The dress, however masculine, could not disguise the swelling hips, the soft outlines of the rounded legs, the swell of the splendid bosom which had seduced Lucien Fairleigh from his fidelity.

"Is it indeed you, my lady?" cried Brandon, still almost doubting his senses.

"Yes, it is I. Enter the carriage. I will accompany you, and at the corner of the Palace Yard you can drop me."

"To Whitehall," cried Brandon, as he sprang in after the marchioness.

The coachman, impatient at having waited so long, obeyed quickly.

"Brandon," said the lady, laying her soft hand upon his, "though you have failed *this* time fear not. You will succeed next."

Brandon answered gloomily.

"I am always unfortunate," he said. "Fate seems against me. I shall fail again, and the reward I was promised—where will that be?"

"It shall still be yours," murmured the marchioness, leaning forward and pressing her lips to his, clasping him so tightly to her that her warm breasts palpitated against his bosom.

Brandon returned her caresses eagerly.

His gloom quickly dispersed as he pressed to him her soft and glowing form, and pressed again and again hot kisses on her eager mouth.

At the place indicated the carriage stopped.

Here the marchioness got out, and soon disappeared in the dark night.

As to the coach with the padded wheels, it rolled on noiselessly towards the Cross at Charing like a fairy car that does not touch the earth.

CHAPTER XV.

DREAMS OF LOVE—A RUDE SURPRISE — THE COMMISSION—THE CONSULTATION—AN ABRUPT BREAK IN THE SUNLIGHT.

BRANDON, after having placed his hat and cloak on a chair, his pistols on the table, and his sword under his pillow, threw himself dressed upon the bed and dreamed pleasant dreams.

Dreamed of the marchioness with whom on the next evening he had an assignation—one not of business but of love.

When he awoke it was broad daylight.

As the evening before he had forgotten to close his shutters, the first thing he saw was a ray of sunshine playing joyously across the room.

He had hardly time to rub his eyes when a knock was heard at the door.

"Who is there?" asked Brandon, in a voice of emotion.

"A friend," answered the voice.

He knew it well.

It was the voice of Lord Gilbert Clifton, an intimate of Royalty, through whom the marchioness had described to King George the events of the preceding evening.

He at once opened the door.

"What is the matter?" cried Lord Clifton, smiling with pleasant malice. "What has happened that you are shut in with bolts and bars? Is it a foretaste of the Tower?"

"No such jokes," exclaimed Brandon, "I beg of you, my lord. They might bring misfortune."

"But look! look!" said Clifton, casting his eyes round him, "would not any one guess you were a conspirator? Pistols on the table, a sword on the pillow, and a hat and cloak on the chair! But, come, I bring you news."

"As to last night's work?"

"All has gone well. The noise of that *private brawl* is silent now. The king *from over the water*, dreaming last night that he was King of England, has already forgotten that he was nearly the prisoner of a highwayman. Now, so are my orders, we must begin work at once again."

"Pardon, my lord," said Brandon; "but, with your permission, it is some one else's turn; I shall not be sorry to rest a little myself."

"That suits ill with the news I bring you. It was decided last night that you should leave for the coast this morning."

"For the coast?"

"Yes."

"What to do there?"

"You will know when you are there."

"And if I don't wish to go?"

"You will reflect and go just the same."

"On what shall I reflect?"

"That it would be the act of a madman to interrupt an enterprise near its end for the love of one whose love will keep; to abandon the interests of an empire to gain the good graces of a very frail marchioness."

"My lord!" cried Brandon, deprecatingly.

"Oh! we must not get angry, my dear Brandon, we must reason. You engaged voluntarily in the affair we have in hand, and promised to aid us in it. You know how much better it would be for our cause if we were to crush this embryo rebellion without coming to a battle. Would it be loyal to abandon us now? No, no, my friend, you must have a little more connection in your ideas if you mix in a conspiracy."

"It is just because I *have* connection in my ideas," replied Brandon, "that this time, before undertaking anything new, I wish to know what it is."

"I doubt the connection!"

"Well, I offered myself to be the arm, it is true; but before striking the arm must know what the head has decided."

"True!"

"I risk my liberty, I risk my life. I will risk them still, with my eyes opened—not closed. Tell me first what I am to do on the coast, and then, perhaps, I will go there."

"Your orders are that you should go to Truebridge on the Essex coast. There you will unseal this letter and find your instructions."

"My orders! my instructions!"

"Are not these the terms which a general uses to his officers? and are they in the habit of disputing the commands they receive?"

"Not when they are in the service. You forget I am in it no longer. The king's ministers took from me my commission, and drove me out upon the world."

"It is true; you were not in the service. I forgot to tell you that you had re-entered it. Yes, you. I have your brevet in my pocket."

As he spoke Lord Clifton drew from his pocket a parchment, which he presented to Brandon, who unfolded it slowly.

"A commission!" cried he. "A commission as a colonel in the Light Dragoons! Whence comes it?"

"Look at the signature."

Brandon looked.

"It is the king's!" he cried.

"Well, is there anything astonishing in that? He gives you one to replace that which was taken from you, and, as your king and commander, he sends you on a mission. Is it customary for soldiers to disobey their chief?"

"No, by no means. Shall I see the king and thank him?"

"No, there is no necessity."

"When must I start?"

"This instant."

"You will give me half an hour?"

"Not a second."

"But I have not breakfasted."

"You shall breakfast with me."

"I have no money."

"You will find a year's pay in your saddle-bag."

"And clothes?"

"Your men will carry plenty."

"At least tell me when I may return."

"In six weeks to a day the king will expect you."

"At least you will permit me to write a couple of lines?"

"Certainly. To refuse would be too exacting."

The newly-made colonel sat down and wrote:

"My dear Marchioness,—I am forced by the king's orders to leave this instant without seeing you—without bidding you adieu. I shall be six weeks absent, and on my return will claim my reward.

"BRANDON."

This letter written and folded, Brandon was ready.

He put his pistols in his pocket, fastened on his sword, took his hat and cloak, and followed Lord Clifton.

When they had breakfasted at Clifton's splendid house, a saddled horse was led into the court-yard, followed by two hundred and fifty dragoons, whose bright uniforms flashed in the noonday sun.

"See, there is one party of your men—another follows," said Lord Clifton.

"In command of whom?"

"In command of Sir Percy Delaine."

Brandon started, and a flush overspread his usually pallid features.

"Do you know him?" asked Lord Clifton.

Brandon quickly recovered his composure.

"Yes," he said, "we were once good friends."

"I trust you will renew your friendship then," said Clifton; "yours is a service which should unite all hearts."

"True," said Brandon, "I trust you are right."

Nevertheless, as he rode out of the court-yard, he muttered to himself,

"Ah! Sir Percy Delaine!—we shall meet in the field. You cannot escape me there!"

As the cavalcade neared Shore Ditch, a boy who had for some time been loitering about, shouted and waved his hand to Brandon.

It was Jonathan Rasper.

Brandon at once stopped and beckoned him to approach.

Young Rasper came forward eagerly.

"My lord," he said, "are you leaving London a prisoner?"

Brandon smiled.

"No, boy; but as commander of these men. Do you know the 'Nailer's Arms?'"

"Yes."

"You know Darley well?"

"Yes, my lord."

"Go thither then and tell him to accompany you to-night to Deerfoot Rise. I shall stop there to-night and camp. Bid him be there by midnight. Here is money to assist you."

He unbuttoned his saddle-bags and took out two guineas.

There were gold coins as well as notes in them.

Jonathan clutched the gold eagerly.

"I will do your bidding, my lord," he said, "fear not. We shall be there before midnight."

He then darted away.

"Treacherous offspring of a treacherous father," muttered Brandon as he moved away, "think not I will trust thee *too* much. Deadly as is my purpose, I shall use you but as a vile instrument. Ah, Ella! when you yielded yourself to the arms of another, you little thought how fearful would be the doom of the husband who, after three trials, you have succeeded in saving."

On the next night Sir Percy Delaine followed with *his* men.

Little did he think upon whose treacherous track he was following, or the *doom* which was held in store for him.

CHAPTER XVI.

MR. RICHARDSON, THE MERCHANT OF CHEAPSIDE — CREDULITY AND SENTIMENT — THE FRENCH NOBLEMEN—THE NIGHT AT RANELAGH—THE FLIGHT OF THE TWO GIRLS—THE ATTACK BY THE POLICE—THE ESCAPE OF THE THIEVES—THE OLD JEW—THE SLEEPING BEAUTIES—THE DARING LOVERS — THE OLD HOUSE AT EDGWARE — THE MARRIAGE INTERRUPTED — HOW LUCIEN RESTORED THE TWENTY POUNDS.

THOSE of our readers who have carefully followed the thread of our story from the first will remember Mr. Richardson, the merchant whom Lucien Fairleigh robbed on the highway, and to whom he presented a ring as a token in the future.

Mr. Richardson had, at the time we again introduce him, two persons staying in his house—a Count de Tourville, and the Chevalier Horace de Beaufort.

He had had excellent letters of recommendation with them from Paris, and he had not only given them all necessary funds, but had asked them to remain at his house.

They had made themselves very agreeable, and had expressed the most ardent admiration for Rosalie and Stephanie, the two daughters of the retired Hamburgh merchant, and on the morning when we introduce them to our readers, they were in Mr. Richardson's drawing-room with the ladies, dressed in the extreme of fashion, though, to one accustomed to society, somewhat awkward in their manners.

These two worthies were no other than Captain Maclean and Peter Rose, two of the most blood-thirsty and vile characters in the band which the death of Gordon had aided in dispersing.

"Let me have a cheque for a hundred pounds, if you please, Mr. Richardson," said Maclean, on this eventful morning, after he and his friend had passed the usual courtesies.

Richardson opened his pocket-book, and taking out a note, presented it to Maclean, who expressed his thanks.

"I am much obliged to you," he said. Then, turning to Mrs. Richardson, "Well, ladies, do you intend to honour the Ranelagh Gardens with your presence this evening? They tell me the *fête* will be most superb."

"I should so like to go," said Rosalie, "but cruel mama won't allow me."

"Isn't it cruel of her?" said Stephanie. "She won't let us leave home."

"Shocking!" said Maclean. "Pray, madam, allow me to intercede for the young ladies. What objection can you have to their enjoying themselves in so harmless and innocent a manner?"

"You don't understand me, my dear count. I should be very sorry to deprive them of any amusement which is consistent with propriety; but the fact is, we have no gentlemen to escort us, as Mr. Richardson will be compelled to go somewhere on most important business this evening, and of course people would say that it was not correct, nor would it be proper for two such angelic girls as mine to be seen at such a place without a gentle-man to protect them. You know, count, young men will be young men, and I couldn't answer for the consequences."

"Quite right, madam; I like your spirit. But are there no other cavaliers to be found?"

"I don't know where to find any that suit my fancy."

Mrs. Richardson said this pointedly, as though she expected the count to offer his services.

Nor was she disappointed.

"Let's go with the girls, and have a jolly lark!" he whispered to his friend.

"All right," was the response.

"If I might venture," said Maclean, "on so short an acquaintance, to offer the services and company of myself and my illustrious friend, we should feel extremely happy and honoured."

He said this with a most magnificent bow.

Mrs. Richardson smirked most condescendingly and blushingly.

"We should feel most highly honoured by your kindness," she said. "Both myself and my daughters will consider your company a pleasure and a con-descension."

To the Ranelagh Gardens they went.

The gardens looked infinitely beautiful.

The weather was extremely fine, and the lights were dazzling, bright and frequent.

The visitors poured in as abundantly as the pro-prietors would have desired in their most avaricious moments, and ere our two thieves and their com-panions reached the place of pleasure, there was the usual array of bright eyes, laughing lips, and gleaming shoulders, with the usual accompaniment of tall cavaliers, with fierce moustaches and brilliant clothes.

Mrs. Richardson was rather oddly garbed, but

with the two daughters no one could have found fault.

They were attired with that modest simplicity which makes women, in ball-rooms, look so infinitely attractive.

They were dressed alike, in pure white; their robes being very low in front, so as to display the bosom, the only ornament being a red rose placed between the breasts.

Their eyes sparkled with pleasure, their very forms seemed impregnated with it, and as they moved about the grounds, leaning upon the arms of their cavaliers, they seemed the perfect pictures of innocence.

"'Pon my life this is like fairy-land! The most superb fête I ever have assisted at!" cried Maclean, as he lounged along, eyeing the dancers through an opera-glass. "Even at the Court I have seen nothing to surpass it."

"It's really quite *magnanimous!*" said Peter Rose. "Quite superior to anything *I* have ever seen in any court, *except the Judge's face when he sentenced us to the noose!*"

Maclean eyed him fiercely.

"Madman!" he whispered, in slang language. "Are you at your foolish tricks again?"

"As you say," returned Peter Rose, "it is mag-nificent. I feel quite *dérangé, distrait,* and so on."

"You are right, sir. It is quite unnerving. It's absolutely entrancing, quite exhilarating!"

"I say," resumed Peter Rose, "I wish I could get rid of this stupid old woman. I am skewered to her side like the wing of a trussed goose."

"I fear," said Mrs. Richardson, "I fear Chevalier, I lean too heavily on you?"

"*Au contraire,*" returned Peter; "you are as light as a feather —— she only weighs about two tons."

"This is indeed a most enchanting scene!" said Maclean, as he paused with Rosalie and Stephanie on either side of him. "I can almost fancy myself in Mohammed's paradise, where love and pleasure ever reign; where all is gay, bright, and beautiful. How delightfully Ovid has it."

Then the clever thief recited to her some verses, which might have been Dutch for all that she understood of them.

If she understood them he did not.

The fact was, that they were merely a mass of slang flung adroitly together.

"How charming," she cried. "The ancient poets were sublime. I doat on the classics, and you speak Latin like an aborigine, count."

Maclean bowed.

"Ah," he said, "a quadrille is being formed. Beaufort, do the amiable, and dance with Step-hanie. Rosalie, my angel, allow me the tips of your pretty fingers. Mrs. Richardson will you join us, or will you look on?"

"I will look on, if you please, count," returned the merchant's wife, curtseying; "my dancing days are over; I would rather watch the young people."

Maclean and Peter Rose accordingly waltzed off with their respective partners, and, having gone through the dance, conducted them to a point the furthest removed from their mother.

Both Peter and his bolder friend had conceived a violent passion for the two girls, and they had resolved, if possible, to induce them to quit London with them.

"My dearest Rosalie," said Maclean, as he sat down with her on a bench beneath the trees, and kissed her fondly on her unresisting lips, "you must by this time have learned how I love you ; and I am about to ask you to give me a proof that you respond to my devotion."

"How am I to do this, count ?" asked the blushing girl, casting her eyes upon the ground.

"By consenting to leave London with me, my sweet girl," he said. "I have anticipated your consent. A carriage will await us ; your sister will accompany you as the betrothed of M. de Beaufort. You will be happy, and your parents will surely forgive us."

This was rather awkward for Rosalie.

She was quite well aware that neither of her parents would object to their union with the Count de Tourville and M. de Beaufort ; but the question was, how she was to tell him so without admitting that those parents had been preparing a grand scheme of match-making.

"I do not think," she said, tremblingly, "that either my father or my mother would object to our marriage."

Maclean heaved a sigh.

"Alas !" he said, "you are wrong."

"I think not," ventured Rosalie.

Maclean sighed again.

"Ah !" he said, "you do not know all. Your father *does* object."

"He does ?"

"More ; he has refused his consent."

"Impossible !"

"It is so indeed."

"I can scarcely believe it."

"And why not ?"

"Because—because he has always expressed himself so great an admirer of you and your friend."

"Well," said Maclean, in a voice as of deep emotion, "I suppose I must confess all. Your father has involved himself in difficulty. He left home to-day on business, he told you ; but, alas ! it was not so."

Rosalie clasped her hands and looked up imploringly in his face.

"My poor father !" she cried, "my poor father ! What has happened to him ? Oh, tell, for pity's sake !"

Maclean took her hand gently in his, and spoke in a low voice of kindness.

"My dear girl," he said, "you must prepare yourself for something unpleasant ; you must promise to receive what I have to say calmly."

"Oh, yes, I will promise. I can readily understand what you mean ; he has—I know his generous heart—made himself responsible for some friend, and has been thrown into prison."

Maclean shook his head gravely.

"It is worse than that," he said. "He has fled from justice !"

"What crime has he committed, then ?"

"I know not ; I only know that he has fled from fear, as he told me, of a prison or death ; that he said he would not disgrace me by allowing his daughter to become my wife ; and no entreaties of mine could induce him to alter his determination."

"My poor father ! It must have been something very sudden. He seemed all life and spirits this morning."

"Yes, indeed, poor man, that was put on to conceal his sorrow. But, my lovely Rosalie, is it to be as I wish ? Will you consent to fly with me this night, and trust me, as your sister has consented to trust my friend ?"

Peter Rose was, about this time, using the same arguments to Stephanie.

Rosalie blushed more deeply than ever.

"You forget our circumstances, count," she said.

"In what way ?"

"As regards marriage."

"I do not understand you."

"You forget that unless we are married with the consent of our parents we lose our fortunes."

The count smiled.

"I have not forgotten that," he said ; "but I can provide for it ; I engage that the ceremony shall be performed, for when your father learns that you have fled with us, and that I am resolved to make you the Countess de Tourville, he will no longer refuse to consent."

By arguments such as these, he at length succeeded in overcoming Rosalie's scruples, and while her enraptured lover pressed her yielding form fondly in his arms, he explained to her his proposed plan.

It was that she should proceed in a Hackney coach with Stephanie to the Cross at Charing, and there await the arrival of Maclean and Peter Rose.

Just as this arrangement was agreed upon Peter Rose appeared with Stephanie leaning on his arm.

The sisters at once rushed to each other, and held a whispered conversation.

The two thieves also spoke together in an under tone.

Then Maclean turned to the girls.

"Come," he said, "let us proceed to the gate and procure a cab. No time must be lost."

"May we see mother first ?"

"You cannot now ; at least, if you wish to come with us. Your mother will join us in three days, bearing your father's consent to our marriage. Come, let us lose no time, or we shall be discovered."

So saying, he hurried the foolish, doubting girls towards the gate of the gardens, and placed them in a cab.

"To the Cross at Charing ; wait at the sign of the 'Red Pullet,' cried Maclean. "Farewell, ladies, we shall soon join you."

And as the cab drove off and the two girls flung themselves into each other's arms in mingled hope and fear, the two villains, *par excellence*, returned towards the spot where they had left Mrs. Richardson.

"Well, Peter, how do you like this game ?" asked Maclean. "It's better than beating hemp in Newgate, eh ? Don't you think so ?"

Peter laughed loudly.

"I should rather say so, my friend," he said. "We are going it in prime style. Ha, ha ! we are, I believe, such out and out swells that our mother even would not know us."

"Are you sure of that ?" asked a voice.

They started in alarm.

On turning round they saw a body of constables, headed by a man, who, although disguised, was easily recognisable as a police spy.

They immediately pounced upon the pretended Frenchmen.

It was a dear struggle for life with the thieves, and, after a desperate encounter, they contrived to break away, Maclean with his coat torn, Peter Rose with his wig in his hand, and only one whisker and half a moustache left.

"Oh, my precious nerves ! oh, my precious nerves !" groaned he, as he fled with Maclean towards their lodgings. "We're done at last ! We're boned and killed !"

"Don't make such a noise, but run," said Maclean, as he dashed on at full speed.

MOONLIGHT JACK

OR THE KING OF THE ROAD

MOONLIGHT JACK.

"It's getting very late," growled Mr. Richardson, as he sat in his dressing-gown and night-cap in an easy chair in his bed-room awaiting the return of the party from the gardens, "it's getting very late. I wish Mrs. Richardson would come home; I am getting very sleepy; I can hardly keep my eyes open."

He stopped to yawn.

"Oh, I wish I had a peep at them," he continued. "I dare say my old fool of a wife is dancing and capering like a two-year-old colt. Ha, ha! I should like to see the old girl in a gallopade."

With this he seemed to go off into a dreamy state of delight at his own joke, and went fast asleep.

In a few moments after the window was cautiously opened and Maclean and Peter Rose entered.

"Be careful," said the former, in a low tone, "we'll slip into our room for our valuables and be off. The devil," he added, as he saw the merchant

No. 16, April 21, 1866.]

Two Numbers and Two Tales every week for One Penny.
THE WORK GIRLS OF LONDON, and THE CRUSADER; OR, THE WITCH OF FINCHLEY.

Price One Penny.

asleep in his chair, "here's the old boy returned; we must secure him. Come on, Peter."

With this they seized upon the sleeping merchant.

"Holloa, holloa!" he cried, waking up with a start; "what's the matter? Count, Chevalier, what's the meaning of this? Why are you here?"

"Our lives are in danger! We are pursued by the soldiery! Conceal us and aid our escape."

"You alarm me," cried Richardson; "why, what—what——"

"Ask no questions; conceal us, and send away the soldiers."

"The soldiers! why, what on earth have you been doing?"

At this moment the voice of the lady was heard without.

"Oh, my poor husband, where is he?"

"Ah!" cried Maclean, "here is your wife. I will not hurt you; give me your cap and dressing-gown."

"But, my dear count, just stop to consider."

"Not a word; give them to me."

The transfer was made too late.

As it was effected the door opened and Mrs. Richardson entered.

Maclean glanced at her for a moment in rage and astonishment.

Then he cried,

"Come, Peter, let us fly."

"No, no!" cried the lady, seizing Maclean's left arm as Peter reached the corridor; "no, no! you shall not escape me! Help, help!"

"Fly, Peter," again cried Maclean; "I will settle her!"

With these words he drew his knife, and, with his right arm, drove it into her bosom.

Then, with a sudden rush, he reached the window and sprang into the street just as the soldiers rushed into the room.

The latter also leaped out into the street, but they were too late.

In the darkness the forms of the thieves could not be distinguished.

Once more they had escaped!

They halted on the other side of the square, underneath the great archway, in order that they might consult.

They wisely conjectured that to appear before Rosalie and Stephanie in this dilapidated condition would be to cause them at once to suspect something wrong.

The signs of a struggle they had no desire to hide, because that could be accounted for, but half Peter's whiskers and moustache had disappeared.

In spite of the deed of blood he had just perpetrated, Maclean could not resist laughing at the comical figure cut by his friend, who had not yet discarded the night cap and dressing-gown which he had caught up in his hurry.

"My worthy friend," he said, "when you think fit to take off your dressing-gown I will explain to you how to get out of our scrape."

"It would be as well, as you say, to put on another dress," returned Peter, laughing rather dolefully, as he flung away the clothes he had adopted as a disguise. "Well, what is your plan?"

"We must go to Moses, the old clothesman, wake him up, renovate ourselves, and proceed post haste to the sign of the 'Red Pullet.'"

"Very well, on's the word, and the further the distance I place between those cursed red jackets and myself, the better it will be for my nerves."

Moses, the old clothesman, as Maclean called him, was nothing more or less than a receiver of

stolen goods of all kinds, and kept a dark-looking little shop in a dark-looking street near the Strand lane.

Thither the two friends betook themselves in a cab, and found the house in darkness.

They knocked loudly and impatiently.

It wanted now but a short time to day-break, and the light would prove their destruction.

Old Moses poked his long nose out of an upper window to have a good look at them.

He always scrutinised his customers carefully before admitting them to his sanctum.

"Who's there?" he cried.

"Captain Maclean," replied that worthy, loudly.

"Stop!" cried Peter, "are you mad?"

"No; no one is near, and time must not be lost. Our object is to get our things quickly and be off, and not to stand here an hour consulting at the door. See, the name is a good pass-word."

So it seemed, indeed, for the old Jew now presented himself at the door and admitted them, closing it carefully afterwards.

He grinned at their strange appearance.

"You've been in a nice mess, my darlings," he said. "Are there any followers?—we don't like 'em here. By followers, we mean the gentlemen in red."

"No: we cut their acquaintance almost at starting. But, come, let us to business. We want fitting out from head to foot—something stylish, tip-top, fashionable jewellery, and so forth, and half a moustache or a new one, and a pair of whiskers for my friend here."

"Very good, very good," said the Jew, as he bustled about, getting a light, and showing them into a room where clothes of every description were hanging round the walls.

"Here you are," he said, after a moment, as he issued forth from behind a mass of clothing which seemed truly large enough to furnish forth an army.

He then spread out upon the table two coats somewhat similar to one another, and both made in the extreme of fashion.

Then he produced pantaloons to match, and light boots and hats, and wigs and moustaches, ad lib., and displayed them to his customers. After which came jewellery of all kinds, good, bad, and indifferent.

Both of the thieves at once donned their new suits, and having chosen some of the real jewels, proceeded to the necessary but unpleasant act of paying.

The Jew exacted, of course, an exorbitant price for his goods.

He knew his customers.

Good pay and no questions asked.

This he was aware was the motto.

Captain Maclean did not hesitate at the price asked, but taking out the pocket book stolen from Mr. Richardson on the day before, he paid in bank notes.

His willingness is easily to be accounted for.

Peter stood behind the Jew during the payment.

Naturally, therefore, the money was transferred from the Jew's pocket into that of the timid confederate in about a minute after the transfer from Maclean's hand.

"Well," cried the latter, after a wink from Peter had assured him of this transaction, "well, Moses, you are a friend in need, and that you know is a friend in deed."

"Indeed," mimicked Peter, flourishing the bank notes behind the Jew's back.

"Well, well," said Moses, returning the captain's hearty grasp in that greasy slipshod way in which Jews generally shake hands. "Well, well, though we prey on one another we still pray for one another. That's good, eh? Dam'me, good night!"

"Good night," cried Maclean, laughing as he issued from the door; "but, I say," he added, looking grave and stopping, "be careful about the notes; don't change them yet."

The Jew put his finger to his nose.

"Leave Moses alone," he said, "he knows what's what," and he tapped his pocket significantly.

Maclean roared with laughter when they reached the corner of the street, and entered a Hackney coach.

At the sign of the "Red Pullet," where they soon arrived, they saw a cab waiting.

"See, here we are!" cried Peter, "here is the tavern, and no doubt that coach there belongs to our patient friends."

The cab containing the friends drew up at the door of the "Red Pullet," as near as the other cab would allow of it, and the thieves alighted impatiently.

The cabman was asleep on his box, but his ready ear caught the sound of wheels.

Starting up he espied our friends.

His surly look, expressive of his real feelings, changed into a bland smile, expressive of his business feelings.

"Ah, gentlemen," he said, "I am glad you have come at last. I thought you were never coming."

"Where are the young ladies?" asked Maclean.

"They are upstairs asleep, I should fancy."

Maclean slipped a gold piece into his hand.

"Do you understand your business, mon garçon?" he asked, aping the Frenchman.

"I fancy so," said the man, with a grin.

"Then take your horse on about half a mile, and there wait—wait even if we are a long time—we are certain to come."

The man touched his cap, and resuming his position on the box, drove off as desired.

Captain Maclean then knocked loudly at the door.

A sleepy waiter opened the door.

"Where is the countess?" asked the robber, magnificently.

The waiter bowed.

"I do not know, sir," he said.

Maclean eyed him fiercely.

Peter whispered,

"They've bolted!"

A kick on the foot kept his tongue quiet.

"Madame la Countess de Tourville and Madame de Beaufort arrived here some time since," resumed Maclean. "Where are they?"

The waiter bowed again.

"I beg pardon, my lord, the two young ladies who came in the cab?" he said. "I wasn't aware——"

He did not stop to explain of what he was not aware, but at once led the way upstairs to a large room where a scene presented itself, which would have been charming in its simplicity to any one less hardened than our thievish companions.

The two girls had discarded the greater part of their travelling clothes, and had fallen to sleep on the big sofa, clasped to each other's breasts, lying with their bright eyes closed, their cherry lips half parted, their white bosoms fully revealed by their low ball dresses, heaving regularly, and throbbing one against the other.

"Egad," cried Maclean, as he entered, "they are two rosebuds, and no mistake."

So saying, he approached the sofa, and patted Rosalie lightly on the shoulder.

"Rosalie," he cried, "wake, my darling!"

The girl glanced up with a half-stupid, half-frightened stare.

Then she recognised him, and sprang into his arms.

"Oh! count," she cried, "we have been so frightened. "We thought some terrible accident had happened to you, and you could not come."

Maclean smiled gallantly.

"Could not come? My dearest, nothing could keep me from you. Ah! Mademoiselle Stephanie, you, too, seem surprised. You would more so were you to know all we have endured ere we could reach you."

"What, then, has delayed you, dear count?" asked Rosalie.

"A few bottles of champagne, waiter. Thank you, yes," said Maclean to the waiter, who was rubbing his eyes, and otherwise denoting his sleepiness; then, turning to the two girls, "I fear to tell you."

"Oh! what is it, count? Another misfortune?"

"Yes, indeed, a sad one. Do you not perceive we are in other dress?"

"Yes, indeed!"

"And we are compelled to fly from London also."

"For what?"

Maclean sighed.

"For your father's sake," he said.

Rosalie burst into tears.

"My poor father!" she said; "in his downfall he involves others."

Peter sighed deeply.

"Yes, indeed," he murmured, plaintively; "he foolishly returned home to fetch something, and the watch saw him. I and my friend here saved him at the imminent risk of our lives. We were sadly torn to pieces, and were obliged to rehabitate ourselves before presenting ourselves here."

So saying, he gallantly kissed the cherry lips of his fair inamorata.

"And why are you compelled to fly?" inquired Rosalie.

"Because we were denounced by the police as his friends, his assistants, his fellow conspirators, and we fled at once to you. Even now we must continue our flight. A carriage is in readiness. Let us go at once; at Edgware we can stop and sleep."

After partaking of the cakes and champagne brought in by the now less sleepy waiter they paid the bill and departed.

The coach was in readiness at the appointed spot, and into it they ascended.

"Drive on, without stopping at Edgware," cried Maclean.

The cabman stared.

"That's miles away, my lord," he suggested, humbly.

"I know that," cried Maclean. "What of that, I will give you three guineas for your trouble. Drive on."

And so the cab drove on, the tired girls sleeping in the arms of their lovers, who in the first instance bestowed literally those caresses which lovers, and amorous lovers such as these, would bestow under such circumstances; but afterwards relapsed also into sound slumber.

At Edgware they stopped, and, dismissing the coach, proceeded to the inn.

"Here," said Maclean, "we must stay a day; there is a house in this neighbourhood which I should wish to take. It would just suit us, and it would be one which your dear father would approve of. I have told him of it, and he proposes to come and see us."

"But he will be taken," said Rosalie.

"Not so; he will not come for some weeks, not till suspicion is lulled," returned Maclean; "meanwhile, I have his consent in writing, attested by two witnesses.

Rosalie and Stephanie gazed at him in delight.

"Oh! count! how kind—how provident of you!" cried both. "You are indeed one whom every one must admire."

Maclean bowed.

"I am working for my own good as well as yours," he said. "Our marriages can now be solemnised at once, and so all question will be avoided."

Peter Rose took him by the arm as he quitted the room and eyed him seriously, if not angrily."

"I say, captain," he cried, deprecatingly.

"Well, what now?"

"About those girls?"

"Well, what of them?"

"Are you really going to marry then?"

"Yes; why not?"

"They'll be a nuisance."

"Then we can leave them."

Peter shook his head.

"That's not the thing," he said.

"No: perhaps not; but it may be necessary sometimes."

"Then why marry them?"

"Because we must."

"Why?"

"Because we must, I tell you."

"I dont understand."

"If you want to live with those girls happily you must marry them."

Peter laughed.

"What!" he cried, "have you grown squeamish all of a sudden?"

"No."

"What then?"

"Why, this! I know the difference between a respectable girl and one that is not respectable; and I tell ye—mind, I, who know something of the world—that these girls will live with us, will make us happy, will make us a little better, will make us forget something of our detestable past, if we behave well and honourably to them."

He spoke with real emotion.

Peter looked at him at first in surprise, and then laughed outright.

"What ails you?" asked Maclean.

"You make me laugh."

"Why?"

"Because you moralise."

"Why should I not?"

"You are married."

"Yes."

"You have just killed a woman who was loved, and wished for happiness as you do."

Maclean shook his head.

"No," he said, "you are telling a lie."

"I am not."

"You are. I saw the deed."

"You saw me plunge my knife in her bosom; you did not see her die."

"No, but she must have died."

"Not so; there again you are at fault. The blow was scientific. She will not die; she will live to haunt us yet."

The words were given solemnly.

He little knew that they were prophetic!

"So you propose to marry these girls, and settle down as true married men?"

"Yes; why not? Let us go and see our new house."

The house, Laurel Lodge, as it was called, was situated about half a mile from Tanpit.

It was a pretty place, and Peter Rose was delighted.

"Well, dam'me, Maclean!" he cried, "I think even my nerves will get strong here. There's a keenness about the air much preferable to the keenness of the soldiers' swords, eh, my friend?"

Maclean laughed heartily.

"Yes, I fancy you will like this a little better than the Tower or Newgate," he said. "But the next difficulty will be about the girls."

This conversation took place on the evening after their arrival, when the tired girls had retired to bed.

"In what way?" asked Peter.

"There must be some sort of ceremony of marriage."

"Yes, there must; but who will perform it?"

Maclean shook his head.

"That's a question I can't answer," he said. "I feel considerably down in that respect."

"Will a written consent do?"

"It might."

"Good, then; I will manufacture one," said Peter.

And sitting down, he concocted the necessary document, and handed it to Maclean.

"You're a man of genius," said the latter when he had perused the document; "and now you had better carry out the affair to the end."

"How?"

"By fetching the priest, and having the ceremony performed this very night."

"To-night?"

"Yes; why not? Delays are dangerous."

"Well, they may be; but they are necessary in this instance. How can we go and drag the girls out of their beds to make them go through a marriage ceremony? First of all, they would smell a rat, and, if not, they would think us mad. Secondly, the priest would smoke us, and all would be spoiled. Let them rest where they are, and wait till to-morrow."

"Well, my philosopher, so let it be," said Maclean. "Meanwhile, go to the priest's house and explain matters to him, that he may be ready to come in the morning."

Peter Rose accordingly left the Lodge, and proceeded to the village inn, where they told him the way to the priest's house.

The worthy man was at home, and he eyed his visitor curiously, and the document still more curiously.

"You have lately arrived here, M. de Beaufort?" he said, seeing the name, with that of the count, on the consent.

"But yesterday."

"Why have not the parents of the young ladies accompanied you?"

Peter Rose affected to hesitate.

"Shall I be plain with you?" he said, after a moment.

"It would be better," said the priest.

"Well, then, we desired them not to. Our families are noble; our friends who will be present at the ceremony are gentry. This is a *marriage de convenance*, but we are not compelled to have retired tradesmen at the wedding."

"I see—I understand," said the priest.

Peter Rose turned and took out his purse.

"My friend, the count, desired me to present you

with the fees in advance. There are twenty guineas."

The priest stared, but placed the coins in his purse, which at once found its way to the pocket of Peter Rose.

"You are most polite, M. de Beaufort," he said. "At what time do you wish the ceremony to take place?"

"To-morrow, at noon."

"To-morrow, at noon, then, it shall be," returned the curé. "My respects to M. le Comte; adieu, until then."

On the next day at noon, the two girls, with Captain Maclean and Peter Rose with two witnesses in the persons of two maid-servants, who had been engaged for them on the previous afternoon, waited in the drawing-room of the Lodge for the arrival of the priest.

At length he came; he bowed to all present, made no remark as to the absence of the noble company spoken of by Peter Rose, but eyed the two Richardsons curiously.

The ceremony began; the blushing brides were almost wives.

Suddenly a noise was heard without, and, to the confusion of Maclean and Peter Rose, in rushed Mr. Richardson and four strangers, headed by two whom they knew well—Lucien Fairleigh and Moonlight Jack.

Neither of the friends were taken off their guard in such circumstances as these.

On quickness depended the success of their theft, on quickness their escape.

Dropping the hands of their astonished brides, they dashed, bare-headed as they were, through the window and were off ere the highwaymen could reach them.

The latter fired through the window and saw Peter drop.

In another instant he rose again and dashed off towards the river.

Lucien Fairleigh and Moonlight Jack hesitated not.

"Come, my men," cried the latter, "let us pursue them. No time is to be lost."

The pursuit was brisk.

The thieves knew that they were flying for dear life.

They knew both pursuers well.

Neither Moonlight Jack nor Lucien Fairleigh were men to be trifled with.

So they fled apace.

Into a boat on the dark river they at length sprang.

The night was black.

The clouds hung heavily.

Not a ray of moonlight could be seen.

As fortune would have it there were two boats.

Into the second sprang the highwaymen with all speed.

Neither knew well their way.

The fugitives and their foes, therefore, were compelled to be cautious.

Presently a rumbling sound was heard in the distance.

It was like far off artillery.

A vivid flash, however, proclaimed its real nature.

It was a thunder storm, coming headlong against the wind.

Peal after peal rattled over the darkening earth.

Flash after flash dashed from one horizon line to the other.

It was a changing scene.

Now the boats dashed onwards along a stream black as ink.

Then the sky, and the waving trees, and the rushing water, and the nodding reeds upon the bank were lit up by a violent flash, which illumined, too, the faces of the eager men.

Presently a roaring noise was heard in the lull of the storm.

It was the noise of the water falling over the rock just above the old mill.

"We must strain every nerve," cried Moonlight Jack, "or they will land ere they reach the fall."

The second boat, containing four men, now began to tell upon the other.

They had got well to their work and came along at a swinging pace.

In a few minutes they were abreast with their foes.

"Surrender!" cried Moonlight Jack.

"Never!" cried Maclean. "Honour let there be among thieves. We know you well; let us go in peace."

"We have no affinity with you," cried Moonlight Jack; "we rob the rich, and give to the poor. We meet men on the highway, and, face to face, man to man, demand their purses. We do not try to ruin helpless girls or to murder heart-broken parents. We do not steal, but fight for money."

Maclean saw that there was no chance of parley.

So, ere our hero could observe his actions, he raised his pistol and fired.

There was a flash!

But that was all.

It was a flash in the pan.

"Coward, knave!" cried the king of the road, as he dashed the hilt of his sword in his mouth. "Follow me, my men."

Into the frail boat he leaped.

His men followed.

They were now nearing the fall.

"Pull back," cried Lucien, as he forced Peter Rose upon a seat.

The two men pulled back strongly.

The highwaymen, meanwhile, still struggled with their foes.

The boat rocked to and fro as the strong men struggled eagerly.

As they passed away there was a roar and a crash.

The boat had gone over the fall.

They had checked their onward course only just in time.

The battle continued for some time.

All four were strong men, yet they knew their danger.

"Pull for land!" cried Moonlight Jack.

The rowers obeyed.

In a few moments the keel of the boat grated against the pebbles, and one of Jack's followers, Hardman, jumping out, secured it.

"Now, my men, assist me," cried Moonlight Jack.

Maclean and Peter Rose had no longer a chance.

After a brief struggle, they were lying helpless on the ground, while their hands were being tied behind their backs.

"If it had been a struggle for life," said Moonlight Jack, "I should have asked no aid against you. But it was not so: I have followed you that I may give you up to those whom you have injured."

"Bring them along," added Lucien; "if they refuse to come quietly, give them a prick with your swords."

The thieves saw there was no use in attempting to escape.

So they went away quietly.

When they reached the house where Mr. Richardson was anxiously waiting their return, Lucien Fairleigh delivered up to him their prisoners.

"When we are gone," he said, "send for constables, and give these wretches into custody. As for us, we are due upon the coast, a hundred miles away, and must quit you."

Mr. Richardson seized his hand.

"Sir," he said, "you will at least tell me your name?"

"It is needless; it is one which you have never heard."

"It is *not* needless. You have saved the honor of my two girls—you have saved me from dying of a broken heart. Tell me, at least, how it was that you gave up to me time which is valuable, and risked life which is priceless?"

Lucien smiled.

Then taking out his purse he counted out twenty gold pieces, and gave them into Mr. Richardson's hands.

"We are now quits!" he said, to the astonished merchant. "You must remember, that some long time ago, when you were a solitary traveller, you quitted an inn where you had boasted of your money, and were robbed upon the road by a highwayman."

"I do. I do remember."

"He told you he had need of twenty pieces, and would take no more. He gave you in exchange a ring, which I see now sparkling on your finger. He has claimed the ring now. I am he."

The merchant for a moment stood spell-bound.

In the darkness he had not seen the highwayman's face.

So recognition was impossible.

"I remember your voice," said Mr. Richardson: "but, of course, your face I know not. Your remembrance of the ring, however, and your story convince me that you are he whom I met on the highway."

"I am he—of that you may be certain."

"While thanking you from my very heart then for your courage and your bravery, let me hope that good fortune has returned to you, and enabled you to quit your dangerous trade."

The old man spoke with much emotion.

Lucien was affected.

"Sir," he said "Fortune is still at odds with me. In future days when I can assure you of my return to society, you will know me by a different title to that which I now tell you. Lucien Fairleigh is my name. Remember it, and some day we may meet in better and more equal positions."

He grasped the worthy merchant's hand in an eager grasp.

Then he turned to his daughters.

"Ladies," he said, as he raised their hands to his lips in turn, "ladies, let me trust that your late danger will be a warning to you. Adieu, till better times."

Moonlight Jack took a similar leave of all present, and then, passing out into the high road, they mounted their horses, and rode off towards the sea coast.

CHAPTER XVII.

THE CAMP BY THE SEA—THE SMUGGLERS—THE REFUGE OF A DEPOSED KING — MOONLIGHT JACK AND THE SIREN OF THE SEA—THE SUBTERRANEAN RETREAT—THE NARROW PASS—ONE AGAINST MANY—TREACHERY—THE BATTLE —BRANDON IS WOUNDED—SIR PERCY TO THE RESCUE!—MEETING OF SIR PERCY AND MOONLIGHT JACK — MUTUAL REVELATIONS — SIR PERCY'S RETREAT—DEFEAT OF THE KING'S TROOPS BY JACK TYRRELL AND LUCIEN FAIRLEIGH.

ON the margin of the broad and ever-restless sea the royal troops pitched their camp.

They were not many in number, yet their halting place presented an imposing appearance.

The white tents dotted the green slopes on the cliffs; the standard waved merrily in the breeze.

Horses grazed here and there, fully equipped for action.

Sentinels walked slowly to and fro.

On their arms and the stocks of weapons—disposed here and there—the bright sun glinted in the daytime, and the silver moonlight crept brightly at night.

But they were useless.

Their very brilliance destroyed their efficacy.

Their camp, by day, could be seen far out at sea.

At night, too, the fires shone out upon the ocean.

Near the very spot where the royal troops were located was a huge cave, which, from time immemorial, had been the resort of smugglers.

Some six months before the time of our story a gang had been dispersed by a force of coast-guard.

They had been gathered together by a man called Black Donald, who, for years before, had been a pirate of desperate character.

They would probably have been able a longer time to resist the efforts of the authorities to repress them had not Black Donald's atrocious crimes roused the anger of the whole neighbourhood.

A band, composed of the inhabitants of the vicinity and the coast-guard, rushed in upon them one night while the band was sleeping.

The sentinel was shot down.

The noise awoke the rest.

Black Donald, whose head was pillowed on the bosom of his mistress, a lovely girl of not more than eighteen summers, was one of the first to rouse himself.

A fearful combat ensued.

Though in their own den, the pirates found they were getting the worst of it.

Then, suddenly, as sudden and desperate, they gathered in a mass at the extreme end of the cave, Black Donald whispered to his mistress.

She rushed towards the barrels containing the powder.

"Hold!" she cried, in a loud, ringing voice, "hold! friends and foes!"

The combatants paused.

They gazed admiringly at the beautiful girl, who, half-undressed, and with dishevelled hair, looked, as she stood there pistol in hand, like some wrathful divinity.

"I will save Black Donald!" she cried, "or ye shall all perish with him."

"What mean ye?" cried the chief of the coast-guard.

"I mean this," cried the intrepid girl. "These barrels contain powder; this is touch paper. See, I light it! If, in five minutes, you are not out of this cavern, it will set fire to the powder, and we shall meet our doom together!"

As she spoke, she lit the paper!

There was a dead silence.

Her assailants did not like to retreat.

Black Donald stood, with folded arms, calmly regarding them.

At length, when one of the fatal minutes had passed, one of the coast-guard rushed forward towards the powder barrels, as if with the intention of extinguishing the touch paper.

He never reached it!

A shot from the girl's pistol laid him dead on the floor of the cave!

The touch paper burned on!

The attackers moved not!

They disbelieved the girl's words.

They disbelieved the assertion that there was powder in the barrels.

Well they might!

Such courage is not proved every day.

More especially among women.

Still it burned on!

The pirates moved not.

"Fire!" cried the chief of the coast-guard, just as the touch paper neared the edge of the barrel, "fire, and——"

He never finished the sentence!

Ere he could do so there was a terrific explosion!

Those who were not killed were thrown upon their faces.

The noise was deafening.

The earth seemed to quake, and the cliffs to rock.

A few of the coast-guard escaped.

Those who did so returned after awhile, with torches, to carry out the bodies of the dead.

Many of the pirates lay strewn about, stiff and stark.

But they sought in vain for Black Donald and his mistress.

They had fled, or Death had claimed them for its own!

One report said that, being so near to the powder barrels, they were blown to atoms.

Another report—a better authenticated one, too—declared that they had, that very evening, embarked in a fishing-smack, with the remainder of their band, and fled to the Orkney Isles.

However this may have been, it is certain that a band, similar in nature and headed by such a chieftain, was long the terror of the Orkneys.

In the cave vacated by these desperate men another band had formed.

It was a band, however, of a different character.

Lawless, and bold, and fearless they were, but not absolutely criminal.

They were banded together—not to plunder or thieve—not to prey upon society, but to defeat the government.

They were smugglers!

Their chief, John Lawless, was a man of gigantic stature, who had earned a reputation in his younger days as one of the cleverest poachers on the country side.

He had been noted for nothing more, however.

He had been a good son and a good friend, and his poaching had been begun because he had seen his brothers and sisters starving.

Those who had *no* game loved him.

Those who *had* game admired him, though they feared him and watched him well.

With him in his cave were more than twenty

followers, who venerated him as men of old venerated their kings, and who would have sacrificed life to save him.

There too lived a gentle being whom they called Eola—a being to whose lips when, storm-lost on the angry sea, he had held the cup of mercy—who, after what she had deemed her agony, had opened her straining eyes, and beheld a being bending over her beautiful in his roughness, gentle in his manly strength.

A being she was, born on the ocean—a waif and stray whom no one claimed—for he who had smiled proudly at her birth, and she on whose breast she had nestled, lay fathoms deep beneath the rolling waves which rolled and rolled and swayed to and fro as they marched in endless ranks above their graves.

"Mercy!" says one we remember, "mercy falleth as the gentle dew from heaven."

So fell the presence of Eola upon the band who had gathered in the mermaid's cave.

She made them better men, because she seemed more beautiful and more good than other women.

Among these smugglers, aided by this man and strengthened by this woman, had retreated the Jacobite leaders.

The conspiracy was growing.

Princes, as a rule, had failed in their promises, as they generally do to those who most need their fulfilment; one only had kept to the semblance of his word.

Those who had sworn to provide arms and money now met their engagements by swearing again to provide them in the future.

Thus James II., instead of invading England with a fleet and an army, came to these shores as the mere plaything of that class who were always ready to follow in the wake of a pretender.

A man fighting for a less stake than for a kingdom would have been ready to abandon his enterprise where James II. only became more desperately determined.

A king who had received the adulations of a court should have known that a kingdom was not to be recovered by a few reckless soldiers and lawless plunderers of the very crown he sought.

But at any rate James II. was glad to accept their adhesion.

More than this, John Lawless was known to be a Jacobite at heart, and was able to influence hundreds on the country side.

The Jacobite leaders, therefore, welcomed their co-operation gladly; and even now in that strange cave were many who reckoned themselves among the noblest in England.

On the night on which the last detachment of the royal troops arrived at Trueford, there was a grand meeting in the cavern to consider what steps were to be taken towards marching upon London when the ship which they expected from France arrived with the supplies.

In the midst of the conference a man entered among them.

"There are three strangers at the door," he said.

"What want they?" demanded John Lawless.

"They ask admittance."

"Do they give the sign?"

"Yes. *From over the water.*"

"And the countersign?"

"Yes. *Moonlight till the dawn.*"

"Good! then admit them."

The man retired, and in a few moments returned with three companions.

They were masked and cloaked.

"Whom have we here?" demanded John Lawless.

"THE KING!" cried a voice.

And James II. unmasked.

The assembly rose.

To them he was a king—though deposed and a fugitive.

His companions unmasked likewise.

These were Moonlight Jack and Lucien Fairleigh.

"We bring you ill news, my friends," said James II. "The troops are surrounding this place; a secret avenue, which my companions here have spoken of as leading hither, and affording a sure mode of retreat, is now in their hands. We must stand to our arms, for though they fear to attack us openly they may by treachery be at any moment in our midst."

As the king spoke and when the assembly had hardly gained their breath after the announcement, there was heard a rumbling sound at the furthest end of the cave.

"To arms, my men!" cried Lawless.

Then came a curious scene.

From every dark and shadowy nook sprang forth an armed man.

John Lawless then led the way towards the passage whose other end led out into the woods.

His gigantic form seemed to fill the passage.

But one pressed on by his side.

This was Eola.

After her came two others.

Lucien and Jack Tyrrell.

The king, too, would have come had they let him.

But he was held back.

To these men—honouring royalty as they did, and as enlightened men will never do again—his person was sacred.

So they piled huge stones at the entrance of the cavern, and placed James where he could not be seen.

Meanwhile the troops without had found the entrance to the cave.

It was well hidden.

Dense bushes obscured it.

Many a time the coast-guard had tried to use it in order to steal a march upon the desperate gang of Black Donald, and had failed.

But no one can fight against treachery.

It was a traitor who had now revealed it.

In a few minutes the royal troops and John Lawless stood face to face.

Like Horatius Cocles defending the bridge over the Tiber against Lars Porsenna's army, the giant stood before them.

Suddenly something caught his eye which made him start back.

A large gun was planted opposite the entrance to the cave.

He drew back a moment.

"Eola," he said, "you must retire to the cavern. The danger here is too great."

"Have I ever shrunk from danger?" cried the intrepid girl.

"No; but this is danger which neither man nor woman can combat. A cannon points towards this entrance. One discharge would destroy both you and me together. Retire back into the cave, and we will sally forth and drive these fellows back to their camp. Tyrrell, see that she does this. I cannot leave my post."

Eola moved not.

"If John Lawless was compelled to head his band in a sally upon the enemy, why should she not be by his side?"

Such was her question.

Moonlight Jack soon answered it.

"Madam," he said, "this is no place for you."

"I share all his perils."

"Not such as this."

"Yes, ten times greater."

"But your remaining here will be his destruction. Come, let me lead you back."

"No; you say this to save me. I will not go!"

Moonlight Jack argued no longer.

It was time to act.

Already was heard the voice of Brandon speaking to John Lawless and proposing a surrender.

There was not a moment to lose.

Grasping her tightly round the waist he raised her soft and glowing form in his arms and bore her swiftly to the cave.

Here he confided her to the care of some of the smugglers' mistresses, and then rushed back to the point of conflict.

John Lawless had waited for him.

He knew well the worth of this redoubted champion.

As soon, however, as Moonlight Jack made his re-appearance, the band of smugglers rushed forth.

Little cared they for the bayonets of the soldiers or the volleys which they poured in.

Better acquainted with the ground, knowing well every projection in the rock, every tree trunk, every inequality in the ground, they could attack the troops where the troops could not touch them.

So the battle did not last long.

Brandon, wounded in the leg, was borne off by his officers.

The troops wavered, and glanced back.

When troops look behind them all hope of victory is gone.

THE MARCHIONESS OF LOUDAN.

"On, on!" cried Moonlight Jack, crossing swords with an officer.

But his sword dropped.

He uttered a cry of surprise.

His antagonist was Sir Percy Delaine.

"You here, Sir Percy?" cried Jack Tyrrell.

"Yes, indeed. But to remain here is impossible. I cannot fight against one who saved my life. The day is lost. I will surrender. See, the troops are flying."

His words were true.

The soldiers, bewildered amid the trees, and scared by the fall of their leader, fled away.

The victors did not pursue.

They returned to fortify their cave.

That same night saw Sir Percy Delaine return towards London, to throw up his commission.

He could not, he said, continue in a service where he would each day be liable to meet in battle his best and staunchest friend.

What a terrible trial awaited him when he reached London, we shall describe hereafter.

No. 17.—April 28, 1866.

Two Numbers and Two Tales every week for One Penny.
THE WORK GIRLS OF LONDON, and THE CRUSADER ; OR, THE WITCH OF FINCHLEY.

Price One Penny:

CHAPTER XVIII.

THREE DAYS OF IDLENESS—" A SAIL ! A SAIL !"
—THE ARRIVAL OF THE "GOLDEN FLEECE "—
THE BATTLE ON THE SANDS—DEFEAT OF
BRANDON—HIS TROOPS FLY AWAY ALONG THE
LONDON ROAD--HE IS LEFT PENNILESS AND
WITHOUT A HORSE—TOM DIBBS—HIS STORY—
WHO'S BORN TO BE HANGED WILL NEVER BE
DROWNED—A LIFE ON THE HIGHWAY—OUT OF
LUCK—THE PROPOSED CRIME—THE MISER'S
COTTAGE--THE TREACHEROUS GUEST—THE OLD
MAN'S FEARS—THE DARK LANE—A NIGHT FOR
CRIME.

THREE days passed.

Three days, during which the pirates rested after
their severe battle, tending the wounded, gathering
strength, too, for coming strife.

On the third night the " Golden Fleece " was expected to arrive from Scotland, with a supply of
arms and men.

During the idle interval, the king was desperately impatient.

He spent most of his time with Jack Tyrrell,
Lucien, Lawless, and Eola, upon the last of whom
he often cast admiring glances, which made the
pirate's mistress blush crimson, and brought the
tell-tale blood to the pirate's cheek.

The most of his time, however, was occupied in
vain regrets, in misty outlines of future campaigns,
in imprecations against the ruling powers.

At length the third day came.

Towards evening all eyes were strained out to
sea.

Towards evening came the wished for sight.

Far out upon the rolling waves came the plunging form of the good ship, bearing straight for
shore.

The ex-king's heart beat high with hope and
fear.

" They will oppose the landing of our friends,"
he said. " Let us hope they will have no rein-
forcements."

" I have well ascertained that," returned John
Lawless. " My scouts have been on the look-out
day by day. The troops have as yet *not* been reinforced, and they are demoralised and far from
anxious to renew the fight. Our men will beat
them again, sire. Let us hope that when the great
battles come we shall have an equal share of victory
as I feel assured we shall claim this night."

Cruising lightly along the coast till the dusk
came on, the " Golden Fleece " made at once for
land when the darkness had fallen over the earth.

Then there was an evident movement in Brandon's camp.

The men mustered to arms, and slowly filed the
steep declivities to the beach.

Some planted themselves behind rocky projec-
tions, or lay behind bunches of dense furze, where
they could fire upon their enemy, and remain themselves in safety.

The smugglers appeared not.

Their plan was to wait.

John Lawless was on the look out.

At nine o'clock a bright light shone for an instant
over the dark waters.

" That is the signal that the boats are about to be
lowered," said he. " My men, stand ready."

The smugglers understood the order.

A long line stood, musket in hand, at the broad
entrance of the cavern.

Others lay at their feet, while some, climbing up
the rock, stood upon the ledges, near enough still

to John Lawless to hear his sonorous voice when he
issued his orders.

The forms of the approaching boats were soon
discernible, moving measuredly over the silent sea.

In an instant the royal troops received orders to
fire.

A long line of fire for an instant illumined the
scene, then the rattle of musketry, and then a repetition from the boats.

Again the soldiers fired.

This time they received a twofold answer.

There was a sharp volley from the boats, and a
volley, too, from the smugglers.

Then, from every ledge of rock came stray shots,
lighting up the darkness at momentary intervals,
and making sad havoc among the soldiers, who
were drawn out in an exposed position on the
sands.

The boats still came on.

In a few minutes more they were struggling amid
the surf, and the Scotchmen, leaping into the
water, waded their way to land, firing as they
came.

They were raw-boned, half-naked Highlanders,
used to rough work, and brave to the backbone,
and they dashed in among the royal troops like an
avalanche.

Brandon's men wavered.

John Lawless saw this at once.

" Now, my brave friends," he cried.

And the smugglers rushed down at a run from
the mouth of the cave upon their already half discomfited foes.

Brandon was once more foiled.

The bad man who had espoused a bad cause
found that even when he battled for another his
avenging fate followed him.

" *Sauve qui peut !*" (Save himself who can).

So goes the French proverb, and certainly, in
this instance the royal troops acted up to it. Away
they ran, breaking anyhow, and leaving Brandon
and his officers to get away as they best could.

The pirates this time followed in pursuit, and in
less than an hour the tents of the camp had formed
a huge bonfire, a passing memorial to a king's folly,
while all the valuables it contained, including the
money belonging to Brandon, fell into the hands of
the victors.

With Brandon was left only one man, Tom
Dibbs by name, one of the most depraved fellows
who ever left thieving for the glorious profession of
arms.

Being left entirely without money this party proposed to Brandon to commit a murder.

There lived in the neighbourhood a man whose
son had gone away some years before—a man well
up in years, whose whole life had been spent in
amassing money.

It was, decided, then, between these partners in
crime, that the miser, Laurence Masters by name,
should be inveigled out of his house and disposed
of by Tom Dibbs, while Brandon went to the cottage, and robbed it of its contents.

They were then to meet at the Chequers Inn, at
Newton.

Before describing the details of this terrible
drama we must give a short account of this Tom
Dibbs, the neplus ultra of rogues and villains.

He was the son of a farmer at Hampton, and was
sent at an early age to the care of his cousin, who
was a haberdasher.

At school he distinguished himself by his cunning ; when he quitted it he became equally
noticeable for the way in which he escaped every
danger.

During the hard part of the winter he was sliding with other boys on the canal in St. James's Park, when the ice broke under him, and he sank.

The ice immediately closed over him, and he would certainly have perished had not the ice near him broken again under the weight of another boy.

Precisely in this spot Tom Dibbs rose and was saved, while the other was drowned.

In the summer following this singular escape, he was trying to swim with corks in the Thames, when they slipped from under his arms, and he sank.

A waterman, however, soon got him out, and he recovered.

Going up the river with a pleasure party, about five years after, the boat was overset with him and several other young men on Chelsea Reach, and every one was drowned except Tom Dibbs.

Eighteen months had scarcely passed when he had another miraculous escape.

On a voyage to Scotland the ship in which he sailed foundered in Yarmouth Roads, and most of the people on board perished ; but another vessel, observing their distress, sent out a long boat, by the help of which Dibbs and two others were saved.

His relation, the haberdasher, employed him in his shop ; but he did nothing but attend to his dress.

He was such a consummate coxcomb that he was perpetually employing tailors to alter his clothes to any new fashion he had seen.

This being discovered his cousin directed the tailors in the neighbourhood not to receive his orders.

Thus foiled, Tom Dibbs procured a dark lantern which he secreted under his bed, and when all the family were asleep he used to alter his clothes to make them resemble the prevailing fashions.

His relation, observing this propensity to be a coxcomb, abridged him of his money allowances.

This was the "beginning of the end."

Tom Dibbs now robbed the till.

The first offence of this kind he committed for the purpose of discharging a pretended debt for which a woman with whom he was acquainted had been arrested by a fellow who was connected with her.

The robbery was not discovered for some days.

When it was, all the servants were taxed with it, but Tom Dibbs was not even suspected.

On his simple denial the affair was suffered to rest, though fifteen pounds had been stolen.

The linendraper, however, with a view to discover the thief, marked several guineas which he put into the till, and they were soon after taken out by Tom Dibbs.

The money having been missed the master went to the bedchamber of every servant at night, and finding them in Tom's pocket he immediately turned him out of the house.

Finding himself alone thus in the streets of London he at once repaired to the house of his female acquaintance, who, as usual, received him with caresses.

Immediately, however, that she found he had no money she caused some one even to drive him out of the house, saying that it was no receptacle for thieves.

Having tried, without success, to obtain money from his relations, he at length joined a company of strolling players.

Among these he remained for some time, but at length was turned out of the company for coming dead drunk upon the stage.

About this time there was a great noise in regard to two daring highwaymen, who had kept the neighbourhood of Bath in a state of terror for some time.

This made him conceive the idea of going out upon the highway for a living.

His first expedition was upon the Kentish Road ; and meeting the Canterbury coach near Shooter's Hill he robbed the passengers of money and watches to the extent of thirty pounds, and then riding through a great part of Kent he took an observation of all the cross roads.

He now took lodgings near Grosvenor Square, and frequenting the billiard tables won a little money, which, added to his former stock, prevented his having recourse to the highway again for a considerable time.

At length, meeting with a gambler who was cleverer than himself, who stripped him of all his money, he turned out again and rode towards Richmond.

Meeting a post chaise near Hampton Court he stopped it, and robbed a lady and gentleman of ten guineas and their watches.

He took also a valuable diamond ring from the gentleman, which he afterwards returned upon a reward of fifteen guineas being offered for it.

By this time Tom Dibbs had drawn from his own observation and for his private use a map of all the roads for twenty miles round London, and as he always drove out in a phaeton and pair he was never suspected of being a highwayman.

In his excursions for robbery he used to dress in a laced or embroidered frock, and wear his hair tied behind.

When at a distance from London he would turn in some unfrequented place, and having disguised himself in other clothes, with a grizzled wig, he saddled one of the horses, rode to the main road, and committed a robbery.

This done he hastened to his carriage, resumed his former dress, and drove back to London.

One evening, having robbed a gentleman near Putney, some persons came up and pursued him so closely that he was obliged to cross the Thames.

In the meantime some haymakers, finding his carriage, carried off his clothes, and the persons who had pursued him meeting them, charged them with being accomplices in the robbery.

Tom Dibbs, however, throwing his clothes into a well, went back nearly naked, claimed the carriage as his own, and declared that the men had stripped him, and thrown him into a ditch.

The poor haymakers were committed for trial, but as Tom Dibbs did not think proper to appear against them they were fortunate enough to be set at liberty.

About two months before his meeting with Brandon at Truebridge he had met at Ranelagh Gardens a lady, of whom he became desperately enamoured, and whom he accompanied home, under the impression that she was some frail lady of title.

He had in his pocket at the time that he entered her house a hundred pounds in gold and notes, but when he left the place in the morning he discovered, to his dismay, that it had all been stolen.

The woman, who had thus duped him, was found upon the following morning lying dead in her bed with her throat cut, and Tom Dibbs disappeared upon the same night.

Having taken this hideous revenge upon the woman who had deceived him, he thought it prudent to absent himself from London for some time.

He it was who had entered the smuggler's band,

and having partaken of their bounty, betrayed them to Brandon.

Gifted with elegant manners and a handsome person, Tom Dibbs had always been a favourite with the women, and being possessed of a persuasive eloquence he had found it a matter of comparative ease to inveigle men into aiding his abominable schemes.

*   *   *   *   *   *

Towards the cottage of the old miser, therefore, Brandon and his accomplice took their way upon that memorable night.

Ere they reached it they parted company.

Then Tom Dibbs advanced alone.

In about a minute after his knocking, the door of the humble dwelling was opened, and a strong light gleamed from the interior of the dwelling—a light which must have fallen full upon the countenance of Dibbs, and enabled those within to get a very perfect view of him, for he felt his eyes dazzled with it coming so suddenly as he had done within the sphere of its influence from the cool damp freshness of the night air.

Hastily stepping inside the cottage, he shaded his eyes with his hand as he said,

"Is this Laurence Masters'?"

"It is," said a woman's voice, "what is it you want, sir?"

Before he could reply, an old man of tall proportions, and who had evidently in youth been very powerful, advanced towards him, saying,

"Sir, I am Laurence Masters. What may be your pleasure?"

"I want," said Dibbs, "to speak with you alone."

"Alone?"

"Yes; concerning matters which are of great importance."

"I have no secrets, sir. Say what you have to say. I never yet kept a secret from my wife, and I'm not going to begin now."

"Be it so," said Dibbs, "the secret is yours, not mine, if indeed it be secret at all. I have come to ask you if you think anything of your son?"

"My son?—yes, yes," said the old man, struck with a sense of coming misfortune by the affected solemnity of Dibbs's manner.

"I grieve to say that—"

The old man sank into a chair.

"God help us!" he cried. "We are childless."

"Oh! my child, my child!" cried the mother, wringing her hands.

"You are wrong," said Dibbs, "he lives."

"Lives? My son lives? Do you tell me that?" cried the old man, starting to his feet.

"I do."

"Then d——n thee, why did thee pull such a long face, eh? Why did thee speak like a mute at a funeral?"

"Don't be violent. I have bad news."

"Out with it, then, like a man. My son lives, and little care I then."

"You shall judge for yourself—listen!"

"Go on, go on."

"There are some soldiers at Truebridge."

"At the 'Half-Moon,' yes. But they do not belong to my son's regiment."

"True; but he deserted, and after a long wandering, enlisted in the regiment which is now at Truebridge."

The old man sprang to the door.

"Wife! wife! he's here—our boy—"

"Hush!" cried Dibbs. "Would you betray him?"

"Betray?"

"Yes; a word of recognition—the pronunciation of his name—the merest accident in the world, would be his death!"

The old man looked aghast.

The mother clasped her hands in silent terror.

"What I tell you is true," said Dibbs; "he and I by chance became acquainted. He was able to do me some service which I am anxious to repay. He is now, as I say, at Truebridge."

"And now—"

"He is at the inn. He came there with his companions, and I met him by appointment. Then, while they were drinking, he stole out with me, and placing his military wallet in my hands, he said, with emotion,

"'Go to my father and mother. Show them this wallet as a proof you are not deceiving them, and implore the old man to come and see me if but for a moment.'"

"Yes, yes," said Laurence Masters, "directly. Come wife, we will both go."

Dibbs objected to this.

It suited not his plans.

One he could deal with.

Not two!

"No," he said, "danger attends such a proceeding. We will return with him."

"We must yield to you," said the father. I will bring our boy home, wife. And now that we know he lives, it will be worth while our looking at the prospect we have neglected. Are you in the army, sir?"

He addressed Dibbs.

"I am."

"Have you the wallet you spoke of? Anything belonging to our son is a welcome sight."

"It is outside. I will bring it in."

Dibbs stepped out and brought in the wallet; and as he re-entered the cottage, the mother said, anxiously,

"What name does my son go by now, sir?"

"What name? His assumed name?"

"Yes."

"Why, he was at a loss for some time," said Dibbs, as he turned the wallet over to see if any name was on it.

There, written in one corner, he saw the name of Gerald.

"After consideration," he added, "he made up his mind to take some common name, so he chose that of Gerald. I dare say it is marked on the wallet somewhere. See, here it is."

If the old couple had had any suspicion of the good faith of their visitor, this dispelled it.

The old man was now anxious to proceed.

"Keep up your spirits, wife," he said, "I shall soon be back—very soon be back, and bring our boy with me. A welcome sight he will be to our eyes!"

He walked to the door.

Then, as if actuated by some sudden impulse, he returned and held out his hand, saying,

"Wife, good bye."

Tears came to her eyes.

"Why say good bye?" she said.

"Did I say good bye? Did I? Well, farewell, wife, farewell!"

He cast a strange look round the well-known house where he had lived so many years.

A deep sigh came from his heart, and then, with Dibbs, crossed the threshold.

His wife watched him from the door, and then he turned to look back.

Dibbs placed his hand in his and led him quickly away out of the town.

Temerity and avarice were struggling together in his breast.

He had resolved to do a deed he shrunk from.

And the night had risen bright in its beauty to welcome him, the second Cain.

Twice the old man had spoken to Dibbs.

He had received no answer.

Now at length he paused.

He spoke tremulously,

"Where are we going? How far are we going? Where is my boy?"

"Down the next lane," said Dibbs, recovering his self-possession. "The distance now is but short. You surely would not have him endanger his safety by meeting you too near the town?"

"No, no; but we have come more than a mile, and I am anxious to see my son."

"He's getting suspicious," thought Dibbs; "I must see that he does not turn back."

He quickened his pace and turned down a lane on the right hand side of the road, which looked very dark and very deserted.

He hesitated as he did so, and such superstitious fears came over him that he felt himself compelled to speak, even to his intended victim.

"We are near at hand," he said.

"Thank God!" replied the old man, solemnly. What a dark lane this is, to be sure! The moonlight is completely obscured by the trees. It is like going into some cavern. What a place this would be, now, for some dreadful murder."

Well might Dibbs start at the remark of the old man.

He staggered back a few paces, as if the intended victim of his mad designs had read the murderous intention of his heart in his face.

"What, what?" he gasped.

"I said it would be a fit spot for a murder," added the old man. "God save us all!"

Dibbs laughed.

"Don't laugh," said the other, "it's just as much out of place here as if we were in a cathedral."

"I dislike this deed," muttered Dibbs to himself, "no good will come of it."

"What did you say?" asked Masters.

"I did not speak."

"I thought I heard some voice."

"A voice? No, surely we are alone; there is no one here but ourselves. What voice do you mean?"

"It might have been my son's. I hope he is near us."

"Yes, true, true. I was abstracted. I feel somewhat confused in this dark lane. Are we near the middle of it?"

"Yes, we are."

"Listen if you can hear anything."

They both stopped and listened.

All was as still as the grave at first.

Then there was a strange rustle, and a harsh, hooting scream came upon their ears from near at hand.

"Great God!" cried Laurence Masters, "what is that?"

"An owl," said Dibbs. "Come, you are easily alarmed. See yonder stile? Get over it and place your back against it on the other side. You will then see your son coming over the adjoining meadow. I have a whistle, which will warn him you are here. You will hear me blow it, and when he hears it, he will come straight over the meadows towards you."

"With pleasure," said the old man.

He advanced to the stile.

The moonlight came from the direction where Dibbs told him to look, so that all the abrupt dark shadows were thrown in the other direction, which made the lane seem dense and black.

The shadow of the stile fell with wonderful clearness and precision right across the lane.

In fact it was only this shadow that had told Dibbs that the stile was there at all.

The old man clambered over, and placed his back against it as directed by Dibbs.

The moonlight fell upon his face, and, as if impressed with the holy stillness of the scene, he took off his hat, and let the gentle breeze that swept over the meadows play with the few straggling silver locks that age had left upon his brow.

"Wait patiently," said Tom Dibbs.

He waved his hand in reply.

Then the wretch, who had such guilt in his heart, crept trembling away from the spot, shaking in every limb, parched with a sudden and unnatural thirst, and his heart beating with such fearful violence that each moment it seemed as if it must burst its bounds.

"It must be done—it must be done," he murmured; "this man must be put out of the way. I can then return, and, as his son, claim his property. Of this Brandon need know nothing."

As he had passed down the lane Dibbs had seen by the dim light which would occasionally—where the vegetation was not so thick—force its way among the trees, a hedge partly composed of living wood, and partly of knotted heavy stakes driven into the earth.

A rank, noisome ditch was close to them.

From the manner in which the stakes bent forward he thought they had but a slight hold of the saturated soil into which they had been thrust.

One of these stakes he now wished to procure, and he soon reached the spot where he had seen them.

Suddenly, however, he paused, and muttered to himself,

"I have forgotten to whistle, and he may, if he hears not that promised sound, become suspicious, and leave the spot."

Taking from his pocket a key, he blew into the barrel of it, producing a loud, shrill sound.

This he repeated thrice, and then he replaced the key in his pocket with trembling hands.

"That will satisfy him," he said; "and now, courage for the deed."

He jumped across the stagnant ditch, but found that what by the faint light he had thought a hard piece of ground was treacherous and weak.

It slid away with him, and he was over his ancles in the ditch.

That, however, was no time for hesitation.

He laid hold of one of the stakes, and tore it from its weak hold in the rotten soil.

It was heavier than he expected, and, as he poised it in his hand, he felt, no doubt, that it was sufficient for his purpose.

He splashed through the ditch, and stamped on the hard ground to get free from the black mud that clung to his feet.

"Confound this part of the business!" cried he. "I must, before I leave this place, get free from this mud. People have been betrayed before this by such trifling things."

On he crept.

The old man was speaking.

Murmuring a hope that he would soon see his son, impatiently expecting his well-known form.

On crept the assassin.

Now, as he neared the stile, he could see the doomed man standing erect.

He stood for an instant to think.

Then he raised the stake, and let it fall over his back to give greater force to the blow.

He hesitated a moment.

The old man moved.

" He will see," thought Tom Dibbs.

With a whistling sound through the air came the heavy piece of wood, then there was a heavy blow.

Then came a ringing shriek, and Dibbs crouched down half dead himself with terror.

The hedge stake had left the hands of Tom Dibbs, but another cry from his victim made him spring to his feet.

He sprang up himself with an answering cry, and glanced over the stile.

" D——n !" he cried, " not dead yet ?"

The sight of horror which met his eyes transfixed him for a few moments.

The old man was battling with death.

He grasped with his two hands at the long, rank grass that fringed the meadow.

He tried to speak, but only a strange gurgling sound came from his throat.

The moonlight fell strangely upon him, and from the frightful wound in his head a stream of gore was running.

" I must strike him again," said Tom Dibbs, " and this time it will be a mercy."

He could not withdraw his eyes from the face of his victim.

Not for the world at that moment could he have taken his gaze from that countenance, distorted as it was in the pangs of death, and speckled with blood.

He tried to look for the hedge stake, and at last, without taking his eyes from his victim, he succeeded.

But death saved him from the last act of merciful atrocity.

A gasping for breath, a convulsive movement, and Laurence Masters was dead.

His murderer stood gazing at him still.

Blood still flowed from the victim's head, and collected around the body in a ghastly, dreadful pool.

The surface of this pool assumed a glassy hue, and Dibbs could see his own face reflected in it.

With a shudder of horror he now roused himself to the necessity of taking some means of self-preservation.

For the first time he withdrew his eyes from the awful sight.

But a new result ensued.

He had been so long looking at the blood that now, let him turn where he would, upon trees, or a road, a meadow, or distant spire, or sky, everything was of the same blood-red hue.

This to him, in his excited state, was a fearful discovery to make.

He closed his eyes.

Yet he still saw blood.

The same frightful, glassy-looking pool of gore was between him and everything.

Hardly knowing what he did he fled away.

Then, as he stood for a moment undecided, he heard footsteps as of some one coming from Truebridge.

Whoever it was, the new comer was a prodigious walker, for he had been going at a great pace, and yet he was being gained sensibly upon.

He mended his pace.

Still on came the man behind him, and he felt convinced that, unless he ran, he would be soon overtaken.

The spot where he was to meet Brandon lay to the right.

He kept straight on.

He had now changed his tactics.

" Let Brandon seize what gold is in the village," thought he ; " I will return as heir."

" Shall I," he asked himself—" shall I take to flight ? No, there can be no danger. The body cannot have been discovered yet."

On he went at a rapid walk.

But it was of no avail.

The faster he walked, the faster came the stranger behind him.

At length, when the perspiration was streaming from his brow, he resolved to slacken his pace, and allow the stranger to pass him.

" He is only some chance passenger," thought he, " and, by the fiend, if he tries to stop me I have a knife, and he will find me a desperate man !"

Tom Dibbs had in his pocket a large clasp-knife, which, when open, was well secured in that position by a spring at the blade.

This he made up his mind to make immediate use of if the man exhibited any token of sinister intentions.

He paused to listen for a moment, and he fancied that, now he had ceased to make such speed, the man who stood towards him had slackened his pace also.

But of this he could not be sure, and he resumed his walk again, although much slower, for, after all he had gone through, he felt much exhausted.

It was just at the corner of a steep and somewhat narrow turning that the stranger gained so far on Tom Dibbs that the latter expected every moment that he would pass him.

To his great terror, however, he did not do so, but, accommodating his pace to Dibbs's, drew a long breath, and in the most unconcerned manner in the world, said,

" A fine night, sir, for a constitutional walk."

Tom Dibbs would have answered with a deep curse.

But he feared now to make this man his enemy.

So he answered merely,

" Yes."

" You are a good walker," said the stranger ; " so am I."

Tom Dibbs made no reply whatever.

The stranger, however, was not at all abashed.

After a short pause, he continued,

" Are you going to town ?"

" I have not the honour of your acquaintance, sir," said Dibbs, " and you must be really aware that in common courtesy you should not be too inquisitive."

" Not at all, not at all ; I am a man of the world, a cosmopolite."

" Curse you !" muttered Tom Dibbs between his clenched teeth.

" Sir ?"

" Nothing, nothing."

" Very good ; I have been out for a constitutional walk, and have had it, so I can afford now to accommodate myself to any respectable companion I may meet with on the road. Don't you think twenty miles in three hours very tolerable going ?"

" Very."

" I have done it. You step out, too. I heard you ; but, then, you got blown soon. I could hear you puffing and wheezing a mile or two down the road."

" You heard me ?"

" Yes, I did. I listened attentively, and knew you were getting winded."

"And pray, sir, what is it to you whether I am winded or not?"

"Nothing at all."

"Then why at:end to it?"

"Because, from being nothing to me it became a matter of some interest and curiosity. If you had been ever so winded I should not have cared, and hence it was that I had the occupation and amusement without any alloying anxiety upon the results, you see."

"Indeed!"

"Yes. Which way are you going? Right on? To the right, or the left? or back again? All's one to me."

Tom Dibbs came to a dead stand-still, and looked at his intrusive companion.

He was a tall man, and had a singular white coat buttoned up to the chin.

Over one eye was a singular-looking patch, which gave his face a very odd look, and imparted some degree even of ferocity to it.

By the firmness of his tread, and the general carriage of his person, it was evident he was a powerful man, although rather ungainly in his build.

In a personal encounter with him Tom Dibbs would not have stood the slightest shadow of a chance.

When Dibbs paused the stranger paused likewise, and regarded him fixedly.

They could both see each other very well indeed, for the sky was completely cloudless, and although the moon's rays were now slant, they were still bright and full.

Everything in fact was as clear as day.

"Do you think you shall know me again?" said the stranger.

"I don't want to."

"I thought you did, as you looked upon me so earnestly."

"Can you not understand that I have an objection to making an acquaintance in this manner?"

"An aversion! I go far beyond you; I have a horror of it. I wouldn't do it on any earthly consideration. Don't fancy it."

They now moved on again.

Dibbs was tremulous with fear and anger.

"Then why do you speak to me?" he cried, in a voice which plainly showed how angry he was.

"Why, what has that to do with it? You don't call this, I hope, making an acquaintance? If you do you are confoundedly mistaken. The next time I meet you I shall think nothing more of cutting you dead than I do of now conversing with you."

"Then allow me to cut you dead now, for I don't want your company."

"Explicitly?"

"Explicitly."

"And no mistake?"

"None whatever."

"Then I want yours."

"Why?"

"Never mind; we won't part yet."

"To all bargains, two consenting parties are necessary."

"I know it; but I admire your candour, and will walk with you."

"Do you mean to tell me that you will walk with me whether I like it or not?"

"Precisely; only you put it in more forcible language than I do."

"Then give me leave to tell you, sir, that you are the most impudent fellow I ever met."

"I know it. I pride myself on it. It's seldom I meet a man that I take such a fancy to as I do to you. Say what you will—do what you will—but while you live you shall *never* shake me off—never! Do you quite clearly understand that?"

Tom Dibbs stopped in amazement.

An unknown, undefined dread crept over him, and he asked himself,

"Is this a madman or the devil?"

"Now, what do you think of me?" said the stranger, assuming an air of defiance.

"Good God!" cried Tom Dibbs. "Why have you picked me out for such a system of persecution?"

"Persecution?"

"Aye."

"Why do you call it so?"

"By what other name can I call it? It wants no conjuror to tell me you are the stronger man, and doubtless you presume on that fact to persecute me with your odious company."

"And this," said the stranger, "this is human gratitude!"

"A mad man, clearly," thought Tom Dibbs. "What a happy stroke of policy it would be, if, by some means or another, I could fix on him the murder. How admirable and safe a thing for me. Perhaps, after all, my being connected with this fellow, whom I have been so anxious to get rid of, may turn out to be one of the most fortunate circumstances that could possibly have by chance occurred to me."

This view of the subject restored Tom Dibbs very much to his equanimity, and much he wished his mad companion would continue silent for some time to allow him to arrange in his mind some plan by which he could involve him in suspicion as to the murder.

The stranger was not much disposed to allow him leisure for much consideration.

"You will take a better thought concerning me," he said, "before we reach London, I could swear."

"Shall I?"

"Of course you will. Nobody likes me at first; but when people find that I know everybody—"

"Know everybody?"

"Yes. And I make it the whole business of my life to ferret out everything that concerns everybody—family secrets, engagements, crimes—they are all food for me."

"A troublesome personage!"

"Not all."

"Well, then, since you know everybody; do you know me?"

"Yes."

"Indeed!"

"Know *you!*—ha, ha! Do you doubt it?"

"In truth I did and do."

Tom Dibbs trembled as he spoke, notwithstanding that he strove to put on an air of indifference.

"Then you must be convinced."

"I shall believe you when I hear you."

"Come, come, Master Tom Dibbs, that will not do!"

"Tom Dibbs! How came you by my name? Who *are* you?"

"Never mind *who* I am. You see very plainly that I know you."

"Mysterious man! Is it for good or evil that you thus assail me?"

"For your own good."

"Tell me, I implore you, who you are?"

"Is it possible you do not suspect?"

"None—none—unless—"

Tom Dibbs shuddered.

The stranger laughed loudly.

"Unless I am the devil, eh?"

"I did not say that."

"But you thought it?"

"I did."

"Well, I keep you no longer in suspense. Look!"

Tom Dibbs eyed him eagerly.

One by one the stranger removed his disguises. The stains left his cheeks—the patch his eye.

It was Brandon!

"Is this possible?" exclaimed Tom.

"Well, it *is* so, as you see."

"You were well disguised."

"I was. I pride myself on it."

"And why practise on me?"

"Cannot you guess?"

"Not I."

"Tax your memory. You will not go far back."

"I do not understand you."

"You do; but are afraid to confess."

"To you I could confess nothing. The murder you know of, since we planned it together."

"We also planned another thing."

"What is that?"

"A meeting."

"I know it. I was hurrying thither when you overtook me. It was to shake off one I knew not that I kept straight on."

Brandon laughed.

"I disbelieve you. You had other thoughts in view; but at any rate you are defeated if you meant to cheat me."

"In what way?"

"The money in the cottage; a large sum, by the way, is in my possession."

"Well?"

"And hardly had I quitted the cottage than I discovered that the son who was expected was dead."

"Dead?"

"Yes; the man was hurrying to them with the news. He is dead, and the only living heir to the property now is an old maiden aunt."

Tom Dibbs uttered a hollow groan.

He had committed the murder for nothing!

At the next inn they took the coach.

No more was said as to the murder.

When at length they *did* part company Tom Dibbs parted company with Brandon.

"To-morrow, at our old place, I will meet you," he said, as they parted in the city.

He went through Cheapside, and passing the Mansion House, he took his way towards the Minories.

Down this sufficiently notorious thoroughfare he walked for some distance till he came to a narrow paved court with an arched entrance, which was, however, a thoroughfare, and boasted several shops.

That is to say there was a beer shop, three marine store dealers, a chandler's shop, and a variety of nondescripts.

Tom Dibbs passed two of the marine store shops; but into the third he dived at once.

A stranger would hardly have believed that prior to so doing he had touched, as he passed the window, a little projecting knob.

But he did so, and the sharp ring of some small but clear-sounding bell immediately sounded within.

The moment he went into the shop a part of the counter was opened by a man who was there, and Dibbs passed behind it.

He was at once out of sight of the street.

"Tom Dibbs, as I'm a sinner!" cried the man.

"Not much doubt of that, old boy. How are ye?"

"Tolerable as things go, Tom Dibbs; "but they *is* hard, you knows."

"Well, they *may* be harder; and that's what I've come to tell ye, or ye wouldn't see *me* here at *this* time of day."

"Indeed!"

"Yes; there is a sneak among you. You'd have been all sold if it hadn't been for me. Are there any of the fellows here?"

"Yes; two or three down below. What is it?"

"I'm always on the watch, and I've found that Jonathan Rasper is trying for a price."

"D———n!"

"It's a fact. Fifty pounds placed in his hand and he peaches. I know it. I know what I'd do."

"You know what we *will* do, Tom Dibbs. The lads will believe you where they won't me. Hold hard."

There was a rope fastened in some manner which was not visible, and which went from the floor to the ceiling.

Dibbs at once, when his companion said "Hold hard!" laid hold of the rope with one hand.

Then the man gave two distinct stamps with his foot.

In about a minute the floor under them began to descend.

They had been standing on a trap-door about three feet square, and it went down as easily as any theatrical affair of the same sort could have done.

The rope, as well as steadying the machine, had something to do with the means by which it was made to descend.

The depth was not considerable, being only sufficient to enable a tall man's head to clear the flooring of the shop when the trap-door on which he descended reached its lowest point.

That lowest point was at the bottom of a strange cavernous-looking place, half cellar, half vault.

MOON-LIGHT JACK

OR THE KING OF THE ROAD

GIPSY BESS.

The floor was of common earth, with only here and there a stone laid in where some hollows had formed themselves in consequence of the yielding nature of the soil.

It had a strange smell, that place; a mixture of tobacco smoke, ardent spirits and burnt bones.

The latter arose from the constant use of a large gridiron, which even now, with some steak or chop on it, was spitting and spluttering over a fire in the corner, which every now and then emitted smoke in dense volumes.

Upon the table was a bottle, in the neck of which was stuck a candle that, in consequence of being all on one side, had distributed its grease down the side of the bottle and on to the table.

To judge from the first glance at the place any one would have supposed it to be of rather limited extent; but such was not the case.

It went a long way back.

The further end, indeed, was completely lost in gloom and obscurity.

"Where are they?" asked Tom Dibbs, as he stepped off the trap-door on which he and his companion had descended.

"Asleep, I suppose," said the other, as he pulled the flooring up to its proper place.

"All but me," cried a young lad, coming forward. "I heard ye knock and shot the bolt."

"Ah, you're the man for my money," cried Tom Dibbs. "Who's here besides you?"

"Only three."

"Which three?"

"The Screamer, Bungy Bill, and the Nonpareil."

"Is that all?"

"Yes."

"Where are they?"

"They're asleep. I was cooking something 'cos I was hungry, or I should have been asleep too."

"Why don't you sleep at night?"

"Can't do it, there's allers somebody here a kicking up a row. The day time's quiet."

"Well, wake 'em up. There's something wrong that they must know."

"All right!"

He went into the darker part of the cellar.

Then there was heard such a grumbling and growling and swearing as would have been almost enough to make one's hair stand on end who was unused to such company.

Tom Dibbs rather liked it.

Use is second nature.

He commenced whistling a popular air, while the old man who had brought him down the trap looked anxiously in the direction the boy had taken who had gone to wake the sleepers at the other end of the cavern.

"What's the row?" said a hoarse voice. "What the devil, can't we sleep night or day?"

"I don't know," replied the boy; "something's wrong, and you'd better all get up."

"Eh! something wrong?"

The fellows now roused themselves.

Half stupefied with drink and tobacco, and having been suddenly aroused from sound sleep, they now staggered forward, winking and blinking at the candle like owls.

"What is it, eh?" cried one.

"A very few words can tell you that," said the old man. "Jonathan Rasper's going to peach. Mr. Dibbs has come to tell us, boys. I always *did* suspect that fellow."

"No, no!" cried the boy. "You can't mean my cousin, Jonathan."

"Yes," said Dibbs, "Brandon heard him. That should be enough. Where he is now, I don't know. He offered, for fifty pounds, to blow the last affair altogether. He must be found, and that to-night, too, or all will be lost. It must be so; there is no help for it. Before to-morrow morning I should recommend——"

Tom Dibbs pointed to the earthen floor at his feet.

"Yes," said one of the men, "that's the only way. He must be killed then, before he is four-and-twenty hours older, or we shall be done for. I always suspected him."

"And *I*," said another.

"No, no! Don't say so," said the boy. "It may be a mistake, you know, after all."

"You stick up for him," remarked the old man, "because he's your cousin."

"Not entirely, for *he* made me what I am."

"Well, and a very genteel thing you've dropped into, Ned, only don't interfere."

"You'll find that men can't be played with so easily. Leave this affair alone, and take care of yourself; it's our business."

"But you will not condemn him unheard?"

"Of course not."

"We'll be off at once, and find him out," said the three fellows who had been sleeping.

"And I too," said the boy.

"No," cried the old man. "You stay here. We have found you faithful, Ned, on more than one occasion. Don't you *now* go in the way of being

suspected. Stay here, and then no one can say a word against you."

"As you please," said the boy. "I didn't mean wrong. If he was ten times my cousin, and played false to his comrades, I wouldn't say a word for him."

"We know that, Ned. You're a good fellow; but stay here, let me advise you."

The boy sat down despondingly.

The three men moved towards the ascending and descending trap-door.

"I shall be home at twelve to-night," remarked Dibbs. "Don't do anything till *I* come, mind."

"No, no."

"Good. But by fair means or foul, bring Jonathan Rasper here."

"Never fear!" cried the desperadoes.

The trap-door was made to descend, and one by one they went up.

Dibbs lingered till the last, and before he left the place, he whispered,

"Whatever you do, keep a sharp look out on the boy. Mind that; I never trust anybody. Kill him rather than let him leave the place."

"All right," said the other.

CHAPTER XIX.

THE PURSUIT OF THE TRAITOR.

THE men who had gone in pursuit of Jonathan Rasper knew well where to find him.

It was in a low inn.

Having ascertained at the bar that he was there, they held a consultation, and then one of the three went into the room where he was as if he had strolled in accidentally.

The moment he saw Jonathan he saluted him with the usual cordiality, as if nothing had happened; but he observed the haste with which the traitor huddled up the paper on which he had been writing.

It was a note to Mr. Bosworth the chief inspector of police.

Something to drink was proposed, and into that something was placed a powerful narcotic, the use of which was well known to the whole gang.

He saw Jonathan drink unsuspectingly; but the other, although he placed the glass to his lips, avoiding doing so.

In the course of a quarter of an hour the narcotic drug began to exercise its baneful influence.

Then so rapid was its effect, that although the youth might well have suspected what had occurred, he was in a state of insensibility before he could make the least movement to save himself from the fate that awaited him.

The other two men were called in.

The people of the house were told that Jonathan had drank too much, and that they, as his friends, would see him home.

A coach was procured, and the doomed traitor placed in it.

A short time sufficed to reach the court in the Minories, and so, within one hour, the pursued deceiver was lying in a corner of the cellar with handcuffs upon him, there to remain until the effects of the drug that had been administered to him had gone off, and he was able to hear and understand the charge against him.

About half-past eleven on the same evening Tom Dibbs, wrapped up in an old faded cloak, took his way again towards the Minories.

What reflections were passing through the mind

of the man might have been guessed by the expression of his face.

He guessed the nature of the scene to which he was hastening.

The cavernous-looking abode of the thieves was now lighted by several lamps which hung by chains from the ceiling, and cast a ruddy glare upon the countenances of those, who, like demons, flitted hither and thither beneath them.

There were now about twelve men present.

Some were smoking, some eating.

There was but little conversation going on, and what *did* proceed was almost in a whispering tone.

In a corner, lying on an old rug, was Jonathan Rasper, and, from the strong odour of vinegar close to him, it was clear that it had been administered to him as an antidote.

"Give him some more vinegar," said one of the men; "he will soon come round, and it's only a quarter to twelve now."

Another stooped down by him, and taking a bottle in which was some strong vinegar in one hand, while he raised Jonathan's head with the other, he poured the stimulating liquid into his mouth.

The youth was forced to swallow, or he would have been soon suffocated; for after every dose the man who administered to him the antidote closed his mouth, and held it shut till he felt convinced the potion was fairly taken.

When he had repeated this operation three times he let his head down, and went and joined the low conversation that was going on among some of the others.

"Is he better, Joe?" said one.

"Oh! he's coming round; he'll be right enough presently."

"D—n him! Where might we have all been to-morrow if such a sneak had had his own way?"

"In Newgate, to be sure."

"Not a doubt of it. Whenever a feller begins to talk of what he oughtn't, he never knows when to stop."

"Sartinly not," said another ruffian, who, judging by his countenance, had not been shaved nor washed for a month or two, "sartainly not. When a fellow once peaches he tells all he knows, and when he gets to the end of that he tells a little more."

"Bill's right there," said one of the previous speakers; "I'd take the life of such a one as I would the life of any vermin in the world. How would blessed security go on, if so be every one was to tell all they knows of everybody?"

"Ah! jest so. How, indeed?"

"Nohow, as you all knows as well as me. You know what a precious row there is, time and time agen, among the nobs in the House of Commons, and them kind o' places, whenever by any kinder sort of an accident it really comes out what they really is."

"Jest so; quite right."

"In course I is, or any other man," said the fellow, severely. "There's every one turns out to be an out-and-out rogue. That's what comes out then; the very honourable member is found out to be a swindler, and the gallant captain a common cheat."

"I say," said one, "how werry severe and strong Joe is a coming out to-night."

"Rather. He's a imitating of the parsons; but I say, there's Tom Dibbs' knock."

"Yes; I'd lay a guinea on it."

Then came two distinct taps at the trap door above.

Then one of the men removed the fastenings which kept it in its place, and it slowly descended.

When it reached within a few inches of the floor Dibbs stepped from it, and throwing off his cloak showed that he was dressed in the very height of fashion.

"My eyes, guvner!" said one of the men, "you *do* come it strong now and then."

"What do you mean?"

"I mean in the way of togs."

"Mind your own business, and leave me to mine if *you* please. Now let's to business."

"I moves as Joe takes the chair," said one.

This proposition met with general applause, and Joe accordingly was installed in a large arm chair.

The remainder of the men grouped themselves around him quickly, and Tom Dibbs stepped forward to an open space which was left in front.

Before he could speak, however, the boy came forward, and cried eagerly.

"You won't try him *now*, surely. He don't know what you are about, and can't say one word for himself. Put it off till to-morrow night."

"D—n that!" cried Tom. "I never put off till to-morrow what can be done to day."

"He's well enough. Get him up," said the chairman. "Look at him; he knows what's going on as well as we do, I'll be bound. Get him up."

Two of the fellows went, and lifted up Jonathan Rasper from the corner in which he lay, and when he was on his feet he betrayed, by his fears, that he was sufficiently recovered to know what was going on, for he said, faintly,

"What's it all about? Who's done anything wrong? I haven't. Don't say it's me. I'd die to save any of you."

"You'll run a good-chance of doing that," said one. "You never spoke a truer word."

"Bring him this way," said the chairman.

The trembling, unhappy wretch was brought forward, and confronted with Tom Dibbs.

The youth eyed him with a glance of great distrust.

"Oh! Mr. Dibbs," said he, with an effort at composure, "is that you?"

"Yes; I think it is."

"What's this all about?"

"You'll soon see," said Dibbs. "Gentlemen," he added, glancing round him upon the assembled company, "I have to accuse Jonathan Rasper here of having offered for fifty pounds to sell us all to a Mr. Bosworth, the chief of the watch."

There was a short pause.

Then Jonathan spoke.

"My good friends, and old pals," he said, "it's all a mistake on the part of Mr. Dibbs; I assure you quite a mistake."

"As how?" asked Joe, "as how? Let's hear that."

"He's mistaken some one for me."

"What hour of the day was it?" asked Joe.

"Half past one," said Dibbs.

"Can you prove you were anywhere else?"

"I can't; but I was asleep on a bench in the park till later than that."

"How much later?" asked Tom.

"Oh, till five."

"When was he brought here?"

"Before four," said one of the men, who had gone in search of him.

The prisoner gave a deep groan.

"Then I can't remember everything," he said, "I'm as weak as a cat, and all in a flurry."

"Now, look here," said Tom Dibbs, "I don't want

to accuse anybody here—as you may be all well aware—wrongfully, because what the devil but trouble should I get by that ?"

" True, true."

" If there was any difficulty about the proof in this case I should say wait till to-morrow ; but there's no mistake. Brandon saw him talking to Bosworth at 'one time, and I at another, and he offered to take fifty pounds to sell us."

" A mistake ; it wasn't me. I was not there. By to-morrow I can find evidence to prove it."

" How and where ?"

" You will let me go, and find some one who saw me in the park during the time I name."

" Is that all you have to say for yourself ?" said the chairman.

" Is not it enough ?"

" I can tell you it is not. Do you know this letter ?"

Jonathan trembled.

He knew the letter well.

It was the one he had commenced writing to Mr. Bosworth.

He saw all was hopeless.

He glanced round.

All was stern rebuke mingled with ferocious glances of anger.

Dropping on his knees, he said, in a thick guttural tone.

" Have mercy upon me ! Oh ! have mercy upon me ! I will confess. I meant to get the money because I wanted to leave the country. I wouldn't have told anything ; I meant to get the money, and tell nothing for it. Have some pity for me, old pals."

" Them 'ere things always begin at home with us," said the chairman.

" Mr. Dibbs, I've done you and Captain Brandon good service before this. Won't you say something for me ?"

" You've always been paid for what you did," said Tom Dibbs. " I've got nothing to do with it. You are in the hands of your comrades."

" But they will listen to you."

" I cannot interfere."

" Old pals—old friends, you won't send me adrift from you like this ? What is to become of me if you do ? You know how I like you all ; I can't live anywhere but among you."

" Why, confound your lies," said the chairman, " you said, just now, that you wanted fifty pounds on purpose to leave us."

" No, no, did I ? I didn't mean that. No ; I did not."

" You are making a nice mess of it," said one man. " I think the less you says the better."

" Yes, yes, perhaps so ; but don't banish me from your society, and turn me into the streets. You won't do this, now, will you ?"

" No, oh, no," said the chairman. " We won't do that."

" Thank you, thank you. Now, the first money I get you shall spend it all in drink—every drain. It's a blessing it's all over. The idea of suspecting me."

" What do you say gentlemen ?" asked the chairman. " Guilty or not guilty ?"

The word " guilty " came from every tongue.

" Good night," said Tom Dibbs, " good night. I am not now wanted any longer. Gentlemen all, I wish you good night."

" I will go with you," said Jonathan Rasper. " I'll walk with you, for I've something very particular to say to you."

" I am afraid," said Tom Dibbs, with mock civility, " that these most worthy friends of yours cannot very well spare you at present ?"

" Oh, yes, yes."

" Nay, they would be dull without you."

Jonathan Rasper saw that there was something wrong.

He trembled violently, and reeled back till he came to the wall, against which he leaned.

" How—how very facetious you all are," he said. " But come, now, the joke has lasted long enough."

" That's just as it suits *you*," said the chairman. " Good night, Tom, good night."

Tom Dibbs got on the trap-door.

" Don't you mean to let me go ?" cried Jonathan.

There was no reply.

Tom Dibbs waved his hand, and in another moment he was gone.

There was a deathlike stillness among those desperate men.

It was broken by a shrill laugh from young Rasper.

" Ha ! ha !" he cried, " you carry out your jokes, comrades. But let one of you take off these ' darbies ;' I'm getting tired of them, I am, upon my soul."

There was no answer.

Only a whispered conversation went on.

" Come, come," said Jonathan, " won't any of you speak to me ?"

The mysterious whispering continued.

Jonathan turned paler than before, and the perspiration, cold and profuse, poured off his face.

He had now in his own heart a full conviction of the fate which awaited him, and yet so dreadful was it that he scarcely dared confess it to himself.

At length suspense was no longer one of his sufferings.

The men seemed to have come to a sudden determination.

" Agreed, agreed !" he heard said on all sides.

Joe the chairman turned to him.

He was pale and grave.

"Jonathan Rasper," he said, " you have been found guilty of treachery."

" No, no !" he cried.

" We say yes ; but we don't, of course, expect you to say so. I say you have been found guilty. Once before a man betrayed us. What became of him ?"

Jonathan shuddered.

" He was hanged," he muttered, " and buried in the cellar."

" You have a good memory. Remember also that you, young as you were at the time, clapped your hands and applauded the sentence."

" He was guilty. I am not."

" We say you *are*. The same fate as was given to that man will be given to you."

" Oh, mercy !"

" You know your doom !"

The boy flung himself on his knees.

" Oh, friends," he shrieked, " you cannot mean, it ! Consider how long I have been among you and how I have served you. I will serve you faithfully again ; but forgive me, for the love of Heaven, forgive me."

As if now with one accord they remained silent.

They allowed him to go on speaking without paying the least attention to the purport of his words.

He, too, found out this himself.

It was in broken accents, and long pauses between, that he now implored them to pay some attention to him.

" Speak to me some of you ! Why don't you

speak to me? How can I hope to defend myself if you won't speak to me? Is this like Englishmen?"

There was no reply.

"If I have done wrong among you, why do you not turn me out? That is surely sufficient punishment, and a great humiliation. Turn me away, and leave me to starve, as you then know I must."

Still no reply.

"And you, Ned, too, you don't say a word, though I am your cousin. One *would* think *you'd* speak to me."

Ned shook his head.

He made no reply in words to the appeal which the shivering, anxious wretch made to him.

One of the men now pulled down the trap door, and then ascended upon it to the shop above them, and a noise was heard as if he were searching among heaps of old iron.

During his absence the men idled listlessly about.

Nobody took any notice of the prisoner.

Jonathan began at length to get desperate.

He ran among them.

He turned to one and the other, and implored them to speak to him.

It was in vain.

Every one turned away.

Not a word did he get, good, bad, or indifferent, from any one.

The probability is that he had, by the great notice he had at first taken of their silence towards him, contributed very much to the making of their determination not to speak with him.

Certain it is they seemed fully resolved on the subject.

In a few minutes more he who had ascended by the trap-door at once came down again.

In his hand he carried half-a-dozen second-hand spades which he found among the miscellaneous matters in the shop.

These spades he distributed among the most robust and hardy-looking of his fellows.

Then, without a word of explanation, they proceeded to the further end of the cellar, and after a glance above them, as if their object was to be under some particular spot, they commenced digging up the ground with a strength and energy which spoke well of their resolution.

Did Jonathan guess it was his grave they were digging?

Yes.

He knew well it was.

Too well he knew it.

The spades had told the tale.

None knew better than he for what they were meant.

Despair took possession of him.

He wept, raved, blasphemed, and prayed by turns.

No one heeded him. It was horrible to hear him.

So anomalous a state of things is seldom presented by human nature as the agitation of this youth and the calm of those surrounding him.

It was evident these lawless fellows had made a desperate resolve.

The question was would they swerve from it?

CHAPTER XX.

THE BRAND OF SIN.

THE men now dug up the earth in the cellar as if their lives depended upon their getting the work done in a certain time.

They had arranged themselves in the best manner for their work.

No one interfered with the other.

So, in a short space of time, they had a trench made six feet long and two in width.

Whenever they had this fairly made about the depth of a spade they set about deepening it in the quickest and most systematic manner.

The whole job was completed in less than half an hour.

A considerable quantity of earth was thrown up on each side.

The grave then seemed quite four feet in depth.

Towards the latter part of their operations Jonathan had become more silent.

He now walked up to the spot where the fearful preparations for death were being made.

He stood for some time as still as a statue.

Then when the men threw down their spades and paused from their labour he held up his manacled hands, and in a wild, shrieking voice that rung through the place, he cried.

"Mercy! mercy! have mercy upon me! Do not take my life! Will you murder me in cold blood? No, no, you will not, you cannot! Mercy! mercy! mercy! Help! help! Murder! help! Here are murderers! Help! help!"

One laid hold of him by the throat.

The sudden loud sounds were stopped.

He could scarcely breathe, much less make the alarm which he had conceived possible.

He who had laid hold of him relaxed his grasp in about a minute, and then the shrieking wretch was silent.

He seemed to have a full impression that it was madness to expect help from without.

Again he cast himself on his knees.

Again he clasped his hands in a last appeal for mercy.

The appeal we cannot record.

Words—articulate, consecutive words—could convey no idea of the horrible agony in which he spoke.

Tears gushed from his eyes.

Sobs burst from his bosom.

He prayed for life.

"Life! life! life!"

On any conditions!

This was all he asked.

To live, to breathe, to grovel through his existence!

Anything but death!

They paid no heed to him.

No more than to a yelping, complaining dog.

They went on with their fearful operations as if he had been the guiltiest and most quiescent malefactor that ever came to a dreadful death.

Immediately over the grave which they had with so much persevering labour, and in so short a space of time dug in the cellar, was a massive beam.

Projecting from this beam was a hook of immense strength, capable of supporting almost any weight that could be suspended to it.

Over this hook they now threw a rope, and two of them held it, while another, with great rapidity, converted the other end of it into a running noose.

Jonathan Rasper did not see these advanced preparations for his death, for he had knelt down.

His back was towards the grave.

Soon, however, he was made perfectly cognizant of them, for while he was yet speaking and imploring those of the party who were nearest to him for mercy, he who had made the noose at the end of the rope came behind him, and placed it over his head before he was aware.

Then he drew it tight round his neck so that he was, no doubt, half strangled before he got exactly under the hook.

He screamed once or twice in a strange, smothered tone of voice, and that was all.

The body tumbled partially into the grave, but then the man who had hold of the rope, by a sudden pull, which was aided by three or four more pairs of hands, run Jonathan close up to the ceiling, and there he hung, plunging and kicking, and the whole body subjected to the most frightful contortions.

There was one who watched painfully.

He expected to see a tragedy.

He did not.

Jonathan Rasper was at length let down.

But this one, Ned, did not expect this.

He watched the screaming youth.

When he was dragged along the floor he had removed his hands from before his face, and then suddenly he had noted everything with a soul-absorbing interest which was not natural.

He had shed no tears.

He had uttered no cry.

For all the feeling which he displayed on the occasion he might have been a statue placed there to *seem* to look on the dreadful scene which was now being performed.

Jonathan, when let down, was seized by a man, and according to the orders of Joe, the chairman, seated in a chair.

A red-hot iron was then brought from the fire.

"Jonathan Rasper," cried Joe, "you were convicted of treachery. We have changed the sentence of death into branding. This is done only on account of your youth. Johnny, do it!"

The man who held the red-hot iron advanced.

Jonathan sat still.

He was stupefied.

The half hanging had outmatched his powers.

The man leaned over him.

The red-hot iron scorched and seared into his flesh.

He sprang up with a yell.

BRANDED FOR EVER !

T.

The first letter of the word "Traitor" was on his brow.

A tell-tale to all.

With a wild yell he sprang on the platform of the ascending machine.

"Am I free now ?" he yelled.

"Yes, traitor !" cried Joe. "Go forth to the world and publish your crime and its punishment !"

There was a hush among the thieves as he went up.

Then a man said, suddenly,

"Where's Ned ?"

"Ned ?" exclaimed another. "I have not seen him for this half hour or more."

"Why, there he is," said another; "he's been a staring at Jonathan. I dare say he's in a nice taking now."

The man went up to the lad, and laid his hand upon his arm.

"Come," he said, "what's the use of sitting there ? Come away, you can't keep it no more than any one else. He has himself to thank for what's come over him."

The boy rose mechanically.

Then he spoke.

His tone was so odd that the man started again.

"When are you going to do it again ?"

"Do what ?"

"That."

He pointed to the spot where Jonathan had disappeared.

"Why, what the deuce do ye mean ?"

"It's all the same," said the boy, "we are all dead now; what a strange feeling it is. Ha! ha! ha! I wonder who it was now, and what he had done to come to such a dog's end as that, eh? Do you know ?"

"D—n me if I can understand you !"

He led the lad forward among other men.

They were collected under one of the lights at the other part of the cellar, and pushing him in among them, said,

"Here's Ned; I think he's taken leave of his senses altogether by what he says."

The light fell full upon the boy's face.

"Oh ! what a wondrous change was there."

"There's many a true word spoken in jest," said one of the men; "what he has seen to-night has turned his brain, poor fellow, look at him."

It was too true !

The boy's reason had given way.

He was an idiot.

The most remarkable change had taken place in his countenance.

All the sharp intelligence, which so short a time before had characterised his features, had completely vanished.

There was *no* mistake.

He *was* the same person.

Else they might truly have doubted it.

"God bless me !" said one, "it is strange."

"It is, indeed."

The lad broke in,

"When are you going to do it again ?"

They answered not.

"What's the time ? Ain't you going to hang him again ?"

He spoke in the strange tone of voice which had so much astonished him who had lifted him from his crouching posture.

"What does he mean ?"

"He means the branding and the sham execution."

"A sad sight," said the boy. "But I want to know what it's all about, and why the thunder was so loud when there was no cloud in the sky ?"

"Mad as a March hare," exclaimed one.

"And no mistake," said another. "Well, who'd have thought it ?"

"I was mad once, I know," said the boy, "if you mean me, but something took place in my head; all of a sudden something came boiling and swelling up, up, up, and then I came to myself again."

The men looked at each other in amazement.

Then they were silent for several minutes.

"What's to be done ?" said one at length.

"Aye, what's to be done wi' the lad ?"

"He seems harmless," said a third, "perhaps after a good sleep he'll come to."

"He may. Look at him."

The men were filling up the grave.

"Let me see, let me see !" cried Ned, eagerly, "we don't see such sport every day. Do you think he'll kick again ?"

"I should think not," said one.

"Come," cried another, "let's get the boy away."

Ned skipped up.

"Oh !" cried he, "are you going to take me to another hanging ?"

"Yes," said the man who had last spoken, knowing it was best to humour him, "yes, you shall see another hanging."

"And will he kick like him, and make faces ?"

"Yes, yes, come away."

The grave was now full.

The men leaned upon their spades.

"Well, what's to be done now?" said one.

"Take the boy away, and drive out the other."

So it was done.

Ned was taken tenderly away by one of those men whose passions when roused were hideous to a degree.

After him Jonathan Rasper was taken up, and out into the dark night, which had now clouded the city, with the BRAND OF SIN upon his brow.

Out into the city where he knew none.

Out into the city, bleeding and burning and in pain.

Out into the city, with the terror yet in his mind and strengthened hate in his heart.

Out into the city, to crouch in dark corners and hide from the light till the damning evidence of his guilt should be wiped away by Time.

BOOK III.
THE DEAD HAND.

CHAPTER I.

AN OLD FRIEND WITH A NEW FACE—THE GLOVER'S NIECE—THE MYSTERIOUS STRANGER—THE MAN IN THE BLACK CLOAK—THE DISCOVERY—THE BRAWL—ST. VALENTINE'S DAY.

IT was the eve of St. Valentine.

Young and old, rich and poor were paying their addresses to their patron saints, and not least noticed of the crowds that thronged the streets were old Robert Damer and his niece, Bessie, the former a glover in good position in London, the latter, his niece, in whose beautiful features one could not have failed to recognise the long-lost smile and expression of Gipsy Bess.

Bess, long since deemed dead by the lover who had deemed her false, had fled to London, and for two years she had heard nothing of Moonlight Jack.

His son Harry was with her in the disguise of an apprentice.

Wars and rumours of wars had prevailed during this time.

The Pretender had fled after a bloody and disastrous battle, while those who had befriended him were compelled to fly also or conceal themselves.

So far away from the gipsy haunts and forest scenes she loved, Bessie Clive remained in town, petted by the old man, her uncle, courted by all, and taught by her guardian to believe herself the betrothed of Hubert Dorstone.

This, of course, she knew to be impossible.

Pledged, as she believed herself to be, to Moonlight Jack, all other men were as nothing to her.

Harry Tyrrell she loved because he was the son of him who was more to her than all the world besides; and he returned her affection with an ardent devotion which some would have believed to be scarcely brotherly.

He was now a fine tall youth of sixteen, well proportioned and manly-looking, and was the best protector which Bessie Clive could have desired.

Old Robert Damer knew nothing of Moonlight Jack's betrothment to his niece, nor did he understand where she had been sojourning during her long forest days.

That a country friend, a near relation to her on her mother's side, had afforded her a shelter was his belief, and the difficulty of intercommunication between town and country in those days fully kept up the illusion.

Well, on this memorable St. Valentine's Eve, Gipsy Bess and her uncle proceeded towards the Monastery of the Black Friars, receiving on their passage homage from young and old.

As they moved along arm-in-arm, they were followed by a tall, handsome young man, well, though plainly, dressed. This was Harry Tyrrell.

He had no weapon but a stick.

The apprentices, to which class he was supposed to belong, were not permitted to wear swords.

The retainers of nobility alone assumed this privilege.

The streets in holiday time was scarcely pleasant for the passage of pretty girls.

Orderly citizens took no further heed of Bessie than was due to her extreme beauty and her generous youth.

But with soldiers or gallants of higher grades it was different, and blood was often shed in the struggle for a kiss.

Harry, therefore, whose place was behind his master, felt less annoyed at the enforced indignity, because it enabled him to watch over the safety of the one he loved.

Presently the party was overtaken by a tall young man, wrapped in a cloak which obscured or muffled a part of his face, a practice often used by the gallants of the time, when they did not wish to be known, or were abroad in quest of adventures.

He seemed, in short, one who might say to the world,

"I desire for the present not to be known, but if I *am* no matter."

He came on the right side of Gipsy Bess, who had hold of her uncle's arm, and slackened his pace as if joining the party.

"Good evening to you," he said.

"The same to your worship, and thanks. May I pray you to pass on? Our pace is too slow for that of your lordship, our company too mean for that of your father's son."

"My father's son can best judge of that, old man. I have business to talk with you and my fair saint here."

"With deep reverence, my lord," said the old man, "I would remind you that this is good St. Valentine's Eve, which is no time for business, and I can have your worshipful commands by a serving man as early as it pleases you to send them."

"There is no time like the present," said the persevering youth, whose rank seemed to be of a kind which set him above ceremony. "I wish to know whether the buff doublet be finished which I commissioned some time since; and from you, sweet Bessie (here he sank his voice to a whisper), I desire to be informed whether your fair hands have been employed on it agreeably to your promise. Ah! you cannot think how my poor heart has been tortured this long while."

"Let me entreat you, my lord," said Gipsy Bess,

"to forego this wild talk ; it becomes you not to speak thus or me to listen. We are of poor rank but honest manners ; and the presence of my uncle ought to protect me from such expressions from your lordship."

She spoke these words in so low a tone that neither her uncle or Harry could hear her.

"Well, tyrant," answered the persevering gallant, "I will plague 'you no longer now, providing you will let me see you from your window to-morrow, when the sun first peeps over the eastern hills, and give me right to be your Valentine for the year."

"Not so, my lord ; my uncle but now told me that hawks, far less eagles, pair not with the humble linnet. Seek some court lady, to whom your favours will be honour ; to me—your highness must permit me to speak the plain truth—there can be nothing but disgrace."

As they spoke thus the party arrived at the gate of the church.

"Your lordship will, I trust, permit us here to take leave of you," said Robert Damer. "I am well aware how little you will alter your pleasure for the pain and uneasiness you may give to such as me. But, from the throng of attendants at the gate, your lordship may see that there are others in the church to whom even your grace must pay respect."

"Yes, but who pays respect to me?" said the young noble, haughtily. "A miserable artizan and his niece, too much honoured by my slightest notice, have the insolence to tell me that my notice dishonours them ! Ah ! my fine lady, I will teach you to rue this."

As he muttered this the old man and his niece entered the church, and Harry Tyrrell, in an attempt to follow them, closely jostled—it may be, not unwillingly—the young nobleman.

The gallant, starting from his unpleasant reverie and looking on the act as an intentional insult, siezed the young man by the breast, struck him, and threw him from him.

His irritated opponent recovered himself with difficulty, and grasped towards his own side, as if seeking a sword or a dagger in the place where it was usually worn ; but, finding none, he made a gesture of disappointed rage and entered the church.

During the few seconds he remained, the young nobleman stood with his arms folded on his breast, with a haughty smile, as if defying him to do his worst.

When Harry had entered the church, his opponent, adjusting the cloak 'yet closer about his face, made a private signal by holding up one of his gloves.

He was instantly joined by two men, who, disguised like himself, had watched 'his motions at a little distance.

They spoke together earnestly, after which the young nobleman retired in one direction, his friends or followers going on in another.

The night had fallen dark and the way was solitary, when Gipsy Bess and her uncle returned along the streets towards their own dwelling.

Most persons had betaken themselves home to bed.

They who still lingered in the streets were night walkers or revellers, the idle and swaggering retainers of the haughty nobles, who were wont to insult the peaceful passengers, relying on the impunity which their masters' court favour was too apt to secure them.

MOONLIGHT JACK

OR THE KING OF THE ROAD

THE CONFERENCE.

It was, perhaps, in apprehension of mischief from some observation of this kind, that Harry, stepping up to the glover, said,

"Sir, walk faster; we are dogged."

"Dogged, sayest thou?"

"Aye, truly."

"By whom and by how many?"

"By one man muffled in his cloak, who follows us like a shadow."

"Then will I never mend my pace in the street for the best man that ever trod it."

"But he has arms," said Harry.

"And so have we, and hands, and legs, and feet. Why, sure, Harry, you are not afraid of one man?"

"Afraid?" cried Harry, indignant at the insinuation; "you shall soon know if I am afraid."

"Now you are as far on the other side of the mark, thou foolish boy; thy temper has no middle course. There is no occasion to make a brawl, though we do not run. Walk thou before with Bessie, and I will take thy place. We cannot be exposed to danger so near home as we are."

The old man fell behind accordingly, and certainly observed a person keep so close to them as, the time and place considered, justified some suspicion.

When they crossed the street he also crossed it, and when they advanced or slackened their pace, the stranger's was in proportion accelerated or diminished.

The matter would have been of very little consequence had Robert Damer been alone.

But the beauty of his niece might render her the object of some profligate scheme in a country where the laws offered such slight protection to those who had not the means to protect themselves.

Harry and his fair charge, having arrived on the threshold of their own house, which was opened to them by an old female servant, the citizen's uneasiness was ended.

Determined, however, to ascertain, if possible, whether there had been any cause for it, he called out to the man whose actions had occasioned the alarm, and who stood still, though he seemed to keep out of reach of the light.

"Come, step forward, my friend, and do not play at bo-peep. Knowest thou not that they who

No. 19.—May 12, 1866.

Two Numbers and Two Tales every week for One Penny.
THE WORK GIRLS OF LONDON, and THE CRUSADER; OR,
THE WITCH OF FINCHLEY.

Price One Penny.

walk like phantoms in the dark are apt to encounter the conjuration of a cudgel? Step forward, I say, and show us thy shapes, man."

"Well, so I can, Master Damer," said one of the deepest voices that ever answered question. "I can show my shapes well enough, only I wish they could bear the light something better."

"Body of me!" exclaimed Damer, "I should know that voice! And is it really you in very truth, Hubert Dorstone? The devil catch me if thou passest this door with dry lips! What, man, is it time for strong hearts like thine to think of turning into the soft couch? If you were married I might understand it well; but now, enter, and old Kate shall get us something to eat and drink. Bessie will be right glad to see you."

By this time he had pulled the person whom he had welcomed so cordially into a sort of kitchen, which also served upon ordinary occasions as a parlour.

Its ornaments were trenchers of pewter, with a silver one or two, which, in a high state of cleanliness and brightness, occupied a range of shelves.

A good fire, with the assistance of a blazing lamp, spread light and cheerfulness throughout the apartment.

A savoury smell of some provisions which Kate, the servant, was preparing, did by no means offend the unrefined noses of those whose appetite they were destined to satisfy.

Their unknown attendant now stood in full light among them, and though his appearance was neither dignified nor handsome, his face and figure were not only deserving of attention, but seemed in some manner to command it.

He was rather below the middle stature, but the breadth of his shoulders, length and brawniness of his arms, and the muscular appearance of the whole man, argued a most unusual share of strength, and a frame kept in vigour by constant exercise.

His legs were somewhat bent, but not in a manner which could be said to approach to deformity.

It seemed, indeed, to correspond to the strength of his frame, though it impaired in some degree its symmetry.

His dress was of buff hide, and he wore in a belt round his waist a heavy sword.

His head was well proportioned, round, and curled thickly with black hair.

There was daring and resolution in the dark eyes, but the other features seemed to expresss a bashful timidity, mingled with good humour, and obvious satisfaction at meeting with old friends.

The glover and his niece seemed well pleased with the unexpected appearance of an old friend.

Robert shook his hand again and again.

Katie made her compliments, and Bessie herself freely offered her hand, which Hubert carried to his lips, while her face flushed crimson.

Not that there was any resistance on the part of the little hand, which lay passive in his grasp, but there was a smile mingled with the blush on her cheek, which came to increase the confusion of the gallant.

Her guardian on his part called out frankly, as he saw his friend's hesitation,

"Her lips, man, her lips! and that's a proffer I would not make to any one who crosses my threshhold. But, by St. Valentine (whose holiday will dawn to-morrow), I am so glad to see thee in the bonny city of London, that it would be hard to tell the thing I could refuse thee."

The smith, for as has been said, such was the craft of this sturdy artizan, was encouraged to salute the red lips of Gipsy Bess, who yielded the courtesy with a smile of affection which might have become a sister.

"I welcome you back," she said, "a better man, I hope, than when London saw you last."

He held her hand as if about to answer.

Then, suddenly, as one who lost courage at the last moment, relinquished his grasp.

Drawing back, as if afraid of what he had done, his dark face glowing with bashfulness, mixed with delight, he sat down by the fire on the side opposite to that which Bessie occupied.

"Come, Katie, speed thee with the food, old woman; and Harry—where is Harry?"

"He is gone to bed, sir, with a head-ache," said Katie, in a hesitating voice.

"Go. Call him," said the old man. "I will not be used thus by him. His blood is too gentle to lay a trencher or spread a napkin, and he expects to enter our ancient and honourable craft without duly waiting and tending upon his master and teacher in all matters of lawful obedience. Go, call him I say; I will not be thus neglected."

Katie was presently heard screaming upstairs, or more probably up a ladder to the cockloft to which the recusant apprentice had made an untimely retreat.

A muttered answer was returned, and soon after Harry appeared in the eating apartment.

There was a gloom of deep sullenness on his haughty though handsome features, and as he proceeded to spread the board and arrange the trenchers with salt, spices and other condiments—to discharge, in short, the duties of a modern domestic, which the custom of the time imposed upon all apprentices—he was obviously disgusted and indignant with the mean office imposed upon him.

Gipsy Bess glanced with some anxiety at him, as if apprehensive that his evident sullenness might increase her uncle's displeasure.

But it was not until her eyes had sought his a second time that he condescended to veil his dissatisfaction, and throw a greater appearance of willingness and submission into the services which he was performing.

"Well, now," cried old Robert, "we will e'en drink to thy coming back to us. Harry, bestir thee. Let the cans clink, lad, and thou shalt have a cup of the nut brown for thyself, my boy."

Harry poured out the good liquor for his master, and for Gipsy Bess.

But that done he set the flagon on the table, and took a seat.

"How now, sirrah; be these thy manners? Fill to my guest, boy."

"Master Dorstone may fill for himself if he wishes for liquor," answered the lad; "the son of my father has demeaned himself enough for one evening."

"That's well crowed for a cockerel," said Hubert; "but you are so far right, my lad, that the man deserves to die of thirst who cannot drink without a cupbearer."

Old Robert did not take the refusal so kindly.

He turned angrily to Harry.

"Now, by my sacred word," he cried, "thou shalt help him with that liquor and that cup, or we part on the moment."

Gipsy Bess glanced pleadingly at the son of Moonlight Jack.

His eyes met hers.

They seemed to say,

"For my sake *do* as you are bid!"

Harry rose sullenly at this.

Approaching the smith, who had just taken the

tankard in his hand, and was raising it to his head, he contrived to stumble against him and jostle him so awkwardly that the foaming ale gushed over his face, person, and dress.

Good-natured, as Hubert had the reputation of being, his patience now failed him.

He seized the young man's throat, being the part that came readiest to his grasp, as Harry arose from the pretended stumble, and pressing it severely as he cast the lad from him, exclaimed,

"Had this been in another place, young gallows bird, I'd have put out your eyes for you."

Harry removed his feet with the activity of a tiger, and exclaimed,

"Never shall you live to make that boast again."

So saying, he drew a short, sharp knife from his bosom, and springing on Hubert Dorstone attempted to plunge it into his body over the collar-bone, which must have been a mortal wound.

But the object of this violence was so ready to defend himself by striking up the assailant's hand that the blow only glanced on the bone, and scarce drew blood.

To wrench the dagger from the boy's hand, and to secure him with a grasp like that of his own iron vice, was for the powerful smith the work of a single moment.

Harry felt himself at once in the absolute power of the formidable antagonist whom he had provoked.

He became deadly pale, as he had been the moment before glowing red, and stood mute with shame and fear, until relieving him from his powerful hold, the smith quietly said,

"It is well for thee that thou cannot make me angry; thou art but a boy, and I, a grown man, ought not to have provoked thee; but let this be a warning."

Harry stood an instant as if about to reply, and then left the room ere Robert had collected himself enough to speak.

Kate was running hither and thither for salves and healing herbs.

Gipsy Bess had swooned at the sight of the trickling blood, and it was some time ere she recovered.

When she did she was conveyed to her room, and the glover and his friend remained for some time over their glasses talking of the turbulence of the times and the means by which Hubert could win the heart of the fair girl.

"Let us finish our flask now," said old Robert, at length, "for I reckon the church clock is tolling midnight. And hark thee, friend Hubert, be at the lattice window on our east gable by the very peep of dawn, and make me aware thou art come by whistling the smith's call gently. I will contrive that Bessie shall look at the window, and thus thou wilt have all the privilege of being a gallant valentine through the rest of the year, which, if thou canst not use to thine own advantage, I shall be led to think that for all thou be'st covered with the lion's hide, nature has left on thee the long ears of the ass."

"Well, a hearty good night to you," said the armourer, "you shall hear my call by cock crowing."

So saying, he took his leave, and went his way towards his own home.

CHAPTER II.

THE COMBAT—THE MEETING BETWEEN MOONLIGHT JACK AND GIPSY BESS—THE FLIGHT—THE WEDDING IN THE CAVERN.

THE sturdy smith was not slow in keeping the appointment assigned by his intended uncle.

But there was one who hurried before him towards the house of the glover.

This was one who had heard the parting words of the uncle of Gipsy Bess and the smith, one who had lingered long near the house, and who had paced to and fro long in the dark desolation of the night.

The sky was yet dark when this stranger passed on towards the rendezvous.

He was passing slowly under the wall of St. Anne's chapel, when a voice, which seemed to come from behind one of the flying buttresses of the chapel, said,

"He lingers that has need to run."

"Who speaks?" said the stranger, looking around him.

He was naturally startled at an address so unexpected, both in its tone and tenor.

"No matter who speaks," answered the same voice. "Do thou make great speed, or thou wilt scarce make good speed. Bandy not words, but begone."

"Saint or sinner, angel or devil," said the stranger, "your advice shall not be neglected. St. Valentine be my speed."

So saying, he instantly changed his loitering pace to one with which few people could have kept up, and in an instant was in the street where lived the glover.

He had not made three steps towards Robert Damer's house, which stood in the middle of the narrow street, when two men started from under the houses on different sides, and advanced as it were by concert, to intercept his passage.

The imperfect light only permitted him to discern that they wore heavy swords.

"Clear the way, fellows," cried the stranger, in a deep, stern voice.

They made no verbal answer, but he could see that they drew their swords.

This was enough to show that they intended withstanding him by force.

Conjecturing some evil, though of what kind he could not anticipate, the stranger instantly determined to make his way through, whatever odds.

Just as he came to this determination he was joined by another, whose form was as broad, though not so tall as his own.

This was the smith.

"We are well met, friend," cried he. "For whom do you fight these roysterers?"

"For a lady whose Valentine's morn they would deluge with tears—for Bessie Clive."

The smith muttered an oath.

Nevertheless, there seemed no time for asking questions.

"We fight, then, for one and the same," cried he. "Have at ye, cowards! There are two now to two."

Casting their cloaks over their left arms, so as to form a kind of a shield, the two newly-made comrades advanced towards their enemies.

The combat was not long, though quick and desperate thrusts and parries were made, and both parties seemed skilful swordsmen.

The smith at length gave one of their antagonists a severe fall on the causeway, while almost at the same moment his strange companion cut down the other.

They then pressed on in alarm, keeping on the side opposite to Bessie's house, that they might reconnoitre.

During their passage the smith and his companion had time for a mutual explanation.

But the opportunity was scarcely taken advantage of.

The stranger explained that he was a friend to Gipsy Bess, and that was all—an old friend, long lost.

This produced an intolerable amount of jealousy in the smith's breast, and brought forth an answer which made the stranger start.

"The glover has betrothed his niece to me," he said, "and I come to be her valentine ; another is striving to take my place. We will see how he will fare."

They now heard a bustle and a whisper beneath Bessie's window, and two of the party, observing them, crossed the street, and taking him, doubtless, for one of the sentinels, one of them said in a whisper to the smith,

"What noise was that yonder, Cuthbert ? Why gave you not the signal ?"

"Villain," said Hubert, "you are discovered, and you shall die the death !"

As he spoke he dealt the stranger a heavy blow with his weapon which would probably have made his words good had not the man, raising his arm, received on his hand the blow meant for his head.

The wound must have been a severe one, for he staggered and fell, with a deep groan.

Without noticing him further, Hubert Dorstone sprung forward upon a party of men who seemed engaged in placing a ladder against the lattice window in the gable, the tall stranger following him, after disposing likewise of his adversary.

Shouting out aloud for the watch, they rushed on the night walkers, one of whom was in the act of descending the ladder.

The smith seized it by the rounds, threw it down on the pavement, and placing his foot on the body of the man who had been mounting, prevented him from regaining his feet.

His accomplices struck fiercely at the smith and the stranger to extricate their companion.

But the two new friends in arms repaid with interest the blows aimed at them.

"Help ! help, brave citizens ! They break into our houses under cloud of night !"

These words, which resounded far through the streets, were accompanied by as many fierce blows, dealt with good effect among those whom the armourer and his friend assailed.

In the meantime the inhabitants of the district began to awaken, and appear in the streets in their shirts, with swords and targets, and some of them with torches.

The assailants now endeavoured to make their escape, which all of them effected excepting the man who had been thrown down along with the ladder.

Him the man in the cloak had caught by the throat in the scuffle, and held as fast as the greyhound holds the hare.

The other wounded men were borne off by their comrades.

"Here are a set of knaves breaking the peace of the city," said Hubert, to the neighbours who began to assemble. "Make after the rogues ; they cannot all get off, for I have maimed some of them. The blood will guide you to them."

"Some robbers, no doubt," said the citizens. "Up and chase, neighbours."

"Aye, up and chase ; leave me to manage this fellow," continued the armourer.

The assistants dispersed in different directions, their lights flashing, and their cries resounding through the whole adjacent district.

In the meantime the armourer's captive entreated for freedom, using both promises and threats to obtain it.

"As thou art a gentleman,"_he said, "let me go, and what is past shall be forgiven."

"I am no gentleman," said Hubert. "I am Hubert the smith, and I have done nothing to need forgiveness."

"Villain, thou hast done thou knowest not what ! But let me go, and I will fill thy bonnet with gold pieces."

"I shall fill thy bonnet with a cloven head presently," said the armourer, "unless thou stand still as a true prisoner."

"What is the matter, my friend ?" said old Robert, who now appeared at the window. "What is all this noise ? Why are the neighbours gathering to the affray ?"

"There have been a set of thieves about to scale the windows, Master Damer," exclaimed Hubert Dorstone.

"Hear me, Master Damer," said the prisoner. "Let me but speak but one word in private, and rescue me from the gripe of this iron-fisted and leaden-pated clown, and I will show thee that no harm was designed to thee or thine, and, moreover, tell thee what will much advantage thee."

"I should know that voice," said Robert Damer, in a strange tone, as he came to the door with a dark lantern in his hand. "Hubert, let this young man speak with me ; there is no danger in him, I promise you. Stay but an instant where you are, and let no one enter the house, either to attack or defend. I will be answerable that this gallant meant but some Saint Valentine's jest."

So saying, the old man pulled in the prisoner, and shut the door, leaving Hubert and his friend a little surprised at the unexpected light in which old Damer had viewed the affray.

"A jest ?" the latter said. "It might have been a strange jest if they had got into the maid's sleeping-room. But here come lighted torches and drawn swords. Ah, they are our friends."

"We have been bootless hunters," cried the townsmen. "We followed by the tracks of the blood into the church burial-ground, and we started two fellows from amongst the tombs, supporting between them a third, who had, probably, got some of your marks about him, Master Hubert. They got to the postern-gate before we could overtake them, and rang the sanctuary-bell. The gate opened, and in they went ; so they are safe in sanctuary, and we may go to our cold beds and warm us."

"Hullo !" cried one of the citizens, holding up a bloody hand, which he had picked up from the ground. "Where did such a hand as that wield the trowel or spade ? It is large and bony, too ; but as fine as a lady's, with a ring that sparkles like a gleaming candle. Robert Damer has made gloves for this man before now, if I am not mistaken, for he is a courtier, I have no doubt."

The spectators here began to gaze on the bloody token with various comments.

"If that is the case," said one, "Hubert had best show a clean pair of heels of it, since it will go hard with any one who cuts off a gentleman's hand to protect the house of a citizen. The laws are hard against mutilation."

"Fie upon you, that you will say so, Michael Dorne," answered the other. "Are we not representatives and successors of the stout old Romans who helped to build our city? Do you think we will suffer an honest citizen's house to be assaulted without seeking for redress?"

"And how can we help it?" said a grave old man. "What would ye have us do?"

"Go to the king! Wake him out of bed, show him this bloody token, and push our cause warmly."

"Warmly, sayest thou?" cried the other. "Why, we are so warmly now discussing it that we shall die of cold before the porter turn a key to let us into the royal presence. Come, friends, the night is bitter, we have kept our watch and ward like men, and our jolly smith hath given warning to those that would wrong us, which is worth twenty proclamations of the king. To-morrow is a new day; we will consult on this matter on this self-same spot, and then think what measures may be taken for the discovery and pursuit of the villains. So let's dismiss before the heart's blood freeze in our veins."

"That's right," cried old Robert the glover, as, seizing the smith by the hand, he pulled him into his house.

"Where is the prisoner?" asked Hubert, as he drew his new friend in with him.

Robert Damer seemed dazed and confused.

"He got out at the back door, and so through the little garden. Think not of him; but come and see her who should have been your valentine this morn."

"Let me but sheathe my weapon," said the smith. "Let me but wash my hands."

"She can yet be your valentine, man; but there is no time to lose. She is now up, and nearly dressed. Come on man. She shall see thee with thy good weapon in thy hand, and with villians' blood on thy fingers that she may know what is the value of a true man's service. I would have her know what a good man's love is worth. But what is here?—whom have we here?"

He turned towards the cloaked stranger.

The smith turned also.

He recognised at once his strange companion.

"Oh! he said, "my friend here I have wrongfully overlooked. He was my brave seconder and comrade. I must introduce him to Bessie."

As they entered the room, and the glover was yet thanking the new comer for his aid, Bessie entered.

Her first glance fell upon the cloaked stranger.

"I am your Valentine, fair lady," he said.

As he spoke he removed his hat.

It was Moonlight Jack!

With a wild cry she sprang forward and threw herself into his arms.

"Oh! Jack, Jack!" she cried, "thank Heaven! we have met once more!"

The glover and the smith looked aghast.

Had a thunderbolt fallen from the skies, and rent the earth at their feet, they could not have felt more wonder-stricken.

Not only were they surprised.

There was another reason.

The meeting, rapturous and loving, was the downfall of all their hopes.

It meant the reunion of two loving hearts.

Therefore the severance of others.

"What have we here?" cried Robert Damer, sternly.

Moonlight Jack released partially his hold upon Gipsy Bess.

"I am an old friend, sir," he said; "ask *her* whom I am."

"I will tell you, dear uncle," cried Gipsy Bess, whose face was irradiated with a smile of extreme happiness, "he is not only an old friend, but my betrothed—my husband."

Robert Damer scowled sternly upon the speaker.

Then he pointed to Hubert, the smith.

"Here is your betrothed," he said, "the one whom your smiles and words have led on. *He* is your husband."

"No, no—never! This is the one whom I have loved since youth. Jack Tyrrell, I am yours for ever—long-lost love—never, never again will I put you to such a trial."

"Let us leave this place," cried Moonlight Jack, not taking further notice of the smith or Damer, "dangers here surround you everywhere. Not a mile hence a priest awaits us—the marriage service shall make us one, love, and give me right to defend you."

The smith upon this broke in furiously.

"You move not hence," he said, turning to Moonlight Jack, "you move not hence with Gipsy Bess. She is *my* betrothed—*my* affianced, and shall never be wife of thine!"

The glover in his heart acquiesced in these words, spoken with so much fire.

But he feared discord in his house.

"Stay! Thirst not for each other's blood. My niece will answer this braggart lover. Bessie, tell him how Hubert loves you, and that you cannot leave him."

Gipsy Bess moved not.

She loved her uncle well for all his kindness; but she loved Moonlight Jack more than all the world.

"Uncle," she cried, "Jack Tyrrell is all the world to me. I am his affianced bride, and I will go with him wheresoever he bids. Jack, I will go *now* if you wish me."

The smith drew his sword.

Still red with the blood of his enemies, it was waved around his head.

"Never," he cried, "never shall he wrest you from me! Release her, man, or my sword shall drink your blood!"

Moonlight Jack released her.

Not as the smith meant it, however.

He did it that he might defend her better.

At one glance he took in the positions of those in the room.

Then, pouncing forward, he seized the old man, and swinging him into the adjoining room, locked him in.

This was done before the smith could stir to prevent him.

Then Jack Tyrrell faced his foe.

"Now," he cried, in a voice of thunder, "understand me. Gipsy Bess, my affianced wife, is going away with me now. Strive not to prevent me, or by Heavens my sword, kept for more glorious battle, will lay you dead at my feet."

The sneer conveyed in these words roused the smith to fury.

His face grew purple.

His eyes glared.

His teeth gnashed together with rage.

"Never," he yelled, in a voice rendered husky with rage, "never, until this heart has ceased to beat, shall you take her from me."

So saying, the smith drew towards the door.

In his hand his strong sword was held firmly.

Moonlight Jack gazed resolutely in his eyes.

Then he advanced.

Gipsy Bess kept behind him.

She knew a deadly struggle was imminent.

Yet, strange to say, she feared not for Moonlight Jack.

She was *so* convinced that he was capable of fighting his own battles that she never once dreamt of his being worsted.

So she watched him calmly.

Her own fear was, that he might meet opposition from without.

The battle, however, did not last long.

The smith fought furiously.

His passion spoiled his courage.

It interfered with his action, and, ere long, he lay unarmed, and at the mercy of his foe.

Moonlight Jack sought not his life.

A brave and straightforward enemy he never took advantage of.

So, throwing himself at once upon him, he held him down while Gipsy Bess tied his ancles and his wrists.

Then, quick as thought, they fled from the room.

In the chamber below was a confused and motley crowd.

They had been drawn together by the clash of arms.

They glanced at Moonlight Jack with no friendly eye.

They had seen him in the company of the smith.

They had seen him fighting by his side for their privileges.

But this was not enough.

The smith was their known and trusted friend.

This man was a stranger.

Naturally, therefore, their sympathies were with the armourer.

A murmur ran through the crowd.

Then there was a movement towards the door.

Jack saw plainly that they intended to stop him.

He smiled graciously.

" My friends," he said, " I am in haste. Let me pass."

They moved not.

A frown replaced the smile.

" Come, come," he cried, " let's have no nonsense here. I *must* pass, as well now as at last."

One bolder than the rest now stood forward.

" We don't know you, my fair sir," he said. " Whence came you with your sword steeped in blood ?"

" You *should* know me," he cried. " I have been defending your liberties. I have fought and bled for them, and the reward I have obtained. I desire to go. This is the glover's niece ; she will tell you I am her friend."

Gipsy Bess was now agitated in truth.

She saw the danger of delay.

Delay meant the rush of the people upstairs, the discovery of the smith bound and helpless, the furious rage of her uncle, the seizure of Moonlight Jack.

So she advanced towards the man who had spoken.

" Sir," she cried, " let my husband pass."

The man drew back.

Drew back in sheer astonishment.

" Your husband ?" he cried.

" Yes, yes," said she. " Let us pass. Danger threatens those dear to us far from hence."

The crowd opened.

As usual, the tact of a woman cleared the way where force would have failed.

They reached the door in safety.

The throng still pressed and jostled and murmured without.

But no one opposed their progress.

Seeing that the fugitives passed the crowd within, those without thought it best to let them proceed.

Moonlight Jack hurried Gipsy Bess forward eagerly.

He knew how fickle a multitude is under such circumstances.

Arrived at the corner of the street, he took one rapid glance back.

Then he said,

" Come, Bess, we must fly swiftly now. They have ascended the stairs."

So saying, he raised her in his arms, and ran hastily towards a spot where a high archway admitted them into a courtyard, which, even in this early hour in the morning, was dark from its narrowness and the height of the surrounding houses.

Passing through this, and emerging into a second street, Moonlight Jack signed to a man with a cloak, who was pacing to and fro impatiently.

In another instant a coach drove up.

Into this they ascended.

It drove off rapidly.

" Whither are we going ?" said Gipsy Bess.

Jack smiled and took her in his arms.

" We are going," he said, " to a place where you can fulfil your words."

Bessie blushed.

But she made no reply.

She knew well what he meant.

" You called me your husband," he said, " in a few hours, Bessie, you shall be my wife. Tell me, dearest, shall it be so ?"

Need we tell the answer.

She pressed him in her arms.

" Dear Jack !" she said, " my heart is full. Oh ! I wish you had come before ! But tell me are we going to the old place—is it safe to go there ?"

" It is not ; we shall not go there, though Lucien wishes it."

" No wonder. Poor Grace ! I pity her indeed."

" Yes, truly ; but things will yet be right with him. We shall not, however, go near the house of old Cormorant. We are going to Northumberland."

" Why so ?"

" Because, in a place called Rombolton, in Northumberland, the Huntleys have another place of residence, and Lady Edith is now there. Soft Sam is there also ; and Lucien hopes, from the folly of the one, or the fear of the other, to extract the papers he so much desires to obtain. But see, here are our horses."

The coach stopped.

It was near the Cross at Charing.

Here two high-spirited steeds awaited them, and four men as escort.

Gipsy Bess at once sprang upon the saddle, and in a few minutes they were all dashing off towards the North Road.

Arrived, after a long and tedious journey, in the neighbourhood of Rombolton, they made their way towards a place, which Jack Tyrrell's band had selected as a place of refuge.

Here, within a few hours of their arrival, they were made man and wife.

It was a strange and imposing ceremony.

In a vast cave, hewn out of the bowels of the earth, the members of Moonlight Jack's band were assembled with torches.

Ranged round the great vault, supported by huge pillars, a strange light was reflected on their faces.

A strange light thrown upon them by the irradiations of a thousand glittering particles.

They were in a deserted coal-mine ; and though they were not begrimed and black, like the workers in these strange labyrinths of latent fire, they seemed dusky and unearthly.

The bride looked excessively beautiful.

Always lovely, her blushes heightened her usual charms.

Moonlight Jack, calmly happy, forgetting now the grave and its terrors, looked just the fine, manly, brave, handsome fellow, he was.

At his side was his son, leaning against a pillar of coal and striving to look back into the distance and fancy that scene when his own mother stood as Gipsy Bess stood, by the side of his father.

Lucien Fairleigh, pale and full of emotion, gave the bride away.

He could not be said to envy Jack Tyrrell.

Too just for this, he only wished and hoped that the day would soon come which would see him standing, as Jack did with Bessie, by the side of Grace Dashwood.

A grand banquet, in which the highways and their danger were forgotten, occupied the time until the hour which gave Gipsy Bess up to the arms of her enraptured husband.

CHAPTER III.

THE SOLITARY WALKER — THE BROAD MOOR — THE STORM—THE HEATH ON FIRE—TERRIBLE PERIL OF THE TRAVELLER — THE WELCOME RAIN—THE SUDDEN LIGHT—THE VOICE FROM THE EARTH.

WE must now pass over a fortnight—a fortnight of delight for Jack Tyrrell and his bride ; but at the end of which he had been compelled to leave Rombolton and proceed to some distance.

It was the period of his expected return ; but a long delay had occurred.

On this sultry evening in July, soon after the sun had gone down, a man, with a large stick in his hand, was seen making his way in great haste over this moor, one of the vastest of those sterile tracts which form so large a portion of the county of Northumberland.

Except one blood-red streak extending far along the edge of the horizon, separating the dark clouds below from the darker clouds above, you could discover nothing in sky nor earth but gloom.

Against that blood-red streak the man's figure, as he suddenly stopped to gaze upward and around him, stood strikingly relieved.

He was about the middle size and rather slightly made, but in the first flush of youth, and full of energy and activity.

From his dress, scrupulously elegant, it seemed clear that he belonged to the rank of gentlemen, though what business he could have in that wild region it would have been difficult to say.

Any one who should have marked his countenance would have discovered much to perplex, and perhaps some little to alarm him.

His mouth expressed strong disdain and wilfulness, and there was an angry flashing in the eye indicating a fierceness approaching to cruelty.

Still the general expression of the face was winning rather than otherwise, though it might have been doubtful whether its fascination, like that attributed to some inferior animals, was not exercised the more effectually to destroy.

Not without reason did he peruse the aspect of the heavens.

It seemed clear that a thunder-storm was approaching.

The previous summer two men had been struck dead by lightning on that desolate track, and the wayfarer, aware probably of the circumstances, appeared anxious to discover some place of shelter to which he might betake himself should the fires of heaven burst forth before he could reach the place, wherever it might be, towards which he was journeying.

As he stood still in the attitude we have described, his figure looked only like a dark line dropped across the crimson patch of sky, which became narrower and narrower every moment as the dusky rock pressed down towards the hills to canopy the whole hemisphere of darkness.

Having swiftly reconnoitred the country, he pushed forward with renewed vigour, following, however, a zigzag course, now verging towards the left and now towards the right, as if he constantly discerned something to be avoided.

And so evidently he did.

Above all things, he steered cautiously clear of certain low, incipient copses, now half scorched and dry, which generally skirted or overspread flattened mounds, composed of a substance resembling the scoriæ of a burning mountain.

As the light faded his terror of these spots increased.

Slackening his pace, therefore, and carefully feeling before him with his stick he still kept advancing, for no place of shelter presented itself.

At length the thunder began to growl in the distance.

Then one pale, livid flash passed over the heath, revealing in its way a thousand yawning pits black as the entrance to hell.

Upon whatever errand he might be proceeding, and whether accompanied by a good or evil conscience, he felt startled at the threatening aspect put on by nature.

He would gladly have hidden himself anywhere till the storm was over.

But as the lightning grew brighter and brighter, it only strengthened the conviction that there existed nothing for miles round behind which any creature larger than a rat could ensconce itself.

Neither tree, nor rock, nor wall, nor ruined habitation rose to break the dreary uniformity of that limitless waste.

Once or twice he fancied he could discern a ruddy glow, which shot upwards from the earth in streaks, slightly diversifying the overpowering darkness which had now settled upon everything.

They who dwell in towns and cities scarcely know what it is to become familiar with the elements under such circumstances, when nature seems as it were desirous to expand to its utmost dimensions the idea which man has formed of her.

There is grandeur in sunrise, grandeur in the accidents in which day extinguishes its glories ; but there is no grandeur like that of night, when the bare face of this planet is kissed by the tempest, and kindled by the lightning as by a smile.

Thunder has always appeared to me as an effort of the elements to articulate and reveal some inexpressible throes or pangs which rack their organic structure.

It addresses itself to the mind ; though from the beginning of time until now man has sought in vain to interpret it.

The person whose movements we have been observing, felt he was alone in that wild place.

He had now been walking for hours, and had not met one living creature, either man or beast.

There was a suffocating heat and closeness in the atmosphere.

The earth was dry and chapped.

The furze-bushes around him seemed as if they had already been placed in the mouth of an oven, and to lie there as it were inviting ignition from the lightning.

The thought several times crosses his mind that if they should by chance take fire, the whole heath would at once be in a blaze, and escape impossible.

The next flash was so vivid that in passing through the withered bushes near him, its brightness appeared to kindle them as it played round their shoots and irregularities, and for an instant revealed them painfully to his sight.

It directed his eye likewise to the large patches of tinder-like heath which lay around, the ready materials of a conflagration.

The darkness which ensued seemed tenfold more pitchy ; but on straining his eyes, as men often do under such circumstances, to discover something, no matter what, he perceived, far to the right, a small pillar of flame which rose and spread as he gazed upon it.

A sickening shudder passed through his frame.

He understood what had happened, and saw every probability that he should be roasted alive, as the moor extended for miles on all sides, and was everywhere covered with dry furze bushes, which he foresaw would be shortly all on fire.

His first thought was to take to his heels and run for his life, but the whole plain was studded with pits many hundred feet deep, and the idea of falling down and being dashed to pieces in one of these, induced him to take in preference the chances of the conflagration above ground.

Meanwhile a breeze had sprung up, and the flames advancing with miraculous swiftness, spread right and left, cracking, hissing, and roaring fearfully.

The whole sky above now seemed like a dull mirror, reflecting back the dark red glow to the earth.

But the thing which most confused him was the noise.

A short time ago there had not been a sound along the whole face of nature in the interval of the thunder claps.

Now the voice of heaven was deadened in the turmoil of earth.

The flames towered aloft in pyrimidal tongues, as if eager to lick the clouds and render them also combustible.

Nothing travels like fire.

While the wayfarer was considering what course he should take and endeavouring to make up his mind to run, at the risk of tumbling headlong into a coal pit, the choice was no longer left him.

Under the influence of circumstances which he could not explain, the space on which, by chance, he stood, offered less food to the flames than that bordering on it, so that to the right and left the fire marched on and met in front while he was deliberating.

What character his feelings then assumed it would be difficult to say.

Despair was in his heart and in his looks.

Had he been engaged in the performance of any great duty, the thought of it might have nerved him and given him courage to meet death.

But it is to be feared the errand he was bent on lay under no benison, but the contrary.

Moon-Light Jack

OR THE KING OF THE ROAD

LADY EDITH HUNTLEY.

Still there is a power of resistance in man's nature, which, after recoiling for a moment before danger, rouses itself and comes to his relief.

He did not stay to analyze his motives, but as if about to combat with some mortal foe, buttoned his coat close up to his chin, pulled down his hat a little in order to set it more firmly on his head, grasped his stick, and faced about towards where the flames burnt hottest.

It was no attitude of theatrical defiance he assumed.

He acted in obedience to a powerful instinct which induces us to struggle with everything and fall, if we fall, in the midst of strenuous exertion.

Still, as the flames mounted and drew nearer, uttering those horrible sounds which the voice of fire only can give forth, his very flesh seemed to creep upon his bones with terror.

The circle around him narrowed.

The heat increased.

He felt his cheeks burning as if half roasted.

The lightning and thunder of heaven itself were unheeded in the presence of far more threatening agencies.

By degrees he retreated towards a sandy patch too sterile to support vegetation.

But it was small; and when the flames encompassed it, he feared he should lie or stand there as on a spit, and, if not scorched, must be stifled to death.

Up at length rushed the flames to the edge of the sand, projecting themselves forward before the wind, and forming over head a fiery canopy.

Had this continued for many minutes he must have perished.

All the blood in his body seemed to be dried up.

No. 20.—May 19, 1866.

Two Numbers and Two Tales every week for One Penny.
THE WORK GIRLS OF LONDON, and THE CRUSADER; OR,
THE WITCH OF FINCHLEY.

Price One Penny.

His mouth was parched, and his eyes were ready to start from their sockets.

Of moments so terrible scarcely any record remains in the consciousness.

We almost dwindle into mere material agents.

Our whole being is absorbed by our sensations, and the mind undergoes a temporary dethronement.

Tortures of all kinds carried beyond a certain pitch defeat the intentions of their inflictors, and deaden the senses they were meant to agonize.

But the fuel supplied by the furze and heath was speedily consumed, and the conflagration swept on before the wind, leaving behind it an interminable bed of hot and sparkling ashes.

The breeze, however, still seemed impregnated with fire; but the clouds came at length to his relief, and the rain, descending in a deluge, soon converted that which had previously been a sheet of flame into an endless succession of pools and diminutive brooks.

Nothing is more changeful than the moods of nature in summer.

The moon now shone forth in all her mild majesty upon one of the most extraordinary scenes the eye ever witnessed.

Far and near nothing was visible but piles of black ashes, divided from each other by small sheets of water now placid and shining like silver; for the breeze soon departed with the clouds, and left the air hushed and deliciously cool.

The stranger moved forward now, though exceedingly uncertain whether he was advancing in the right or the wrong direction.

But in the midst of his uncertainty he discovered far to the left a small bright blaze, which, after continuing for a few minutes, was extinguished.

His spirits, which had begun to flag, were once more roused.

Knowing now his way, and convinced that he was not going on a bootless errand, he quickened his pace, and in a short time drew near the spot where he had beheld the fire.

Here he stopped and threw a scrutinising look around him, but could perceive on the surface of the heath no guiding object.

He gave a low whistle, and then listened attentively; but hearing no answer he began to fear that his evil genius had after all led him wrong.

Presently, however, by the light of the stars, a head was seen rising from the earth, and the stranger heard words of welcome pronounced in a low sweet voice.

He then hurried forward, descended into the opening, and disappeared.

CHAPTER IV.

GIPSY BESS AT HOME—THE WARNING—PREPARATIONS FOR BATTLE—GIPSY BESS AND VICTORY—THE BATTLE ON THE HEATH—THE TRAITOR IN THE CAMP—DEFEAT AND FLIGHT—THE SNAKE AND THE DECEIVED—THE SECRET PLOT AGAINST MOONLIGHT JACK.

THE cheery voice which welcomed the stranger was that of Gipsy Bess.

She had imagined, and no wonder, that the new-comer was Moonlight Jack.

He had promised to return home on that day.

He had even said, in fact, that the sun of the yesterday would not set before he came back.

But on this night of storm and rain he was still absent.

The new-comer was Lucien Fairleigh.

Gipsy Bess turned deadly pale when she saw who it was.

"Where is Jack?" she asked.

"He is safe," said Lucien, "and will be here to-night."

"Why, then, does he delay?" she asked, hurriedly.

"Dangers threaten us all," said Lucien. "Brandon has found our retreat."

"Through whom?"

"Through Jonathan Rasper."

Bess shuddered.

"I fear that youth," she said.

Lucien smiled.

"Why so?" he asked.

"Because, if he befriends Brandon, after the terrible punishment of which he was the author, how fearful must be his enmity against us! How awful must be his spirit of revenge when he can smother his hatred of those who have maimed and injured him! But tell me what danger threatens, and why you have come in secret and disguise?"

"I will tell you," said Lucien: "Jonathan Rasper has followed in our wake; he has discovered the exact point at which we have fixed our retreat. Spies tell us that he knows the pit's mouth, and thither, to-night, he will bring his men. Jack has kept behind, that he may follow in his wake, and surprise him."

Gipsy Bess clenched her hands.

"Why is this enmity?" she cried. "What does Brandon want of Moonlight Jack? Why does he follow him thus, when he has done him no injury?"

"I fancy I know the clue to his actions," said Lucien. "He imagines that Sir Percy Delaine and his wife are with us. Ella Huntley he has not and never will forgive."

He stopped suddenly.

The spot where they were standing in the deserted coal-mine was far below the surface of the earth, and reached by a series of long ladders.

But nevertheless they could hear sounds from above.

A long, shrill whistle resounded over the dusky heath.

"That's Jack's signal," said Lucien. "I must assemble the men."

He left her side, and hurried to the huge "banquetting hall," hewn out of coal, where the wedding feast had taken place.

Here the men were carousing.

They stopped singing and drinking as he entered.

Next to Moonlight Jack, he was their captain.

Next to him they respected Fairleigh.

"Well, Captain Fairleigh," cried Hardman, "what cheer?"

"To arms, my men!" he cried. "Our enemies are approaching. Follow me."

He had not long to wait.

In a few minutes the men were armed and ready.

"And what am I to do?" cried Gipsy Bess.

"You had best remain here."

"Remain here, in the bowels of the earth, while Moonlight Jack is in trouble? No, Lucien, no; you have not learned to know me yet. Stay, only one moment, and I will accompany you."

She waited for no answer.

Off she flew like a lightning flash.

She knew well that danger waits for no man.

In a few minutes she returned.

In those few minutes a great change had been effected.

She had donned male attire.

From her face nothing could take its exquisite female grace.

The rounded outlines of her form could with difficulty be compressed within the male habiliments.

The large breasts, the swelling hips, the rounded lower limbs, could belong to none other than a woman.

Neither Lucien nor any of the highwaymen, however, paused to gaze at her beautiful form as she ascended the steep ladders.

Their thoughts were busy with the coming fray.

When they reached the surface of the earth the night was heavy over the dusky heath.

Yet they could see afar off some objects moving over it.

"They come," said Lucien. "Gipsy Bess, where will you wait?"

"I will go with you."

"Why needlessly expose yourself to danger?"

"It is not needless; Gipsy Bess has sworn to be by the side of Moonlight Jack in safety and in danger, and that oath she will keep. Come, let us march onwards; let us not compromise his safety by delay."

Lucien saw it was useless any longer to resist it.

Young and gentle as she was she was determined enough in cases where her love was concerned.

So they all advanced together.

The opposing party drew near.

They came within a few yards of one another.

"Halt!" cried Lucien Fairleigh.

They halted.

"What want ye?" cried a loud voice.

It was the voice of Brandon.

"That is the question I would ask of you," said Lucien.

"Wherefore?"

"I desire to know."

"Then I refuse to tell."

"Then perhaps you will answer one other question, asked civilly?"

"It depends upon its nature."

"Whither go you?"

"Towards the north."

Lucien laughed aloud.

"Your fence of words is good, Harry Brandon," he said, "but shall I tell you your object?"

"If it please you," returned Brandon, then, turning to one of his men, he added, "retire for a hundred yards, and keep a look-out."

"You are travelling towards the north," said Lucien, "yet you send out scouts behind you. I will tell you whom you seek. It is Moonlight Jack!"

Brandon was silent a moment.

"And what if it is?" he said, "what if it is? I seek him man to man, not by stealth or treachery."

"True, but it is from information given you by a traitor."

"His name?"

"Jonathan Rasper."

"He is dead."

"That is false!"

"Ha! say you so?"

"I repeat it."

"How know you it?"

"That is my secret. But, still, let it suffice that I do know it. Upon his forehead he bears the everlasting brand of treachery. He is not dead, but lives to destroy all with whom he comes in contact.

However this may be, Moonlight Jack is not here, and so I beg you to pass on."

Brandon laughed scornfully.

"Why should I?" he said.

"Because I ask it."

"Because you ask it, forsooth. Is this wild moor your own?"

"It is not, but it belongs to one you do not serve; William of Orange is no longer your master. But I do not wish to bandy words with you; Sir Percy Delaine and his wife, whom you seek also, are far away. Turn back, therefore, since you cannot pass here."

Brandon drew back a few paces.

"This mad-brained fool, Lacy," he cried, turning to a man who appeared to act with him in the character of a lieutenant, "this mad-brained fool is intent on shedding blood. Keep the men to their work."

Then he spoke to our hero once again.

"Lucien Fairleigh, my battle is not with you. Let me pass, therefore, and let no needless blood be shed."

"Words are useless," cried Lucien, "strike now, and your blood and the blood of those that fall be upon your head."

These sentences were received by Jack Tyrrell's men as the order of command.

They at once rushed towards Brandon and his troop.

The battle became general.

Over the silent heath, so lately the scene of a terrible conflagration, the sounds of deadly strife rolled loudly.

Brandon's men were in greater numbers than those of Fairleigh.

Though the latter, therefore, pressed vigorously forward; though they exerted their strength to the utmost; though they never dreamed of flying, but gave way what ground they did yield inch by inch; though Lucien urged them on by words and actions; though Gipsy Bess fought with them, all seemed in vain.

The men under the command of Brandon steadily gained ground.

Lucien had already begun to despair.

Already he had whispered to Gipsy Bess,

"For Heaven's sake fly!"

Suddenly, in a slight lull in the battle, was heard the trampling of horses' feet.

"Aid comes, my men!" shouted Lucien, "Moonlight Jack to the rescue!"

The words had a magic effect.

The men no longer gave ground even by the inch.

They knew that succour was at hand, and, as in all fields of battle, the men from this knowledge seemed to receive renewed strength.

Brandon's followers, on the other hand, began to waver.

Down now like an avalanche came the men with Jack Tyrrell at their head.

From this moment Brandon's case was hopeless.

His men, attacked on both sides, fled in disorder.

Moonlight Jack did not pursue them.

He went on towards home exultingly by the side of his newly-made bride.

Brandon could not rally his men until they arrived at the edge of the burnt heath.

Then, when they stopped in their flight, a gliding form, snake-like, crept up to the side of Brandon.

It was Jonathan Rasper.

"Moonlight Jack," said he, "will attack the Northern mail to-morrow night. Let us stay here to thwart him."

Brandon had the spy in his camp ; yet knew it not.

He was so disguised so that he seemed a man.

"Good," cried Brandon, "we will wait in the neighbourhood. If I cannot capture him I will spoil his sport."

CHAPTER V.

THE NORTHERN MAIL AND ITS STRANGE FRIENDS.

It was about nine o'clock on the following evening that Moonlight Jack and Lucien Fairleigh went out to stop the Northern mail.

They were accompanied by six of their followers.

Little dreaming that Brandon and his men were lurking in the neighbourhood to waylay them, they had not deemed it necessary to take a larger number.

The others, therefore, had remained behind in the deserted coalpit with Gipsy Bess.

The night was favourable to such an enterprise.

The spot chosen by them for their venture was well selected.

About midway between two of the stages at which the mail coach took its relay of horses, the road wound rather abruptly round the edge of a thick copse of brushwood and stunted hazel bushes, forming an admirable shelter for an attacking party.

Two of their six followers were told off to rush forward and secure the leaders.

The other four, with their pistols in hand, were at the same time to form a line across the road a few yards in advance.

Jack himself, with Lucien, undertook the remainder of the work.

They anticipated but little difficulty, still less any danger from those they would have to encounter.

The information they had received as to the hour was so accurate that they had barely sufficient time to carry out their plan of concealment within the shadow of the plantation ere a signal from their leader warned them of the approach of the prize.

Every eye was on the look-out at once, and every hand ready.

Moonlight Jack passed rapidly by the spot where his followers lay in waiting.

"Don't waste a shot," he whispered, with his usual caution. "Should it be necessary, I will fire, and then you may follow suite."

He waited for no reply, quickly disappearing behind the trunk of a pollard willow which grew out of the morass which skirted the road.

The heavy bank of dark clouds which had, up till this moment, obscured the moon's light, seemed suddenly to be lifted up, disclosing to view the clumsy vehicle which in those days carried his majesty's mail, descending the hill at rather a rapid pace.

As it approached the hollow where Moonlight Jack and his men were in ambush, the driver, apparently, was in some difficulty, one of his leaders having entangled his near hind leg in the traces.

The whoop of an owl was heard repeated three times.

The third still reverberated on the night wind, when, as if by a stroke of magic, four dark figures with masks appeared to rise out of the road, debarring his further progress.

At the same moment his horses' heads were seized on either side, and thrown back upon their haunches by a violent effort.

The moon's ray glancing down the barrels of two long horseman's pistols pointed at him from the right hand of each of the men who had thus taken possession of his charge.

"You had best get down and see to your horses' trace," said Jack, who had proceeded to open the door, requesting the occupants to alight.

Lucien Fairleigh had, in the meantime, disposed of the guard.

The latter's first thought was a bag of gold, with which he had been entrusted to convey to the bank at Newcastle.

Springing from his seat on the first alarm, he fled at his best speed across the field on the right hand side of the road.

Quickly as his movements had been made, they had not escaped the eye of Lucien.

Dismounting in an instant, he was on his track in pursuit.

Young and well skilled in all things approaching agility and strength, the race was over ere well commenced.

With a smart blow from his riding-whip (for Lucien had no other weapon with him, his pistols being left in the holsters with the saddle) across the thigh, he was soon brought to the ground, and the bag which he held in his hand secured, and himself brought back to the scene of action.

Things had not progressed there so peaceably as they had expected. Amongst the inside passengers was a young cornet of dragoons about to join his regiment in the north, to which part he was also conducting his bright-eyed lady love.

Stung to the quick at being ordered to leave the coach, and at Jack's hand being applied to his collar to expedite his descent, he flung himself unexpectedly on his assailant.

With one hand at Moonlight Jack's throat, the other grasped the pistol Jack held in his hand, and a violent struggle began between them.

Being a powerful young fellow, and withal well trained in wrestling, it would doubtless have been not an unequal match had they stood alone.

The pistol, in their striving who should obtain possession of it, went off unexpectedly, the ball nearly ending Jack's career for ever. On his attempting to bring it to bear on his opponet, the latter, by a strong effort, threw his arm upwards.

In its course the ball passed obliquely through the embroidered border of Moonlight's Jack's hat, carrying away part of the feather.

"Too near to wish a repetition of it," he muttered.

The report of the pistol produced two results.

One was, it brought assistance to Jack, for Lucien, on his return with the captured guard, having his attention drawn by it to the position of his friend, at once proceeded to relieve him by pinioning the arms of the young soldier.

The other was, it brought to the coach's side the four men who had been stationed across the road in front.

Simultaneously with their approach the sound of advancing horsemen was heard.

It was evident, by the noise of the horses' feet, that they were a considerable number.

"Call the lads off, and form to the front. Quick, Lucien, we shall have them on us like a thunder cloud ! Hark ! what word was that ? Yes, by G—d, 'twas Brandon. To the rescue !"

Moonlight Jack had spoken truth.

With the skill of an able general Lucien Fairleigh had drawn his men together so as to be in some sort prepared for the attack of their enemy, which he expected justly would be quick, if not decisive.

As the dark forms of the approaching party came

into view they seemed to number double the followers of Moonlight Jack, if not more.

By a rapid change Jack moved his men to the left side under the shadow of the wood.

Brandon's troop dashed past them at full speed.

" Fire !"

Following, or rather accompanying the word, the report of six pistols was heard from the road side.

More than one of Brandon's horses were riderless.

Taking advantage of their unexpected assistant's diversion in their favour, the occupants of the mail prevailed on their guard and driver to leave the scene at once.

In the confusion, and being too much engaged with each other, their escape was not noticed by the fighting parties.

The firing having disclosed the position taken up by Jack's men the attack was begun in earnest.

It was a desperate hand to hand encounter ; if Brandon possessed the advantage in men it was almost counterbalanced by the skill and daring of the other side.

Suddenly, when the strife was at the hottest, Brandon's men made a quick detour to the left across the meadows.

Lucien Fairleigh remained master of the field.

But Jack was not to be seen, having been taken off by the retreating party.

    *   *   *   *

On the 26th of August, 1717, the gates of Newcastle were, contrary to custom, still closed at half-past ten in the morning.

A quarter of an hour after a guard of twenty Dutch, the favourite troops of William of Orange, passed through these gates, which were again closed behind them.

Once through they arranged themselves along the hedges which, outside the gates, bordered each side of the road.

There was a great crowd collected there, for numbers of peasants and other people had been stopped at the gates on their way into London.

They were arriving by three different routes.

The crowd was growing more dense every moment.

Women seated on pack-saddles, and peasants in their carts, and all by their questions more or less pressing, formed a continual murmur, while some voices were raised above the others in shriller tones of anger or complaint.

There were, besides this mass of arrivals some groups who seemed to have come from the city.

These, instead of looking at the gate, fastened their gaze upon the horizon as though they were expecting to see some one arrive.

These groups consisted chiefly of citizens warmly wrapped up, for the weather was cold, and the piercing north-east wind seemed trying to tear from the trees the leaves which the first symptom of autumn had begun to brown.

Three of these were talking together, that is to say, two talked, and one listened, or rather seemed to listen, so anxiously did he look towards the horizon.

Let us turn our attention for a moment to this last.

He was a man who must have been tall when he stood upright.

But at this moment his long legs were bent under him, and his arms, not less long in proportion, were crossed over his breast.

He was leaning against the hedge, which almost hid his face, before which he also held up his hand as if for further concealment.

By his side a little man, mounted on a hillock, was talking to another tall man, who was constantly slipping off the summit of the same hillock, and catching hold of the button of his neighbour's doublet.

" Yes, my friend Marston," said the little man to the tall man ; " yes, I tell you, there will be ten thousand men round the scaffold of this Jack Tyrrell."

" See, without counting those already on the market-place, the number of people here, and this is but one gate out of four."

" Ten thousand ! that is a round number," replied Marston. " To be sure, many people will follow my example and not go to see this unlucky man executed, for fear of an uproar."

" Mr. Marston, there will be none, I answer for it. Do you not think so, sir ?" continued he, turning to the long-armed man.

" What ?" said the other, as though he had not heard.

" They say there will be nothing on the market-place to-day."

" I think, sir, that you are wrong, and that there will be the execution of Jack Tyrrell."

" Yes, doubtless ; but I mean that there will be no noise about it."

" There will be the noise of the blows of the whip which they will give to the horses as they drag the cart up."

" You don't understand. By noise I mean tumult. If there were likely to be any the king would not have had a stand prepared for him and the queen."

" Do kings ever know when a tumult will take place ?" replied the other, shrugging his shoulders with an air of pity.

" Oh, oh !" said Mr. Marston, " this man talks in a singular fashion ; do you know who he is, friend ?"

" No."

" Then why do you speak to him ? I think you are wrong ; he does not like to talk."

" And yet it seems to me," replied John Adlam, in a tone loud enough to be heard by the stranger, " that one of the greatest pleasures in life is to exchange thoughts."

" Yes, with those whom we know well," answered Mr. Marston.

" Are not all men brothers, as the priests say ?"

" They were primitively ; but, in times like ours, the relationship is singularly loosened. Talk low, if you must talk, and leave the stranger alone."

" But I know you so well—I know what you will reply, while this stranger may have something new to tell me."

" Hush ! he is listening."

" So much the better ; perhaps he will answer. Then you think, sir," turning again towards him, " that there will be a tumult ?"

" I did not say so."

" No, but I believe you think so ?"

" And on what do you ground your surmise, Mr. Adlam ?"

" Why, he knows me !"

" Have I not named you two or three times ?" returned Marston.

" Ah ! true. Well, since he knows me, perhaps he will answer. Now, sir, I believe you agree with me, or else you would be there, while, on the contrary, you are here."

" But you, Mr. Adlam, since you think the contrary of what you think I think, why are you not at the market-place ? I thought the spectacle would have been a joyful one to all friends of the king. Perhaps you will reply that you are not friends of the king, but of the Pretender, and that you are waiting here for the rebels, who, they say, are about to enter Newcastle in order to deliver Jack Tyrrell ?"

"No, sir," said the little man, visibly frightened at this suggestion, "I wait for my wife."

"Look, friend," cried Marston, "at what is passing."

John Adlam, following the direction of his friend's finger, saw them closing another door, while a party of Dutch placed themselves before it.

"How ! more precautions ?" cried he.

"What did I tell you ?" said Marston.

A the sight of this new obstacle a long murmur of astonishment and discontent proceeded from the crowd.

"Clear the road ! back !" cried an officer.

This manœuvre was not executed without difficulty ; the people in carts and on horseback tried to go back, and nearly crushed the crowd behind them. Women cried, and men swore, while those who could escape did, overturning the others in their passage.

"The rebels ! The rebels !" cried a voice in the midst of the crowd.

"Oh !" cried Marston, trembling. "Let us fly !"

"Fly, and where ?" said Adlam.

"Into this enclosure," answered Marston, tearing his hands by seizing the thorns of the hedge.

"Into that enclosure ? It is not so easy. I see no opening, and you cannot climb a hedge that is higher than I am."

"I will try," returned Marston, making new efforts.

"Oh, take care, my good woman," cried Adlam, "your ass is on my feet."

"Oh, sir, take care, your horse is going to kick."

While Mr. Marston was vainly trying to climb the hedge, and Mr. Adlam to find an opening through which to push himself, their neighbour quietly extended his long legs, and strode over the hedge with as much ease as one might have leaped it on horseback.

Mr. Marston followed his example, after having considerably damaged his hands and clothes, but poor Adlam could not succeed, in spite of all his efforts, till the stranger, stretching out his long arms, and seizing him by the collar of his doublet, quietly lifted him over.

"Ah, sir !" cried he, when he found himself safely landed on the other side. "On the word of John Adlam you are a real Hercules ! Your name, sir ! —the name of my deliverer !"

"I am called Birkett, James Birkett."

"You have saved me, Mr. Birkett. My wife will bless you !—but *apropos !* Good Heavens ! she will be stifled in this crowd ! Ah, you cursed Dutch are only good to crush people !"

As he spoke, he felt a heavy hand laid upon his shoulder, and upon looking round, and seeing that it was a Dutchman, he took to flight, followed by Marston.

The other man laughed quietly, then turning to the Dutchman, said,

"Are the rebels coming ?"

"No."

"Then why do they close the door ? I do not understand it."

"There is no need that you should," replied he, laughing at his own wit.

CHAPTER VI.

PREPARATIONS FOR THE EXECUTION OF MOONLIGHT JACK.

ONE of the groups was formed of a considerable number of towns-people.

They surrounded four or five of a martial appearance, whom the closing of the doors annoyed very much, as it seemed, for they cried with all their might,

"The door ! The door !"

James Birkett advanced towards this group, and began to cry, also,

"The door ! The door !"

One of the cavaliers, charmed at this, turned towards him, and said,

"Is it not shameful, sir, that they should close the gates in open day, as though a foreign army were overrunning England ?"

James Birkett looked attentively at the speaker, who appeared to be about forty-five years of age, and the principal personage in the group.

"Yes, sir," said he, "you are right ; but may I venture to ask what is their motive for these precautions ?"

"I don't know, except that they may fear some one will eat up this Tyrrell."

"By Heavens !" said a voice. "A sad meal."

James Birkett turned towards the speaker, whose voice had a strong Norman accent, and saw a young man, from twenty to twenty-five, resting his hand on the crupper of the horse of the first speaker.

His head was bare ; he had probably lost his hat in the *melée.*

"But as they say," replied Birkett, "tha this Tyrell belonged to the Pretender——."

"Bah ! they say that."

"Then you do not believe it, sir ?"

"Certainly not," returned the cavalier. "Doubtless, if he had, the Pretender would not have let him be taken, or at all events would not have allowed him to have been carried hither, bound hand and foot, without even trying to rescue him."

"An attempt to rescue him," replied Birkett, "would have been very dangerous, because whether it failed or succeeded, it would have been a mistake. Excuse me, if I insist, but it is not I who invent. It appears that Tyrrell has confessed."

"Where, before the judges ?"

"Yes."

"And what did he say ?" cried the cavalier, impatiently. "As you seem so well-informed, perhaps you can repeat his words ?"

"I cannot certify that they were his words," replied Birkett, who seemed to have a satisfaction in teazing the cavalier.

"Well, then, those they attribute to him ?"

"They assert that he has confessed that he conspired for the Pretender."

"Against the king, of course ?"

"Yes."

"If he confessed that——"

"Well ?"

"Well, he is a poltroon !" said the cavalier, frowning.

"Alas ! but anger makes a man confess many things."

"Ah, sir, that is true."

"Bah !" interrupted the other, "anger be hanged, if Tyrrell confessed that he was a knave and his patron another."

"You speak loudly, sir," said the cavalier.

"I speak as I please ; so much the worse for those who dislike it."

"More calmly," said a voice, at once soft and

imperative, of which Birkett vainly sought the owner.

The cavalier seemed to be endeavouring to controul himself, but at length said,

"Do you know him of whom you speak ?"

"Tyrrell ?"

"Yes."

"Not in the least."

"And the Pretender ?"

"Still less."

"Well, then, Tyrrell is a brave man."

"So much the better ; he will die bravely."

"And know that when the Pretender wishes to conspire, that he conspires for himself."

"What do I care ?"

"What ?"

"Yes, by my faith, what do I care ? I came here on business, and find the gate closed because of this execution ; that is all I care for."

At this moment there was the sound of trumpets.

The Dutch had cleared the middle of the road, along which a crier proceeded, dressed in a flowered tunic, and bearing on his breast a 'scutcheon on which was embroidered the arms of the king.

He read from a paper in his hand the following proclamation :—

"This is to make known to our good people of Newcastle and its environs, that its gates will be closed for one hour, and that none can enter during that time, and this by the will of the King."

The crowd gave vent to their discontent in a long hoot, to which, however, the crier seemed indifferent.

The officer commanded silence, and when it was obtained the crier continued,

"All who are the bearers of a sign of recognition, or are summoned by letter or mandate, are exempt from this rule. Given at the Palace at Whitehall, 20th October, 1717."

Scarcely had the crier ceased to speak, when the crowd began to undulate like a serpent behind the line of soldiers.

"What is the meaning of this ?" cried all.

"Oh, it is to keep us out of Newcastle," said the cavalier, who had been speaking in a low voice to his companion. "These guards, this crier, these bars, and these trumpets, are all for us ; we ought to be proud of them."

"Room," cried the officer in command ; "make room for those who have the right to pass."

"By St. George, I know who will pass, whoever is kept out," said the North-countryman. Leaping into the cleared space, he walked straight up to the officer who had spoken, and who looked at him for some moments in silence, and then said,

"You have lost your hat, it appears, sir."

"Yes, sir."

"Is it in the crowd ?"

"No, I had just received a letter from my sweetheart and was reading it, by St. George ! near the river, about a mile from here, when a gust of wind carried away both my letter and my hat. I ran after the letter, although the button of my hat was a single diamond. I caught my letter, but my hat was carried by the wind into the middle of the river. It will make the fortune of the poor devil who finds it."

"So, then, you have none ?"

"Oh, there are plenty in Newcastle. I will buy a more magnificent one, and put in a still larger diamond."

The officer shrugged his shoulders slightly, and said,

"Have you a card ?"

"Certainly I have one, or rather two."

"One is enough if it be the right one."

"But it cannot be wrong. Oh ! no. By St. George ! is it to Lord Ruthven I have the honour of speaking ?"

"It is possible," said the officer, coldly, and evidently not much charmed at the recognition.

"Lord Ruthven, my compatriot ?"

"I do not say no."

"My cousin !"

"Good. Your card."

"Here it is," and the North-countryman drew out the half of a card carefully cut.

"Follow me," said Lord Ruthven, without looking at it, "and your companions, if you have any. We will verify the admissions."

Henry de Lorton, for such was the North-countryman's name, obeyed, and was followed by five other gentlemen.

The first was unattended, but the second, who was lame, was followed by a grey-headed lackey, who looked like the precursor of Sancho Panza, as his master did of Don Quixote.

The third carried a child of ten months old in his arms, and was followed by a woman, who kept a light grasp of his leathern belt ; while two other children, one four and the other five years old, held by her dress.

The fourth was attached to an enormous sword, and the fifth, who closed the troops, was a handsome young man mounted on a black horse.

He looked like a king by the side of the others.

Forced to regulate his pace by those who preceded him, he was advancing slowly, when he felt a sudden pull at the scabbard of his sword.

He turned round, and saw that it had been done by a slight and graceful young man with black hair and sparkling eyes.

"What do you desire, sir ?" said the cavalier.

"A favour, sir."

"Speak ; but quickly, I pray you. I am waited for."

"I desire to enter into the city, sir. An imperious necessity demands my presence there. You, on your part, are alone, and want a page to do justice to your appearance."

"Well ?"

"Take me in, and I will be your page."

"Thank you ; but I do not desire to be served by any one."

"Not even by me ?" said the young man, with such a strange glance, that the cavalier felt all the icy reserve in which he had tried to close his heart melting away.

"I meant to say that I could be served by no one," said he.

"Yes ; I know you are not rich, Sir Hubert Huntley," said the young page.

The cavalier started ; but the lad continued,

"Therefore, I do not speak of wages. It is you, on the contrary, who, if you grant what I ask, shall be paid a hundredfold for the service you will render me. Let me enter, then, with you, I beg. Remembering that he who now begs has often commanded."

Then turning to the group, of which we have already spoken, the lad said,

"I shall pass ; that is the most important thing ; but you, Hardman, try to do so also, if possible."

"It is not everything that you should pass," replied Hardman. "It is necessary that he should see you."

" Make yourself easy ; once through he shall see me."

" Do not forget the sign agreed upon."

" Make yourself easy about that. Two fingers on the mouth, is it not ?"

" Yes ; success attend you."

" Well, Sir Page," said the man on the black horse, " are you ready ?"

" Here I am," replied he, jumping lightly on the horse behind the cavalier, who immediately joined his friends, who were occupied in exhibiting their cards and proving their right to enter.

" God be praised !" said James Birkett " what an arrival of North-countrymen !"

*   *   *   *   *

The process of examination consisted in comparing the half cards with another half in the possession of the officer.

Henry de Lorton, with bare head, was the first to advance.

" Your name ?" said Lord Ruthven.

" It is on the card."

" Never mind ; tell it to me."

" Well, I am called Henry de Lorton."

Then, throwing his eyes on the card, Lord Ruthven read,

" Henry de Lorton, 26th October, 1717, at noon precisely."

" Very good ; it's all right," said he. " Enter. Now for you," said he to the second.

All passed in safely enough until it came to the turn of Sir Hubert Huntley.

He got off his horse and presented his card, while the page hid his face by pretending to adjust the saddle.

" The page belongs to you ?" asked Lord Ruthven.

" You see he is attending to my horse."

" Pass, then."

" Quick, my master," said the page, " or we shall be late."

Behind these men the door was closed, much to the discontent of the crowd.

James Birkett, meanwhile, had drawn near to the porter's lodge, which had two windows, one looking towards Newcastle, and the other into the country.

From this post he saw a man, who, coming from Newcastle at full gallop, entered the lodge, and said,

" Here I am, my Lord Ruthven."

" Good. Where do you come from ?"

" From the Tyne Gate."

" Your number ?"

" Five."

" The cards ?"

" Here they are."

" Good," said Lord Ruthven. " Now open the gates, that all may enter,"

The gates were thrown open, and then horses, mules, and carts, men, women, and children pressed into Newcastle at the risk of suffocating each other, and in a quarter of an hour all the crowd had vanished.

James Birkett remained until the last.

" I have seen enough," said he. " Would it be very advantageous to me to see this unfortunate Jack Tyrrell strung up ? No, by the saints, I have renounced politics, I will, therefore, go and dine."

CHAPTER VII.

THE RESCUE OF MOONLIGHT JACK.

JOHN ADLAM was right when he talked of 10,000 persons as the number of spectators who would meet in the market-place and its environs to witness the execution of Jack Tyrrell.

All Newcastle appeared to have a rendezvous before the grand hotel.

The spectators who succeeded in reaching the place saw a large number of Dutch and light horse surrounding a little scaffold raised about four feet from the ground.

It was so low as to be visible only to those immediately surrounding it, or to those who had windows overlooking it.

After the scaffold, what next attracted all looks was the principal window of the grand hotel, which was hung with red velvet and gold, and ornamented with the royal arms.

This was for the king.

Half past one had just struck when this window was filled.

First came the king, pale, and with a sombre expression, always a mystery to his subjects, who, when they saw him appear, never knew whether to say " Long live the king !" or to pray for his soul.

He was dressed in black, without jewels or orders, and a single diamond shone in his cap, serving as a fastening to three short plumes.

The only expression visible upon his face was one of satisfaction—a kind of anticipated triumph —a sort of hideous gratification at the loathsome spectacle he was about to witness.

After him came the queen.

Her appearance and expression was very different from that of her husband.

THE PLEA FOR MERCY

She was pale, agitated, and evidently eager for the completion of the execution, simply because she wished to escape from it.

Moonlight Jack having been exalted from the position of highwayman to that of state prisoner, was feared, of course, by the queen as well as by the king.

They both knew that he had a double set of friends.

The rebels came first.

Then came the gentlemen of the road, who would stop at nothing, and who would not have been very particular about stringing up the king himself in Jack Tyrrell's place.

A short distance behind the queen the councillors entered.

"Well, gentlemen," said the king, "is there anything new?"

"Sire," replied the president of the council, "we come to beg your majesty to promise life to the criminal; he has revelations to make, which, on this promise, we shall obtain."

"But have we not obtained them?"

"Yes, in part. Is that enough for your majesty?"

"No," said the queen; "and the king has determined to postpone the execution if the culprit will sign a confession substantiating his depositions before the judge."

"Yes," said the king, "and you can let the prisoner know this."

"Your majesty has nothing to add?"

"Only that there may be no variation in the confessions, or I will withdraw my promise; they must be complete."

"Yes, sire, with the names of the compromised parties."

No. 21, May 26, 1866.]   Two Numbers and Two Tales every week for One Penny.
THE WORK GIRLS OF LONDON, and THE CRUSADER; OR,
THE WITCH OF FINCHLEY.   Price One Penny.

" With all the names."

" Even if they are of high rank ?"

" If they were those of my nearest relations ?"

" It shall be as your majesty desires."

" No misunderstanding, Lord Denman. Writing materials shall be brought to the prisoner, and he will write his confession ; after that we shall see."

" But I may promise ?"

" Oh, yes, promise."

Lord Denman and the councillors withdrew.

" He will speak, sire," said the queen, " and your majesty will pardon him. See the foam on his lips."

" Ah ! he is seeking something. What is it ?"

" By my faith," said the king, " he is looking for his rebel friends. He may look as much as he pleases. If they couldn't rescue him on his road thither there is no chance of their rescuing him on the market-place."

Moonlight Jack had seen the troops sent off for the executioner, and he understood that the order for punishment was about to be given.

It was then that he bit his lips till the blood came as the queen had remarked,

" No one," murmured he, " not one of those who had promised me help. Cowards ! cowards !"

The executioner was now seen making his way on horseback through the crowd, and creating everywhere an opening which closed immediately behind him.

As he passed the corner of a street a handsome young man, whom we have seen before, pushed forward impatiently by a young lad apparently about seventeen.

It was Sir Hubert Huntley and the mysterious page !

" Quick !" cried the page, " throw yourself into the opening, there is not a minute to lose !"

" But we shall be stifled. You are mad, my little friend."

" I must be near," cried the page, imperiously. " Keep close to the executioner's horse, or we shall never arrive there."

" But before you get there you will be torn to pieces."

" Never mind me, only go on."

" The horses will kick."

" Take hold of his tail ; a horse never kicks when you hold him so."

Sir Hubert Huntley gave way in spite of himself to the mysterious influence of this lad, and seized the tail of the horse while the page clung to him.

And thus through the crowd, waving like the sea, leaving here a piece of a cloak, and there a fragment of a doublet, they arrived with the horses at a few steps from the scaffold.

" Have we arrived ?" asked the young man, panting.

" Yes, happily," answered Huntley, " for I am exhausted."

" I cannot see."

" Come before me."

" Oh, no ; not yet. What are they doing ?"

" Making slip knots at the ends of the cords."

" And he, what is he doing ?"

" Who ?"

" The condemned ?"

" His eyes turn incessantly from side to side."

The executioner now began to tie the feet and hands of the prisoner.

Moonlight Jack uttered a kind of a groan when he felt the cord come in contact with his flesh.

" Sir," said Lieutenant Laughton to him, politely, " will it please you to address the people ?" and

added in a whisper, " A confession will save your life."

Tyrrell looked earnestly at him as if to read the truth in his eyes.

" You see," continued the lieutenant, " they abandon you. There is no other hope in the world but the one I offer you."

" Well," said Tyrrell, with a sigh, " I am ready to speak."

" It is a written and signed confession that the king exacts."

" Then untie my hand, and give me a pen, and I will write it."

They loosened the cord from his wrist, and an usher, who stood near with writing materials, placed them before him on the scaffold.

" Now," said the officer, who had before spoken, " state everything."

" Do not fear, I will not forget those who have forgotten me."

But as he spoke he cast a glance around.

While this was passing the page, seizing the hand of Sir Hubert, cried,

" Take me in your arms, I pray you, and raise me above the heads of the people who prevent me from seeing.

" Ah ! you are insatiable, young man."

" This one more service ! I must see the condemned, indeed, I must."

Then, as Huntley still hesitated, he cried,

" For pity's sake, sir, I entreat you."

Sir Hubert raised him in his arms at this last appeal, and was somewhat astonished at the delicacy of the body which he held.

Just as Tyrrell had taken the pen and looked round, as we have said, he saw this young lad above the crowd, with two fingers placed on his lips.

An indescribable joy spread itself instantaneously over the face of the condemned man, for he recognized the signal so impatiently waited for, and which announced that aid was near.

After a moment's hesitation, however, he took the paper and began to write

" He writes !" cried the crowd.

" He writes !" exclaimed the queen.

" He writes," cried the king, " and I will pardon him !"

Suddenly Tyrrell stopped, and looked again at the lad, who repeated his signal.

He wrote on, then stopped to look once more.

The signal was again repeated.

" Have you finished ?" asked Laughton.

" Yes."

" Then sign."

Tyrrell signed, with his eyes still fixed on the young man.

" For the king alone," said he, and he gave the paper to the usher, though with hesitation.

" If you have disclosed all," said the lieutenant, " you are safe."

A strange smile played over the lips of the prisoner.

Hubert Huntley, who was getting tired, now wished to put down the page, who made no opposition.

With him disappeared all that had sustained the unfortunate man.

He looked round wildly, and cried,

" Well, come !"

No one answered.

" Quick ! quick ! the king holds the paper ; he is reading !"

Still there was no response.

The king unfolded the paper.

" Ten thousand devils !" cried Tyrrell ; " if they

have deceived me ! Yet it was she—it was really she !"

No sooner had the king read the first lines than he called out, indignantly,

"Oh, the wretch !"

"What is it, my king ?"

"He retracts all ; he pretends that he confessed nothing ; and he declares that the nobles who have been accused are innocent of any plot."

"But," said the queen, "if it should be true."

"He lies !" cried the king.

"How do you know, sire ? Perhaps the nobles who have been accused have been calumniated ; the judges, in their zeal, may have put a false interpretation on the depositions."

"Oh, no, madam ; I heard them myself."

"You, sire ?"

"Yes, I."

"How so ?"

"When the prisoner was questioned I was behind a curtain, and heard all that he said."

"Well, then, if he will have it, order the executioner to do his duty."

There was no time left them for any dubious conversation as to whether Moonlight Jack would confess or not.

The queen's words had scarcely left her lips when there was a loud roar in the market-place.

The king and queen were looking at the crowd and the scaffold.

They were not left many moments in doubt as to what was to happen.

From among the throng of people were seen flashing swords raised on high, and lanes, as it were, of armed men meandered among the peaceful citizens.

"There is a rescue !" cried the queen.

"Why don't they execute him at once, and so stop this tumult ?" cried the king.

He glanced round him for some one who could bear an order to the executioner.

The councillors around him were horror-stricken.

They knew that the wrath of the excited mob, if it fell upon the king, would fall upon them too.

A popular tumult is a wonderful test of loyalty and courage.

There was scarcely a man present who did not wish himself a hundred miles off.

One of them, a young man, who had but lately been near the person of his majesty—Andrew Burnet, the son of a loyal but poor baronet—at once came to the king's side, when he saw that he was looking for a messenger.

The king seized him by the shoulder.

"See, Burnet," he cried ; "there is a tumult in the market-place. There will be a rescue if we do not look to it at once. Have you courage to carry through this crowd an order to the executioner to do his duty quickly ?"

"Yes, sire," returned Andrew Burnet ; "give me the order, and I will go at once."

In a few moments he had left the stand, leapt upon his horse, and was making his way through the crowd.

He waved a paper in his hand.

This was an act of treachery and deception.

He intended the crowd to believe that he was the bearer of a pardon.

Many were deceived.

But not those whom he sought to deceive.

Those who were there to rescue Moonlight Jack knew well that he had done nothing to merit a pardon.

"A pardon ! a pardon !" cried some one in the crowd.

"A death warrant ! a death warrant !" shouted Hardman and his men, who were attacking the dragoons.

At the same moment the mysterious page made a dash at Andrew Burnet, and snatched the paper from his hand.

Burnet drew his sword and made a cut at him.

But ere the steel had time to strike he uttered a loud cry, and fell back bathed in blood.

A ball from Hardman's unerring pistol had pierced his brain.

The page sprang into the empty saddle.

He waved the paper around his head.

"This is no pardon," he shouted. "It is the king now who is the traitor. He extorts confessions, and rewards them by death warrants. To the scaffold !—to the scaffold, my friends, and let us save the prisoner !"

The fickle crowd responded at once to the appeal.

They had come there to see a man hanged.

They would go home now and boast how they had saved him.

Armed men seemed to spring from the earth.

From behind the companies of soldiers, from the corner of the streets, from knots of people hitherto quiet, from beneath the scaffold, from beneath the very window where the king and queen were standing pale with terror, friends of the condemned man sprang up, shouting the name of Moonlight Jack, and, what was still more vexatious to the royal ears, "Long live King James !"

The soldiers did their best.

Animated by the kind of loyalty which can be bought for a shilling a day, and animated also by that spirit of brutality which inspires the strong and ignorant to attack the weak and defenceless, the dragoons dashed at the crowd, and struck right and left with their swords.

The executioner, seeing what was occurring around him, thought that his better part of valour was discretion, and bolted.

He left the prisoner standing with the rope round his neck.

In a few moments Moonlight Jack was free.

The mysterious page was the first to undo the cords which bound the prisoner's ankles and wrists, the first to take the fatal noose from around his neck.

Then came a curious scene.

Moonlight Jack clasped the page to his heart, and kissed him again and again.

Not more rapturously than he embraced and kissed another light and agile figure which sprang second on the scaffold.

Need we lift the veil which enshrouds the mystery of this page and this boy ?

Need we say that they were Gipsy Bess and Harry, Jack Tyrrell's son ?

Seizing a sword from the man nearest him, Moonlight Jack sprang from the scaffold full upon the head of one of the troopers beneath it, and scrambling upon the saddle thus left empty, put himself at the head of the trusty band of highwaymen who had guarded the steps of the scaffold, and held the horses for Harry and Gipsy Bess.

Amid the tremendous tumult and the bloodshed, few had had time to observe the movements of the king.

When at last they did find time to look, the windows of the grand hotel were empty.

The royal and respectable person who had ordered the execution, had, in the sublime words of the New London Dictionary, "hooked it."

Kings are always fairweather birds.

They are all very well when there is nothing to

do, and plenty of time to do it in—when there is no danger, and no prospect of danger.

When there is, the best thing for them is to be out of the way.

Tradition says that this most potent and wonderful king leapt upon his horse at the door of the grand hotel, and, like Napoleon returning from the Battle of Waterloo, never drew rein till he reached the gates of his palace.

How the queen got to London tradition does not say.

But the probability is that being a less noticeable person, and less hated than the king, she was enabled to proceed to the capital by ordinary routes.

"The king has fled!" cried Moonlight Jack, during a lull in the combat, when the dragoons and the infantry had been driven to one side of the market-place. "Long live King James. Down with the Dutch pensioners!"

The people took up the cry.

The troops saw themselves in the wrong, and showed every disposition to gain the populace.

The officers saw it was time to give in.

The word "retreat" was given.

The soldiers were not slow in obeying.

Down one of the by-streets the dragoons fled apace.

In a few minutes the people and highwaymen had the market-place to themselves.

Moonlight Jack always knew when to profit by a victory.

He was perfectly well aware that in half an hour the place might be swarming with the king's troops.

He soon, therefore, gave the signal to retreat, and it was not long before he and his trusty band were scouring over the sunlit heath towards the deserted coal mine, which was their present place of concealment.

CHAPTER VIII.

AN ACT OF TREACHERY PUNISHED.

IT may be a subject of wonder to our readers why Lucien Fairleigh was not present at Newcastle at the time of the attempted execution of Moonlight Jack.

The fact was, he had gone to London for the purpose of endeavouring to procure for Jack Tyrrell the remission of his sentence.

On arriving at the northern extremity of the city, he entered an inn for the purpose of obtaining refreshment, and also to rest his horse.

Seating himself in the common room, near the open window, he was quietly partaking his supper, when his attention was attracted by an extraordinary circumstance.

A tall man, whose face he could not will discern, issued from the high porch of the tavern, and walked straight into the middle of the road.

He then turned at right angles, and walked ten paces down the road.

Here he halted.

Then a second man issued from another door, and acted in exactly the same manner, except that he walked in an opposite direction.

Then the two men turned so as to face each other, and advancing, said,

"At the door of the church of St. Andrew to-night at ten."

Then the two men walked off by different routes.

"By my faith," said Lucien Fairleigh, "but this is extraordinary. I like the unravelling of mysteries, and I, therefore, rather fancy, my gentlemen, that there will be three at the appointed place to-night."

It was now nine o'clock.

It was impossible to see the king before the morning, and Lucien Fairleigh therefore had the rest of the evening to himself.

After disposing of his supper, therefore, he left the tavern, and proceeded by the nearest route to St. Andrew's church.

St. Andrew's was but a strange old edifice, and cast a phantom-like shadow over a broad waste piece of ground which had been the scene of many a dark crime.

The nearest house was two hundred yards distant from the church, and this was only one of a few straggling edifices which formed the beginning, as it were, of a long street.

On one side of the church there was a row of thickly-planted trees bordering a deep and noisome ditch, and it was at the extremity of this row that Lucien Fairleigh posted himself to watch.

He had not long to wait.

The clock tolled out dismally the hour.

Then a man with a black mask appeared suddenly.

He sprang, as it were, from the shadows.

Casting a rapid glance round him to see if he was watched, he passed into the church porch.

Then down the road came the second figure.

Lucien crept nearer.

Ere the men met he was close beside them.

"The stars shine," said one.

"And the moon," said the other.

"Good; we are well met, Thornley Rowe," said one. "This is the best place we could have chosen. I have not met a soul for miles."

"Nor I."

"Well, then, to business. You have heard that Jack Tyrrell, one of the bravest leaders of the Pretender's army is awaiting death?"

"I have."

"Then, as sure as my name is Henry Elliot, I mean to save him if I can."

"Good," thought Lucien; "these are men of the right kidney."

"What is your plan?" asked Rowe.

"I will tell you. I am commissioned by Lord Thelford to collect arms and men. I have money of his to do so with. There is no fear of not being able to pay any rewards that may be offered. How many men do you think you can collect?"

There was silence for a moment.

Then Rowe said, hesitatingly,

"How much money can you make available for me?"

"What is necessary."

"Have you it with you now?"

"I have some."

"Good; I should wish for some at once. I shall see my men this night."

"How much do you need now?"

"Ten guineas."

"You can have them. Use them sparingly, however."

"Depend upon me for that."

"Well, it is best so. It would not do to pay them all at once. Give them an earnest, and pay them when the work is done."

As he spoke Elliot drew out his purse.

Rowe eyed him eagerly.

In the moonlight Lucien Fairleigh saw the keen flash of his eyes.

He guessed at once the character of the man.

"Here," said Elliot, "here are the ten guineas, use them well."

Rowe grasped them anxiously.

But he made no attempt at reply.

"To-morrow night!" said Elliot, "meet me here with your men."

He then moved away.

The other delayed.

"This is good," he said to himself, with a chuckling murmur, "ten guineas from this rebel, and fifty from the king when Lord Thelford is betrayed. But, stay! he had more. Why not follow him and get the rest?"

The idea seemed to please him.

He drew from his girdle a dagger, and crept away on the track of his friend.

Lucien's mind was made up.

He also drew his dagger, and, making a detour, found himself, after a few minutes, close to Elliot, who was striding along with rapid steps.

To speak to him now would be to ruin all.

To keep quiet and frustrate the schemes of this traitor would be to prevent his success in the future.

So he crept on.

The assassin advanced.

Suddenly Elliot stopped.

This Rowe seized as his opportunity.

But he was wrong.

Elliot turned.

He saw his face.

He saw the flashing of the steel.

There was no time for him to dream of arresting the weapon.

But help was near.

As Rowe's arm was raised there was another flash in the moonlight!

A quickening gleam!

A heavy blow!

Rowe, the traitor, was lying dead and stark on the ground.

Elliot stood aghast.

All had happened so swiftly that he could scarce credit his senses.

In fact he could not understand how it all happened or whether Lucien Fairleigh, who had killed his friend, was friend or foe.

So he still stood on the defensive.

"Who are you?" he demanded.

"A friend."

"Your name?"

"Lucien Fairleigh."

The man stared in silence.

He knew the name.

Lucien proceeded,

"I am doubtless a stranger to you, but I have two claims upon you."

"And those are?"

"First, I have saved your life."

"Granted."

"Secondly, I am the bosom friend of Moonlight Jack."

"Your watch-word?"

"Gipsy Bess and Safety."

Elliot still hesitated.

"A traitor might know this."

"You hesitate," said Lucien.

"Yes; I must know more."

"Good! I approve of your caution. But I will tell you more. I am the leader of Jack Tyrrell's band; I am on my way to the king's palace to demand his pardon. On the other hand I know you; you are commissioned by Lord Thelford!"

Elliot started.

"You know me!" he cried.

"Yes! your name is Elliot; your companion, the dead traitor there, is named Rowe; you are collecting men to save Moonlight Jack. There is yet another sign which I can give you; but I warn you that, if you cannot return the answer, you or I must die, here on this spot."

Elliot started again.

"I am ready," he said; "no traitor lives who knows that last sign. Speak, I accept the chance you offer."

"*For love or for hate?*" said Lucien, with his hand on his sword.

"*Love dies where hate survives*," returned the other, without hesitation. "We had best journey on together, my friend, since we can now understand each other well."

Lucien smiled.

He held out his hand.

Elliot grasped it firmly.

"We fight for a good cause," he said, "and I am sure in you the cause finds a true and faithful servant."

"And in you; but come, let us take from this man his money, and, what are more valuable, his papers."

"True, we may discover some network of villany."

Lucien knelt down by the man's side.

"The last I can answer for," he said, as he dived in the man's pocket, "for I know he was to receive fifty pounds for betraying Lord Thelford into the hands of the king."

On the man's body they found little money beyond the ten guineas which were given him by Elliot.

But of papers they found not a few.

These they placed in their pockets for examination at a future time.

Then they took their way to London.

Their arrangements were somewhat modified by this meeting.

Instead of trusting to the aid of such men as Elliot it was determined to carry the money into the North, and distribute it among those who were still friends to the Pretender, and who would fight to save one who had been to him such a staunch adherent as Jack Tyrrell.

Elliot himself was not to take the money.

He was compelled to remain in London.

But he knew, trusty friend, none other than his own brother.

To him he resolved to entrust the arrangement of his new scheme.

He, however, was not to start until it was discovered how Lucien Fairleigh fared at the king's palace.

On arriving at the inn where they had first met, or rather where Lucien had heard the strange appointment made, they examined rapidly the documents they had taken from the dead body of the traitor.

They were conclusive.

No more was required to prove what a rogue and treacherous slave he was.

There was a letter from Lord Robert Monteagle promising fifty pounds in the king's name for the body of Lord Thelford alive, and thirty for it dead.

There was a copy of a letter of his own accepting the offer, another to Jack Tyrrell promising him help, and another offering to disclose a grand conspiracy for the sum of a hundred pounds, and a pardon for all offences.

"A sorry knave," said Lucien Fairleigh, when they had perused these documents, "and *you*, my friend, were nearly falling a victim to him."

Elliot sighed.

"Aye," he said, "more than you think."

Lucien looked surprised.

"Do you know more of his knavery, then?" he asked, quickly.

The other lowered his voice.

"Not that," he said, "not that. I have a secret to confide to you. I do so because I know you to be honest. Look at me well."

He removed from his face his whiskers.

They were heavy, and had concealed his face greatly.

Lucien glanced at him, and then uttered an irrepressible exclamation of astonishment.

It was Lord Thelford himself.

"My Lord," he said, somewhat piqued, "you disguise yourself well."

Thelford smiled as he replaced his disguise.

"Be not angry with me, my friend," he said, "because my disguise has been impenetrable to you. It should give you pleasure since one of King James's best friends can pass unnoticed and unharmed, therefore, through a crowd. But come, since I have thrown off the mask, I will deal candidly with you in all things. The man whom I shall send to-morrow is named Langley—Royd Langley. He was once my faithful steward. He is a clever man, and as brave as he is clever. He will proceed to Newcastle by way of Leyburne, and keep the road straight on. He will start at noon should you not by that time reach my house with orders to the contrary."

"Good, my lord——"

"Nay, Elliot, if you please."

"Well, then, Elliot, since it must be so," said Lucien, smiling. "I will endeavour to be with you. But where can I meet you?"

"My house, as I style it, is a little room situated at the top of the abode of a worthy farrier named Smythe, residing in Cumberland Street. You know it, doubtless?"

"I do."

"Then we part till to-morrow."

"That is arranged. Good night."

"Good night"

The visit of Lucien Fairleigh to the king we need not speak of.

The king was gone to Newcastle, and at noon Royd Langley started.

He was conscious from the moment he left London that his steps were dogged.

More than once he felt so exceedingly nervous as to the safety of the money and papers confided to him that, brave man as he was, he almost determined to send back to Lord Thelford for an escort.

But as the road to Leyburne was passed without accident, Royd Langley began to think again that it was needless, and that the Pretender would lose his good opinion of him, and also that an escort would be a great trouble.

He went on, therefore, but his fears began to return as evening advanced.

All at once he heard behind him the galloping of horses, and turning round, he counted seven cavaliers, of whom four had muskets on their shoulders.

They gained rapidly on Langley, who, seeing flight was hopeless, contented himself with making his horse move in zigzags, so as to escape the balls which he expected every moment.

He was right, for when they came about fifty feet from him, they fired, but thanks to his manœuvre, all the balls missed him.

He immediately abandoned the reins, and let himself slip to the ground, taking the precaution to have his sword in one hand and a dagger in the other.

He came to the ground in such a position that his head was protected by the breast of his horse.

A cry of joy came from the troop, who seeing him fall, believed him dead.

"I told you so," said a man, riding up with a mask on his face. "You failed because you did not follow my orders. This time, here he is. Search him, and if he moves, finish him."

Langley was not a pious man, but at such a moment he remembered his God, and murmured a fervent prayer.

Two men approached him, sword in hand, and, as he did not stir, came fearlessly forward.

But instantly Langley's dagger was in the throat of one, and his sword half-buried in the side of the other.

"Ah! treason!" cried the chief. "He is not dead! Charge your muskets!"

"No, I am not dead!" cried Langley, attacking the speaker.

But two soldiers came to the rescue.

Langley turned and wounded one in the thigh.

"The muskets!" cried the chief.

"Before they are ready you will be pierced through the heart!" said Langley.

"Be firm, and I will aid you!" cried a voice, which seemed to him to come from Heaven.

It was that of a young man, on a black horse.

He had a pistol in each hand, and cried again to Langley,

"Stoop!—quick!—stoop!"

Langley obeyed.

One pistol was fired, and a man rolled at Langley's feet.

Then a second, and another fell.

"Now we are two to two!" cried Langley. "Generous young man, you take one; here is mine."

He then rushed on the masked man, who defended himself as if used to arms.

The young man seized his opponent by the body, threw him down, and bound him with his belt.

Langley soon wounded his adversary, who was very corpulent, between the ribs.

He fell, and Langley, putting his foot on his sword to prevent him from using it, cut the strings of his mask.

"Lord Robert Monteagle! I thought so," said he.

His lordship did not reply; he had fainted from loss of blood and the weight of his fall.

Langley drew his dagger, and was about coolly to cut off his head, when his arm was seized by a grasp as of iron, and a voice said,

"Stay, sir! One does not kill a fallen foe."

"Young man, you have saved my life, and I thank you with all my heart; but accept a little lesson very useful in the time of moral degradation in which we live. When a man has been attacked three times in three days; when he has been each time in danger of death; when his enemies have, without provocation, fired four musket balls at him from behind, as they might have done to a mad dog, then, young man, he may do what I am about to do."

And Langley returned to his work.

But the young man again stopped him.

"You shall not do it while I am here. You shall

not shed more of that blood which is now issuing from the wound you have already inflicted."

"Bah! Do you know this wretch?"

"That wretch is Lord Robert Monteagle, a noble equal in rank to many kings."

"All the more reason. And who are you?"

"He who has saved your life, sir."

"And who, if I do not deceive myself, brought me a letter from the king three days ago?"

"Precisely."

"Then you are in the king's service?"

"I have that honour."

"And yet you save Lord Monteagle? Permit me to tell you, sir, that that is not being a good servant, according to my ideas."

"I think differently."

"Well, perhaps you are right. What is your name?"

"Lucien Fairleigh."

"Well, Mr. Lucien, what are we to do with this great carcase?"

"I will watch over Lord Monteagle."

"And his follower, who is listening there?"

"The poor devil hears nothing; I have bound him too tight, and he has fainted."

"Mr. Fairleigh, you have saved my life to-day, but you endanger it furiously for the future."

"I do my duty to-day; God will provide for the future."

"As you please, then, and I confess I dislike killing a defenceless man. Adieu, then, sir; but first I will choose one of these horses."

"Take mine; I know what it can do."

"Oh, that is too generous!"

"I have not so much need as you have to go quickly."

Langley made no more compliments but got on Fairleigh's horse and disappeared.

———

CHAPTER IX.

LUCIEN FAIRLEIGH RENDERS A SERVICE TO LORD ROBERT MONTEAGLE.

LUCIEN remained on the field of battle for some time, much embarrassed what to do with the two men, who would shortly open their eyes.

As he deliberated he saw a waggon coming along, drawn by two oxen and driven by a peasant.

Lucien went to the man and told him that a combat had taken place between the rebels and the royalists, that four had been killed, but that two were still living.

The peasant, although desperately frightened, aided Lucien first to place Lord Robert Monteagle and then the soldier into the waggon.

The four bodies remained.

"Sir," said the peasant, "were they rebels or royalists?"

"Rebels," said Lucien, who had seen the peasant cross himself in his first terror.

"In that case there will be no harm in my searching them, will there?"

"None," replied Lucien, who thought is as well that the peasant should do it as the first passer-by.

The man did not wait to be told twice, but instantly turned out their pockets.

It seemed that he was far from disappointed, for his face looked smiling when he had finished the operation, and he drove on his oxen at their quickest pace, in order to reach his home with his treasure.

It was in the stable of this excellent man, on a bed of straw, that Lord Monteagle recovered his consciousness.

He opened his eyes and looked at the men and things surrounding him with a surprise easy to imagine.

Lucien immediately dismissed the peasant.

"Who are you, sir?" asked his lordship.

Lucien smiled.

"Do you not recognise me?" said he.

"Yes, I do now; you are he who came to the assistance of my enemy."

"Yes; but I am he who prevented your enemy from killing you."

"That must be true, since I live, unless, indeed, he thought me dead."

"He went away, knowing you to be alive."

"Then he thought my wound mortal."

"I do not know; but, had I not opposed him, he would have given you one which certainly would have been so."

"But then, sir, why did you aid him in killing my men?"

"Nothing more simple, sir, and I am astonished that a gentleman, as you seem to be, does not understand my conduct. Chance brought me on your road, and I saw several men attacking one; I defended the one, but when this brave man—for whoever he may be, he is brave—when he remained alone with you, and would have decided the victory by your death, then I interfered to save you."

"You know me, then?" said Monteagle, with a scrutinising glance.

"I had no need to know you, sir; you were a wounded man, that was enough."

"Be frank; you know me?"

"It is strange, sir, that you will not understand me. It seems to me that it is equally ignoble to kill a defenceless man as six men to attack one."

"There may be reasons for all things."

Lucien bowed, but made no reply.

"Did you not see that I fought sword to sword with that man?"

"It is true."

"Besides, he is my most mortal enemy."

"I believe it, for he said the same thing of you."

"Do you think me dangerously wounded?"

"I have examined your wound, sir, and I think that although it is serious, you are in no danger of death. I believe the sword slipped along the ribs, and did not penetrate the breast? Breathe, and I think you will find no pain in your lungs."

"It is true. But my men——"

"Are dead all but one."

"Are they left on the road?"

"Yes."

"Have they been searched?"

"The peasant whom you must have seen on opening your eyes, and who is your host, searched them."

"What did he find?"

"Some money."

"Any papers?"

"I think not."

"Ah!" said Lord Monteagle, with evident satisfaction. "But the living man, where is he?"

"In the barn close by."

"Bring him to me, sir, and, if you are a man of honour, promise me to ask him no questions."

"I am not curious, sir, and wish to know no more of this affair than I do at present."

His lordship looked at him uneasily.

"Sir," said Lucien, "will you be kind enough to charge some one else with the commission you have just given me?"

"I was wrong, sir, I acknowledge it. Have the kindness to render me the service I ask of you."

Five minutes after the soldier entered the stable.

He uttered a cry on seeing the wounded man; but he put his finger on his lip, and the man instantly became silent.

"Sir," said Lord Monteagle to Lucien, "my gratitude to you will be eternal, and, doubtless, some day we shall meet under more favourable circumstances. May I ask to whom I have the honour of speaking ?"

"I am Lucien Fairleigh."

"You were going to Newcastle ?"

"Yes, sir."

"Then I have delayed you, and you cannot go on to-night ?"

"On the contrary, sir; I am about to start at once."

"For Newcastle ?"

"No, for London."

Lord Monteagle looked surprised.

"Pardon," said he, "but it is strange that going to Newcastle, and, being stopped by an unforeseen circumstance, you should return without fulfilling the end of your journey."

"Nothing is more simple, sir. I was going to a rendezvous for a particular time, which I have lost by coming here with you; therefore, I return to London."

"Oh, sir, but will you not stay here with me for two or three days? I will send this soldier to London for a surgeon, and I cannot remain here alone with these peasants, who are strangers to me."

"Then let the soldier remain with you, and I will send you a doctor."

"Do you know the name of my enemy ?"

"No, sir."

"What, you saved his life and he did not tell you his name ?"

"I did not ask him."

"You did not ask him ?"

"I have saved your life also. Have I asked you your name? But in exchange you both know mine."

"I see, sir, there is nothing to be learned from you; you are as discreet as brave."

"I observe that you say that in a reproachful manner, but on the contrary, you ought to be reassured, for a man who is discreet with one person will be so with another."

"You are right. Your hand, Mr. Fairleigh."

Lucien did quietly as he was asked.

"You have blamed my conduct, sir," said Lord Monteagle, "but I cannot justify myself without revealing important secrets."

"You defend yourself, sir, when I do not accuse."

"Well, I will only say that I am a gentleman of good rank, and able to be of use to you."

"Say no more, sir; thanks to the master whom I serve, I have no need of assistance from any one."

"Your master? Who is he ?"

"I have asked no questions, sir."

"It is true."

"Besides, your wound begins to inflame. I advise you to talk less."

"You are right; but I wan't my surgeon."

"I am returning to London, as I told you; give me his address."

"Mr. Fairleigh, give me your word of honour that if I can trust you with a letter, it shall be given to the person to whom it is addressed."

"I give it, sir."

"I believe you; I am sure I may trust you. I must tell you a part of my secret. I belong to the private guards of the king."

"I did not know he had private guards."

"In these troublous times, sir, every one guards himself as well as he can, and more than this."

"I ask for no explanations, sir."

"Well, I had a mission to Newcastle; when on the road I saw my enemy; you know the rest ?"

"Yes."

"Stopped by this wound I must report to Lady Monteagle, my sister, the reason of my delay."

"Well ?"

"Will you, therefore, put into her own hands the letter I am about to write ?"

"I will see for ink and paper."

"It is needless, my soldier will get my tablets."

He instructed the soldier to take them from his pocket, opened them by a spring, wrote some lines in pencil, and shot them again.

It was impossible for any one who did not know the secret to open them without breaking them.

"Sir," said Lucien, "in three days these tablets shall be delivered."

"Into her own hands ?"

"Yes, sir."

The marquis, exhausted by talking, and by the effort of writing the letter, sank back on his straw.

"Sir," said the soldier, in a tone little in harmony with his dress, "you bound me very tightly, it is true, but I shall regard my chains as bonds of friendship, and will prove it to you some day."

And he held out a hand, whose whiteness Lucien had already remarked.

"So be it," said he, smiling; "it seems I have gained two friends."

"Do not despise them, one has never too many."

"That is true," returned Lucien, and left them.

MOON-LIGHT JACK

OR THE KING OF THE ROAD

As soon as he arrived in London he went to Monteagle House.

There, after having knocked at the great door, and had it opened, he was only laughed at when he asked for an interview with the Lady Monteagle.

Then, as he insisted, they told him that he ought to know that her ladyship lived at Chelsea, and not at London.

Lucien was prepared for this reception, and therefore was not discouraged.

"I am grieved at her ladyship's absence," said he, "for I had a communication of great importance to deliver to her from Lord Robert Monteagle."

"From Lord Robert Monteagle? Who charged you to deliver it?"

"His lordship himself."

"His lordship? and where, pray? for he is not i London either!"

"I know that, as I met him on the road to Newcastle."

"On the road to Newcastle?" said the porter, a little more attentive.

"Yes; and he there charged me with a message for Lady Monteagle."

"A message?"

"A letter."

"Where is it?"

"Here," said Lucien, striking his doublet.

"Will you let me see it?"

"Willingly," and Lucien drew out the letter.

"What singular ink!" said the man.

"It is blood!" said Lucien, calmly.

The porter grew pale at these words, and at the idea that the blood belonged to the marquis.

At this time, when there was a great dearth of ink, and abundance of blood spilled, it was not uncommon for lovers to write to their mistresses, or absent relations to their families, in this liquid.

"Sir," said the servant, "I do not know if you will find Lady Monteagle in London or its environs; but go to a house in Percival Street called the Red House, which belongs to Lady Monteagle. It is the first on the left going to Whitehall. You will sure to find some one there in the service of her ladyship sufficiently in her confidence to be able to tell you where she is just now."

"Thank you," said Lucien, who saw that the man either could or would say no more."

He found the "Red House" easily, and, without more inquiries, rang, and the door opened.

"Enter," said a man, who then seemed to wait for some pass word, but as Lucien did not give any he asked him what he wanted.

"I wish to speak to Lady Monteagle."

"And why do you come here for her?"

"Because the porter at Monteagle House sent me here."

"Lady Monteagle is not here."

"That is unlucky, as it will prevent me from fulfilling the mission with which the marquis charged me."

"For Lady Monteagle?"

"Yes."

"From Lord Robert Monteagle?"

"Yes."

The valet reflected a moment.

"Sir," said he, "I cannot answer; there is some one else whom I must consult. Please to wait."

"The king is well served," thought Lucien. "Certainly they must be dangerous people who think it necessary to hide in this manner. One cannot enter a house of the Monteagle's as one can the palace. I begin to think that it is not the true king whom I serve."

He looked round him.

The court yard was deserted; but all the doors of the stables were open, as if they expected some troop to enter and take up their quarters.

He was interrupted by the return of the valet, followed by another.

"Leave me your horse, sir, and follow my comrade; you will find some one who can answer you much better than I can."

Lucien followed the valet, and was shown into a little room, where a simple, though elegantly-dressed, lady was seated at an embroidery frame.

"Here is the gentleman from the marquis," said the servant.

"Leave us," said she to the valet.

"You are of the household of Lady Monteagle, madam?" said Lucien.

"Yes; but you, sir, how do you bring here a message from the marquis?"

"Through unforeseen circumstances, which it would take too long to repeat," replied Lucien, cautiously.

"Oh, you are discreet, sir," said the lady, smiling.

"Yes, madam, whenever it is right to be so."

"But I see no occasion for your discretion here, for, if you really bring a message from the person you say—— Pray do not look angry; a lady, you know, may say things which would seem harsh from a gentleman."

The lady threw into those words all the caressing and seductive grace that a pretty woman can.

"Madam," replied Lucien, "you cannot make me tell what I do not know."

"And still less, what you will not tell."

"Madam, all my mission consists in delivering a letter to her ladyship."

"Well, then, give me the letter," said the lady, holding out her hand.

"Madam, I believed I had had the honour of telling you that this letter was addressed to her ladyship."

"But as her ladyship is absent, and I represent her here, you may give me the letter."

"Impossible, madam."

The Unknown seemed trying not to grow angry.

"Impossible?" repeated she.

"Yes, impossible, for I swore to the marquis to deliver it only to Lady Monteagle herself."

"Say, rather," cried the lady, giving way to her irritation, "that you have no letter; that, in spite of your pretended scruples, it was a mere pretext for getting in here; that you wished to see me, and that was all. Well, sir, you are satisfied, you have effected your entrance, you have seen me."

"I have told you the truth, madam."

"Well, you wished for some unaccountable reason to see me, and you have seen me. And now good evening."

"I will obey you, madam; since you send me away, I will go."

"Yes," cried she, now really angry; "that will be the better course, since I do not consider you have behaved like a gentleman."

"Stay, madam, I will not go way from here under the weight of your unworthy suspicions. I have a letter from the marquis for Lady Monteagle, and here it is; you can see the handwriting and the address."

Lucien held out the letter to the lady, but without loosing his hold of it.

She cast her eyes on it and cried, "His writing! Blood!"

Without replying, Lucien put the letter back in his pocket, bowed low, and very pale and bitterly hurt, turned to go.

She ran after him and caught him by the skirt of his cloak.

"What is it, madam?" said he.

"For pity's sake, pardon me; has any accident happened to the marquis?"

"You ask me to pardon you only that you may read this letter, and I have already told you that no one shall read it but Lady Monteagle—"

"Ah! obstinate and stupid that you are," cried the lady, with fury, mingled with majesty. "Can you not see that I am the mistress? Have I the appearance of a servant? I am the Lady Monteagle—give me the letter."

"You the Lady Monteagle?" cried Lucien, starting back.

"Yes; I am. Give it to me. I want to know what has happened to my brother."

But instead of obeying, as her ladyship expected, the young man, recovering from his first surprise, crossed his arms.

"How can I believe you when you have already lied to me twice?" said he.

The lady's eyes shot forth fire at these words; but Lucien stood firm.

"Ah! you doubt still. You want proofs!" cried she, tearing her lace ruffles with rage.

"Yes, madam."

She darted towards the bell and rang it furiously. A valet appeared.

"What do you want, madam?"

She stamped her feet with rage.

"Harcourt!" cried she, "I want Harcourt. Is he not here?"

"Yes, madam."

"Let him come here."

The valet left the room.

A moment after Harcourt appeared.

"Did you send for me, madam?" said he

"Madam! and since when am I simply madam?" cried she, angrily.

"Your ladyship!" said Harcourt, in surprise.

"Good!" said Lucien. "I have now a gentleman before me, and if he has lied, I shall know how to treat him."

"You believe, then, at last?" said her ladyship.

"Yes, madam. I believe, and here is the letter;" and bowing, the young man gave to Lady Monteagle the letter so long disputed.

When she had finished, she gave it to Harcourt to read.

It ran as follows :—

"MY SISTER,—I tried to do myself the work I should have left to others, and I have been punished for it. I have received a sword wound from the fellow whom you know. The worst of it is that he has killed five of my men, among them my best men; after which he fled.

"I must tell you that he was aided by the bearer of this letter, a charming young man, as you may see.

"I recommended him to you; he is discretion itself.

"One merit he will have, I presume in your eyes, my dear sister, is, having prevented my conqueror from killing me, as he much wished, having pulled off my mask when I had fainted, and recognised me.

"I recommend you, sister, to discover the name and profession of this discreet cavalier, for I suspect him while he interests me.

"To my offers of service, he replied that the master whom he served let him want for nothing.

"I can tell you no more about him; but that he pretends not to know me.

"I suffer much; but believe my life is not in danger.

"Send my surgeon to me at once. I am lying like a horse upon straw; the bearer will tell you where.
"Your affectionate brother,
"MONTEAGLE."

When they had finished reading, the lady and Harcourt looked at each other in astonishment.

The lady first broke the silence.

"To whom," said she, "do we owe the signal service that you have rendered us, sir?"

"To a man who, whenever he has the opportunity, helps the weak against the strong."

"Will you give us some details, sir?"

Lucien told all that he had seen, and named the marquis's place of retreat.

Lady Monteagle and Harcourt listened with interest.

When he had finished, her ladyship said,

"May I hope, sir, that you will continue the work so well begun, and attach yourself to our house?"

These words, said in the gracious tone which she knew so well how to assume, were very flattering to Lucien.

"Madam, however," said he, "I have already had the honour of telling Lord Monteagle that I serve a good master who treats me too well for me to desire to seek another."

"My brother tells me in his letter that you did not seem to recognise him. Now, if you did not know him then, did you use his name to penetrate to me?"

"Lord Monteagle seemed to wish to preserve his incognito, madam; and I, therefore, did not think I ought to recognise him. It might also have been disagreeable for the peasants to know what an illustrious guest they were entertaining. Here there was no reason for secrecy; on the contrary, the name of Lord Monteagle opened the way to you; so I thought that, here as there, I acted rightly."

The lady smiled and said,

"No one could extricate himself better from an embarrassing question; and you are, I must confess, a clever man."

"I see no cleverness in what I have had the honour of telling you, madam"

"Well, sir," said her ladyship, impatiently, "I see clearly that you will tell nothing. You do not reflect that gratitude is a heavy burden for one of my house to bear; that you have rendered me now an important service, and that if I wished to know your name, or rather who you are —"

"I know, madam, you would learn it easily; but you would learn it from some one else, and I should have told nothing."

"He is always right," cried Lady Monteagle, with a look which gave Lucien more pleasure than ever a look had done before.

Therefore he asked no more, but, like the gourmand who leaves the table when he thinks he has had the best bit, he bowed and prepared to take leave.

"Then, sir, that is all you have to tell me?" asked the lady.

"I have executed my commission, and it now only remains for me to present my humble respects to your ladyship."

As soon as the door had closed behind him she stamped her foot impatiently.

"Harcourt," said she, "have that young man followed."

"Impossible, madam; all our household is out, I myself am waiting for the event. It is a bad day on which to do anything else than that we have decided to do."

"You are right, Harcourt; but afterwards."

"Oh, afterwards if you please, madam."

"Yes; for I suspect him as my brother does."

"He is a brave fellow, at all events, and really we are fortunate in having a stranger to come and render us such a service."

"Nevertheless, Harcourt, have him watched. But night is falling and James must be returning from Whitehall. It is strange that he goes prowling about his old palace, when at every corner there is danger."

"Oh! we have time before us; it is not eight o'clock, and our men have not arrived."

"All have the word, have they not?"

"All."

"They are trustworthy?"

"Tried, madam."

"How many do you expect?"

"Fifty; it is more than necessary."

"As soon as our men arrive range them up the road."

"They are all ready, madam; they will intercept the way; our men will push the carriage towards them; the gates of the Red House will be open and will have but to close behind the carriage."

"Let us sup, then, Harcourt; it will pass the time. I am so impatient that I should like to push round the hands of the clock."

"The hour will come. Be easy."

"But our men?"

"They will be here; it is hardly eight."

"Harcourt, my poor brother asks for his surgeon; the best surgeon, the best cure for his wound, will be a lock from the Pretender's head, and the man who should carry him that present, Harcourt, would be sure to be welcome."

Harcourt opened the window and tried to look out.

"Oh! what a dark night," said he.

"An excellent night; the darker the better. Therefore, good courage, my captain."

"Yes, but we shall see nothing."

"God, whom we fight for, will see for us."

Harcourt, who did not seem quite so sure of the intervention of Providence in affairs of this nature, remained at the window looking out.

"Do you see any one?" asked the lady.

"No, but I hear the tramp of horses."

"It is them; all goes well."

CHAPTER X.

THE PRETENDER, WITH HIS ARMY, MARCHES ON TO DURHAM.

LUCIEN went away with a full heart but a quiet conscience.

He had had singular good fortune.

He had neither betrayed the Pretender, Lord Monteagle, nor himself.

Therefore he was content, but he still wished for many things, and, among others, a quick return to Whitehall, where the Pretender was concealed in the house of Lord Thelford.

He set off at full gallop, but had scarcely gone a hundred yards when he came on a body of cavaliers who stretched right across the road.

He was surrounded instantly, and half-a-dozen swords and pistols presented at him.

"Oh," said Lucien, "robbers on the road half-a-league from London."

"Silence, if you please," said a voice that Lucien thought he recognized. "Your sword, your arms; quick!"

And one man seized the bridle of the horse, while another stripped him of his arms.

"St. George! what clever thieves. At least, gentlemen, do me the favour to tell me——"

"Why, it is Lucien Fairleigh," said the man who had seized his sword.

"Ah, Hardman!" cried Lucien. "Oh! fie, what a bad trade you have taken up."

"Damn it," growled Hardman, "this is unforseen."

"By me also, I assure you," said Lucien, laughing.

"But this is embarrassing; I was ordered to seize upon all loiterers. What were you doing here?"

"If I asked you that question would you answer me?"

"No."

"Then let me act as you would."

"Then you will not tell me?"

"No."

"Nor where you were going?"

Lucien did not answer.

"Then, sir, since you do not explain, I must treat you like any other man."

"Do what you please, sir, only I warn you that you will have to answer for it."

"To Moonlight Jack?"

"Higher than that."

"To Lord Thelford?"

"Higher still."

"Well, I have my orders, and shall take you to Whitehall."

"That is capital. That is just where I was going."

"It's lucky that this little journey pleases you so much."

Lucien Fairleigh was then conducted by his companion to the courtyard of Lord Thelford's house.

Here he began at once to mount the staircase, which led to the Pretender's chamber.

Hardman followed him with his eyes, and saw Lord Thelford meet him on the stairs and sign to him to come on.

Thelford then descended, and said to Hardman,

"Sir, His Majesty, King James, orders that his guards form themselves into three compact bodies; one to go before, and one on each side of the carriage, so that if there be any firing, it may not reach the carriage.

"Very good," said Hardman, "only that I do not see where the firing is to come from."

"At the Red House, sir, they must draw close."

This dialogue was interrupted by the Pretender, who descended the staircase, followed by several gentlemen.

"Gentlemen," said the Pretender, "are my brave friends all here?"

"Yes, sire," said Thelford, showing them.

"Have the orders been given?"

"Yes, sire, and will be followed."

"Let us go, then."

The Light Horse were left in charge of the prisoners, and forbidden to address a word to them.

The Pretender entered his carriage with his naked sword by his side, and as nine o'clock struck they set off.

Mr. Harcourt was still at his window, only he was infinitely less tranquil and hopeful, for none of his soldiers had appeared, and the only sound heard along the silent black road was now and then horses' feet.

When this had occurred, both Harcourt and Lady Monteagle vainly tried to see what was going on.

At last Harcourt became so anxious that he sent off a man on horseback, telling him to inquire of the first body of cavaliers he met.

The messenger did not return.

Her ladyship sent another, but neither reappeared.

"Our officer," said Lady Monteagle, always hopeful, "must have been afraid of not having sufficient force, and must have kept our men to help him. It is prudent, but it makes one anxious."

"Yes, very anxious," returned Harcourt, whose eyes never quitted the horizon.

"Harcourt, what can have happened?"

"I will go myself, madam, and find out."

"Oh, no, I forbid that. Who would stay with me? who would know our friends when the time comes? No, no, stay, Harcourt! One is naturally anxious when a secret of this importance is concerned; but really the plan was too well combined, and above all too secret not to succeed."

"Nine o'clock!" replied Harcourt, rather to himself than to the lady. "I begin to think something must have happened."

"Listen! cried the lady.

They began to hear from afar a noise like thunder.

"It is cavalry!" cried she. "They are bringing him. We have him at last!" and she clapped her hands in the wildest joy.

"Yes," said Harcourt, "I hear a carriage and the tramp of horses."

And he cried out loudly,

"Outside the walls, my friends, outside! Here are our men coming out of the house, and ranging themselves along the walls.

As he spoke the doors of the Red House opened, and twenty armed men marched out.

Soon the road was illumined by a number of torches, thanks to which Lady Monteagle and Harcourt could see cuirasses and swords shining.

Incapable of moderation, she cried,

"Go down, Harcourt, and bring him to me."

"Yes, madam; but one thing disquiets me."

"What is it?"

"I do not hear the signal agreed on."

"What use is the signal since they have him?"

"But they were to arrest him only here, before the Red House."

"They must have found a good opportunity earlier."

"I do not see our officer."

"I do."

"Where?"

"See that red plume?"

"Ten thousand devils! that red plume ——"

"Well?"

"It is Lord Thelford, sword in hand!"

"They have left him his sword?"

"By George, he commands!"

"Our people! Then there has been treason!"

"Oh, madam, they are not our people!"

"You are mad, Harcourt."

But at that moment Lord Thelford, brandishing his sword at the head of the first body of guards, cried, in a loud voice,

"Long live King James!"

"Long live King James!" replied, enthusiastically, the whole of his partizans.

Lady Monteagle grew pale and sank down almost fainting.

Harcourt, sombre, but resolute, drew his sword, not knowing whether the house was to be attacked.

The cortége advanced, and had reached the Red House.

"Room for the king!" cried Lord Thelford.

Then the Pretender passed the house where his course was to have terminated like a whirlwind of fire, noise and glory, and soon left the place behind him in obscurity.

From her balcony, hidden by the golden scutcheon behind which she was kneeling, Lady Monteagle saw and examined each face on which the light of the torches fell.

"Oh!" cried she, "look, Harcourt, that young man, my brother's messenger, is in the service of the Pretender. We are lost, for the king will never believe that we had him in our house and were not able to detain him."

"We must fly immediately, madam, now the Pretender is conqueror."

"We have been betrayed; it must have been by that young man; he must have known all."

The Pretender had already, with all his escort, passed miles along the northern road.

His destination was Durham.

In that town were stores of ammunition which he coveted much.

Durham once his he could make better terms with his enemy.

On his route thousands joined him.

They seemed to spring from the earth.

The Pretender, on his white horse, marched at the head of a line which increased in length at every step.

There was a constant smile of triumph and satisfaction upon the Pretender's countenance.

He glanced round the country and surveyed the broad fields and villages as if he were already their king.

He was received with enthusiasm even by those who could not join his standard.

His army which, when it reached its destination, had only swelled to five thousand men, was divided into two sections.

One of these sections was commanded by Moonlight Jack, and the other by Lucien Fairleigh.

The Pretender, thus full of eagerness and hope, though trembling inwardly at his own constitutional timidity, hurried on till the walls came in sight.

CHAPTER XI.

THE SIEGE OF DURHAM—LUCIEN FAIRLEIGH A PRISONER.

THE little army advanced near the town.

They then breakfasted.

The repast being over two hours were given for the officers and men to rest.

The Pretender was very pale, and his hands trembled visibly when at three o'clock in the afternoon the officers appeared under his tent.

"Gentlemen," said he, "we are here to take Durham, therefore we must take it by force. Do you understand? Douglas, who has sworn to hang every rebel, is only forty-five miles from here, and doubtless a messenger is already dispatched to him by Colonel Fairthorpe. In four or five days he will be on us, and, as he has ten thousand men with him, we should be taken between the city and him. Let us, then, take Durham before he comes, that we may receive him well. Come, gentlemen, I will put myself at your head, and let the blows fall as thick as hail."

The men replied to this speech with enthusiastic cheers.

"Well," said Lucien, to himself, "it was lucky he had not to speak with his hands, though, or he would have stammered finely. Let us see him at the work."

As they were setting off the Pretender said to Lucien,

"If I am afraid, and you find it out, tell no one."

"If you are afraid?"

"Yes."

"Are you, then, afraid of being afraid?"

"I am."

"But, then, why the devil do you undertake such a thing?"

"I must."

"Colonel Fairthorpe is a terrible person."

"I know it well."

"Who gives quarter to no one."

"You think so, Lucien."

"I am sure of it. Red plume or white, he will not care, but cry—Fire!"

"You say that for my white feather, Lucien."

"Yes, sire; and as you are the only one who wears that colour——"

"Well?"

"I would take it off."

"But I put it on that I might be recognised."

"Then you will keep it?"

"Yes; decidedly."

And the Pretender trembled again as he said it.

"Come, sire," said Lucien, who did not understand this difference between words and gestures, "there is still time. Do not commit a folly. You cannot mount on horseback in that state."

"Am I, then, very pale, Lucien?"

"As pale as death, sire."

"Good."

"How, good?"

At this moment the noise of cannon, and a furious fire of musketry, was heard.

It was Colonel Fairthorpe's reply to the summons to surrender given by Moonlight Jack.

"Then," said Lucien, "what do you think of this music, sire?"

"It makes me cold in the marrow of my bones," replied the Pretender. "Here, my horse!—my horse!" continued he.

Lucien looked and listened, unable to understand him.

The Pretender mounted, and then said,

"Come, Lucien, get on horseback, too; you are not a warrior either, are you?"

"No, sire."

"Well, come; we will be afraid together. Come and see, my friend. A good horse here for Mr. Lucien."

The Pretender set off at full gallop, and Lucien followed him.

On arriving in front of his little army, the Pretender raised his visor and cried,

"Out with the banner!—out with the new banner!"

They drew forth the banner, and unrolled it.

Again the cannon from the walls of Durham were fired, and the balls tore through a file of infantry near the Pretender.

"By the Lord! did you see that?" cried he, as his teeth chattered.

"He will be ill," thought Lucien.

"Cursed body!" murmured the Pretender. "Ah! you fear, you tremble; wait till you have something to tremble for."

And, striking his spurs into his horse, he rushed onwards before cavalry, infantry, and artillery, and arrived at a hundred feet from the place, red with the fire of the batteries which thundered from above.

There he kept his horse immovable for ten minutes, his face turned towards the gate of the city, and crying,

"The fascines!—the fascines!"

Moonlight Jack had followed him sword in hand, and then came Lucien.

Behind them the young scions of the noble houses who had espoused the cause of the Pretender, crying,

"Long live King James!"

Each carried a fascine, which he threw in, and the fosse was soon filled.

Then came the artillery, and with a loss of thirty men succeeded in placing their petards under the gate.

The shot whistled like a whirlwind of iron round the Pretender's head, and twenty men fell in an instant before his eyes.

"Forward!" cried he, and rushed on through the midst of the fire, and arrived just as the soldiers had fired the first petard.

The gate was broken in two places.

The second petard was lighted, and a new opening was made in the road.

Twenty arquebuses immediately passed through, vomiting balls on the soldiers and officers, and the men fell like mowed grass.

"Sire!" cried Lucien, "in Heaven's name retire!"

Moonlight Jack said nothing.

He was proud of his pupil; but from time to time he tried to place himself before him.

Once the Pretender felt the damp on his brow, and a cloud pass over his eyes.

"Ah! cursed nature!" said he, "you shall not conquer me!"

Then jumping off his horse,

"An axe!" cried he, and with a vigorous arm he struck down wood and iron.

At last a beam gave way, and a part of the gate and a portion of the wall fell, and one hundred men rushed to the breach, crying,

"Long live King James! Long live King James! Durham is ours!"

Lucien had not quitted the Pretender.

He was with him under the gate when he entered one of the first, but at each discharge he saw him shudder and lower his head.

"By St. George, did you ever see such a coward, Fairleigh?" he said.

"No, sire, I have never seen such a coward as you."

The soldiers of Colonel Fairthorpe now tried to dislodge the Pretender, and his advanced guards who received them sword in hand.

But the besieged were strongest, and succeeded in forcing the Pretender and his troops back beyond the fosse.

"By St. George!" cried the Pretender, "I believe my flag retreats. I must carry it myself."

And snatching it from the hands of those who held it, he was the first to rush forward again, half enveloped in its folds.

The balls whistled round him and pierced the flag with a hollow sound.

A long hand to hand fight ensued, above all the uproar of which Colonel Fairthorpe's voice was heard crying,

"Barricade the streets! Let trenches be dug, and the houses garrisoned"

"Oh," cried Lucien, "the siege of the city is over!"

And as he spoke he fired at him and wounded him in the arm.

"You are wrong," cried Fairthorpe, "there are twenty sieges in Durham. So if one is over, there are nineteen to come."

Colonel Fairthorpe defended himself during five days and nights from street to street, and from house to house.

Luckily for the rising fortunes of the Pretender he had counted too much on the walls and garrison of Durham, and had neglected to send to Lord Douglas.

During these five days and nights the Pretender commanded like a captain and fought like a soldier; slept with his head on a stone, and awoke sword in hand.

Each day they conquered a street or a square, which each night the garrison tried to retake.

On the fourth night the enemy seemed willing to give some rest to the army.

Then it was the Pretender who attacked in his turn.

He forced an intrenched position, but it cost him seven hundred men.

And nearly all the officers were wounded, but the Pretender remained untouched.

To the fear which he had felt at first, and which he had so heroically vanquished, succeeded a feverish restlessness -- a rash audacity.

All the fastenings of his armour were broken as much by his own efforts as by the blows of the enemy.

He struck so vigorously that he always killed his man.

When this last post was forced the Pretender entered into the enclosure, followed by the eternal Lucien Fairleigh, who, silent and sad, had for five days seen growing at his sides the phantom of a monarchy.

"Well, Fairleigh, of what are you thinking?" said the Pretender to him.

"Sire, that you are a real king."

"And I, sire, that you are too imprudent," said Moonlight Jack, "to put up your visor when they are firing at you from all sides."

As he spoke a dozen arquebuses were fired at them.

One ball struck off a plume from the Pretender's helmet; his horse was killed by another, and Jack Tyrrell's had his leg broken.

The Pretender fell, and there might have ended his career, but Lucien, whirling his sword round to keep off the nearest, helped him up and gave him his own horse.

The siege was soon over; and resolved at once to take advantage of his victory, the Pretender sent Lucien Fairleigh to the Court to see the king.

What was in the dispatches Lucien did not know.

At any rate it did not please the king.

In fact, ere he had been at the palace twenty-four hours, he found himself a prisoner.

He was treated with every distinction; in fact, just as a foreign ambassador would be treated, but he was not suffered to go anywhere except under surveillance.

This was exceedingly irksome.

He could get no answer from the king, nor could he hear any news of the Pretender.

So when on the fourth night he retired to the room which had been fitted up for his reception, he resolved at any risk to escape from a place where he was doing no good, and, perhaps, even prejudicing the Pretender's interests.

CHAPTER XII.

LUCIEN FAIRLEIGH'S INEFFECTUAL ATTEMPT TO ESCAPE FROM THE PALACE.

LUCIEN, having taking taken his resolution, began to prepare his little packet.

"How much time will it take me," thought he, as he did so, "to carry to the Pretender the news of what I have seen and fear? Two days to arrive at a city whence the governor can send couriers. Once there I can rest, for after all a man must rest sometimes. Come, then, Lucien, speed and non-chalance. You thought you had accomplished your mission, and you are but half way through it."

Fairleigh now extinguished his light, opened his door softly, and began to creep downstairs on tiptoe.

He went into an ante-chamber, but he had hardly gone four steps before he kicked against something; this something was the king's page lying on a mat.

"Ah! good evening, Mr. Van Scheldt," said Lucien Fairleigh; "but get out of the way a little, I beg, I want to go for a walk."

"Ah! but it is forbidden to walk by night near this castle."

"Why so?"

"Because the king fears robbers and the queen lovers."

"The devil!"

"None but robbers or lovers want to walk at night, when they ought to be sleeping."

"However, dear Mr. Van Scheldt," said Lucien, with his most charming smile, "I am neither the one nor the other, but an ambassador, very tired from having supped with the king. Let me go out, then, my friend, for I want a walk."

"In the city, Mr. Lucien?"

"Oh, no; in the gardens."

"That is more forbidden than in the city."

"My little friend, you are very vigilant for your age. Have you nothing to occupy yourself with?"

"No."

"You neither gamble nor fall in love?"

"To gamble one must have money, and to fall in love one must find a lady."

"Assuredly," said Lucien, and feeling in his pocket he drew out ten guineas, and slipped them into the page's hand, saying, "Seek well in your memory, and I'll warrant you'll find some charming woman, to whom I beg you to make some presents with this."

"Oh! Mr. Lucien, it is easy to see that this is not the first time you have visited the Court; you have manners to which one can refuse nothing. Go, then, but make no noise."

Lucien went on, glided like a shadow into the corridor, and down the staircase; but at the bottom he found an officer sleeping on a chair placed right against the door, so that it was impossible to pass.

"Ah! little wretch of a page, you knew this," said Lucien.

He looked round him to see if he could find no other way of making his escape with the assistance of his long legs.

At last he saw what he wanted.

It was an arched window of which the glass was broken.

Lucien climbed up the wall with his accustomed skill, and without making more noise than a dry leaf in the autumn wind, but unluckily the opening was not big enough, so when he had got his head and one shoulder through, and had taken away his foot from its resting place on the wall, he found himself hanging between heaven and earth without being able either to advance or retreat.

He began then a series of efforts, of which the first result was to tear his doublet and scratch his skin.

What rendered his position more difficult was his sword, of which the handle would not pass, making a hook by which Lucien hung on the sash.

He exerted all his strength, patience, and industry to unfasten the clasp of his shoulder belt.

But it was just on the clasp that his body leaned, therefore he was obliged to change the manœuvre, and at last he succeeded in drawing his sword from its sheath, and pushed it through one of the interstices; the sword, therefore, fell first on the flag-stones, and Lucien now managed to get through after it.

All this, however, was not done without noise, therefore Lucien, on rising, found himself face to face with a soldier.

"Ah, Mr. Lucien, have you hurt yourself?" said he.

Lucien was surprised, but replied,

"No, my friend, not at all."

"That is very lucky; there are not many people who could do such a thing."

"But how the devil did you know my name?"

"I saw you to-day at the palace, and asked who was the gentleman that was talking with the king."

"Well, I am in a hurry; allow me to pass."

"But no one goes out of the palace by night, those are my orders."

"But you see they do come out, since I am here."

"Yes; but——"

"But what?"

"You must go back, Mr. Lucien."

"Oh, no."

"How, no?"

"Not by that way, at all events; it is too troublesome."

"If I were an officer instead of a soldier, I would ask you why you come out so; but that is not my business, which is only that you should go back again. Go in, therefore, Mr. Lucien, I beg you."

And the soldier said this in such a persuasive tone that Lucien was touched, consequently he put his hand in his pocket and drew out another ten guineas.

"You must understand, my friend," said he, "that as I have torn my clothes in passing through once, I should make them still worse by going back again, and should have to go naked, which would be very indecent in a Court where there are so many young and pretty women; let me go, then, to my tailor."

And he put the money into the man's hand.

"Go quickly, then, Mr. Lucien," said he.

Lucien was in the street at last.

The night was not favourable for flight, being bright and cloudless, and he regretted the foggy nights of November, when people might pass close to each other unseen.

The unfortunate fugitive had no sooner turned the corner of the street than he met a soldier.

He stopped of his own accord, thinking it would look suspicious if he tried to pass unseen.

"Oh, good evening, Mr. Fairleigh," said the officer, " shall we reconduct you to the palace ; you seem as though you had lost your way ?"

"It is very strange," murmured Lucien, " every one knows me here."

Then aloud, and as carelessly as he could,

"No, my friend. I am not going to the palace."

"You are wrong, Mr. Fairleigh," said the officer, gravely.

"Why so, sir ?"

"Because a very severe edict forbids the inhabitants of London to go out at night without permission, and without a lantern."

"Excuse me, sir ; but this edict cannot apply to me, who do not belong to London."

"But you are in London. Inhabitants means, living at ; now you cannot deny that you live at London, since I see you here."

"You are logical, sir ; unluckily I am in a hurry. Make an exception to your rule and let me pass."

"You will lose yourself, Mr. Fairleigh. London is a strange place ; allow three of my men to conduct you to the palace ?"

"But I am not going there, I tell you."

"Where are you going, then."

"I cannot sleep well at night, and then I always walk. London is a charming city, and I wish to see it."

"My men shall conduct you where you please."

"Oh, sir, I would rather go alone."

"You will be assassinated."

"I have my sword."

"Ah, true ; then you will be arrested for bearing arms."

Lucien, driven to despair, drew the officer aside, and said,

"Come, sir, you are young ; you know what love is—an imperious tyrant."

"Doubtless, Mr. Fairleigh."

"Well, then, I have a certain lady to visit."

"Where ?"

"In a certain place."

"Young ?"

"Twenty-three years old."

"Beautiful ?"

"As the graces."

"I felicitate you, Mr. Fairleigh."

"Then you will let me pass ?"

"It seems I must."

"And alone ? I cannot compromise."

"Of course not—pass on, Mr. Fairleigh."

"You are a gallant man. But how did you know me ?"

"I saw you at the palace with the king. Apropos ! which way are you going ?"

"Towards Temple Bar. Am I in the right road ?"

"Yes ; go straight on. I wish you success."

"Thank you," said Lucien, passing on.

But before he had gone a hundred steps he was met by the watch.

"By Jupiter ! the town is well guarded," muttered Lucien.

"You cannot pass," cried the leader, in a voice of thunder.

"But sir, I want—"

"Ah, Mr. Fairleigh, is it you in the street in this cold ?" asked the officer.

"Ah, decidedly, it must be a bet !" thought Lucien, and bowing, he tried to pass on.

"Mr. Fairleigh, take care," said the officer.

"Take care of what ?"

"You are going wrong ; you are going towards the gates."

"Just so."

"Then I arrest you."

"Not so, sir ; you would be very wrong."

"However—"

"Approach, sir, so that your soldiers may not hear."

The man approached.

"The king has given me a commission for the gatekeeper of Temple Bar."

"Ah !"

"That astonishes you ?"

"Yes."

"It ought not, since you know me."

"I know you from having seen you at the palace with the king."

Lucien stamped his foot impatiently.

"That should prove to you that I possess the king's confidence ?"

"Doubtless, Mr. Fairleigh, go on and execute your commission."

"Come," thought Lucien, I advance very slowly, but I do advance. By Jupiter, here is a gate ; it must be that of Temple Bar. In five minutes I shall be out."

He arrived at the gate, which was guarded by a sentinel walking up and down with his musket on his shoulder.

"My friend, will you open the gate for me ?" said Lucien.

"I cannot, Mr. Fairleigh," replied the man, "being only a private soldier."

"You also know me ?" cried Lucien, in a rage.

"I have that honour. I was on guard at the palace this morning, and saw you talking with the king."

"Well, my friend, the king has given me a very urgent message to convey to Whitehall ; open the postern for me."

"I would with pleasure, but I have not the keys."

"And who has them ?"

"The officer for the night."

Lucien sighed.

"And where is he ?"

The soldier rang a bell to wake his officer.

MOON-LIGHT JACK

OR·THE·KING OF·THE·ROAD

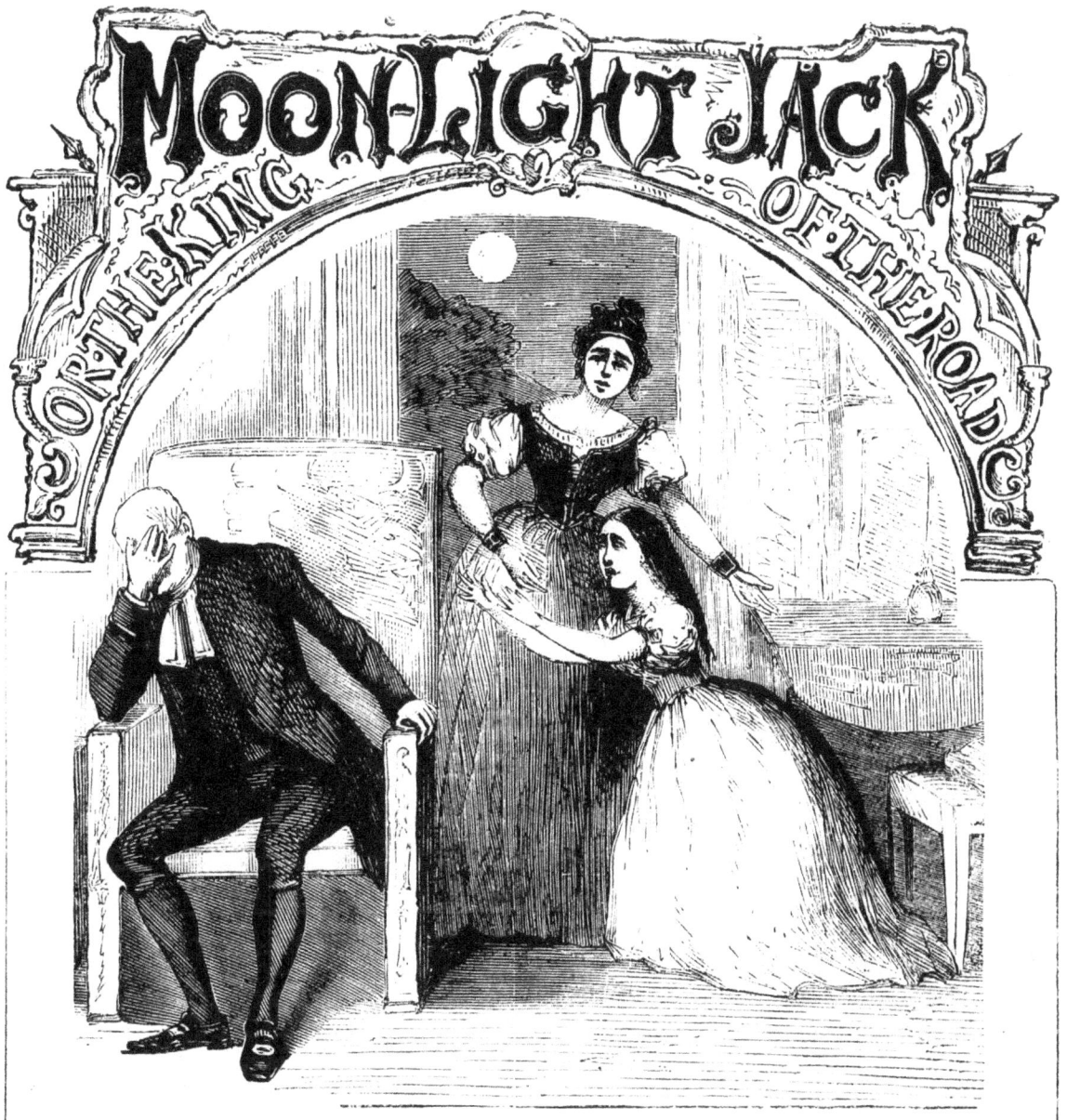

THE RETURN OF THE PENITENT.

"What is it?" said he, poking his head through a window.

"Lieutenant, it is a gentleman who wants the gate opened."

"Ah, Mr. Fairleigh," cried the officer, "I will be down in a minute."

"What! does every one know me?" cried Lucien. "London seems a lantern, and I the candle."

"Excuse me, sir," said the officer, approaching; "but I was asleep."

"Oh, sir, that is what night is made for. Will you be good enough to open the door? Unluckily, I cannot sleep, for the king, whom you doubtless also saw me talking to——"

"Yes, I did sir."

"Of course," growled Lucien. "Well, the king has sent me on a mission to Whitehall. This is the right gate, is it not?"

"Yes, Mr. Fairleigh."

"Will you please to have it opened?"

"Certainly; open the gate quickly for Mr. Fairleigh."

Lucien began to breathe.

The door creaked on its hinges and opened, and Lucien saw liberty through it.

"Farewell, sir," said he, advancing.

"Farewell, Mr. Fairleigh, a pleasant journey; but stay one moment. I have forgotten to ask for your pass," cried he, seizing Lucien by the sleeve to stop him.

"How, my pass?"

"Certainly, Mr. Fairleigh. You know what a pass is? You understand that no one can leave a town like London without a pass, particularly when the king is in it."

"And who must sign this pass?"

"The king himself. So if he sent you he cannot have forgotten to give you the pass."

"Ah! you doubt that the king sent me?" cried Lucien, with flashing eyes, for he saw himself on the point of failing, and had a great mind to kill the officer and sentinel, and rush through the gate.

"I doubt nothing you tell me; but reflect, that if the king gave you this commission——"

"In person, sir."

"All the more reason, then, if he knows you are going out. I shall have to give up your pass to-morrow morning to the governor."

"And who is he?"

"Sir Thomas Gregory, who does not jest with disobedience, Mr. Fairleigh."

Lucien put his hand to his sword; but another look showed him that the outside of the gate was defended by a guard, who would have prevented his passing if he had killed the officer and sentinel.

"Well," said Lucien, with a sigh, "I have lost my game."

And he turned back.

"Shall I give you an escort, Mr. Fairleigh?" said the officer.

"No, thank you."

Lucien retraced his steps; but he was not at the end of his troubles.

He met the chief of the watch, who said,

"What! have you executed your commission already, Mr. Lucien? How quick you are!"

A little further on he encountered the cornet, who cried,

"Well, Mr. Fairleigh, what of the lady? Are you content with London?"

Finally, the soldier in the court-yard said,

"Ah! Mr. Fairleigh, the tailor has not done his work well. You seem more torn than when you went out."

Lucien did not feel inclined to climb back through the window; but, by chance, or rather by charity, the door was opened, and he returned into the palace.

Here he saw the page, who said,

"Dear Mr. Fairleigh, shall I give you the key to all this?"

"Yes, serpent," muttered Lucien.

"Well, the king loves you so well he does not wish to lose you."

"And you knew, and never told me?"

"Oh! Mr. Lucien, impossible! It was a state secret."

"But I paid you, knave."

"Oh! dear Mr. Fairleigh, the secret was worth more than ten pounds."

Lucien returned to his room in a rage, for he saw that without the king's permission there was no possibility of escape.

On the next day a curious event happened.

During his researches in London he had had occasion to penetrate into a convent to watch some suspicious people, and among others he had seen a man dressed in the usual habit of a monk; but whom he recognized as one George Broxfield, a captain in the king's guard, who, under the guise of religion, was in reality organizing a body guard for the king.

On the day after his attempt at escape, this man presented himself before the king, with a letter from Lord Monteagle.

At the same time he dropped upon the floor another one, the superscription of which Lucien Fairleigh took care to observe.

Immediately upon reading the letter, the king said to Lucien,

"You are at liberty to go, Mr. Fairleigh. Return to this Pretender, and tell him that there is no answer to his letter, except these words—'Death to all traitors and their friends!'"

In the ante-chamber Lucien waited.

The captain came out five minutes after him, and went down the steps and across the court proudly, and with a satisfied air, for George Broxfield, be it said, was proud of his person, and he was delighted

too that the king's suspicions had not been raised by the letter he had let fall.

As he passed he heard behind him steps which seemed to be the echo of his own.

He turned and met Lucien.

"Ah, brother Eustacious!" he said, "you are the very man I wished to see. If you have half an hour this evening I will meet you gladly at eight to-night."

"I will come now, if it pleases you."

"I know a quiet little place where we shall be undisturbed; the 'Horn of Plenty' I mean."

"I know it well," said Lucien; "let us adjourn thither at once."

On arriving at the inn they passed into a little private room.

"Now," said Broxfield, "wait here while I avail myself of a privilege granted to the frequenters of this house."

"What is that?"

"To go to the cellar and fetch one's own wine."

"Ah! a jolly privilege. Go, then."

As soon as Broxfield was gone Lucien called the landlord.

"I wish you to understand," he said, slipping some pieces of gold into his hand, "that, whatever noises you hear in this room, you are not to come until I call you."

"Your directions will be easy to obey, since they are exactly the same as your companion has just given me."

"Yes, but if he calls don't come. Send away every one you can from the inn; I will make it worth your while."

We don't know how the worthy landlord managed, but when ten minutes had expired the last customer was seen crossing the threshold of the door, muttering as he did so words indicative of annoyance and disgust.

CHAPTER XIII.

WHAT HAPPENED IN THE LITTLE ROOM.

WHEN the captain re-entered the room with a basket in his hand containing a dozen bottles, he was received by Lucien with smiles.

George Broxfield was in haste to uncork his bottles, but his haste was nothing to Lucien's.

Thus the preparations did not take long, and the two friends began to drink.

At first, as though their occupation was too important to be interrupted, they drank in silence.

Lucien uttered only these words:—

"By my faith, this is good wine!"

They drank two bottles in this way.

At the third Lucien raised his eyes to Heaven and said,

"Really, we are drinking as though we wished to intoxicate ourselves."

"It is so good," said Broxfield.

"Ah! it pleases you. Go on, friend, I have a strong head."

Each of them swallowed another bottle.

The wine produced on each of them an opposite effect; it unloosened Lucien's tongue, and tied that of Broxfield.

"Ah!" murmured Lucien, "you are silent; then you doubt yourself."

"Ah!" said Broxfield to himself, "you chatter; then you are getting tipsy."

He then asked Lucien,

"How many bottles does it take you?"

"For what?"

"To get lively."

"About four."

"And to get tipsy?"

"About six."

"And dead drunk?"

"Double."

"Boaster!" thought Broxfield; "why he stammers already, and has only drank four."

"Come, then," said he, aloud, "we can go on, then," and he drew out a fifth for Lucien and one for himself.

But Lucien remarked that of the five bottles ranged beside Broxfield, some were half full and others two-thirds.

None were empty.

This confirmed him in his suspicions that the captain had bad intentions regarding him.

He rose as if to fetch his fifth bottle, and staggered as he did so.

"Oh!" said he, "did you feel?"

"What?"

"The earth trembling."

"Bah!"

"Yes, by the saints! Luckily the hotel is solid, although built on a pivot."

"Doubtless, since it turns."

"True," said Broxfield, "I felt the effects, but did not guess the cause."

"Because you are not a Latin scholar, and have not read the book which is called 'Concerning the nature of Things.' If you had you would know that there is no effect without a cause."

"Well, my dear captain—for you are a captain, like me, are you not?"

"Yes, from the points of my toes up to the roots of my hair. But tell me why were you disguised as a monk?"

"There were private reasons for it."

"Doubtless. I also was there for private reasons."

"May I ask what they were?"

"I was a spy of the Pretender."

"And did you discover anything?"

"Certainly."

"And what was it?"

"I discovered that Brother Eustacious was not a monk, but a captain."

"Ah! you discovered that?"

"At once."

"Anything else?"

"I discovered that——but give me more drink, or I shall remember nothing."

"Recollect that you are beginning your sixth bottle," said George Broxfield, laughing.

"Did we not come here to drink?"

"Certainly we did."

"Let us drink, then."

"Well," said George, "now do you remember——"

"What?"

"What else you said in the convent?"

"Well, I said that the monks were really soldiers, and, instead of obeying the superior, obeyed you."

"Ah! truly; but doubtless that was not all."

"No; but more to drink, or my memory will fail me."

And as his bottle was empty, he held out his glass for more.

"Well, now, do you remember?"

"Oh, yes, I should think so."

"Well, what else?"

"I saw that there was a plot."

"A plot?" cried Broxfield, turning pale.

"Yes, a plot."

"Against whom?"

"Against the Pretender."

"Of what nature?"

"To try and carry him off."

"When?"

"When he was returning from Whitehall."

"The devil!"

"What did you say?"

"Nothing. And you found out that?"

"Yes."

"And warned the Pretender?"

"Of course; that is what I came for."

"Then you were the cause of the attempt failing?"

"Yes, I."

"Hang him!" murmured Broxfield.

"What did you say?"

"I said that you have good eyes, friend."

"Bah! I have seen more than that; pass me one of your bottles and I will tell you what I have seen."

Broxfield hastened to comply with Lucien's desire.

"Let me hear," said he.

"Firstly, I have seen Lord Monteagle wounded."

"Bah!"

"No wonder; he was on my route. And then I have seen the taking of Durham."

"How, the taking of Durham?"

"Certainly. Ah, Captain, it was a grand thing to see, and a brave man like you would have been delighted."

"I do not doubt it. You were, then, near the Pretender?"

"Side by side, my friend, as we are now."

"And you left him?"

"To announce this news to the king."

"Then you have been at the palace?"

"Yes; just before you."

"Then as we have not quitted each other since, I need not ask you what you have done."

"On the contrary; ask, for that is the most curious of all."

"Tell me, then."

"Oh, it is very easy to say tell."

"Try."

"One more glass of wine, then, to loosen my tongue. Quite full—that will do. Well, I saw, my friend, that when you gave the king Lord Monteagle's letter that you let another fall."

"Another?" cried Broxfield, starting up.

"Yes; it is here."

And having tried two or three times with an unsteady hand, he placed his finger on the coat of his companion, just where the letter was.

Broxfield started as though Lucien's finger had been a red-hot iron, and had touched his skin instead of his coat.

"Ah!" cried he, "there is but one thing wanting."

"And what is that?"

"That you should know to whom the letter is addressed."

"Oh, I know that quite well; it is addressed to Lady Thelford."

"Great heavens! I hope you have not told that to the king?"

"No, but I am going to."

"When?"

"When I have had a nap."

Then he let his arms fall upon the table, and his head upon them.

"Then, as soon as you can walk you will go to the palace again?"

"Yes, I shall."

"You will denounce me?"

"Yes."

"Is not this a joke of yours ?"

"What ?"

"That you will tell the king ?"

"Not at all. You see, my dear friend," said Lucien, half raising his head, "you are a conspirator, and I am a spy ; you have a plot, and I denounce you. We each follow our business."

And Lucien laid his head down again, so that his face was completely hidden by his hands, while the back of his head was protected by his helmet.

"Ah !" cried Broxfield, "you will denounce me when you wake !"

And rising, he made a furious blow with his dagger on the back of his companion, thinking to pierce him through, and nail him to the table.

But he had not reckoned on the shirt of mail which Lucien wore.

The dagger broke upon it like glass, and, perhaps, for the hundredth time, Lucien Fairleigh owed his life to it.

Before Broxfield had time to recover from his astonishment Lucien's right fist struck him a heavy blow in the face, and sent him bleeding and stunned against the wall.

In a minute, however, he was up, and sword in hand ; but this minute had sufficed for Lucien to draw his sword also, and prepare himself.

He seemed to shake off as if by enchantment all the fumes of the wine, and stood with a steady hand to receive his adversary.

The table, like a field of battle covered with empty bottles, lay between them, but the blood flowing down his face infuriated Broxfield, who lunged at his adversary as fiercely as the intervening table permitted.

"Dolt," cried Lucien, "you see that it is decidedly you who are drunk, for you cannot reach me across the table, while my arm is six inches longer than yours, and my sword as much longer than your sword, and here is the proof."

As he spoke he stretched out his arm, and wounded Broxfield in the forehead.

Broxfield uttered a cry still more of rage than of pain, and as he was brave enough attacked with double fury.

Lucien, however, still on the other side of the table, took a chair and sat down, saying,

" By George, how stupid these soldiers are ; they pretend to know how to manage their swords, and yet any tradesman, if he liked, could kill them like flies. Ah ! now you want to put out my eye. And now you mount on the table ; but take care, donkey !"

And he pricked him with his sword in the stomach, as he had already done in the forehead.

Broxfield roared with anger, and leaped from the table to the floor.

"That is as it should be," said Lucien. "Now we are on the same level, and we can talk while we are fencing. Ah ! captain, captain, and so we sometimes try a hand at assassination in our spare moments, do we ?"

"I do for my cause what you do for yours," said Broxfield, now brought back to the seriousness of his position, and terrified in spite of himself at the smothered fire which seemed gleaming in Lucien's eyes.

"So much for talking." said Lucien, "and yet, my friend, it is with no little pleasure I find myself a better hand than you are. Ah ! that was not bad."

Broxfield had just made a lunge at Lucien, which had slightly touched his chest.

"Not bad ; but I know the thrust ; it is the very same you once showed a friend. I was just saying then that I have the advantage of you, for I did not begin this quarrel, however anxiously disposed I might have been to do so. More than that even, I have allowed you to carry out your project by giving you every latitude you required, and yet at this very moment even I have been acting only on the defensive, and this because I have something to propose to you."

"Nothing !" cried Broxfield, exasperated at Lucien's imperturbability. "Nothing !"

And he gave a thrust, which would have run Lucien completely through the body if the latter had not, with his long legs, sprung back a step, which placed him beyond his adversary's reach.

"I am going to tell you what this arrangement is all the same, so that I shall have nothing left to reproach myself for."

"Hold your tongue," said Broxfield ; "hold your tongue, it will be useless."

"Listen," said Lucien, "it is to satisfy my own conscience. I have no wish to shed your blood, you understand, and have no wish to kill you unless driven to extremities."

"Kill me ! Kill me, I say, if you can !" exclaimed Broxfield, exasperated.

"No, no : I have already, once in my life, killed another such a swordsman as you are ; I will even go so far as to say a better swordsman than you. By George, you know him ; he was a lawyer, too."

"Ah ! John Davidson !" cried Broxfield, terrified at the incident, and again placing himself on the defensive.

"Exactly so."

"It was you who killed him ?"

"Oh, yes, with a pretty little thrust, which I will presently show you if you decline the arrangement I propose."

"Well, let me hear what the arrangement is."

"You will pass into the service of the Pretender without quitting that of the king."

"In other words that I should become a spy like yourself ?"

"No, for there will be a difference ; I am not paid, but you will be. You will begin by showing me that letter you have in your pocket ; you will let me take a copy of it, and I will leave you quiet until another occasion. Well, am I not considerate ?"

"Here," said Broxfield, "here is my answer."

Broxfield's reply was a thrust, so rapidly dealt that the point of his sword slightly touched Lucien's shoulder.

"Well, well," said Lucien, "I see I must positively show you John Davidson's thrust ; it is very simple and pretty."

And Lucien, who up to that moment had been acting on the defensive, made one step forward and attacked in his turn.

"This is the thrust," said Lucien, "I make a feint thus."

And he did so.

Broxfield parried by giving way, but after this first step backwards he was obliged to stop as he found that he was close to the partition.

"Good ! precisely so ; you parry in a circle. That's wrong, for my wrist is stronger than yours. I catch your sword in mine, thus ; return to the attack, thus ; I fall upon you, so, and you are hit ; or, rather, you are a dead man !"

In fact the thrust had followed, or had, rather, accompanied the demonstration, and the slender rapier, penetrating Broxfield's chest, had glided like a needle completely through him, penetrating deeply, and with a dull, heavy sound, the wooden partition behind him.

Broxfield flung out his arms, letting his sword fall to the ground.

His eyes became fixed and injected with blood; his mouth opened wide; his lips were stained with a red-coloured foam; his head fell on his shoulder with a sigh which sounded like a death-rattle.

Then his limbs refused their support, and his body, as it sunk forward, enlarged the aperture of the wound, but could not free itself from the partition, supported as it was by Lucien's wrist, so that the miserable wretch, like a gigantic insect, remained fastened to the wall, which his feet kicked convulsively.

Lucien, cold and impassable, as he always was in positions of great difficulty, especially when he had a conviction at the bottom of his heart that he had done everything his conscience could require of him; Lucien, we say, took his hand from the sword, which remained in a horizontal position, unfastened the captain's belt, searched his doublet, took the letter, and read the address—

"Marchioness of Loudan."

All this time the blood was flowing copiously from the wound, and the agony of death was depicted on the features of the wounded man.

"I am dying! I am dying!" he murmured. "Oh, Heaven, have pity on me!"

This last appeal to the divine mercy touched Lucien's feelings, made as it was by a man who had most probably rarely thought of it until this moment of his direst need.

"Let us be charitable," he said, "and since this man must die let him at least die as quietly as possible."

He then advanced towards the partition, and, by an effort, withdrew his sword from the wall, and, supporting Broxfield's body, prevented it from falling heavily to the ground.

This last precaution, however, was useless; the approach of death had been rapid, and had already paralysed the dying man's limbs.

His legs gave way beneath him, he fell into Lucien's arms and then rolled heavily on to the floor.

The shock of his fall made a stream of blood flow from his wound with which the last remains of life ebbed away.

Lucien then went and opened the door of communication and called Joe Ryder the landlord.

He had no occasion to call twice, for the innkeeper had been listening at the door, and had successively heard the noise of tables and stools, the clashing of swords, and the fall of a heavy body.

Besides, the worthy Joe Ryder had, particularly after the confidence which had been reposed in him, too extensive an experience in the character of gentlemen of the sword in general, and that of Lucien in particular, not to have guessed, step by step, what had taken place.

The only thing of which he was ignorant was which of the two adversaries had fallen.

It must, however, be said, in praise of Ryder, that his face assumed an expression of real satisfaction when he heard Lucien's voice, and when he saw that it was he who, safe and sound, opened the door.

Lucien, whom nothing escaped, remarked the expression of his countenance, and was inwardly pleased at it.

Joe Ryder tremblingly entered the small apartment.

"Good Heavens!" he exclaimed, as he saw the captain's body bathed in blood.

"Yes, Joe," said Lucien, "this is what we have come to; our dear captain here is very ill, as you see."

"Oh, my good Mr. Lucien! my good Mr. Lucien!" exclaimed Ryder, ready to faint.

"Well, what?" inquired Lucien.

"It is very unkind of you to have chosen my inn for this execution; such a handsome captain too!"

"Would you sooner have seen Lucien lying there and Broxfield alive?"

"No, oh, no!" cried the host, from the very bottom of his heart.

"Well, that would have happened, however, had it not been for a miracle of providence."

"Really!"

"Upon the word of Lucien, just look at my back, for it pains me a good deal, my dear friend."

And he stooped down before the inn-keeper, so that both his shoulders might be on a level with the host's eye.

Between the two shoulders the coat was pierced through, and a spot of blood as large and round as a silver crown-piece, reddened the edges of the hole.

"Blood!" said Ryder, "blood! then you are wounded."

"Wait, wait."

And Lucien unfastened his coat and shirt.

"Now look," he said.

"Oh, you wore a cuirass! What a fortunate thing, Mr. Lucien, and you were saying that the ruffian wished to assassinate you."

"The devil! it hardly seems likely I should have taken any pleasure in giving myself a dagger-thrust between my shoulders. Now, what do you see?"

"A link broken."

"That dear captain was in good earnest then; is there much blood?"

"Yes, a good deal under the links."

"I must take off the cuirass, then," said Lucien.

Lucien took off his cuirass and bared the upper part of his body.

"Ah! Mr. Fairleigh, you have a wound as large as a plate."

"Yes, I suppose the blood has spread; there is what the doctors call *ecchymosis*. Give me some clean linen, pour into a glass equal parts of good olive oil and wine dregs, and wash that stain for me."

"But, dear Mr. Lucien, what am I to do with the body?"

"That is not your affair."

"What, not my affair?"

"No. Give me a pen, some ink and a sheet of paper."

"Immediately, dear Mr. Lucien," said Joe Ryder, as he darted out of the room.

Meanwhile, Lucien, who probably had no time to lose, heated at the lamp the point of a small dagger, and cut in the middle of the wax the seal of the letter.

This being done, and as there was nothing else to retain the dispatch, Lucien drew it from its envelope, and read it with the liveliest marks of satisfaction.

Just as he had finished reading it, Mr. Joe Ryder returned with the oil, the wine, the paper, and the pen.

Lucien arranged the pen, the paper, and ink, before him and then sat himself down at the table, and turned his back with stoical indifference towards Ryder for him to operate upon.

The latter understood the pantomime and begun to rub it.

However, as if, instead of irritating a painful

wound, some one had been tickling him in the most delightful manner. Lucien, during the operation, copied the letter to the Marchioness of Loudon right through to the end.

"Dear Mr. Fairleigh," Ryder ventured to observe, seeing that Lucien had finished writing, if not thinking, "dear Mr. Fairleigh, you have not told me what I am to do with the corpse."

"That is a very simple affair."

"For you, sir, who are full of imagination, it may be, but for me——"

"Well, suppose, for instance, that unfortunate captain had been quarreling with some street brawlers, and had been brought to your house wounded, would you have refused to receive him?"

"No, certainly, unless, indeed, you had forbidden me to receive him, dear Mr. Lucien."

"Suppose that having been placed in that corner, notwithstanding the care and attention you bestowed on him, he had departed this life while in your charge, it would have been a great misfortune and nothing more, I suppose?"

"Certainly."

"And instead of incurring any blame you would deserve to be commended for your humanity. Suppose again that while he was dying this poor captain had mentioned the name Father Anthony, whom you know well."

"Of Father Anthony?" exclaimed Ryder, in astonishment.

"Yes, of Father Anthony. Very good. You will go and inform Father Anthony of it. He will hasten here with all speed, and, as the dead man's purse is found in one of his pockets——you understand it is important that his purse should be found; I mention this merely by way of advice——and as the dead man's purse is found in one of his pockets, and this letter in the other, no suspicion whatever can be entertained."

"I understand, Mr. Lucien."

"In addition to which you will receive a reward instead of being punished."

"You are a great man, Mr. Lucien; I will run at once to the convent."

"Wait a minute. Did I not say there was the letter and purse?"

"Oh! yes. And you have the letter in your hand."

"Precisely."

"I must not say that it has been read and copied?"

"Certainly not; it is precisely on account of this letter reaching its destination intact that you will receive a recompence."

"The letter contains a secret, then?"

"In such times as the present there are secrets in everything, my worthy Ryder."

And Lucien, with this sententious reply, again fastened the silk under the wax of the seal by making use of the same means as he had done before.

He then fastened the wax so artistically that the most experienced eye would not have been able to detect the slightest crack.

He then replaced the letter in the pocket of the dead man, had the linen which had been steeped in the oil and wine applied to his wound by way of a cataplasm, put on again the safety coat of mail next to his skin, his shirt over his coat of mail, picked up his sword, wiped it, thrust it into his scabbard, and withdrew.

He returned again, however, saying,

"If, after all, the story which I have invented, does not seem satisfactory to you, you can accuse the captain of having thrust his own sword through his body."

"A suicide?"

"Well, that does not compromise any one, my friend. You understand."

"But they won't bury this unlucky fellow in holy ground."

"Pooh!" said Lucien, "will that be giving him much pleasure?"

"Why, yes, I should think so."

"In that case, do as you like, my dear Ryder. Adieu. By the bye I pay since he is no more."

And he laid three guineas down on the table, and then placing his forefinger on his lips in token of silence, he departed.

CHAPTER XIV.

THE LAST HOPE OF THE PRETENDER—THE ATTACK ON TRUEBRIDGE—THE LANDING OF THE FRENCH—THE ADVANCE—HOPES AND FEARS—THE FRENCH FLEET IN THE OFFING—DUC DE LA OMER THE ADMIRAL—THE BATTLE—THE FIRE-SHIPS—THE DEFEAT OF THE FRENCH FLEET—THE LANDING OF THE SAILORS—THE BATTLE CONTINUED—THE BLACK HORSEMAN—THE SINGLE COMBAT—THE TRAITOR—THE RETREAT OF THE REBELS.

WHILE Lucien Fairleigh was endeavouring to aid the cause of the Pretender in London, and worming out the Court intrigues of William of Orange, great events were taking place.

The Pretender had at length induced the French king to aid him.

Marching towards Truebridge, after leaving a strong garrison in Durham, he made a forced journey, and arrived without any one expecting him on the Essex coast.

Here, two days after his arrival, he was joined by a French contingent, who had landed in the dead of night.

The French commander, Monsieur de Croissy, was received by the Pretender with every enthusiasm.

"I should have nothing now to wish for," said James, "if the French fleet were here."

M. de Croissy smiled.

"They *are* here," he said. "The transports which brought us were followed by men of war."

"Good!" said the Pretender, as a bright flash invaded his cheek. "Good! England may yet be ours."

"It will not be my fault, your majesty," said De Croissy, with a bow.

"We will advance at once," said the Pretender. 'Ha! there are lights in the offing. How have you arranged?"

"To advance at once. See, the ships are still in motion."

And so they were little thinking that the English ships in the harbour had been converted into fire-ships, the most deadly instruments of destruction.

So the order was given in the French camp, and the whole rebel force began their march in silence, the French taking the vanguard.

The Pretender was in the centre.

Hardly had they began to move, ere the cannon on the ramparts opened fire.

The artillery surprised the French in their nocturnal march, by which they hoped to surprise the town.

But instead of stopping their advance it only hastened it.

If they could not take the city by surprise they might fill up the moat with fascines, and burst open the gates with petards.

The cannon from the ramparts continued to fire, but in the darkness took scarcely any effect.

After having replied to the cries of their adversaries the French advanced silently towards the ramparts with that fiery intrepidity which they always show in attack.

But all at once doors and posterns opened, and from all sides poured out armed men, if not with the fierce impetuosity of the French, with a firmness which rendered them massive as a rolling wall.

It was the English who advanced in close ranks and compact masses, above which the cannon continued to thunder, although with more noise than effect.

Then the combat began hand to hand, foot to foot, sword to sword, and the flash of pistols lighted up faces red with blood.

But not a cry, not a murmur, not a complaint was heard, and the English and French fought with equal rage.

The English citizens were furious at having to fight, for fighting was neither their profession or their pleasure.

The French were furious at being attacked when they meant to have taken the initiative.

While the combat was raging furiously explosions were heard near, and a light rose over the city like crest of flames.

It was the Duc de St. Omer attacking and lying to force the barrier across the river, and who would soon penetrate into the city, at least, so the French hoped.

But it was not so.

The Duke had weighed anchor, and sailed, and was making rapid progress, favoured by the west wind.

All was ready for action.

The sailors, armed with their boarding cutlasses, were eager for the combat.

The gunners stood ready with lighted matches.

While some picked men, hatchet in hand, stood ready to jump on the hostile ships, and destroy the chains and cords.

The seven ships advanced in silence, disposed in the form of a wedge, of which the admiral's galley formed the point.

St. Omer himself had taken his first lieutenant's place, and was leaning over the bowsprit trying to pierce the fogs of the river, and the darkness of the night.

Soon through this double obscurity he saw the pier extending itself darkly across the stream.

It appeared deserted, but in that land of ambushes there seemed something terrifying in this desertion.

However, they continued to advance, and soon were within sight of the barrier, scarcely ten cable lengths off.

They approached nearer and nearer, and yet not a single challenge struck on their ears.

The sailors only saw in this silence a carelessness which rejoiced them.

But their young admiral, more far-seeing, feared some ruse.

At last the prow of the admiral's ship touched the two ships, which formed the centre of the barrier, and made the whole line, which was fastened together by chains, tremble.

Suddenly, as the bearers of the hatchets received the orders to board and cut the chains, a crowd of grappling irons, thrown by invisible hands, seized hold of the French vessels.

The English had forestalled the intended movement of the French.

The Duc de St. Omer believed that his enemies were offering him a mortal combat, and he accepted it with alacrity.

He also threw grappling irons, and the two lines of ships were bound firmly together.

Then seizing a hatchet he was the first to jump on a ship, crying,

"Board them! board them!"

All his crew followed him, officers and men, uttering the same cry.

But no cry replied to them, no force opposed their advance.

Only they saw three boats full of men gliding silently over the waters like three sea-birds.

The assailants rested motionless on the ships which they had conquered without a struggle.

All at once St. Omer heard, under his feet, a crackling sound, and a smell of sulphur filled the air.

A thought crossed his mind, and he ran and opened a hatchway.

The vessel was burning.

A cry of "To our ships!" sounded through all the line.

Each climbed back again more quickly than he had come in; but St. Omer this time was the last.

Just as he reached his galley the flames burst out over the whole bridge of boats like twenty volcanoes, of which each ship or boat was the crater.

The order was instantly given to cut the ropes and break the chains and grappling irons, and the sailors worked with the rapidity of men who knew that their safety depended on their exertions.

But the work was immense.

Perhaps they might have detached those thrown by the enemy on their ships; but they had also to detach those which they themselves had thrown.

All at once twenty explosions were heard, and each of the French ships trembled to its centre.

It was the cannons that defended the port, and which, fully charged, and then abandoned by the citizens, exploded as the fire gained on them, breaking everything within their reach.

The flames mounted like gigantic serpents along the masts, rolled themselves round the yards, then, with their forked tongues, came to lick the sides of the French vessels.

The duke, with his magnificent armour, covered with gold, giving calmly, and in an imperious voice, his orders in the midst of the flames, looked like a fabulous salamander, covered with scales, and at every moment threw off a shower of sparks.

But the explosions became louder than ever; the gun room had taken fire, and the vessels were flying in pieces.

St. Omer had done his best to free himself, but in vain.

The flames had reached the French ships, and showers of fire fell about him.

The English barriers were broken, and the French burning ships drifted to the shore.

St. Omer saw that he could not save his ships, and he gave orders to lower the boats, and land on the left bank.

This was quickly done, and all the sailors were embarked to a man before the duke quitted his galley.

His *sang froid* kept every one in order, and each man landed with a sword or an axe in his hand.

Before he had reached the shore, the fire reached

the magazine of his ship, which blew up, lighting the whole horizon.

Meanwhile the artillery from the ramparts had ceased, not that the combat had abated, but that it was so close it was impossible to fire on enemies without firing on friends also.

The cavalry had charged, and done wonders.

Before the swords of its cavaliers a pathway opened, but the wounded English pierced their horses with their large cutlasses, and in spite of this brilliant charge, a little confusion showed itself in the French columns, and they only kept their ground instead of advancing, while from the gates of the city new troops continually poured out.

All at once, almost under the walls of the city, a cry of " France ! France !" was heard behind the mass of the English.

This was the duke with his 1,500 sailors armed with hatchets and cutlasses.

They had to revenge their fleet in flames, and two hundred of their companions burned or drowned.

No one could manage his long sword better than St. Omer.

Every blow cut open a head, every thrust took effect.

The group of English on which he fell were destroyed like a field of corn by a legion of locusts.

Delighted with their first success, they continued to push on.

But the cavalry, surrounded by troops, began to lose ground.

Infantry, however, kept their place.

The Pretender had seen the burning of the fleet, and heard the reports of the cannon and the explosion, without suspecting anything but a fierce combat, which must terminate in victory for St. Omer, for how could a few English ships fight against the French fleet ?

He expected, then, every minute a diversion on the part of the duke, when the news was brought to him that the fleet was destroyed and St. Omer and his men fighting in the midst of the English.

He now began to feel very anxious, the fleet being the means of retreat, and consequently the safety of the army.

He sent orders to the cavalry to try a fresh charge, and men and horses, almost exhausted, rallied to attack the English afresh.

The voice of St. Omer was heard in the midst of the mêlée crying,

" Hold firm ! France ! France !"

And like a reaper cutting a field of corn, his sword flew round, and cut down its harvest of men.

He seemed to have put on with his cuirass the strength of a Hercules, and the infantry hearing his voice above all the noise, and seeing his sword flashing, took fresh courage and, like the cavalry, made a new effort, and returned to the combat.

But now the person who had been called the prince, came out of the city on a beautiful black horse.

He wore black armour, and was followed by three hundred well mounted cavaliers, whom the English king had placed at his disposal.

By a parallel gate came out William himself, with a picked body of infantry, who had not yet appeared.

The prince hastened where he was most wanted, that is to say, where St. Omer was fighting with his sailors.

The English recognized him, and opened their ranks, crying joyfully,

" The prince ! the prince !"

St. Omer and his men saw the movement, heard the cries, and all at once found themselves opposed to a new troop.

St. Omer pushed his horse towards the Cavalier, and their swords met.

He was confident in his science, but all his thrusts were skilfully parried, and one of those of his adversary touched him, and drew some drops of blood from his shoulder.

" Ah !" cried the young admiral, " this man is a Frenchman, and what is more, he has studied fencing under the same master as I have."

At these words the unknown turned away, and tried to find a new antagonist.

" If you are French," cried St. Omer, " you are a traitor, for you fight against your king, your country, and your flag."

The unknown replied only by attacking him with redoubled fury ; but now St. Omer was on his guard, and knew with what a skilful swordsman he had to deal.

He parried two or three thrusts with as much skill as fury, and it was now the stranger who made a step back.

" See," cried St. Omer, " what one can do fighting for one's country ! A pure heart and a loyal arm suffice to defend a head without a helmet."

And he threw his helmet far from him, displaying his noble and beautiful head, with eyes sparkling with pride, youth, and anger.

His antagonist forbore to answer, uttered a cry, and struck at his bare head.

" Ah !" cried St. Omer, parrying the blow, " I said you were a traitor, and as a traitor you shall die. I will kill you, and carry off this helmet which hides and defends you, and hang you to the first tree that I see."

But at this moment a cavalier cried,

" Your highness, no more skirmishing ; your presence is wanted over there."

Glancing towards the point indicated, the unknown saw the English giving way before the cavalry.

" Yes," cried he ; " those are the men I wanted."

At this moment so many cavaliers pressed on the sailors that they made their first step in retreat.

The black Cavalier profited by this movement to disappear in the mêlée.

MOONLIGHT JACK
OR THE KING OF THE ROAD

LUCIEN'S INTERVIEW WITH GRACE IN THE PRETENDER'S CAMP.—*See page* 191.

A quarter of an hour after the French began to give way.

They tried to retreat in good order, but a last troop of two thousand infantry, and five hundred horse, came out fresh from the city, and fell on the harassed and already retreating army.

It was the old band of the Prince of Orange.

In spite of the coolness of the chiefs, and the bravery of many, a frightful rout commenced.

At this moment the unknown fell again on the fugtives, and once more met St. Omer with his now diminished band.

The young admiral was mounted on his third horse, two having been killed under him.

His sword was broken, and he had taken from a sailor one of their heavy hatchets, which he whirled round his head with the greatest apparent ease. From time to time he turned and faced his enemy, like the wild boar who cannot make up his mind to fly, and turns desperately on the hunter.

No. 24.—June 16, 1866.

Two Numbers and Two Tales every week for One Penny.
THE WORK GIRLS OF LONDON, and THE CRUSADER; OR,
THE WITCH OF FINCHLEY.

Price One Penny.

The English were active in the pursuit, and gave no rest to the enemy.

Something like remorse seized the unknown at the sight of this disaster.

"Enough, gentlemen," cried he in French. "Ask no more of the God of battles."

"Ah! he is French," cried St. Omer. "I guessed it, traitor. Ah! be cursed, and may you die the death of a traitor!"

This furious imprecation seemed to disconcert the unknown more than a thousand swords raised against him.

He turned, and, conqueror as he was, fled as rapidly as the conquered.

But the retreat of a single man changed nothing in the state of affairs.

Fear is contagious; it seized the whole army, and the soldiers began to fly like madmen.

The horses went fast, in spite of fatigue, for they also felt the influence of fear.

The men dispersed to seek a shelter, and in some hours the army, as an army, existed no longer.

CHAPTER XV.

LUCIEN FAIRLEIGH ON HIS JOURNEY FROM LON-
DON—HIS RECOGNITION OF GRACE DASHWOOD
—THE MEETING—THE FEARFUL NEWS—LOVE'S
LIMIT — THE VOW OF VENGEANCE — THE
LOVER'S ENTREATY—THE FLIGHT—THE SECOND
MEETING—THE PURSUIT—THE STRANGE MAN-
SERVANT—THE CALM BEFORE THE STORM—
THE SOUND OF FAR-OFF BATTLE—THE STILL-
NESS OF DEATH—THE WATER! THE WATER!

ON reaching the neighbourhood of Huntley Castle, where it will be remembered Grace Dashwood lived, Lucien Fairleigh at once proceeded to the house of old Clement Cormorant, determined at any risk to see his betrothed.

He went in disguise, but he found that it was needless.

Cuthbert, the man servant, came to meet him at the door.

His face wore a sombre expression, and he was dressed in black.

"What is the matter?" exclaimed Lucien, in fear.

"Have you not heard, then?"

"No, no; tell me."

"Mr. Cormorant is dead; he has been murdered by the Pretender's orders."

Lucien started back.

"Murdered?"

"Yes, murdered, and you must understand that Miss Dashwood cannot see you."

"Cannot see me? Does she, then, suspect me of complicity?"

"No, no. She loved you well, Mr. Fairleigh, and, as far as she can, loves you still, but her love can take no form in this world. She has vowed vengeance against the Pretender, and when she has effected this vengeance she will retire for ever into a convent."

"This is madness!" cried Lucien. "I must and will see her."

The door, however, was closed in his face.

In vain he knocked.

In vain he wandered to and fro.

Once he caught sight of Grace at a window, and made signs to her.

He was only replied to by a sad shake of the head.

"What folly, what madness is this?" he thought. "Can it be possible that she will sacrifice herself for him? There must be more in this than I am told."

On the second day he was told by a woman servant that Cuthbert and his mistress had departed by a back way and taken the road towards True-bridge.

Lucien at once followed; for some distance it was in vain, but at length he saw before him two travellers, both in male dress, the rounded form of one of whom, however, proclaimed the female sex.

"It must be she," he cried, and, spurring across the country, he dismounted, and lay in wait in a clover field until they passed by him.

When they did so, Lucien recognised her and nearly fainted.

The travellers passed on, and then anger took in Lucien's mind the place of the goodness and patience he had exercised while he believed Cuthbert and the lady sincere towards him.

But after the protestations of Cuthbert this journey seemed to have a species of treason.

When he had recovered a little from the blow, he rose, shook back his long, glossy ringlets, and mounted his horse, determined no longer to take those precautions that respect had made him hitherto observe, and he began to follow the travellers openly and with his face uncovered.

No more cloak nor hood, no more stops and hesitation; the road belonged to him as to them, and he rode on, regulating the pace of his horse by that of theirs.

He did not mean to speak to them, but only to let them see him.

Cuthbert soon perceived him, and seeing him thus openly advance without any further attempt at concealment, grew troubled.

Grace noticed it, and turned also.

"Is it not that young man following us?"

Cuthbert, still trying to re-assure her, said,

"I do not think so, madam. As far as I can judge by the dress, it is some young soldier going probably to Truebridge, and passing by the theatre of war to seek adventures."

"I feel uneasy about him, Cuthbert."

"Re-assure yourself, madam; had he been really Lucien Fairleigh he would have spoken to us, you know how persevering he was."

"I know also that he was respectful, Cuthbert, or I should never have troubled myself about him, but simply told you to get rid of him."

"Well, madam, if he be so respectful you would have no more to fear from him on this road than on the other."

"Nevertheless, Cuthbert, let us change our horses here in order to get on faster."

"On the contrary, madam; I should say do not let us enter the town of Truebridge at all. Our horses are good; let us push on to the little village which is to the right; in that manner we shall avoid the town, with its questioners and its curious gazers."

"Go on, then, Cuthbert."

They turned to the left, taking a road hardly made, but which visibly led to the village.

Lucien also quitted the road, and turned down the lane, still keeping his distance from them.

Cuthbert's disquietude showed itself in his constantly turning to look behind him.

At last they arrived.

Of two hundred houses which this village contained not one was inhabited.

Some forgotten dogs and cats ran wildly about the solitude, the former calling for their masters by long howls.

Cuthbert knocked at twenty doors, but found no one.

Lucien, on his side, who seemed the shadow of the travellers, knocked at the first house as uselessly as they had done ; then, divining that the war was the cause of this desertion, waited to continue his journey until the travellers should have decided what to do.

They fed their horses with some corn which they found at an inn, and then Cuthbert said,

" Madam, we are no longer in a friendly country, nor in an ordinary situation ; we must not expose ourselves uselessly. We shall certainly fall in with some French band, for in the present state of England adventures of all kinds must be rife. If you were a man, I should speak differently, but you are a young and beautiful woman, and would run a double risk for life and honour."

" My life is nothing," said she.

" On the contrary, madam, it is everything. You live for a purpose."

" Well, then, what do you propose? Think and act for me, Cuthbert."

" Then, madam, let us remain here ; I see many houses which would afford us a sure shelter. I have arms, and we will defend or hide ourselves as occasion shall require."

" No, Cuthbert, no, I must go on ; nothing must stop me, and if I had fears they would be for you."

" We will go on, then."

They rode on, therefore, without another word, and Lucien Fairleigh followed.

As the travellers advanced the country took an equally strange aspect, for it was utterly deserted, as well as the towns and villages.

Nowhere were the calves to be seen grazing in the meadows, nor the goats perched on the top of the mountains, or nibbling the green shoots of the briar or young vine.

Nowhere the shepherd with his flock.

Nowhere the cart with its driver.

No foreign merchant passing from one country to another with his pack on his back.

No ploughman singing his harsh song or cracking his long whip.

As far as the eye could see over the magnificent plains, the little hills, and the woods, not a human figure was to be seen, not a voice to be heard.

It seemed like the earth before the creation of animals or men.

The only people who animated this dreary solitude were Cuthbert and his companion, and Lucien, following behind and preserving ever the same distance.

The night came on dark and cold, and the northeast wind whistled in the air and filled the solitude with menacing sounds.

Cuthbert stopped his companion, and, putting his hand on the bridle of her horse, said,

" Madam, you know how inaccessible I am to fear ; you know I would not turn my back to save my life, but this evening some strange feeling possesses me, and forbids me to go further. Madam, call it terror, timidity, panic, what you will, I confess that, for the first time in my life, I am afraid !"

The lady turned.

" Is he still there?" she asked.

" Oh ! I was not thinking of him. Think no more of him, I beg of you, madam ; we need not fear a single man. No, the danger I fear, or rather feel or divine with a sort of instinct, is unknown to me, and, therefore, I dread it. Look, madam, do you see those willows bending in the wind?"

" Yes."

" By their side I see a little house. I beg of you, let us go there ; if it is inhabited, we will ask for hospitality, and if not we will take possession of it. I beg you to consent, madam."

Cuthbert's emotion and troubled voice decided Grace to yield, so she turned her horse in the direction indicated by him.

Some moments after they knocked at the door.

A stream, bordered with reeds and grassy banks, bathed the feet of the willows with its murmuring waters.

Behind the house, which was built with bricks and covered with tiles, was a little garden encircled with a quickset hedge.

All was empty, solitary, and deserted, and no one replied to the blows struck by the travellers.

Cuthbert did not hesitate.

He drew his knife, cut a branch of willow, with which he pushed back the bolt, and opened the door.

The lock, the clumsy work of a neighbouring blacksmith, yielded almost without resistance.

Cuthbert entered quickly, followed by Grace, then closing the door again, he drew a massive bolt, and, thus intrenched, seemed to breathe more freely.

Feeling about he found a bed, a chair, and a table in an upper room.

Here he installed his mistress, and then returning to the lower room, he placed himself at the window to watch the movements of Lucien.

His reflections were as sombre as those of Cuthbert.

" Certainly," said he to himself, "some danger, unknown to us, but of which the inhabitants are not ignorant, is about to fall on the country. War ravages the land ; perhaps the French have taken, or are about to assault the place, and the peasants, seized with terror, have gone to take refuge in the towns."

But this reasoning, however plausible, did not quite satisfy him.

Then he thought,

" But what are Cuthbert and his mistress doing here? What imperious necessity drags them towards this danger? Oh! I will know ; the time has come to speak to this woman, and to clear away all my doubts. Never shall I find a better opportunity."

He approached the house and then suddenly stopped, with a hesitation common to hearts in love.

" No," said he, " I will remain a martyr to the end. Besides, is she not mistress of her own actions? And, perhaps, she does not even know what fable was invented by Cuthbert. Oh! it is he alone whom I hate—he who assured me that she loved no one. But still let me be just. Ought this man, for me whom he did not know, to have betrayed his mistress's secrets? No, no ; all that remains for me now is to follow this woman to the camp, to see her hang her arms round some one's neck, and hear her say, ' See what I have suffered, and how I love you.' Well, I will follow her there, see what I dread to see, and die of it ; it will be trouble saved for the musket or cannon. Alas! I did not seek this. I went calmly to meet a glorious death, and wished to die with her name on my lips. It is not so to be ; I am destined to a death full of bitterness and torture. Well, I accept it !"

Then, recalling his days of waiting and his nights of anguish before the inexorable house, he came to the conclusion that he was less to be pitied now than before.

"I will stay here," continued he and take these trees for a shelter, and then I can hear her voice when she speaks, and see her shadow on the window."

He lay down, then, under the willows, listening, with a melancholy impossible to describe, to the murmur of water that flowed at his side.

All at once he started ; the noise of cannon was brought distinctly to him by the wind.

"Ah !" said he, "I shall arrive too latè ; they are attacking."

His first idea was to rise, mount his horse, and ride on as quickly as possible.

But to do this he must quit the lady and die in doubt ; so he remained.

During two hours he lay there listening to the reports.

He did not guess that what he heard was the blowing up of the ships.

At last about two o'clock all became quiet.

"Now," thought Lucien, "the town is taken, and the Pretender is conqueror. I shall not want an occasion for a glorious death ; but, before I die, I must know what this woman wants in the camp."

He lay still, and had just fallen asleep, when his horse, which was grazing quietly near him, pricked up his ears and neighed loudly.

Lucien opened his eyes.

The animal had his head turned to the breeze, which had changed to the south-east, as if listening.

"What is it, my good horse?" said the young man ; "have you seen some animal which has frightened you, or do you regret the shelter of your stable ?"

The animal stood still, with his eyes fixed and his nostrils distended, and listening.

"Ah !" said Lucien, "it is more serious ; perhaps some troops of wolves following the army to devour the corpses."

The horse neighed and began to run forward to the west, but his master caught the bridle and jumped on his back, and was then able to keep him quiet.

But, after a moment, Lucien himself began to hear an unaccountable noise.

A long murmur, like the wind, but more solemn, which seemed to come from different points of the compass from south to north.

"What is it?" said Lucien ; "can it be wind? No, it is the wind which brings this sound, and I hear the two distinctly. An army in march, perhaps ? But, no, I should hear the sound of voices, and regular marching. Is it the crackling of a fire? No, there is no light in the horizon ; the heaven seems even to grow darker."

The noise redoubled and became distinct.

It was an incessant growling and rolling, as if thousands of cannon were being dragged over a paved road.

Lucien thought of this.

"But, no," said he, "there is no paved road near."

The noise continued to increase, and Lucien put his horse to the gallop, and gained an eminence.

"What do I see ?" cried he, as he attained the summit.

What he saw his horse had seen before him, for he had only been able to make him advance by furious spurring, and, when they arrived at the top of the hill, he reared so as nearly to fall backwards.

They saw in the horizon an infinite body rolling over the plain, and visibly and rapidly approaching.

The young man looked in wonder at the strange phenomenon, when, looking back to the place he had come from, he saw the plain beginning to be covered with water, and that the little river had overflowed, and was beginning to cover the reeds which, a quarter of an hour before, had stood up stiffly on its banks.

"Fool that I am," cried he, "I never thought of it before. The water ! the water !"

He flew to the house and knocked furiously at the door.

"Open ! open !" cried he.

No one replied.

"Open !" shouted he, furious with terror ; "it is I, Lucien Faïrleigh."

"Oh, you need not name yourself, Mr. Fairleigh," answered Cuthbert, from within, "I recognized you long ago ; but I warn you that if you break in the door you will find me behind it with a pistol in each hand."

"But you do not understand !" cried Lucien ; "the water ! it is the water !"

"No fables, no pretexts, or dishonourable ruses, Mr. Fairleigh ; I tell you that you will only enter over my body."

"Then I will pass over it but I will enter ! In Heaven's name, in the name of your own safety and your mistress's, will you open ?"

"No !"

Lucien looked round him and perceived an immense stone.

He raised it, and threw it against the door, which flew open.

A ball passed over Lucien's head, but without touching him ; he jumped towards Cuthbert, and seizing his other arm, cried,

"Do you not see that I have no arms? Do not defend yourself against a man who does not attack. Look ! only look !" and he drew him to the window.

"Well," said he, "do you see now ?"

And he pointed to the horizon.

"The water !" cried Cuthbert.

"Yes, it invades us ; see at our feet, the river overflows, and in five minutes we shall be surrounded.

"Madam ! madam !" cried Cuthbert.

"Do not frighten her, Cuthbert ; get ready the horses at once."

Cuthbert ran to the stable, and Lucien flew up the staircase.

At Cuthbert's cry Grace had opened the door.

Lucien seized her in his arms, and carried her away as if she had been a child.

But she, believing in treason or violence, struggled, and clung to the staircase with all her might.

"Tell her that I am saving her, Cuthbert !" cried Lucien.

Cuthbert heard the appeal, and cried,

"Yes, yes, madam, he is saving you, or rather he will save you. Come, for Heaven's sake !"

Lucien, without losing time in reasoning with Grace, carried her out of the house, and wished to place her before him on his horse ; but she, with a movement of invincible repugnance, glided from his arms, and was received by Cuthbert, who placed her on her own horse.

"Ah !" cried Lucien, "how little you understand my heart. It was not, believe me, for the pleasure of holding you in my arms, or pressing you to my heart—although for that favour I would sacrifice my life—but that we ought to fly as quickly as the birds ; and look at them how they fly !"

Indeed, in the scarcely dawning light were seen large numbers of curlews and pigeons traversing the air with a quick and frightened plight, which in the night usually abandoned to the silent bat looked strange to the eye, and sounded sinister to the ear.

Grace did not reply, but rode on without turning her head.

Her horse, however, as well as that of Cuthbert's, was fatigued with their long journey, and Lucien, as he turned back each moment, saw that they could not keep up with him.

"See, Grace," said he, "how my horse outstrips yours, and yet I am holding him in with all my strength. For Heaven's sake, while there is yet time, if you will not ride with me, take my horse and leave me yours."

"No, thank you," replied she, in her usual calm voice.

"But," cried Lucien, in despair, "the water gains on us ; do you hear ? do you hear ?"

Indeed, a horrible crashing was now heard ; it was the dyke of a neigbouring village giving way to swell the inundation.

Boards and props had given way, a double row of stairs broke with a noise like thunder, and the water rushing over the ruins began to invade an oak wood, of which they saw the tops trembling, and heard the branches cracking as though a flight of demons were passing under the leaves.

The uprooted trees knocking against the stakes, the wood of ruined houses floating on the waters, the distant neighings and cries of horses, and men carried away by the inundation, formed a concert of sounds so strange and gloomy that the terror which agitated Lucien began to seize also upon Grace.

She spurred her horse, and he, as if he understood the danger, redoubled his efforts.

But the water gained on them, and it was evident that before ten minutes it would reach them.

Every instant Lucien turned, and cried,

"Quicker ! for pity's sake ! The water comes ! here it is !"

It came, indeed, foaming and turbulent, carrying away like a feather the house in which they had taken shelter.

Majestic, immense, rolling like a serpent, it arrived like a wall behind the horses of Cuthbert and Grace.

Lucien uttered a cry of terror, and turned on the water as if he would have fought it.

"You see you are lost !" screamed he. "Come, perhaps there is still time ; come with me."

"No, no," said she.

"In a minute it will be too late ; look !" cried he.

"Let my fate be accomplished," said she ; "you fly !"

Cuthbert's horse fell exhausted, and could not rise again, despite the efforts of his rider.

"Save her in spite of herself !" cried Cuthbert.

And at the same moment, as he disengaged himself from the stirrups, the water passed over the head of the faithful servant.

His mistress at this sight uttered a terrible cry, and tried to jump off her horse to perish with him.

But Lucien, seeing her intention, seized her round the waist, and, placing her before him, set off like an arrow.

"Cuthbert ! Cuthbert !" cried she, extending her arms.

A cry was the only answer.

Cuthbert had come up to the surface, and, with the indomitable hope which accompanies the dying man to the last, was swimming, sustained by a beam.

By his side came his horse, beating the water desperately with his feet, while the water gained on Grace's horse, and some twenty feet in front Lucien and Grace flew on the third horse, which was half mad with terror.

Cuthbert scarely regreted life since he hoped that his beloved mistress was saved.

"Adieu, madam !" cried he ; "I go to those who wait for us to tell them that you live for——"

He could not finish, a mountain of water rolled over his head.

"Cuthbert ! Cuthbert !" cried the lady, "I wish to die with you. I will, Mr. Fairleigh, I will go to him ; in the name of God, I will !"

She pronounced these words with so much energy and angry authority that the young man unfolded his arms, and let her slip to the ground, saying,

"Well, Grace, we will all three die here together ; it is a joy I had not hoped for."

As he said these words he stopped his horse, and the water reached him almost immediately.

By a last effort of love the young man kept hold of Grace's arm as she stood on the ground.

The flood rolled over them.

It was a sublime spectacle to see the sang froid of the young man, whose entire bust was raised above the water, while he sustained Grace with one arm, and with the other guided the last efforts of his expiring horse.

There was a moment of terrible struggle, during which the lady, upheld by Lucien, kept her head above water, while, with his left hand, he kept off the floating wood, and the corpses which would have struck against them.

One of the bodies floating past, sighed out "Farewell, madam !"

"Heavens !" cried Lucien, "it is Cuthbert !"

And without calculating the danger of the additional weight he seized him by his sleeve drew him up, and enabled him to breathe freely.

But the exhausted horse now sank in the water to its neck, then to its eyes, and finally disappeared altogether.

"We must die !" murmured Lucien. "Grace, my life and soul belonged to you."

As he spoke he felt Cuthbert slip from him, and he no longer tried to retain him, it was useless.

His only care was to sustain Grace above the water, that she, at least, might die the last, and that he might be able to say to himself, in his last moments, that he had done his utmost to save her.

All at once a joyful cry sounded at his side, and turning he saw Cuthbert, who had found a boat, which had belonged to the little house where they had taken shelter, and which the water had carried away.

Cuthbert, who had regained his strength, thanks to Lucien's assistance, had seized it as it floated past.

The oars were tied to it, and an iron hook lay at the bottom.

He held out the hook to Lucien, who seized it, and, drawing Grace with him, raised her over his shoulders, and passed her to Cuthbert, and then climbed in himself.

The first rays of the rising sun showed them the plains inundated, and the boat swimming like an atom on that ocean covered with wrecks.

Towards the left rose a little hill, completely surrounded by water, looking like an island in the midst of the sea.

Lucien took the oars and rowed towards it, while Cuthbert with the boat-hook occupied himself in keeping off the beams and wrecks which might have struck against them.

Thanks to Lucien's strength, and Cuthbert's

skill, they reached, or rather were thrown, against the hill.

Cuthbert jumped out, and, seizing the chain, drew the boat towards them.

Grace, rising alone, followed him, and then Lucien, who drew up the boat, and seated himself a little way from them.

They were saved from the most menacing danger, for the inundation, however strong, could never reach the summit of the hill.

Below them they could see that great angry waste of waters, which seemed inferior in power only to God himself, and by the increasing light they perceived that it was covered with the corpses of the French soldiers—the allies of the Pretender.

Cuthbert had a wound in his shoulder, where a floating beam had struck against him.

But Grace, thanks to Lucien's protection, was free from all injury, although she was cold and wet.

At last they noticed in the horizon on the eastern side something like fires burning on a height which the water could not reach.

As well as they could judge they were about a mile off.

Cuthbert advanced to the point of the hill, and said that he believed he saw a jetty advancing in a direct line towards the fires.

But they could see nothing clearly, and knew not well where they were; for though day was dawning, it came cloudily and full of fog.

Had it been clear, and under a pure sky, they might have seen the town of Hadleigh, from which they were not more than two miles distant.

"Well, Mr. Fairleigh," said Cuthbert, "what do you think of those fires?"

"Those fires, which seem to you to announce a hospitable shelter, appear to me to be full of danger."

"And why so?"

"Cuthbert," said Lucien, lowering his voice, "look at these corpses—they are all French, there is not one Royal soldier; they announce to us a great disaster. The flood-gates have been broken to finish the destruction of the French army, if it has been conquered; to nullify the victory, if they have been victors. Those fires are as likely to have been lighted by enemies as by friends, and may be simply a ruse on the part of the English troops to draw fugitives to destruction."

"Nevertheless, we cannot stay here; my mistress will die of cold and hunger."

"You are right, Cuthbert. Remain here with her, and I will go to the jetty and return to you with the news."

"No, indeed, Mr. Fairleigh," said Grace, "you shall not expose yourself alone. We have been saved together, we will live or die together. Cuthbert, your arm; I am ready."

Each word which she pronounced had so irresistible an air of authority that no one thought of disputing it.

Lucien bowed and walked first.

It was more calm, the jetty forming with the hill a kind of bag where the water slept.

All three got into the little boat, which was once more launched among the wrecks and floating bodies.

A quarter of an hour after they touched the jetty.

They tied the chain of the boat to a tree, landed once more, walked along the jetty for nearly an hour, and then arrived at a number of little cottages, among which, in a place planted with lime trees, were two or three hundred soldiers, sitting round a fire, above whom floated the French flag.

Suddenly a sentinel, placed about one hundred feet from the bivouac, cried,

"Qui vive!"

"France," replied Lucien.

Then, turning to Grace, he said,

"Now then, Grace, you are saved. I recognise the standard of my friend."

At the cry of the sentinel, and the answer of Lucien, several soldiers ran to meet the newcomers, doubly welcome, in the midst of this terrible disaster, as survivors and compatriots.

Lucien was soon recognised.

He was eagerly questioned, and recounted the miraculous manner in which he and his companions had escaped death.

Cuthbert and Grace had sat down silently in a corner; but Lucien fetched them, and made them come to the fire, for both were still dripping with water.

"Grace," said he, "you will be respected here as in your own house. I have taken the liberty of calling you one of my relations."

And without waiting for the thanks of those whose lives he had saved, he went away to rejoin the officers.

The soldiers of whom our fugitives were claiming hospitality had retired in good order after the defeat, and the "sauve qui peut"* of the chiefs.

Wherever there is similarity of position and sentiment, and the habit of living together, it is common to find unanimity in execution as well as in thought.

It had been so that night with the soldiers.

For, seeing their officers abandon them, they agreed together to draw their ranks closer instead of breaking them.

They, therefore, put their horses to the gallop, and, under the conduct of one of the ensigns, whom they loved for his bravery and respected for his birth, they took the road towards London.

Like all the actors in this terrible scene, they saw the progress of the inundation, and were pursued by the furious waters.

But by good luck found in this spot a position strong both against men and water.

The inhabitants, knowing themselves in safety, had not quitted their homes, and had only sent off their women, children, and old men to Chelmsford.

Therefore the soldiers met with resistance when they arrived, but death howled behind them, and they attacked like desperate men, triumphed over all obstacles, lost ten men, but established the others, and turned out the English.

Such was the recital which Lucien received from them.

"And the rest of the army?" asked he.

"Look!" replied the ensign, "the corpses which pass each moment answer your question."

"But Moonlight Jack?" said Lucien, in a choking voice.

"Alas! Mr. Fairleigh, we do not know. He fought like a lion, but he survived the battle; as to the inundation, I cannot say."

Lucien shook his head sadly; then, after a minute's pause, he said,

"And the Pretender?"

"He fled one of the first. He was mounted on a white horse, with no spot but a black star on the forehead. Well, just now we saw the horse pass among a mass of wrecks; the foot of the rider was

_____
* Save himself who can.

caught in the stirrup, and was floating on the water.

"Great God !"

"Good heavens !" echoed Cuthbert, who had drawn near and heard the tale.

"One of my men ventured down into the water, and siezed the reins of the floating horse, and drew it up sufficiently to enable us to see the white boot and gold spur that the Pretender wore, but the waters were rushing past and the man was forced to let go to save himself, and we saw no more. We shall, therefore, not even have the satisfaction of giving our prince Christian burial."

"Dead ! he also ? What a misfortune !"

Cuthbert turned to his mistress, and, with an expression impossible to describe, said,

"He is dead, madam, you see."

"I praise the Lord who has spared us a crime," she said, raising her eyes to Heaven.

"Yes, but it prevents our vengeance."

"Vengeance only belongs to man when God forgets."

"But you yourself, Mr. Fairleigh," said the ensign to Lucien, "what are you about to do ?"

Lucien started.

"I ?" said he.

"Yes."

"I will wait here till Jack Tyrrell's body passes," replied he, gloomily, "then I will try to draw him to land. You may be sure that if I once hold him I will not let him go."

Cuthbert looked pityingly at the young man, but Grace heard nothing.

She was praying.

After her prayer Grace rose up so beautiful and radiant that Lucien uttered a cry of surprise and admiration.

She appeared to be waking out of a long sleep, of which the dreams had fatigued her and weighed upon her mind ; or rather she was like the daughter of Jairus called from death, and rising from her funeral couch already purified and ready for heaven.

Awakening from her lethargy she cast around her a glance so sweet and gentle that Lucien began to believe he should see her feel for his pain, and yield to a sentiment of gratitude and pity.

While the soldiers, after their frugal repast, slept among the ruins, while Cuthbert himself himself yielded to it, Lucien came and sat down close to Grace, and, in a voice so low and sweet that it seemed a murmur of the breeze, said,

"Grace, you live ! Oh ! let me tell you all the joy which overflows my heart when I see you here in safety, after having seen you on the threshold of the tomb."

"It is true, Mr. Fairleigh," replied she. "I live through you, and I wish I could say I was grateful."

"But, Grace," cried Lucien, with an immense effort, "if it is only that you are restored to those you love ?"

"What do you mean ?"

"To those you were going to rejoin through so many perils."

"Mr. Fairleigh, those I loved are dead ; those I am going to rejoin are so also."

"Oh, Grace !" cried Lucien, falling on his knees, "throw your eyes on me – on me who have suffered so much and love so much. Oh, do not turn away ; you are young and beautiful as the angels in heaven ; read my heart, which I open to you, and you will see that it does not contain one atom of the love that most men feel. You do not believe me. Examine the past hours ; which of them has given me joys

or even hope ? Yet I have persevered. You made me weep ; I devoured my tears. You made me suffer ; I hid my sufferings. You drove me to seek death ; and I went to meet it without a complaint. Even at this moment when you turn away your head —when each of my words, burning as they are, seems a drop of iced water falling upon your heart, my soul is full of you, and I live only because you live. Just now was I not ready to die with you ? What have I asked for ? Nothing. Have I touched your hand ? Never, but to draw you from a mortal peril. I held you in my arms to draw you from the waves, nothing more. All in me has been purified by the devouring fire of my love."

"Oh, Mr. Fairleigh ! for pity's sake do not speak thus to me."

"Oh, in pity do not condemn me. You told me you loved no one. Oh, repeat to me this assurance ; it is a singular favour for a man in love to ask to be told that he is not loved, but I prefer to know that you are insensible to all. Oh, Grace, you, who are the adoration of my life, reply to me."

In spite of Lucien's prayers, a sigh was the only answer.

"You say nothing," continued Lucien. "Cuthbert, at least, had more pity for me, for he tried to console me. Oh, I see you will not reply, because you do not wish to tell me that you came hither to rejoin some one happier than I ; and yet I am young and am ready to die at your feet."

"Mr. Fairleigh," replied Grace, with majestic solemnity, "do not say to me things fit only to be said to a woman. I belong to another world, and do not live for this. Had I seen you less noble— less good—less generous—had I not for you in the bottom of my heart the tender feeling of a sister for a brother, I should say, 'Do not assail with protestations of love ears which only listen to them with horror.' But I do not say so because I suffer in seeing you suffer ; I say more. Now that I know you I will take your hand, and place it on my heart, and I will say to you, willingly, 'See, my heart beats no more.' Live near me if you like, and assist day by day, if such be your pleasure, at this painful execution of a body which is being killed by the tortures of the soul ; but this sacrifice which you may accept as happiness——"

"Oh, yes," cried Lucien, eagerly.

"Well, this sacrifice I ought to forbid. This very day a change has taken place in my life. I have no longer the right to lean on any human arm, not even on the arm of that generous friend—that noble creature who lies there, and, for a time, finds the happiness of forgetfulness. Alas ! poor Cuthbert," continued she, with the first change of tone that Lucien remarked in her voice : "your waking will also be sad. You do not know the progress of my thoughts—you cannot read in my eyes that you will soon be alone, and that alone I must go to God !"

"What do you mean, madam ? Do you also wish to die ?"

Cuthbert, awakened by the cry of the young man, began to listen.

"You saw me pray, did you not ?" said Grace.

"Yes," answered Lucien.

"This prayer was my adieu to earth. The joy that you remarked on my face—the joy that fills me even now is the same you would see in me if the Angel of Death were to come and say to me, 'Rise, Grace, and follow me.'"

"Oh, Grace, do not tell me you are going to die."

"I do not say that," replied she, in her grave voice ; "I say that I am about to quit this world of tears—of hatreds—of bad passions—of vile interests and desires. I say that I have nothing left to do among creatures whom God created my fellow mortals. I have no more tears—no more blood in my heart—no more thoughts; they are dead. I am a worthless offering, for, in renouncing the world, I sacrifice nothing, neither desires nor hopes; but such as I am I offer myself to my God and He will accept me—He who has made me suffer so much, and yet has kept me from sinking under it."

Cuthbert, who had heard this, rose slowly, and said,

"You abandon me?"

"For God," said Grace, raising her thin, white hands to heaven.

"It is true," said Cuthbert, sadly, and seizing her hand he pressed it to his breast.

"Oh, what am I by these two hearts?" sighed Lucien.

"You are," replied Grace, "the only human creature, except Cuthbert, on whom I have looked twice since the death of those who were dear to me."

Lucien knelt.

"Thanks, Grace," he said, "you belong to God; I cannot be jealous."

As he rose they heard the sound of trumpets on the plain from which the water was rapidly disappearing.

The soldiers seized their arms, and were on horseback at once.

Lucien listened.

"Gentlemen," cried he, "those are the French trumpets, I know them. May they announce Moonlight Jack."

"You see that you still wish something, still love something; why, then, should you choose despair like those who desire nothing, like those who love no one?"

"A horse!" cried Lucien, "who will lend me a horse?"

"But the water is still all round us," said the ensign.

"But you see that the plain is practicable; they must be advancing, since we hear their trumpets."

"Mount to the top of the bank, Mr. Fairleigh; the sky is clear, perhaps you will see."

Lucien climbed up; the trumpets continued to sound at intervals, but were seemingly stationary.

A quarter of an hour afterwards Lucien returned.

He had seen a considerable detachment of French troops entrenched on a hill at some distance.

Excepting a large ditch, which surrounded the place occupied by Lucien's companions, the water had begun to disappear from the plain, the natural slope of the ground in the immediate neighbourhood making the waters run towards the sea, and several points of earth, higher than the rest, began to re-appear.

The slimy mud brought by the rolling waters had covered the whole country, and it was a sad spectacle to see, as the wind cleared the mist, a number of cavaliers stuck in the mud, and trying vainly to reach either of the hills.

From the other hill on which the flag of France waved, their cries of distress were heard, and that was why the trumpets had sounded.

The soldiers now sounded their cornets, and were answered by guns in joyful recognition.

About eleven o'clock the sun appeared over this scene of desolation, drying some parts of the plain, and rendering practicable a kind of road.

Lucien, who tried it first, found that it led by a detour from where they were to the opposite hill, and he believed that, though his horse might sink to a certain extent, he would not sink altogether.

He, therefore, determined to try it, and recommending Grace and Cuthbert to the care of the ensign, set off on his perilous way.

At the same time as he started they could see a cavalier leave the opposite hill, and, like Lucien, try the road.

All the soldiers seemed trying to stop him by their supplications.

The two men pursued their way courageously, and soon perceived that their task was less difficult than had been feared.

A small stream of water escaped from a broken aqueduct, washed over the path, and little by little, was clearing away the mud.

The cavaliers were within two hundred feet of each other.

"France!" cried the one who came from the opposite hill, at the same time raising his hat, which had a white plume in it.

"Oh! it is you, Jack Tyrrell!" cried Lucien, with a burst of joy.

"You, Lucien; you, my friend!" returned the other.

And they set off as quickly as their horses could manage to go, and soon, among the frantic exclamations of the spectators on each side, embraced long and tenderly.

They were not long, however, to remain together, for the army being without provisions Lucien was dispatched at the head of a hundred men on a foraging expedition.

He hastened full of joy to Grace Dashwood.

"Get ready for a journey," he said; "in a quarter of an hour we set out on a foraging expedition. You will find two horses saddled at the door of the little wooden staircase. Join my suite, and say nothing."

In half an hour they set out.

Lucien himself did not stay by them, but rode at the head of his company.

Their march was slow, for often the ground nearly gave way under them, and they sank in the mud.

Sometimes figures were seen flying over the plain.

They were peasants who had been rather too quick in returning to their homes, and who fled at the sight of the enemy.

MOONLIGHT JACK
OR THE KING OF THE ROAD

THE AMBUSH.

Sometimes, however, they were unlucky French-men, half dead with cold and hunger, and who, in their uncertainty of meeting with friends or enemies, preferred waiting until daylight to con-tinue their painful journey.

At last they arrived on the banks of the river.

The night was dark, and the soldiers found two men who were trying, in bad English, to obtain from a boatman a passage to the other side, which he refused.

The ensign, who understood English, advanced softly and heard the boatman say,

"You are French, and shall die here. You shall not cross."

"It is you who shall die if you do not take us over at once," replied one of the men, drawing his dagger.

"Keep firm, sir," cried the ensign, "we will come to your aid."

But as the two men turned at these words the boatman loosened the rope, and pushed rapidly from the shore. One of the soldiers, however, knowing how useful this boat would be, went into the stream on his horse, and fired at the boatman, who fell.

The boat was left without a guide; but the current brought it back again towards the bank.

The two strangers seized it at once and got in, somewhat to the astonishment of the ensign.

"Gentlemen," said he, "who are you, if you please?"

"Gentlemen, we are marine officers; and you are French soldiers, apparently?"

"Yes, gentlemen, and very happy to have served you. Will you not accompany us?"

No. 25, June 23, 1866.]   Two Numbers and Two Tales every week for One Penny.   Price One Penny.
THE WORK GIRLS OF LONDON, and THE CRUSADER; OR,
THE WITCH OF FINCHLEY.

"Willingly."

"Get into the waggons, then, if you are too tired to ride."

"May we ask where you are going?" said one.

"Sir, our orders are to push on to Colchester."

"Take care," answered he, "we did not pass the stream sooner because this morning a detachment of English passed, coming from Truebridge. At sunset we thought we might venture, for two men inspire no disquietude; but you, a whole troop—"

"It is true. I will call our commander."

Lucien approached and asked what was the matter.

"These gentlemen met this morning a detachment of English following the same road as ourselves."

"How many were they?"

"About fifty."

"And does that stop you?"

"No, but I think it would be well to secure the boat in case we should wish to pass the stream; it will hold twenty men."

"Good. Let us keep the boat. There should be some houses at the junction of the rivers."

"There is a village," said a voice.

"Then let two men descend the stream with the boat while we go along the bank."

"We will bring the boat if you will let us," said one of the officers.

"If you wish it, gentlemen; but do not lose sight of us, and come to us in the village."

"But if we abandon the boat some one will take it."

"You will find ten men waiting to whom you can deliver it."

"It is well," said one, and they pushed off from the shore.

"It is singular," said Lucien, "but I fancy I know that voice."

An hour after they arrived at the village, which was occupied by the fifty English; but they were taken by surprise when they least expected it, and made little resistance.

Lucien had them disarmed and shut up in the strongest house in the village, and left two men to guard them.

Ten more were sent to guard the boat, and ten others placed as sentinels, with the promise of being relieved in an hour.

Twenty of the others then sat down in the house opposite to that in which the prisoners were, to the supper which had been prepared for them.

Lucien chose a separate room for Cuthbert and Grace.

He then placed the ensign at table with the others, telling him to invite the two naval officers when they arrived.

He next went out to look for accommodation for the rest of the men, and when he returned in half an hour he found them waiting supper for him.

Some had fallen asleep on their chairs, but his entrance roused them.

The table, covered with cheese, pork, and bread, with a pot of beer by each man, looked almost tempting.

Lucien sat down and told them to begin.

"Apropos!" said he, "have the strangers arrived?"

"Yes; there they are at the end of the table."

Lucien looked and saw them in the darkest corner of the room.

"Gentlemen," said he, "you are badly placed, and I think you are not eating."

"Thanks, Mr. Fairleigh," said one; "we are very tired, and stand more in need of rest than food.

We told your officers so, but they insisted saying that it was your wish that we should sup with you. We feel the honour, but if, nevertheless, instead of keeping us longer, you would give us a room——"

"Is that also the wish of your companion?" said Lucien, and he looked at his companion, whose hat was pushed down over his eyes and who had not yet spoken.

"Yes, Mr. Fairleigh," replied he, in a scarcely audible voice.

Lucien rose, walked straight to the end of the table, while every one watched his movements and astonished look.

"Sir," said he, to the one who had spoken first, "will you do me a favour?"

"What is it, Mr. Fairleigh?"

"Tell me if you are not Courtney's brother, or Courtney himself?"

"Courtney!" cried all.

"And let your companion," continued Lucien, "raise his hat a little, and let me see his face, or else I shall call him prince and bow before him."

And as he spoke he bowed respectfully hat in hand.

The officer took off his hat.

"His Majesty King James the Third!" cried all.

"Indeed, gentlemen," replied he, "since you will all recognise your conquered and fugitive prince, I shall not deny myself. I am your prince."

"Long live the prince!" cried all.

"Oh, silence, gentlemen," said the prince. "Do not be more content than I am at my good fortune. I am enchanted not to be dead, you may well believe, and yet, if you had not recognised me, I should not have been the first to boast of being alive."

"What, your highness," cried Lucien, "you recognise me? You found yourself among friends, and would have left us to mourn your loss without undeceiving us."

"Gentlemen, besides a number of reasons which made me wish to preserve my incognito, I confess that I should not have been sorry, since I was believed to be dead, to hear what funeral oration would have been pronounced over me."

"Your highness!"

"Yes, I am like Alexander of Macedon. I make war like an artist, and have as much self-love, and I believe I have committed a fault."

Unluckily for Lucien, the prince required him almost at once to go with a message for him.

During his absence the Pretender's secretary, Daniel Courtney, had informed him that Lucien had a lady—a pretty lady, too—in his charge.

The ensign had unwittingly betrayed the fact.

The Pretender's curiosity was at once awakened.

"Where is this lady?" he said.

"Upstairs."

"Upstairs? What, in this house?"

"Yes, your highness! But, hush, here is Mr. Fairleigh."

"Hush!" said the prince, laughing.

Lucien, as he entered, could hear the laugh of the prince, but he had not lived long enough with him to know the danger that lurked in his laugh.

Besides, he could not suspect the subject of conversation, and no one dared to tell him in the Pretender's presence.

Besides, the Pretender, who had already settled his plan, kept Lucien near him until all the other officers were gone.

He then changed the distribution of the posts.

Lucien had established his quarters in that house, and had intended to send the ensign to a post near the river, but the Pretender now took Lucien's place, and sent him where the ensign was to have been.

Lucien was not astonished, for the river was an important point.

Before going, however, he wished to speak to the ensign, and recommend to his care the two people under his protection, and whom he was forced, for the time, to abandon.

But at the first word that Lucien began to speak to him the Pretender interposed.

"Secrets ?" said he, with his peculiar smile.

The ensign had understood, when too late, the fault he had been guilty of.

"No, your highness," replied he, "Mr. Fairleigh was only asking me how much powder we had left fit for use."

This answer had two aims.

The first to turn away the Pretender's suspicions, if he had any, and the second to let Lucien know that he could count on a friend in him.

"Ah !" said the Pretender, forced to seem to believe what he was told.

And as he turned to the door, the ensign whispered to Lucien,

"The prince knows that you are escorting some one."

Lucien started ; but it was too late.

The Pretender remarked the start, and, as if to assure himself that his orders were executed, proposed to Lucien to accompany him to his post, which he was forced to accede to.

Lucien wished to warn Cuthbert to be upon his guard, but it was impossible ; all he could do was to say to the ensign,

"Watch well over the powder ; watch it as I would myself, will you not ?"

"Yes, Mr. Fairleigh," replied the young man.

On the way the Pretender said to Lucien,

"Where is this powder you speak of ?"

"In the house we have just left."

"Oh, be easy, then, Fairleigh. I know too well the importance of such an article in our situation to neglect it. I will watch over it myself."

They said no more until they arrived, when the Pretender, after giving Lucien many charges not to quit his post, returned.

He found Courtney wrapped in an officer's cloak, sleeping on one of the seats in the dining-room.

The Pretender woke him.

"Come," said he.

"Yes."

"Do you know what I mean ?"

"Yes ; the unknown lady—the relation of Mr. Fairleigh."

"Good ; I see that your intellect is not clouded."

"Oh, no, your highness, I am more ingenious than ever."

"Then call up all your imagination and guess."

"Well, I guess that your highness is curious."

"Ah, exactly ; I always am. But what is it about just now ?"

"You wish to know who is the brave creature who has followed Mr. Fairleigh through fire and water ?"

"You have just hit it. *Apropos*, have you written to her, Courtney ?"

"To whom, your highness ?"

"To the Marchioness of Loudan."

"Had I to write to her ?"

"Certainly !"

"About what ?"

"To tell her that we are beaten—ruined."

"Ah ! true."

"You have not written ?"

"No."

"You slept ?"

"Yes, I confess it ; but, if I had thought of it, what could I have written with, when we have neither pens, ink or paper ?"

"Well, seek."

"How, in the devil's name, am I to find it in the hut of a peasant, who probably does not know how to write ?"

"Seek, stupid ! if you do not find that you will find——"

"What ?"

"Something else."

"Oh, fool that I was !" cried Courtney, "your highness is right ; I am stupid, but I am very sleepy, you see."

"Well, keep awake for a little while, and, since you have not written, I will write ; only go and seek what is necessary. Go, Courtney, and do not come back till you have found it ; I will remain here."

"I go, your highness."

"And if, in your researches, you discover that the house is picturesque—you know how I admire English interiors ?"

"Yes."

"Well, call me."

"Immediately ; be easy."

Courtney rose, and, with a step as light as a bird, went up the staircase.

In five minutes he returned to his master.

"Well ?" asked he.

"Well, your highness, if I may believe appearances, the house is devilishly picturesque."

"How so ?"

"Why, because one cannot get in to look."

"What do you mean ?"

"I mean that it is guarded by a dragon."

"What foolish joke is this ?"

"Oh, your highness, unluckily it is not a joke, but a sad reality. The treasure is on the first floor, in a room in which I can see light through the door."

"Well ?"

"Well ! before this door lies a man, wrapped in a grey cloak."

"Oh, oh ! Mr. Fairleigh puts a soldier at the door of his mistress."

"It is not a soldier, your highness, but some attendant of the lady's, or of Mr. Fairleigh's."

"What kind of a man ?"

"It was impossible to see his face, but I could perfectly see a large knife in his belt, and his hand on it."

"It is amusing ; go and awaken the fellow."

"Oh, no."

"Why not ?"

"Why, without counting the knife, I do not wish to amuse myself by making a mortal enemy of Mr. Fairleigh, who stands so well at Court. If you had been king of this country it might have passed, but now you must be gracious, above all with those who saved you, and Tyrrell did save you. They will say so whether you do or not."

"You are right, Courtney, and yet——"

"I understand ; your highness has not seen a woman's face for fifteen mortal days. I do not speak of the kind of animals who live here ; they are males and females, but do not deserve to be called men and women."

"I must see this lady."

"Well, your highness, you may see her, but not through the door."

"So be it then ; I will see her through the window."

" Ah ! that is a good idea, and I will go and look for a ladder for you."

Courtney glided into the court-yard, and, under a shed, found what he wanted.

He manœuvred it amongst the horses and men so skilfully as to wake no one, and placed it in the street against the outer wall.

It was necessary to be a prince and sovereignly disdainful of vulgar scruples to dare, in the presence of the sentinel who walked up and down before the door, to accomplish an action so audaciously insulting to Lucien Fairleigh.

Courtney felt this, and, pointing out the sentinel, who, now observing, called out,

" Qui vive !"

The Pretender shrugged his shoulders, and walked up to him.

" My friend," said he, " this is the most elevated spot in the village, is it not ?"

" Yes, your highness," said the man, " and, were it not for those lime trees, we could see over a great part of the county."

" I thought so, and, therefore, I have brought a ladder," said the Pretender. " Go up, Courtney, or, rather, let me go up ; I will see for myself."

" Where shall I place it ?" said the hypocritical follower.

" Oh, anywhere. Against that wall, for instance."

The sentinel walked off, and the Pretender mounted the ladder, Courtney standing at the foot.

The room in which Lucien had placed Grace was matted, and had a large oaken bed with serge curtains, a table, and a few chairs.

Grace, whose heart seemed relieved of an enormous weight since she had heard the false news of the death of the Pretender, had, almost for the first time since her uncle's death, eaten something more substantial than bread, and drank a little wine.

After this she grew sleepy, and Cuthbert had left her and was sleeping outside her door, not because he had any suspicions, but simply because it had been his custom to do so ever since they had left her uncle's house.

Grace herself slept with her elbow on the table, and her head leaning on her hand.

A little lamp burned on the table, and all here looked peaceful where such tempestuous emotions had raged and would soon again.

In the glass sparkled the Rhine wine, scarcely touched by Grace.

She, with her eyes closed, her eyelids veined with azure, her mouth slightly open, her hair thrown back, looked like a sublime vision to the eyes that were violating the sanctity of her retreat.

The Pretender, on perceiving her, could hardly repress his admiration.

He leaned over to examine every detail of her ideal beauty.

But all at once he frowned and came down two or three steps with a kind of nervous precipitation, and leaning back against the wall, crossed his arms and appeared to reflect.

Courtney watched him as he stood there, with a dreamy air, like a man trying to recall some old souvenir.

After a few minutes he remounted and looked in again, but Courtney called out,

" Quick, quick, your highness ! Come down, I hear steps !"

The Pretender came down, but slowly.

" It was time," said Courtney.

" Whence comes the sound ?"

" From there," said Courtney, pointing to a dark street. " But the sound has ceased ; it must have been some spy watching us."

" Remove the ladder."

Courtney obeyed.

However, no one appeared, and they heard no more voices.

" Well, your highness, is she beautiful ?" said Courtney.

" Very beautiful," answered the prince, abstractedly.

" What makes you sad, then ? Did she see you ?"

" No, she was asleep."

" Then, what is the matter ?"

" It is strange, but I have seen that woman somewhere."

" You recognized her, then ?"

" No, I could not think of her name, but her face gave me a fearful shock. I cannot tell how it is, but I believe I did wrong to look."

" However, just on account of the impression she has made on you, we must find out who she is."

" Certainly we must."

" Look well in your memory. Is it at Court you have seen her ?"

" No, I think not."

" In France ?"

" No."

" A Spaniard, perhaps ?"

" I do not think so."

" An English lady ?"

" No, I seem to know her more intimately, and that she appeared to me in some terrible scene."

" Then you would have recognized her at once ; you have not seen many such scenes."

" Do you think so ?" said James, with a gloomy smile. " Now," continued he, " that I am sufficiently master of myself to analyze my own sensations, I feel that this woman is beautiful, but with the beauty of death ; beautiful as a shade, as a figure in a dream, and I have had two or three frightful dreams in my life, which left me cold at heart. Well, now I am sure that it was in one of those dreams that I saw that woman."

" Your highness is not generally so susceptible, and but that I believe we are watched from the street, I would mount in my turn and look."

" You are right, Courtney."

Courtney made a step forward to obey, when a hasty step was heard, and Lucien's voice, crying,

" Your highness ?"

" You here ?" said the Pretender, while Courtney bounded back to his side, " you here, Mr. Fairleigh ? On what pretext have you quitted your post ?"

" Your highness," replied Lucien, firmly, " you can punish me if you think proper ; meanwhile, my duty was to come here and I came."

The Pretender glanced towards the window.

" Your duty, Mr. Fairleigh ? Explain that to me," said he.

" Horsemen have been seen on the other side of the river, and we do not know if they are friends or enemies."

" Numerous ?" asked the prince, anxiously.

" Very numerous,"

" Well, Mr. Fairleigh, no false bravery ; you did well to return. Awake the soldiers and let us decamp, it will be the most prudent plan."

" Doubtless, my prince ; but it will be urgent, I think, to warn Moonlight Jack."

" Two men will do."

" Then I will go with a soldier."

" No, no, Fairleigh, you must come with us. It is not at such a moment that I can separate from a defender like you."

"When does your highness set out ?" said Lucien, bowing.

"At once, Mr. Fairleigh."

"Some one comes," cried Lucien.

The young ensign came out immediately from the dark street.

Lucien gave his orders, and soon the place was filled with soldiers preparing for departure.

Among them the Pretender talked with his officers.

"Gentlemen," said he, "the Prince of Orange is pursuing me, it seems ; but it is not proper that your true king should be taken prisoner. Let us, therefore, yield to numbers, and fall back upon Colchester. I shall be sure of life and liberty whilst I am among you."

Then turning to his secretary, Courtney,

"You remain," said he. "This woman cannot follow us. Fairleigh will not dare to bring her in my presence ; besides, we are not going to a ball, and the race we shall run would fatigue a lady."

"Where are you going, your highness ?"

"I must remain in England ; I think my business is here."

"But what part of England ? Does your highness think it good to return to London ?"

"No, I shall stop at Darnley House."

"Has your highness decided on that ?"

"Yes ; Darnley House suits me in all respects. It is a good distance from London, about twenty-eight miles ; so bring the beautiful unknown to Darnley House."

"But, your highness, perhaps she will not be brought."

"Nonsense ; since Lucien Fairleigh accompanies me, and she follows him, it will be quite natural."

"But she may wish to go somewhere else if she sees that I wish to bring her to you."

"But I repeat that is not to me that you are to bring her, but to Mr. Fairleigh. Really one would suppose that this was the first time you had aided me in such circumstances. Have you money ?"

"I have the two rouleaux of gold that you gave me when you left the camp."

"Well, by any and by every method, bring me the lady to Darnley House ; perhaps, when I see her nearer, I shall recognize her.

"And the man also ?"

"Yes ! if he is not troublesome."

"But if he is ?"

"Do with him as you would a stone that is in your way. Throw it away."

"Good, your highness."

While the two conspirators formed their plans, Lucien went up and awoke Cuthbert.

He knocked at the door in a peculiar fashion, and it was almost immediately opened by Grace.

Behind Cuthbert she perceived Lucien.

"Good evening, sir," said she, with a smile, which had long been foreign to her face.

"Oh ! pardon me, Grace," said Lucien, "for intruding on you ; but I come to say farewell."

"Farewell, Mr. Fairleigh ? Are you, then, going to leave us ?"

"Yes."

"And you will leave us ?"

"I am forced to do so ; my duty is to obey the prince."

"The prince ? Is there a prince here ?" asked Cuthbert.

"Yes, the Pretender, who was believed dead, and who has been miraculously saved, has joined us."

Grace uttered a terrible cry, and Cuthbert turned as pale as though he had been suddenly struck with death.

"The Pretender living ?" cried Grace. "The Pretender here ?"

"Had he not been here, Grace, and ordered me to follow him, I should have accompanied you to the convent into which you tell me you are about to retire."

"Yes, yes," said Cuthbert.

And he put his finger on his lip.

"I would have accompanied you the more willingly," said Lucien, "because I fear that you may be annoyed by the prince's people."

"How so ?"

"I believe that he knows there is a lady here, and he thinks that she is a friend of mine."

"And what makes you think so ?"

"Our young ensign saw him place a ladder against this window and look in."

"Oh !" cried Grace, "we are discovered."

"Re-assure yourself, madam. He heard him say he did not know you ; besides, the Pretender is going to set off at once. In a quarter of an hour you will be alone and free. Permit me to salute you with respect, and to tell you once more that till my last sigh my heart will beat for you and with you. Farewell, madam," and Lucien, bowing, took two steps back.

"No, no !" cried Grace, wildly, "this cannot—this cannot be ! Heaven cannot have given this man his life again. No, sir, you must be wrong ; he is dead."

At this moment, as if in reply, the Pretender's voice was heard calling from below.

While the grey mists of a February morn still hung heavily on the summits of the surrounding hills, or rolled lazily away before the earliest rays of the rising sun from the rich valleys at their feet, Moonlight Jack and Lucien Fairleigh might have been seen making their progress slowly down the narrow steep bridle road which, from its direction, would seem to lead over to the neighbouring sea coast of Sussex.

Making their way towards the small hamlet that had grown around the old collegiate church of Lingfield in Surrey.

The square tower of the building could be just discerned by them ever and again as the wreaths of fog were broken or up-lifted by the coming breeze, at, perhaps, somewhat less than a mile's distance from them.

The difficulties of the unfrequented path they travelled had been lately increased by heavy floods, sweeping down much of the lighter soil from the hills on either side.

They were both too much occupied by their own secret thoughts, as well as speculating on the success of the enterprise they had in hand, to notice the lovely prospect before and around them, reaching distant as the eye could penetrate the mists over bright fertile meadows and rich clumps of standing oaks.

Having with some difficulty gained the more used and better road that skirted the base of the hill they had descended, they paused for a short time, as though in doubt which road to follow.

"We were to look for Hardman at the 'Star,' were we not, Lucien ?" asked Jack. "If so, we must take the road on the right-hand side."

"Yes, at the 'Star,' where we are to breakfast at nine, and, by my faith ! I shall not be displeased. The keen air over these hills has given me an appetite which will do justice to it, so, if you are sure of your road, let's push forward, as it must be already past the hour."

A firmer footing having now been obtained for their horses, but a short time elapsed ere they drew up at the door of the little inn.

Dismounting and leading their horses into the stable, at the door of which stood an old helper rubbing down a horse, they gave him charge to see to them carefully as they had sharp work before them.

Making their way into the little parlour they found it already occupied by two travellers, who had apparently, like themselves, ridden far.

"I trust our presence may not be considered any intrusion here," said Moonlight Jack, bowing slightly; "we had expected to meet an attendant, who has doubtless been detained by the bad state of the roads.'

"The devil take such roads and those who are fools enough to travel by them," said the elder of the two; "that is, saving your worthy presence, gentlemen. I found it plaguing hard to get here even by the shortest cuts; every other mile being like charging up to your saddle-girths in a morass. The devil take such roads, I say again!"

"But, be seated, gentlemen. We will soon have an addition to our table, for I can assure you our worthy host, old Reuben Hardness, is no niggard."

"We will accept your hospitable welcome willingly," said Lucien, taking his proffered hand, which was again extended to Moonlight Jack, who did not fail to notice the costly diamond ring that graced his little finger.

The substantial meal over, Jack, always with an eye to his vocation, was not long in asking the road his companions travelled.

They were going to the neighbouring house of Starburgh—Starburgh Castle, as it was called, out of respect to the ruins of an old family residence of the Howard's, and no great distance from the inn, and which latter took its sign of the "Star" from the house. The present proprietor had been keeping great state there of late, and much good company was yet expected from town.

Declining an invitation to accompany them, for reasons of their own, Lucien and Jack bade them farewell.

"We should be only too happy to have been with you," said Jack, as their breakfast companions mounted their horses at the door; "but our movements must be entirely regulated by the letters brought us by our man. We may, however, meet again; but, for the present, God speed you."

Returning to the house they were soon joined by Hardman, who brought them the welcome intelligence that a rich booty might be expected.

The old Marquis of Brassington might be expected at the castle towards the evening; and, as it was well known he never travelled with an empty purse, our heroes made up their minds to await him on the road, more especially as by doing so they would rather serve the secret mission on which they were engaged. Whiling away the day as best they could, they took their departure from the house at dusk, having previously despatched Hardman to keep a look-out upon the road, and give them timely warning of the advent of the lumbering vehicle in which the nobleman travelled, which he, very well mounted, could easily do.

"Boot and saddle! we shall be in the nick of time; the old boy is about the middle of the high road leading to the house; in ten minutes we can be upon him."

"How many are there in all?" said Jack.

"Only two; the old rogue has muslin with him. A young face, and well-looking, too, popped from the window to ask me the way, and how far they were from the house."

"Only two servants with him again?" asked Moonlight Jack. "Did they seem armed?"

"Two in the rumble behind; the coachman counts for nothing."

"As for their arms," broke in Lucien, for the first time taking part in the conversation, "never heed them. We are three to three, if we reckon the driver as one."

"And the old boy and his girl will want a good deal of their help to keep them from fainting."

"Forward, then, at once."

Donning their masks they soon reached the high road.

"Hardman, look to the horses; Lucien and myself will make the meeting agreeable to the travellers."

The sound of approaching wheels was soon heard.

With a sudden spring of his horse Hardman's left hand was on the reins, his pistol at the same time levelled with his right, pointed direct to the coachman's head.

At the same moment, Lucien's pistols, one in each hand, covered the servants.

The faint cry from within the coach evidenced more of surprise than fear on the part of the female inmate.

"We will trouble your lordship to alight," said Moonlight Jack, bowing respectfully to the luxurious nobleman.

"As faithful subjects to the 'king of the road,' we are bound to make a strict search of any vehicle travelling between sunset and morning."

"What if I object to the jurisdiction? What if I oppose force by force?"

"An unpleasant result," said Jack, smilingly, and in his softest tones.

"I should first have to remove your fair companion; in our king's court or presence scenes of violence are never enacted before the gentler sex."

"Well, and then?"

"Then having given your lordship fair time to consider the question——"

"On my refusal?"

"On your refusal I should find myself under the disagreeable necessity of placing a 'brace of balls' through your lordship's head, 'pon my honour."

To guard against any sudden surprise Moonlight Jack produced his weapon, passing it quickly before the nobleman's eyes that he might see he was in earnest and prepared.

"You are an impudent scoundrel," said his lordship, struck by the extreme coolness displayed by his assailants; "but I suppose there is no help for it."

With the air of a polished courtier Jack received the well-filled purse handed to him.

"Thanks! Your lordship's small trunk, the end of which I see projecting from beneath your seat, shall receive due attention immediately.

"Nothing but a change of linen, I assure you."

"Probably; but even that must be examined."

"Your lordship's ring? Thanks again! Gold snuff-box and eye-glass," continued Jack, removing the different articles as he spoke.

"And, now, if your lordship will be pleased to alight until we have paid attention to your fair companion?"

But this proceeding met with his lordship's most strenuous objection.

"The lady is an invalid; in fact I am escorting her to the residence of her medical adviser. You will scarcely be so ungallant as to endanger her life?"

"Her life? In truth, no. I trust your lordship is indulging in needless alarm. I have some skill in the profession myself, and, under the circumstances, must insist on examining the case. You must get out."

The voice in which Jack had uttered the order convinced the marquis that he had gone far enough in his refusal.

In anything but a pleasant mood he obeyed.

"Now, your ladyship," commenced our hero.

His further speech was drowned in a loud laugh, as the lady removed her veil.

"Betsy Watson, the ballet-girl, by Gad!"

"Ha, ha! Lucien, his philanthrophic lordship conducting the invalid lady to her medical adviser! I shall not cease laughing for a month, at least," cried Moonlight Jack, politely handing out the "fascinating Elizabeth."

"Be under no alarm; as his lordship's companion ought to be her ladyship, so she shall be treated."

"I trust your illness is not of a serious nature," said Lucien, stepping up to the fair one with a smile, and at the same time taking her hand. "What does your Majesty prescribe?" he continued, turning to Moonlight Jack. "I am sure the noble marquis will be very grateful for your services."

"Yes, faith!" said Jack, "I had almost forgotten. Allow me to look at your ladyship's tongue; now the pulse, if you please? Feverish; decidedly too much ease and indolence, added to too much high living and rich wines. His lordship is slightly touched with the same complaint; strong exercise much wanted in both cases."

"Why not commence at once, then," suggested Lucien Fairleigh. "Hardman plays indifferently well on the fife, and, I'll be sworn, has one with him. What says our worthy doctor, a merry tune and a lively jig in the moonlight will not be a bad commencement?"

"Strike up at once, Hardman; and now, my lord, do your best; you have a good partner, we know, and you owe us a forfeit for the cheat you tried to put on us."

The marquis, finding himself so fairly caught, and having the fear of his wife before him should his present adventure become known, was fain to comply.

It was not until nearly exhausted with his unusual exertions that his tormentors allowed himself and party to proceed.

Moonlight Jack, Lucien, and their follower retraced their steps to the "Star," where they had decided on remaining for the night.

The amusing incident of meeting with the old marquis formed a subject of conversation for their supper-table.

In addition to their frolic of making the old man dance, they had every reason to be pleased with the spoil they had stripped him of.

The purse contained over a hundred and sixty guineas in notes and gold.

The ring, massive gold, with a large cluster of diamonds of the first water, and the gold box, with a jewelled border, would realize not much less than the like amount.

Having examined and carefully put away their gains, Lucien and Jack settled themselves quietly down to drink and talk over their plans for the future.

Their follower had found other occupation for himself.

The daughter of the landlord of the inn, Bridget Hardness, was a fine, showy, country lass, thoroughly English both in form and feature.

The rosy cheeks had make an impression on Hardman when he had seen her some weeks since on his first visit to the neighbourhood.

This had, in a great measure, induced him to name the house to his chiefs as well suited for their purpose, being quiet and at the same time good.

Taking advantage of the absence of the old man, her father, who had gone to witness the gay doings at the castle, he had cunningly insinuated himself into the little bar parlour, so as to enjoy, to the utmost, the presence of his fair enslaver.

His courtship progressed favourably.

The soft heart of the country girl was not proof against the dashing, off-hand manner and flattering tongue of the knight of the road.

"And you really will not deceive me?" she said, in answer to one of his fervent declarations of constancy and love. "Yet, how can I expect you will even remember a poor country girl like me when you are with your gay town folks?"

"And why not, my darling? why not think of my blooming Sussex rose? We do not always wear a flower in our breast, yet we do not forget that flowers do grow and smell sweet, and are lovely, too, like my own Bridget. Come, let me kiss away the cloud, and have the sunshine."

As he spoke he drew her to his side, and, clasping her round the waist, laid her head upon his shoulder.

She soon started up again.

"Fie, Master Ralph; I declare I had well-nigh forgotten where we were. You had better pass out at the side door, and go round by the stables. I must to the parlour at once, or I shall have been missed. Go now, there's a dear fellow."

But Hardman was not to be so dismissed.

"It is easy to say go," he said, squeezing her hand, and forcibly detaining her. "It is easy to say go, but in my case how hard to do it."

"Do let me go; we shall be found out, and I at least shall be almost killed."

"I cannot," he said, shaking his head, and pressing her to his side; "nay, I will not, until I have your promise."

"My promise for what? Oh, I will promise almost anything, only let me go now, for I am sure we shall be found out."

He caught her to his breast, and whispered in her ear.

"Yes," she answered, "I will—I will, indeed, if you let me go."

"At what time, then?"

"At about half-past twelve I will be at the door."

"And you may be sure I shall not fail to keep the appointment."

After sealing the bargain with more than a dozen kisses, Hardman made his way to the stables to look to their horses, and Bridget not without a slight pricking of her conscience to think over her plans for successfully carrying out the appointment she had made with him for to-night.

Lucien and Jack still occupied their private room.

They had fully discussed and arranged their plans, and only waited the return of day to recommence their journey.

"Have you ever been over this part of the country before?" asked Lucien of Jack, as if to start a conversation, for they had both been silent some time.

"I once had rather a startling adventure betwixt this and the next county," replied the latter.

"Was it in connection with our present vocation?"

"Oh, no; strictly private."

"Tell it then, Jack; it will pass away an odd half-hour."

"It was when quite a youngster. I had been travelling through Surrey and Sussex on some business concerning land or some other thing in which I took no interest.

"It was a job entrusted to me by my granddad.

"In my journeying I chanced to stay for one night at this very same house, the 'Star.'"

"After a ramble about the old church here, close by, at an early hour in the morning, I was returning to breakfast, when my attention was drawn to a man on horseback, making towards the house as hard as his horse could lay legs to the ground.

"My curiosity was excited, and quickening my steps, I was soon at the inn door.

"Not so soon as he was, however, for I found he had entered the house some few minutes, in fact he was coming from the house as I approached it.

"His anxious, hurried look told at a glance that his errand was of importance.

"'As you are a man, tell me if he has been here this morning, and if he has left the house long. Life and death, nay, even what is dearer than either to him, rests upon his safety.'

"'I do not even known of whom you speak,' I answered. 'I noticed a party of horsemen leaving the house about two hours since, when I was on the hill behind the church, but whether they were the ones you seek I cannot tell.'

"'Too late—too late! my poor good master,' he cried, wringing his hands, 'to be caught and sold by such treachery—even perhaps to his death.'

"'There yet may be time to help him,' I said, (You know, Lucien, I was always quick enough for anything that promise life and excite.) 'I have a good horse in the stable and a good sword at my side, and though not very old or strongly built, I have struck a good blow before now in a just cause.'"

"And since then, may I add, Jack, in an unjust one too,' said Lucien, with a laugh; "but go on, I am interested in the story."

"Thanking me heartily," continued Jack, with a smile, at the interruption, 'I fear it will be too late, their plan was so well laid that I do not think, if we do our utmost, we shall be able to rescue him.'

"'We'll try hard, however. Help yourself to a fresh horse; you will find one in the stable belonging to the house. Don't waste a moment for sanction or denial. I will be ready in an instant.'

"Calling to the old landlord, who had bustled to the door as I leapt into the saddle,

"'Here, Reuben, you will find we have taken one of your horses on a work that would not stay the asking. We leave you a better one in its stead. You need not fear us though; we shall be back again, perhaps before nightfall.'

"'And now forward with our best speed,' I cried to my companion, 'and in God's name spare not horseflesh,' as we galloped out of the yard together.

"The finish of the story had better be given in the words of the man we rode to help," said Jack.

"You saved him?" said Lucien.

"Yes; but not without a bit of a tussle.

"I do not rightly remember the exact case, but at all events the young nobleman was the son of one of our own best patrons. He had been carrying off some great prize in the way of a wife. The girl was under the protection of the crown. He had made his escape, and might easily have got out of the country, but one of his old chums had, for a large sum, agreed to deliver him up, bound hand and foot, to his enemies.

"I knew them both, prisoner and traitor, and felt not a little pleased at having the chance to pay out the treacherous hound who had before been guilty of behaving badly to myself.

"It seems, by his account (I mean the man we

went to serve) that after imposing on him by a false tale to the effect that they would lead him to the place of his wife's confinement, and, setting her at liberty, restore her to him, they had journeyed for some time pleasantly enough, his suspicions not being excited by anything that had taken place.

"When they had arrived at a part of the way where the path led through a thick plantation of young firs, on a signal given by the scoundrel to his servant, the latter gradually lessened the distance that had hitherto been between them until he was nearly abreast of their victim on the opposite side to his employer.

"The latter repeating his signal (merely a slight motion of his hand) and at the same time giving a shrill whistle, laid hold of his unsuspecting companion's bridle, and forcing his horse upon his haunches with all his strength, threw the rider back almost into his follower's arms.

"Quickly as the fellow cast himself around him he still had time to draw his pistol; but his aim was disturbed by his horse's plunging violently.

"The capture thus safely made, and the victim secured, their route was at once changed. Leaving the Kentish land, on which the capture had been made, they took their way by Mereworth and Bradbourne House, back again into Surrey. As they neared the long downward shoot of hill that carried them over by Bradbourne Wash, Godwin, the servant, rode forward to find out the track.

"The two men who had joined them in answer to the whistle, whose presence I had forgot to mention, bringing up the rear, when about half way down the hill, one of the men had moved forward to help Godwin in keeping in the road as the darkness increased.

"'What stops the way now?'

"'In the devil's name! your horse is down, you clumsy fool!' cried the leader of the party to the foremost man. 'Get him on his legs again at once. We shall have night set in on us before we get out of this cursed lane.'

"The job was not so easily done.

"A long slip and then a sudden rise in the road had thrown the poor brute off his balance, and his leg falling outwards as it were, its own weight had broken its thigh.

"'Out with your hunting knife, and slash it across the throat, Jasper,' he said. ''Tis a good horse lost, but the day's gains may well stand a heavier loss.'

MOON-LIGHT JACK

OR THE KING OF THE ROAD

THE ADVANCE OF THE PRETENDER'S ARMY.

"Instead of obeying him, Godwin was listening to some sounds that seemed to come down the hill behind him.

"'Look to yourselves!' he cried. 'We are pursued! Have with the prisoner through the hedge; there is our best chance of safety, for we cannot pass that kicking brute as he lays in the road there.'

"While he was speaking he seized the bridle of the captive's horse, and, in spite of the efforts of its rider, was forcing his way through the hedge, closely followed by his superior.

"At this instant the flash of two pistols was seen.

"With a short convulsive sob Godwin fell d from his saddle.

"Before the surprise of the attack had passed the least from their leader, I had forced my through the hedge to his side, and ere he co command his pistol or draw his sword, I grappled him firmly by the throat, and throw him backwards over his horse's back had car him to the ground."

"'Twas well and bravely done, Jack," Lucien. "And what was the result? How di fare with the bride and bridegroom afterwar Did they live happy to the end of the chapter?"

"In faith, Lucien, I hardly took the pains

No. 26.—June 30, 1866.

Two Numbers and Two Tales every week for One Penny.
THE WORK GIRLS OF LONDON, and THE CRUSADER; OR, THE WITCH OF FINCHLEY.

Price One

enquire. I quietly took myself out of the county till my share in the circumstances had grown out of men's memories ; and now I think, as it's past midnight, we'll think of a little slumber. Another glass, and then good night."

But a short time elapsed before they both slept soundly.

Hardman had found the time hang heavily indeed upon his hands.

He had lingered in the stable until the last moment, then he had tried smoking and gossiping with the old farm labourers in the tap until the last one had left him to himself, even in spite of the offered bribe of another " quart of zidu."

When quite alone he had again sauntered up to the bar. This time he was successful.

He had just caught old Reuben on his return from the castle, but the old man was in no hurry to leave him—the good cheer had opened his heart and made him talkative.

"They do keep a good home up there, my word, Muster Hardman. Right down good English livin'— beef, ale, and zidu, and none of yer wishy-washy stuff, neither, the real good barleycorn ; some on't has a-been in the house over a fifty year, and is now stronger nor brandy, I've hearn say. But, law a marcy ! warn't there a row about an old lord as comed down to-day. He was stopped and robbed of all his money ; yes, and made to dance, too, for near an hour."

"Made to dance ! That's a rum freak for the thieves to take into their heads. I'll be bound it was some one that knew his lordship."

"He dun'no' who 'twas ; leastwise, so he says ; but if he could on'y ketch 'em in Lunnon they'd know who to stop, I'll warrant."

At length, to Hardman's great relief, the old man's gossip was done, or rather his powers of speech were drowned for the time in old ale, three or four horns of which he had added from his own cellars to the store he had brought from the castle.

When all had been some time in bed in the little inn, Hardman crept cautiously from the chamber assigned to him to keep his appointment with the fair Bridget.

He found her to her word awaiting his arrival at the door of her own room.

"Hush !" she whispered. "I think they are all asleep. Did you hear or see anything as you came through the passage ?"

"All as still as the grave, my sweetest. This is in truth kind of you."

Again she cautioned him.

"For God's sake be careful and let not a soul know of your being here. I should be killed outright."

Carefully bolting the door, he led her to a chair by the window and commenced calming the fears in which she had indulged.

"What was that ?"

Again it was repeated.

"It is surely some one tapping at the window. Hush ! for mercy's sake go to your own room ! My God ! I made sure that Stephen would not return until to-morrow."

"Bridget, unlatch the window, there's a darling," a voice whispered outside. "It's only me, your own Steve. I've given them the slip up at the house, and can safely stop for an hour."

"Oh ! run to your room. In pity, spare me !" cried the frail Bridget, sinking on her knees before Hardman. "There will be murder done if he finds you here !"

"Murder or not, I don't stir from here till I have a better cause than the fear of a dozen Stephen's !"

cried Hardman. "So you would fool me by making me play second fiddle to your Stephen's toy, Mistress Bridget ? Well, open the window, and let's see this living wonder."

"Mercy ! mercy ! Oh ! do not expose me again !" cried Bridget, piteously ; "not for fear of him, but in pity to me. Oh ! do go !"

"Well, for your sake, I will, then ; but mind, I will return and claim my reward."

"Too late !"

"Oh ! too late !"

The window was dashed in by a powerful blow of a fist.

And a tall, strongly-built young fellow sprang on to the floor from the outside.

At a glance Hardman saw he had no mean antagonist to meet.

No word was spoken by either.

They glanced at each other as two wild beasts.

Bridget, in piteous accents, tried to appease them in vain.

"Back to your kennel !" cried Stephen, fiercely to her. "I will reckon with you by-and-bye. As for you, sir," he continued, turning to Hardman, "follow me to the courtyard, we have light enough to settle our quarrel there."

This challenge was at once accepted.

Though greatly superior in point of strength, Stephen was but as a mouse to his opponent in the use of his sword.

Their combat was not of long continuance.

Bridget, who had followed them from her chamber, became seriously alarmed when she saw the blood flowing from a wound in her old lover's arm.

"Help ! part them ! Stephen will be murdered !" she shrieked out.

A few moments served to thoroughly rouse the inmates of the house.

Two or three of the servants, hearing the clashing of swords and the cries of Bridget, made in at once to secure Hardman.

"Back !" he cried, keeping them off at his sword's point. "Within there, Moonlight Jack and Lucien, to the rescue !"

His call for assistance had not been made too soon.

Pressed as he was on all sides by the servants, he had found it no easy task to avoid the angry attack of his opponent.

The appearance of Moonlight Jack and Lucien on the scene soon changed the aspect of affairs.

Ranging themselves on the side of their follower they effectually kept back the attacking party by the sight of their pistols ; gradually retreating towards the stables they fought their way to the door, Jack and Hardman keeping the crowd at bay, whilst Lucien prepared their horses.

Leading them forth when ready the three were soon in the saddle, and a short time sufficed to place them in perfect safety.

We must now return to the time when Lucien Fairleigh quitted the old inn, and left behind him Grace Dashwood and old Cuthbert the servant.

To the confusion occasioned by the departure of the troops, a profound silence succeeded.

When Cuthbert believed the house to be empty he went down to prepare for his departure and that of Grace, but on opening the door of the room below, he was much surprised to see a man sitting by the fire, evidently watching him, although he pretended to look careless.

Cuthbert approached, according to his custom, with a slow halting step, and uncovering his head bald, like that of an old man.

He could not, however, see the features of the man by the fire.

"Pardon, sir," said he, "I thought myself alone here."

"I also thought so," replied the man, "but I see with pleasure that I shall have companions."

"Oh, very sad companions, sir, for except an invalid young man, whom I am taking back to his native place——"

"Ah!" said Courtney, "I know whom you mean."

"Really?"

"Yes, you mean the young lady."

"What young lady?"

"Oh, do not be angry, my good friend; I am the follower of Lucien Fairleigh, and at his departure he recommended to my good offices a young lady and an old servant who were returning to London."

As he thus spoke, he approached Cuthbert with a smiling and affectionate look.

But Cuthbert stepped back, and for an instant a look of horror was painted on his face.

"You do not reply; one would say you were afraid of me," said Courtney, with his most smiling face.

"Sir," said Cuthbert, "pardon a poor old man, whom his misfortunes and his wounds have rendered timid and suspicious."

"All the more reason, my friend, for accepting the help and support of an honest companion; besides, as I told you just now, I speak on the part of a master who must inspire you with confidence."

"Assuredly, sir," said Cuthbert, who, however, still moved back.

"You quit me," said Courtney.

"I must consult my mistress. I can decide nothing. You understand?"

"Oh, that is natural; but, permit me to present myself. I will explain my directions in all their details."

"No, no, thank you; my mistress is, perhaps, asleep, and her sleep is sacred to me."

"As you wish; besides, I have told you what my master wished me to say."

"To me?"

"To you and the young lady."

"Your master, Mr. Lucien Fairleigh, you mean?"

"Yes."

"Thank you, sir."

When he had shut the door, all the appearances of age vanished, except the bald head, and Cuthbert mounted the stairs with an agility more like a young man of twenty-five than the old man he had appeared to be but a few minutes before.

"Madam, madam!" cried he, in an agitated voice.

"Well, what is it Cuthbert? Is not the Pretender gone?"

"Yes, madam; but there is a worse demon here, a demon on whom, during six years, I have daily called down heaven's vengeance, as you have on his master."

"Courtney?"

"Yes, Courtney; the wretch is below, forgotten by his infernal accomplice."

"Forgotten do you say, Cuthbert? Oh, you are wrong, you who know the Pretender, know that he never leaves to chance any evil deed, if he can do it himself. No, no, Cuthbert, Courtney is not forgotten, but left here for some bad design, believe me."

"Oh, about him, madam, I can believe anything."

"Does he know me?"

"I do not think so."

"And did he recognise you?"

"No, madam," returned Cuthbert, with a sad smile, "no one recognises me."

"Perhaps he guesses who I am?"

"No, for he asked to see you."

"I am sure he must have suspicions."

"In that case, nothing is more easy, and I thank God for pointing out our path so plainly. The village is deserted, the wretch is alone. I saw a poignard in his belt, but I have a knife in mine."

"One moment, Cuthbert. I do not ask the life of that wretch of you; but, before you kill him, let us find out what he wants of us; perhaps we may make his evil intentions useful. How did he represent himself to you, Cuthbert?"

"As an old servant of Mr. Fairleigh."

"You see he lies; therefore he has some reason for lying. Let us find out his intentions, and conceal our own."

"I will act as you wish, madam."

"What does he ask now?"

"To accompany us."

"In what character?"

"As Mr. Fairleigh's servant."

"Tell him I accept."

"Oh, madam!"

"Add, that I am thinking of going to London, where I have relations, but have not quite decided; lie like him, Cuthbert; to conquer we must fight with equal arms."

"But he will see you."

"No, I will wear my mask. Besides, I suspect he knows me."

"Then if he knows you there must be a snare."

"Let us pretend to fall into it."

"But——"

"What do you fear, we can but die? Are you not ready to die for the accomplishment of our vow?"

"Yes, but not to die without vengeance."

"Cuthbert," cried Grace, her eyes sparkling with wild excitement; "we will be revenged! you on the servant, and I on the master."

"Well, madam, then so be it."

And Cuthbert went down, but still hesitating.

The brave fellow had, at the sight of Courtney, felt, in spite of himself, that nervous shudder that one feels at the sight of a reptile; he wished to kill him because he feared him.

But as he went down his resolutions returned, and he determined, in spite of Grace's opinion, to interrogate Courtney, to confound him, and if he discovered he had any evil intentions to kill him on the spot.

Courtney waited for him impatiently.

Cuthbert advanced, armed with an unshakeable resolution, but his words were quiet and calm.

"Sir," said he, "my mistress cannot accept your proposal."

"And why not?"

"Because you are not the servant of Mr. Lucien Fairleigh."

Courtney grew pale.

"Who told you so?" said he.

"No one; but Mr. Fairleigh, when he left, recommended to my care the person whom I accompany, and never spoke of you."

"He only saw me after he left you."

"Falsehoods, sir, falsehoods!"

Courtney drew himself up.

Cuthbert looked like an old man.

"You speak in a singular tone, my good man," said he, frowning; "take care, you are old and I am young; you are feeble and I am strong."

Cuthbert smiled, but did not reply.

"If I wished ill to you or your mistress," continued Courtney, "I have but to raise my hand."

"Oh," said Cuthbert, "perhaps I was wrong, and you wish to do her good."

"Certainly I do."

"Explain to me, then, what you desire."

"My friend, I will make your fortune at once, if you will serve me."

"And if not?"

"In that case, as you speak frankly, I will reply as frankly, that I will kill you; I have full power to do so."

"Kill me," said Cuthbert; "but if I am to serve you, I must know your projects."

"Well, you have guessed rightly, my good man; I do not belong to Mr Lucien Fairleigh."

"Ah, and to whom do you belong?"

"To one more powerful."

"Take care; you are lying again."

"Why so?"

"There are not many people above the house of Huntley."

"Not that of England?"

"Oh! oh!"

"And see how they pay," said Courtney, sliding into Cuthbert's hand one of the rouleaux of gold.

Cuthbert shuddered and took a step back, but controlling himself, said,

"You serve the king."

"No; but the Pretender."

"Oh, very well, I am his highness's most humble servant."

"That's excellent."

"But what does his highness want?"

"His highness," said Courtney, trying again to slip the gold into Cuthbert's hand, "is in love with your mistress."

"He knows her, then?"

"He has seen her."

"Seen her, when?"

"This evening."

"Impossible; she has not left her rooms."

"No, but the prince by his conduct has shown that he is really in love."

"Why, what did he do?"

"Took a ladder and climbed to the balcony."

"Ah, he did that?"

"Yes; and it seems she is very beautiful."

"Then you have not seen her?"

"No; but from what he said I much wish to do so, if only to judge of the exaggeration of his love. Thus, then, it is agreed; you will aid me?" and he again offered him the gold.

"Certainly I will, but I must know what part I am to play," said Cuthbert, repulsing his hand.

"First tell me is the lady the mistress of Lucien Fairleigh, or of whom?"

The blood mounted to Cuthbert's face.

"Of neither," said he; "the lady up-stairs has no lover."

"No lover! But then she is a wonder. By jove, a woman who has no lover! We have found the philosopher's stone."

"Then," said Cuthbert, "what does the Pretender want my mistress to do?"

"He wants her to come to Darnley House, where he is going at his utmost speed."

"This is, upon my word, a passion very quickly conceived."

"That is like his highness."

"I only see one difficulty," said Cuthbert.

"What is that?"

"That my mistress is about to proceed to London."

"The devil! this, then, is where you must beg to aid me."

"How?"

"By persuading her to go in an opposite direction."

"You do not know my mistress, sir; she is not so easily persuaded. Besides, even if she were persuaded to go to Darnley House instead of London, do you think she would yield to the prince?"

"Why not?"

"She does not love him."

"Bah! Not love a prince of the blood?"

"But if the Pretender suspects my mistress of loving Mr. Fairleigh, how did he come to think of carrying her off from him she loved?"

"My good man," said Courtney, "you have trivial ideas, and I am afraid we shall never understand each other; I have preferred kindness to violence, but if you force me to change my plans, well I must change them."

"What will you do?"

"I told you I had full powers from the Pretender to kill you and carry off the lady."

"And you believe you could do it with impunity?"

"I believe all my master tells me to believe. Come, will you persuade your mistress to come to Darnley House?"

"I will try, but I can answer for nothing."

"And when shall I have the answer?"

"I will go up at once, and see what I can do."

"Well, go up; I will wait. But, one word, you know that your fortune and your life hangs on your answer?"

"I know it."

"That will do. Go and get the horses ready?"

"Do not be in too great a hurry."

"Bah! I am sure of the answer; a woman is never cruel to a prince."

"I fancy that might happen sometimes."

"Yes, but very rarely."

While Cuthbert went up, Courtney proceeded to the stables, without feeling any doubt as to the result.

"Well!" said Grace, on seeing Cuthbert.

"Well, madam, the Pretender has seen you."

"And——"

"And he says he loves you."

"Loves me? You are mad, Cuthbert!"

"No, I tell you that he—that man—that wretch Courtney, told me so."

"But then he recognised me?"

"If he had, do you think that Courtney would have dared to present himself, and talk to you of love in the prince's name? No, he did not recognise you."

"Yes, you must be right Cuthbert. So many things have passed during the last year through his infernal brain, that he has forgotten me. Let us follow this man."

"But this man will recognise you?"

"Why should his memory be better than his master's?"

"Oh! it is his business to remember, while it is the Pretender's to forget. How could he live, if he did not forget? But Courtney will not have forgotten; he will recognise you, and denounce you as an avenging shade."

"Cuthbert, I thought I told you I had a mask, and that you told me you had a knife?"

"It is true, madam, and I begin to think that Providence is assisting us to punish the wicked."

Then, calling Courtney from the top of the staircase,

"Sir," said he, "my mistress thanks Mr. Fairleigh for having provided thus for her safety, and accepts with gratitude your obliging offer."

"It is well," said Courtney; "the horses are ready."

"Come, madam, come," said Cuthbert, offering his arm to Grace.

Courtney waited at the foot or the staircase, lantern in hand, all anxiety to see the lady.

"The devil!" muttered he, "she wears a mask; but between this and Darnley house the silk cords will either wear out or be cut."

They set off.

Courtney affected the most perfect equality with Cuthbert, and showed to Grace the profoundest respect.

But this respect was very interested; indeed, to hold the stirrups of a woman when she mounts or dismounts, to watch each of her movements with solicitude, to let slip no occasion of picking up her glove, is the business either of a lover, a servant, or a spy.

In touching Grace's glove, Courtney saw her hand, in clasping her cloak he peeped under her mask, and always did his utmost to see that face which the Pretender had not been able to recognize, but which he hoped to recognize himself.

But Courtney had to deal with one as skilful as himself.

Cuthbert claimed to perform his ordinary services for Grace, and seemed jealous of Courtney, while Grace herself, without appearing to have any suspicions, begged Courtney not to interfere with the services which her old attendant was accustomed to render to her.

Courtney was then reduced to hoping for rain or sun to make her remove her mask; but neither rain or sun had any effect, and whenever they stopped Grace took her meals in her own room.

Courtney tried to look through the key-holes, but Grace always sat with her back to the door. He tried to peep through the windows, but there were always thick curtains drawn, or if none were there, cloaks were hung up to supply their place. Neither questions, nor attempts at corruption succeeded with Cuthbert, who always declared that his mistress's will was his.

"But these precautions then are only taken on my account?" said Courtney.

"No, for everybody."

"But the Pretender saw her; she was not hidden then.".

"Pure chance; but it is just because he did see her, that she is more careful than ever."

Days passed on, and they were nearing their destination; but Courtney's curiosity had not been gratified.

Already Yorkshire appeared to the eyes of the travellers.

Courtney began to lose patience, and the bad passions of his nature to gain the ascendant. He began to suspect some secret under all this mystery.

One day he remained a little behind with Cuthbert, and renewed his attempts at seduction, which Cuthbert repulsed as usual.

"But," said Courtney, "some day or other I must see your mistress."

"Doubtless," said Cuthbert, "but that will be when she likes, and not when you like."

"But if I employ force?"

"Try," said Cuthbert, while a lightning glance which he could not repress shot from his eyes.

Courtney tried to laugh.

"What a fool I am," said he. "What does it matter to me who she is? She is the same person whom the prince saw!"

"Certainly."

"And whom he told me to bring to Darnley House?"

"Yes."

"Well, that is all that is necessary. It is not I who am in love with her, it is the prince, and provided that you do not seek to escape or fly——"

"Do we appear to wish to do so?"

"No."

"And she so little desires to do so, that were you not here we should continue our way to Darnley House; if the Pretender wishes to see us, we also wish to see him."

"That is capital," said Courtney. "Would your mistress like to rest here a little while?" continued he, pointing to an inn on the road.

"You know," said Cuthbert, "that my mistress never stops except in towns."

"Well, I, who have made no such vow, will stop here a moment; ride on, and I will follow."

Cuthbert rejoined Grace.

"What was he saying?" asked she.

"He expressed his constant desire——"

"To see me?"

"Yes."

Grace smiled.

"He is furious," continued Cuthbert.

"He shall not see me; of that I am determined."

"But once we are at Darnley House, must he not see your face?"

"What matter, if the discovery comes too late? Besides, the Pretender did not recognise me."

"No, but his follower will. All those mysteries which have so annoyed Courtney for eight days had not existed for the prince; they had not excited his curiosity or awakened his souvenirs, while for a week Courtney has been seeking, imagining, suspecting; your face will strike as a memory fully awakened, and he will know you at once."

At this moment they were interrupted by Courtney, who had taken a cross road, and came suddenly upon them, in the hope of over-hearing some words of their conversation.

The sudden silence which followed his arrival, proved to him that he was in the way, and he therefore rode behind them.

He instinctively feared something, as Cuthbert had said, but his floating conjectures never for an instant approached the truth.

From this moment his plans were fixed, and in order to execute them the better, he changed his conduct, and showed himself the most accommodating and joyous companion possible during the rest of the day.

Cuthbert remarked this change not without anxiety.

The next day they started early, and at noon they were forced to stop to rest their horses.

At two o'clock they set off again, and went on without stopping until four. A great forest was visible in the distance.

It might have been about six o'clock in the evening when they entered the forest, and after half an hour's journey the sun began to go down.

A high wind whirled about the leaves, and carried them towards a lake, along the shore of which the travellers were journeying. Grace rode in the middle, Courtney on the right, and Cuthbert on the left. No other human being was visible under the sombre arches of the trees.

From the long extent of the road one might have thought it one of those enchanted forests, under whose shade nothing can live, had it not been for the hoarse howling of the wolves waking up at the approach of night.

All at one Grace felt that her saddle, which had been put on by Courtney, was slipping.

She called Cuthbert, who jumped down, and began to tighten the girths.

At this moment Courtney approached Grace, and while she was occupied cut the string of silk which fastened her mask.

Before she divined the movement, or had time to put up her hand, Courtney seized the mask, and looked full at her.

The eyes of these two people met with a look so terrible that no one could have said which looked most pale and menacing.

Courtney let both the dagger and the mask fall, and clasping his hands, cried,

"Heavens and earth ! Grace Dashwood !"

"It is a name which you shall repeat no more," cried Cuthbert, seizing him by the girdle and dragging him from his horse.

Both rolled on the ground together, and Courtney stretched out his hand to reach his dagger.

"No, Courtney, no," said Cuthbert, placing his knee on his breast.

"Cuthbert," cried Courtney. "Oh, I am a dead man !"

"That is not yet true, but will be in a moment," cried Cuthbert, and drawing his knife he plunged the whole blade into the throat of the secretary.

Grace, with haggard eyes, half turned on her saddle, and leaning on the pommel shuddering, but pitiless, had not turned her head away from this terrible spectacle.

However, when she saw the blood spirt out from the wound, she fell from her horse as though she were dead.

Cuthbert did not occupy himself with her at that terrible moment, but searched Courtney, took from him the two rouleaux of gold, then tied a stone to the neck of the corpse, and threw it into the lake.

He then washed his hands in the water, took in his arms Grace, who was still unconscious, and placed her again on her horse.

That of Courtney, frightened by the howling of the wolves, which began to draw nearer, had fled into the woods.

When Grace recovered herself she and Cuthbert, without exchanging a single word, continued their route towards Darnley House.

On reaching their destinations they reconnoitred the mansion with the object of discovering how best to obtain access to the Pretender.

They were saved the trouble of much manœuvring, for the Pretender met them on the very threshold.

Regarding the prince as the destroyer, not only of her uncle, for whom she had possessed no affection whatever, but also as the destroyer of friends whom she had loved, and of the innocent and helpless family of Cuthbert, Grace Dashwood gazed at him with a heart brimful of hate.

But the suddenness of his appearance overwhelmed her, and prevented her accomplishing at once the object of her long and weary mission.

"Madam," said the Pretender, "information as to the object of your pursuit has reached me. You have come hither to destroy me. I shall be able to prove to you my innocence. One of the assassins whom you sought has already fallen by Cuthbert's hand. The other, whose right hand was cut off by Jack Tyrrell when defending his wife, is a friend, not to me, but to the king. That my secretary was in league with him I have discovered by the confession of an accomplice—a confession which will prove to you my innocence and the necessity of a search elsewhere. Allow me, madam, to bid you welcome to Darnley House."

With these words he offered his arm, and led her beneath the high porch into the old building.

Here, in the web spread for her by this strange man who loved her in so strange a manner, we must leave her for a time, and turn to another personage in our story doomed to achieve his hideous purpose in a manner he little suspected.

BOOK IV.

THE HEADSMAN'S DAUGHTER.

CHAPTER I.

THE MURDER IN THE WOOD.

JONATHAN RASPER, amid all his knavish transactions, had found time to fall in love. The object of his affection was far above him in rank ; but from among his numerous thievings he had picked up enough money to make a pretty good display before his fair one.

Ellen Greenlay was the daughter of a rich farmer who had pitched upon one of two officers from the neighbouring garrison as the future husband of his only daughter and heiress.

With these two officers Ellen used to flirt and amuse herself a little, but somehow or another she had taken an unaccountable fancy to the tall lanky youth who had inherited so much of his father's knavery and craft.

One evening, soon after the attack of Brandon upon Moonlight Jack and Lucien Fairleigh, he passed into a little road just behind the farm where he had arranged to meet his fair one.

The farm of Mr. Greenlay was situated about a mile from the town of Uxbridge, and the wood lay half way between.

For some time Jonathan sat there on a fallen tree amusing himself by cutting his name with an ivory clasped knife, which had been given him by one of his friends, and wondering by what means he could mollify the heart of the farmer who was so inveterate against him.

An hour had thus elapsed when suddenly he was roused from his dream of bliss by tones of loud and vehement contention at no great distance from the elm.

Prompted by his natural cowardice he concealed himself behind the tree, from whence he was enabled to discern his two military rivals, out of uniform, approaching the elm, and indicating by furious tones and gestures feelings of mutual and deadly animosity.

Jonathan, whose sense of the awkwardness of his situation was increased by his timidity, fancied that he should be discovered listening to their conversation, and, retreating unobserved into the wood, he had gained the high road before he recollected that he had left his knife on the seat of turf.

Ashamed of his cowardice, he determined to return and claim it in the event of its having been discovered and taken by one of the contending parties.

He was solicitous also to complete the intended cipher on the bark of the elm while there was light enough for his purpose.

Concluding that his angry rivals had walked on in another direction, he hastily retraced his steps.

Looking over some tall evergreen shrubs, which were separated by a footpath from the elm, he observed that the turf seat was unoccupied.

Supposing, from the total silence, that the hostile youths had quitted the grove, he emerged from the evergreens with confidence, and approached the tree, but recoiled in sudden horror as he almost stepped upon the body of one of his rivals, who lay dead on his back, while the blood was issuing in torrents from a wound in his throat, inflicted by the knife given him by his friend Eustace, the remarkable handle of which protruded from the deep incision.

His blood froze as he gazed on this spectacle, and, covering his face with his hands, he stood for some moments over the body in stolid and sickening horror.

Soon, however, his strong aversion to scenes of violence and bloodshed impelled him to rush in headlong precipitation from the fatal spot.

Leaving his knife in the wound, he darted forward through the wood, and fortunately without meeting any one in or near it.

When he reached the high road, the darkness had so much increased as to render his features undistinguishable to the passengers, and, running towards the city, he soon reached the public promenades, where he threw himself upon a bench, exhausted with terror and fatigue.

Looking fearfully around him through the darkness, he endeavoured to collect his reasoning faculties, and immediately the recollection that he had left his knife in the throat of the murdered man flashed across him.

With this fatal weapon were connected many old associations, which now crowded with sickening potency upon his memory.

Again he saw the sarcastic grin with which his friend had said,

"What we most carefully shun is most likely to befall us."

And would not this remarkable knife, too, probably verify the malignant prophecy of its owner?

Forgetful of the improbability that any one had seen in his possession a knife, which, before that evening, he had never used, his senses yielded to an irresistible conviction that this instrument of another's guilt would betray and lead him to the scaffold.

Immediate flight was the only resource which presented itself to his bewildered judgment, and, rising from the bench, he hastened to his lodgings to complete his preparations for departure the following morning.

After a sleepless night, during which he started at every sound with apprehension of a nocturnal visit from the constables, he proceeded at daybreak with a heavy heart to the post-house, where, observing a carrier's waggon on the point of departure for the north, he availed himself of the opportunity to facilitate his escape by putting a few essentials into a cloak bag, and forwarding his heavy trunk by the carrier.

After some delay, of which every moment appeared an age, the coach departed, and when the church towers were lost in distance the goading terrors of the unhappy fugitive yielded for a time to feelings of comparative security.

His apprehensions, however, were renewed by every rising cloud of dust behind the coach, and by every equestrian who followed and passed the vehicle.

Busily did the frenzied fancy of the unhappy youth call up a succession of imaginary terrors, until at dusk the coach stopped at a solitary inn, and Jonathan heard, with new alarm, that there the passengers were to remain the night.

"And here," thought the timid fugitive, "I shall certainly be overtaken and arrested."

A traveller, who arrived soon after the coach, and supped with the passengers, afforded him, however, another chance of escape.

This man was lamenting that at a neighbouring fair he had not been able to sell an excellent horse; and Jonathan, watching the opportunity, concluded the purchase with little bargaining.

Pleading the necessity of going forward on urgent business, he mounted his purchase, and quitted the inn-yard with a heart lightened by the certainty that he should gain a night upon his pursuers.

On the fifth morning he found himself in a fertile district of central England, and considering himself safe from all immediate danger, he pursued his journey more leisurely between the gently swelling hills until the noon-day heat and dusty road made him sensibly feel the want of refreshment.

While gazing around him for some hamlet or cottage to pause at, his attention was caught by sounds of lamentation at no great distance, and a sudden turn in the road revealed to him a prostrate mule, vainly endeavouring to regain his legs, one of which was broken.

A tall boy, in peasant garb, was scratching his head in rustic embarrassment at this dilemma, and near him stood a young and very lovely woman, wringing her hands in perplexity, and lamenting over the unfortunate mule, a remarkably fine animal, and caparisoned with a completeness which indicated the easy circumstances of the owner.

Jonathan immediately stopped his horse, and dismounted to offer his assistance.

The young woman said nothing as he approached, but her beautiful dark eyes appealed to him for aid and counsel with an eloquence which reached his heart in a moment.

Examining the mule, he said, after some consideration,

"There is no hope for the poor animal, and the most humane expedient will be to shoot him as soon as possible. Your side saddle can be strapped on my horse, which shall convey you to the next village, or as much further as you like, if you have no objection to the conveyance."

Expressing her thanks with engaging frankness and cordiality, the fair traveller told him that she was returning from a visit to some relations, and that she was still some miles from her father's house.

She would gladly, she said, avail herself of his kind offer, but insisted that her servant should not kill her favourite mule until she was out of sight and hearing.

Then, turning briskly towards Jonathan, she told him that she was ready to proceed.

Finding all opposition fruitless, Jonathan remounted, and, with the assistance of a servant, the fair unknown was soon seated behind him.

Blushing and laughing at the necessity, she put an arm around his waist to support herself, and then begged him to proceed without delay as she was anxious to reach home before night.

Conversing as they journeyed onward, their communications became every moment more cordial and interesting, and, as Jonathan felt the warm hand of his lovely companion near his heart, he began to feel a soothing sense of gratification which cheered and elevated his perturbed spirits.

He had never before found himself in such near and agreeable relation to a beautiful and lively woman, and, whenever he turned his head to speak or listen, he found the finest black eyes, and the most lovely mouth he had ever seen, within a few inches of his own.

So potent, indeed, was the charm of her looks and her language that he forgot for a time the timid graces and less sparkling beauty of her he had lost for ever, and was insensibly beguiled of all his fears and sorrows as he listened to the lively sallies of this laughter-loving fair one.

Meanwhile they had quitted the cross-road in which he had discovered her, and pursued by her direction the great road from London to the east of England.

Here, however, he remarked with surprise that she invariably drew the large hood of her cloak over her face when any travellers passed them, and his surprise was converted into uneasiness and suspicion when, after commencing the last mile of their journey, she drew the hood entirely over her face, and her conversation, before so animated and flowing, was succeeded by total silence, or by replies so brief and disjointed as to indicate that her thoughts were intensely pre-occupied.

The sun had reached the horizon when they arrived within a short distance of the town before them, and here she suddenly asked her conductor whether he intended to travel further before morning.

Jonathan, hoping to obtain some clue to her name and residence, replied that he was undetermined.

Upon which she advised him to give a night's rest to his jaded horse, and strongly recommended to him an hotel, the name and situation of which she minutely described.

He promised to comply with her recommendations, and immediately, by a prompt and vigorous effort, she threw herself from the horse to the ground.

Hastily arranging her disordered travelling dress, she approached him and clasped his hand in both her own, thanking him, in brief but fervent terms, for the important service he had rendered her.

"And now," added she, in visible embarrassment, as she raised her head, and looked fearfully around, "I have another favour to request. My father would not approve of your accompanying me home, nor must the town gossips see me at this hour with a young man and a stranger; you will, therefore, oblige me by resting your horse here for half-an-hour that I may reach the town before you. Will you do me this favour?" she repeated, with a pleading look.

"I will," replied the disappointed Jonathan.

"Farewell, then," she cordially rejoined, "and may heaven reward your kindness."

Bounding forward with a light and rapid step, she soon disappeared round a sharp angle in the road occasioned by a sudden bend of the adjacent river.

Jonathan, dismounting to relieve his horse, gazed admiringly upon her elastic step and well-turned figure until she was out of sight.

He recollected, with a sigh of regret, the sprightly graces and artless intelligence of her conversation.

Again the sense of his desolate and perilous position smote him.

While thus painfully musing the time she had prescribed elapsed.

Jonathan, remounting, let the bridle fall upon the neck of the exhausted animal, which paced towards the town as deliberately as the unknown fair one could have wished.

At a short distance from the town gate the high road passed under an archway, composing part of a detached house of ancient structure.

On the town side of the arch was a toll bar, at which a boy was stationed, who held out his hat to Jonathan, and demanded a penny.

"For what?" asked Jonathan.

"A long-established toll, sir," said the boy, "and if you have a compassionate heart you will give another to the condemned criminals," he continued, as he pointed to an iron box placed near the house door.

Shuddering at the words, Jonathan threw some copper coins into the box; and, as he hastened forward, endeavoured to banish the unpleasant association of ideas, by fixing his thoughts upon the mysterious fair one.

Suspecting from the pressing manner in which she had recommended a particular hotel to his preference, that if he went there he might possibly see or hear from her in the morning, he proceeded to the "Stag's Head," which proved to be an hotel of third-rate importance, but well suited to his limited means, and recommending itself by an air of cleanliness and comfort.

MOON-LIGHT JACK

OR THE KING OF THE ROAD

The evenings, at this season were cool, and as it would have required some time to heat the parlour, the landlord proposed to him to sit down and take some refreshments in his well-warmed kitchen.

Jonathan complied with this invitation; but not without some apprehension of the presence of strangers; and, stepping into the kitchen, was relieved by the discovery that it was occupied only by servants, who were too busily engaged in preparing supper to take notice of him.

Sitting down in a corner near the fire, the combined effects of a genial warmth and excessive fatigue threw him into a sound sleep which lasted several hours, and would have continued much longer, had he not been roused by the landlord, who told him that his supper had been ready some time

but that he had been unwilling to disturb a slumber so profound.

In fact the repose of the unfortunate fugitive had not for a long time been so continuous and refreshing, so free from painful and menacing visions.

Rising drowsily from his chair he followed the landlord to a table, where a roasted capon and a glass jug of bright wine waited his arrival.

The servants had all retired for the night.

The landlord quitted the kitchen, and Jonathan, busily engaged in dissecting the fowl, thought himself the sole tenant of the spacious apartment, when, looking accidentally towards the fire, he saw, with surprise, that the chair he had just quitted was occupied.

Looking more intently he distinguished a short

No. 27, July 7, 1866.]   Two Numbers and Two Tales every week for One Penny.
THE WORK GIRLS OF LONDON, and THE CRUSADER; OR,
THE WITCH OF FINCHLEY.   Price One Penny.

man, of more than middle age, whose square and sturdy figure was partially concealed by a capacious mantle.

His hair was grey, his forehead seamed with broad wrinkles, and his bushy brows beetled over a set of features stern and massive as if cast in iron.

His eyes were small and deep-set, but of a lustrous black, and Jonathan observed with dismay that they were fixed upon his countenance with a look of searching scrutiny.

It was near midnight, and in the deep silence which reigned through the house, this motionless attitude, and marble fixedness of look, gave to the stranger's appearance a character so appalling that had he not broken the spell by stooping to light his pipe, the excited Jonathan would ere long have thought him an unearthly object.

The stranger now quitted his seat by the fire, took from a table near him a jug full of wine, and approached the wondering Jonathan.

"With your leave, my good sir," he began, "I will take a chair by your table. A little friendly gossip is the best of all seasoning to a glass of wine."

Without waiting for a reply the old man seated himself directly opposite Jonathan, and again fixed a scrutinizing gaze upon his countenance.

The conscious fugitive, who felt a growing and unaccountable dread of this singular intruder, muttered a brief assent, and continued to eat his supper in silent but obvious embarrassment.

Stealing now and then a timid look at the stranger, but hastily withdrawing his furtive glances as he felt the beams of the old man's small and vivid eyes penetrating his very soul.

He observed that the features of his tormentor were cast in a vulgar mould, but his gaze was widely different from that of clownish curiosity: and there was in his deportment a stern and steady self-possession which suggested to the alarmed Jonathan a suspicion that he was an agent of the police, who had probably tracked him through the cross-roads he had traversed in his flight.

The rich colour of his cheeks turned to an ashy paleness at this appalling conjecture, and, leaving his supper unfinished, he rose abruptly from the table to quit the room, when the old man, starting suddenly from his chair, seized the shaking hand of Jonathan, and, looking cautiously round him, said in subdued but impressive tones,

"It is not accident, young man, which brings us together at this hour. I came in while you were asleep, and begged the landlord would not awaken you, that I might say a few words to you in confidence after the servants had gone to bed."

"To me?" exclaimed Jonathan, in anxious wonder.

"Hush!" said the old man, again looking round the kitchen. "My object is to give you a friendly warning; for, if I am not for the first time mistaken in these matters, you are menaced with a formidable danger."

"Danger?" repeated Jonathan, in a voice which was scarcely audible.

"And have you not good reason to expect this danger?" continued the stranger. "Your sudden paleness tells me that you know it. I am an old man, and my life has been a rough pilgrimage: but I have still a warm heart, and can make large allowances for the headlong impetuosities which too often plunge a young man into crime. You

may safely trust me," he continued, placing his hand upon his heart, "in whose bosom the confessions of many hapless fugitives repose, and will repose, so long as life beats in my pulses. I betray no man who confides in me, were he even stained with blood."

Pausing a little, he fixed a keenly searching look upon the shrinking youth, and then whispered in his ear,

"Young man, you have *murder* on your conscience!"

"It is false, old man!" he cried: "I swear I am innocent of this crime!"

"I shall rejoice to learn that I am mistaken," replied the old man, with evident gratification, as again he fixed his searching orbs upon Jonathan. "If you are innocent, it will be all the better for both of us; but," he continued, after a hasty look around him, "the danger I alluded to still hangs over your head; I trust, however, that I shall be able to shield you from it."

Jonathan, too much alarmed to reply, looked at him doubtingly.

"I will deal candidly with you," resumed the old man, after a pause of reflection. "When you rode by my house this evening——"

"Who and what are you?" exclaimed Jonathan, in new astonishment.

"Have a little patience, young man," replied the stranger, while his iron features relaxed into a good-natured smile. "Do you recollect the tall archway under an old house, where a toll of a penny was demanded from you? That house is mine, and I was sitting by the window, when you threw alms into the box for the condemned criminals. Had you then looked upward you would have seen a naked sword and a bright axe suspended over your head."

At these words Jonathan shuddered, and involuntarily withdrew a few paces from his companion.

"I see by your flinching," sternly resumed the old man, "that you guess who is before you. You are right, young man, I am the town executioner, but an honest man withal, and well inclined to render you essential service. Now mark me! When you stopped beneath the broad blade, it quivered, and jarred against the axe. Whoever is thus greeted by the headsman's sword is inevitably doomed to come in contact with it. I heard the boding jar, which every executioner in England well knows how to interpret, and I immediately determined to follow and warn you."

The unhappy Jonathan, who had listened in dismay to this strange communication, now yielded to a sense of ungovernable terror.

Covering with both his hands his pallid face, he exclaimed, in nameless agony,

"Oh, mercy! mercy!"

"Hah!" ejaculated the headsman, sternly; "have I then roused your sleeping conscience? However, whether you conclude to open or shut your heart is now immaterial. In either case I will never betray you: for accusation and judgment belong not to my office. Profit, therefore, as you best may, by my well-intentioned warning. Alas! alas!" he muttered between his closed teeth, "that one so young should dip his hands in blood!"

"I swear," exclaimed Jonathan, with trembling voice, "I am innocent of this murder; and yet, so disastrous is my destiny, that I am beset with peril and suspicion. You are an utter stranger to me, but you appear to have benevolence and worldly wisdom. Listen to my tale, and then, in mercy, give me aid and counsel."

He now unfolded to the executioner the extraordinary chain of circumstances which had compelled him to seek security in flight, and told his tale of trials with a pretended simplicity and artlessness, which carried with it an irresistible conviction of his innocence.

The rigid features of the headsman gradually relaxed, as he listened, into a cheerful and even cordial expression.

Then warmly grasping the hand of Jonathan, as he concluded, he said,

"Well, well; I see how it is. In my profession we learn to read human nature. I will yet save you from this peril; and, indeed, had you killed your rival in sudden quarrel, I would have done as much for you, for I well know that sudden wrath has made many a good man blood-guilty. There was certainly some danger of your being implicated by the singular circumstances you have detailed; but the real and formidable peril has grown out of your flight. That was a dreadful blunder, young man; but I see no reason for despair. It's true, the broad blade has denounced you, and my grandfather, and father, as well as myself have traced criminals by its guidance; but I trust that the sword will speak alike to its master and its victim. You have yet to learn, young man, that in this life every man is either an anvil or a hammer; a tool or a victim; and that he who boldly grasps the blade will never be its victim. Briefly, then, I feel a regard for you. I have no sons, but I have a young and lovely daughter. Marry her, and I will adopt you as my successor. You will then fulfil your destiny by coming in contact with the sword, and if you clutch it firmly, I will pledge myself that you will never die by it."

At this strange proposal Jonathan started to his feet with pretended abhorrence.

"Hold!" continued the headsman, coolly. "The night is long and favourable to reflection. Bestow a full and fair consideration on my proposal, and recollect that your neck is in peril, and that all your prospects in life are blasted; that my offer of a safe asylum and competent support can alone save you from despair and destruction. The sword has sent you a helper in the hour of need, and if you reject the friendly warning, you will soon discover that the consciousness of innocence will not protect a blushing and irresolute fugitive from the proverbial ubiquity and prompt severity of the police."

The headsman now emptied his glass, and, with a friendly nod, left the kitchen.

Soon after his departure the landlord appeared with a night-lamp, and conducted Jonathan to his apartment.

Without undressing, the youth extinguished the lamp, hoping that the darkness would accelerate the approach of sleep, and of that oblivion which accompanies it.

Vain, however, for some hours was every attempt to lull his senses into forgetfulness.

The terrible proposal of the old man haunted him incessantly.

"I become an——" he muttered, but could never utter the word.

The cowardice, which had been a fertile source of difficulty to him through his life, had been increased tenfold by recent calamities.

He felt that he should never have resolution to grasp the sword which was to save him from being numbered with its victims.

The broken slumber, into which he fell before morning, was haunted by bodings, forms and tragic incidents.

The sword, the axe, the scaffold, and the rack flitted around him in quick succession, and seemed to close every avenue of escape.

He awoke from these visions of horror at daybreak, and left his bed as wearied in body, and as irresolute in mind as when he entered it.

Dreading alike a renewal of the executioner's proposal, and the risk of being arrested and tried for murder, he saw no alternative but flight—immediate flight beyond the bounds of England.

While pondering over the best means of accomplishing this non-settled purpose, the tin weathercock upon the roof of his bed-room creaked in the morning breeze.

Jonathan, to whose excited fancy the headsman's sword was ever present, thought he heard it jar against the axe, and started in sudden terror.

"Whither shall I fly?" he exclaimed, while tears of agony rolled down his cheeks. "Where find a refuge from the sword of justice? Alas! my doom is fixed and unalterable. Anvil or hammer I must be, and I have not courage to become either."

Again the weathercock creaked above him, and more intelligibly than before.

Jonathan, discovering the simple cause of his terrors, rallied his drooping spirits and hastened downstairs to order his horse, that he might leave the hotel and the town before the promised visit of the fearful headsman.

Notwithstanding his urgency he found his departure unaccountably delayed.

The servants were not visible, and the landlord, insisting that he should take a warm breakfast before his departure, was so dilatory in preparing it that a full hour elapsed before Jonathan rode out of the stable-yard.

His officious host then persisted in sending a boy to show him the nearest way to the town gate, and the impatient traveller, who would gladly have declined the offer, found himself obliged to submit.

His guide accompanied him to the extremity of the small suburb beyond the eastern gate and quitted him, while Jonathan, whose ever ready apprehensions had been roused by the tenacious civility of the landlord, rode slowly forward, looking round occasionally at his returning guide, and determining to take the first cross road he could find.

A little further on he discovered the entrance of a narrow lane shaded by a double row of lofty chestnut trees, and, as he turned towards it his horse's head, he saw the old man, whose promised visit he was endeavouring to escape, issuing from the lane on horseback.

"I guessed as much," said the headsman, smiling, as he rode up to the startled fugitive; "I knew you would try to escape me, but I cannot consent that you should thus run headlong into certain destruction. Fear not that I shall either repeat or allude to my last night's proposal; my sole object is your immediate protection at this critical period when you are doubtless tracked in all directions by the bloodhounds of the police. At the frontiers you will inevitably be stopped and identified, but under my roof you will be safe from all pursuit and suspicion. I live secluded from the world, I have no visitors, and your presence will not be suspected by any one ; in a few weeks the heat of pursuit will abate, and you may then take your departure with renewed courage and confidence."

"Courage and confidence!" repeated the cowardly dastard to himself, "would I had either."

The good sense, however, of the old man's advice was so obvious that he determined to avail himself of so desirable an offer.

Pressing his hand with apparent sincerity, he said,

"I will accompany you. May Heaven reward you for your kindness."

"We must return by the road I came," said the headsman, turning his horse ; "it will take us outside the town to my house, and at this hour we shall arrive there unperceived. Your landlord, who is under obligations to me, sent you this road at my request ; he supposes that you are my distant relative, and that, unwilling to appear in public with the executioner, you had made an appointment with me for this early hour on your way homeward."

After a ride of half-an-hour through the shady lanes which skirted the ramparts they reached the back entrance of the building before mentioned, and Jonathan entered this singular sanctuary with emotions not easily described.

The old headsman was in high spirits, and the blunt but genuine kindness and cordiality of his manners soon removed from the mind of his guest every lurking suspicion that some treachery was intended.

The table was promptly covered with an excellent breakfast, and the old man sent a message to his daughter requesting that she would bring a bottle of the best wine in the cellar.

Jonathan fixed his eyes on the door in shrinking anticipation.

He suspected new attempts to ensnare him to the headsman's purpose, and, notwithstanding his firm determination to resist them, he recoiled with his usual cowardice from the anticipated conflict.

How widely different were his emotions when the door opened and his lovely travelling companion, whom, in the terrors of the past night he had forgotten, entered in blushing embarrassment with the bottle of wine.

In a tumult of mingled apprehension and delight, he started from his chair, but the cordial greeting he intended was checked by a significant wink from the lively fair one as she passed behind her father to the table.

It was obvious to Jonathan that she wished to conceal their previous acquaintance, and, with a silent bow, he resumed his seat, while the smiling maid, whom her father introduced to his guest by the name of Geraldine, took a chair between them, and the conversation soon became general and exhilarating.

The continued fever of apprehension which had almost unhinged the reason of the miserable Jonathan, now rapidly subsided.

The cordial hospitality of the old headsman soon made him feel at home, in an abode which he had once contemplated with horror, while the artless attentions and fascinating vivacity of the pretty Geraldine soon wove around him a magic spell, and invested the chambers of her father's antique mansion with all the splendours of Aladdin's palace.

Motherless from the age of fourteen, and secluded by her father's vocation from all society save occasional intercourse with relatives of the same degraded caste, the headsman's daughter had been early accustomed to rely upon her own resources.

The intercourse of Jonathan and Geraldine we need not describe minutely.

We need only say that he forgot the girl who had been, as it were, one cause of his flight, and surrendered all his sympathies to his fair companion before he was aware of the consequences which must inevitably follow, while she also seemed influenced by some unaccountable attraction.

Some weeks after his arrival in this asylum, the headsman had advised him to prolong his stay until all danger of pursuit was over, and the fears of the fugitive soon gave way to cheering sensations of security and confidence.

To lovers the present is everything.

Jonathan forgot alike the trying past and the menacing future.

Weeks and months flitted past unobserved by the youthful pair, while the crafty headsman, who had silently watched their growing intelligence, crowed in secret over the now certain success of his stratagem.

Several months had thus elapsed, and the old man, after ascertaining from his daughter that the affections of Jonathan were irredeemably plighted, took an opportunity to address him one morning as soon as Geraldine had quitted the breakfast-room.

"I think it is high time, young man," he said, smiling, "that you should proceed to business. Come along with me into my workshop."

Jonathan looked at him in silent wonder, but unhesitatingly followed him into the capacious cellar, where the old man unlocked a door which his guest had never before observed.

Jonathan entered with his conductor ; but started back in dismay as he saw a number of executioners' swords and axes hanging round the walls of a low vaulted room, in the centre of which several cabbage heads were fixed with pegs upon an oblong block of wood.

The headsman took one of the swords from the wall, drew it from the scabbard, carefully wiped the glittering blade, and then offered it to Jonathan.

"Now, my son," he said, "try your strength upon these cabbage heads. It is easy work, and requires nothing but a steady hand."

"Good lord ! you cannot be in earnest !" exclaimed Jonathan, retreating from him in deadly terror.

"Not in earnest?" rejoined the headsman, sternly. "I consider your compliance as a matter of course. You love my daughter—you have won her affections, and surely, Jonathan, you will not play her false ?"

"Not I," exclaimed Jonathan. "I seek no greater happiness than to become her husband."

"I offered her to you, my son.!" said the other, with returning kindness ; "but you did not like the conditions, and declined her. You have, since, without my permission, sought and won her affections, and you have no right to flinch from the implied consequences. It is high time to come to a conclusion, and to apply yourself in good faith to the only pursuit through which you can ever obtain my Geraldine."

"The only one ?" repeated Jonathan. "I have, it is true, abandoned everything for your daughter's sake ; but I am young, and may find some employment which will maintain a wife and family."

"And my daughter?" exclaimed the headsman, with loud and bitter emphasis. "What is to become of *her?* If even you could step back within the pale of society, *she* would for ever be excluded; but you have neither moral courage nor animal bravery enough for any worldly pursuit. Your original station in society is irrecoverably gone, and if you attempt to leave this safe asylum, the sword of justice will face you at every turn. No, no, Jonathan, I love my son-in-law too well to expose him to such imminent and deadly peril. There," he continued, "read that paper; perhaps that will bring you to your senses."

With these words, which struck like a wintry chill into the heart of Jonathan, he took an old newspaper from his pocket.

The fugitive received it with a shaking hand, and read a judicial 'summons from the authorities of S—— seeking intelligence of one who had, on a certain day, unaccountably disappeared.

His Christian and surname, with an accurate description of his dress and person, were appended.

Glancing fearfully down the pages, he distinguished some particulars of a murder.

His sight grew dim with terror.

After a vain attempt to read further, he dropped the fatal document, and reeled back breathless, and almost fainting against the wall.

"He is the very man," muttered the headsman, whose keen eye had been intently fixed upon him during the perusal. "I never asked your real name, young man," he continued; "but now I know it. Your terrors would betray it to a child. How, then, are you without fortitude to face the common evils of life, and bearing in every feature a betrayer, to escape the giant grasp of the police? Believe me, Jonathan, here and here only will you find safety, support, and happiness."

The headsman proceeded then to draw a glowing picture of the benefits he now received from his employment, of all of which he would be deprived if he could find no one to follow his vocation; and he then described to him the terrible risk he would run by placing himself in the power of the authorities.

The appalling alternatives held out to Jonathan by the politic headsman, and the consciousness of his own inability either to escape the police, or to steer his way successfully through the shoals and quicksands of life, rendered him incapable of either argument or reply.

He had for some months been cut off from all that freedom has to bestow.

He had neither relations or friends on whose interposition he could rely.

He recollected, with agony, that every heart beyond the limits of his present home was steeled against him.

That every hand was ready to seize and betray him.

Should he quit this safe asylum, and even establish his innocence of the imputed murder, his cowardice would make him a prey to every kind of misery and fear.

His despair and timidity worked upon him strongly; the headsman overpowered him by continual arguments, the beauty of the fair Geraldine overwhelmed him in another way, and, at length, therefore, he yielded to the old man's proposal, and commenced training for his terrible vocation.

The time passed wretchedly for the coward who had thus dropped into the jaws of the serpent.

Meanwhile, the old man had quietly made every requisite preparation, and, a month after the assent of Jonathan to his proposal, the lovers were united.

The official appointment of Jonathan, as adopted successor to the headsman, took place some days before the marriage, and it was stipulated by the town authorities that, on the next ensuing condemnation of a criminal to death, he should prove, on the scaffold, his competency to succeed the executioner.

For many months after this appointment, every arrival of a criminal in the town prison struck terror into the heart of Jonathan.

He enjoyed, however, for some time, domestic happiness, disturbed only by apprehensions which he could never subdue, that sooner or later the evil he so much dreaded would certainly befal him.

His father-in-law received one morning at breakfast an order from the town authorities to repair early on the following day to a city at ten miles' distance, and there to behead a criminal whose execution had been delayed by the illness of the resident headsman.

At this unexpected intelligence the features of Jonathan were blanched with terror, but the iron visage of the old executioner betrayed not the slightest sign of emotion.

Regardless of the terrors of his son-in-law, he viewed this unexpected summons as a fortunate incident, and maintained that any unskilfulness in decapitation would be of less importance at a distance than in his native town.

He regarded, also, this brief summons as more favourable to Jonathan's success than a longer fore-knowledge; and urged, in strong and decisive terms, the necessity of submission to the call of duty.

The blood of Jonathan froze in his veins as he listened, but he acquiesced, as usual, in timid silence.

In the afternoon he yielded to the old man's wish, that he should give what the headsman termed a master proof of his skill in the science of decapitation, and with a cold sweat on his brow severed a number of cabbage heads to the satisfaction of his teacher.

Meanwhile, the sympathising but energetic Geraldine prepared a palatable meal, and endeavoured, more successfully than her uncompromising parent, to sustain and cheer the drooping spirits of her husband.

She could not, however, always repress her starting tears; and, as the night approached, even the firm nature of the old headsman betrayed symptoms of growing anxiety, notwithstanding his endeavours to exhilarate himself by deep potations of his favourite wine.

After a night of wearying vigilance and internal conflict, the miserable Jonathan entered at daybreak the vehicle which awaited him and his father-in-law under the arched gateway.

With a view to prevent his trembling substitute from witnessing all the preparations for the approaching catastrophe, the old man so measured his progress as to enter the city a few minutes before the appointed hour, and drove immediately to the scene of action without pausing at the church, to attend, as customary, the service then performing in presence of the criminal.

Soon after their arrival the melancholy procession approached, and Jonathan, unable to face the criminal, turned hastily away, ascended the ladder with unsteady steps, and concealed himself behind the massive person of the old headsman, as the victim of offended justice, with a firm and measured step, mounted the scaffold.

The old man felt for his shrinking son-in-law, but kept a stern eye upon him, in hopes to counteract the disabling effects of his rising agony.

When, however, the decisive moment approached, he whispered to him, encouragingly,

"Be a man, Jonathan. Beware of looking at the criminal before you strike; but when his head is lifted look him boldly in the face, or the people will doubt your courage."

Jonathan fixed on him a vacant stare, but these kindly meant instructions reached not his inward ear.

At this moment, his attention was caught by the admiring comments of the crowd upon the courageous bearing, and firm, unflinching features of the criminal.

Roused by these exclamations to a stinging consciousness of his own unmanly timidity, he made a powerful effort, and rallied his expiring energies into a temporary life and action.

The headsman now approached him with the broad axe, and whispered,

"Courage, my son! 'tis nothing but a cabbage head."

With a desperate effort, Jonathan seized the weapon, fixed his dim gaze upon the white neck of the criminal, and, guided more by long practice than by any estimate of place and distance, he struck the death stroke.

The head fell upon the hollow flooring of the scaffold with an appalling bounce, which petrified the unfortunate executioner.

This terror for some moments deprived him of all volition, and he stood in passive stupor, gazing wildly upon the blood which streamed in torrents from the headless trunk.

Immediately, however, his father-in-law approached him, with a whisper,

"Admirably done, my son! I give you joy! But recollect my warning, and look boldly at your work, or the mob will hoot you, as a craven headsman, from the scaffold."

The old man was obliged to repeat his admonition before it reached the senses of his unconscious son-in-law.

Long accustomed to quiet unresisting obedience, Jonathan slowly raised his eyes at the moment when the executioner's assistant, after showing the criminal's head to the multitude, turned round and held out to him the bleeding and ghastly object.

Gracious heavens! what were his feelings, when he encountered a well-known face, when he saw the yellow, pock-marked visage of his cousin Ned, whose widely opened milky blue eyes were fixed upon him in the glassy dim and vacant stare of death?

Paralysed with sudden and overwhelming horror, he fell senseless into the arms of the headsman, who had watched this critical moment, and, with ready self-possession, loudly attributed to recent illness an incident so puzzling to the spectators.

He succeeded ere long in rousing Jonathan to an imperfect sense of his critical situation, and, supporting his tottering frame, led him to the house of the sick executioner.

For an hour after their arrival the unhappy youth sat mute and motionless, the living image of despair.

Agony in him had passed its wildest paroxysm

and settled down into a blind and mechanical unconsciousness.

The old man, who began to suspect some extradinary reason for emotion so excessive compelled him to swallow several glasses of wine, and anxiously besought him to explain the cause of his impassioned deportment.

It was long, however, before the disconsolate Jonathan regained the power of utterance.

At length a burst of tears relieved him.

"I knew him!" he began, in a voice broken by convulsive sobs. "He was once my greatest friend. Oh! my father! there is no hope for me! I am a doomed man—a murderer! He stands before me ever, and demands my blood in atonement for his destruction. How can I justify such guilt? I never knew his crime. I cannot even fancy him a criminal; but I well remember that he loved and cherished me. Away, my father, if you love me, to the judges! I must know his crime, or the pangs I feel will never depart from me."

The executioner, in whose stern and inflexible nature feelings of pity, and even of repentance, were now at work, hastened to obtain some information, and returned in half an hour with indications of anxiety and doubt, too obvious to escape Jonathan, who exclaimed,

"For heaven's sake tell me all! I must know it sooner or later. Your anxiety prepares me for the worst. If you, a man of iron, are thus shaken——"

"I! nonsense!" retorted the old man, somewhat disconcerted. "The fellow was a notorious villain, and was executed for two murders."

Jonathan, relieved rather by this intelligence, began to breathe more freely, and gazed upon the headsman with looks which sought for further explanation.

"Jonathan," continued the old man, fixing upon him his stern and searching look, "when you told me the tale of your calamities, did you tell me all? Had you no reservation?"

"None, father, by all I hold most sacred," replied Jonathan, with emphatic earnestness.

"One of the crimes of the man you have beheaded," resumed the headsman, "is connected with your story. He is said to have slain the officer in whose murder you thought yourself implicated by suspicious appearances."

"He?" exclaimed Jonathan, gasping with horror. "No, he did not slay him! I have beheaded an innocent man, and the remembrance will cleave to me like a curse!"

"Can you prove that he had no share in that murder?" now sternly demanded the headsman, whose suspicions had been roused by Jonathan's acknowledgment of former intimacy with Ned.

"I can swear to his innocence of that murder," vehemently replied Jonathan, whose energies rose with his excitement. "And the other crime?" he eagerly continued. "In mercy, father, tell me whom else he is said to have murdered?"

"*Yourself!*" said the old man, turning pale, as he anticipated the effect of this communication; "if the name inserted in the judicial summons was really yours."

For some moments Jonathan gazed upon him in speechless despair.

His eyes became fixed and glassy.

His jaw dropped, and he would have fallen from the chair, had not the old man supported him.

The headsman looked with anxious and growing perplexity upon his unfortunate victim.

"After all," he muttered, "he is my daughter's husband, and a good husband. I forced him to the task, and must, if possible, save him from the consequences."

By an abundant application of cold water to the face of Jonathan, he succeeded at length in restoring him to consciousness.

The miserable youth opened his eyes, and when in some measure tranquillised, the headsman asked him soothingly, "if he felt sufficiently collected to listen to him?"

"Yes, father, I am," he replied, with an effort.

"Recollect, then, my son," continued the old man, "that you are under the assured protection of the sword; and that you may open your heart to me without fear of consequences. Say, then, in the first place, who are you?"

"I am no other, father," answered Jonathan, with energy, "than I have already acknowledged to you, and I was the cousin of the man whose blood I have shed upon the scaffold. But I must and will have clear proof of every crime imputed to him," he exclaimed, in wild emotion. "Again, I see his large dim eyes fixed on me in reproach, and if you cannot give me evidence that he deserved his fate, my remorse will goad me on to suicide or madness."

It was now evident to the old man that the suspicions he had founded on Jonathan's acknowledged intimacy with Edward Forsyth were groundless.

He went to bed that night resolved on the next day to obtain every information respecting the criminal.

He little knew how his son-in-law would be engaged on that night.

His game was now played out.

He had obtained possession of the headsman's lovely daughter.

It was indeed a marriage; but what cared he for that?

He had discovered another fact.

The headsman was wealthy.

Hidden away in his chamber were bags of gold.

For a time Jonathan Rasper had consented willingly to abide in this part of England, where the axe was used as often as the cord, and to fulfil the hideous office of public executioner.

But now there was no object in remaining.

His own innocence of the crime, from the consequences of which he had fled, was now clearly established.

He had begun to tire of the person of his lovely young wife.

He had a chance of obtaining a large sum of gold, and flying to a distant part.

All these considerations weighed heavily with him.

Of course he expected impunity.

In those lawless days crime was only punished severely from a spirit of vengeance.

Every town was an Alsatia, for, in the absence of anything like telegrams, penny posts, steam engines and newspapers, one half of England knew not how the other half lived.

So, on this night he determined to quit the house, taking with him the headsman's gold, and, proceeding to the neighbourhood which he had quitted so abruptly, pay his court once more to the farmer's pretty daughter.

The dark night came.

The young husband and his wife retired to rest.

Geraldine seemed overwhelmed by some hideous presentiment.

Taking her treacherous husband in her arms, and drawing his head upon her breast,

"I know not what ails me," she said. "I feel as if I were about to lose you."

He pressed her fondly to him.

"Fear not," he said. "Sleep dear one, and, believe me, it is but an idle dream."

In half an hour he had kissed and caressed her to sleep.

Then he rose gently.

One parting look he gave her when he had dressed himself and was ready for departure.

She was lying with her bright hair in black disordered coils on the white pillow.

One soft arm was thrown above her head.

The clothes, disordered by his quitting the bed, disclosed the whole of the other arm and one rounded breast, which fluttered with the pulsations of her heart.

"She is devilish pretty," murmured Jonathan, "and I am sorry to leave her. I would gladly take her with me, but I know her too well. She would not consent to rob her father."

So he glided away.

She slumbered heavily.

Though he stumbled at the door she moved not.

The headsman's room was close to that of the young couple.

The door was ajar.

A light burned within.

Jonathan crept in.

Like a snake he glided along—noiselessly, slimingly.

The old man slept heavily.

"I am in luck," murmured the traitor.

He approached the bed.

Turning the light of the dark lantern he carried full upon the face of the headsman, he assured himself that he was asleep.

Seeing that all was safe, he advanced towards the door which led to the inner chamber where the old man kept his treasure.

There was no key in the lock.

He pressed heavily against the bar.

It gave no signs of yielding.

He pressed still more violently.

The wood began to yield with a loud crash.

The old man started in his sleep.

The robber paused a moment.

But there was at present no fear of his being disturbed by the headsman.

The old man was but moving uneasily in his sleep.

Jonathan Rasper, coward as he was, trembled, nevertheless, with deadly fear, and grasped tightly the dagger which he had concealed beneath his vest.

However, his object was one—infamous, truly, yet calculated to lead on a far less courageous man than he.

So, placing his shoulder against one of the panels of the door, he pushed vigorously.

The wood yielded.

The aperture he had made was large enough for him to creep through, and in another moment he was within the room where the treasure was concealed.

The headsman sprang up in his bed.

"Who's there?" he cried.

There was no answer.

The headsman laid down again.

There were a few moments of silence, and Jonathan Rasper, thinking that all now was safe, turned on the light of the dark lantern once more and began his search for the gold.

The headsman, however, was not asleep, and the first glint of the light upon the wall opposite his bed roused him to a sense of danger.

He leaped from his bed.

Rushing to the door of his treasure room he peered in.

There was no misunderstanding the scene which met his gaze.

Jonathan Rasper had discovered the place where the gold was concealed, and was now counting out the glittering coin upon the table.

The headsman, seizing a pistol from the place where he always kept it in readiness, leapt through, and had seized the robber by the throat before he was aware that the thief was his own son-in-law.

It was but an instant, however, before he recognized the features of Jonathan Rasper.

He glanced horrified at the face of the traitor.

Then he loosed his hold and staggered back, exclaiming,

"You, Jonathan !"

The coward saw that it was necessary for a time to cast aside his cowardice.

It was one of those supreme moments when the danger lies in timidity, and safety in a bold and resolute attack.

Jonathan dropped upon the table the glittering coins which he had been admiring and examining, and turned towards his father-in-law.

"Yes," he said, "it is I. What then ?"

Then, for the first time, he saw the pistol glittering in the headsman's hands.

He saw, or thought he saw in the old man's face a look of unutterable hatred.

No time was to be lost.

Either he or the headsman must die.

Of this he was convinced.

So ere the old man could frame a reply he sprang upon him.

The headsman was unprepared.

He was down on the floor in a moment.

"Yield !" cried Jonathan.

"Yield what ?"

"Your gold."

"Never !"

"Then I will have your life."

"I knew it ! I knew it ! The axe and the sword said so. Doomed—doomed to the scaffold !"

Although he said these words, however, he was not undisposed to battle against the very fate he spoke of.

He made a determined effort to fire the pistol, which, in spite of his fall he still grasped in his hand.

There was a flash and a report, and Jonathan felt himself wounded in the side.

"Curse you !" he cried, "I will pay you for this," and with the words he drove his knife deep into the old man's skull.

The headsman uttered no sound.

He died without a struggle.

Jonathan Rasper sprang from the ground, and seizing the two bags of gold crammed them into his pocket.

As he glared about in search of more he heard a light step entering the adjoining chamber, and a gentle voice calling,

"Father ! father !"

He knew it to be his wife who was approaching, and fearing to meet her amid such a scene of blood he rushed to the window, flung up the sash, and scrambled out into the back garden.

Flying away at headlong speed he had before him the vision of the hideous scene at the place of execution ; the vision, too, of the fair Geraldine, as he would have seen her had he remained bending in tender fear and sorrow over her father's murdered body, while the words, the last words of the headsman, rang like a death knell in his ears—" Doomed, doomed to the scaffold."

CHAPTER II.

JONATHAN RASPER'S REVENGE UPON BRANDON.

ONE of the principal objects which Jonathan Rasper had in view, when he first contemplated escaping from the house of the public executioner was, as I have said, a return to the fair daughter of the farmer.

The crime into which his filthy greed had led him, prevented, of course, any idea of such a proceeding ; and he, therefore, resolved for the present to turn his attention to an object which he had for a long time deferred, which was revenge upon Brandon for the part he had taken in his punishment as a traitor.

Accordingly, instead of making his way towards the neighbourhood where the crime had been committed, he proceeded towards London, and took up his lodgings in close proximity to Brandon's house.

He knew well that constantly intriguing, as Brandon was, he would be sure either in one way or another to betray the interests of his party, either through self-interest or conceit.

It was not long before he discovered a weak point, where his old enemy could be assailed.

He found that Brandon, who up to this time, as we have seen, had been a staunch adherent of the Royalist party, and had carried arms in the king's cause against the Pretender, had failed now in his fealty, and was secretly plotting the return of James to England.

Jonathan had money, as we know.

In all ages men have been accessible to bribes.

MOONLIGHT JACK
OR THE KING OF THE ROAD

INTERVIEW BETWEEN GRACE DASHWOOD AND THE MONK.

Through them he discovered more than the mere fact of the correspondence between Brandon and the Pretender.

He discovered its contents.

He found that Brandon had offered to arrange for a descent, on the condition that neither Moonlight Jack or Lucien Fairleigh were allowed to have any command in the rebel army.

Overjoyed at a discovery which promised him immediate revenge upon the man whom, of all others, he most hated in the world, Jonathan Rasper at once set to work to take advantage of it.

Communicating at first, of course, with those about the royal person, and receiving from the king himself money wherewith to work out his treachery, Jonathan was enabled to offer larger bribes than ever.

Before he had been in London a month he had in his possession documents which criminated Brandon to such an extent that there was no possibility of evading the truth.

In the midst of what he had hoped would prove to be the inauguration of a great triumph, Brandon was arrested.

Brought up to trial at once without being allowed any time to prepare his defence, he was proved guilty beyond all shadow of doubt.

In the fury occasioned by his unlooked-for discovery, he declared that the judges on the bench were as guilty as he, and members of the same conspiracy.

No. 28, July 14, 1866.]   Two Numbers and Two Tales every week for One Penny. THE WORK GIRLS OF LONDON, and THE CRUSADER; OR, THE WITCH OF FINCHLEY.   Price One Penny.

But he alarmed none of them.

Sentenced to death, he had not even the doubtful honour awarded him of being executed by the axe.

He was condemned to die, within three days after the trial, the death of a dog, by hanging.

The day at length arrived.

The cart in which the state criminal was conveyed to the place of execution was followed by a large number of citizens.

A clergyman was seated in the same cart with the traitor, who did not hesitate to repeat the same false assertion which he had made in the court of justice that his judge, Lord Falconby, was one of the leaders of the conspiracy against the king.

The same falsehoods he disseminated amongst the crowd, averring with unblushing effrontery to those who were nearest to the cart, that he owed his death to his having been too willing to execute Lord Falconby's pleasure.

For a time he repeated those words sullenly and doggedly, in the manner of one reciting a task, or a liar, who endeavours by reiteration to obtain a credit for his words which he is internally sensible they did not deserve.

But when he lifted up his eyes and beheld in the distance the black outline of a gallows at least forty feet high, with its ladder, and its fatal cord, rising against the horizon, he became suddenly silent, and, brave as he was, trembled.

He glanced round the large assembly with an agonized countenance.

The faces around him were unfriendly.

He had been led to believe that even at the last moment efforts would be made to save him.

Naturally enough, therefore, he gazed eagerly into every face, and longed for delay, which might bring him help in his extremity.

His doom, however, was sealed, and there was no escaping from it.

They slowly approached the fatal tree, which was erected on a bank by the river's side, about half a mile from the walls of the city.

A site chosen in order that the body of the wretch, which was to remain food for the carrion crows, might be seen in every direction.

Here the priest delivered Brandon to the executioner, by whom he was assisted up the ladder, and, to all appearance, despatched according to the usual forms of the law.

He seemed to struggle for life for a minute, but soon after hung still and inanimate.

The executioner, after remaining on duty for more than half an hour, as if to permit the last spark of life to be extinguished, announced to the admirers of such spectacles that the irons for the permanent suspension of the carcase, not having been got ready, the concluding ceremony of attaching it to the gibbet would be deferred till the next morning at sunrise.

Notwithstanding the early hour which he had named, Master Chokum had a reasonable attendance of rabble at the place of execution to see the final proceeding of justice with its victim.

But great was the astonishment and resentment of these amatuers to find that the dead body had been removed from the gibbet.

They were not, however, long at a loss to guess the cause of its disappearance.

Brandon had numerous friends.

What more natural, therefore, than that these friends should have clandestinely removed his body from the place of public shame ?

The crowd vented their wrath upon Chokum for not completing his job on the preceding evening, and had not he and his assistant betaken themselves to a boat and escaped across the river, they would have run some risk of being pelted to death.

The event, however, was too much in the spirit of the times to be wondered at.

Its real cause we shall explain.

The incidents of a narrative of this kind must be adapted to each other, as the wards of a key must tally accurately with those of the lock to which it belongs.

The reader, however gentle, will not hold himself obliged to rest satisfied with the mere fact that such-and-such occurrences took place, which is, generally speaking, all that in ordinary life he can know of what is passing around him.

But he is desirous, while reading for amusement, of knowing the interior movements occasioning the course of events.

This is a legitimate and reasonable curiosity, for every man has a right to open and examine the mechanism of his own watch, put together for his proper use ; although he is not permitted to pry into the interior of the time-piece, which, for general information, is displayed on the town steeple.

It would be, therefore, uncourteous to leave my readers under any doubt concerning the agency which removed the assassin from the gallows.

An event, which some of the citizens ascribed to the foul fiend himself, while others were content to lay it upon the natural dislike of Brandon's men to see him hanging on the river side, as a spectacle dishonouring to their province.

About midnight succeeding the day when the execution had taken place, and while the inhabitants of London were deeply buried in slumber, three men, muffled in their cloaks, and bearing a dark lantern, descended the alleys of a garden which led from the house occupied by Lord Bowden to the banks of the Thames, where a small boat lay moored to a landing-place or little projecting pier.

The wind howled in a low and melancholy manner through the leafless shrubs and bushes, and a pale moon forced its way with difficulty through drifting clouds, which seemed to threaten rain.

The three individuals entered the boat with great precaution to escape observation.

One of them was a tall powerful man.

Another short, and bent downwards.

The third middle-sized, and apparently younger than his companions, well made and active.

Thus much the imperfect light discovered.

They seated themselves in the boat, and unmoored it from the pier.

"We must let her drift with the current till we pass the bridge," said the most youthful of the party, who assumed the office of helmsman, and pushed the boat off from the pier, whilst the others took the oars, which were muffled, and rowed with all precaution till they attained the middle of the river.

They then ceased their efforts, lay upon their oars, and trusted to the steersman for keeping her in mid channel.

In this manner they passed unnoticed or disregarded beneath the old bridge.

Although they heard the voices of a civic watch, which, since these disturbances commenced, had been nightly maintained, no challenge was given, and, when they were so far down the stream as to be out of hearing of those guardians of the night, they began to row, but still with precaution, and to converse, though in a low tone.

"You have found a new trade, comrade, since I left you," said one of the rowers to the other. "I left you engaged in tending a sick boy, and I find you employed in purloining a dead body from the gallows."

"A living body, so please you, master, or else my craft has failed of its purpose."

"So I am told ; but begging your pardon, unless you tell me your trick, I will take leave to doubt of its success."

It would be tedious to the reader to explain in the precise words of surgeon Macfarlane, who accompanied the two men sent by Lord Bowden to rescue Brandon, the method in which they had contrived the trick.

The surgeon, however, had procured some bandages, made in a manner similar to horse girths.

Especial care was taken that they were not likely to shrink.

One loop of this substance was drawn under each foot, and passed up the leg to a girdle, with which they were united.

This cincture was connected by several straps down the breast and back in order to divide the weight.

The chief of all the contrivances, however, was a broad steel collar turning outwards, and having a hook or two for the better security of the halter, which the friendly executioner passed, of course, round that part of the machine instead of round the neck of the patient.

Thus, when thrown off from the ladder, the sufferer finds himself suspended not by his neck but by the steel circle which supports the loops in which his feet are placed, and on which his weight really rests, diminished a little by similar supports under each arm.

Thus, neither vein nor windpipe being compressed, the man will breathe as freely, and his blood, saving from fright and novelty of situation, will flow as temperately as any one else's.

"Well, that is a clever scheme !" cried George Marchant, Lord Bowden's page, "is it not, friend Tristram ?"

"Aye, that it is, indeed !" returned the other.

"It is, truly," said Macfarlane, "and is well worth learning by such mounting spirits as you, for there is no knowing to what height Lord Bowden's pupils may arrive. If it is necessary to descend from it by a rope, you may find my mode of management more convenient than the common practice, only you must wear a high-collared coat to conceal the ring of steel."

"Base vendor of poisons !" cried Marchant, "men like us die on the field of battle."

"I will save the lesson, however," cried Tristram, laughing, "for it may be useful in the future. But what a night Brandon must have had of it, dancing in mid air to the music of his own shackles, as the night wind swings him to and fro."

"It would be a devilish good thing to leave him there," said Marchant, "for his descent from the gibbet will but encourage him to the perpetration of fresh crimes. Lord Bowden, by the way, looked deuced black to-night ; can you guess the reason of his anger ?"

"I think I can do so without much cost of wit," said the surgeon. "But yonder I see in the pale moonlight our dead alive. Should he have screamed out to any chance passenger it were a curious interruption to a night journey, to be hailed from the top of such a gallows as that. Hark ! I think I hear his groans amid the whistling of the wind and the creaking of the chains."

"So fair and softly ! Make fast the boat with the grappling and get out the casket with my matters. We would be better for a little fire, but the light might bring observation on us. Come on, my men of valour, and march warily, for we are bound for the gallow's foot. Follow with the lantern ; I trust the ladder has been left. Sing—

"'Three merry men, and three merry men,
And three merry men are we.
Thou on the land and I on the sand,
And Jack on the gallow's tree!'"

As they advanced to the gibbet, they could plainly hear groans, though uttered in a low tone.

Macfarlane ventured to give a low cough once or twice by way of signal, but received no answer.

"We had best make haste," said he, to his companions, "for our friend must be in the last agonies, as he makes no answer to the signal which announces the arrival of help. Come, let us to the gallow's tree ! I will go up the ladder first, and cut the rope ; do you two follow me one after another, and take fast hold of the body, so that he does not fall when the halter is unloosed. Keep sure gripe, for which the bandages afford you convenience. Although he plays an owl's part to-night, he has no wings, and to fall out of a halter may be as dangerous as to fall into one."

While he spoke thus assuringly, he ascended the ladder, and, ascertaining that the men-at arms who followed him had the body in their hold; he cut the rope and then gave his aid to support the almost lifeless body of the criminal.

By a skilful exertion of strength and address, the body of Brandon was placed safely on the ground, and the faint yet certain existence of life having been ascertained, it was thence transported to the river side, where, shrouded by the bank, the party could be best concealed from observation, while the leech employed himself in the necessary means of recalling animation with which he had taken care to provide himself.

For this purpose he first freed the recovered person from his shackles, which the executioner had left unlocked on purpose, and at the same time disengaged the complicated envelopes and bandages by which he had been suspended.

It was some time ere his efforts succeeded, for, in spite of the skill with which his machine had been constructed, the straps designed to support the body had stretched so considerably as to occasion the sense of suffocation becoming extremely overpowering.

But the address of the surgeon triumphed over all obstacles.

And after sneezing and stretching himself, with one or two brief convulsions, Brandon gave decided proofs of re-animation by arresting the hand of the operator as it was in the act of dropping strong waters on his breast and throat, and directing the bottle which contained them to his lips, he took, almost perforce, a considerable gulp of the contents.

"It is spiritual essence double distilled," said

the astonished operator, " and would blister the throat and burn the stomach of any other man ; but this extraordinary beast is so unlike all other human creatures that I should not wonder if it brought to the complete possession of his faculties."

Brandon seemed to confirm this.

He started with a strong convulsion, sat up, stared round, and indicated some consciousness of existence.

" Wine ! wine !" were the first words which he articulated.

The surgeon gave him a glass of medicated wine mixed with water.

He rejected it, and again uttered the words, " Wine ! wine !"

" Nay ; take it then, in the devil's name !" said the doctor, " since none but he can judge of your constitution."

A draught long and deep enough to have discomposed the intellect of any other person was found effectual in recalling those of Brandon to a more perfect state ; though he betrayed no recollection of where he was or what had befallen him, and, in his brief and sullen manner, asked why he was brought to the river side at this time of night.

" Hush !" interrupted Marchant, " and be thankful, I pray you, if there is any thankfulness in you, that your body is not crow's meat, and in a place where water is too scarce to duck you."

" I begin to think," said the ruffian.

And raising to his mouth the flask, which he saluted with a long and hearty kiss, he set the empty bottle on the earth, dropped his head on his bosom, and seemed to muse for the purpose of arranging his confused recollection.

" We can abide the issue of his meditations no longer," said Macfarlane ; " he will be better after he has slept. Up, sir ; you have been riding the air these last few hours. Try if the water be not an easier mode of conveyance. You must lend me a hand here, gentlemen ; I can no more lift this mass, than I could raise in my arms a slaughtered bull."

" Stand upright on your own feet, Brandon, now we have placed you upon them," said Marchant.

" I cannot," answered the patient. " Every drop of blood tingles in my veins as if it had pin points, and my knees refuse to bear their burden. What can be the meaning of all this? This is some practice of yours, doctor."

" Aye, aye, so it is, honest Brandon," said Macfarlane, " a practice you will thank me for when you come to learn it. In the meanwhile, stretch down in the stern of the boat, and let me wrap this cloak about you."

Assisted into the boat accordingly, Brandon was deposited there as conveniently as things admitted of.

He answered their attentions with one or two snorts, resembling the grunt of a bear who has some food which is particularly agreeable to him.

" And now, Tristram," said the surgeon, " you know your charge. You are to carry this lively cargo by the river to Chelsea Reach, where he is to await Lord Bowden, at the ' King's Head.' "

" Aye, aye, sir," said Tristram.

" Meanwhile," continued Macfarlane, " here are his shackles and bandages, the marks of his confinement and liberation ; bind them together and fling them into the deepest pool you pass, for found in your possession they might tell tales against us all. This low, light breath of wind from the west

will permit you to use a sail as soon as the light comes in and you are tired of rowing. Your other friend, Master Marchant, must be content to return to London with me on foot, for here severs our company. Take with you a lantern, for you will require it more than we."

As the pedestrians returned to London, Marchant expressed his belief that Brandon's understanding would never recover the shock which terror had inflicted upon it, and which appeared to him to have disturbed all the faculties of his mind, and in particular his memory.*

In Brandon's case Marchant was wrong.

The breeze that fanned his cheek while Tristram pulled strongly up the river recalled him to that consciousness which he had not attained before the surgeon and the page had left him.

He arose from his recumbent posture as soon as the boat began to move, and looked around him.

The night was dark.

The moon only showed itself at intervals.

Through the drifting clouds she peeped ever and anon, and lighted up fitfully the river and its verdant banks.

As he glanced towards the Middlesex side of the Thames, just as they started, the fickle goddess cast a flood of light upon the gallows.

Brandon shuddered.

The sight recalled him to himself.

" I have had a narrow escape," he said to Tristram.

The man was pulling laboriously at the oars

The tide, running strongly down the stream, offered an unexpected resistance.

He made, therefore, but little way, in spite of all his efforts.

" Yes, you have," he said, surlily.

" Where are we going ?" asked Brandon.

" You had better take a turn at the oars," replied Tristram, " and you will get there and find out quicker."

Brandon laughed gloomily.

" I have no objection," he said.

" No ; I don't know that a man who has just been hanged will be of much use."

He took the oars, however, and pulled sturdily.

The steady sweep serving to take much of the stiffness and cramp from his arms.

On nearing Chelsea Reach, Tristram stopped rowing suddenly.

" What is the matter ?" said Brandon.

" Hush !" said Tristram, " and listen."

---

* Marchant was by no means wrong in his surmise. The memory of criminals is lost often when executed. In Paris once, a criminal was condemned to die by the halter. He suffered the sentence accordingly, showing no particular degree of timidity upon the scaffold, and behaving and expressing himself as men in the same condition are wont to do. Accident did for him what a little ingenious practice did for Brandon. He was cut down and given to his friends before life was extinct, and a surgeon restored him. But though he recovered in other particulars, he remembered but little of his trial and sentence. Of his confession on the morning of his execution he remembered not a word. Neither of leaving the prison, nor of his passage to the Place de Greve where he suffered, nor of the speeches he made, nor of his ascent of the fatal tree, nor of taking the fatal leap, had this restored man any recollection whatever.

An incident similar to this occurred within the present century at Oxford, in the case of a young woman who underwent the last sentence of the law for child murder. A learned professor of the university has published an account of his conversation with this girl after her recovery.

Brandon listened.

A sound floated on the waters.

It was the sound of voices.

But where they were they could not tell.

The breeze had lulled.

The clouds consequently had gathered thickly, and over land and river darkness hung like a pall.

"There'll be a smash," said Tristram, "so let's lie on our oars. At any rate that will be better than running right into them."

"They may be on land," said Brandon.

"Not they ; they are on the river. Look out, here they come ; there we have it."

There was a rushing sound of water, and then a shout, and a heavy boat ran into them.

A terrible smash followed.

The boat in which Brandon sat, weaker and more loosely made than the other, gave way at once, and Brandon and his companion only saved themselves by leaping into the other wherry.

"This is a rude welcome, my friends," said the resuscitated man.

One of those he addressed started on hearing the voice, and held a lantern to Brandon's face.

"Brandon !" he cried ; "by all the powers this is a strange meeting !"

Then turning to the two fellows with him he said—

"Turn towards shore, my men."

Brandon at once recognised his voice.

It was that of Sir Robert Panton, once a staunch adherent of the Pretender, but now suspected of being a secret friend of the King.

"Sir Robert," cried Brandon, "this is, indeed, as you say, a strange meeting. Whither are you bound ?"

"To Darnley House," he said. "There will be strange doings there soon, I think. If you have a mind to help me, there are plenty of treasures in store for both of us."

They soon reached the shore.

Until they did so, there was no further talk as to their arrangements.

When they landed, however, Sir Robert Panton took Brandon aside.

A long whispered conversation ensued.

The result of this was that Brandon's companion went off in search of Macfarlane, and at twelve next day the two worthies were joined by the doctor at the "Talbot Inn."

That day they set out in company for Darnley House, where the Pretender still was, and where Cuthbert and Grace Dashwood still rested after hard fatigues.

In the evening the Prince summoned Sir Robert Panton to his table, and even admitted Macfarlane to the same honour.

The conversation was of a lively and dissolute cast, a tone encouraged by the Prince, who, although he had behaved with such respect towards Grace Dashwood, was a well-known admirer and follower of the fair sex.

The banquet, notwithstanding the indifferent health of the Pretender, was protracted in idle wantonness, far beyond the rules of temperance ; and, whether owing simply to the strength of the wine which he drank, or the weakness of his constitution, or, as it is probable, that the last wine which he quaffed had been drugged by Panton, it so happened that the Prince, towards the end of the repast, fell into a lethargic sleep, from which it seemed impossible to rouse him.

The next morning, it was announced that the Prince was taken ill of an infectious disorder ; and, to prevent its spreading through the household, no one was admitted to wait on him, save Panton and Macfarlane, one of whom seemed always to remain in the room, while the others observed a degree of precaution in their intercourse with the rest of the family so strict as to maintain the belief that he was dangerously ill of an infectious disorder.

Far different had been the fate of the Pretender from that which was publicly given out.

His ambitious uncle had determined on his death as the means of removing the first and most formidable barrier between himself and the throne.

Panton's views of aggrandisement, and the resentment which he had lately entertained against his master, made him a willing agent.

Macfarlane's love of gold, and his native malignity of disposition, rendered him equally forward.

It had been resolved, with the most calculating cruelty, that all means which might leave behind marks of violence were to be carefully avoided, and the extinction of life suffered to take place of itself, by privation of every kind acting upon a frail and impaired constitution.

His bedchamber was well adapted for the execution of such a horrible project.

A small, narrow staircase, scarce known to exist, opened from thence by a trap-door to the subterranean dungeons of the mansion, through a passage by which the feudal lord was wont to visit, in private and in disguise, the inhabitants of those miserable regions.

By this staircase the villains conveyed the insensible prince to the lowest dungeon of the mansion, so deep in the bowels of the earth that no cries or groans, it was supposed, could possibly be heard ; while the strength of its door and fastenings must for a long time have defied force, even if the entrance could have been discovered.

Brandon, who had been saved from the gallows for the purpose, was the willing agent of this cruelty to his misled and betrayed patron.

This wretch re-visited the dungeon at the time when the Pretender's lethargy began to wear off, and, when awaking to sensation, he found himself deadly cold, unable to move, and oppressed with fetters, which scarce permitted him to stir from the damp straw on which he was laid.

His first idea was that he was in a fearful dream.

His next brought a confused augury of the truth.

He called and shouted.

Yelled at length in frenzy.

But no assistance came.

He was answered only by the vaulted roof of the dungeon.

The agent of Hell heard these agonising screams.

When, exhausted and hopeless, the unhappy youth became silent, the savage resolved to present himself before the eyes of his prisoner.

The locks were drawn.

The chain fell.

The Prince raised himself as high as his fetters permitted.

A red glare, against what he was fain to shut his eyes, streamed through the vault.

When he opened them again he beheld the ghastly form of one whom he had reason to think dead.

He sank back in horror.

"I am judged and condemned!" he exclaimed, "and the most abhorred fiend in the infernal regions is sent to torment me!"

"I live, my lord," said Brandon; "and, that you may live and enjoy life, be pleased to sit up and eat your victuals."

"Free me from these irons!" said the Prince; "release me from this infernal dungeon, and, dog as thou art, thou shalt be the richest man in England!"

"If you would give me the weight of your shackles in gold," said Brandon, "I would rather see the irons on you than have the treasure myself. But look up! you were wont to like delicate fare. Behold how I have catered for you!"

The wretch, with fiendish glee, unfolded a piece of raw hide covering the bundle which he bore under his arm, and passing the light to and fro before it showed the unhappy Prince a bull's head recently hewn from the trunk.

He placed it at the foot of the bed, or rather lair on which the Prince lay.

"Be moderate in your food," he said; "it is likely to be long ere you will get another meal."

"Tell me but one thing, wretch!" said the prince. "Does Panton know of this?"

"How else were you decoyed hither? Poor woodcock, you are snared," answered the murderer.

With these words he closed the door, the bolts resounded, and the unhappy Prince was left to darkness, solitude, and misery.

"Oh! my father! my prophetic father! The staff I leaned on has, indeed, proved a spear!"

We will not dwell on the subsequent hours, nay, days of bodily agony and mental despair.

But it was not the pleasure of heaven that so great a crime should be perpetrated with impunity.

Grace Dashwood and Cuthbert, neglected by the other inmates, who seemed to be engaged with the tidings of the Prince's illness, were, however, refused permission to leave the house, until it should be seen how this alarming disease was to terminate, and whether it was actually an infectious sickness.

They lived in this manner four or five days, and in order to avoid as much as possible the gaze, and perhaps the incivility, of the menials in the offices, Cuthbert prepared their food in his own apartment, always taking upon himself the trouble of getting from the butler the materials for the slender meal.

He had been abroad for this purpose on the sixth day, a little before noon, and the desire for fresh air, or the hope to find some salad or pot herbs, or, at least, an early flower or two, with which to deck their board, had carried him into the small garden at the back of the mansion.

He re-entered Grace's apartment in the tower with a countenance as pale as ashes, and a frame which trembled like an aspen leaf.

His terror instantly extended itself to Grace, who could hardly find words to ask what new misfortune had occurred.

"Is the Prince dead?"

"Worse! They are starving him alive!"

"Madness!"

"No, no, no, no," said Cuthbert, speaking under his breath, and huddling his words so thick upon each other that Grace could hardly catch the sense. "I was looking for flowers—because you said you loved them yesterday—when my poor little dog, thrusting himself into a thicket of yew and holly bushes that grew out of some old ruins close to the wall, came back whining and howling. I crept forward to see what might be the cause, and heard a groaning as of one in extreme pain, but so faint that it seemed to arise out of the very depths of the earth. At length I found it proceeded from a small rent in the wall covered with ivy, and when I laid my ear close to the opening I could hear the Prince's voice distinctly say, 'It cannot now last long,' and then it sunk away in something like a prayer."

"Gracious heaven! did you speak to him?"

"I said, 'Is it you, my lord?' and the answer was, 'Who mocks me with that title?' I asked him if I could help him, and he answered in a voice I shall never forget, 'Food! food! I die of hunger!' so I came hither to tell you. What is to be done? Shall we alarm the house?"

"Alas! that would more likely destroy than aid him!" said Grace.

"And what, then, shall we do?" asked Cuthbert.

"I know not yet," returned Grace, prompt and bold in cases of emergency, though yielding to her companion in ingenuity of resource on ordinary occasions; "I know not yet; but something we must do. He shall not die unaided!"

So saying, she seized the small cruise which contained their soup, and the meat of which it was made, wrapped some thin cakes which she had baked, in the folds of her cloak, and beckoning her companion to follow with a vessel of milk, also part of their provisions, she hastened towards the garden,

"So our fair vestal is stirring abroad," said the only man she met, who was one of the menials; but Grace passed on without notice or reply, and gained the little garden without further interruption.

Cuthbert indicated to her a heap of ruins, which, covered with underwood, was close to the wall.

It had probably been originally a projection of the building; and the small fissure which communicated with the dungeon, contrived for air, had terminated within it.

But the aperture had been a little enlarged by decay, and admitted a dim ray of light to its recesses, although it could not be observed by those who visited the place with torch-light aids.

"Here is dead silence," said Grace, after listening attentively for a moment. "Heavens and earth, he is gone!"

"We must risk something," said Cuthbert, singing a few notes of an old familiar glee.

A sigh was the only answer from the depth of the dungeon.

Grace then ventured to speak.

"I am here, my lord; here with food and drink."

"Ha! the aid comes too late. I am dying!" was the answer.

"His brain is turned, and no wonder," thought Grace; "But while there is life there is hope."

"It is I, my lord, Grace Dashwood. I have food if I could pass it safely to you."

"Heaven bless you, maiden! I thought the pain was over, but it glows again within me at the name of food."

"The food is here; but how, oh! how shall I pass it to you? The chink is so narrow, the wall is so thick. Yet there is a remedy; I have it. Quick, Cuthbert! cut me a willow-bough, the tallest you can find."

Her companion obeyed, and by means of a cleft in the top of the wand, Grace transmitted several morsels of the soft cake steeped in soup, which served at once as food and drink.

The unfortunate young man ate but little, and with difficulty; but prayed for a thousand blessings on the head of his preserver.

"I had destined you to become the slave of my vices," he said, "and yet you try to become the preserver of my life! But away, and save yourself."

"I will return with more food the first opportunity," said Grace, just as Cuthbert plucked her sleeve, desiring her to be silent.

Both crouched away among the ruins, and they heard the voices of Sir Robert Panton and the doctor in close conversation.

"He is stronger than I thought," said the former, in a low croaking voice.

"Would it not be better to end the matter more speedily? Lord Thelford comes this way. He is not in this secret. He will demand to see the Prince, and all must be over before he arrives."

They passed on in their dark and fatal conversation.

"We must gain the tower now," said Grace, to her companion, as she saw they had left the garden. "Amid these strange doings I had resolved to escape, and had contrived a plan for so doing; I will turn it into one of rescue for the Prince."

"Escape for you?" said Cuthbert. "We are not prisoners here."

"Yes, yes," said Grace, "we are no better. But listen. An old woman enters the house about dark, and usually leaves her cloak in the passage as she goes into the butler's room with the milk. Take the cloak, muffle yourself closely and pass the warder boldly. He is usually drunk at that hour, and you will go as the dairy-woman unchallenged through the gates, if you do so with confidence. Then you may away to meet Lord Thelford, who is our nearest and only ally."

The bell of the village church at length tolled eight o'clock.

"Go," said Grace; "and heaven be with you. If you find me dead upon your return, give to Lucien Fairleigh a lock of my hair, and tell him that Grace Dashwood died in endeavouring to save the blood of the Prince she had falsely accused."

In a few moments after the dairy-woman entered with her pails and delivered the milk for the family and to hear and tell the news stirring.

"If you see Lucien or Moonlight Jack," said Grace, as Cuthbert was leaving the room, "wait not for Lord Thelford, but tell them to hasten hither."

The next hour was an anxious one for Grace.

It was, however, quite an hour before the escape of the fugitives was known; as soon, however, as it was discovered, a strict search was set on foot, and as Cuthbert could nowhere be found, suspicion at once fell upon him.

The steward at once went to inform Sir Robert Panton and Macfarlane, who were now scarcely ever separate, of the escape of one of the captives.

Everything awakens the suspicions of the guilty.

They looked on each other with faces of dismay, and then repaired together to the apartment of Grace, that they might take her as much as possible

by surprise, while they enquired into the facts attending Cuthbert's disappearance.

"Where is your companion, young woman?" said Sir Robert Panton, in a tone of austere gravity.

"I have no companion here," answered Grace.

"Trifle not," replied the baronet. "I mean your servant, who was here with you."

"He is gone, they tell me," said Grace, "about an hour since."

"And whither?" said Macfarlane.

"How," answered Grace, "should I know which way a professed wanderer should choose to travel? He was tired, no doubt, of a solitary life, and is gone. The only wonder is that he has stayed so long."

"This, then, is all the information you can give us?" said Sir Robert.

"All that I have to tell you, Sir Robert," answered Grace, firmly; "and, if the Prince himself should inquire, I can tell him no further."

"There is little danger of his again doing you the honour to speak to you in person," said Sir Robert Panton.

"Is the Prince, then, so very ill?" asked Grace.

"There is no help for him, save in heaven," said Sir Robert, looking upward.

"Then may there yet be help there," said Grace, "if human aid prove unavailing."

"Amen!" said Macfarlane, with the most determined gravity, while Sir Robert Panton adopted a face fit to echo the feeling, though it seemed to cost him a painful struggle to suppress his sneering, yet soft laugh of triumph, which was peculiarly excited by anything having a religious tendency.

"And it is men—earthly men, and not incarnate devils, who thus appeal to Heaven, while they are devouring by inches the life blood of their hapless master," muttered Grace, as her two baffled inquisitors left the room. "Why sleeps the thunder? but it will roll ere long; and, oh, may it be to preserve as well as punish."

The hour of dinner gave Grace an opportunity of venturing to the breach in the wall.

In waiting for the hour she observed some stir in the house, which had been silent as the grave ever since the seclusion of the Pretender.

Rushing to the window she saw that the court yard was full of armed men.

At their head was Lord Thelford, and by his side the welcome forms of Lucien Fairleigh, Moonlight Jack, and Cuthbert.

The safety of the Prince was soon assured.

There was no resistance offered to the entry of Jack Tyrrell's band.

A rush was made by Brandon and Sir Robert Panton to the cell where they had placed their captive, in order to conceal the evidence of the cruel punishment to which they had subjected him.

But it was in vain!

Led on by Grace Dashwood they caught the traitors in the very act of removing the hideous and bleeding head.

"Seize these ruffians," cried Lord Thelford, to the men at his back, "and hang them up over the walls."

Sir Robert Panton drew back, pale and ghastly, and trembling.

"I am of gentle blood," cried he: "a dog's death is not for me!"

"To the devil with your blood," exclaimed Lord

Thelford, "traitors and dogs die the same death. To the walls with them!"

They were hurried away at once to the walls of the house, and there the last sentence of the law was carried out upon them.

This time there was no machinery to save Brandon.

A few struggles, a few convulsive clutchings, and the two traitors were lumps of lifeless clay.

———

CHAPTER III.

THE ESCAPE OF THE DOCTOR—HE RESOLVES TO SEEK REWARD—HURRIES TO LORD MONTEAGLE—THE NIGHT FETE AT RICHMOND—THE GLITTER OF GEMS AND THE BEAUTY OF WOMEN—THE AWKWARD ARRIVAL—THE INTERVIEW—OUT IN THE GROUNDS—THE TWO SHADOWS—THE AVENGERS—THE BOAT ON THE RIVER—THE DARK ISLAND—THE DEATH OF A TRAITOR.

THE doctor, Macfarlane, not having rushed, like Brandon and Sir Robert Panton, into the very jaws of the lion, resolved at once to make good his escape.

He saw how matters stood.

To remain was death.

So he watched his chance.

At one time he thought of turning round and accusing his two associates of forcing him into a scene of blood.

But of this he thought better.

He was not quite certain of the reputation he had acquired among the gentlemen of the road.

So he watched his time.

At the very first sight of the armed band he concealed himself in the chapel of Darnley House, and when all had sought the tower, he made the best of his way into the open country, determining to seek Lord Monteagle, announce the Pretender's *death*, and claim a reward in the name of himself and the other two conspirators.

On arriving in the vicinity of Monteagle House, he heard there was to be a gala in the evening, and he resolved to be there.

The villa of Lord Monteagle, where the night fête was to take place, was situated on the side of the Thames, below Richmond.

A long cottage residence, fronted by a smooth, springy lawn that sloped to the water's edge, and half washed by the graceful foliage of some weeping willows, the ends of which quivered always in the tide that rippled amongst them.

Dark, fragrant cedars broke the light upon the close turf, shading the rustic seats beneath their low, flat branches, and throwing out the bright petals of the flowers that were glowing in the sun beyond in the large baskets of fir.

Delicate creeping plants appeared to support the light verandah ere they bordered the upper window, for the villa was only one story high.

Festoons of vines, and clusters of twisting hops stretched from tree to tree over the walks, and from one of the wings of this conservatory extended, sheltering the rarest scent-laden plants, in the midst of which a fountain rose like a dome of water plashing musically as it fell back into the basin of

shells and corals, within which a few pale water lilies were floating.

The interior of the house was fitted up with the most exquisite taste.

Nothing was obtrusively prominent, and yet nothing could have been added to improve the graceful effect of the whole.

In the same uniform spirit of elegance had the arrangements for the intended fête been made.

Every point on which the eye could be expected to rest had some subject for its admiration to dwell upon.

And when night came, and the thousand lamps twinkled from the trees and flowers, and trembled by reflection in the river from the illuminated boats moored in the stream opposite ; when that delicious *ensemble* of transparent gleaming windows, faint sounds of waltzes from a well-conducted band, fresh odours of flowers, rustling dresses, bright eyes, perfumed tresses, and white shoulders were perfected, the effect was most bewildered.

It equalled the most gorgeous scenes of Eastern festivities ever described, with all their orange and citron thickets, and flaming tapers, and Persian girls, and marble stairs, and nightingales, and diamond-studded rivers, that held their mirror to the stars.

It was long since the road leading to the villa had been in the state of turmoil that disturbed it on the evening in question.

For vehicles of all description, from the London chariot and the heavy country family carriage to the provincial fly of the neighbouring petty gentilities, kept unceasingly arriving even from the first moment specified in the note.

In fact, Lord Monteagle and his lady were scarcely ready to receive their guests when the first carriage drew up at the door.

And from that moment the sound of the falling steps were never hushed.

The country folks came first.

It is the habitude of some always to do so.

———

Moonlight Jack

OR THE KING

OF THE ROAD

GERALDINE, THE HEADSMAN'S DAUGHTER.

Their imaginations, in fact, are literal, and they believe that nine of the clock means an hour after eight, and so they start betimes.

Richmond itself sent its undeniable gentry, people who looked as if they lived on maids of honour, always so courtly is their bearing.

Hampton Court turned out its dowagers in the brocade of other days, around which the cardinal spiders of the palace might have spun their webs for years.

Mortlake and Barnes provided some oscillating respectability which a breath might have inclined to the patrician or parvenu rank.

Twickenham came out strong in Tritons amid the neighbouring minnows.

Kingston sent substance, Sunbury beauty, and Kew staid propriety.

So, altogether, there was a good mixture.

The arrivals were at their height, and the hall was filled with company on their way, when, as the newspapers would say, "considerable excitement was caused in the neighbourhood of the gates" by the approach of a four-wheel chaise, which cut in before a post-chariot and stopped at the door.

Nothing of its inmates was visible in consequence of an immense umbrella that rose from the front seat.

"Hulloa, waiter! anybody! here some of ye!" cried a voice.

But nobody appeared disposed to move.

| No. 29.—July 21, 1866. | Two Numbers and Two Tales every week for One Penny. THE WORK GIRLS OF LONDON, and THE CRUSADER; OR, THE WITCH OF FINCHLEY. | Price One Penny. |

" I say, you sir," repeated the voice, to a very pompous butler, who was just inside the door, " where can my horse go, eh ? "

" I think you must have made a mistake in the house, my good man," replied the butler, " this is not an inn."

" Who the devil do you call a good man ? " exclaimed the other ; " don't good man me. Whose house is this ? "

" My Lord Monteagle's," answered the grave retainer.

" Well, that's where I want to go. I'll trim all you flunkeys' jackets for you, you rascals. Go and tell his lordship that I'm here—Dr. Macfarlane. Tell him my horse is here, and no one to hold it."

" Now, then," cried the post-boy of the chariot behind, not exactly comprehending the scene, " go on with that hutch."

This was too much.

The umbrella which Macfarlane had held over him to keep the dust from his dress costume was suddenly closed, and the rascally doctor appeared in the full blaze of the evening attire of that period.

Turning round, and, in accents of fearful excitement, he cried,

" If you move an inch your pole will be through my back boot, and I'll pull you up for it, as sure as your name's——. D—n your name ! I don't care what it is ; only look out, that's all. Now mind, I warn you before witnesses."

" There's no place nearer than the inn," said the butler.

Not knowing who the strange visitor might be the man thought it best to say something.

" Oh, yes, the inn, I should think so," said Macfarlane. " Fancy coming back half-a-mile over that gravel, and with these new boots. There, look at them—satisfy yourself."

He put his foot out in the light of the lamp as he spoke, and was exhibiting it to the butler, when he caught sight of the marquis.

" Ha ! there's my lord. Hi ! my lord, my lord ! " he shouted ; " here, half a minute. I'm sorry to trouble you."

Lord Monteagle was passing with a lady from the drawing room to the conservatory.

He started as the tones of Macfarlane's voice reached him, but directly recognizing them he hurriedly found a seat for his companion, frowned and bit his lip until the blood almost started from it, and then, assuming a smiling face, came to the door.

" So, Mr. Macfarlane, it is you. You have caught me just in time to be present at my fête."

" Yes, I heard of it ; so here I am, as right as twenty trivets. But, if I had not seen you, I should have had very little chance of getting any further. What am I to do with my horse ? "

" Well, I really don't know, Macfarlane ; I'm afraid we cannot accommodate you, and you see my servants are all engaged."

" Ah ! " said Dr. Macfarlane, " so they are. They were not so much so that night when we were escaping from——"

" Hush ! " cried Monteagle, hurriedly, " hush ! Here, Darton, take the gentleman's horse round."

Then he added,

" I suppose you have important tidings to communicate ? "

" I have."

" Excuse me now, half a minute ; I will see you directly."

Dr. Macfarlane, having used his handkerchief with the noise like an ophecleide, and brushed up his hair, was announced, and entered the drawing-room.

Lady Monteagle was talking to some of her visitors—one or two that she especially venerated—and would rather that any one else in the world but her had seen the arrival of the doctor.

But there was no help for this.

So she bowed very distantly, and then went on with her conversation.

But Mr. Macfarlane was not so easily shaken off.

" Uncommon pretty to be sure, my lady ! " he exclaimed, as he gazed about him ; " quite bangs Ranelagh ; no cheap suppers here, too, I'll be bound. No, no ; my lord always does the right thing when he does do it."

Dr. Macfarlane finished with a pleasant laugh in which nobody joined.

Lady Monteagle would have rejoiced at an earthquake, and was ready to faint.

She knew, however, how her husband was mixed up with this man, and how dangerous it would be to offend him.

In high life this is often the fate of women.

They have to put up with low society because by the labour of this low society their husbands live !

Fortunately there was a little diversion very soon in the position of things, as the company thronged round one of the guests who was about to sing.

It was now that Lord Monteagle slipped away, and drew Dr. Macfarlane into the grounds.

Here the doctor rapidly told the story of the attempt on the Pretender's life.

Lord Monteagle listened attentively.

" We must start at once for Leaskton," he said ; " the king is there. Remain here a moment ; I will order the carriage, and rejoin you at once."

Then he muttered, as he moved away,

" This man *must* be disposed of, or *I* shall be ruined."

He hastened to Lady Monteagle, and told her all.

This designing woman was in all her husband's secrets.

" I am going to Leaskton, now," he said ; " I must return ere morning. Let no one know I am absent ; let every one suppose I am in my study."

In a quarter of an hour the two men had issued from a private postern, and entering a post-chaise, dashed away at headlong speed.

After passing through two villages they traversed a low road by the side of a canal, whose water was roaring through the locks above the roar of the storm which had now burst.

After a time they turned off on to what was almost a by-path, and where their progress along a thoroughfare, if such it could be called deep in ruts, and bordered on either side by a water-course, became one of no common difficulty.

At length they could perceive a glimmering light reflected on the rain-laden ground, and towards this doubtful beacon Lord Monteagle now directed the postillion.

The man blundered on as well as he was able, and finally stopped at the door of what was evidently a beer-shop on the side of the canal, for over the bit of red curtain in the window several rustics could be seen drinking, and the light streamed up upon a rude sign that overhung the entrance.

As the chaise stopped a man came to the door, whom Lord Monteagle at once recognised, and called by his name, Dawson,

There was a good deal of private confabulation, and then Monteagle invited Macfarlane to enter the house for refreshment.

The doctor assented at once, and they passed into the house together, and entered a little room with a rough sanded floor.

Once here glasses of spirits were brought, and Lord Monteagle said, with an effort,

"Macfarlane, this affair in which we have been engaged is a dangerous one. We may chance to get into sore trouble through it.

"But the king is on our side."

Monteagle shook his head.

"Kings are not understood by every man," he said. "If we had succeeded we should have been his friends. We have failed, we are the reverse ; you had better go abroad, I will find you the means."

Macfarlane was taken aback.

"Go abroad ?" he repeated.

"Yes, for a time."

"I cannot."

"Why ?"

"Because I cannot leave my family."

Monteagle laughed.

"Pooh ! pooh !" he cried, "let us have no foolish excuses. You must go, it is my wish, my determination ; you *must* go. It is for that purpose I brought you hither. Say at once, will you accept the money and go ?"

Macfarlane sprang up.

"No, my lord," he said, resolutely ; "no, I will *not* go. I will keep your secret, be assured, but I will *not* go."

Monteagle rose also and whistled.

"I have prepared for your refusal," he said, as the door opened, and four men entered—four as savage and as fierce-looking men as could well be found.

"Treachery !" cried Macfarlane, springing back, and drawing a pistol from his girdle.

"No, a method of smothering a traitor. Giles and Mordaunt, you know where he is to go. Down the canal first, and then to the mines. He'll never be found there."

"Murderer !" cried Macfarlane, and raising his pistol, he fired at the nobleman's head.

But it was in vain.

There was a flash—a flash in the pan, and Lord Monteagle stood unharmed.

"Seize him !" he shouted, and the four men at once precipitated themselves upon the unfortunate man.

In a few moments he was bound and helpless.

"Carry him away !" cried Lord Monteagle, "let me not see his face again."

The poor wretch was dragged at once away.

Lord Monteagle remained until he was gone.

Then after sending out some drink to the post-boy, he departed.

He enjoined silence respecting the scene which had just taken place, which was hardly necessary.

Then throwing himself back in his carriage he directed the man to proceed at once to his house at Richmond, telling him his haste was most urgent,

and that in consequence, not being near a posting-house, he must contrive to make the same horses do for the remainder of the journey.

Stimulated by the brandy, and a promise of reward if he reached "The Elms" by a certain time, the man commenced to re-trace the road by which they had arrived at the beer-shop.

But this was by no means an easy task.

Dawson ran in front of them a little way with a lantern to get them clear of the canal bank ; but his progress was soon stopped.

Torrents of rain had so swelled the water courses which intersected the low ground in every direction that scarcely anything was visible but a sheet of water, from which a few pollards rose, gaunt and scathed, as the only guides to the edge of the road, and these were not to be discerned in the intervals of the lightning, for the lamps of the carriage were now burning dimly, and threatened shortly to go out.

But the postillion kept on spurring and thrashing the horses, which, what with their punishment, their uncertain footing, and the thunder and lightning, were snorting and quivering with fright until they got upon the regular road again, when, feeling their way once more comparatively safe before them, they started off almost at a gallop.

Lord Monteagle, who, during the journey across the wilder tract, had been directing the man as well as he was able, now put up the glass of the window again, and once more gave himself up to his thoughts, which were confused and almost bewildering.

Still there was a feeling of satisfaction as he felt tolerably assured, if all went as he had pleased, that Macfarlane was safely disposed of until further arrangements could be made.

And this was increased by the rapidity with which, in spite of the previous work, the horses were being urged along.

At last they came to a high wooden bridge of an irregularly steep and unsafe build, over which the road was carried in an awkward turn, and which spanned the junction of the canal with the river Wey before they fell into the Thames.

As the horses, without relaxing their pace, almost climbed up the slope, just as they reached the top of the arch a vivid flash of lightning that for the moment lighted up everything with dazzling clearness broke full on their faces, closely followed by a clattering peal of thunder, which appeared to shake the very earth.

Already frightened, they backed suddenly, and before the postillion had the least mastery over them they drove the hind wheels of the chaise against the wooden post and rails on the top of the bridge, which were rotten and insecure from age.

These gave way in an instant, and as Lord Monteagle started from his seat to learn the cause of the check, the whole equipage was precipitated into the dark foaming water of the lock directly underneath them.

The heavy chaise had, of course, dragged the horses after it, and still fastened to the pole they fell kicking and struggling fearfully half across the top of the flood gate.

The pole directly snapped, and the horse which the postillion was riding got free, as his harness was torn away by the weight, and fell into the comparatively shallow water below the pound of the lock.

But the other was pulled, battling with his hoofs

against the timbers, after the chariot, until he hung suspended as it were by the chain and the entanglement of the broken pole and harness in the woodwork.

For a second or two, and no more, the interior of the post chaise remained dry, for the windows were still up.

But as the animal in a frantic plunge kicked in the front glasses the water rushed in, and it filled immediately, settling down in the deep enclosure of the lock, and drawing the horse after it.

———

CHAPTER IV.

THE GOOD CITY OF DURHAM—THE IRON GATE—THE MAYOR'S DAUGHTER—THE YOUNG ARMOURER—KISSING IN THE DARK—THE CAPTIVE—THE PLAN OF ESCAPE—THE PREPARATIONS FOR THE WEDDING—THE STEEL BOX—THE SECRETED LETTER—THE BALL—THE FLIGHT—THE DENOUEMENT.

WE must turn now to Moonlight Jack and Lucien Fairleigh, who, after releasing Grace Dashwood and the Pretender from the hands of their bloodthirsty enemies, proceeded by pre-arrangement towards Durham.

Fine old city of Durham!

It is like a memory of the past, a living page in the history of England.

It seems to have defied time, or to have stood so sturdily against its attacks that the old gentleman had at length got tired of assaulting it any further.

Its old sandstone walls, and its old towers; its old black beams and carved, uneven gables; its quaint supports, and discoloured panes of glass, quivering and blinking in the wide, ricketty casements; its overhanging floors, and rude steps and pavements, make up a scene which few will forget who are in search of pictures of old England.

One of the curiosities which has now faded away—or rather, we may say, rusted away—into the past, was the iron gate, about which there has been told, by one of our greatest historians, a strange and romantic tale.

This tale—which is one of the days of yore, and treats, in fact, of love and other things as they existed six hundred years ago—runs, according to our best records, as follows:—

"THE STORY OF THE IRON GATE OF DURHAM.

"We are going a long, long way back into the chronicles of the past, for the events on which the following legend is founded.

"You might search in vain for any tangible memorials of the persons who were the principal actors in its story.

"Everything has crumbled away except the city walls, and with them the old red blocks catch the rays of the rising sun, and afterwards doze away in the deep shadows of noontide, just as they used to do six hundred years ago.

"But all else connected with their being has long since passed.

"Where the broad ancestral oaks cast the shadow of their deep green summer leaves upon the daisy-spangled turf beneath them, only allowing loopholes for the noontide sunlight to dance and quiver in ever-flitting patches of brilliancy, there are now streets, and houses, and clusters of life.

"And, on the other hand, the broad pastures and wild, open wastes have been cultivated and enclosed; and, where the clear water of the river rolled over the pebbles of its bed, there are cornfields and pleasant courses of green turf.

"Forests, whose trees are already old, have risen on other tracts; streams have silently worn fresh channels through the meadows, and the old beds of tributary rivulets have turned to hollows filled with brambles, and tossing, waving honeysuckles, with delicate hare-bells quivering on their edges, and their banks gleaming with the golden blossom of the furze, or laughing as their thousand blades and petals ripple in the summer air.

"You must go back with us, against the stream of time, to the period of the Crusades.

"Do not fear that the epoch will be too by-gone for you to feel interested in the flirtations of those who lived in it.

"The passions of men were the same then as now; their outward costumes and the usages of their social life were different, but every chord of their hearts vibrated as with us at the present hour.

"The time, then, is that of the sixth Crusade against the infidel possessors of the Holy Land, and the scene passes at Durham, when the outlines of the old tower rose sharp and freshly chiselled in the clear air, when the mailed knight and the man-at-arms came hither for accoutrements, and the tramp of horses and the blast of clarions echoed throughout the city and the wooded tracts surrounding it.

"The anvils of the armourers rang from morn until night in their ceaseless labour to accomplish the fittings of the eager aspirants to glory in the East; and the state of the entire place reversed the common order of improvement, having possibly somewhat degenerated from its comparative importance in the middle ages.

"There were a great many pretty girls in Durham then.

"There are faces to be seen there now equally fair; in less number, though, and, moreover, they bear that sober sadness in the streets which all nice-looking girls adopt—we never could make out why.

"But of all the fair ones who then lived within the walls, there was not one to compare with Marian Winstanley, the pearl, or daisy, or whatever other pretty synonyme you like to give her, the only child of Master Hugh Winstanley, the mayor.

"It would have done you good for a long time if you were ever so deeply in love to have seen her, for she had such speaking bright eyes, and such marvellously red, pouting lips, that, both together, they gave her face a come-kiss-me-sort-of expression, that quite drove the young men mad.

"But they would have been terribly taken to task had they attempted it.

"And she had, moreover, a white, smooth forehead, and dark, silky, braided hair, with rounded ivory shoulders, and small delicate hands; so that altogether you may readily understand that she had plenty of suitors, and more squabbles, not to say fights, took place about her amongst the gallants of the town, than about any other disputed point of dissension.

"But private affairs are as well known in the

country to everybody else as they are to those whom they mostly concern ; sometimes better. It was the same in the times of the Crusades as at present.

"And as the gossips of the city said that Marian Winstanley cared more for young Harry Barnes, the armourer, outside the gate, than anybody within it—nay, they went so far as to declare that a jolly miller, who lived down the river, returning late one evening from a pottle carousal at his favourite haunt, had seen Harry and his lady on the walls with their faces certainly much closer together just before he bade her good-night than the brawling of the river rendered necessary for the mere purpose of hearing each other's words.

"There was no post at the time, and so no kind friend of the mayor sent him an anonymous letter to tell him this news ; but Mark Trouncewell, the son of the baron justice, heard of it, and as Master Winstanley had selected him for his son-in-law, he did not take much time in telling the mayor all about it.

"Marian always thought that she did not like Mark Trouncewell much, and you would not have liked him either if you had seen him.

"He was short and awkward, with stubby light hair, and a low forehead, and always appeared to be scowling at everybody.

"But his father was a potent man in Durham, and a brave one, too—much braver than his son— for he had been beseiged for two months without effect in the castle during the baronial wars ; he owned ten mines, too, in distant counties, and as such was an eligible relative.

"And, therefore, Master Winstanley told his daughter that if ever she dared to think of the armourer again, a worthless, common fellow, who spent all his time in thumping red hot steel into swords and bassinets, he would put her for ever in a convent.

"And he was the man to keep his word.

"Harry Barnes, however, was not to be so lightly given up, for Marian loved him deeply, and when a pretty girl loves a handsome young man deeply it is either very delightful or very awkward, as circumstances may be.

"In her case it was the first.

"She loved his fine manly figure and good-tempered intelligence, and clever handiwork, for many of the productions of his hammer and anvil might have rivalled those of Benvenuto Cellini.

"But the Mayor of Durham had no appreciation of high art, as he often observed the wrought steel of Harry Barnes was nothing to the ready tin of Mark Trouncewell.

"He, therefore, settled the time of the marriage himself, and told Marian that she must never stir from home without her maidens, and that when she did, on her peril, she was not to go beyond the city gates in any direction.

"Young ladies had not much to amuse themselves in those days beyond embroidery, which was a pleasant excuse for doing nothing. It is curious how the custom has been preserved.

"So Marian took to working a scarf, and used to go and sit, surrounded by her fair playmates, on a pleasant green plot, shadowed by leafy waving trees at the foot of Curzon Street, as it was then called.

"And here she was always gazing up over her work, through the gate, making such strange shots in the colours, and sewing so many wrong needle-fulls in all sorts of odd places that the pattern became at last the wildest thing imaginable.

"Sometimes she saw Harry pass, and then the young couple looked very tearfully and very wistfully at one another, for they did not dare to speak ; if they had the mayor would have heard of it, and the consequence would have been dreadful.

"The wedding day came very near, and the lovers got desperate.

"In those times the bride did not make many purchases before her wedding.

"The wardrobes of young ladies about to marry did not then appear to be in that extremely destitute state which they appear to be in at present, when everything in the way of clothes, from top to toe, from little fly-away caps to trim kid slippers, has to be purchased bran new.

"No, she had only to sit amongst her maidens, and look pretty, and receive whatever presents her intended chose to send her, or play at ball with them for kisses, which, as they were all girls together, and not even Mark Trouncewell was admitted to the game, was slow enough even then.

"But they had little enough to do, for as few but the monks could read or write, it followed that there were not many circulating libraries ; and as nobody went to the sea side because, for one reason there was no railways, and for another it had not become the fashion, they had nothing but ball and tapestry to occupy their minds with.

"Mark Trouncewell sent a great many presents, and was cruel enough to order Harry Barnes to make a coffer of steel and brass and green velvet for the bride.

"He did this to annoy the armourer, being perfectly aware of the attachment.

"It did not do to refuse the order, although poor Harry set about it with a heavy heart at first, but, as he went on, it became, apparently, a labour of love for him.

"He was employed at it morning and night, and, at last turned out a piece of work that would have shaken Wardour Street to its very foundation if ever it appeared there.

"But it has long since rusted away.

"Harry was very particular as to the exact time it was to be sent home, and he kept it to the minute, charging Mark Trouncewell a good round sum for it—half as much as an old curiosity dealer would have asked at the present day—no trifle, as you may imagine.

"The intended bridegroom examined it closely both inside and out to see that Harry had not locked up all his love and allegiance to go with it ; and then it was sent off to his betrothed.

"Marian was sitting alone in her room that day, listening to the murmuring of the river, and looking abroad at the beautiful scenery up its banks, glittering in the afternoon's sun, when the coffer came.

"It was placed before her, and, as the messenger left, she thought still more of Harry Barnes, and how much she loved him, and how soon the time would come when to think kindly of him would be a crime, until her heart was so very, very full that, if she had not burst into tears to have relieved it, it had well nigh broken.

"She cried a long time, until the sun went down, and the calm twilight, still blushing with its rays, stole up along with the stars over the heaven.

"And then she would have fairly sobbed herself

to sleep, if she had not been suddenly startled with a whirring noise inside the box, like that which impetuous folks of the present time are familiar with when they over-wind their watches.

"The noise continued, and presently a false lid of the box flew open, and she saw a scrap of paper lying beneath it.

"For Harry had contrived and wound up a cunning piece of machinery, which he meant should just go off when there was a chance of Marian's being alone.

"It was a risk, to be sure, and a very great one; but she was so watched, and all her maidens were so very proper that he had no other way of communicating with her.

"Marian seized the paper, and, with some difficulty read——no matter what, but it appeared satisfactory to her.

"For her pale face flushed, her bosom moved quickly, and her red lips parted and almost smiled; one or two sobs, remnants of the old stock, rose every now and then, but even these soon stopped, and she went to bed and dreamed of Harry Barnes.

"The next afternoon she went with her maidens as usual to the green sward in Curzon Street to play at ball, and Mark Trouncewell was half bewildered with joy at being allowed to join in the games for the first time.

"He could not make it out at all, but of course came to the conclusion that at last the eyes of Marian were opening to his merits.

"The old mayor came down, too, and sat under the trees to watch them.

He would have had a pipe, only tobacco was, at that time, confined to an undiscovered world, so, instead he had a posset, and administered justice to all who came before him, very properly allowing wealth and power to weigh down the scale.

"Marian caught the ball and threw it here and there, contriving to make Mark look for it in all sorts of uncomfortable places.

"At last she said that she would throw it somewhere, and if her intended got it he should have a kiss from all her maidens—she was not jealous, not she; but that, if they got it first, then he must give them all a heart cake to ransom it.

"They agreed, and she at once pitched the ball very carefully on the top of the city walls.

"There was a terrible scuffle at the old steps by the side of the gate after it, and Mark was quite smothered up by the veils and dresses of the pretty girls, as they all crowded up towards the top.

"At last they all got there, and the instant they were all fairly on the ramparts Marian darted through the gate into the open country, where Harry Barnes was waiting for her on a stout black horse.

"He caught her up in his arms and gave her such a kiss, and the chronicles say it was returned before Mark Trouncewell's own face!

"And then, shaking the heavy purse which had been given in payment of the coffer, he struck spurs to his horse, galloped off along the right bank of the river and was out of sight almost before any of the astounded gazers could have called upon Jack Robinson, had that person lived in the middle ages.

"Where they went to was not known for a long time.

"But Marian had taken all her jewels with her, and Harry had all his wealth buckled about him

so that their prospects were not so hopeless as those of runaway couples in general, and they settled down in a leafy inland county, as happy as it was possible to be, and a great deal happier than the king, who, one way and another, was badgered into having a very sorry time of it altogether.

"They did not appear again in Durham for four years, at the end of which time the armourer came back as Sir Henry Barnes, with a title won by himself in stalwart fight, and Lady Marian so very beautiful that it was quite a treat to see her.

"In fact the old acquaintances could not have kept their eyes from her fair face had it not been for the beautiful three-year-old cherub who dragged her point lace into holes all day by trying to climb upon her knees.

"Mark Trouncewell, as the chronicles say, took to drinking, and becoming a graceless bird was one day happily knocked on the head in the Welsh wars.

"But what of the mayor?

"He was a long time calming his anger.

"He was, however, resolved that no other such elopement should ever happen.

"The very next day after the flight he had the Iron Gate shut up, which was of little use then, seeing that the mischief was done.

"This gave origin to the Durham proverb which the good citizens still use: 'When the daughter is stolen, shut the Iron Gate;' an adage, by the way, which, by varying the positions to that of a steed and a stable door, is not unknown all over England."

CHAPTER V.

MOONLIGHT JACK AND LUCIEN FAIRLEIGH AT DURHAM—THEIR ADVENTURE WITH THE BEAUTIFUL WOMAN.

"What do you say to a walk?" said Moonlight Jack, addressing his companion, Lucien Fairleigh.

"Nothing would suit me better. I should, above all things, like to see the ancient city of Durham by moonlight."

"Though, perhaps, you have a still greater desire to behold some of the fair ladies of Durham by candlelight."

Lucien shook his head with a half-serious, half-amused look.

"At all events, on such a fine evening as this, we shall be pretty certain to meet a few of the fair; so on with your hat, put a couple of pistols in your belt in case of emergency, and let us be going."

In a few minutes the two friends stood at the door of the house in which they had taken up their abode, and a guinea was spun in the air to decide whether they should turn to the right hand or to the left.

Lucien won, and elected to walk towards the noble cathedral, whose solemn-looking towers were looking calmly down upon the silent town like a giant sentinel.

The night air was balmy and cool, the bright moon shed a silver radiance on the scene, lighting up the old houses and their gable ends till they seemed more like the choice efforts of the painter's brush than real houses of brick, stone, and timber.

Far away might be heard the rushing sound of the river as it glided away on its course towards the sea; and that was nearly the only sound that fell upon the ears of the two friends.

Not long, however, was this deep silence to last.

As they passed by a house, the general aspect of which betokened wealth and luxury on the part of its owner, a guitar was heard.

Both Lucien and Moonlight Jack paused to listen to the silvery sounds, which so well accorded with the calm beauty of the scene.

The house from whence the sounds proceeded was one that had apparently been built in the reign of Queen Elizabeth. It had all the characteristics of that period—deep bay windows, high gables, and arched doorway.

It stood in the midst of a garden which was enclosed by a low brick wall.

"Shall we enter?" asked Lucien.

Moonlight Jack replied by laying his hand upon his sword, as though in expectation of an immediate assault.

"Why, what is the matter?"

"Some one threw a stone at me."

"Nonsense."

"I tell you it struck me on the arm."

"Then where is it? I won't believe it without you can show me the stone."

Moonlight Jack stooped down and lifted something from the ground.

It was not a stone, but a small piece of metal, to which was attached a slip of paper.

"A letter, by all that pertains to Venus! from yonder fair musician, I doubt not. Ha! ha! now I know why you were so anxious to walk this way, Master Lucien."

"Is it addressed to me?" asked Lucien.

"No; no name on it."

"Then as you received the letter it shall be yours, unless the contents prove that it was intended for me. I disclaim all knowledge of the fair musician, though I should have no objection to become acquainted with her."

Moonlight Jack unfastened the paper from the weight to which it was attached, and opened it.

The light of a lamp which stood over a surgeon's door near at hand enabled him to decipher the contents with ease.

It was as follows :—

"GENTLEMEN—Whoever you be I appeal to your generosity and honour. For six days and nights I have been imprisoned in my chamber by my father, who wishes to force me to wed a distant relative of mine—an old man, and one whose reputation is none of the best. I love him not, and would sooner die than submit to such an odious tie. Pray aid me in my adversity, and my prayers shall for ever be yours. I will pass a light three times across my window, that you may know where I am imprisoned."

The letter bore no signature, but a crest engraved at the top of the paper told the friends that the lady who implored their aid was no lowborn damsel.

"Well, Lucien, it seems this concerns both of us. What do you say to the adventure, shall we undertake to rescue the lady?"

"With all my heart."

"I am glad to have a chance of doing something. I haven't drawn my sword all day, and I am glad of an adventure which promises to drive away melancholy thoughts."

"Ah! my friend, then you propose to repay yourself for the trouble and risk of carrying off the lady from her ugly lover by enjoying her smiles and kisses yourself; but this is not fair, my friend, we are partners in this adventure."

"Then the lady shall choose between us."

"Agreed! And now watch for the signal."

In a minute a light was seen to cross one of the upper windows slowly, and then disappear.

Three times did this occur, and then the casement was thrown open.

"Here goes," exclaimed Moonlight Jack, as he vaulted lightly over the wall.

"And here follows," whispered Lucien, as he leaped into the enclosure, and stood by the side of his friend and companion.

"The next question is, how are we to reach the lady's chamber? The door appears to be fastened."

"I see a way," replied Lucien.

"Lead on, then; I'll follow thee."

"Then lend me your shoulders for a minute. Stand here by the door."

Moonlight Jack placed himself in the position indicated by his friend, and Lucien scrambled nimbly as an acrobat over his shoulders till he was able to climb on to the portico over the door.

"This is all very well," exclaimed Moonlight Jack; "but I am like the goat in the pit after the fox had made his escape. I can't very well follow you."

"Hush! here, join your sword belt to mine, which I have fastened to this pipe, and you can follow me in an instant."

Moonlight Jack did so, and in a few seconds stood on the platform above the door.

There was barely room for both on the narrow space.

Lucien tapped gently against the window, which was only a few inches over his head.

A beautiful female face looked out upon him, and by a gesture enjoined silence.

It was a face for which a man might have foresworn himself and sold his soul—an oval face, with eyes of deep blue, which sparkled like diamonds in the moonlight. The features were regular, the lips full and of a rosy hue, the complexion a pure white and red, without spot or imperfection, and the beautiful face was shaded by long golden curls, more resembling floss silk than human hair.

"Hush!" whispered the owner of all this beauty. "My father and cousin are in the room beneath. Enter as quietly as you can."

Lucien clambered into the room without making the slightest noise, and Moonlight Jack followed him.

The latter whispered—

"You do all the love making, Lucien. I'll attend to the fighting department."

When both were in the room the lady closed the window, and, turning to the two friends, said—

"Gentlemen, I shall never be able to thank you sufficiently for your kindness in venturing here to my assistance."

"Madam, to be of service to one so lovely is in itself a sufficient reward," said Lucien.

"Sir, you flatter me," replied she, blushing, and hanging her head.

"No, on my word, as a gentleman. I am a devoted servant to the fair sex, and am never so happy as when employed on the behalf of a lady."

"I am sorry to put an end to all your fine speeches and compliments," said Moonlight Jack, "but allow me to suggest that, as the lady wishes to leave this place as quickly as she can, you should propose some plan by which we can lift her to the lawn below; for I presume that the door of your prison is secured."

"It is, alas! locked. The key——"

"Ah, where is the key?" asked Lucien.

" My father has it, or my cousin, I know not which."

Moonlight Jack laid his hand upon his sword, and said—

" Would it not be a good plan to make a noise so as to attract their attention, and then disarm them, and take the keys from them."

" No, no, no!" exclaimed the lady ; " he has half a dozen servants with him, strong ruffians who would shrink from nothing. Pray do not rush into such fearful danger."

" But we are used to fight against odds," said Lucien, in a calm tone.

" You know not these men. Pray don't seek an encounter with them, for my sake."

" Then for your sake, fair lady, I will not ; but what and who is your father that he should thus treat you like a tyrant ?"

" My father is a rich man, though I know not how he obtained his wealth. I can recollect, when I was a child, we lived in the greatest poverty, till suddenly he removed to this house, where he seemed surrounded by riches."

" And his name ?"

" He is called Reginald Hallom."

" And now pray tell me what you are called, fair one ?"

" My name is Laura."

" Then, sweetest Laura, I will rescue you from your ugly lover and tyrannical parent, though he had a dozen servants at his call.

" You had better commence by fastening this rope round the lady's waist," said Moonlight Jack, who had been looking about for means of escaping.

" Good heaven ! surely I am not to trust my life to that cord ?" said Laura.

" Even so."

Lucien took the end of the rope in his hand, and began to fasten it round the lady's waist.

But he was a long time about it, and it seemed to Moonlight Jack an unnecessary time, neither did it appear absolutely necessary that Lucien's face should approach so close to the lady's.

At length the task was completed, and Lucien led Laura to the window.

It must be confessed that she looked much more red in the face than when the two gentlemen entered, but, doubtless, it was nervousness at the thought of dangling from the end of a cord.

Lucien carefully lifted her through the window, and then lowered himself on to the portico by her side.

" I will be on the ground to receive you, and protect you against danger should any threaten you."

It was well he took the precaution.

Scarcely had Laura Hallom's feet touched the ground when the door was thrown open, and two men made their appearance.

" Hullo ! what is all this ?" exclaimed one, who fully bore out Laura's assertion that he was old and ugly.

Without replying, Lucien Fairleigh cut the rope from around the young lady's waist, and throwing himself before her drew his sword.

" Ho ! within there, Giles, Tomkins, your weapons, lads !" shouted the other individual, who was Laura's father.

At the sound of the outcry two stout fellows in a gaudy livery rushed out with drawn swords in their hands.

" Cut him down ! cut him down !" shouted the angry parent. " No mercy."

Their weapons clashed as Lucien swiftly parried their strokes, and rather astonished at his skill the two servants drew back.

" Upon him ! cut him down ! we are four to one ! What are you afraid of ?" exclaimed the ugly lover of pretty Laura.

" Sir, you lie !" exclaimed Moonlight Jack, leaping to the ground. " If you feel insulted by my words I shall be most happy to give you instant satisfaction.

" You see we are two to four, which makes a great difference," he continued, crossing swords with the hump-backed lover, and at the same time keeping his eye upon the man in livery, who stood next him.

The ringing of the blades sounded clearly in the still night air, but in those times battles with sharp weapons were of too frequent occurrence to attract any special attention.

But the two friends had all their time engaged in warding off the furious assaults of the enraged parent and the lover.

" I must put an end to this !" muttered Moonlight Jack, as with his left hand he felt in his pocket for a pistol.

He cocked the weapon, and taking careful aim at one of the servants, fired.

The man dropped his weapon, as well he might, for the bullet had pierced his shoulder.

Lucien at once followed the example of his friend, and winged the other flunkey.

" Murder ! murder ! watch ! watch !" shouted Laura's ugly cousin.

" We must bolt, Lucien !" cried Moonlight Jack ; " you run on with the lady while I keep these two fellows at bay for a few minutes."

Lucien caught up Laura Hallom in his arms, and darted down the street, while Moonlight Jack prolonged the contest.

By a sudden thrust in *tierce* the King of the Road gave the lover a severe wound, while, before the father of Laura could lunge, *his* sword was wrested from his grasp.

Moonlight Jack then followed Lucien.

But as he ran along the street he heard Reginald Hallom ordering his servants to follow.

MOONLIGHT JACK
OR THE KING OF THE ROAD

The retreat which Moonlight Jack and Lucien Fairleigh had now secured for themselves was an old house outside the walls of Durham.

It was situated near a spot called Darton's Tarn.

The tarn was nothing more nor less than a deserted quarry.

It had been dug out irregularly, so that here and there was a sheer precipice, and there a ledge, and there a slope, and at the bottom was a green and stagnant pool, the gatherings of innumerable storms.

The edges of the quarry were overhung by trees and straggling undergrowth, while here and again were jagged places as if murder had run riot there,

and desperate hands had clutched them in a dying fall. It was a strange, dark, ill-looking spot.

There were strange stories about the pool in the Tarn.

Voices of lost people were said on still nights to be heard calling upon their friends for aid.

But the wind had, no doubt, much to do with it.

The rustling trees above, and the nodding reeds below; the falling of pebbles from the rock-side, and the starting of rabbits from their lairs; the chirping of birds, the hum of insects, and the whirr of the swooping bat, all these are strange and unwelcome sounds at night, and form the foundation of a hundred tales of *diablerie*.

Nevertheless it was so.

The old quarry, rough, unvegetated, wild, and weird, had its traditions of assassination and self-murder, and on one of its ledges, shaded from the bleak winds of heaven, stood the old wooden house where the highwaymen had taken up their abode.

They were once more Knights of the Road.

The cause of the Pretender was now a mere shadow.

He himself had forsaken all hope of the English throne.

So, as Lucien was in no fair way of recovering his estate and title, and as Moonlight Jack, too, was without funds, they took once more to their old business.

The old house by the quarry was just the place for concealment.

It had two advantages.

It was hidden away.

And then——

It was haunted!

Nothing could be better.

There is no greater covering for rascality than superstition.

Half the "haunted houses" have served as places of concealment for desperate thieves.

Thither the two highwaymen sped with their new charge.

They were not, however, destined to arrive there unmolested.

The pursuit came fast and furious.

The pursuers had a great advantage over them.

They knew the town better than either Jack Tyrrell or Lucien.

So, ere the latter reached the gates, they found that the men who followed were upon their heels.

Spurring their horses they plunged through the gate, Laura Hallom clinging to her preserver in terror.

Ere they had proceeded fifty yards, however, they halted.

They determined to run the risk of a battle.

Their reasons were obvious.

They desired to drive off their pursuers, and thus prevent the discovery of their secret abode.

Danger there was both in flight and in halting.

But discovery meant death, or the dispersion of their band.

The latter was but a peril such as a thousand times they had braved before.

Laura turned more deadly pale still as she saw four of her father's servants plunging towards them.

"Oh, why do you wait?" she cried, pressing herself so close to Moonlight Jack that her soft breast palpitated against his bosom. "It is death to meet them."

Jack laughed.

"We fear no one," he said.

She gazed wistfully in his face.

"But what of me?"

She asked it timidly.

"We will save you."

"But in your arms I shall only embarrass you."

"We will place you on the ground. Descend quickly, and conceal yourself behind yonder bush."

She slid to the ground.

There was no need to ask her twice to fly.

She fled like the wind.

But not far.

Behind the bush she crouched.

Just in sight of the combatants.

Hardly had she placed herself in concealment when the opposing parties met.

It was a bright moonlight night.

They at once could reckon their numbers.

There were four pursuers against our two heroes.

This was nothing.

Men who had fought single-handed against a score, were not likely to be dismayed by less odds.

"Stand here!" cried a voice.

"We are doing so. What want you with us?"

"The restoration of Laura Hallom," returned the other.

"Of whom?" asked Moonlight Jack, drawing his sword.

"Of Laura Hallom."

The highwayman laughed.

"You are jesting, my friend," he said, "but such jests are ill-timed."

"You are wrong," returned the other; "there is no jest in us. We are in search of our master's daughter, Laura Hallom, whom you have taken forcibly with you. So give her up to us or prepare to die."

At these words the highwaymen both laughed loudly.

"We are not here to die," cried Lucien. "Our time, please God, has not yet come. If we have Laura Hallom with us we have her here to save her from the cruelty and tyranny of those who should protect her. *So*, let us pass, my worthies. Ha! then, since you will have it, here we try you."

With these words, he attacked his adversary.

Jack did the same.

In a moment it was a deadly fight.

A deadly, silent fight.

Laura watched it in terror.

She had never before seen so hideous a spectacle as these six men gliding around one another in the dark night eager for one another's blood.

The difference in their mode of fighting soon, however, made itself apparent.

Lucien Fairleigh and Moonlight Jack fought for life and their own honour.

The hired servants fought for their master's child.

They were, therefore, though superior in number, scarcely equal to the two brave men.

They fought certainly, and shed their blood and still stood their ground for a time.

But the inevitable result followed.

The hirelings fled, and, desperately wounded, left Lucien and Jack Tyrrell masters of the field.

Laura at once crept out of her concealment when she saw the flight of her father's servants.

"Let us fly at once," she cried, "or fifty will be at our heels."

Jack at once lifted her on to his horse, and in five minutes after the flight of the servants they were all three spinning away towards the quarry.

Here they arrived duly, and Laura Hallom slept a safe sleep beneath the ancient rafters of the "haunted house."

———

CHAPTER VI.

LUCIEN AND JACK QUIT HOME — HARDMAN IN CHARGE — THE YOUNG BEAUTY'S TALE — A QUIET CORNER—A LITTLE LOVE-MAKING—NOT TO BE RESISTED—LAURA LOVES IN EARNEST—THE FACES AT THE WINDOW—THE THREE AVENGERS — THE FATE OF HARDMAN, THE ROBBER.

ON the evening following Laura Hallom's introduction to the "Haunted House," Lucien Fairleigh and Jack Tyrrell issued forth from their retreat with their band, to try their luck upon the road.

Hardman alone was left in charge of the habitation and its fair occupant.

It was a night calculated in every way to induce a feeling of loneliness.

It was very dark.

The moon set early.

Scarcely a star was visible in the sky.

The wind, too, howled dismally and plunged furiously into the quarry, whistling round the old house, and shaking its ricketty walls.

Hardman sat for some time smoking and drinking, until at length he became lonely.

His fair neighbour in the room next to him was evidently awake.

He heard her moving about.

"Perhaps she is lonely too," thought he. "I will see."

So, rising, he knocked at the door.

"Come in," said a gentle, lazy voice.

He entered.

A beautiful vision met his eyes.

Laura Hallom was lying on the sofa.

She had discarded her heavy travelling dress, and had now nothing on but a light, gauzy gown, tied in at the waist by a girdle of silk.

It was a dress which this beautiful daughter of love always carried with her.

The extreme heat of the weather of course warranted a very light covering, but her dress was something beyond this.

She blushed, and affected a pretty surprise when Hardman appeared.

A proud consciousness of beauty swelled her heart as he stood there gazing at her, his eyes wandering in wonder over the white shoulders, and the maidenly breasts, which were nearly naked, and the outlines of the splendid limbs, whose rounded proportions and delicate texture were scarcely concealed.

"What do you wish for, sir?" she asked, timidly, finding he did not speak.

"I was lonely, miss, and thought you might be lonely also."

She smiled.

"I *was* lonely," she said. "Sit down and remain. I am glad of some one to speak to."

Hardman was not at all a faint-hearted cavalier.

He closed the door, and sat down near the lady.

"How long shall you remain here?" asked he.

"I scarcely know," she said. "I suppose I *must* remain here until the search for me has ended."

"And why are you so eager to avoid your father?"

Hardman asked the question, gazing into her eyes fixedly as he did so.

"Because he wished me to marry one who, besides being as ugly as sin, was a desperate and infamous character. Three times I have been engaged to men, young, handsome, and intellectual. They have been driven away always, perhaps disposed of by treachery, and this hideous ruffian pressed upon me. Alas!" sighed the beauty, "I shall never taste real happiness, for it seems my fate to be the victim of this loathsome wretch. But, there, I bore you."

Hardman seized her hand.

"Oh, no," he cried. "I love to hear your voice."

She glanced at him.

Their eyes met.

"Oh, you put me so much in mind of Charles," she said, flushing.

In an instant he leaped to her side.

His arm glided round her warm, soft waist.

His lips were pressed to hers, her bosom panted against his.

"Fancy me Charles," he said, as she responded eagerly to his caresses.

*   *   *   *   *

An hour passed.

The lovers were still engaged in love-making.

They had not yet tired of the delirious intoxication of passion, and Hardman's lips were still clinging to those of his newly-made mistress, when a slight scratching noise was heard at the window.

They started and glanced up.

Laura still clung to her lover.

Now it was in fear.

Well might she hide her face in his breast.

At the window were two dark faces.

The one was that of her father.

The other the hideous face of her would-be lover.

One look was enough.

The diabolical look upon their features proved to her they had seen all, and she fainted away with shame and fear.

In another moment the door was burst open, and the two infuriated men rushed into the room.

Hardman sprang to his feet and drew his sword.

He saw at once the meaning of the situation.

"What is the meaning of this intrusion?" he cried. "How dare you thus break into my house?"

"Villain!" said Hallom, "that is my daughter!"

"Well, and what then?"

"What then? Ten thousand furies! Ruffian that you are, you have ruined her, and shall die the death of a dog!"

The two men, who were nearly foaming with rage, advanced to the attack.

By this time Laura had somewhat raised herself.

She knew well what she had to fear.

Her father and her would-be lover meant Hardman's death.

For her there was the choice of death or public shame.

She chose rather to risk the former.

Rushing from the room she returned in a few moments with a long sword.

"Now, then," she cried, "the odds are more even!"

The combatants paused.

Her father and her hideous pursuer gazed at her in wonder.

She looked splendid, standing there with her form dilated, her bosom heaving with excitement, her legs planted firmly on the ground in the position of a clever fencer.

But their rage was not thus to be appeased.

"Girl, stand aside," cried her father, "or death will be your fate!"

Hardly had the words left his lips when a lunge from Hardman's sword wounded him, and he was compelled to turn his attention to his more formidable foe.

Thus Laura was left to the mercy of her lover.

She attacked him vigorously.

Of course she had no science.

This for a time was to her advantage.

The man could scarcely tell how to parry the blows which fell upon him on all sides.

But at length, though severely wounded, he contrived to weary her out.

Her blows became fainter.

Then, with one gloating glance at the fair bosom where he had seen another's head reposing, he made a desperate lunge.

She uttered a loud cry.

It was her last !

The remorseless steel had passed like lightning between her quivering breasts.

She fell dead !

Her last glance fell upon her destroyer.

A glance he never forgot.

It was one full of hate, brimful of silent curses.

The sight of the bleeding corpse of the beautiful girl whom he had held in his arms, but a few moments before, completely overwhelmed Hardman.

He struck wildly right and left.

No longer using care, seeming, in fact, reckless of consequences, he delivered blows at random at both his adversaries.

They soon, therefore, had him at his disadvantage, and it was not long before, with savage exultation, the men who thirsted for his blood saw him stretched in death by the half-naked form of her whose cause they pretended to uphold.

The lover, Gerald Dorling, was the first to recognise the extreme peril of their position.

"We must fly now," he said.

Hallom glanced at him hurriedly.

The blood-thirsty wretch was now pale and trembling.

"Fly ?" said Hallom. "Why ?"

"Because these two dead persons will be avenged."

"You say rightly," cried a voice.

They started.

It was that of a woman.

Gipsy Bess stood before them !

In her hands were pistols.

"Stir not," she cried ; " whoever moves is a dead man !"

For a moment the men were taken by surprise.

That surprise was fatal to them.

Like a sudden avalanche, Moonlight Jack and his men sprang into the room and surrounded them.

"What means this hideous scene ?" cried Jack Tyrrell, in a loud and commanding voice.

"A hideous scene it may be to those who do not understand its import," cried Hallom, with as much calmness as he could assume. "This man seduced my daughter. I caught them in the very act of caressing as only lovers will. I have killed him— her lover here has killed her ; it was our right."

"Your right, say ye," cried Lucien Fairleigh, "to destroy my friend and murder his mistress ? We will try you for it, nevertheless, and if we find you guilty, you shall die, both of you, the death of dogs."

"Have a care, young sir," cried Laura's father, "have a care. Do you know that I am Sir Reginald Hallom—that I am of noble blood ?"

"If you were the king himself you should hang for this," cried Moonlight Jack. "Bind them, my men, and let us to our work."

CHAPTER VII.

THE TRIAL—THE DISCOVERY—THE SENTENCE—A
STRONG BOUGH AND A LONG ROPE—THE BURIAL
—THE EXECUTION—"IN THE NAME OF THE
KING, FIRE !"—UNEXPECTED AID—THE ROYAL
TROOPS FLY.

RESISTANCE to a host of men of course was useless, and in a very few minutes both Gerald Dorling and Sir Reginald Hallom were prisoners at the mercy of Moonlight Jack's band.

The trial was a short one.

There could be no doubt that the attack of the two men upon Hardman was little less than murder, while the killing of Laura Hallom was a cowardly assassination.

So there was but one response when Moonlight Jack asked,

"Guilty or not guilty ?"

"Guilty !"

"And what death ?"

"Death by the rope !"

"I protest against this," cried Sir Reginald Hallom.

Some of the men smiled and others laughed aloud.

"A seemly court of justice," added Sir Reginald. "I protest against the sentence of death passed by marauders."

"Your protest will avail you nothing," said Moonlight Jack, sternly. "You have confessed to a murder, and you must die the death allotted to murderers."

"At least, then, let me die by shooting—let me not die a dog's death. You cannot condemn me, a knight, to such a death as this."

"I can and will," said Moonlight Jack. "This judgment is one you little comprehend the significance of ; your judges are of a rank you little suspect. I, Lord Henry Mountjoy, Earl of Drerewater, and Lucien, Marquis of Huntley, have condemned you to die the death of a dog, and so you shall die. Fancourt, strike off his spurs."

The order was promptly obeyed.

The robbers, seizing the astonished knight, tied his hands behind him, and then, with a heavy sword, Fancourt struck off his spurs.

"And now," said Moonlight Jack, as we must still call him, "since it is not our interest to be discovered in this place of concealment, we must bury poor Hardman and Laura in the old quarry. Their murderers shall see their burial, and be hung above their graves."

The two bodies, having been wrapped in sheets, were taken up tenderly by the highwaymen and borne out into the dark night.

Torches were lit, and the two condemned men, being placed in the midst with long stout ropes around their necks, the procession took its way down the rocky slopes to the bottom of the old quarry.

Here, by the side of the water, they dug the graves.

It was a solemn scene.

On the one side the torch-bearers holding aloft the lights to enable the grave-diggers to do their work.

The two dead bodies, lying extended silent on the ground, were just at the feet of the condemned.

The ropes around the necks of these latter were drawn over the strong bough of an old oak which bent over the Tarn.

As soon as the dead bodies were placed side by side in the grave, and before the earth was thrown over them, the robbers began forming a kind of extempore scaffold.

They brought out a large table, and on these they placed two chairs.

Then the ropes were made fast above, and the condemned men were forced to mount the chairs.

"Now," cried Moonlight Jack, "all is ready. Reginald Hallom and Gerald Dorling, there are your victims. If you deem yourselves right you are not afraid to die. Comrades, remove the chairs."

At these words the table was at once upset, and

the wretched men fell heavily, breaking their necks at once.

Hardly had they fallen—hardly had the graves begun to be once more filled up—when the sound of approaching feet was heard.

The labour was now hurriedly completed, and each man stood to arms, Gipsy Bess retreating by Jack's orders to the concealment of the old house on the ledge.

In a very few moments the cause of the sounds was explained.

A company of soldiers were approaching.

"We are betrayed !" cried Jack Tyrrell ; "conceal yourselves. There is no knowing the number of our enemies."

The torches would at once have been extinguished.

But there was no time.

The soldiers, who had evidently had good information from some source or another, poured in on all sides.

They were in strong force.

About a hundred men, besides their two officers, entered the quarry.

Moonlight Jack's band numbered but twenty men.

"In the King's name, fire !" cried the chief officer.

The soldiers did so.

They asked not for surrender.

Their orders were evidently to exterminate all they fell upon.

But in this object they failed utterly.

The ledges of the rocks and the huge trunks of the trees concealed the dark forms of the highwaymen, while the torches glared vividly upon the redcoats of the soldiery.

Armed only with pistols, the robbers, nevertheless, made terrible havoc among the troops.

What was the object or origin of the fight, it was hard to say.

The only interpretation which seemed feasible was, that after the attack they had that night made upon the mail coach, some one had tracked them to their quarters, and given information to the authorities.

However, whatever the cause was, the battle waxed fast and furious.

Now and then a well-aimed volley disconcerted the soldiers.

Then again a stray shot laid one of Jack's men low.

It was evident that by morning the band would lose some of its best men.

Yet they fought well.

And all this time the two dead men swung to and fro in the breeze amid the smoke and the glare.

At length Jack resolved to make a flank movement.

Collecting his men, he bade them creep up under shadow of the trees, and await him on the margin of the quarry.

This they contrived to do by degrees, and ere long the band—now reduced to sixteen—was gathered near the old house.

From this vantage ground—the soldiers being now some distance below them—they poured down a sudden volley, which had a murderous effect.

The soldiers were for a moment taken aback, and huddled together like frightened sheep.

But at a word from their commanding officer they once more drew themselves into order, and running up the slope with that discipline and pluck which are the combined characteristics of the English soldier, they attacked the highwaymen fiercely.

For the first time for a long time the heart of Moonlight Jack was assailed by unwelcome fears.

Gipsy Bess was alone in the old house.

His men were falling around him.

A superior and disciplined force was pressing them.

To retreat was impossible.

Had he felt disposed to fly the danger of Gipsy Bess would at once have precluded all such ideas.

Just as amid his prodigies of courage he was considering whether it would not be better to make for the old house, and barricade themselves there ; just as he was about to give the order, an unexpected assistance came.

A loud shout was heard.

A report of fire-arms and a number of shaggy, ragged forms rushed from among the forest trees.

Their strange appearance was easily accounted for.

They were some of the great, disbanded, and routed army of the Pretender.

"Moonlight Jack for ever !"

Such was the cry which resounded through the night air.

The tide was turned at once.

The soldiers were attacked front and rear.

In vain their officers shouted to them.

In vain they urged them almost by blows not to turn.

After a gallant resistance, after the decimation, in fact, of their number, already half destroyed in the quarry, they fled, pursued for some distance by the disbanded soldiery, who seemed anxious to pay off old scores.

Moonlight Jack and Lucien hastened to the old house where Gipsy Bess tremblingly awaited them.

They had issued forth from that house twenty in number.

They returned—ten !

A melancholy departure that was from their newly-made home, each man leading the horse of his dead comrade.

They proceeded hurriedly along the road in a direction opposite to that which led to Durham, and hurried sad and weary towards London.

CHAPTER VIII.

GRACE DASHWOOD'S NEW HOME—LONELY HOURS —THE SILENT NIGHT—THE FALLING RAIN—THE TAPPING LEAVES—THE STRANGE INTRUDER— THE INTERVIEW—PASSION v. HONOR—LUCIEN AND THE PRINCE— PREPARATIONS FOR A COMBAT—HOW IT ENDED.

WHEN Grace Dashwood left Darnley House in company with Lucien Fairleigh and Moonlight Jack, she proceeded by their direction more towards the north, and took up her abode in a cottage situated in the slope of a hill near Demstead.

Near it waved the leaves of a dense wood, and a few trees which seemed as if they had straggled away from the forest, waved against the back of the house and overhung the windows.

It was not a place well calculated to impress the mind with any very great amount of cheerfulness.

But it suited the occasion.

Grace Dashwood was very still that evening on which we proceed to her new home.

Her life had been strangely purposeless of late.

She had imagined that the Pretender had caused the death of her uncle, and of two other beings who were more dear to her still.

She had followed him like a fate.

She had pursued him to the uttermost parts of the country, and found him.

How?

Only to discover that he was innocent of all that she had attributed to him.

Thinking over the past—thinking over the time when she was happy in her furtive meetings with Lucien Fairleigh—Grace fell almost into a slumber.

So soundly did she slumber that she did not hear a noise without like the pattering of rain, did not observe a shadow fall on the ground, did not see a face peering in.

Presently starting from her sleep, she glanced around.

"I will sleep awhile," she murmured. "This night Lucien promised to return to me. I will wait for his coming."

So saying, she divested herself of her outer garment and lay down upon the couch in a lovely deshabille, exhibiting her naked shoulders warm and white, and her splendid bust firm and rounded as the breasts of the Venus de Medicis.

Lying thus her light under-garments gave a full display of her glorious limbs, for the gauzy materials of her summer clothing served rather to exhibit than to disguise the proportions of her form.

Nothing is so conducive to slumber as the languor of love.

Long she dreamed thus.

She was rudely awakened.

It was by the impress of a passionate kiss upon her lips.

She woke at once.

Woke to find a man leaning over her, his arm around her waist, his eyes gleaming admiringly as they wandered over her exquisite beauties.

"Release me, sir!" she cried, attempting to spring up.

The man permitted her to do so.

She then saw who it was.

The Pretender!

The man she had saved!

"Sir," she cried, "this is unmanly!"

"Madam," he said, as he still held her hand, "it may to you appear unmanly; but it is natural, from my love. I have long tried to conquer it. I have failed. Saved by your hand from a shameful death I love you more than ever. I have tracked you hither, and finding you at length, I am here on my knees to tell you how much I adore you."

He flung himself on his knees at her feet.

"Rise, my prince," cried Grace. "Rise, this is no position for you. I forgive you your unfortunate passion; but leave me now in peace. I expect in this place to-night those who would not thank you for your company, prince as you are."

The prince rose.

"Is this, then, all my reward?"

"Indeed, yes. I can give no other. I am the pledged wife of another. To him my heart is given, and to you, as to any other man, I refuse to be a toy."

"You wrong me, dearest girl," cried the prince, eagerly. "I mean you not to be a toy. You shall be my wife. I will——"

Grace interrupted him,

"Nay, my prince," she cried. "Nay; do not, for my poor sake, perjure yourself; but hark! they come! For my sake, and your own, fly!"

He hesitated.

But the sound of horse's feet was in the courtyard.

He gave her one despairing glance.

Then he seized her in his arms, and covered her neck, her lips, her bosom with passionate kisses.

Having done this he rushed away, and Grace Dashwood saw him no more.

She had scarcely time to readjust her dress, when Lucien Fairleigh and Moonlight Jack stood before her.

With happy tears the lovers were clasped in each other's arms.

"Stay," cried Jack Tyrrell, "stay, my young people. Allow me to introduce you to one another."

"We scarcely need that," said Grace Dashwood, with a smile.

"Nay, then, you do," said Jack Tyrrell. "I introduce you, Miss Grace Dashwood, to Lucien, now acknowledged Marquis of Huntley."

"Is this true, Lucien?" she asked, regretfully.

"Yes, indeed. Are you, then, sorry that I have secured my rights?"

"No; but I would love you to be always Lucien, not Lord Huntley."

"To others I am Lord Huntley, to you I am ever Lucien Fairleigh," he answered; "but can you dream as to who had these papers?"

"I cannot, indeed."

"It was Soft Sam. He secreted them somewhere on the night of the great fire at Huntley Castle, and until three days since, when he lay on his death-bed, he never confessed it. However, all is now settled, and what remains to be done now is to lead you to Huntley Castle as its mistress and my wife."

The marriage of Lucien Fairleigh, fourth Marquis of Huntley, with Grace Dashwood, took place on the next day.

After this the band dispersed.

Jack Tyrrell, having also obtained his rights, and performed his vow to Lucien's parents, quitted the road, and as Moonlight Jack was heard of no more.

As Lord Drerewater he was long known and respected, and among the firmest and fastest of friends were Lucien and Jack, and Grace and Gipsy Bess with Sir Percy and Lady Ella Delaine.

As for Jonathan Rasper a hideous fate awaited him.

Hearing of Jack Tyrrell's and Lucien's happiness, he made his way into the vaults of the new Huntley Castle, for the purpose of burning it down like the old one.

Here he was, by some means or another, wedged in by the falling of some masonry he had displaced, and was eaten alive by rats.

His skeleton was in after years discovered with some writing which proved who he was.

[THE END.]

www.ingramcontent.com/pod-product-compliance
Lightning Source LLC
Chambersburg PA
CBHW080733250626
47170CB00010B/2816

* 9 7 8 1 5 3 5 8 0 7 4 8 7 *